Athalie

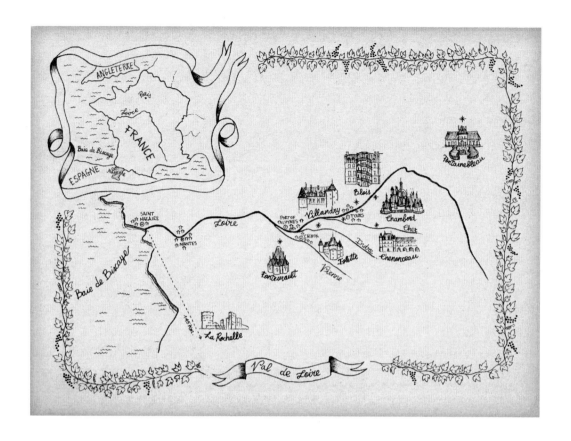

Athalie

Caroline Marie Martin

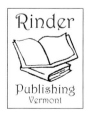

Rinder Publishing
Vermont

Nod to the Author

Caroline Marie Martin uses the general term "Protestant" to refer to those in 16th-century France who joined other Europeans in breaking away from the Roman Catholic Church. This movement, known as the Protestant Reformation, was triggered by Martin Luther in Germany in 1517 and grew exponentially. Protestants emphasized the authority of the Bible over the authority of the Pope, and "protested" – hence, the term "Protestant" – the corruption of the Catholic Church as seen in the debauchery of its clergy, the sale of indulgences, the Inquisition, and other horrific abuses of clerical power rampant in that era.

In some chapters, the author refers to branches within the larger Protestant group as those of the "Reformed" faith, or "Reformed Religion," "Religionists," or "co-Religionists." Those who followed John Calvin of the French Reformed Church were called "Calvinists." French Protestant "Huguenots" followed Bezanson Hugues of Switzerland and evolved into the Reformed Church of southern and western France.

"Heretics" was an inflammatory term used by Catholics for Protestants, while Catholics were held in contempt as "papists" by their Protestant countrymen.

The various references augur the challenges Protestantism fomented in European kingdoms as it began to spread throughout the Christian world.

* * *

The author often chooses to use the more formal European pronoun "which" instead of "that" as she describes objects and places in her narrative. This bow to Continental tradition adds to the appeal of her book.

* * *

ATHALIE © 2022 by William Barrett. ISBN: 978-1-7369033-1-5
All rights, including the right of first publication, reserved to William Barrett.

Published by Rosemary Rinder of Rinder Publishing, Bomoseen, Vermont.

Foreword "A Letter to Our Readers" by Rosemary Rinder.
Cast of Characters prepared by Rosemary Rinder.

Edited by Christine Cash Gilroy, DeWitt, Iowa.

Painting of Château Chenonceau on cover by Caroline Marie Martin, ca. 1980.
Cover painting photograph by Caleb Kenna Photography, Middlebury, Vermont.
Back cover photograph of Caroline Marie Martin by William Barrett, ca. 1978.

Map of France drawn by Violeta Terroba Souto, Madrid, Spain.
Drawings of Abbey Fontevrault and châteaux Chenonceau, Fontainebleau, Blois, Chambord, Islette, and Villandry by Violeta Terroba Souto.

For Virginia Deming Barrett

Cast of Characters

BOLDFACE TYPE indicates a historical figure. *Italic type indicates a fictional character.*

ADMIRAL: See Coligny, below.

ÁLAVA: See Francisco de Álava, below.

ALENÇON: See Hercule-François, below.

ALBERT GONDI: Count de Retz. Son of an Italian merchant banker, uses the Count de Retz name based on the title of his wife, Catherine de Clermont-Tonnerre, baroness of Retz.
In the novel, Gondi is the manipulative, self-serving uncle and guardian of Athalie.

ALVA, DUQUE DE, FERNANDO ALVAREZ DE TOLEDO: Brutal Spanish ruler of the Netherlands. Known in Spain as Duke de Alba, Alva in the Netherlands.

AMBROISE PARÉ: Doctor in the court of King Charles.

Anne de Revillars: Pierre de Galle's bride. Dies after giving birth to Pierre's son, Gatien.

ANJOU: See Henri, Duke d'Anjou, below.

ANTOINE DE GRÈVE: Friend and adviser to Admiral Coligny.

ARÉTIN, PIERRE: Italian author of lewd humor and biting satire.

Athalie de la Roque: Orphan daughter of Blaise, Duke de la Roque, and Alicia Gondi. She is the only heir to the great house of la Roque; she is half-French, half-Italian, like the Queen Mother.

Blaise de la Roque: Duke, head of a great noble family, father of Athalie. Friend of Raymond de Galle, Pierre's father. Married Alicia de Gondi, fictional sister of Albert Gondi, who died giving birth to Athalie. Dies from injuries fighting Protestants at Battle of Moncontour.

BRANTÔME: See Pierre de Bourdeille, below.

CARDINAL DE BOURBON: Henri of Navarre's uncle, conducts marriage of Henri to Margot.

CATHERINE DE MEDICI: Queen Mother. Half-French, half-Italian, regent to her sons for many years, dominates the court. Her daughter Elisabeth is married to King Felipe II of Spain. Her husband, King Henry II, died after a jousting accident.

Chabannes, also called Charbonneau. Trusted agent of Gondi, sent to Protestant stronghold of La Rochelle to gain information. Hanged for a spy by the Admiral.

CHARLES IX, KING OF FRANCE: Young king with tuberculosis. His brother the Duke of Anjou would inherit the throne should Charles die without a male heir.

CHARLES DE TELIGNY: Nephew of Coligny.

CHRISTOPHE DE THOU: Prominent president of the Parliament of Paris, judicial official.

COLIGNY, GASPARD DE: The Admiral. Key leader of the Protestant Reformed Religion in France. Killed in St. Bartholomew's Day massacre. *In the novel, Coligny is admired by Pierre de Galle.*

CONDÉ: See Louis de Nassau, below.

DIEGO DE ZÚÑIGA, DON: New Spanish ambassador to France, spring 1572. Replaces Álava.

Eleanor d'Avrillac: Also known as Elie. Mistress of Raymond de Galle, mother figure to Pierre.

ELEANOR DE BOURBON: Prioress at the abbey Fontevrault, niece of the Abbess. Later, Abbess.

ELISABETH OF AUSTRIA: Wife of Charles IX, King of France.

FRANCISCO DE ÁLAVA: Francés in French. Spanish ambassador, discredited, replaced by Zúñiga.

FRANÇOIS: Name given to Hercule, Duke of Alençon, upon his Confirmation.

GENLIS: Jean de Hangest, Seigneur d'Yvoy. Protestant. Led French expedition to invade the Netherlands to begin The Enterprise.

GODEFROI DU BARRY, SEIGNEUR DE LA RENAUDIE: Protestant. Executed after his role in the 1560 Conspiracy d'Amboise. *In the novel, father of Maurice de La Renaudie.*

GONDI: See Albert, above.

GUISE FAMILY: Powerful arch-Catholic family seeking to purge France of the Protestant Reformed Religion. Princess Marguerite de Valois (Margot) was in love with Henri, Duke de Guise, but the Queen, her mother, arranged a marriage to Protestant Henri of Navarre instead, as a political move to try to unite France and prevent civil war.

HENRI, DUKE D'ANJOU: Brother of the king, later King Henri III; close to Catholic Guises.

HENRI II: Previous king, died 1559 from jousting wounds, leaving Queen Mother regent.

HENRI OF NAVARRE, PRINCE: Protestant. Scion of then-powerful ruling family of Navarre. The Queen Mother and others hoped that his marriage to Princess Margot would foster peace between Catholics and Protestants in France. He later became King Henry IV (Good King Henry), the first of the Bourbon dynasty in France.

HERCULE-FRANÇOIS, DUKE D'ALENÇON: Youngest of the Valois, brother of King Charles IX.

JEANNE D'ALBRET, QUEEN OF NAVARRE: Protestant, mother of Henri of Navarre; visited the Queen Mother in Paris in 1572, was taken ill (or poisoned?), died returning to Navarre.

JÉRÔME DE GONDI: Young cousin of Gondi, possibly spying for the Spanish ambassador.

Julio de Gondi: Gondi's cousin and secretary.

LOUISE DE BOURBON: Abbess at Fontevrault. *In the novel, great-aunt of Athalie.*

MARGUERITE DE VALOIS, PRINCESS: Also called Margot. Daughter of Catherine de Medici and the late King Henry II, sister of King Charles IX. Her mother aims to marry her to Protestant Henri, Prince of Navarre, despite her love for Catholic Henri, Duke de Guise. *In the novel, Margot and Athalie become friends.*

MARGOT: See Marguerite, above.

MARIE TOUCHET: Mistress of King Charles IX.

Mathilde: Nurse and caretaker of Athalie.

Maurice: See Renaudie, below.

NASSAU, LOUIS DE: Also known as Ludovic of Nassau, Louis I of Bourbon, Prince de Condé. Uncle of Prince Henri of Navarre. Protestant leader. Proposes King Charles invade the Netherlands to free them from the Spaniards. Brother of William of Orange.

Pascal family: Artus Pascal is Gondi's banker and friend; he's an important banker who lends substantial sums to Gondi to be passed on to the Queen Mother. His warm and hospitable wife is Amelie. Aimeri is the older, scholarly son of the family, who is in love with Athalie. A younger son, Augustin, looking for notice at Court, is a skilled swordsman who duels with Pierre.

PIERRE DE BOURDEILLE: Abbé and Seigneur de Brantôme. Courtier with wide experience in war and diplomacy, friend to Hercule-François, Duke d'Alençon.

Pierre de Galle: nicknamed Blondel. Son of Raymond de Galle and heir of an important landed family. Marries Anne de Revillars, who dies after childbirth. Lover of Athalie.

QUEEN MOTHER: see Catherine de Medici, above.

Raymond de Galle, Duke de Touraine: Pierre's father. His first wife died, leaving Pierre motherless. Now he is married to Maurice's mother, whose husband was Godefroi du Barry, above.

Renaudie, Maurice: fictional son of Godefroi du Barry, above. Nicknamed Noiret. His mother is now married to Raymond de Galle, so he and Pierre are stepbrothers. Spies for Gondi at La Rochelle.

RENÉE DE RIEUX DE CHÂTEAUNEUF: Maid of honor to the Queen Mother and mistress of the queen's son Henri, Duke d'Anjou.

Trophime Daudet: Protestant friend of Augustin Pascal and later of Pierre.

VALOIS: The royal house of France from 1328 to 1589. Junior members of the family founded cadet branches in Orléans, Anjou, Burgundy, and Alençon.

WILLIAM OF ORANGE: also called William the Silent. Protestant. Wishes to deliver the Netherlands from Spanish Catholic tyranny. Brother of Louis of Nassau.

ZÚÑIGA: See Diego, above.

And a note on locations: Many of the novel's locations are real châteaux of the Loire region in France. The drawings of Violeta Terroba Souto represent several of them. Key action in the novel occurs at the famous thousand-year-old Abbey of Fontevrault, also known as Fontevraud, whose monastic order was dispersed during the French Revolution. France declared Fontevrault a major cultural center in 1963.

—Rosemary Rinder

A Letter to Our Readers

The Story Behind the Story

Caroline Marie Martin, my dear friend and Manhattanville College roommate, was a brilliant scholar of history and literature before taking to the law. Her mother was English, her father French, thus the traditional French pronunciation of her name – Caro-"leen" – rather than Caro-"line." Though she was born and bred in New York City, she spent all summers her whole life with godparents in France. Her engrossing novel features political and romantic intrigue in 1570s France.

Sadly, Caroline died in 1982 at the age of 34. Once she received the diagnosis of terminal leukemia (these were other times – no bone marrow transplants, alas), she quit her lucrative legal job to do what she'd always wanted to do: write a novel – or a series of them – and paint. She devoted her last couple of years to this.

Readers, indulge me while I tell you about two regrets. Caroline and I first met as we settled into our shared freshman dorm room. At her bedside, Caroline placed a memorable photo of a beautiful woman. I asked who it was. She told me it was her mother, who had died when Caroline was 13. I was aghast, and I said something like, "How horrible." But, thinking that Caroline was probably "over it" after four or five years, I never asked or said anything more about this terrible loss. How little I knew! My own mother has been gone for 40-plus years, and I am not "over it."

Much later, after Caroline's diagnosis, when I was already the enchanted mother of my delicious little first girl, Caroline told me she thought she would also love to have a "little puffin," but she'd consulted with her doctor, who recommended against it. Why? Because he didn't approve of motherless children. Oh, my God, we were both being stoic and trying to use humor to cope. I said something like, "Gosh, he doesn't sugarcoat things, does he?" How often, in later years, I have regretted not throwing my arms around Caroline and sobbing with her about all she and we were losing.

Caroline's widower, Bill Barrett, tried to get her novel published during the mid-1980s, but got worn out after speaking with several agents and publishers. The manuscript, written in longhand by Caroline on yellow legal pad paper, was laboriously typed and retyped and retyped yet again by Bill's mother, Virginia Deming Barrett, and languished on our various bookshelves (another Manhattanville classmate, Molly Noonan, also had a copy) for decades. Once I retired, determined to get this book published, I re-read it, loving the feel of having a nice long visit once more with Caroline. And I took up the subject with Bill.

A galvanizing catalyst came at our 50th Manhattanville class reunion. Molly and I spoke with and gained the extraordinary support of classmate Christine Cash Gilroy, who, after teaching high school English and journalism for many years, has built a second career consulting and editing for self-published books. Bill has told me that Caroline hoped the book would be a commercial success and would likely be embarrassed at the idea of it as some kind of a monument to her. So here it is – just a story for all of us to enjoy.

–Rosemary Rinder
Bomoseen, Vermont
January 2022

Athalie

Death at Moncontour

The surgeon and his assistant wiped the saw and scalpel on some burlap and began to pack them into a wooden box. "If the cauterizing iron is cool enough, put it away," the surgeon snapped. The other nodded and wearily wrapped the heavy bar in its leather cover. The surgeon took the burlap, and finding a more or less unstained corner, cleaned the blood from his hands, one finger at a time. As he finished, two men came through the tent flap. Dropping the cloth, the surgeon rushed forward, hurriedly straightening his attire. In the press of the day's emergencies, he had hitched up the long robe of his profession and tied it with cord; now, he let the creased skirt drop to hide his muddy hose.

"My lords," he said, and bowed deeply.

The two bore the marks of recent battle. Though they had removed their heavy outer armor, they still wore mail and quilted tunics; mud and blood bespattered them; fatigue bleared their eyes.

Their mail sparkled in the brazier's wavering light, while on the tent wall, their shadows jumped and loomed.

The taller of the two, Raymond de Galle, Duke de Touraine, a giant, auburn-haired man, gazed with disdain at the surgeon's bent shape.

"How is he?" he asked.

"I took the leg off below the knee," the surgeon replied. "I could do nothing else. The spear pierced the calf. I suppose it penetrated the horse's side, and the beast must have fallen on him. Everything was crushed and mangled."

"Was he conscious?"

"I could not make him swallow the eau de vie before surgery, so I supposed he was out."

The redhead looked at his silent companion. Albert de Gondi, Count de Retz, was a man in his prime, strong and well proportioned, with brown hair, a golden beard, and penetrating, clear eyes.

Responding wearily to the unspoken query, Gondi shrugged and said, "I don't know, de Galle. I suppose we should come back later. There doesn't seem to be much we can do. Marcel will call us if there is any change." He indicated a manservant who stood in the shadows twisting his cap round and round from pent-up emotion.

Turning on the surgeon, de Galle said sharply, "You understand, he is to get the best of care?"

"But of course, Monsieur." The robe folded in yet another deep obeisance.

"You are to stay with him at all times, you understand?"

The figure shot upright. "But Monsieur, there are many wounded. I cannot stay. I cannot even leave my assistant. We have much work still to do."

"Never mind the others. The Duke de la Roque is worth an entire army."

The surgeon rubbed his hands together. They were hard and callused, and caked blood was still visible in the wrinkles. He made a last attempt to sway the Duke. "I would remain gladly, if it would help, but really, there's nothing I can do."

"No doubt," de Galle replied, his mouth curling, "but you will stay anyway."

The surgeon shrugged helplessly. The noblemen left. The figure on the couch stirred and moaned softly.

Several hours later, the same group gathered around the camp bed. Silence had fallen after the customary cursory exchange of information, the nervous silence that comes to people forced to stay where they cannot help. The surgeon had put pillows under his patient's torso to assist his labored breathing. The wounded man's head lolled aimlessly, as if he lacked the strength to lift or even move it. His body, which that very day had stood massive and proud in its armor, seemed to have crumpled together. Even his cheeks had sunk in the short period of his infirmity, giving the face an old, frail look. From time to time, his feverish eyes opened and darted about the tent.

"Testament." It was barely a whisper, but everyone started and turned toward the bed. The manservant looked at the two noblemen, and then at his helpless master, and finding no guidance, went to a small casket and took out a piece of parchment.

"This is his will, Messieurs. He made it years ago, and it is in order."

De Galle stood in the center of the tent, where the roof was highest, and still he looked oversized and awkward. He bent his gaze on Gondi.

"This is family business, Albert. You had better deal with it."

Taking the will from the servant, Gondi went down on one knee next to the bed and said, "Blaise, we have your testament. Everything is as it should be." The eyelids fluttered, and the ghastly white face shook slowly.

Gondi looked about helplessly, then leaned over the prone figure.

"Here, I shall read it for you, shall I?"

Gondi unfolded the unsealed parchment and began:

To my noble liege Lord and Master, his gracious Majesty, King Henry, the Second of that name, I address my last will and Testament: That my lands and property, howsoever situated, realty or personalty, shall be held by my gracious liege Lord or his chosen representative in trust and wardship for my only daughter, Athalie, until such time as she shall marry, whereupon they shall, at my Lord's pleasure, be granted and bestowed upon her absolutely. Until that time, I ask that his gracious Majesty provide for the guardianship of the person and property of the said Athalie by such action and appointment as to him shall seem appropriate.

Made this 15th day of May in the year of our Lord 1559.

Signed, Blaise, Sieur de la Roque

The wounded man's eyes had closed during the reading. De Galle and Gondi looked at each other. De Galle's husky voice broke the silence.

"Other than that it's the wrong King, it's fine. The responsibilities will simply devolve on King Charles; there's no problem. The King will obviously appoint you as the girl's guardian. You're her closest relative, so it's only right. Plus, it's a way he can reward your services that doesn't cost him anything." De Galle smiled grimly.

"If he dies," the other said.

"Of course." De Galle shrugged.

The wounded man opened his eyes and fixed them on Gondi.

"Albert. Athalie," he murmured.

De Galle leaned far over and patted de la Roque's shoulder.

"That's just what we were saying, old man. Gondi here will take care of your girl 'til she is properly married, if you don't make it. You don't have to worry. You can relax and rest. Build up some strength, and Albert's services won't be needed."

The dark eyes wavered and returned to Gondi, and the hoarse voice came again. "Testament."

Gondi stood up and said to de Galle, "I can't tell what he's thinking. I can't even tell if he's thinking at all. Coherently, I mean."

Blaise de la Roque looked up at the two shapes silhouetted against the charcoal fire. Despair filled him. He was thinking, but he did not know how to tell them what he was thinking. He wanted to shout, and instead he pushed and pushed and a mumble came out. Sweat beaded his dark hairline. He closed his eyes again. The testament. It was not what he wanted. As long as his friend, the late King Henry, had been on the throne, it had been what he wanted, but now it should be more detailed, more formal; it should give Athalie more independence and more safeguards.

Why hadn't he rewritten it? He had never thought it would come to this. He had never really cared.

Athalie! Slim, dark, quiet Athalie. He hardly knew her. Her birth had killed his dear, gentle wife, and he had never forgiven her. Even as she grew older and began to resemble her mother — the coloring, the nose, a gesture, a tone of voice — these subtle reminders of his wife did not endear his daughter to him. Instead, they seemed by their inadequacy to mock his loss. It was not the child's fault, he knew, and he should have done more — so much more.

The images of his daughter and his wife fused in his mind. It seemed to him suddenly as if there were only one person and she were about to die — instead of two, one dead and one full of life. And it was he who was dying, he suddenly remembered. Tears overflowed and trickled toward his ears. He could not say whose death he was weeping for.

He had not cried since his wife died. Not even yesterday, or whenever it was that they had cut his leg off. They had amputated, hadn't they? He thought he could feel the leg, though the terrible crushing pain in the bone and muscles of his calf had miraculously stopped. The thought that perhaps he would live to ride again crossed his mind.

He sighed as if a weight had been taken from his mind. Then he remembered that it was not just the will he had wanted to discuss. He looked around feverishly for his tall friend.

His fading eyesight could make out only his brother-in-law, Gondi. Panic seized him.

"De Galle," he cried. "Raymond de Galle."

To the listeners, the cry came as a muffled roar, but it had the desired effect. De Galle bent over to stroke the short, grizzled hair with a delicacy surprising in one so big.

Blaise's black eyes caught and held de Galle's hazel eyes. "Pierre," he muttered. "Pierre," he repeated with suddenly clear articulation.

"Pierre? Stone? What is made of stone? What does he mean?" de Galle asked, bewildered.

Blaise closed his eyes, anger and despair clutching his throat. Stone! He didn't mean pierre, he meant Pierre. The only stone involved was de Galle's thick skull.

For years, he had meant to talk to de Galle about marriage between his son, Pierre, and his own daughter, Athalie. It would be a most fitting match. They were of similar age and rank, strong, healthy, and comely. Each was the only heir to a tremendous estate. It was his dream that they should join and multiply, that with their children, his descendants, they should possess the earth. It could be arranged quite soon. Athalie was already fourteen. Had she reached puberty yet? He should know, but he didn't. In any event, it could be soon, that was sure. Still, it seemed likely that he would not be there. But were he not, it would never come to pass, he realized abruptly, remembering again that he had never talked to de Galle. God in Heaven, why hadn't he?

He had done so many things, many that seemed folly to him now. Dying like this was foolish. To die fighting the enemies of France was glorious, but this? To die at the hands of a fellow Frenchman because of some doctrinal difference in religion that he, Blaise, did not understand, did not care about, could not even remember! There was no glory in this death. He saw it all now. He had spent his life fighting and had left the important things, the lasting things, undone.

Blaise opened his mouth to try again. This time, no sound at all came out. His eyes stared vacantly. He no longer saw de Galle or Gondi. He realized then that he could not see anything.

Blaise de la Roque died without speaking again. It was October 3, 1569, the night of the Catholic victory over the Protestants at Moncontour. The surgeon opined that he had bled to death, which was ironic, since bleeding was believed to alleviate most ills.

Part I

Chapter I

The Cathedral of St. Gatien retained its chill on this Saturday, April 28, 1571, despite the crowd rustling and jostling beneath its high-flown arches. Angling rainbow-like through the brilliant hues of the high choir windows, the sunlight still had a wintry weakness, pale and slow to warmth. Motes of dust stirred by hundreds of feet mingled with smoke from incense and candles and filtered the noon light through a pale golden haze. Where patches of brightness caught the crowd, gowns and doublets echoed the riot of color in the windows above. The dais of the royal family in the south transept facing the altar was not in the path of the sun. The faces looking out over the motley mass of courtiers were only dimly discernible.

The narrow, bearded heads of King Charles and his brother, Anjou, were indistinguishable in the half-light; the soft shadows masked equally the gaunt frailty of the one and the febrile vitality of the other. The dark bulk of Catherine, the Queen Mother, disappeared into the gloom and only her pale, puffy face could be seen behind the slim shape of her daughter-in-law, Elisabeth of Austria. Below the royal entourage, hundreds of bodies shifted and swayed, courtiers, retainers, palace guards, clergymen, the elite of the traveling society of which the King was the heart and purpose. Kaleidoscopically, the forms rippled and settled, shimmered and gleamed, dazzling in their pearls, their gold filigree, their satin, their damask, their white ruffs, their curled hair. In the midst of this brilliance stood the two whom King and Court honored by their presence.

Two people, now a couple, heads bowed together, gravely pronounced the prayers and solemn promises of the long matrimonial Mass. The bride, Anne de Revillars, was slender, long of leg, waist, and neck, perfectly proportioned, and graceful of movement. Her delicate body supported an elaborate gown, pale grey satin laden with hundreds of pearls caught in webs of silver filigree. A white ruff and a lace veil held captive a heart-shaped face. Hair of palest gold trapped in a net of silver and pearls encased her small, proud head. Her eyes gleamed sapphire-blue, cold and bright, as she looked up at her new husband.

Though Anne was six years his senior and tall for her sex, Pierre de Galle towered above her. At seventeen, he was prodigiously tall, as tall as the late King Henry, almost as tall as his own father, who was a giant among men. Though he lacked, as yet, his father's bull neck and massive shoulders, his muscular arms and broad back rippled with lithe strength. Above this full-grown warrior's body, the face, clean-shaven despite the fashion for beards, seemed oddly vulnerable in its youthfulness.

The sun hit Pierre's red-blond hair, striking gold from the short, bronze curls. The tawny velvet of his doublet was slashed with yellow satin insets edged with gold, and his long, well-formed legs were hosed in yellow ending in the

9

ceremonial, bejeweled velvet slippers. Together, Pierre and Anne were like a display of precious metals. Their dress unconsciously mimicked a famous Gobelin tapestry, where Apollo, a bronzed youth against a blazing sky, battles Diana, the silver queen of the night. But the bride's expression, though mature, had neither the wisdom nor the serenity of Diana's arch smile.

Hands joined, they knelt for the final blessing. The Latin phrases came to most only as a sonorous intonation, almost drowned in the roll of the organ. The Archbishop of Tours sprinkled holy water over them; his coadjutor incensed them, standing on the balls of his feet to heave the heavy, gold censer. Then he stepped forward to incense the congregation. The spicy, evocative perfume drifted into the vast interior to lose itself among the lilies, the candle smoke, and the close-pressed bodies. The ceremony was ended, the union made; nothing but the recession remained.

In the parvis before the Cathedral, Pierre and Anne made obeisance to their sovereign. Standing on the Cathedral steps, slightly apart, in white satin and gold shining in the sun, the King had the advantage of height even over Pierre, and managed to achieve an appearance of majesty, which his unhealthy spareness normally prevented. A hush fell on the crowd. The King spoke to be heard by all, not just by the pair that he addressed.

"I came from Normandy not only to escort your queens, my mother and my wife, to their summer lodgings. It was also my wish to be present at this glad and important occasion. To show my joy and to honor you and your families, my faithful subjects, I will hold, two nights hence, a feast in celebration of your union, to which I bid you come." Cheering filled the square, repeating and echoing back on itself.

Horses and litters were brought. The monarch, his brothers, his queens, and the lords and ladies of his court clattered from the square, surrounded by the colorful retinue of his guards, the Hundred Swiss in gleaming white, the Scottish archers in white and red, and the French archers in red, white, and blue.

Attention returned to the wedding couple. Pierre handed Anne into a gilded litter supported by pure white mules, then swung effortlessly into the ornate saddle of a bay stallion, whose immaculately groomed hide shone bright in the sun. The bridal party completed its mounting up, formed itself into a loose procession, and moved along the base of the Cathedral steps, past the chapterhouse, and out into the street going toward the Tour de Guise and the river. Cheers of admiration and approval resounded through the square, until a cacophony of bells rang out and drowned the talk and the laughter. As the last rider disappeared, the mass of spectators broke into eddies and streams, swirled through the open place, and drained into the dark streets and alleys surrounding the Cathedral.

* * *

The vast hall of the castle of Plessis Gaillard rang with the din of merrymaking. Two canopies faced each other across the breadth of an immense table. Under the first sat the bride. Vivacious as always in company, her pale, clear skin flushed with excitement, Anne talked animatedly to her new father-in-law on her right, ignoring for the most part her own father on her left. Opposite, his eyes never leaving her, Pierre sat beneath the second canopy, flanked by his stepmother and Albert de Gondi on the one hand and his father's mistress and his stepbrother on the other. A jumble of nobles, retainers, clerics, and remote relatives crammed the long table. Their age and importance diminished toward the ends, where young men joked, shouted obscenities, and broke into occasional choruses in time with the minstrels. The hubbub of laughter, clinking tableware, and shuffling feet drowned most conversation, and the guests, with more gusto than refinement, grabbed eagerly for the spicy quails and liver pasties of the first meat course.

Anne chattered brightly about how long the ceremony had seemed, how near she had come to laughing at the Archbishop and his coadjutor, the one like an egret, the other like a toad, and how gracious the royal family had been. Duke Raymond de Galle grunted amiably, but listened with only half an ear. He was not interested in women for their gossip. Wishing to be pleasant, however, he refrained from cutting her off sharply, as he did his wife when she plagued him.

The Duke was well satisfied with his new possession, so he viewed Anne, for to his mind nothing in or of the family existed except to serve him. He glanced across the table at Gondi, and nodded to himself. It was right that Gondi should occupy a place of honor at this feast, for he had done much to bring about the marriage: Gondi had suggested that de Galle send out feelers to Anne's father, without even waiting for the mourning period for her first husband to end; he had shown de Galle how to overcome the old man's feigned reluctance; and together, they had bargained as hard as the prize was valuable.

They had done exceedingly well. Gondi is a clever one, thought the Duke, and no mistake: Anne had brought not only her first dowry, but also her deceased husband's domain, and even some additional lands they had been able to extort from her father as a second dowry. It was a fine deal, which pleased de Galle greatly, and they had very much bested the Count de Revillars, which pleased him even more.

De Galle sloshed some wine around his mouth and glanced at Anne's father. The Seigneur de Revillars was a hawk-like man, narrow and bent, with hooded eyes and thinning hair brushed straight back. De Galle, feeling a wave of graciousness to a vanquished opponent, leaned forward to propose a toast, extending his arm past his daughter-in-law. The older man looked up slowly and clinked his tumbler. De Galle laughed quietly as if at a private joke, and brushing against Anne's full bosom with a grunt of satisfaction, dropped back into his seat. With any luck, he thought, she'll bury the old vulture before she's even whelped.

He looked across at Pierre. Though not sharp enough to value the alliance at its true worth, the boy at least hadn't fought it. Wouldn't have had the guts even if he'd wanted to, thought the Duke, forgetting that he had never brooked opposition on any subject. But indeed, he mused, why should Pierre have wanted to fight it?

The Duke bent his ruddy head to smile into the eyes of his daughter-in-law. His great paw held a tiny pasty for her, which she took with a laugh suddenly gone high and nervous.

The Duke was not an original thinker, and his thoughts continued down familiar paths. Our great families are failing: I've an only child (thank God, a son), my wife's first marriage made only one, that old miser a single daughter. The wars are partly responsible — killing the best of the men. Look at Blaise de la Roque, dead with no descendants but a daughter, and didn't I hear she's gone to be a nun? What's left are a queer lot, not worth the hindquarters of a sow.

He stared across at his son so balefully that Pierre flushed suddenly and dropped his knife onto his trencher. The Duke reflected sourly on the many of his son's habits that irritated him — his courtesy to servants and peasantry; his refusal to spur his horses; his reluctance to fight, even in games, or at least with those smaller than himself, which since adolescence had included almost everyone. The list went on and on. Christ's body, he'd even caught him pressing flowers in his prayer book.

It's not that he doesn't have what it takes, the Duke thought. God knows, he's built like an ox and he's had nothing but the best of training, and a lot of it. In fairness, what he is willing to do, he does well. It's just that he doesn't go about it in the right way; he doesn't approach it like a real man.

He's better than the other one, at least, the Duke thought.

The Duke never spoke the name of his stepson, Maurice de La Renaudie. Indeed, he never addressed him or looked at him if he could avoid it. "Your son," he would say to his wife on those occasions when it was necessary to mention him. Chewing slowly and narrowing his eyes, Raymond looked across at the Duchess. She had kept the brat out of the way when they were courting. Well, he thought, she was desperate.

Although not normally a sensitive man, the Duke knew, and had understood at the time, what her position had been — widowed by that fool, La Renaudie, who'd gotten himself, and hundreds of better men than he, butchered like common herd animals. And for what? He belched reflectively. The great Calvin? She hadn't even gotten the body back, not even the head. They threw it into the river when the skin decayed and stank. Yes, she had been desperate. She had dropped her Protestant cant quickly enough. The quick and the dead, he smiled.

He would never have married her for pity, though. He had sensed that her frenzy had a part of pent-up passion. The passion and the panic had enhanced each other in a most attractive way. Even now, a decade later, the memory of those mad months aroused him.

He remembered when he had first seen her son, fourteen but still a puling brat, clinging to his mother like a toddler. He remembered the day he had found him fawning over his mother and had kicked him in his soft buttocks. When she had risen to defend him, he'd slapped her around the head, although he was not normally given to brutality where women were concerned.

To give the bastard credit, her son had learned fast to keep out of sight. He's no idiot, the Duke thought. Drawn in spite of himself to stare at his stepson, he noted the redness of his wet lips against their frame of black hair, observed the nervous flutter of his hands, and listened to the nasal resonance of his voice. God, I would kick him again, he thought, if I wasn't afraid he'd enjoy it.

The Duke stuck a huge finger back into his mouth and pried loose a piece of gristle lodged in the space of a missing tooth. Leaning over, he spat the morsel onto the floor. His great head rubbed against his neighbor's satin shoulder. Gazing down at her breasts, he chuckled cheerfully as she broke off a description of some fancied change in necklines.

The Duke's voice broke into the conversation, booming across the table. "Well, the King's still as knobby in the knees as an underbred cow, and the thinner he gets the more he looks like a pack-ass," he exclaimed. His wife glanced furtively to left and right, a shadow of fear in her eyes.

"I used to think he'd grow into it," the Duke continued. "God knows, his father was built and his grandfather, now, there was a man." He sputtered slightly, and took a gulp of wine to wash down the meat. "Hard to say the Italian ruined the stock," he resumed loudly. "She's not much for looks, but she's tough as a nut." He laughed harshly as the thought of nuts suggested pastimes other than eating. He placed a hand briefly on his daughter-in-law's arm, leaving a mark on the sleeve. The Duke's mistress glared across at him. Anne dropped her hands into her lap. Her lashes fluttering nervously, she hurriedly resumed the conversation.

"I thought His Majesty looked stronger. He carries himself like a King."

"His Majesty." The Duke mimicked her high-pitched inflection so perfectly that even his mistress laughed. Eleanor d'Avrillac, a buxom woman with ruddy, curly hair and intelligent brown eyes, was generally quiet and good-humored. She had kept her position longer than her predecessors by giving generously and asking little.

She turned now to Pierre. "You're going to be kept busy, I suppose, managing your wife's estates," she observed quietly. Her words woke Pierre from what seemed to him a state of enchantment.

The wine and music had cast a dream-like aura over him, but had done so without muting the passionate excitement he felt at his very core. She is so beautiful, he repeated to himself, so beautiful!

Taking his eyes from his wife, Pierre turned and replied. "I think not. My lord father has appointed a steward who will look after them, Herve Dubois, old Herve's son."

Eleanor smiled at him gently. "Well, these burdens will fall on your shoulders soon enough. You're not even eighteen, after all."

Pierre's rejoinder was so sharp it surprised her. "The King reached his majority at thirteen. I didn't know it was a royal prerogative."

She nodded, sympathetic but unwilling to encourage him to complain of his father.

"I don't think I would look to His Majesty as a model of independence," she said. "After all, you know the old saw, 'The King reigns but his mother rules.'"

Pierre laughed. "I thought it was ruder than that, Aunt."

"There are quite a few versions," she said, indicating by her straight stare that she did not intend to recite them for his benefit.

Pierre could not have said precisely why he called her Aunt. It emphasized that she was his dead mother's distant relation and dear friend, instead of highlighting her present tie to his father. Her closeness to his mother, and to himself, which filled his earliest recollections, counted for so much more to him than her later involvement with his father that he had never really focused on the latter.

Although her presence at the Plessis Gaillard of his childhood had been intermittent, her influence had rivaled his mother's — no, not rivaled, but fused with — for she and his mother had complemented each other and set each other off as sun and shadow dance together under breeze-ruffled summer leaves: one with wiry brown hair, the other with a head of fine flax; one impulsively warm, the other gently self-restrained; one with a hearty, earthy voice, the other with a voice like a slow stream, trickling and bubbling through a sunny plain. Eleanor was truly Gallic, while his mother had been essentially English, but whatever their differences, they had had in common an abiding affection and a bond of laughter, lilting infectious laughs which blended together and became indistinguishable.

"They say the King is showing a lot more spunk lately. The boys," Pierre said, gesturing toward an unruly group of youths in russet and chartreuse livery, "were talking to some people in Monsieur's entourage, who said the Queen Mother and Monsieur are furious with the King. They said he handles most of his own correspondence now, without even consulting them. He has even held Council meetings without them."

"They said. He said." Eleanor leaned forward and gripped Pierre's arm. "Listen, Pierre. Everything they say may be true, but you must remember something when you're at Court. Don't gossip with the underlings. Don't believe everything you hear. Don't even listen. The Court's full of people with nothing much to do, people who aren't involved in anything except the mischief they can make. They watch and speculate and talk. It makes them feel grand and it fills up their days. It was all right when you were younger, though, thank God, your father saw to it that you had better things to do than hang around making trouble, but those boys down there aren't fit companions for you any more. You are, or you will be, an important person. Your father's lands and your wife's together are a small kingdom. You are the King's friend. Look for yourself. See what *you* see and hear what *you* hear and make your own judgments. Well, that's my speech for tonight."

They both laughed to relieve the tension. The Duke clapped his hands sharply to hasten the second meat course. The room hushed. With a fanfare of trumpets, a procession of servants entered, dividing to approach the two sides of the table. The files were headed by two servers, each carrying, on a great gilded tray, a marvelous golden beast. The fantastic creations were presented with deep bows: to the bride, a cockatrice constructed of a pig's front and a chicken's back, baked in batter and adorned with golden hooves and claws; to the groom, the reverse image, a gold-trimmed bird with a pig's rear. A rumble of appreciation spread through the room as servings of roast chicken and suckling pig were deftly distributed.

Albert de Gondi watched the uproar with a tolerant smile. He was bored, but would not make the mistake of showing it. The Duchess, at whose right hand he sat, was an odd woman, at once intense and evasive. Conversation with her was more difficult than amusing, but he had done his best by it, as anyone in his position would have. Gondi was acutely conscious of the honor the Duke had paid him, embracing him in the bosom of his family. Though he had worked hard to earn this mark of esteem, it would have been impolitic folly not to appear thankful for it.

He had, as it were, paid his way, no doubt about it. There would have been nothing to celebrate had he not made the marriage his business. The Duke was grateful, and had cause to be: It was a good match, not the best the boy could have made, but good. The Revillars girl made up in money what she lacked in standing, and for all their standing, the de Galles could use the money. They had immense wealth, yes, but like that of so many old families, it was burdened with immense obligations. Moreover, the Duke was an old-fashioned man, who would not bleed his lands for all they were worth.

This is a bastion of the old school, Gondi reflected; we are aeons apart. As the thought passed through his mind, it filled him with an old anger. They are rich without culture, high-handed without merit, brutal without ruthlessness. That man, Gondi viewed the Duke through veiled eyes, that man despises me, I know how much, but he will never know that I despise him.

The rage tide ebbed. Gondi smiled across at the Duke, who answered with a half-wink of pleased complicity. Funny people, these, Gondi thought, with a contrary impulse of affection. Their impervious complacency sometimes awed him, even while it always annoyed him. Worlds came and worlds went, but de Galle always stood for de Galle, and the Duke obviously thought that it always would — if he thought about it at all.

Take this barracks of a castle — Gondi looked about at the cavernous hall, at its vaulted roof, its squat pillars, its irregularly placed windows, narrow and deep in the thickness of the wall. It was so different from the light elegance that Gondi loved. Massive, austere, unrelieved by decoration, ungraced by symmetry, there

15

was no concession here to the dawning of a new age. And yet, daily, the Duke was exposed to the finest in art and architecture, and he had the means to patronize the new styles, if he wished. He simply saw no need to change his ways, or rather, the ways of his forebears.

At Gondi's elbow, the Duchess murmured vaguely, as if proposing an idea to which someone might object, "It is a happy day, isn't it? And we see the future here, before our very eyes."

"Yes, indeed, Madame," Gondi replied convivially, hiding his exasperation and wry amusement behind a gracious look.

The sunlight waned as course followed course. The pauses grew longer between each round. At last, the group broke from the table, which was rapidly cleared and pushed back to make room for the dancing. Torches were thrust into wall sockets; the musicians retuned their instruments; the under-stewards passed among the guests with bowls of fermented cider.

At nine, the flushed group gathered around the table, which had been set for the final collation. A "surprise" dominated the elegant array of cold foods and pastries, a great cake decorated with colored sugar sculptures of the emblems of the two houses — the cerf gallant of Galle, a leaping red hart with a tiny heart between his antlers, and the porcupine of de Revillars. The latter wore a coquettish expression, but the chef had been unable to make its quills look inviting.

Anne laughed and admired, making herself pleasant to everyone, while enjoying the freer atmosphere of the evening buffet. As she exclaimed over the setting for the benefit of her belle-mère, she wondered, inwardly, that the repast, complicated, huge and filling as it had been, should also have been so uninspired. She and her husband — her first husband, she meant — had had a chef, who, though not stylish, had at least known that cockatrices were passé and would never have used as a subtlety something as banal as heraldic symbols. She shrugged and puffed out her lips very slightly. Given the wealth of the family, it must be the fault of the mistress of the house. Ah, well, in time, things would be to her own liking. She would see to that.

As the evening drew to a close, the Duchess and her ladies escorted the bride to her chamber, ceremoniously removed her gown and underclothing, and draped her in a shimmering white nightdress. Nodding gravely, they left her, taking the lamps with them.

She lay staring blankly at the casement, her eyes gradually discerning in the silvery light arches of stone and elaborately carved shutters. She was not afraid. She had been taken before, often, and none too ceremoniously. Her former spouse had been a rough man, strong and confident, not unlike her father-in-law. No wonder they call Raymond de Galle the Red Ox, she thought.

She had not married for this, she reflected, wondering with a touch of disdain whether her boy-husband had deserted his duties. She knew she had been sold by a calculating father to a grasping father-in-law, but it had not been against her will. In a rising mist of somnolence, she cogitated bitterly that with all the possessions in the universe, a woman alone was nothing. Nothing.

He approached the bed where she lay as though unaware, dropping his loose robe from his shoulders. There was a tension in his movements unlike anything he had ever felt or seen, unless it was the convulsions of the cat before it leaps. His legs and arms ached as if a hand in his groin were pulling the nerves and muscles to a converging point, a confluence of singing tributaries roaring toward a dam. The trembling control he exercised over this tumult of sensations sharpened the voluptuousness which pervaded him.

He leaned over and pulled back the heavy coverings. In the faintest of visible light, he could see the curves of her shoulder, her torso, her hip, her thigh, to where her leg disappeared beneath the rough sheets. He ran his hand down her arm, feeling through the satin sleeve the musculature of the upper arm, the knobbiness of the elbow, the hardness of the forearm. Leaning over and parting her hair from the soft lace collar, he pressed his lips against her neck. He gently pulled her over on her back, and his shaking hand slid her gown up to reveal the darkness of hair against her white limbs.

Suddenly overcome, he grasped her shoulders and half fell, half jerked himself across her body. Anguish and joy surged through him as the hot liquid spurted against their bodies and into the folds of her gown. He clung to her shoulders and let the course of feeling flow and ebb. Only as coherence returned to his thoughts did the noise he had hardly heard penetrate his consciousness, the mocking ring of her laugh.

He fell back, a flush of humiliation replacing the passion which had suffused his face. Lowering his gaze self-consciously, he attempted to control his breathing before glancing across at her. Her face was half turned away and wore an expression that even in his confusion he recognized as more sardonic than sensuous. His fading recollection of pleasure was overcome by an indefinable emotion, a bitter mix of injured pride, self-ridicule, and anger.

He lay awake contemplating his resentment until it merged with his returning desire. When he leaned over her again, she seemed asleep. He turned toward the unlit side of the room and gazed into the blackness, filled with a disquiet more piercing than any he had known before.

Chapter II

At the end of the orchard was an apple tree which Athalie visited most evenings at dusk. It was not really unusual in appearance, being the last in a long line of similar shapes, whose grotesqueness became banal through sheer repetition; slightly, but only slightly, out of step with its companions; wicked-looking in its gnarled nakedness, but no more so than the others. A casual passerby would never have remarked on it, but Athalie knew that it had an extraordinary quality, a magnetism which drew all the birds of Fontevrault, it seemed, into its branches at dawn and at dusk. Athalie imagined the old tree in human terms, as the church where the birds said their offices, the marketplace where they gossiped, the dormitory where they whispered after dark. The pictures she created amused her without deceiving her; she knew this was no human phenomenon, nothing that people could explain and so dismiss.

It was a magic place, and it drew her as it drew the birds. Nearly every evening, as the light faded, she walked through the lengthening shadows down to the old tree. She would turn and rest her head, eyes shut, against its trunk, she would press her hands against its rough, cold bark, and she would listen intently to the insane, enthusiastic, optimistic medley of chirping, warbling birds. Eventually, some need satisfied, she would relax, open her eyes, and watch the last sun rays disappear behind the Abbey.

The orchard was long and inclined downward from the Abbey's main buildings. It faced the wall of the great cloister, the bulbous apse of the Abbey Church, and the high, sturdy bell tower. All that spring, as the days had grown longer, Athalie had watched the light and shadow that played on the buildings change in color and intensity, the massive, clustered forms looming black against a varying sky, their bulky silhouettes broken by unexpected bars of slanting luminosity. As the sun set behind them one fine evening in late April, she marveled again at the mass of stone on which the light broke like waves on a rock.

Though familiarity had in no way cheapened its grandeur, the Abbey was by now a familiar sight. It seemed to Athalie, on this lovely spring evening, a different place entirely from the cold shelter she had come to that wintry day almost a year-and-a-half before, when she had seen it for the first time. Nor was it simply that the seasons had changed; she realized that it was principally she herself who had changed. She looked back at the child she had been then with sympathy and a certain detachment. The child had had much to cope with, and she had coped indeed, Athalie thought, with such a touch of pride as a mother might feel for a precocious offspring.

After her father's death at Moncontour, Athalie had arrived at Fontevrault in December 1569, just before Christmas. Rising stark from a denuded, hostile landscape, the Abbey had seemed alien and unwelcoming, crowded yet solitary, huge yet cramped and wall-bound. She had seen Christmas celebrated through the restrained glories of the endless liturgy, sung out by hundreds of voices, full of a genuine gladness in which she had no part. Her longing to join in the monastery's solemn, ethereal, but ever joyful spirit had been unable to overcome the frozen numbness that had possessed her, preventing all feeling. Christmas here had seemed such worlds apart from the gorging, uproarious, chaotic feasting which those outside the cloister waited for eagerly all year long.

Not that Athalie was accustomed to the normal Christmases of the big family at the heart of the big household making merry together with lots of siblings, much giving and getting, many games and tricks and jokes, and, above all, feasting and dancing. Her Christmases had been quiet and somewhat — well, artificial was perhaps the best word. Since she belonged to no family circle of her own, she had celebrated Christ's birth with her father's steward, a good man, and his family, whom she had joined not as a member, but as a guest of honor. Throughout the year, they prayed and ate and played together, she and the steward's numerous children, and each Christmas she gathered with them to feast and receive her presents, better presents than they received. In the early years, she had not questioned the source of the presents. Later, she had realized that though they purported to come from her father, they were the work of the steward or his wife, part of the household duties for which they were duly remunerated.

She had realized other things as she grew older. On the eve of the Epiphany, everyone gathered to cut the great traditional cake and see who would receive the charm and become Monarch for a night. As long as she could remember, Athalie had always found the charm in the crumbled remains of her piece of cake. She had thought, at first, that it was destiny or magic; finally, she had seen how the household conspired to make the master's daughter Queen of the Epiphany. It was a kind sham, but a sham nonetheless.

Athalie remembered her sadness when the magic of the moment had been lost. She smiled wryly. She had been silly, she thought, to have taken seriously something which was only a game, and yet, even though what was lost was an illusion, the loss had been real.

Shaking her head, Athalie brought back other memories to dispel the bittersweet taste. She remembered the time when, as Queen of the Epiphany, she had chosen as her King old Benjamin, the gatekeeper, who was eighty-two and had no teeth and was considered by the assembled party as a very funny match for a fresh young girl.

Another time, she had picked the steward's oldest boy. She remembered the embarrassment which had come over the company, which she had recognized, but had not understood. Whenever her father had been present, she had, of course, picked him.

He had been there the Epiphany before his death. She had, as ever, found the coin in her cake, had been duly crowned, and had in turn crowned her King. How incongruous the gay, beribboned confection had seemed above his eyes, which stared out constrained, sad, and strangely absent, as if intent on a vivid past which made the present seem pale and distant. His manner had cast a pall on the gaiety of the evening. Athalie had not been surprised, for she had known there would be no joy in the exercise. Still, it would have been wrong to pick anyone else.

When news of his death had come one-and-a-half years earlier, she had felt it keenly, not so much in a personal way, for they were almost strangers, but as one would a major, irreparable loss which affects more than oneself alone. Her father was something grand and powerful, magnificent in stature, majestic in bearing — altogether regal, that was the word. She had been to Court, but so long ago, she did not remember King Charles. Her visit was only a haze in her mind; she assumed he must be like her father, younger of course, but splendid and terrible. But there couldn't be many other men like her father; she, at least, had never seen any. His death was to her not an intimate loss, but a tragedy on a grand scale.

She had felt his death in another way, too. Since he was her only direct relative, his death had made her feel that she had been cut adrift from her moorings and that she had lost whatever stability and significance and individuality she had ever had. And then she had come here to Fontevrault, and had felt at first almost devoured by this great, strange warren of a place. By a cruel mischance, her menses had begun at that time, an event she had not known how to anticipate, which had brought her some terror and much discomfort. The place was strange, her body was strange, everything was strange.

Athalie shuddered, partly from the poignancy of her memories, partly from the damp chill of the now dark orchard. She looked up at the buildings, distant in a darkness lit only by the faintest of fading light, and realized that even if she hurried she would not be home before nightfall. Pulling her thick shawl tight, she started up the incline, directed more by instinct than by sight. The ground was soft and damp and gave slightly under her feet. The orchard was quiet now; the birds had long since scattered. A single, wailing voice came through the dark. An owl? Athalie wondered, stopping to listen. She stood still, and the dank, musty, rich spring smell of the earth overwhelmed her, filling her with an almost painful feeling of vitality and promise. The mud is alive and I am alive, Athalie thought. She started up the slope, hopping occasionally from exuberance. Yes, she thought, I am alive and well. I can think back now to those painful, difficult times, because they are gone, and therefore harmless. I have a place and a purpose.

She came out from under the last of the apple trees onto a dirt road which led past the Madeleine and around the Abbey church. Looking up, she stopped, struck suddenly by the unexpected sight of Fontevrault glimmering in the silver light of the moon. Joy and pride clutched at her, joy because this was her home, and pride because, though she knew its homely secrets, it was still glorious.

She knew the long, dusty corridors, the steaming laundry room, the bustling new kitchens, and the draughty old smokehouse. She knew the people, too, the round, red cheeks and redder hands of the cook, the fine, long hands and parchment skin of the librarian, the unformed faces of the novices, the sculptured, timeworn face of her great-aunt, the Abbess. It was all so comfortably familiar, yet out of it rose this otherworldly thing of beauty. Home and heaven, too? Athalie cocked her head, wondering if her elation was not carrying her too far. Both aspects were real, Athalie felt sure, and if she could, she would seize and hold them both.

Athalie hurried up the path, around the apse, and through a narrow corridor into the cloister. Lights wavered through the refectory windows and with the moonlight revealed the outlines of the square, more by darker darknesses than by light. She crossed and took the stairs to the second floor and the Abbess's quarters. Once arrived, she paused outside the low door. A torch in a wall bracket gave off a flaring, uncertain light. Athalie looked up at the flamboyant arch over the door and its ornate stone initials, L B, Louise de Bourbon, Abbess of Fontevrault, ruler of the bodies and souls of hundreds of men and women and of one of the greatest abbeys in France.

The Abbess, Athalie knew, was a personage not to be lightly disturbed. Still, she felt somehow that she had a claim of right on the Abbess's time. The Abbess was Athalie's great-aunt, but it was not just because of kinship or even affection that this was so; there was another reason that she did not fully grasp. She knocked and entered the anteroom, where the Abbess's secretary, Dame Thérèse, sat to screen visitors and answer the Abbess's call; her kind, old face broke into a smile of welcome, as she waved Athalie through.

Louise de Bourbon was seated at a candlelit table, hunched over the Abbey's great book of accounts. As Athalie entered, she straightened her stooping shoulders, left her worktable, and gestured to Athalie to join her by the window. She was of medium height with a lean, sunken frame, which only sparingly filled her black-and-white wool robes. Her face was angular, with a slightly hooked nose, ageless skin and a thin mouth. In stillness, it was an old, hard face, but now, pleasure warmed it and hid its age.

The two sat together on the window seat. The Abbess shut her eyes. The close work over the lists and figures was especially tiring by candlelight. Athalie's shadowy green eyes contemplated the older woman with tenderness.

The Abbess turned slowly to meet her gaze. "I've been so busy, child. I've hardly given you a thought, which is far more my loss than yours." The corners of her eyes creased in a smile.

"Somehow, since Lent, I haven't found my old energy," she continued. "Each year, it takes more out of me."

"Mother, you should not fast so severely. At your age, it is not demanded."

Louise de Bourbon straightened. "I am the ruler of this House and the model God has placed before his people. The Rule says that I must do no less than I ask of my children, and I will live by that law so long as I have breath. But this isn't talk for you."

Unable to contain her emotions any longer, Athalie broke in, "Indeed, what you say is full of interest for me. Indeed... indeed, there is nothing that could interest me more. For I have come, Reverend Mother, to receive your permission to become a postulant in this Order."

"May God blast me for a silly old fool!" The words burst from the Abbess's mouth.

Louise de Bourbon stood and paced across the room; tumultuous thoughts stormed through her mind — anger at her own thoughtlessness in failing to foresee the event and bitterness now that it had come to pass. She had not taken the child at Fontevrault with this in mind. It had been her intention to give her the formation appropriate for a lady of her rank and to send her out to take her place in the world. But now, this other alternative filled her with a deep longing. Would it not be a wondrous thing if Athalie in time assumed the leadership of Fontevrault? To become Abbess was to attain stature beyond anything society could offer and for a better purpose. Yes, she mused, my niece, Eleanor, will follow me, and my great-niece, Athalie, will come after. I am barren, but shall have had my dynasty.

With sudden shame, she turned on herself: Is this for God? Or is it even for Fontevrault? Isn't it rather for the greater glory of Louise de Bourbon? Black resignation etched itself around her pursed mouth. This was an ancient battle in a new form; she had long ago accepted that it would neither be won nor lost in her lifetime.

Resolutely turning back, she met Athalie's puzzled, but trusting gaze. "I should, of course, have seen it coming. Well," she sat down, "it is not too late. The decision is mine, and I say 'nay.' Do you understand me?

"Athalie," she resumed more gently, "I know we have done you much good in your time among us, and truly you needed our help. Your mother loved learning. Her French was as good as her Italian, and I believe she could have conversed in Greek or Latin as well as in either. What she would have thought of your education when you came here, I shudder to think. But you are quick and have learned more than most people consider necessary, especially for a woman. Now you have the tools; you can continue without help as far as your curiosity will take you. My child, though you think you need us, you do not need us anymore. This desire of yours tells me what I should have seen without being told. I have kept you long enough. Indeed, I have kept you too long."

They watched each other warily, each waiting now for the other to break the silence. Finally, Athalie shifted and looked down.

There was a pain in her throat which made her voice tight and strained. "Reverend Mother, why do you think I should leave? Why should I ever leave?" She stared at the blue-and-white tiled floor, blankly noting the hundreds of initials, L B, L B, L B, which testified to the position and power of the Abbess. "How can my decision be wrong?" she asked again.

"Because you are not fit to make such a decision," the Abbess answered, watching a flush of anger suffuse the girl's face.

"Yes," she continued, "I said before that you have acquired the rudiments of an education, but I did not mean to imply that you yet possess any real judgment. Don't be offended, my Athalie," she smiled with sudden tenderness as she saw the girl's eyes fill with tears of pain and rage.

"I don't mean that you have less judgment than is proper at your age. Indeed, you have led a solitary life which has made you thoughtful for your years. But it is your very ignorance of society that makes you too young for the choice you wish to make."

Athalie broke in, "Since I've been here, I've seen people, many people. I've seen the goodness of the people here and their love of God. I know what I want. I want to try to be as good, and I believe that God will help me, as He helped them. Mother, what more do I need to know than that?"

Realizing that the girl was now more bewildered and frightened than angry, the Abbess pondered what to say.

"Yes, you are a reflective child. You have observed the people around you. You have seen the goodness, even the holiness in some, and you have concluded that goodness and Godliness are the same. Though in some cases you may be right, there is more to it than you understand. What you are doing is like trying to tell the colors of a stained glass window from the outside.

"I know many people whose natural, easy goodness makes them effortlessly better than others who expend lifetimes of prayer to improve an intractable bad disposition. Who is the holier, there, is not for us to say. Nor should you conclude that the rigidity of the monastic life will make people good. We are a little universe with a monarch, an aristocracy, tradespeople, serfs. All the struggles and

23

failings you will see outside you would observe here, if you knew what you were looking at.

"Indeed, the fact that there is even less escape from life here than there is elsewhere intensifies faults and often stifles qualities. I could not even say for sure, and may God forgive me for it, that the one true Faith leads to either sincerity or good works. There are snobs, gossips, sluggards, even perverts, who have taken vows in this Abbey, while there are those who do good who look to Calvin for the truth, or even who have no religion at all, God forbid.

"What I'm saying, Athalie, is that what you think you have understood of a neat relationship between a certain belief, a certain life, and a certain way of behavior, is no understanding until you can find your own way, judging yourself rightly, in all paths of life. You see things in an intellectual way, which is normal for someone your age. You have to live longer, and you will come to see that life is not principally a question of belief."

Unconvinced and defiant, Athalie burst out, "No, you haven't understood. This isn't something I have reasoned out. I love this place with my heart; it is my heart that tells me it is right for me. Besides, you were not much older, Madame, when you made the same decision."

The Abbess's face contorted.

"I never made such a decision, or at least not at the time you are referring to. I was put here, whether I wanted or no. Your grandmother was a holy woman." She lingered with a suggestion of sarcasm over the word *holy*. "She believed the second daughter should be the Bride of Christ. My father was only too happy — there was less dowry to pay."

Athalie turned a horrified gaze on the Abbess; an unpleasant, arch expression crossed her face. "Is that why you will stop me from doing what I want with all my heart, because they made you do something you didn't want?" she asked.

The Abbess looked tired. "No, Athalie. You know — I have been happy here. I did not choose it, and God knows at times I've wanted other things, what other women have." She glanced at the girl, wondering whether she could understand what it felt like to be deprived of something that, so far, she seemed not to know existed. "But I have done good work, and have come to love my God. And strangely, though I had no freedom in coming here, yet once I accepted the life, I had more freedom than I would have had elsewhere. Had I stayed home, my father would have married me to some stranger, whose bidding I would have done and whose children I would have borne.

"Whereas, here," she smiled with unmalicious pride, "I am the monarch. As God's representative, I rule women and men alike, which few women outside these walls have done."

Athalie started again, "Mother, then you can understand me when I say that my aim has been to decide what to do with my own life.

"All my life," — the Abbess smiled at Athalie's view of her own longevity — "all my life, I have been thrown here and there as others wanted, with no rhyme or reason. This was the only decision I could make of my own free will." She stopped in an anguish of inchoate emotion.

The Abbess leaned forward and clutched Athalie's wrist.

"I know better than you, child, that a person can decide freely to do the only thing possible, but to do so blindly is mere self-delusion. You must go away, Athalie, and perhaps make the choice when you see that you have more options than just one. Then I will respect your decision."

Athalie did not look up for her final argument, for although she could not give up, she knew she would not prevail. "You let other girls, even younger than I, become postulants. Why not me?"

Louise de Bourbon leaned back. "I cannot stop the families of France, high and low, from ridding themselves of unwanted daughters by sending them to the nunnery. At least by taking those from the poor families I will have saved them from starvation, and the rich, well, I cannot stop them. I do not have to take you."

"Why are you so careful of me?" Athalie asked, wishing for the first time that she had come to Fontevrault with the shield of anonymity.

The old nun's shrewd eyes held Athalie's. "Don't you realize, my girl, that you are not an abandoned farm wench or the dowry-less daughter of a minor nobleman? What you choose, or what is chosen for you, is important. You are an eminent young woman, and when you marry, you will be a very rich one."

Silence fell between them, a tangible, palpable silence, cutting them apart, Athalie felt, pushing them out of reach of each other. When at last she spoke again, it was no longer to persuade, but merely to maintain, through opposition, some contact with the other.

"My uncle, my guardian," she stammered, "he will have something to say." She hesitated, feeling she could say no more. Though she believed her uncle had sent her to Fontevrault for more than mere education, she had no concrete proof that he wished her to take the veil.

The Abbess stiffened and her eyes narrowed. "Yes, your uncle will be disappointed." Athalie was startled at the certainty in her aunt's voice. "I will write to him and explain what is necessary."

As she spoke, the Abbess stood abruptly, her tone and manner signaling that the interview was over. Athalie, too, stood up, and so dominated her aunt by several inches. The realization of defeat filled her, but she remained, despite the unspoken dismissal, wordless, but stubborn in her opposition to the older woman's dictate.

In a harsh voice, the Abbess said, "Send me Dame Thérèse when you leave." The Abbess turned her back and did not watch the girl hurry from the room. Her heart was as heavy as Athalie's.

The secretary entered and stood at the escritoire. Still without turning, the Abbess said, "This letter will go to Sieur Albert de Gondi, Count de Retz. 'Monsieur de Retz...'"

Chapter III

uffled noises drifted from the courtyard into Gondi's apartments. It was the evening of Their Majesties' feast in honor of Pierre de Galle and his new wife, and the castle of Tours hummed with preparations. Gondi paid no attention to the bustle. He stood by the window, his eyes turned inward rather than focused on the scene below, his fingers drumming lightly on the rough sill. The heavy arras at the end of the room was pulled back, and a youth not yet twenty entered the room. Despite their difference in age, Gondi's secretary and cousin, Julio de Gondi, shared with his eminent employer a common look of eager alertness and some small similarity of nose and chin which confirmed their remote kinship.

To that relationship, however distant, Julio owed his position and his presence at Court; the ancestry that allowed him to link his fate to the Count's rising star filled him with pride and gratitude.

Silenced by Gondi's inhospitable look, Julio merely stood aside, waved in the awaited visitor, and withdrew. As the curtain fell into place, Gondi and Maurice Godefroi du Barry, Seigneur de la Renaudie, faced each other across the room. A brief ceremony of salutation was curtly concluded, followed by a few moments of quiet appraisal.

The two were dissimilar in aspect, with the one exception that both took care with their dress, though for different effects. Gondi's clothing was rich and artful — his golden-green brocade and fox fur set off his light brown hair; his well-cut doublet emphasized his trim, athletic figure; and his discreet jewelry suggested rank and opulence. He was a man in whom personal charm, fine health, and distinguished good looks, enhanced by wealth, formed a nearly perfect ensemble.

Maurice, at twenty-five, was half Gondi's age, but though muscular and fit, he did not give the same impression of supple strength. Today, as always, he wore black velvet, unrelieved by colored trim or golden jewelry. It was a manner of dress which should have appeared sober and restrained. Instead, it drew unnecessary attention to his physical attributes and created a curiously sensuous impression.

The doublet, cinched tight above the puff of his pants, accentuated the breadth of his shoulders and hips. Its color echoed his dark eyes and smooth black beard. While Maurice was handsome in a theatrical way, his movements and expressions seemed always to camouflage and deform his basic physique. Indeed, it was difficult to focus on anything about La Renaudie other than his restlessness — the hunching and shifting of his body, the fluttering of his eyelids, and puffing and pursing of his mouth. His hands moved constantly to touch and feel the objects and people around him, to caress his own beard and hair, and to find their way into his mouth. Yet, Gondi wondered, some people find him attractive.

Gondi waved at a straight, narrow chair, which had been placed near the quite unnecessary fire, while remaining himself by the window. La Renaudie slid cautiously onto the hard seat, perspiration rising in his beard. His eyes wandered over the luxurious details which made the room comfortably elegant, but returned irresistibly to Gondi's motionless silhouette. Gondi left the window, settled against the great table, and crossed his arms in easy repose.

"You are always at Court, Monsieur," Gondi said. "For many, many years, I have seen you prominently among the courtiers."

Maurice raised his shoulders and lowered his eyebrows before responding. "Why would I leave, Monsieur? For one such as myself, to be away from Court is to be nowhere."

"Of course, there is no reason why you should have considered leaving." Gondi's voice was pleasing. Unlike the Queen Mother, he had no noticeable Italian accent. His parentage, half Italian, half French, had enabled him to become perfectly bilingual, and yet, he spoke French with a difference. It was as if the Italian in his background had softened and rounded his well-articulated French, giving it a smooth, lilting delivery, which did not startle or offend.

"The past has been forgiven," Gondi resumed, "many times, in fact. And no Christian visits the sins of the father on the son. Still, I wonder that you are satisfied to live quietly in the bosom of the royal family. Especially here, on the Loire, which has seen such horrible things. Even Tours has lived its bloody days; they did not concern you, perhaps. It is Amboise that I am thinking of most of all. It puzzles me that you can frolic with the living at Amboise without feeling the eyes of the dead upon you."

A flash of red rage ripped through Maurice's head, as it always did whenever anyone mentioned, however fleetingly, the now famous Conspiracy of Amboise. Maurice had been fourteen that day in March 1560, when his father's plan to kidnap the young King François had led to the massacre of all the conspirators. The boy had only known that his father had disappeared in circumstances which left his mother speechless with terror and which threatened their property, their rank, their very lives. But later, when his mother's remarriage had guaranteed their personal safety and his title, Maurice had satisfied his curiosity. Then, he had eavesdropped and pried, interrogated and reconstructed. He had seen, as with his own eyes, the tortures, the hangings, the drownings, had heard the screams, and had breathed the stench. From the first confusion to the aftermath of decay and epidemic, he had relived each terrifying instant through the memories of a hundred onlookers and participants. Every retelling brought him a queer satisfaction, a kind of climax and a release. At first, the process was only partly understood, but later he recognized and cultivated the brilliant flash of red, the exquisite tingling in his groin, and the shuddering, buzzing sensation in his head and shoulders.

As the throbbing subsided, he looked up to find Gondi gazing thoughtfully at him. His eyes are quite mad, Gondi noted to himself, wondering uneasily whether the condition they indicated would help or hinder his plans. Maurice swiveled on his seat, savoring his now subsiding emotions. His pleasure and anger abruptly flickered out, leaving him sweaty and tired. He wondered what he was expected to say.

"As Monsieur knows, my stepfather's presence on the Royal Council requires his attendance at Court, and it is natural that I should be here, as a member of his family."

"Yes, I know your situation. What I was asking was how you yourself feel about your situation, which is less obvious. But no matter."

Suddenly afraid that his loyalty to the Crown was in question, La Renaudie protested earnestly, "I am honored beyond my deserts by the opportunity of companionship, dare I say friendship, with the King and his brothers. I know, of course, that I owe all this to the position and loyalty of my stepfather and to the generosity of the royal family, for which I am most grateful to them all, but particularly to the royal family. I can assure you that my gratitude, my devotion is all the more in light of, in light of — the past."

He wriggled and smiled wetly in so creditable an imitation of a lap dog that Gondi could barely contain his amusement.

Truly, this young man has excellent possibilities, he thought. "Believe me, La Renaudie, I don't doubt for a second that you appreciate your opportunities. I have long admired how you have turned to advantage your proximity to the royal brothers to create an intimacy with them — or at least with the Duke d'Anjou — which neither your position nor your background justifies. In years gone by, when Anjou was but a boy, I wondered why a man of your years preferred his company to that of men — or women — of your own age.

"Even now, your friendship would puzzle the casual observer. You are twenty-five and Anjou is barely twenty. But I am no longer bemused. I have come to understand or at least to imagine what his attraction is for you. People of your type like them young, the younger the better, I am told. And that, of course, is to speak only of your physical pleasure, which I am confident matters less than your ambition.

"No, indeed, what concerns me is that you have become so attractive to him. The son of a Protestant traitor could hardly become the favorite of so Catholic a Prince, unless... you have taught him to look to you for something which he believes he cannot find elsewhere. Now, perhaps you have certain qualities which are, in fact, irreplaceable — that I do not know. The point I am making is that you have taught the Queen Mother's dearest son habits — shall we say — which she would hardly appreciate."

La Renaudie lifted his hands to smooth down his beard. Sweat ran down his palms into his cuffs. How could Gondi know, he thought frantically. Though Maurice could think of no act of indiscretion, yet he could not be sure that Gondi or his spies had not seen something, sometime, somewhere, and yet... maybe it was a bluff.

Time stood still. Absurdly, a childhood memory flashed through Maurice's mind: his first joust against a man instead of a target. How the minutes had become hours as he had rolled and thundered toward the massive figure of his opponent and the terrifying point of his lance.

It had seemed then, as now, as if time had simply stopped.

He jerked his mind back to his present peril. He should say something, argue, shout denials, perhaps even hit the man. Seconds passed in an agony of indecision.

The seconds were enough for Gondi to know that he had discovered the truth. Careful to keep the satisfaction from his voice, he said sternly, "Don't try to deny the obvious. You are indeed lucky that, so far, I alone know the truth."

La Renaudie looked at him with glazed, bewildered eyes.

"You can imagine what the Queen Mother would do to you, if she even suspected. Anjou is her pride. The idea of sharing him in marriage, even in the most advantageous of marriages, fills her with terror. Only ambition for him and the belief that she can control another woman bring her even to contemplate it. But to share her son with you," he paused contemptuously, "a man whose, whose dowry — What shall I call it? — would be nothing but perdition, dissension, and shame, well, such a liaison, as you can imagine, would not survive an instant beyond the moment she learned of it. Your father's death would seem merciful compared to the fate she would arrange for you. You know," he paused in mock reflection, "she watched while your father's body was quartered and hung on the gates of Amboise. She might make young Anjou watch while your miserable carcass was similarly distributed." The thought that Anjou might enjoy it darted across Gondi's mind, and he laughed abruptly.

For once, La Renaudie's body was completely still. He had passed beyond thoughts of denial, paralyzed by a confusion of images of himself dying, Anjou laughing like Gondi, his father's corpse in pieces, the Queen Mother, his stepfather and all the Court applauding. He covered his eyes, but his ears continued to ring with the applause.

"But," said Gondi, "the Queen Mother does not yet know."

La Renaudie straightened, feeling his wet clothing rub under his armpits, and looked at Gondi with great, mournful, staring eyes. A muffled bell rang six-thirty. Maurice started.

How little time had been required to blight his harvest. He could still save himself. If worst came to worst, he could burst from the room now, and make a run for it. He could disappear into the Southwest, wait for a renewal of civil war, and throw his lot in with the Protestants. They would almost surely welcome him. He was, after all, the son of their hero, the first Calvinist to break the chains of passive resistance, the father of this endless struggle.

Yes, that would be possible. But deep in his heart, La Renaudie doubted that the Protestants would prevail. He had said what he believed: Court was the only place for someone with long-term ambitions and no wealth.

For years now, he had studied to further those ambitions. He had watched the decline of the King from pale, scrawny adolescence to his present skeletal imitation of manhood. He had observed the comparative robustness of Anjou and the esteem in which he was held because of his wit, his culture, and his supposed military prowess. He had given Anjou odds on becoming king against the chance of his brother's surviving or procreating. It was a careful study to pick the winner and to exploit his one great weakness, which his family and courtiers ignored, which no one but he, and now this cunning schemer, had yet recognized, and all for nothing. The years of patient work, artful cajolery and exquisite flattery, the delicate balance of self-assertion and self-effacement, the model courtship, all were lost, lost if he stayed and lost if he left.

Gondi strode out of the shadows to stand by the fire, his figure suddenly a blaze of color. He spoke down at the hunched black shoulders and averted dark head.

"The question is, What should be done? I have considered all the alternatives, starting of course with the obvious one of destroying you. That is certainly what my mistress, the Queen Mother, will require, if she ever learns of what you have done. But considering further, I am not sure that the interests of the Crown, or even her own interests, would best be served in that way.

"It would be a most wasteful solution. Obviously, you cannot remain here to complete Anjou's education in perversion, but what he has already learned from you, he will not forget, even if we cut you into pieces and scatter you over France. Moreover, I think we would have destroyed a potentially useful servant of the Crown."

La Renaudie looked up at Gondi, desperate entreaty flooding his face.

"So," Gondi continued, "I have devised a plan which will remove you from Anjou's orbit and will give you the opportunity of showing some of that gratitude you spoke of earlier." Gondi smiled grimly.

"This opportunity arises because I need information about the Protestants. Whatever your virtues and vices, you have one asset which only death can destroy. You are La Renaudie. Because of your name and blood, there is a bare chance that they will admit you to La Rochelle, and perhaps even to their councils. Though I have many servants more worthy and more reliable than you, none has such an advantage. So, it is to you that I have decided to confide a delicate mission. If you perform well, I will feel justified in keeping your secret. If not... " Gondi shrugged. Maurice dropped his gaze, and Gondi continued smoothly.

"You will go to La Rochelle, where you will find the Admiral de Coligny and his followers. You will send me accurate, complete, and absolutely confidential information. What I will require further, I will let you know in due course. In order to be accepted by the Protestant leaders, you will, of course, have to convince them that you have returned to the religion of your fathers, or your father at any rate. Your departure from Court will follow as the natural consequence of your relapse. Your safety, once among the Huguenots, will require that absolutely no one know that you are engaged in my service. They make short work of spies."

Though moments before he himself had thought of fleeing to the Protestants, hearing the idea from Gondi terrified La Renaudie. "Monsieur, you must know that what you ask is impossible. Why, since I came here, since I came to Court, my bread and butter, my name, indeed my life, have depended on my practicing the religion of Rome."

Suddenly suspecting a trap, he added, "Which, of course, I have adopted in full sincerity."

"Come, come," said Gondi. "My loyalty to Rome is well known. I would not ask you to go against your conscience, and I am not trying to make converts for Monsieur Calvin. I am sure that you will be able to serve not only the King, but the Church itself, while in my service. True, your apparent relapse into heresy will not sit well here at Court, but there is no real danger, I shouldn't think. We are, after all, at peace with the Protestants. At any rate, I thought we had agreed that you are to leave soon, one way or another."

"What of my stepfather? What of Anjou?"

"Your departure will save you from harm here, and if it becomes desirable for you to return, I will try to see to it that you can come in safety. I can do no more for you."

"It will be the end of everything with Anjou."

"The penance suits the offense," Gondi replied dryly.

"But how can I persuade the Protestants to welcome me with open arms and to take me into their confidence? I abjured their faith eleven years ago, and have, of course, never looked back."

Gondi shrugged. "The prodigal son's return I leave to your paternity and your obvious abilities at dissembling. There really is no alternative, you understand. Leave soon. I will find a way to give you instructions on how to communicate your reports. Don't come to me again, unless I send for you. Now, you must rejoin your stepfamily. The feast will be beginning, and you'll be missed."

* * *

The castle at Tours was not a festive place. Rising from the Loire's banks, it had been built to defend a major river crossing. Its military function had determined its nature. Plain, old, and monumental, it was a medieval fortress, not a palace. Though it had served well enough as a royal residence in ruder times, its shabby austerity and comfortless disorder oppressed and repelled eyes grown accustomed to the grace and symmetry of the Renaissance.

Notwithstanding the castle's forbidding aspect, the servants of the Crown had proved equal to the task of transforming it into a fitting site for the great feast the King had ordered for Pierre and Anne. Torches on stands and in wall brackets dispelled the gloom of its passages and stairways and illuminated, with blasts of light, the vast cavern of the great hall. There, long tables placed around three sides of the room left ample room for dancing. Their Majesties' best and richest tapestries covered the walls, concealing most of the dark, rough stone and framing

31

the gaping white maw of the huge mantel with somber greens and browns. In the fireplace, an immense blaze, capable of roasting two stags end to end, not only radiated a heat that was intolerable close up and uncomfortable even at several meters, but with the hissing of its logs, whispered promises that tonight the horn of plenty would flow for all. The weather had crowned these efforts with a still, clear night. The window slits gave glimpses of a glory of shimmering starlight multiplied by the river's reflections.

So large was the crowd of guests that the royal cutlery was quite depleted. The great among them received individual knives, spoons, and goblets; the lesser gentry were satisfied to use their own knives and to share their jugs of wine. These were the old ways, and gave no cause for shock or injury. Indeed, the stewards agreed among themselves, the new luxuries of individual place settings not only drained the royal treasury, but encouraged theft and drunkenness. Be that as it may, the crowd enjoyed its meats, whether nibbled or wolfed, fingered or pronged. It was the general consensus that the digestion of so copious a meal would require many hours of dancing.

As the last dish was cleared away, King Charles led out the lovely bride to open the dancing. In a gown which shimmered like topaz, Anne blazed in golden glory, quite eclipsing the thin, dark monarch. As the slow steps of the pavane brought them together, she flashed him a brilliant smile, full of a joy that was entirely unfeigned.

The moment seemed to her a lofty, dizzying peak, the culmination of her desires. Its symbolic significance far outweighed its objective importance, for it was not only an achievement in itself, but it held out a promise for the future. A door had opened, through which she thought she glimpsed an avenue of escape from the eternal rhythm of householding, birthing, and dying.

Anne could not remember when she had first perceived life as a pallid, tasteless travail. It was a vision born from watching her mother's tired face and listening to her dull talk. The young Anne had seen, stretching before her as before her mother, a multitude of days which would be indistinguishable but for the weather and a handful of years which would only seem different as age and illness narrowed the slender scope of life. In fear and loathing, she had sought a remedy for life's implacable, insipid repetitiveness, and with the coming of maturity, she believed she had found it in novelty, beauty, and success. What she had now, she vowed, she would never lose.

She curtseyed low at the dance's end. As the King raised her and led her to Pierre, her hand fluttered in his, lingered a moment, and reluctantly withdrew. Charles' face had an unaccustomed rosiness, and his voice was cheerful and strong as he addressed the groom.

"This union of two great and loyal families honors both and strengthens our realm. It pleases us greatly."

He leaned forward and patted Pierre's shoulder. "She is a wonder to behold," he said, "and dances like a queen. I wish you both much joy. I know you will grace our Court in happy times and fight for it in hard times. And may God give you many strong sons, loyal subjects for my service."

The surrounding guests laughed and clapped. Pierre doffed his plumed cap for a deep bow. His mouth smiled, but his eyes looked blank and dazed.

"Come, Pierre," the King said, prodding him with his fist. "Take out your beautiful wife, and I will escort my Queen."

The two couples weaved, circled, and cavorted in a brisk galliard. Anne guarded her face, schooling it to show the emotions a young bride should feel: demure admiration for her King and bashful amorousness for her husband. The room buzzed with approval.

Eleanor d'Avrillac, standing next to Raymond de Galle, watched Pierre and Anne alternatively, as the dance swung them around.

"Though he hardly knows her, he seems already to love her," she observed.

"Why should he not?" grumbled de Galle, his eyes following Anne's slim figure. Elie smiled at the Duke. They were old lovers, and she did not delude herself that de Galle's eyes had not wandered and he after them in the years of their liaison. But surely not here, she thought with a sudden frown.

"Raymond," she said, "now that Pierre is married, shouldn't you give him some responsibility? Someday, God willing, many years from now he will have great responsibilities indeed. It would be best if he were prepared. Forgive me. I only say what I think his mother would say were she alive. Perhaps it is not my place." She dropped her head uncomfortably.

De Galle looked down from his great height. "Responsibility," he replied, "is not something that is given; it is taken. The boy is not ready. He is a dreamer, which is the same as saying that he is still a child." His eyes returned to Anne, and took on a distant look. "He should make sons on her," he said, as if to himself.

The dance concluded in a long, sweet harmony of lute and oboe.

The musicians struck up a new tune, and lords and ladies filled the floor. Raymond said curtly, "I must dance with my wife. I will come for you anon." With a half-bow, he left her. Eleanor stared again at Anne and Pierre, as they took their places in the dance line. She felt strong, if undefined, misgivings which bewildered and troubled her. The match was so perfect as to appear foreordained, yet she knew that the pleasure she felt obliged to express was far from genuine.

She watched Anne curtsey deeply and poise herself for the dance, one delicate hand hovering over Pierre's arm. She is fair as a goddess, Elie thought. No wonder both father and son are besotted by her in their different ways. Yet, to dispassionate eyes, she seems cold, metallic almost, like a burnished mirror which reflects the viewer instead of giving of itself. Or are you jealous, she asked herself mockingly, because she is more beautiful than you ever were and twenty years your junior? She shook her head.

That isn't it, she thought. I never envied Pierre's mother, who was even lovelier to look at than Anne, and unlike Anne, was as good as she looked. Giving up on the puzzle, she let her eyes wander idly over the silks and velvets, seeing colors rather than faces, until a black spot arrested them. Focusing on the face above the dark figure, she saw it was La Renaudie's. Maurice was looking out over the dancers with a fixed stare. His expression startled Eleanor. She groped for what it conveyed, and concluded with a shock that he looked terrified.

In fact, the emotion Maurice was experiencing, whose reflection Eleanor saw expressed in his face, was not unalloyed terror, but terror submerged in seething resentment. The glitter of the ball, crowning his stepbrother's happiness, momentarily epitomized the unfairness of life. Pierre had everything, however little he deserved; he, Maurice, had nothing, however much he merited. From the time his father's fall had annihilated his boyish hopes, nothing had gone right. God knows how many times he had fought against the paralysis of envy, but it seemed that every time he made the effort to struggle from one of life's troughs, some implacable force toppled him from his precarious perch into a yet more fearful abyss, leaving him with little hope and much hatred.

He had never forgiven his father for ruining them all. He despised his name and what the name stood for, and it galled him unspeakably to be forced by Gondi to rely on them for his present salvation. From the ruins his father had left, his mother had salvaged what she could, but only at the cost of their dignity. Instead of thanking her, Maurice blamed her, laying his own subservience at her door. None of her achievements, or even his warped affection for her, had succeeded in softening his contempt for her.

Despite the adversity of his early years, he had never completely abandoned hope. The blows that had laid him low had been suffered indirectly, and he had consoled himself with the idea that once he was master of his own destiny, he would be free to climb life's peaks unimpeded. But now, he was down again, his delicately nurtured schemes brutally uprooted. He would have felt that it was useless to go on, but his hatred — for Gondi, for Pierre, for everyone who possessed the power and fortune he longed for — triumphed over his despair.

He caught Elie's eyes fixed on him, and rubbing the back of his hand wearily over his forehead, turned away. Her puzzled gaze followed him until it lost him in the crush.

"Madame," Gondi's smooth voice broke into Eleanor's reflections. "Will you honor me?" With an amiable smile he extended his arm in a courtly gesture of welcome.

Gondi admired Eleanor d'Avrillac's honest good looks. While it was not his practice to poach on another's domain, at least in matters of the heart, he felt that brief, innocent contacts such as this were among the simpler and more legitimate pleasures of Court life.

An allemande swept them up in a breathless whirl, and they continued together as the music melted into the slow ballet of another pavane. On the third round, de Galle loomed up to assert his rights of possession. He led Eleanor away, leaving Gondi to savor an instant of solitude before plunging back into the overwhelming press of company. The solitude was so relative as to be illusory, and knowing it would last mere moments, he relished it all the more. The role he had created for himself — the affable courtier, the able politician — required that he be sociable, but he had an affinity for aloneness that few would have suspected. These days he was more vulnerable than usual to the claims of others, his wife, who was sometimes a buffer and sometimes a refuge on occasions like this, being too pregnant to be at Court.

He lingered on amidst the spectators, watching the flushed, concentrated faces of the dancers. Although more people were dancing than the area could comfortably hold and many of these had drunk to excess, the discipline of the dance imposed a semblance of order on the scene. The two lines of bodies weaved around the floor, marching rhythmically to the music's cadence, bowing and swirling to its flourishes. It was a fair sight, albeit a familiar one, and it lightened his heart. Well, he thought with more cheerfulness than resignation, I may as well get to it.

He danced dutifully, or warmly, as the occasion warranted, with wives and daughters of various notables, before escaping again, this time to a corner of the now stuffy room. The hall's multiple odors — pungent sweat and acrid meat overlaying the original bittersweet mélange of herbs and smoke — oppressed him; for relief, he approached a nearby window, where, wooden shutters pulled back, the cold night air poured through unimpeded. Stretching his neck, he could see highlights of moonlit water below. The rushing and eddying interplay of dark and light showed plainly how the river ran high and fast tonight. Fickle bitch of a river, he thought with wry fondness. You're quiet enough now, but tomorrow, rainstorms or melting snow may turn you loose on our towns like a mad dog. And then, in summertime, you will dry up 'til you look like a row of sandbanks with puddles in between, instead of a royal riverway.

Gondi shook his head and inhaled deeply. The heavy dinner and the constant noise had made him befuddled, stale, and tired. As the biting breeze washed over him, he recognized his discomfort for what it was, boredom. It was all too much — too much gourmandise, too much drink, too much gaiety. What was worse, it surfeited him in exactly the same way as a hundred other soirées which had glittered and ultimately palled just as this had. How well he remembered his first ball, he thought. The last detail of its menu, its conversations, and its music had impressed themselves indelibly on his adolescent mind. But this? He doubted he would remember it had happened a week from now.

He turned to rejoin the revelers and nearly collided with the Spanish Ambassador. Don Francés de Álava lifted an eyebrow at Gondi, and said, "Your mien is uncommonly serious for so festive an occasion. What is worrying you, my friend, or shouldn't I ask?"

Gondi gazed warily at his interlocutor, but answered pleasantly enough, "I had absolutely nothing on my mind, Signor, which is precisely what was bothering me. My stomach is too full and my head too empty for me to be content. I was reflecting sadly that in years gone by I would have been ecstatic over an occasion like this. A person who has lived through too many 'evenings' to enjoy another must be getting old, don't you agree?"

Álava's throat rumbled in a harsh imitation of laughter. "Are you fishing for compliments, my dear de Retz? I watched you dance earlier. I thought how dapper and elegant and healthy you look." There was envy, bordering on malice, in his tones, which robbed the words of their graciousness.

"The expression is 'well-preserved,'" Gondi interjected, his eyes twinkling.

The tirade which followed was delivered in the grating, priggish manner which had made the Ambassador the object of almost universal dislike. "Stop your foolery," he said. "I am old. I feel it when I wake, I feel it at meals, I feel it at every time of day. I am stiffening in the joints. I cannot digest my food or void myself. I cannot sleep and I cannot get up. I have no sympathy for the troubles of those younger than myself. Their ills seem inconsequential next to the ruthless scourge of old age."

Moved in spite of himself, Gondi answered rapidly, "Come, Don Francés, don't talk so. Why man, you're hale enough by the look of it."

But he knew, as he watched Álava, that his statement was only half true. Though there was no visible mark of illness, the older man appeared worn, though as much by cares as by age. His skin was finely lined and seemed transparent about the eyes, his hands were thick-jointed with arthritis, and his calves showed thin and stringy through his wrinkled hose.

Indeed, Álava had not exaggerated his feelings. He often felt, as he did now, that he was beyond enduring the hard life his post imposed. It was a privileged life, he knew, but demanding and often unrewarding. Privy to vital secrets and intimate with the great, an ambassador was also the butt of the petty spite of kings and the jealousy of commoners. Added to the hardships suffered by all who lived at Court — the constant traveling, the scramble for lodgings, the irregular and basically unhealthy regimen — were burdens peculiar to being a foreigner, indeed, at times, an enemy. Moreover, there were no periods of escape to the sovereignty and comfort of one's own hearth. Álava sighed. If it were not for the trust King Philip placed in him, which filled him with a fierce pride, he would have retired years before.

That he himself, by his impatience and his intransigence, made his own life more difficult was something which he did not have the honesty to recognize. Álava collected his wandering thoughts to focus on the present conversation.

"I have been wanting to talk with you, Albert," he said to Gondi, "about matters of concern to us both."

Gondi's look darted apprehensively around the room and settled on Álava's face. "Unless my instincts lie, such a conversation would be inappropriate at any time and in any place, and certainly this is neither the time nor the place for anything but frivolous chatter."

"On the contrary," Álava said, purposely disregarding the first part of Gondi's objection, "in my experience, there is no place like a crowd for a private

36

conversation. All observers are persuaded of its innocence, and none can overhear."

The Ambassador settled back against the shutter to ease the weight on his legs during what he hoped would be a long and fruitful discussion.

"You misunderstand me deliberately," Gondi said. "To be seen with you at all is dangerous. The Queen Mother was not overly fond of you before, but when she saw your letter accusing her of conceiving a child by the Cardinal de Châtillon, and her son, the King, of falling into bed dead drunk every night, well, since then she hates you with an implacable hatred."

"You wrote that letter. It was a vicious forgery!" Álava sneered.

"So you would say."

"So you know!"

The two men glared at each other, then Álava continued more quietly, "I don't know why you wish to foster hatred between my master and your mistress. You are making a terrible mistake. This is what I must make you understand. I am even willing to forget the past. We should work together. There is so much to be gained by working together, and it is so stupid to give up the gains for nothing. It surprises me, de Retz, because you are not a stupid man. You Italians are too subtle to be wrong-headed or to let profit slip through your fingers."

Álava permitted himself an acid smile and shifted uncomfortably on his spindly legs.

"I am not Italian, Ambassador," Gondi hissed. "I am a servant of France."

"Believe me," Álava resumed sharply, "it is as a servant of France that I address you, as you will see if I am permitted to continue. What I wish to say is that I believe we, that is, our respective monarchs, have many interests in common, which have been hidden or forgotten as a result of the long hostility between our countries. Times change. The Peace of Cateau-Cambresis is now more than a decade old. There is no longer any necessity for us to continue to act like two boxers circling to land a punch."

"Forgive me, Ambassador," said Gondi, "I wonder, is the hostility between France and Spain of which you and I are both so much aware, imaginary, as you claim, or real, as our recent history would seem to indicate? True hostility between nations cannot be willed or wished away by a couple of well-meaning individuals."

"Precisely, precisely, my boy," Álava said, ardor for his argument beginning to animate his face and gestures. "It is necessary to distinguish between true and imagined hostility. I say that France has a mentality of enmity to my country which flows from our past regrettable conflicts, but which does not in fact reflect present realities.

"Now, it is the job of statesmen and rulers to discern their people's true interests through the fog of hysteria and confusion which commonly passes for public opinion and to guide the actions of the State accordingly. In that manner, public opinion itself is slowly brought around to a truer appreciation of the affairs of the nation."

Gondi's eyes gleamed. There were few things he loved more than an argument, and he had met few people who could argue with greater conviction than Álava.

"The only problem with what you say is this: that the premise has not been established. You have not shown me how I have failed to grasp that France's welfare is tied to Spain's favor."

Forgiving the irony, Álava exclaimed, "This is exactly the purpose of our talk. Now, let me explain why you, Albert, are so uniquely qualified to see my point. First, I do not think that you share the prejudices of some of your colleagues. We have understood each other in the past, despite certain misunderstandings, shall we say. Second, you are as capable a diplomat and courtier as anyone at Court."

Gondi bowed sardonically and interjected, "Barring yourself, of course."

"No, no," the old man said, waving both hands angrily. "Attend to my words."

"Believe me, I am." Something cold in Gondi's voice brought home to Álava that Gondi was, indeed, attentive, and that realization stilled his agitation. After a moment's pause, he resumed quietly, "Third, and most important, I believe that you are uniquely qualified among all who hold power in France to understand why the fates of France and Spain flow down the same course.

"You are not just a diplomat. You are a businessman, a banker, and a merchant. You know that peace is essential to wealth and that wealth is the font of a nation's welfare. Is it not true, Alberto?"

"You speak truly," Gondi replied in a low voice.

"Now, there can be no peace in enmity with Spain. You will soon see the Turkish infidels receive their just deserts. France has favored the Turkish Empire for years just to keep us occupied in the East. I tell you now as a certainty that it will be to no avail. Once that situation is corrected, we shall be free to crush the revolt in the Low Countries. Let there be no misunderstanding — my master, King Philip, intends that all Dutch folk be loyal Catholic subjects of His Majesty, or dead. We will brook no interference in the Netherlands.

"But," he smiled wanly, "I digress. What I want you to understand is that there is no reason why you should not be as pleased as King Philip at these results. France is the eldest daughter of the Church, it has always been said, and France will rejoice with Spain to see a Pax Christiana restored to our poor, torn, confused world."

Gondi leaned forward to speak, but stopped at the sight of the Ambassador's face. Álava's eyes shone with fanatic ardor. Gondi understood suddenly that it was not good birth or uncommon abilities which had ensured Álava's success with his monarch, but his gift of seeing the world through the same eyes and speaking with the same voice as his master. It was principally this same attribute that made the French Court hate and fear him.

"You see, de Retz, if you help us, or at least if you do not hinder us, we will be able to do much for you. For one, there will be peace among the lands of Europe. For another, your own Huguenots, who are a viper in the bosom of France, take solace and aid from the Protestant and infidel forces. They will collapse if they can no longer get that support, and if you act strongly against them. Indeed, Spain will gladly help you to crush them, with money, arms, and soldiers, if need be."

"Signor," Gondi broke in, but Álava continued unheeding. "Then there will be peace in France, and France will once again be great."

"Ambassador," Gondi said sharply, "to listen to such talk is treason, as you well know. You do me no service to speak to me in this manner."

"Nay, Monsieur, you misunderstand my gist. I am talking about assistance, not aggression. It was my belief that, if you knew what I know, you would see more clearly to guide the destinies of France."

The Ambassador's features sank into an expression of injured melancholy. "I have been very candid with you, Albert, perhaps more than I should, but it is because I trust you and respect you."

Gondi stood silently, lost in thought. After a few moments, he turned slowly and said, "I don't disagree with your logic. There is no doubt that strife — internal and external — has sapped the great strength and richness which is the heritage of this country.

"I would be a fool to pretend it is not so. Even though, of course, I would prefer you to believe otherwise, I know you are too astute and too well informed not to see the stark facts which are obvious to all thinking observers of my country.

"First, our wars with Spain, then our civil wars, have wreaked havoc in the farmlands, have killed too many of our able young men, and have depleted the treasury to an alarming point. We both know all this. It follows, then, that peace in which to rebuild our lost prosperity is what we need. Moreover, I am well known for my Catholic sentiments, so you knew you could arouse my sympathy for your goals by suggesting that it would be to our benefit to obtain peace at the expense of the Protestants." He smiled wryly, and Álava beamed back encouragingly.

"But," Gondi paused and raised a finger, "but, I am still not persuaded that Spain can accomplish all you say it can. We bankrupted ourselves fighting you, it is true, but Spain, too, defaulted. You remember, I'm sure, that we were both unable to meet our obligations in 1557. That's not so long ago. Let me see," he calculated quickly, "fourteen years — it is an instant in the history of a nation. Why are you so cocky now?"

Álava ran his hand feverishly through his thin white hair so that it stood up wildly from his forehead. "My dear Gondi, must I remind you of a source of wealth which Spain and only Spain has — American gold, and even more, American silver. That is a well which will never go dry. We can accomplish anything — anything, I tell you true.

"Fourteen years is nothing in normal times, but these times we live in are like no other. Things change daily, for better, and sometimes for worse in Spain's case, for better. Spain has caught hold of the good part of the changes these years have brought. The sun never sets on our Empire," (Gondi smiled at the cliché), "and wealth pours into our coffers. But a greater source of strength, I believe, is that Spain has cast aside the evil changes to which this century has given birth. We are strong because we know what we believe. We have held firm to our Faith, whereas France is a country divided against itself, weakened not just by the devastation of man, but by spiritual corruption. My master would see Christendom strong again, in the strength of the Faith."

As the Spaniard broke his tirade to take a breath, Gondi interjected, "And what of England, brother Álava? How will Spain bring England back into the fold, now that Elizabeth rules instead of Mary? Or was England on your laundry list with Turkey and Holland and France?"

Álava's face closed up tight. He replied with unaccustomed brevity, "We will take care of that, too. I can say no more."

The two men stood silent for a while. "Well," Gondi resumed. "I am still in the dark as to what you want of me. Perhaps it's just as well."

"I don't want anything, Alberto. Nothing, except that you see where your own best interests lie. If peace comes, commerce will flourish. Why should you and your children not reap the fruit of your labors? Hurricanes in nature cannot be prevented, but hurricanes in the affairs of men can be forestalled. I only ask that you think about what I am saying and that you keep your mind open to me. I believe I can be useful to you."

"Really, Don Francés, you're impossible. What you mean is, I can be useful to you."

"And so?" replied the old man, without the slightest discomfiture. "Why should we not be useful to each other? We each have our country's best interests at heart, and I say those interests are the same. As for your own interests, you must know that my King does not forget his friends. Your cousin, Jerome, has had reason to be grateful for his good will."

"I was going to ask you, Álava. Why are you coming to me, instead of to Jerome?"

Álava paused, wondering how to say as little as possible about Jerome without appearing disingenuous. He finally chose the course long experience had taught him was the wisest — to tell the truth to one who already knows it.

"Your cousin, Jerome, is a useful tool. I would be a fool to deny it since you obviously follow his activities closely." Indeed, thought Álava, Jerome's main limitation is that he is so well known as an informer that very likely he supplies only information which is fed to him. "But he does not have your stature, my dear de Retz. He is still a callow youth, after all."

"You mean that he is too obvious an ally," riposted Gondi, laughing.

"No," Álava lied with stern dignity. "I mean what I say.

"Now, if you will excuse me. Age must have some privileges. I will congratulate the Queen Mother on this splendid reception, and will request her permission to withdraw."

The old man bent in a half-bow to Gondi, and walked stiffly away, his gaunt black figure contrasting uncomfortably with the crowd of gay revelers. Gondi watched him go with narrow eyes.

He is a fanatic, he thought, but does that mean he is wrong? We have seen eye to eye on occasion. Perhaps this is such a time again. He sighed, and left his seclusion to resume an attitude of merrymaking which was a far cry from his true state of mind.

An undertow of feeling, which, if Gondi had analyzed it, he would have recognized as guilt, moved him momentarily to speak to the Queen Mother, but he resisted the impulse. He did not wish to give his shrewd mistress further cause to associate him in her mind with the Ambassador, who was even then making his adieux.

Instead, he looked around for a likely way of passing the time until it would be politic to withdraw. As he did so, a perspiring, red face loomed out of the room's smoky haze.

Hugues de Tournelle boomed over the music, "Well, Gondi, how are you enjoying this fête? I must say I enjoyed the meal greatly. You know how exercise gives an appetite. That's what I like, riding out to hunt, then coming home to a good meal. They go so well together, complement each other, you know. But this dancing, it seems a shame to get so hot without any sport, you know? Of course, you're a fine dancer, I can see, though I'm not an amateur of the art. I don't see you hunting very often? Don't you hunt? I can't understand men who don't hunt. Why, what's the matter, man? What are you staring at?"

Gondi said with a grave expression, "I didn't know it was possible to project the human voice for such an extended period without pausing to breathe, and, indeed, Monsieur, you look quite apoplectic."

"Oh, really?" said de Tournelle in an anxious tone. He rubbed his sleeve roughly across his forehead. "Just that one would like to go to bed.

"No, I feel fine. It's, you know, hunting is quite hard work. I'm surprised the King is as lively as he is tonight. He ran a fine course today. We started a stag near Pouillé and followed him across the Bigot woods quite off the beaten path, you know, lost him once at the stream that runs into the Choisille, practically lost ourselves in a ravine, couldn't tell you where that was. Well, it was a fine chase, I mean seven horns. I was in at the kill with his Majesty." De Tournelle beamed across at Gondi, creasing several unshaven chins. "Did you say you hunt? I don't often see you."

"I enjoy the sport, and I make it a point to hunt with the King when I can. But even when my work prevents me from joining in the fun, I find the sport has value for me.

"You see, it creates long peaceful periods, during which I can accomplish a great deal, while everyone else is running around."

"I see," mumbled de Tournelle, who plainly did not see.

"How is Madame la Comtesse?" Gondi forced himself to ask.

"Ah, my wife is well, Monsieur, very well. She is very animated on these occasions. You see, she doesn't get up until the noonday meal, unless the Court is traveling, so she's still spry at the witching hour. You might do a turn with her on the floor. She loves to dance, and as I was saying, I'm not much for it myself."

De Tournelle yawned and looked distractedly around the room. "Ah, there she is, talking to that fine doe young Pierre has married."

Gondi inwardly considered whether dancing with Elise de Tournelle would be more unpleasant than conversing with her husband was tedious. Shrugging at the fates, he nodded and strolled in the indicated direction.

Madame de Tournelle was a large lady with an aggressive nose and a tight, sour mouth. Chance had left Anne beside her on one of the few occasions when neither of them was dancing. Although she had been disposed to dislike the young bride, who was too fetching by far for her taste, their awkward initiation at conversation had revealed common interests which neither had suspected. The two women were now deep in a conversation whose gist was that the attractive women at the gathering wore unattractive clothes and vice versa. By judiciously overlooking the exceptions to their newly articulated rule, they were finding good cheer communing together.

Seeing them so engaged, Gondi believed he could slip by, in dereliction of his duty, until Anne looked up, curtseyed, and batted her eyelashes at him with inviting coyness.

Gondi bowed deeply, and proclaimed himself glad for an occasion to offer his best wishes again "to the lovely lady who is the reason and heart of this delightful celebration." He smiled engagingly at Madame de Tournelle as he ended his speech.

That lady sniffed injuredly. She had been in the midst of a particularly sharp remark about the style prevalent among the personal ladies-in-waiting of the young Queen ("How they must dress at the Austrian Court, my dear, one can only imagine, but you'd think that a year with us would have shown them how it's done..."), when Gondi's appearance in Anne's line of vision had taken the younger woman's attention quite away from Madame's remarks.

The Countess could recognize a snub almost before it had happened, and had never forgotten or forgiven a perceived slight to herself. Considering all women superior to men and herself superior to all women, she was never more injured than on occasions like this, when a younger woman preferred a flirtation to receiving her sage instruction.

The Countess sniffed mightily, muttered about needing to speak to her husband, and took herself off. Gondi and Anne were left in an unexpected tête-à-tête.

Gondi smiled at her with that warmth and humor which almost never failed to endear him to the fair sex. "We must have offended her, though I don't know how," he said. "Madame la Comtesse has never been known to converse with her husband, except when strict propriety required it."

"I'm sure I don't know how." Anne had lowered her head, and now looked up at him in a provocative way, which was all the more sensual for its mimicry of childhood.

As a current passed between them, Gondi saw at the same moment the reason for the Countess's displeasure and that Anne had intentionally provoked it. He stepped back slightly and looked appraisingly at his companion.

Essentially a controlled man, far more interested in political power than carnal conquests, Gondi satisfied his desires principally with his wife and only on a small scale with casual mistresses, whom he required to be unencumbered by uneasy consciences, powerful families, jealous husbands, or other inconveniences. Given his fear of damaging imbroglios, he seldom bedded women, though he often used them, manipulating them by means of an attentive, supportive charm which gave him lasting successes that mere sexual prowess would never have yielded. He immediately took Anne's measure as the type of woman who could be handled more easily in the absence of romantic involvements.

"To have driven the Countess to the refuge of her husband's arms is no mean feat," he resumed, "for a more tedious man never existed, and that is something which his devoted wife realized a quarter of a century ago."

Anne laughed delightedly, breaking the momentary tension which had come between them.

"Whatever the cost to that good woman," Gondi continued, "I say I have done right by society. At midnight, the star of the firmament should shine for all to see, not fade into the horizon as though dawn were upon us. Come." He placed his fingers gently under hers and led her out onto the dance floor.

Anne looked at Gondi with open admiration. She had long known that he was a man whose position was higher than many of better birth would ever willingly acknowledge. Moreover, she had picked him out earlier in the evening as the most attractive man at the night's revels. Now, she felt for the first time the full effect of his charm, and her mind fairly buzzed with seductive ideas.

As Anne rose from a deep curtsey at the end of their dance, she found Pierre beside them. She opened her mouth to vent a sudden annoyance, but closing it, forced a sweet smile to her lips. By no word or gesture would she mar the perfect image she had conveyed to all through the long celebration.

"This is as it should be," said Gondi, and he took Anne and Pierre by the elbows and urged them together. "Now, go out and show us what we have come for." He watched the handsome couple glide onto the floor, gave a bemused shake of his head, and cast his eyes around for the Queen Mother.

Finding her by the great door, he weaved through the crowd to her side. He took her hand and bowed deeply and slowly, with an emphasis which only she would recognize as a means of holding that hand longer than etiquette permitted. Rising, he looked into her face, observing the annoyance and fatigue expressed by the tight mouth.

"Monsieur has certainly been busy tonight," the Queen Mother remarked.

Gondi wondered anxiously whether Catherine was angry as a woman who has been neglected or as a queen who has been betrayed.

"Madame," he replied, "though the evening has been a delight, as are all your fêtes, it has seemed long to me because the demands of your guests have kept me from your side."

"And what, pray, did my most eminent adviser have to say to the Spaniard?" she asked in a voice that was half-whisper and half-snarl.

So, the wind blows that way, he thought. God damn Álava for an old fool!

"Madame, even when others are at their amusements, I am at my work. It is unwise not to listen to one's adversaries."

"Keep your wisdom, sirrah," she muttered so only they could hear. Shifting suddenly into Italian, she said more audibly, "I was a statesman before you were housebroken. I am wise enough not to be made a fool of by you."

Gondi drew himself up, and coldly replied, "Madame, if I am not trusted, I am a useless tool indeed." He continued in French, "I will not trouble you further."

The hard eyes looked at him speculatively, then the face around them crinkled into a hint of a smile. "Well, well, this is not the time for such talk." The mobile face now pouted. "The evening lacked savor because we lacked your company. But now it is too late. I must bid my guests farewell, and you among them. I will speak with you further tomorrow." She briefly extended her hand, while her eyes looked by him with expressionless dignity at the growing group of guests waiting to take their leave of her.

With a mixture of relief and anxiety, Gondi slipped past her and away.

Chapter IV

aurice awoke late to find himself alone in an unfamiliar room. At first he felt lost and bewildered, just as he used to feel as a child waking in a new place and unable to remember how he had come there. Recollection came to him suddenly that he was in the château of Tours and this was the bedchamber he had been assigned to share with two other bachelors. He now had the room to himself; the tumbled, scruffy bedding of his absent companions gave it a disheveled, somewhat disreputable air, which matched the musty, confused, and insalubrious state of his head.

He rolled over and tried to coax a little order out of the muddle of his ideas. Reluctantly, the previous evening returned to him in vivid images tarnished by the bile of too much drink. He isolated the picture of Pierre and Anne dancing, turned it over in his mind, and felt it give new life to his old discontentment, the way a sudden movement jabs at an old wound. He could always revitalize himself by recalling his grievances against Pierre — Pierre, who had been given everything, Pierre who had now received the culminating gift, a wealthy goddess for a wife, Pierre.... The itch of envy tormented him so, he wished he could physically cut it out of himself.

But what good would that do? he asked himself. Better to strike outward than inward was one of his guiding principles; its familiarity comforted him now as in the past. Feeling slightly more awake, he sat up and glanced through the narrow window. The clear night had become a heavy, hazy morning. Where is Paul? he queried in silent irritability. The manservant's pallet at the foot of his bed was empty. Always there when he's in the way and never there when you need him, he grumbled to himself. He swung his bare feet to the floor, flinching from the cold stones and wondering vaguely what the day would hold.

A flash of recall, unexpected and unwanted, blasted his raw nerves: Gondi, Gondi and his vicious dilemma, it all came back to him. He suffered again the sensation he had felt immediately after Gondi's attack: He was cut off, adrift, powerless to arrest the current or turn back the tide, a bark sailing toward the horizon and into the unknown beyond. The situation was inconceivable, yet it existed and was every bit as fearful as it seemed. A new passion possessed him: Gondi will pay for this, he thought, if it takes a hundred years! He let the rage for vengeance push out all other emotions; beside its lusty vigor, his old disgruntlement against Pierre seemed feeble, worn, paltry, and childish.

As quickly as the burst of venom had animated him, however, as quickly it spent itself. With a dull ache of fear, he thought, if it must be, let it be soon. I'll simply slip away; that's the easy way. How he longed for something to be easy! But he knew there was never an easy escape. Though fear made him long to flee, fear also prevented him from simply fleeing. The customary farewells, however much they would expose him to heartache or even danger, could not be safely ignored.

Grudgingly, he heaved himself up from the bed. At least, he thought, I can start with the easy part. Leaving his mother would distress her far more than himself, he knew, and the thought was vaguely consoling.

Rummaging among the neatly folded clothes at the foot of the bed, he suddenly remembered Paul and bellowed for him bad-temperedly. His head emerged from his shirt to face the old servant, who was watching his struggles with tolerant contempt. With Paul's help he continued to dress, all the while sputtering out garbled instructions.

"An early departure for a long journey," Paul summarized, roughly brushing the white specks off Maurice's dark doublet. "Is my young Lord sure of what he is undertaking?"

"Yes, yes, man. Now, take me to my mother, and then go immediately and request an audience for me with His Majesty."

Minutes later, a calmer Maurice strode purposefully into his mother's chamber. Ignoring her startled look, he waved her waiting women away, glaring imperiously as they curtseyed respectfully and withdrew. His mother's eyes softened as he ceremoniously took her hand and raised it to his lips, but the wariness had returned to them by the time he had straightened.

"Mother," he said, "I have come to kiss you goodbye, perhaps forever."

"What?" she exclaimed, her hands unconsciously flying together. "Where could you possibly be going? Everyone is here."

He stiffened theatrically.

"You needn't remind me that there is nothing to keep me from the quite useless life I lead here, playing jester to your husband and lackey to his golden-haired boy. Let me remind you, instead, that even the poorest knave can call his life his own, and I must tell you that I intend to begin to lead my own as I please. Jesu knows, I am old enough."

"What are you going to do?" she asked, her voice scratching with emotion.

"I intend to offer my services to Monsieur the Admiral de Coligny in furtherance of the cause for which my father died. I'm told he's at La Rochelle."

She sagged as if struck with a heavy blow. In a valiant effort at self-control, she pressed her trembling lips together. Reaching for his hand, which hung close to her shoulder, she spoke as calmly as she could.

"Maurice," she said, "I understand how hard it has been for you. If your father had lived and prospered, your life would have been so different. He threw everything away, his life and everything else, on a foolish gamble. I have done my best to preserve something for you out of the shambles he left behind. And have I not succeeded?

"Your life here is secure, your position in a great household is no small thing, you have an entrée at Court and a future. Your stepfather, my husband, will assist you, should you seek a worthy marriage. For God's sake, don't throw all this away for some delusion about your father. To honor his memory is a blameless thing, but to adopt his follies as your own is another matter."

"Do you understand?" he asked rhetorically. Her words were an unfortunate reminder of his newest grievance against his stepfamily: There was a worthy match, the likes of which he'd never see!

He met her ardent gaze with a scowl. "It ill suits you, Mother, to talk of my father's follies. You were a Protestant until your fear of this world overcame your terror of the next."

She dropped her eyes, distraught. Her hands clutched and unclutched the thick folds of her skirt. Maurice watched them unmoved. His gaze wandered slowly up to the coils of her hair, showing agate through a gold filigree net. How black, he thought. With a flash of insight, he saw that they were too flawlessly black for her age. He whistled merrily at her unrecognized coquettishness, put his hand under her chin, and pushing her head roughly back, kissed her lustily and fully on the lips. Numbly, she watched him prance from the room, her eyes filling slowly with tears.

Though he swaggered to conceal his fear, he could not stop himself from glancing warily up and down the corridor when he left her room, or from letting out a breath of relief on finding the hall empty. At the corridor's end, he collided with Paul, who reported, "His Majesty is in council, but he would probably receive you after the session, if there's time before the noonday meal."

"Good, Paul, good. Now, where is everyone?"

"Monsieur Pierre and his lady are up on the battlements. The Duke is in council with the King."

Nodding a curt dismissal, Maurice turned into the tower stairway and started up the winding steps, running his left hand along the inner column and his right along the rough wall. Every fifty steps or so, he stopped to catch his breath and peer out through the slit windows into the morning mist.

The haze blocked out the usual sights — the tangle of roofs, the lower fortifications, the great stone bridge, and the river's currents, islands, and sandbanks — but it did not filter the city's smells, which in the dampness seemed all the more pungent. After several pauses, Maurice emerged onto the battlements. The castle's two other principal towers were visible ahead, and behind, he could barely make out the beginning of the ring of lesser fortifications which encircled the city.

Screwing his eyes up against the glare, he stared down the wide walk and terrace which ran inside the ramparts between the towers. In the distance he could make out a tall, broad-shouldered figure. Blondel, he thought. Many years back, the young blades of de Galle's retinue had nicknamed his stepbrother Blondel, and himself Noiret, in recognition of their coloring. Farther away, he could barely discern a group of figures, some on the walk and some on the terrace below. Maurice sauntered toward his stepbrother.

Pierre was looking down at the golden shards of landscape, now clear, now obscure in the haze, which appeared where breaks in the mist gave glimpses, here and there, sometimes meaningless, without reference points, of water, sand, or stone. Swallows ricocheted across the rents in the billowing whiteness, screaming their shrill cries.

With the practiced eye of one who has been brought up to take account of the weather, Pierre assessed the uncomfortable stillness and unsuitable warmth of the air as the prelude to a storm. Bad weather, he thought, when the swallows fly low.

He glanced over his shoulder at his companions, who seemed, through the distorting light, to be far distant, and then turned resolutely back to his contemplation of the mists. Try as he would, Pierre could not completely ignore the giggles and shrieks from the joyous band on the terrace. It was beyond his power to ignore his wife's high-pitched laugh, which pealed incessantly above the accompanying raucous confusion.

Most of the young people were playing a kind of tag that involved staying within certain boundaries and avoiding being touched by the last person in the chain of people who had already been caught. Others were yelling advice and insults from the walk above. It annoyed Pierre that he could not leave the group completely without emphasizing his poor humor, nor because of that humor could he join in the fun.

He tried to concentrate on his thoughts, or rather on his feelings, for his thoughts were essentially an attempt to grasp and define his feelings. His wedding celebration seemed like a dizzy dream, bewildering and stupefying. Moments only stood out, dancing through his mind without ever assembling as a whole. The wedding night, yes, that stood out. Each night since, too, was a distinct phase of a separate life that seemed to have nothing to do with his daytime existence.

His wife's tantalizing displays of a carnal knowledge he had never even guessed at, her sudden, rough rebuffs to his timid advances, her sharp riposte and piercing laughter as she toyed with him, these memories were lost in others more vivid — the torture of unsatisfied lust and the writhing glory of satisfaction. He flushed with shame and desire.

But the days? They were a tumult and a contradiction. The festivities which had celebrated their union seemed to Pierre only to highlight their separateness. Anne still seemed to him as unattainable as a statue and as errant as a butterfly. He saw her gliding about the men of his father's entourage, indeed all the men of the Court, curtseying to this one, laughing with that one, dancing, smiling, touching. He saw her still as he had seen her one afternoon, silhouetted against the setting sun in a glorious crimson robe, one white hand resting on his father's arm, a look in her eyes which a week ago he would not have understood, which even now he could barely comprehend. His bile rose dangerously.

"Ho, Blondel!" A nasal inflection broke his reverie. Startled, he looked around to find the smirking face of his stepbrother barely inches from his own. Maurice's habit of getting as close as possible to his auditor and pinning the unfortunate against the nearest wall had always annoyed Pierre. He slid sideways and stepped back, as Maurice put out a hand to obstruct his retreat.

"How's married life?" Maurice asked with uncharacteristic jocularity. "Your face would provide a fine model for a statue of St. Sebastian, but hardly suits a newlywed. Come, come! It can't already be that bad."

"I have a headache," Pierre rumbled.

Maurice's grin broadened. "Better a headache than a heartache, eh? Though, I must say, la belle Anne does not strike me as exactly a bed of roses, or perhaps she is, if you mean the thorny reality rather than the rosy image."

He laughed and shook Pierre by the shoulder. Pierre grimaced with distaste and twisted free.

"If you ask me," continued Maurice in a confidential tone, his mouth almost touching Pierre's ear, "what she needs is a real man, one who can master her and ride her, if you take my meaning. Fortunately, you have a lifetime to grow into the role." His chortle died out as he caught in Pierre's look a vivid and painful reminder of his stepfather's hostile gaze.

"Well, Blondel, actually, I've come along to bid you farewell. I've asked audience of the King as soon as the Council breaks, and I intend to get His Majesty's permission to leave Court at once to join the other Protestants with Coligny at La Rochelle. So, this is goodbye for a while."

Pierre looked, and was, thunderstruck. "Does father know?" he asked.

"Not yet. I'm not obliged to request permission to withdraw from your father. He's not my sovereign. My life's my own, and he's done little enough to buy it if he could. I doubt he'll miss me, anyway. Nor will you, eh?" He bared his teeth unpleasantly.

Pierre did not bother to confirm or deny Maurice's statement, but stood lost in thought. It surprised and pained him that his principal reaction was envy at La Renaudie's freedom to leave everything behind and ride off to adventure, however disreputable his pursuits might ultimately be. Pierre felt saddled with the restraints of responsibility without its freedom.

"Why now, Noiret?" he asked suddenly.

"That's for me to know, boy," answered the other. With a movement so quick that Pierre could not escape, Maurice grasped him by the shoulders and sarcastically smacked each of his cheeks with a kiss.

As he loped off, Maurice called back, "Try to give your ravishing bride the farewell my absence will deprive her of." Pierre's cheeks flamed and he gritted his teeth until the pain became intolerable.

Maurice made his way down through another tower to the royal apartments and entered the Guard's Hall. He exchanged banalities with those of the men who spoke French, watched two French guards fleece a Swiss at a fast dice game which apparently only the winners understood, and finally dropped down on the window seat to wait for the Council to end, hoping against hope that it would break before dinner.

* * *

Gondi sat by the window holding the letter out of the fierce morning glare and giving it his fullest concentration.

Monsieur de Retz,

I am writing you concerning the one bond between us, Athalie, your niece and my great-niece. You confided the child to me after her father's death, and my constant joy in her presence here has only now been marred by the knowledge that her stay in this House has set her on the wrong path, to her detriment and my chagrin. Briefly, Athalie believes that she has a vocation to live forever the life she has seen, and in part shared, during her days among us. Because of your well-known devotion to our Faith and Church, it may at first seem to you that such an inclination should receive the most ardent encouragement. Indeed, I do not doubt that that will be your wish. However, I trust that further thought, to which I add my arguments for your consideration, will show you that this choice is not a suitable one given Athalie's position.

It has been God's will, to which we must sorrowfully bow, that of the de la Roque line, none remains save Athalie. Her name is a proud and noble one, and the extent of her fortune I need not describe to you, since unforeseen tragedies have placed her inheritance in your hands until her marriage.

Thus, you and I stand guard over the destiny of the last member of a good and prominent house. Although I myself have by my vows relinquished the position and wealth which such a heritage entails, and have taken God for my family, yet it grieves me to see such a family, to which I feel strong ties, die out.

My sister's blood and my nephew's cry out that the line must continue. I would be shamed to confess to what may seem a loyalty divided, even torn, between my family and my God, or to advance such worldly arguments, if I did not know that each soul reaches salvation in its own way and no path can be considered more sure of its destination, at least by those of us who are still seeking our own ways in this earthly maze, and if I did not know further that the family is one of the sure values in this changing world and one which God knows and blesses.

Of course, if it is God's will that the line should perish entirely and its great property, so carefully amassed and conserved, should pass into other hands, if such should be the Divine will, I would not set myself against it. Indeed, for the joy of my declining years and the good governance of this house, for Athalie would surely follow in the steps of the Prioress, my niece, Eleanor, to become Abbess in the fullness of time, I would not wish to turn her from her chosen way were it not for the considerations which I have attempted to describe. No matter whether you have been swayed by my poor contribution to your thoughts, I am confident that you will agree that a decision which affects such interests cannot be made by one so uninformed as to ignore their very existence, much less their merits.

Thus, I shall send this dear child from my House that she may be with you, her guardian, and may acquire in your company the worldly knowledge that I cannot impart to her. By the same post, I am writing Madame the Queen Mother to add my introductions to your own.

I await your word as to where your ward should rejoin you, or your own arrival, which would honor this Establishment.

Louise de Bourbon, Abbesse de Fontevrault

Gondi glared at the interlocking loops of the great signature which dominated the tightly woven text. Fierce anger burst through his customary composure and for an instant, masked his charming, courtly mien with a grimace like a snarl. "Proud and noble name," "inheritance and great property," "good and prominent house," "position," "wealth," and "heritage." The phrases leapt up at him and pricked old sores on the all-too-thin skin of his self-esteem. With what condescension she views the world, he thought. No family is as proud and noble as hers, not even the de la Roques, blood nobility though they be. And the rest of us? Well, we are a separate race, scarcely human.

Gondi stood abruptly, knocking aside his cushioned armchair.

He leaned up against the cold stone wall, stared blindly through the window, and ground his right fist into the open palm of the other hand. "Relax, relax, relax," he murmured to himself. Shaking his head vigorously several times, he turned back and picked the letter up from the table. Once again, anger overcame him, and he slammed his hand and the letter against the heavy mahogany.

How her kind despise all who are not of their race, he resumed, tasting again the bitter remembrance of that chilly reception for his sister's wedding. No one had understood how a nobleman like Blaise de la Roque could have married the daughter of a Florentine merchant banker when he did not really need to. Yes, they all understood marrying for money, he smiled sarcastically, but though she had brought a fine dowry, he had had money enough not to marry for that. It had so riled his august relatives that one of theirs should breed with a commoner for no good reason, that their eyes had been blinded. Stern, humorless, and thickheaded soldier though Blaise had been, he had seen the deep spring of sweetness in Alicia de Gondi's character, which they had never troubled to look for.

Gondi thought wistfully of his little sister. She had been so pretty, so winning, so quick to learn, so full of grace. De la Roque had made her pregnant within weeks, and she had died within the year. Gondi exhaled sharply to loosen a constriction in his chest. And Blaise de la Roque had never married again. Gondi smiled. How ironic for Alicia's daughter, Athalie, to inherit everything; how much more ironic if it all came to him, as it should, if she became a nun.

It would make up for a lot to get his hands on the property of the de la Roques and, above all, on the title that went with it. He would be paid back for the insults, the shame, he had suffered all his life. He had been treated like dirt by people with half his wit, all because he had been born with less. But if his plan came off, he would be a duke, and they would have to kiss his feet.

He remembered his own wedding, celebrating the union that had made him Count de Retz. He had married the most eligible widow in France, and how they

51

had gasped and looked askance. "He should remember his origins," everyone said. "He aspires to too much."

His wife's family had fought him; only his money and his position with the Queen Mother had made them see where their own advantage lay. Even now, his wife refused to bear his name. He was Count de Retz, as her husband before had been; she was not Madame de Gondi.

His thoughts came back to the matter at hand. She is a shrewd one, the old Abbess, he reflected. She knows I want the girl to take the veil, and she knows why. This — he looked with disgust at the letter — is clear notice that she will fight me to keep their precious estates from my tainted mercenary hands.

We shall see, he mused, we shall see. Gondi's blue eyes had regained their normal, dispassionate clarity. He stroked his beard pensively, a calculating smile etching itself across his mouth.

His thoughts were suddenly interrupted by rustling, pattering noises, whose cause became apparent as the arras was thrown back to admit the Queen Mother. With astonishing speed, the bulky figure burst into the study, accompanied rather than announced by Gondi's flustered secretary. Startled and perturbed, Gondi bent in a respectful bow as Catherine de Medici snapped at the bewildered youth. "Go, and don't hang around the door."

As the arras fell into place, she said in throaty Italian, "Does he speak our language?"

"Of course, Your Majesty," Gondi replied suavely. "He is a cousin, albeit several times removed. For my business affairs, I need a well-educated secretary and preferably a member of the family." As she lowered herself heavily into a straight-backed armchair, despond clouded her face and caused her to forget to extend the privilege of being seated to Gondi, who perforce remained standing.

"I came here thinking we would be more private than in my own apartments, where every lady-in-waiting asks nothing more than to sell my secrets to my enemies, but I don't know that this is any better. That boy is probably a tool of the Spanish, like your cousin, Jerome."

She eyed Gondi narrowly. "I do not expect your business affairs to jeopardize the affairs of state."

She shrugged and waved the subject aside, as if it were of no further consequence in the context of matters of greater import.

"Alberto, Alberto," she repeated, honoring him as she sometimes did with the intimacy which first names implied. "This situation with my son cannot continue."

"What situation, your Majesty?" he asked carefully.

"Really, Sir, you play me for an idiot, when you play the fool. What situation, except the state of my son's government! Sit down! Why are you standing like that?"

She leaned forward and continued in a confidential tone. "It grows worse and worse. I thought at first that he was merely expressing a desire natural at his age for fuller participation in our decisions. But he has gone far beyond mere consultation with me about the affairs of the country. Indeed, he has come to decide alone; he does not consult with me at all. He is too young, Alberto; he lacks the experience to judge the terrible results his acts can have. He cannot yet appreciate that every act of statecraft has incalculable consequences, which still we have to strive to consider and which can be weighed only on the scale of long experience.

"He has no judgment, and the proof that he has no judgment is that he turns his back on everything we have to offer, everything I have done to try to keep this poor kingdom together for him. There will be a disaster, I tell you. There is just no controlling him. He abuses his brother, Anjou; he favors all advisers over his family; he visits me rarely and discusses nothing in my presence. Why, even now, he is in a Council meeting to which I was not summoned. A Council, indeed! No meeting without me, without you and me, is a Council meeting. I cannot allow it."

"What do de Galle and the others on the Council say? Where do the Guises stand?"

"Misericordia, man, how should I know? No one talks to me!"

"Still, I know the Guises are beside themselves. Young Guise sulks on his estates and talks of being a foreign power instead of a vassal, which I ought to treat as treason, and I would if I had the force to make the point stick. The Cardinal de Guise talks only of stamping out heresy — and that means more fighting. My poor son cannot understand men or control them. He hates them all because he believes they prefer Anjou to him. But they are only using Anjou because they think Charles favors the Protestants too much. But does Charles see this? No!

"Charles even thinks that I favor Anjou, I who have never favored any of my children over the others. I believe that's why he avoids me. It's all emotion on his part."

Gondi cleared his throat gently, since for many years he had made his own observations of the Queen Mother's relations with her children. Her protestations of impartiality, which he had heard before, did not arrest his thoughts.

"What of Raymond de Galle?"

"I could not say. He always appears so much simpler than he is. But he has nothing to lose here. He believes in moderation, in avoiding bloodshed and bankruptcy. He looks to use the King's sentiments against Anjou and the Guises for his own purposes. At any rate, Raymond de Galle has always thought my sons but pale shadows of their father and grandfather. But he will not succeed," she finished fiercely.

"Yes, Raymond is unpredictable about the religious situation," Gondi answered obliquely. "He does not understand the principles involved. With all due respect, Madame, you, too, have been guilty of a failure of leadership on this question. We have talked of this before. Your subjects will not fight for a principle when their sovereign vacillates."

The Queen Mother faced him, eyes blazing. "Yes, Sir, and I have as often told you that I do not feel that I have benefited from your best advice on this issue. You treat it far too much as a question of theory, a religious question, a Catholic question, but it is not so.

"This State is mine, and my son's, and its problems — yes, even the religious question — must be settled so as to keep the State whole and strong. And I tell you, Sir, that continuation of these endless internal wars can benefit no one except the enemies of France, and particularly the Spanish. Three wars and three "peaces" — only a little less bloody — in just ten years: It cannot be tolerated, no matter what principles are involved.

"Since the death of my husband, the late King Henry, there has been no real peace. It breaks my heart to see this rich and welcoming land, the heritage of my sons, wasted and torn by war. The people are poor, their farms burnt, their villages pillaged. The bravest men are dead. And we have been punished. Think back to the summer of '68, the wind that flattened the grain to rot in the fields, and never was there a winter so bitter, so angry, so desperate. You cannot have forgotten. I shall remember it always." She shuddered as if with cold.

"That was surely a punishment. At least if I believed that God involved Himself in our pathetic squabbles, I would think it a punishment, for I know it cannot please a rational Being that we should kill each other like dogs fighting over garbage."

She stopped, looking puzzled and bereft, then finding her train of thought again, she resumed. "We have had peace now since last August, but if it were eight years rather than eight months, it could not restore the country to itself. The misfortunes of this decade have tarnished the glory of France and set us back a generation.

"And it is not only death and destruction which distress me. The controversies have rotted men's souls more than the heresy that engendered them. Men's spirits are poisoned by distrust. Because of old Guise's death at Protestant hands — no, Sir, I never wish to know your part in it, although it served me well to be rid of so impertinent and powerful a rival and to have no suspicion fall on the Crown — yet I suspect that you did not serve me in that matter as well as I might have wished, for the result is that the Protestants are called assassins and the Guise family has vowed to avenge his death with Protestant blood. You alone know the truth of it, but blame cannot be taken from the Protestants without it falling elsewhere and that risk we cannot run. And so, we are trapped in this vicious quarrel — Guise against Châtillon — to the death. But the Protestants are as full of hate and fear as the Catholics.

"My meeting in Bayonne, which you arranged, with my dear daughter and the emissaries of my son-in-law of Spain was six years ago, but will the Protestants never forget? What do they think I did in Bayonne? Sold them to the Spanish for Peruvian silver? God knows, I could use the money, but I would not sell my people — even heretics — to the Spaniard. In any event, Philip is a mule with

54

whom no one can do business. No, I will not sell them to Spain. But you, Sir, delight in the disaffection of the Protestants."

She continued after a moment's pause, "I am not fond of them myself. Their cant revolts me even when it is just talk, and when they act on it to tear down the art and culture of centuries, I could wish them in the Hell they preach so much about. No, I cannot forget how they tried to kidnap my son at Amboise. They have only themselves to blame for what followed. Worse, they are traitors, open traitors, bartering French soil for English support.

"But are their Catholic opponents so much better? I am not blind, like you and others of your ilk. I do not view life from the inside of a confessional. Your co-Religionists, and mine, think nothing of arson, pillage, rape, and revolt, and their dealings with Spain are no less treasonous because Spain is Catholic. Remember that, Sir. We will not brook divided loyalties on a matter so close to our heart as the peace and unity of this kingdom."

"Madame," Gondi interjected nervously, "you cannot question my loyalty. If I have failed you, it is because my abilities were not equal to your demands. How can you doubt the loyalty of one who does not hide his thoughts from you, even for fear of displeasing you."

The Queen Mother smiled suddenly at her adviser. Just as suddenly, the old look of worry clouded her expression.

"What shall we do about Charles?" she resumed almost petulantly.

"Madame, I would be glad to govern France for you, nay, even Europe for you, but I cannot govern your own family."

"How does that pretty answer serve me? Think again, Sir!" The Queen's eyes flashed her fury, and she stood and whirled as if to push physically away the implication that her children were beyond her control. Stopping in mid-turn, she gazed blankly out at the wall of mist beyond the window. When she turned back, distress had softened her firm mouth. "Alberto," she said, "who else will try to help me?"

"My Queen," Gondi smiled, and leaned forward with a suggestion of gallantry. "I will advise you as best I can, but I fear you will not like what you hear and will question my motives."

The Queen answered with no resentment. "I have never rejected advice because it was hard to follow, and I do not question the motives of my advisers because they make mistakes."

"Then, Madame," he said, "I advise you to hide your feelings from your son, and to encourage, even admire, his independence. If Charles is left to steer his own course, I believe he will soon sail out so far that he will be unable to return to port without calling for your assistance. When that time comes, we do not wish his pride to keep him from turning to you until it is too late."

Catherine's gaze returned to the window and she was silent for several moments. Finally, she said wearily, "Perhaps you are right. I only hope that in the meantime he will not wreck us all."

She exhaled softly and glanced at Gondi. "How glad I will be to leave this place! The gloom of Tours depresses me even more than the ghosts of Amboise. There is mildew on the wall behind my bed. We have hidden it with tapestries, of course, but the damp remains. When I return to my lovely Chenonceau, I will know the summer is near."

She turned to go, but stopped and looked back. "You will let me know what transpired at the Council?"

Gondi rose. "Your Majesty, you see me here before you. I was not invited. Indeed, His Majesty's dislike for your humble servant is at least equal to his feelings against the Guises."

"No, but people talk to you. Everyone talks to you. I, alone, now, am kept in the dark by all." She turned and slowly left the room. Gondi's deep bow hid his profound relief that the ordeal was over.

* * *

Maurice had almost despaired of his audience with the King, when, suddenly, the heavy Council Room doors swung open, all in the antechamber leapt to their feet, and Charles IX entered. There followed a motley group of notables, led by the King's brother, Anjou, looking flushed and angry, and Maurice's stepfather, the Duke de Galle, wearing a serious, preoccupied expression. Faced with this imposing gathering, Maurice was struck with something akin to stage fright. The enormity of the step he was about to take overwhelmed him again, dispelling the carelessness of his earlier farewells. It came to him that he had done nothing irrevocable, so far.

If he never spoke to the King, life would go on as before, except.... Desperation filled him.

The King waved nonchalantly to his entourage, and turned toward the smaller door leading to his private apartments; his Councilors bowed deeply. Maurice edged toward him, hoping to catch his attention before he disappeared, but finding himself instead fixed by his stepfather's hostile gaze. He shifted irresolutely, tempted once again to withdraw.

When at last Maurice heard the young King's puzzled greeting, his relief was much dampened by uneasiness. Bowing and mumbling, he requested a brief audience; the King granted it with aloof courtesy; and Maurice followed him from the antechamber, feeling every eye in the room bore into him.

The King led Maurice into his sparely furnished bedroom and perched on the edge of the bed. Fatigue etched lines in a face that seemed both old and immature. With a formal smile, he gestured to the bowing Maurice to be seated. An awkward silence fell.

At last, the King said, "I was greatly pleased to consent to a marriage which links two such fine and loyal families as the de Galles and the Revillars. Though I could not share the joy as one of the family could, it brought great delight to me and mine."

"Your Majesty is most gracious," said Maurice in a tone which belied his words.

"You are older than your brother — er, stepbrother — by how much?"

"Seven years, Your Majesty."

"It would have been natural for you to have been the first wed. Perhaps you wished to discuss such a matter with me?"

"Well, no, Your Majesty."

"I believe you are a companion of my brother, Anjou." The young King's narrow, dark eyes swiveled to stare at La Renaudie.

"Monsieur has honored me with his friendship. Of course, I rejoice at every opportunity for closeness with Your Majesty. But I fear," Maurice inhaled deeply and plunged ahead, "I fear that there are differences which may separate me from Monsieur's good graces, but not, I hope, from Your Majesty's."

Charles' attentive look contained more sympathy than heretofore.

"You see, Your Majesty," Maurice continued, "I have come to ask Your Majesty's permission to take a step which is surely as important as marriage. I wish to leave Court, but not, I assure you, for any reason of disloyalty. I wish to travel to La Rochelle to receive instruction in the religion in which I was raised."

Maurice ran a tongue around his lips and hunched down for the inevitable reaction. The King's face had, indeed, closed up like a box. The odd, almond-shaped eyes watched him fixedly, as seemingly endless seconds passed. When it came, the amused note in the King's voice reassured Maurice more than his words.

"Well, how amazing!"

The young King paused, then continued in a serious tone. "I have just spent several hours discussing with my Councilors the fact that I feel it is high time for myself to have gentle speech with Monsieur de Coligny. There are weighty matters which could best be resolved in man-to-man conversation."

The King straightened his narrow shoulders. "I need hardly tell you that my suggestion met with a very mixed reaction, but I will not let the die-hards discourage me. I am King, and I believe I know best.

"As you know, I am leaving for Normandy to hunt. I will tell you in confidence what I told the Council: That I plan to return through Brittany to give the Admiral the chance to come to me. And now, I find you are going to La Rochelle! I must think on this, for it may be that you can do me service there. If my plan to receive Coligny personally comes to nothing, your observations may provide the best substitute for firsthand impressions."

Charles got up, and waving Maurice to stay seated, strode slowly across the room and back. "Have you told Anjou yet?"

Maurice shook his head.

"He will, indeed, be beside himself," Charles continued. "You should have heard him at the Council meeting just now. I'd like to be there when you tell him, but it wouldn't be the same if I was." Charles' laugh had a sharp edge.

"Well, La Renaudie, you certainly have my permission to go, and if all remains calm, as it is my earnest desire that it should, you may return at will. Indeed, I hope you may return with the Admiral himself. But, of course, you must not breathe a word of that to anyone. If the die-hards choke over the idea of a casual meeting between Coligny and myself, you can imagine they would become apoplectic at the thought of my receiving him back at Court. It will all take a great deal of planning."

The King sighed, then roused himself to wave dismissal to an astonished La Renaudie.

* * *

The main meal of the day interrupted Maurice's pilgrimage, and it was mid-afternoon before he gained admission to the apartments of the Duke of Anjou. This was the interview he dreaded most; it was with a heavy heart that he penetrated into the Prince's bedroom.

The room was stuffy. One half of the high window had been pulled wide open, giving a now clear view of the Loire running grey under a heavy overcast. In black velvet with white hose, Monsieur's figure stood out trimly against the grey, layered landscape. Maurice doffed his cap, bowed, and waited tensely for his friend's greeting.

Anjou turned abruptly, his normally pale face tinged pink with the effects of emotion and drink. The face was plumper, more regular and handsomer, though not necessarily more attractive, than that of his brother, the King.

"You ingrate," Anjou sputtered abruptly. "You squirming, slimy, slithering, slobbering, sniveling, sneaking, slavering serpent of a man. You..." The tirade continued in a crescendo of wet eruptions. La Renaudie reflected sourly that the gossip of this inbred Court had guaranteed that Anjou had received news of his departure before he could announce it himself and had given him ample time to prepare this outburst.

The noise abruptly desisted. Anjou wiped a trickle of saliva from his brown goatee, and glared balefully at La Renaudie.

"I don't understand. Unless you mean it as a gratuitous affront, I just don't understand," Anjou picked up, a note of whining in his voice.

"How could you think that, Your Highness?" asked La Renaudie in dulcet tones. "Your esteem..."

"How could I think that, you driveling idiot!" interrupted Anjou.

"Because you haven't had a thought of God since the Serpent ate your infant heart out. When I remember how often you have mocked my prayers as childishness, how often you have told me that whatever man can do he is permitted to do, how often you have said that popish nonsense is merely paganism reborn and Huguenot cant is an edema for the frustrated..." He paused with sudden shock. "Unless you truly are a heretical minister sent to tempt me from my sworn duties."

Anjou shook his head. "No, I don't think you believe in anything. I don't understand. You are too ambitious to throw your chances to the wind for no purpose. Maurice, tell me, please."

La Renaudie felt an impulse of pity for the younger man, but not enough to give himself away.

"I'm bored," he said finally.

"Bored," yelled Anjou. "Bored," he repeated, with genuine hurt in his voice.

Maurice hastened to cut in. "Your companionship gives the only meaning to my life here. If I could be with you always, I would be satisfied. But as it is, I am one of a hundred who wait on your pleasure. We can grab only minutes in a week, and they are all I have. Your life is full of purpose, but mine is not."

Moving gracefully on the balls of his feet, Anjou approached La Renaudie. He ran a finger around Maurice's ear, then cupped the back of his close-cropped head in his hand.

"Stay, Maurice," he said softly.

"I cannot," mumbled La Renaudie.

Anjou turned sharply and went back to the window. He ran his fingertips inside his ruff to air his hot neck.

"What are you up to? Why can't you tell me?" he asked. "I don't know who you're working for, or why. You'd best think to tell me when next we meet." He turned a direct gaze on La Renaudie. "Whatever you're cooking, think on this. I would like to see the Admiral and his henchmen back at Court. Tamed rabbits are easier potted than wild ones. You could render me service in preparing that stew, if you can reach the Admiral's long ears.

"Of course, that's between us two. My reputation would be ruined if it got around Court that I was in favor of bringing the Protestants back. I don't know why I should trust you at this point," he murmured almost to himself. "Well, one more secret between us can hardly make things worse."

La Renaudie's astonishment at this discourse quite took away his speech, and he bowed himself out in silence. He made for the stairs to join the de Galle retinue in the courtyard for the ride back to Plessis Gaillard. On the landing, he was accosted by a dapper young man, whom he recognized, after a moment's hesitation, as Gondi's secretary.

Julio put a hand on Maurice's arm and spoke quietly. "You are leaving tomorrow." It was more a statement than a question, but Maurice nodded.

"So are we, weather permitting. Meet me at daybreak at the boat landing. I'll have something for you."

Without a farewell, the young man hurried off down the corridor.

* * *

De Galle and his retinue rode slowly along the river in the grey dusk. No sunset was visible; the landscape stretched far away, dreary and barren under the lowering clouds. Maurice rode most of the way alone, lost in thought of his recent interviews and his coming adventures. On reflection, he had become more thrilled than terrified by his prospects, casting his situation in a heroic light and feeling an intense satisfaction with himself that almost superseded his fears and resentment.

Shortly before they reached home, Maurice looked up to find his stepfather riding beside him. Maurice rode on silently, uncomfortable under the Duke's level stare.

"So you're leaving," said de Galle. La Renaudie was far more astonished by the quiet tone of the statement than by the knowledge it indicated.

"Yes, Sir."

"I would like to see the Admiral come here himself. Communicating by third parties is an invitation to poisoning, and we are in a situation where communication has become a matter of life and death. But direct speech cannot be for the time being. If you could indicate to their leadership that there are those here who wish them well, provided that they wish us well, you would perform an unlooked-for service. If not, keep your mouth shut. Do you understand?"

"Yes, Sir."

"I would not tell you my thoughts if you were staying at Court. See that you don't repeat them to anyone before you're well away from here. I am a realist surrounded by people who don't understand realities. If they got the impression that I have any Protestant sympathies, it would only cause trouble."

The Count abruptly spurred his horse, leaving his dumbfounded stepson to mull over his words. How bizarre life is, Maurice reflected. By becoming a renegade, he had in a day gained more intimate insight into the minds of the great men of the kingdom than he had achieved in years of apparent respectability. And he had been given a piece of information which could not help but be useful: That unknown to each other, the most significant men at Court wanted the Protestants to return, albeit for drastically different reasons.

Should he tell Gondi? He would love to impress him with his ability and usefulness. But, he thought spitefully, it would be fun — and prudent — to keep a card or two up his own sleeve. It would be enough to tell Gondi of the King's plans for a casual encounter with Coligny in Brittany. This had been openly discussed in Council and he would hear of it from others, but he would still be impressed that Maurice knew of it. After all, Maurice mused with malicious satisfaction, Gondi had been excluded from the council whereas Maurice had learned of the King's scheme from the King's own mouth. Yes, make him worry and impress him, but give him nothing: That was the best plan.

Chapter V

he impenetrable obscurity of the starless night grudgingly yielded to a brooding grey. The fickle wind from the west blew fitful, unreliable, full of vagaries and bluster. Despite the gusts in its face and its furled sails, the shallow-bottomed sloop kept a good speed, more from the strong current than from the oarsmen's work. At the stern of the boat, Gondi huddled under a rickety, tent-like shelter, clutching about him some dank hides in a feeble attempt to ward off the dawn's damp chill. A sour smile at the hopelessness of this effort creased his lips.

Long use had worn the coverlets down to a layer of thin, cracked leather on which only dirt-stiffened patches of matted fur remained. They smelled so strong and gave so little comfort that Gondi wondered if they did not belong to that rare category of objects about which it is not possible to say that they are better than nothing.

Next to Gondi, thighs partly covered by one of the hides, calves and feet protruding from their cramped quarters, squatted Julio. A restless shift and a bump reminded Gondi of his presence. He turned and eyed Julio with weary distaste.

"Well, what did La Renaudie say?" he forced himself to ask.

Julio squirmed around to face Gondi, tucking his chilled legs up against Gondi's under the paltry covers.

"We didn't have much conversation. He had a boat lined up to leave shortly before dawn, and I didn't want anyone to see us. Not that there was much danger at that hour."

"Right," mumbled Gondi.

"Anyway, I told him how to get his reports through to you. As you expected, he said he could use a little money, as he had barely enough to get to St. Nazaire and he'd need something to take another boat to La Rochelle. He made a snide remark to the effect that if he walked, the King would get there before he would."

"What?" asked Gondi, his interest suddenly aroused.

"My reaction exactly. It seems he had an interview with His Majesty yesterday, and the King told him he was going to use the hunting trip to Normandy as a pretext for getting close to La Rochelle, so the Admiral would have a chance to meet with him on the sly. Something like that. It all seemed a bit vague, as he described it. Apparently, it was all discussed at the Council meeting."

"Was it indeed. No wonder it was such an exclusive party."

"La Renaudie was terribly puffed up about being in the King's confidence. Quite insufferable about it, really."

"So would you be, if you had the chance."

"All right, all right. I tossed the purse you gave me over to him, and for all his airs, he took it like a varlet. And that was all."

Gondi mulled over the news. He would send a rider back to inform the Queen Mother. No, he thought, he would wait. He would send someone to La Rochelle immediately — a reliable agent, not some madcap like La Renaudie — and on his return to Court, or soon after, there would be dependable information with which to decide what to do about the young King's impetuosity. When he had come to some kind of decision himself, there would be plenty of time to discuss the matter with the Queen Mother.

If only he did not feel so dull-witted this morning. The short night had left him unrefreshed, and the weather depressed him. This cursed trip to the abbey at Fontevrault had been inflicted on him against his will and for an end which he deplored. The additional burdens of discomfort and fatigue merely added fuel to the fire of his irritability. An irresistible, if irrational urge to vent his spume on his companion overwhelmed him.

"I can't imagine why you couldn't find something better than this," he snarled at Julio. "No doubt it's adequate by your standards, but I'm not accustomed to traveling like cattle. If you don't know my style by now, I doubt you'll ever know it."

"It looked all right," Julio replied petulantly, adding as a second thought, "I'm sorry."

In fairness, Gondi admitted reluctantly, its gaudy paint and heavy carvings gave the boat a grand enough look, and the obvious failings of its fittings would not have been striking on a fine day.

He shrugged resignedly. It seemed he would have to keep a private ship available at all times and avoid the commoner means of transport, which so often proved unfit for a man of his dignity.

Vallières and port of Luynes slid by in the penumbra. With uncharacteristic sentimentality, Gondi reflected that their clusters of houses looked pathetic, huddled within low fortifying walls, tight-shuttered under thatch. How illusory was the shelter provided by those walls! A few years of peace, a few bountiful harvests, and people took heart again and looked for easy times, but he, Gondi, knew better. Shaking himself mentally, he broke off from his morbid musings. He turned to Julio.

"And what did you think of yesterday's tirade from our Royal Mistress?" he asked in a bantering tone.

The youth rearranged his legs awkwardly and stared resolutely ahead. "I, Signor?" he mumbled.

"Come, come, Julio. You're an astute young man, well aware of the use to which an arras can be put. I'll give you some advice. You should never attempt to conceal something which is already known. That is a truth of general applicability. I would add further that in your case in particular, you should lie as little as possible, because you're not at all good at it."

Noticeably pink, the young man's face assumed a mulish look, as he turned away from Gondi's direct gaze.

"I would be a tyro indeed," Gondi continued, "if I had failed to discover that my cousin Jerome is paying you an allowance in return for tidbits which he can feed to the King of Spain. I have no objection to the arrangement or believe me, you would have heard about it before now. Your snooping does not interfere with your work. Everyone spies for someone, after all. Personally, I'm just as glad to keep my secrets in the family, as much as possible."

The pink passed up Julio's neck and cheeks to the very roots of his hair. Gondi could see only the back of the young man's head, but even so, the scarlet tip of his left ear, exposed by the jaunty angle of his cap, told eloquently of his embarrassment. Gondi smiled maliciously.

"To demonstrate my trust in you," Gondi continued, "I will tell you what I think yesterday's discussion amounted to.

"I have always thought that the Queen Mother's great strength is that she will fight like a wolf, fierce and shrewd, for her cubs, but alas, as always, a great weakness is the other side of the same coin. Whatever affects her children's attachment to her attacks her where she is most vulnerable. She lives through them more than she lives for them. Charles is, after all, King, and her power is only as great as his obedience.

"The advice I gave her was good advice, though it may serve other ends as well as her own. If encouraged, her pup will indeed get in over his head and cry for his mother, but with luck and planning, we can manage that the mother's need for succor at that moment will be no less than the son's, and both will sink or swim as we tell them.

"However, we must play our hand cautiously. Her Majesty has never had a tantrum, but for a purpose. We cannot safely ignore this sermon on peace, and we should attend especially to her denunciation of the treachery of dealings with Spain. King Philip should appreciate the fact that, were we as devoted to his cause as Álava, it would still be necessary to act against the Protestants with subtlety, and therefore with less speed than he would hope. Feel free to pass that thought on."

Gondi reached over and pushed Julio's cap forward over his eyes.

"Have you ever been to Fontevrault, Julio?" he asked. Taking the young man's fumblings with his headgear as a shake of the head, Gondi continued, "It's an amazing place. They say it has had as many as four thousand monks and nuns in its time. I've always found that claim a bit fanciful, but there's no doubt it was once a very great foundation. It's Benedictine, but in part its rules are absolutely original. You see, they provide for men and women alike to be governed by a woman. 'Mother, behold thy son. Son, behold thy Mother,' that's the Abbey's motto.

"It fell on hard times, like everything else, but the main house became a center of reform and revival, and now, it's thriving. The recent Abbesses, you see, have been Bourbons of the highest rank, who've used that rank to make their Abbey great again. Funny, really, when you consider that the Bourbons are now of the Reformed Religion.

63

"I saw a curious thing years ago: The King stopped at Fontevrault during his royal tour, and I saw the Abbess Louise fall on her knees before him and beg him to punish her own great-nephews, Condé and Navarre, for their heresy."

He paused, thinking of the strength and audacity of the great Abbess. "The other odd thing is that those of the Reformed Religion have largely spared the Abbey, even though it stands for everything they despise."

Interest had overcome Julio's pique, and he turned to face Gondi again. At this point, he interjected, "The prioress, Eleanor — She's the Abbess's niece, isn't she? — has Huguenot sympathies, or at least that's something I've heard. That might explain it."

Gondi looked at his cousin sternly, but amusement soon softened his regard. "So, the little pitcher's ears are long enough to catch conversations other than my own. Really, though, you should show more respect. Louise de Bourbon is a very great woman, and should not be scoffed at by the likes of you.

"Even if she is a pain in the..." he bit back the last word, so it was inaudible to his listener.

"At any rate," Gondi recollected himself, "it's a huge place — four monasteries really, one for monks, one for nuns, one for fallen women, and one for lepers.

"Last time I was there was five years ago. I was with the Queen Mother," he added unnecessarily. "That was the time she donated 10,000 pounds for their new dormitory. And you know, though you should not know, what a sum like that means to her." Gondi smiled at Julio.

"Forgive me, Uncle," Julio said, falling back into the time-honored form of address for older relatives, "but why are we going to Fontevrault?"

"We are going to Fontevrault to see about my ward, your cousin, Athalie."

"What's to see about?" the young man asked glibly. "Athalie's going to be a nun, isn't she? Cousin Jerome says you sent her to Fontevrault to become a nun so her inheritance would come to you."

A dark hue suffused Gondi's rosy cheeks. "By God, I'll not be party to this womanish tale-telling. You and Jerome, you spy for a living and you gossip for fun. It's revolting."

Julio resumed his former unsociable position, his back to Gondi, his legs stretched out on the deck, his gaze fixed on the hull of the boat. As he watched, the rain began to fall. As best he could, he pulled his legs under cover, hugging his knees for warmth.

At first, the water fell only in bursts and gusts, blowing under the flimsy canopy, slapping a loose sail end in an irritating cadence, playing at being a mere spate. The gay feather in Julio's cap wilted sadly; drops fell from its tip onto his cheek. Gondi removed his own sodden velvet headgear, and hid his face in the crook of his arm.

By noon, the downpour was heavy, steady, and impenetrable. The boat slipped eerily through a grey isolation into which murky outlines intruded, distorted shapes that threatened rather than welcomed. The storm's medley of rushing, gurgling, slapping noises did not synchronize with the boat's jerky, bumpy progress. Queasiness added itself to the passengers' other discomforts.

Draping one of the hides over his head and shoulders, Gondi struggled to his feet and staggered to the bow, where the Captain stood peering down at the river's dark flood. Without waiting for Gondi to speak, the Captain burst out, "I tell you, Sir, I'm afraid.

"I know the river well, my Lord, but now, when I'm close to one bank, I can hardly see the other. I'm afraid for my ship, I tell you. This current is so damned fast, you'll pardon me, and will be faster when the Indre joins in. You can't see the islands 'til you're on top of them, and you can't see the sandbars at all. Normally, I don't like to leave the steering to someone else, but I figure I have to stand up here and try to make our course and signal as best I can."

Gondi's curtly sympathetic shrug was lost on his companion, so he cleared his throat and yelled a reply, "You're in charge on board. What should we do?"

"To tell you true, my Lord, I'm afraid to try for La Chapelle. We just passed where the Cher comes in, and I figure the town's not far, but I could be wrong, and who knows what we'll run into between here and there! I'm afraid for my ship," he repeated miserably.

"Well?" asked Gondi.

"It's a tricky maneuver, but with your permission, I'd like to tie up and take shelter 'til this filth blows over."

Gondi looked out at the sheets of rain, and felt a numbing certainty that the storm was not about to blow over. Impressed with the look of fear in the Captain's eyes, he said resignedly, "Do as you wish. We are in your hands."

The Captain yelled a command, incomprehensible to Gondi, and miraculously, it seemed, the small crew materialized from behind crates and under tarpaulins. Apparent pandemonium followed, the illusion which the crisp execution of complex maneuvers often creates in the minds of bystanders.

Gondi, who knew a thing or two about ships, was both impressed and terrified, as he watched the little ship execute a gut-wrenching turn, which brought it broadside to the current, where it seemed to hang suspended for an eternity before gliding around to bump into the shore. Sweating despite the cold, the hands made fast the ship's ropes to some trees, and the party went ashore.

They sought an uncertain refuge under the same barren trees.

A rough meal from the crew's supply of victuals — cold sausage, bread (stale, but, miraculously, only slightly damp) and wine — was shared out among them. Equals in the face of adversity, they overlooked distinctions of rank. The wet hides were distributed as evenly as possible, the food was divided equally, and the wine flasks were passed from mouth to mouth.

Gondi found a strange comfort in the press of bodies, the coarse food, and the sharp, young wine. It seemed to remind him of something he had known and lost. Thinking back, he recognized this solidarity in the face of the storm's mindless hostility as akin to the virile, sometimes brutal, camaraderie of his soldiering years in Italy. He had been younger then — years younger — fighting, like all the others, for glory, for money, for fun. There had never been anything like it since that time. The civil wars of later years had yielded only dreary, half-suppressed memories, tinged with bitterness, anxiety, and loneliness, which were but shadows of his exciting recollections of the battles of his youth.

He took a gulp of wine, which burned his throat and made his nose tingle, and passed the flask to the Captain. The uniqueness of the occasion struck him suddenly. Routine dealings with servants and utilitarian exchanges with common strangers, these were ordinary, but to sit down man-to-man with one of that class, that was unusual.

Would conversation with such a person prove amusing? He looked at the Captain's dour, lined face, cracked, dirty and expressionless, and thought not. Eventually, however, his irritation at the silent munching of his companions prodded him into speech.

"Where are you from, Captain?" he asked.

"I'm from Kervoyal originally, my Lord," the other replied. "That's south of Vannes." Gondi, thinking of the bleak, harsh Atlantic shore of southern Brittany, understood the man's grim, worn face.

"I learned my trade off the coast there, and there's no teacher like the ocean. This river is treacherous, with its currents and shifting sands and spring floods, but I still say it's child's play compared with the ocean. We were a fishing family, but the village had too many children and not enough boats, so I went inland and had a bit of luck. I worked as a hand for the owner of this boat and married his daughter. The old man died five years ago, and now the boat's mine. We also got a little land, two strips you'd hardly call a farm — in Rochecorbon, the other side of Tours, and that's my home, when I'm not on the boat."

"I know Rochecorbon. It's a narrow town that goes north from the riverbank, with a very old church that looks like a bulwark built into the hillside."

"Well, yes, my Lord, that's the place, though I don't know what you'd say about the church. It's old all right, and not much to look at, not like some of the other parishes have. It's a poor place really, but what can you expect? That's what was there, and you can be sure the curé doesn't have money to spend on the church."

"He has the tithes, doesn't he?"

"I don't rightly know how that works. It seems a lot of the money goes to the Abbey, you know, at Marmoutier. And anyway, you see, the tithes don't get paid regular by everyone." His expression made it clear that he felt he had volunteered enough information on that score.

"Well," Gondi said tactfully, "with the cost of everything so high, it must be hard to find an extra tenth to give to the Church, however much people may want to."

"That's just it, my Lord. We're sorry for Father Michel. He's not a bad man, and we don't like to see him starve. But the cost of everything keeps going up, and then they keep increasing the tithes, too, like they don't understand." The Captain's grizzled eyebrows ran together into a thick line.

"Surely, it's not a question of starving, your priest, I mean."

"Not to say starving, no, but he'd be hard up if he hadn't kept his hand in the tanning business."

At Gondi's look of frank astonishment, the creases around the Captain's eyes deepened with a hint of amusement.

"Well, Sir, you mustn't think it's like what you're used to.

"I've been to St. Gatien at Tours, and I know what it's like," he said, a trace of pride warming his voice, "but Father Michel?" He snorted suddenly. "I mean, your bishops, they wouldn't claim him for a cousin, if you know what I mean.

"Don't take me wrong, my Lord. He does all right, given who he is. He was the tanner's son, and our old curé, Father Alphonse, taught him his letters and all that Latin, and when he showed an interest, well, he got the post. There weren't exactly a lot of other people interested. So he says the Masses, he baptizes, and he buries. I guess he gets some money from that. And for the rest, he does a little tanning on the side to help out his old man in exchange for some extra food and maybe a few sous. He lives mostly with his family anyway. The curé's house is really just a shack. What's more, I've a feeling he's got something on with his sister. She's not married, so it doesn't bother anyone."

At this, he lowered his voice. "I don't hold with Protestants, my Lord, that I don't, but I sometimes think they've got a point about priests getting married. No one's the better for it. It's a lonely life, after all, and..."

Taking Gondi's shocked look for disapproval, the Captain subsided into silence. The two men sat speechless, listening to the mingled rushing of rain and river water. A recollection flashed through Gondi's mind — a Sunday, years ago when he had been on the road and had stopped for Mass in a little village in the Auvergne.

He remembered the stink of matted rushes, the noise of mangled Latin, barely audible for the stirring and coughing of the congregation, and, most of all, the sight of the priest's broken, black fingernails against the whiteness of the host.

"What does he preach about, your tanner?" Gondi resumed quietly.

The Captain picked at a scab on his hand, while he reflected. "Oh, I don't know. The Blessed Virgin, sometimes."

"Does he preach the Immaculate Conception?"

"No," he replied hesitantly, then with fervor, "Certainly not! He doesn't preach any heresy, our curé." Gondi's brows shot up.

"We wouldn't stand for it. To give Father Michel credit, he's very strong against Protestants, my lord, and like I said, we're all with him on that."

"Are there no Protestants in Rochecorbon?"

"Only one household, and that's one household too many, say we all. You'd think they owned the place," he continued in a bitter tone. "Of course, they've got so much money they could own it.

"Why, I guess if they called in their loans they'd have half the town overnight. But I'm telling you, my Lord, they'll get it in the end, they will; they'll get it for sure." The man's low voice vibrated harshly.

"Like that time at Tours in '62. I was there. I was young and new-married then, and working alongside my father-in-law. It was July, I remember, normally our busiest time, but with all the fighting along the river, there wasn't much business. Things were tight. My wife and I already had one child, that's why we got married, see, and we had another on the way, and the old man still had two living at home. We were having a hard time and we were in Tours, trying to pick up some business — cargo out the coast, or even a short ferrying job.

"I don't know how it started, but suddenly I hear yelling and see smoke over by the Place Plumereau. So I leave the old man with the boat, and the rest of us, we run over to the market and there's the merchant's lane, see, with a whole mob of people waving staves and axes — anything they could get their hands on. I didn't have anything like that, so I figured I'd better get something. There was this old wheel lying in the gutter. I smashed the rim, and me and the boys, we each took two spokes. It wasn't much, but it was better than nothing. I still didn't know what was going on, but then the crowd started kind of chanting, 'Heretics'll burn, heretics'll burn,' so I got the idea. Most of those merchants, see, were Protestant, or that's what we figured, anyway. It was scary, even to me, that chanting, over and over, louder and louder, and the square was so tight packed I thought it would burst. It did, in a way, because we started breaking into the shops. Me and my boys, we took what we could carry. So did everyone else, I guess.

"The people inside, the heretics, I mean, they got dragged out and clubbed or carved up. I guess they drowned quite a few of them. I didn't get involved in all that. What I was really interested in was getting some stuff to live off. That kept me busy, or I'd have been happy to lend a hand.

"They didn't get more than they deserved, that's for certain. I wasn't there when the heretics went around pillaging and looting the churches, but I saw what they did to St. Martin's. They broke everything they could break. Every statue had its head smashed off. The windows were all shattered. The place was a wreck. No one could ever use it again. So I guess everyone was just waiting to get back at the swine. Bloody infidels, no better than Moorish heathens. Anyway, see, I was sick and tired of breaking my back for nothing, while they all ate white bread and kept their hands clean."

The man paused, then resumed with less fervor. "They say the Loire ran red with blood that day I was telling you about, but I don't know about that. People always like to say things like that, to make a thing sound important.

"Here," the Captain broke out savagely, "lay off that, you scum." He reached out roughly and grabbed the wine flask from his youngest oarsman, a wiry youth, whose thin limbs protruded from his worn clothing. The Captain glanced a mute query at Gondi; at his silent headshake, he poured the remaining wine down his throat.

"There's peace now, or so they say," he resumed. "But they'll still get it, I tell you. If not today, then tomorrow."

The rain cleared slowly. The voyagers resumed their course, and reached La Chapelle without further ado.

Gondi's group put up at the tiny village inn. There was no room for the others, and Gondi did not know or care where they spent the night. The privileges of rank had reasserted themselves.

* * *

Morning broke clear, sunny, and cold, transforming all objects, great and small, natural and man-made, into sharp, glistening wonders. The wind had come around; together with the swollen current, it made short work of the last ten miles of the river trip. The travelers left La Chapelle at dawn, quickly passed the gentle influx of the Indre, moss green in the morning light, and came at last to where the Loire and the Vienne meet and the greater river absorbs the lesser, and thus swelled, flows on to the sea.

At Candes, Gondi, Julio, and their party debarked and equipped themselves for the ride inland to Fontevrault. Gondi, impatient, soon found their slow pace irksome and split the group in two, riding ahead with Julio and some of his men-at-arms, leaving the rest of the escort with his manservant and the baggage. Thus liberated, he pushed his mount, rushing at the steep hills and sharp ravines which rose from the river bank to the inland plateau as if they were enemy fortifications to be attacked and overcome. He felt the nervous energy from the previous day's confinement and the anxious tension over his coming interview with the Abbess charge through him into his horse, which skittered and bounded like a creature in torment. Unaware of what drove his companion, Julio joined in the race with all the joyful abandon of youth, while their guards clambered to keep them in sight.

At midday, they reached the summit of their climb and paused.

After the shadowed gully they had left behind, the sun seemed bright on the level land ahead. They saw a narrow, rutted track winding through a rough land, overgrown with wind-blown gorse and brush.

There was but little cultivation. Here and there, where scattered plots had been cleared for a vineyard or a wheat field, the land was rich and rewarded those bold enough to till it — but as a rule, people preferred the river towns to the vulnerable loneliness of open country. Of human habitations, there were none in sight.

They rode on, halting in a clearing for a meager, cold lunch. The exuberance of the morning ride exhausted, Gondi ate without appetite, lost in apprehensive musings over the coming ordeal. Gondi was accustomed to confrontations. Indeed, his greatness lay in his ability to do in politics and commerce what others did in war: to ambush the unsuspecting, to browbeat the weak, and to trick the strong. By careful planning and sheer force of character, he would — as a rule — have his way. It was not simply that he had great abilities, though, indeed, he did;

it was that he wanted what he wanted more than those who stood in his way wanted to oppose him.

Gondi, however, never approached the task of imposing his will on others without suffering all the nervousness of a star performer before his entrance. Today, especially, he was filled with foreboding.

He had not seen Louise de Bourbon for years and had never spoken to her alone, but he knew her. He knew the power of her rank and connections, because he always knew such things, and he knew by instinct that her character was as great as her position. He feared to find her too strong to be bullied and too wise to be deceived. His stomach churned, his upper lip beaded with sweat, and his hands felt wet and cold.

After their brief pause, they made good time, and came, sooner than they had hoped, to Fontevrault's civilized lands, where fields and orchards, meadows and vineyards checkered the plain which spread away from the Abbey's grey walls and slate roofs. The road, now wide and smooth, went forward through a countryside hazed and silver green with the tender colors of spring, through the town gate, and through the humble village, straight to the massive archway in the Abbey's claustral wall.

In the dusty, sunlit courtyard, they dismounted and gave their horses to a group of anonymous, silent monks. A brisk, spry nun, one of the lay religious, greeted Gondi, and showed him into the parlor, a starkly elegant room with a vaulted ceiling and a tiled floor, cool and dim. The change from the glare outside made Gondi walk slowly, almost timidly, down the long room toward the erect, black-clad woman awaiting him at the end.

As he approached the Abbess, his eyes now accustomed to the light, he saw at once her alertness, her tautness, her vibrant intelligence. Louise de Bourbon was almost thirty years his senior, but she was strong from half a century of disciplined, hard living. Never had she failed to break the night with prayers or to rise again to chant the day in. He recognized in her a quality that he had found before only in dedicated soldiers. At the same time, he sensed that her discipline extended to the mind as well as the body. He realized gratefully that he felt fit and ready for the encounter. Energy surged through him.

He bent gracefully over the Abbess's ring. With apparent calm, he stood quietly under her long, appraising stare, waiting respectfully for her permission to sit. When they were settled at last, he took the offensive.

"Madame, I came as soon as I could in response to your letter, which I must say distressed me greatly. Now that I am here, I am confused as to how to proceed. I do not wish to seem to imply reproach to someone whose position places her above reproach." He inclined slightly from the waist.

Speaking for the first time, the Abbess said slowly, "No one is above reproach."

"Well, then, I take courage," he resumed. "Both as a devout Christian and as a loving kinsman, I am greatly upset by what seems to me, forgive me, as a thwarting of God's will for my niece. We are all so aware, in these days of trouble, of the need for vocations, true vocations, especially in those whom God has chosen to lead, as he has chosen the noblemen and noblewomen of this country.

"We are all aware," he repeated, "that Calvin's successes have multiplied now that he has recruited the nobility of France — or some of its weaker members. Our only defense is to arouse similar ardor in the stronger members of that same class. Thus, Madame, that you, in your position, should discourage our young kinswoman from taking up cudgels for her Faith came as a disappointment, indeed, Madame, I cannot say otherwise, as a shock."

A stiff smile crossed Louise de Bourbon's white face. "It pleases me to find, Monsieur, that one in your position," and she imitated him by also bowing slightly, "can spare time for such earnest thought on the future of our beleaguered Church from your numerous political and domestic duties. These thoughts will no doubt have led you to conclude that the battle against those of the so-called Reformed Religion must be fought on many fronts — by true reform of the Church itself, by military strength, and, most importantly, by building strong, faithful, ardent families, who will support Church, Crown, and Country."

"Madame, the way you have chosen, giving thus the example my niece wishes to follow, is the way that God has declared to be the highest form of devotion to our causes. Who are we to gainsay His Word?"

"It is the highest way for those who are called to it. For others, different ways are better."

"Lesser ways, Madame, lesser ways. For my sister's daughter, I look for the highest way."

"Only if she has a true vocation."

"She says she has. Why should we question it?"

"It seems to me, Count," the old Abbess smiled shrewdly, "that it depends on one's perspective whether one should question it."

"How so?" he asked haughtily and immediately regretted giving his adversary the opportunity to explain.

"Monsieur knows I have no interest in this matter," Louise de Bourbon replied. "Indeed, my interest would, if anything, run to keeping Athalie for Fontevrault, for God, and for myself. But, if it is not best for her, it will not be best for God. On the other hand, you have nothing to gain and much to lose if Athalie returns to Court and discovers that her apparent calling is not genuine."

Gondi stood abruptly and looked down at the Abbess. "What do you wish to say, Madame? That I would ignore my duty?"

The Abbess smiled the smile of a leader who for forty years had winnowed the truth from the evasions and prevarications of her countless charges. Gondi was surprised and oddly touched by the kindly understanding in that smile, but he knew that he would find no quarter. He sat down.

"I have watched your progress with great interest, Monsieur. I am locked away from the world, but you must not think that my physical seclusion prevents me from observing it with interest. And how could one fail to be fascinated by your achievements — and your acquisitions? I am not speaking only of material possessions; even more, I am talking of power and prestige, things that usually require generations or even centuries to be acquired, but which you have amassed in a matter of years. You possess the magic formula. Some men have only greed, or ambition, or what shall we call it? Others have only ability, without the force, whatever we have decided to call it, that makes them invincible. You have everything — brains and will, shrewdness and courage, charm and ruthlessness. But you shouldn't overreach. It is not becoming in you."

She took a breath, and continued as if on a new subject. "You have surely merited recompense from the monarchy. Your advice to the Queen Mother has assisted her in times of great need, and I doubt not will do so again." He bowed gravely. "Still," she continued, "it must be difficult to reward one who is already so well situated, especially in these times of need. It has occurred to me, as it must have occurred to you, that our kinswoman's estate, should she no longer need it, would be a dazzling reward, even for someone like yourself. You must understand, Monsieur, that I could not stand by quietly for such an arrangement, unless I were convinced that Athalie's vocation were absolutely unswerving."

"Madame, I do not need my niece's money."

"That is certainly true, Monsieur. Your wealth is famous. But I have never noticed that the possession of wealth, however great, diminished the possessor's desire for more. Those who care enough to accumulate money usually continue to care after they no longer need to.

"Moreover, Monsieur, I do not imagine for a moment that it is money that you are principally after." She leaned forward, and spoke harshly. "If you came into her possessions, you would come into her land, and with her land, her title. That is the important thing, is it not?"

Gondi's face reddened and he raised his voice, expressing outrage to conceal his dismay. "I have done nothing for which the law does not provide. I will not have you suggest the contrary. I have used the income from my niece's property to maintain and increase its prosperity. I have provided for her proper education and her spiritual and physical welfare. Any profits beyond these needs are mine by right. As for the future, if she wishes to give her all for the Kingdom of Heaven, I neither can nor should stand in her way.

"What happens to her worldly goods thereafter is not in my hands, but in the King's."

"Count," Louise de Bourbon retorted, frost in her eyes and voice, "do not pretend to misunderstand me. I know that you commit no crime, but I believe you may wish to commit a sin. As Athalie's guardian, your actions are above reproach and your motives are irrelevant. As her religious counselor, which is what you now presume to be, your motives become important, and to me they appear most questionable. To offer spiritual guidance, where the end is not God's glory but your own advancement, would be a grievous fault."

He could think of no answer which would deceive or dissuade her, so he blurted out stupidly, "You will get your dowry, never fear."

"No doubt," and she waved that substantial sum aside as if it were nothing.

"She is, at any rate, too young to give what she does not know she has," the Abbess continued. "I do not mean only her riches, I mean also her life as a woman. The Church speaks of a nun as the Bride of Christ, but a bride is not a wife, not a mistress of a home, not a mother. She must know what she is giving before she gives. She has a great heart and a great mind. When she is older and has had experience, she will herself choose, and such is her wisdom and goodness that she will choose better than you or I could ever choose for her."

"Many give up what you speak of before they know of it. Surely you do not mean that their gift is meaningless."

"Athalie is not like other people."

The Abbess stood, her dark eyes holding his light ones.

"She is great in her own right, and she is my child, my sister's granddaughter, as much as she is your child, your sister's daughter. I am the ruler of this House; here, it will be done as I say."

"I trust," he bowed sardonically, "I trust you will allow me to speak to her myself?"

"Of course. It is my wish that she should be your ward and companion for many months or years, however long it takes for her to find her true path. You may see her now, if you wish. Adieu, Monsieur."

The Abbess clapped her hands and instructed the portress who answered to conduct Gondi to the guesthouse and to summon Athalie to him.

As the girl entered his room, he sought briefly a glimpse of her mother's charm, and was relieved not to discern it. Athalie curtseyed, her face lowered, not to express modesty but to conceal her distress and confusion.

"Child," Gondi gestured to the window seat opposite his.

"Child, you have chosen a noble road, and I am most gratified."

She glanced up at him, pain in her eyes. "Madame the Abbess does not feel I am ready, Monsieur, so it cannot be as yet."

"There are other houses, niece. You may enter anywhere."

She looked at him with shock and wonder in her face. "How should I be ready elsewhere, if I am not ready here?"

"Well, your aunt, your great-aunt, has an idea that you are not ready, but you look to me as a grown girl would. Your mind is your own."

Athalie gazed blankly at her uncle. She did not know him, and by some undefined instinct, she did not trust him. Though she heard what she wished to hear from his mouth, she did not believe it. It merely intensified her anguish. She remained mute and troubled.

Gondi sensed her resistance. It puzzled and annoyed him. Women normally responded to his charm as a thoroughbred to its trainer's hand. The anger he felt at his setback by the Abbess was intensified by a feeling of frustration. How to penetrate this alien, adolescent intellect? He curbed his desire to lash out at the girl and resumed pleasantly.

"I do not believe that you wish to go to Court."

"No, no. I don't. I want to stay here," she pleaded.

"Well, you cannot stay here. The Abbess is mistress of her House. But there are other houses. Do you understand me? Other orders. Active orders. Contemplative orders. You may choose."

Her lip curled sarcastically. "I have chosen. If I cannot have what I have chosen, I will wait. This is not an auction."

Gondi stared at the young girl, feeling her covert violence, wondering where she had found the power to speak up to her elders, recognizing her stern, forbidding father in her look.

"Then pack your bags, niece," he said sharply. "We will leave tomorrow, and you will go with me where I will, as befits a girl of your age."

Returning to her little room, Athalie lay down diagonally across the bed furs, her head twisted to avoid the mound of pillows. Ignoring the bells for supper, she watched the evening light slant across the ceiling.

Her old nurse entered, carrying a wooden platter with a hunk of dark bread, a slab of paté, and a mug of spicy bouillon, still steaming slightly. The reflected light picked out the promontories of her craggy face. She was in her fifties and already her face was developing the hollow temples, eye-sockets, and cheeks that would mark her in time as truly and venerably old. Without looking at Athalie, she deposited the platter on the table and said, "Whatever's eating you, it won't get any better for your starving."

When this brought no response, she crossed and perched next to the pillows, looking down tenderly. She said, without much conviction, "If you talked to me, maybe it would help."

Athalie turned her head toward the wall. She knew the old woman approved of the Abbess's decision, of the return to Court, of the resumption of ordinary life. Athalie blamed her irrationally for her troubles.

The nurse got up, shaking her head with a mixture of annoyance and worry.

"Well, I certainly can't help if you shut me out, and I may as well take care of myself instead."

She paused for a reply, but none was forthcoming.

She left abruptly. Moments later, Athalie swung her legs over the edge of the bed, hesitated, then went to the food, hunger overcoming her distaste for life.

Chapter VI

At dawn, the little group clattered through the Abbey's great gate, Gondi and his nephew riding ahead, his manservant, Athalie, and the old nurse following in the baggage cart, and the escort lined up behind. Just before leaving, Gondi had said to Athalie, "We have no saddle for you. You could ride behind your cousin, but you'd be better off with the baggage." She had assented, inwardly relieved at not being asked to handle a horse alone, but hurt nonetheless by Gondi's indifference and most of all by his curt tone. The old nurse had cushioned the cart's rough boards with bedding, and she and Athalie now sat together, facing back, watching as Fontevrault dwindled and disappeared from sight.

The morning was cool but held a promise of warmth. As the sun cleared the horizon, the air about the travelers vibrated with the calling of birds. Flocks of them, little brown specks, sparrows and starlings mostly, scattered in rough rambunctious clusters across the dewy fields. The earth was dark from the spring rains, and the vineyards beside the road were a flush of baby green against the black loam. In spite of herself, Athalie responded to the lovely morning.

Like that evening in April when she had stood in the orchard cherishing its new life, she felt a mysterious bond with the rich earth, the running sap, and the glowing greenery. She would have liked to jump down from the cart, to lay her palms and her cheeks against the soil and to absorb the moist life-giving strength of the earth through her pores. Her apprehension evaporated like the dew, and a feeling of excitement swelled deep inside her.

On the plateau, the roads were soft, and progress, though slow, was not uncomfortable. As the decline toward the river steepened, the track became harder, rocky in places, and ravaged with cuts where the rains had wrought their damage. The cart bumped and thumped on its wooden wheels, jarring its passengers with every creaking jolt. Progress was even slower and had become very uncomfortable.

Gondi and Julio now rode slowly behind the lurching vehicle. Athalie saw with resentment the ease with which they navigated the ruts and gullies, riding cool and relaxed high above the dust.

She looked down, and watched the road streaming out from under the cart. The sight brought an odd sensation, similar to a childhood experience, when once she had stood above an old mill wheel looking down at the Indre flowing ceaselessly below. It had seemed then as if the mill platform that supported her moved, while the water stood still; she had been so caught up in the illusion that she had fallen forward as if thrown by its motion, and only the quick catch of some grown-up had saved her from tumbling into the paddles. The same confused, dizzy feeling overcame her, as, hypnotically, she watched the pebbles, mounds, and furrows flow beneath the cart, borne on the road's strong current.

She clutched the side of the cart and closed her eyes, suppressing the hungry queasiness of her empty stomach.

The mill of her near mishap had belonged to one of her father's smaller residences — Islette of the verdant park, Islette of the cool, shadowy waters, Islette, the only dwelling before Fontevrault she had recognized as home. She saw it now through her closed eyes, basking in the eternal summertime of childhood memories. Here she was, she thought, leaving another home, uprooted and cast adrift, just like the little girl who had loved Islette. When would she be old enough to do as she chose, instead of being trucked around like baggage in someone else's life? Her mouth twisted sarcastically at the aptness of the image.

She opened her eyes and stared up at her uncle. Gondi's horse was directly behind the cart, so close she could have stroked its nose had she dared. It was a large animal, and mettlesome, but Gondi controlled it effortlessly, even thoughtlessly. Athalie sensed his power and resented it.

And if he died? The question popped up unbidden; it shocked her and it fascinated her. She had no thought of hastening the event. She merely recognized that what seemed indestructible could suddenly be destroyed. It was not really his demise that she wanted, merely his removal from her life; she used the image of death to make his disappearance seem possible.

Suddenly, in her imagination, he was dead, and no sense speculating about the consequences. If he died, would she still have a guardian? Would it be the Abbess? Or was guardianship reserved for men? If he died, her fancy ran on, she would throw herself at the King's feet and beg him to take her property but leave her free in her own person. She pictured the scene in the most romantic terms, the tall and shining monarch stooping over her, setting her on her feet, and bestowing on her, with royal prodigality, full liberty to dispose of her self and her possessions. What were her possessions? she wondered. The Abbess had said she would be very rich one day, as her father had been, but Athalie's inexperience made it difficult for her to visualize what that meant. She remembered well the family seat. "Rocher de la Roque" it was called — "Rock of the Roques" — and a great rock it was, a bastion built on the summit of one of the few real promontories overlooking the Loire. It was a good place for fortification, and over the centuries, the opportunity had not been wasted by her family. Was this fortress hers? Would it ever be? Would lovely Islette ever be hers? She looked down at the thin, small hands fingering the plain, dark stuff of her dress. It seemed inconceivable.

Her head buzzed so! She shook it sharply, and the bright figments of imaginings crumbled and disappeared, leaving a curiously empty, dazed feeling. The cart gave a thunderous crash. Athalie thought desperately, I can't stand it, I'm going to cry; I would rather die, but I'm going to cry. She suddenly realized that the pink nose of Gondi's horse was nearly in her lap and that the cart had stopped moving. Startled, Athalie looked over her shoulder and gasped at the sight she beheld. They were on a spit of sand overlooking the meeting of the Loire and the

Vienne. The two rivers joined in a placid expanse of slowly flowing water, deep, calm, and strong. As the men dismounted, Athalie and the old woman scrambled from the cart; together, they walked to the water's edge. In the quiet of full noon, the current was the only sound, a celestial-seeming music that imposed a momentary silence on the group.

The illusion of eternal harmony was broken by Julio stretching, waving his arms, and loudly demanding food. The others turned back; only Athalie remained, dreamily watching the blue mirror of the river's surface slip over its silty depths.

The group ate heartily. Athalie found, as she finished the robust meal of spicy meat and coarse bread, that its solid comfort had crushed the airy hallucinations of the morning. Gondi and the two young people sat in sleepy silence, squinting in the bright light.

Julio lazily twirled his cap in his hands. It was of the newest style, in patterned green velvet. He had tenderly brushed and re-blocked it after its wetting, so that it would lose none of its elegance; now, he stroked its long, fluffy feather with a rapt and innocent pleasure.

Occasionally, he sent Gondi veiled glances, which spoke eloquently of his admiration and timidly sought the affirmation of reciprocated approval. Gondi, oblivious, leaned back against the sandy bank, his half-closed eyes looking off into the distance.

At length, he roused himself and smiled merrily at his nephew, who responded on the instant with a grin of dog-like adoration.

"Tell your cousin how Court strikes a newcomer. You're still one yourself, eh, paisano?" Gondi reached over, and pulled Julio's earlobe affectionately, as the pleased expression disappeared from the young man's face. Julio thought himself the model of a dapper young courtier, with sophistication and polish beyond his drab cousin's imagining. With the deliberation of one who has done with frivolities and is prepared to continue with the work of the moment, he set his beloved cap carefully on his curls and moved to rise.

Swiftly grasping his arm, Gondi pulled him back to earth. "I'm quite serious, you little peacock. Your cousin, here, is going into an unknown world, and she's terrified, just as you were when you came to me not so long ago."

Far from appreciating her uncle's apparent concern, Athalie fiercely resented having her unacknowledged fear held up for display, and she in turn looked coldly away.

"You can do her a service by telling her what to expect, what life there is like, how it differs from life elsewhere." Having with lofty adult disregard for adolescent sensibilities offended both of his young companions, Gondi leaned back with an expression that was at once complacent and expectant.

Intrigued in spite of himself, Julio mentally withdrew from the headlong process of living and tried to look at his life as a spectator instead of a participant. Such detached introspection was not a common activity with him; the effort it entailed puckered his brow, giving him an intent, questing expression, like a hunting dog pointing.

Life at Court was certainly different from life at home, a different world, but he could not bring together all the elements of excitement, novelty, and intrigue which set it apart. Proceeding with uncharacteristic logic, Julio asked himself which aspect of Court life was the most striking, and the answer came in a flash.

It was, of course, the women, nubile young attendants, eager like himself to learn every twist in the road of love, but, unlike himself, unwilling to arrive at its inevitable destination; courtesans who would come readily enough, but rarely for a price he could afford; and bored wives, older women to his young eyes, for whom it seemed that the rites of initiation were as pleasing as the climax itself. The women came in all sizes, shapes, and dispositions, but all were elegant, most were beautiful, all were tantalizing, and many were willing. The images and memories thus conjured up exploded Julio's careful analysis and filled him with acute enjoyment and frustration. He sat with mouth parted and quickened breathing, perspiration moistening his downy beard. Gondi's renewal of conversation brought a sudden return to reality. Julio noted gratefully that his stylishly puffy breeches concealed the evidence of his distraction.

"Well, if you won't talk, then I shall," Gondi resumed. "Court life and life away from Court? It's the difference between the animation of market days and the dullness of other days. It's always market day at Court, with the crowds, the shows, the gossip, the display. For the lords, it's the difference between merely having wealth and showing others that they have it. Somehow, possessions are always more exciting if someone else is envying them, especially if you're pretending to have more than you do. For the have-nots, it's the chance — a bare chance, but a chance nonetheless — of getting ahead in a way that they never could if they stayed on the land."

Gondi paused, thinking of the meteoric flights to fame and fortune he had seen, including his own — and the crashes that had sometimes followed. Royal favor? A castle built on sand.

"It will be very different from what you are accustomed to," he continued, turning to Athalie. "No quiet contemplation in shady gardens, no privacy of any kind — there are too many people for that. People will watch everything you do and listen to everything you say. What's worse, they will read their own meanings into every word or glance. I don't think you'll like it."

Athalie's mouth was set in a firm line; she stared resolutely ahead at the scene which earlier had filled her with such pleasure. Annoyed by her lack of response, Gondi shrugged and rose, curtly signaling their departure.

"We will ride on, now, to Chinon," he said, "and will spend the night with my friend, banker Pascal."

The afternoon passed more quickly than the morning. They traveled on the south bank of the Vienne along a narrow road which followed the course of the river. Julio, soon over his fit of pique, sang bits of song that were popular at

78

Court. He had a pleasing, lilting voice, which could barely be heard over the river's burbling and the clopping of the horses.

Dismayed and angered by the conversation at lunch, Athalie was at first oblivious both to Julio's melodies and to the passing countryside. As the afternoon waned, however, her spirits rose slightly. The birds in the bare trees beside the water began their evening festival, and Athalie suddenly awoke to notice how the band of light that was the river gave life to the barren landscape which still languished in winter's dead grip. Her senses newly heightened, she strained to make out Julio's fragments of song. The words were unknown to her; they mingled in a formless harmony with the music of the birds and the river.

As night's shadows fell, they turned north over the bridge into Chinon, gaining admission through a squat entrance in the fortifications just short of closing time. The transition from the clear, golden evening by the river to the rank obscurity of winding, dark, smelly streets brutally affronted Athalie's tender sensibilities; nor was she reassured when she saw their destination. In the dim light, she made out a narrow, beamed house, crammed between similar buildings, and overhanging the road. It looked as though, crushed by its neighbors, it was bursting forward to meet the house opposite. In a state of nervous excitement and intense fatigue, Athalie stumbled from the cart, landed with one foot in a gutter, whose noisomeness defied her to imagine its contents, and stood, shivering slightly, while her uncle rapped sharply on the inset door.

Athalie had never visited the house of an untitled person. Her town-dwelling experience was limited to castles, which were, in every town, the pinnacle and the place of security. From there, she had looked down at hovels such as she imagined this to be; she could not conceive that anyone respectable could live this humbly.

The heavily barred and studded door opened inward; a streak of light struck the travelers, who in a single, spontaneous rush pushed through the entrance. Crowding around the door to greet them was a representative portion of the numerous Pascal family, whose cheerful gabble made a warm and welcoming commotion around them.

"At last, my dear Sir, at last — come in! You must be exhausted." Their host's words gushed out in a hospitable torrent, while his hands mimed the intent of his words.

At fifty, Artus Pascal was only months older than Gondi, yet his garb and manner contrasted with his guest's emphatic youthfulness. His long, heavy robe emphasized, deliberately it seemed, his middle-aged bulk. He was as solid as the massive furniture which embellished his home — an armoire bursting with valuable possessions.

Gondi stood debonairly, one hand on his sword's intricate basket hilt, the other on the inset waist of his crimson doublet, and listened with a slightly ironic smile to his colleague's greetings. He is a barge, not a sloop, thought Gondi; nonetheless, he always reaches his destination. Thinking back to his recent tumultuous river trip, Gondi confessed to himself that he was not sure that, in navigation at least, the slow and steady way was not superior to the swift but perilous. And in men? The unabated civilities drew him back from his digression.

"You must come this way, my friend. I have had a table set privately in my chambers. We will dine as soon as you have recovered from your trip, and then we can take up our business at our leisure. And these charming young people?"

Pascal waved a chubby hand at Athalie and Julio, who had assumed discreet places by the wall.

Gondi bowed slightly. "I apologize, my dear Pascal, for being so slow with my introductions," he began. The plain truth is, I couldn't get a word in, he thought. "This is my cousin from Lyon, young Julio de Gondi." Julio bowed deeply to meet Pascal's gracious nod. "And this is my niece, the Duchess de la Roque." Athalie stepped forward and wondered suddenly whether she should curtsey. Was she a child or a Duchess? The question, which had never before occurred to her, was resolved by the banker's conduct. Artus bowed as quickly and as deeply as his corpulence permitted, and his wife and children followed his example with alacrity.

"My house is honored, Madame, most honored. I hope our simple arrangements will not offend you; I hardly dare hope that they will please you." He broke off and exchanged confused glances with his wife. Gondi, though noble, was after all an old friend, a sometime colleague, and a present customer of Pascal's. His occasional visits, which were part personal and part business, gave no cause for consternation. In contrast, the family had never had or hoped for the visit of a scion of the highest nobility. The sudden and unannounced arrival of such a person, however youthful and modest her appearance, bred panic in their comfortable breasts.

Resolving to make the best of it, Pascal carried on as planned. "Now, as I was saying, if these charming young people, er, our honored guests, er, will accompany my wife — they will share suitable refreshments with my family in the, er, kitchen. Amelie?"

Artus and Amelie Pascal shared a look of misery, as the latter began shepherding her guests and three of her children along a narrow hallway. The kitchen was the heart of their house, but was it adequate for nobility? She shot Gondi a reproachful glance; he smiled broadly.

As Athalie followed her hostess, she assessed her surroundings. The building was narrow and low-ceilinged, not spacious like the residences she was accustomed to, and the wavering, shadowy torchlight gave the hall where she stood a dim, cavern-like appearance, but even so, she could tell that she was in no mean or tawdry abode. Her feet slipped slightly on an immaculate floor, neatly tiled with blue and white ceramic squares. Between the windows' intricate mullions and elaborate double shutters, thick glass panes sparkled and caught her eye. She noticed with sudden surprise that the odors she smelled were neither pungent nor unpleasant. She passed the banker's quarters to the right and glimpsed a large fireplace with a fine marble mantel, a richly carved settee, and a massive table, laid now for dinner with clean linen and crystal goblets. Though Pascal's house was not on a scale with what she was accustomed to, she could not deny that in basic cleanliness and certain details of luxury it outshone many grander edifices.

It was with a mild sense of wonder that she left the hall to follow Amelie through a low door into the kitchen. As she crossed the threshold, her ruminations on the quality of her hosts vanished, as her senses were buffeted by heat, light, and noise. Though a large room, the kitchen seemed too small to contain the energy generated by the huge blaze that occupied the entire far wall and by the bustling activity of its occupants — several serving women, who were preparing the platters for their master and his guest; two more "charming young people" who were teasing a compact rat terrier; and the dog himself, who was jumping up and down, yapping incessantly.

Amelie Pascal raised her hands for silence; magically, the din subsided, slowly at first, tailing off at last into a single whine from the now neglected terrier. Athalie looked more closely at the mistress of the house, lit now by the fire's brilliant glow. Amelie Pascal was a big woman, with a calm mien that bespoke competence and authority. She had salted blond hair, pulled back in a messy but pragmatic bun, the waistline of a childbearer past her prime, and kind, strong hands, round, clean and pink. On the whole, Athalie thought she would like her.

Amelie paused, as if puzzled at how to proceed. "If you wish, Madame," she began hesitantly, "I will present the children to you."

One by one, the blond, rosy-cheeked, well-scrubbed tribe stepped forward. "This is Alphonse, he is 15 and deep in his studies; Alice, 16, and I don't know what I would do without her; Armelle is 14; there's Andrée, she is 13; Abel is 7 — now bow properly, you rascal. My oldest boys are away. Aimeri will finish his law at the Sorbonne. He's already 22. Then, there's Augustin, who has run away to Court. Well, perhaps I shouldn't put it that way. Augustin is 21. Perhaps you know him?"

Athalie hesitated, then responded, "No, Madame, I haven't been to Court since I was a child."

"Ah?" the older woman said, sending the girl a quizzical look, which took in her unassuming garb and plainly dressed hair. Athalie felt suddenly mortified.

The decorous interlude now over, the children rushed toward the table and scrambled onto the benches. No one stood on ceremony; Athalie and Julio, hungry from their trip, dipped into their bowls of milk and bread porridge with as much abandon as all the seemingly ravenous Pascals. With half her attention, Athalie listened to the din of talking, laughing, slurping children, so different from the silence of mealtime at Fontevrault, which was broken only by the voice of the week's reader drifting down from the rostrum high above the refectory.

A constant string of queries and commands came from Amelie at the head of the table. "Did you finish your translations, Alphonse?" "Alice, you know that your housework does not excuse you from your readings. Alphonse helps me, too..." "Andrée, you must sit up straight at the table."

Athalie was suddenly struck to the heart by the constant care and comfort that emanated from the mother to the children, who seemed to bask and glow in the rays of her affection. They will be paragons of virtue and knowledge, she thought with a pang. What would I have been had I been raised like this?

The din continued. "Mummy, can I...?"

"Do you remember when Augustin pushed Roger into the horse pond?"

"No, stupid, the black and white cat wasn't called Tiger!"

"Mummy, can I...?"

"Roger was a pimple. I'm glad the plague took him."

"Not the plague, Jesu! It was the pox." This from Alice, who crossed herself demurely. "And you shouldn't say things like that."

"Well, I'm glad anyway. Mummy, can I be excused?"

A wave of sadness soured with envy swept over Athalie as she looked around the bright room at the excited, happy faces.

They all have each other, and so their lives are richer than mine, she thought. I have memories, too, but I don't have any shared memories. No one knows the tiny moments that make up my existence, so it is as if I didn't exist.

Athalie could not shake her despond. It followed her into the night, into her dreams.

* * *

Far into the evening, Pascal and his guest sat opposite the spacious fireplace Athalie had glimpsed in the banker's study. They had eaten a copious repast, the noonday meal which had been postponed in honor of Gondi's arrival. The table — now cleared of the remains of the dinner — and the armchairs on which they sat crowded the small room with more furniture than was elegant, yet the effect was not displeasing. The well-buffed paneling and polished furniture gave back a hundred glimmering reflections as the firelight struck the shiny knobs and recesses of the carvings.

Gondi felt slightly suffocated, as a man dressed for the outdoors feels sitting by a blazing fire, a sensation provoked as much by the bourgeois gentility of Pascal's home as by the heat of the room. He despised this complacent atmosphere of literate, moneyed respectability, and had dedicated his life to escaping from it. His father had been a banker like Pascal, and a foreigner to boot, but he had married small nobility, and that had given Gondi the chance he had needed. Having left it behind, he did not relish returning to the milieu that Pascal had remained in, but ties of business and of friendship, too, brought him to Pascal's home from time to time. It was true, he thought, that though he now outclassed Pascal in every way, he still considered him a friend, and God knows, friends were rare enough in the jealous little world he had chosen to conquer.

Well fed and a little sleepy, the companions exchanged pensive, peaceful talk, while thinking of other things which seemed too weighty to bring up in the first phases of digestion. Gondi wrestled inwardly with a difficult tactical problem:

Should he broach the subject of the Queen Mother's outstanding notes? Over the past year, he had taken discounted notes from the Queen Mother in exchange for substantial sums and had rediscounted them to Pascal. They were now coming due; indeed, some were already overdue. Recently, Her Majesty had coolly informed him that she expected him to extend the time to pay, since as he obviously knew, she did not have the funds handy right at the moment. Unable, himself, to raise so much money on such short notice, Gondi was caught between her default and his own joint liability to Pascal. It was a most embarrassing predicament and a worrisome one.

He hated to be at any man's mercy and abhorred the idea of putting his reputation for financial integrity or the inviolability of his assets into another's hands, even those of a friend. He dreaded to discuss the outstanding obligations and wondered whether, if he let the matter go, he could treat Pascal's silence as a tacit extension of their due dates. After all, there wasn't any real problem — money came in as fast as it went out, or almost. He wondered uneasily why the banker had not mentioned the subject; he was kindly, but not sentimental. Was some shrewd overreaching in the offing? He glanced at Pascal's placid face — there is a visage that gives nothing away, he thought.

Artus sat, hands folded over his belly, gazing into the flames with an apparent somnolence which quite belied his inward state. Since early evening, he had suffered from the most tantalizing, the most excruciating, the most perplexing of emotions. Gondi, his old friend Gondi, had a niece and ward who was a de la Roque!

This simple truth, which the evening's encounter had brought home to him, raised possibilities which in his wildest dreams had never before occurred to him. Did he dare suggest an alliance between his son and this blooded aristocrat? It was unthinkable, it was madness, but could it just barely be possible? After all, he would offer Gondi a better deal than anyone more appropriate would be willing to make. He looked across at Gondi's suave expression — there is a visage that gives nothing away, he thought.

While these inner struggles took place, the effortless banalities flowed blandly on.

"How is the family, Artus?" asked Gondi. "You are blessed with most attractive children."

"I have indeed been lucky. Seven healthy children, none lost or deformed, and Amelie none the worse for it. I thank God daily."

Gondi grunted appreciatively.

"It's a miracle, and they're good children," Pascal continued, "all getting ahead in their own ways. My oldest boy, Aimeri, is finishing his law and will be coming down from Paris when the term is over. He has worked very hard. I think no one would contradict me when I say he is a scholar, a good scholar — and, er, a gentleman." Pascal paused, then resumed less aggressively. "He will help me with my affairs for a little while. It will do him good, and me, too. But I'm going to set him up on his own fairly soon, give him some prospects. Then he'll have to manage for himself. In fact, I was going to talk to you about that." Pascal faltered.

"Mine are still too young for me to worry about their prospects, thank God!" Gondi broke in airily. "Instead, I've got all my relatives' children clamoring for advancement."

"That's the trick at Court, of course," said Pascal, almost relieved at the change of subject. "You've got to get somebody's attention, don't you? It's not enough to be shrewd and hardworking and have a little capital, as it is in business."

"My second boy, I was going to tell you, he's at Court. When he was still quite young, he decided that the profession at arms was the only way for a gentleman. Of course, it's true if you're born to it. Otherwise, I've always felt that intellectual puissance led more surely to advancement than physical prowess. I'd pick mind over body any day; of course, the old mule has to be able to carry its rider, but that's about it. But then, I would never have been a good soldier. Not like you. You've got the brains and the brawn, too." He looked at Gondi with frank admiration.

"My oldest always liked books," he continued, "and he could never have been a soldier, his eyesight is too bad. You can't very well wear a helmet over spectacles."

"You'd be surprised," Gondi said, "I've seen it done. You can't see anything out of a lowered visor in any event."

"My second boy stutters, and the other students used to laugh at him during their repetitions. I think that's why he dropped everything to become a soldier."

"Yes," mused Gondi, "it's odd how minor accidents of birth can alter the course of a lifetime."

"They didn't when I was a boy! We learned to overcome, you and I. That's why we've arrived where we are."

The two men looked at each other, each reviewing in his own mind the status and achievements of the other. Was this a good time? Artus asked himself.

Cowardly, he merely said, "If you could look out for my boy, Augustin, I would consider it a favor."

Is this what he's been leading up to? Gondi wondered. "Of course, Artus, I'll see what I can do." It's little enough considering what I owe, Gondi thought to himself.

An uncomfortable silence fell. Both men sensed that something else had to be broached, something important enough to alter their longstanding relationship.

"Albert," said Pascal, advancing friendship over rank, "I won't beat around the bush. Seeing you here with your niece, the young Duchess, I have a proposal to make to you, just a suggestion, something we should think over and talk over..."

"Well, man?" Gondi queried.

"She's of marriageable age, and she's your ward..." He paused.

"Old friend, come now," the other interrupted hastily, "don't go any further. The Duchess is nobility of the blood. If you are hinting at what I think, a link between her and one of your brood, you're mad. Even if I would agree, which I couldn't in conscience, the Queen Mother would never accept it, and the royal will must prevail in such a matter. Come, you'd do better not to even mention the matter."

Piqued by Gondi's absolute rejection, Pascal rallied himself to the attack. "It's not as preposterous as you depict it. We are closing on a piece of property at the end of the month. It's the château of Beaumont. You probably know it. We will be noble, and we deserve to be noble."

"You know as well as I do that you will never be noble, so long as you carry on in trade. Frankly, friend Pascal, I can't see you giving up the business."

"Well, as a matter of fact, what I had in mind was to give the land and a suitable endowment to my son. I'm talking of my eldest boy, now, Aimeri. I bought Augustin a little fief after he insisted on going to Court, so he could wear a sword and not be treated like a lackey. Aimeri, now, he'll be the Sieur de Beaumont, and quite a substantial landowner to boot. That's not as fancy as being a de la Roque, but it's not nothing either."

"Of course, Pascal, but overnight nobility won't qualify your boy for the likes of Athalie. France is swarming with newly acquired titles. No one seriously believes them the equivalent of genuine aristocracy. Why, Athalie's father had in mind a match like Pierre de Galle."

Gondi stopped. In the heat of the argument, he had blurted out something he had never before alluded to; it was an intuition he had hardly even admitted to himself.

The banker glared at Gondi with eyes of steel. "Frankly, friend Albert, I don't see that what I propose is any different from what you've done yourself. Your father was just as grubby a commercial type as I am, if you like. He was only able to call himself the Sieur du Perron because he bought himself a little land outside Lyon and the name went with the land. Nonetheless, as Sieur du Perron in your turn, you married the most eligible widow in France, and became Count de Retz in the bargain.

"It's all recent enough that I'm not likely to have forgotten, you know. So you see, perhaps I wouldn't have set my sights so high, if you yourself hadn't shown me the way."

Gondi could not deny the truth of his friend's words, but they angered him, more for the bitter memories they revived than for any other reason. Gondi did not find Pascal's implied claim of equality nearly as humiliating as the assumption of superiority which was so common among the nobility whom he frequented. He had felt the initial haughty indifference of France's proud and mighty families, then their dismay that he, by marriage, should presume to come among them as an equal, and finally their unshakable conviction that he would never be worthy of the position and honors which had come his way. He had been the butt of their covert ridicule, and even of their open insults, often enough that his resentment was like a canker at the heart of the pride and pleasure he felt at his successes.

Even his wife, he thought bitterly, had not put away her class feelings in marrying him.

Embarrassed, and afraid that Pascal would notice his discomfiture, Gondi replied to the banker's argument in as reasonable a tone as he could muster.

"You must admit, my dear Pascal, that the situations are really not comparable. Your son, whatever his merits, is a callow youth, just out of school, whereas when I married my dear wife, I had by my own efforts and abilities reached a position of preeminence which my marriage merely confirmed.

"Anyway, this discussion is not only inappropriate; it is also academic. The girl wants to be a religious, and I have no intention of discouraging her. True vocations are few enough. I don't believe any Christian should stand in the way of one."

Pascal's shrewd eyes rested appraisingly on his friend's face. "Surely Their Majesties will have something to say about that! But, though you say new titles are running the streets," he continued, "you will admit that not all of them are as well-endowed as my son. I don't, of course, mean looks or intellect, but, to speak plainly, money. On the one hand, I can afford to be generous, and on the other, I have every reason not to be demanding. To the contrary, if your ward marries someone like a de Galle, that's the end of your revenues."

"I could make a lucrative deal with any bourgeois-cum-nobleman," Gondi replied.

"Ah, but I would not only guarantee you an adequate percentage of the revenue from the estate, or a lump sum, if you prefer — I have the capital — but would also be accommodating about, or perhaps even forgive, certain past debts — past-due as well — which, I imagine, would be of assistance to both you and your royal mistress."

The two men stared at each other coldly.

"As you say," Gondi replied slowly, "we can think it over, and maybe talk of it again on one of my next visits."

"I thought, perhaps, I might bring Aimeri to Court, when he returns in early summer?"

"Yes, yes, if you want to come then, we'll set something up. Of course, my niece may be back in the nunnery — or married — by then, but you must come anyway. I'd be delighted to see you."

An uncomfortable pause followed, broken at last by Gondi clearing his throat.

"About the notes: Her Majesty, the Queen Mother, has asked me to grant her an extension, and I fear I am obliged to couple her request with a similar one of my own to you. Your interest is safe, and your capital, too, but she did not, alas, vouchsafe me enough notice to raise the money, and..."

"I understand. I would lend the money again, if you asked for it, so there is no reason for me to refuse you additional time to pay. I'll send the papers along by the next post. You needn't delay your departure tomorrow for them to be prepared."

"That's most accommodating of you," Gondi replied with a bow. "I hate to impose again, but speaking of mail, there is something else I wanted to ask you, a small service you could do for me and for my people. There is a man going to La Rochelle who may be able to provide me with some useful information. But as you can imagine, it can only be done in confidence. If anyone suspects a link between him and me, well, the link will instantly be broken. Do you see?"

"I would be more than happy to provide a conduit, if that is what you wish."

"Precisely," Gondi nodded, "and I would be more than grateful." The men rose, happy to end their discussions with a semblance of harmony restored.

"His name, by the way, is La Renaudie," Gondi added.

"Is it indeed?" Pascal exclaimed.

Chenonceau

Chapter VII

thalie could hear none of the comments that hummed around her as she waited to be presented to the royal family, but she could feel them. She felt as lonely and desperate as a stranded mariner whose rock is disappearing beneath the waves. It seemed as though the murmurs were eddying and flowing through the room, washing around her, threatening to submerge her in a swelling tide of curiosity and criticism.

"Who is she?"

"Don't you know? I heard from my chambermaid, who overheard Madame de Luynes, who had probably been told by the Queen Mother herself."

"Funny, I thought she was dead. Ah... the convent."

"Well, look at the dress. My dear, she can't have been born when that dress was made!"

"Too thin."

"That's a criticism that can't be made of enough people."

"We can't all have tiny waists, however much Her Majesty likes them."

Her ears buzzed and roared. She realized the sensation came more from inside herself than from her surroundings; it was only one of the many symptoms of her acute nervousness.

Though she tried to stand with quiet dignity, her knees wobbled and knocked together.

Cold as ice, her hands were nonetheless clammy, and she did not dare wipe them on her dress for fear of staining the delicate material.

It was such pretty material — a ruby satin that showed off her pale skin and dark hair, so unassuming, she had always thought, as though they were as matchless as ivory and ebony. She had never worn such a dress; its grandeur elated her, even as its novelty frightened her.

Inwardly, Athalie blessed the Abbess for having insisted on the dress. Twirling the embarrassed and sulky girl around to check the fit of the garment, the old woman had said, "It will have to do. It hasn't been the height of fashion since King Henry's time, but it's the only one here that's even possible. You're so slender for your height, that's the problem. Fortunately, Dame Elizabeth, who wore it when she came to Fontevrault, was thin like you, though you'd hardly know it now. It's a good Court dress, good quality and attractive, too. The Queen Mother would be rightly put out if she were asked to receive you in your country woolens."

Athalie was as grateful now as she had been restive then. Though she was too nervous and preoccupied to take in the details of dress of those around her, she could not fail to perceive that she was in the midst of finery that was splendid beyond her imagining. She had had no idea. The condescending indifference, so typical of adolescence, with which she had greeted the news of her unwanted trip to Court gave way now to an equally typical reaction upon arrival: stupefied, star-struck shyness. The minutes seemed like hours. Athalie lowered her eyes to avoid the solecism of staring at the three seated women who were the object of her attention. Still, though she wished to appear respectful, she could not stop herself from casting sidelong glances in their direction.

Seated directly ahead of her was a heavyset woman, dressed in sumptuous widow's weeds. A black coif framed a sallow face; intelligent, dark eyes looked out above a prominent nose and a narrow, hard mouth. This, Athalie was sure, must be Catherine, the Queen Mother, the famous Florentine, who still wore mourning for King Henry, twelve years dead. To Catherine de Medici's left was a laughing, chubby-cheeked girl in her late teens, whose features closely resembled the older woman's, though the expression they bore was quite different, being more vivacious, but less intelligent. This, Athalie deduced, must be Princess Marguerite, the present King's sister and Catherine's youngest daughter. The two talked to the various courtiers and ladies-in-waiting who hovered about them, the Queen Mother in a deep, authoritative voice, which seemed to Athalie to grate harshly on the ear, her daughter in lively tones, broken by peals of high-pitched laughter, which, on occasion, drowned out the stern voice of her mother in incongruous merriment.

Opposite the young Princess, on the Queen Mother's other side, there sat silently a fair, pale girl, whose timid, reticent look was as different as it could be from the robust, somewhat domineering manner shared by the other two. Athalie was entirely at a loss as to this person's identity, until, to her amazement, as the

Queen Mother gestured to Gondi that he should proceed, she found herself being presented to her, rather than to Catherine, as she had expected. So this is our new Queen, she thought, and the idea shocked her, for she saw that Elizabeth of Austria was hardly older than herself, and Athalie seemed to see her own shyness mirrored in the other's blue eyes. So interested was Athalie in her inspection that she almost forgot to lower her eyes respectfully as she curtseyed. As she rose, the King's absence suddenly struck her.

Though Athalie had been consumed with curiosity, diffidence and wariness had prevented her from asking her uncle who would be present and what would transpire when she was received at Court. Gondi, of course, had volunteered nothing. Thus, her preparation had consisted of speculations and daydreams. A hundred times, she had conjured up the scene as she had thought it would be — a glittering bustle, surrounding a silent center, at the heart of which stood the monarch of her fantasies, regal in every sense of the word. But now, though the ensemble was grandiose enough to exceed her naive dreams, the King's absence transformed the pomp and finery into an empty charade.

In fact, though Athalie did not know it, she was not at Court in the true sense of the word. To the extent that there was such an entity, it consisted of a gathering of the great around their King for the purpose, ostensibly at least, of governing the country. But these were days of leisure; His Majesty was hunting, and those who did not wish to accompany their monarch in simple play were excused to attend to their own affairs. In the absence of the King and much of the nobility, Athalie beheld only a truncated version of the famed spectacle of royal pageantry. Even with fewer than the normal complement of courtiers and ladies present, the room which held them was almost oppressively crowded. Though Chenonceau was the gem of the Queen Mother's many houses, it retained the character of a private home, rather than a royal residence, and its rooms, though elegant, were small. But the rich and lovely setting for the bedizened intimates and favorites of the Queen of France would have more than met Athalie's expectations, except that her King was not there.

A sharp tug on her arm broke into her reflections, as Gondi steered her around to face the Queen Mother and abruptly pushed her into a curtsey. Catherine de Medici leaned forward and examined the girl's face with keen interest. Then, to Athalie's surprise, she held out both arms and grasped her hands tightly in her own. The babble of a score of conversations faltered and stopped.

"This is a great pleasure, my dear," she said, and Athalie wondered how she could ever have found her warm, throaty voice harsh or forbidding.

"I knew your father well. He was a fine soldier and a fine man. His death was a great loss to me. He was a friend and a statesman, and God knows how much I need both in these difficult times.

"I knew your mother, too, of course. She was most lovely, as you are, my dear. Only her untimely death stopped her from becoming one of my closest companions. But now, you have come to replace them both. You will have your work cut out for you, but I can tell that you will be more than capable of it."

Inexperience kept Athalie from observing that all the Queen Mother's talk revolved around her own losses and gains, taking no account of how Athalie might have been affected; Athalie was quite simply awestruck to be the object of so much graciousness from so great a lady.

Keeping Athalie's left hand in her grasp, the Queen Mother stood, looking more rotund than ever next to the slim, tall girl. She raised her voice and proclaimed, "The Lady Athalie, the Duchess de la Roque, will be my lady-in-waiting. I claim her for my own." With a glance back at her daughter-in-law, the Queen, she stated rather than asked, "You will not begrudge her to me." The young Queen shook her head silently. Then, still holding the girl's hand, Catherine gestured to her daughter, as if to show Athalie further honor by completing the introductions herself. Wordlessly, Gondi stood to one side, his guarded expression revealing none of his surprise.

After Athalie's curtsey, Catherine continued, "My daughter will take you under her wing, won't you, Margot?" Impishly, the Princess wrinkled her nose, then her face broke into a mocking, but nonetheless welcoming, grin. "I suspect that there is much that each of you can teach the other," the Queen Mother concluded, appraising the two girls' dissimilarities with a shrewd, if kindly, glance. To Athalie's relief, this comment marked the end of the ceremony, whose brevity seemed ridiculous in comparison with the lengthy anguish of anticipation which had preceded it. After a few more exchanges with those around her, the Queen Mother withdrew, accompanied by the Queen.

Princess Margot lingered only long enough to grab Athalie by the arm and drag her away, without so much as a glance at Gondi. "We might as well go, too," she said, or else you'll get stuck here, and end up black and blue from having long noses poked into you. I ought to know. I have one of the longest noses around." Margot hastened away; Athalie followed, holding up her heavy skirt to avoid tripping.

They crossed the room at such a pace that, once again, Athalie had no time to reflect on the bewildering array of staring faces that followed her progress, but even so, she realized that there was a different quality to the murmurs of the onlookers, an undercurrent of awe, curiosity, and astonishment.

Once outside, Margot stopped. "I'll show you where you'll sleep, shall I?" At Athalie's nod, she hurried across the hall and started up the main staircase. Athalie followed more slowly. Escape from the brutal inquisitiveness of the crowded room left her free to marvel at the things around her. She longed to linger and appreciate them in their fullness — the elaborate vaulting of the hallway, the delicately tiled floor, and the straight stairway with its coffered ceiling. Especially the stairway! She had never seen such a stairway, rising in straight ramps instead of circling upward, yet it was not its novelty but its beauty that struck her. Its stone was white and so cunningly worked that fruits, flowers, and even human figures nestled in every angle. Its vaults and keystones caught the light reflected up from the river through the tall windows that ran its full length. Athalie dawdled on the steps, craning back to gaze at the carvings, while on the landing between floors, in a little loggia with a balustrade, Margot waited for her, somewhat impatiently. When Athalie finally reached her, she was still unable to bring her mind back to Margot and Margot's interests, but instead, looked past the other girl, through the window, to the valley of the Cher stretching away all yellow-green and bright beneath a delicate spring sky.

"How lovely!" she exclaimed.

"Yes," Margot replied without much interest. "Mother always calls Chenonceau her 'jewel'– and when I say 'always,' I mean, I can't tell you how often I've heard it. There's no doubt she loves it, loves the building, and the park, and the river, as she'll tell you any time she has a chance, but still, part of her enthusiasm comes from the fact that she wrested it from the ravishing Diane. Revenge is sweet, after all.

"But come along. We're not halfway there yet. You'll be up with the other ladies-in-waiting, which will be more fun than staying with your uncle. They're a good group — lots of fun, when they can get out from under Mother's thumb. When she doesn't have a lot of other things on her mind, Mother loves to think up things for her ladies to do, so as to keep them out of mischief. Whatever she dreams up, I have to do it, too. Things like sewing lace on underskirts and cutting off dead roses and praying." Athalie, who had not been brought up to look on praying as busywork, favored Margot with a scandalized look, which was entirely lost on her companion. "You'd think," Margot continued, "that we didn't have servants for that sort of thing."

"For praying?" asked Athalie.

"Well, no, I suppose not." Margot's doubtful look managed to convey the impression that, even if she had never thought of it before, she found the idea of having the servants say her prayers quite appealing.

On the third floor, they paused in a narrow corridor, and Margot threw open a door. The two girls entered a small, bright room.

"This is where you'll be," announced Margot. "I know, because it has the only free bed."

It was a pretty room, though tiny and cluttered. The shutters were pulled back from the dormer window, and there again was a dazzling view of the Cher. Sunlight glinted off the water, dappling the beams with brightness.

On this occasion, however, Athalie ignored the beauty beyond the window, because the room itself took all her attention. What preoccupied and dismayed her was the sight of the four beds occupying its corners, with hardly space enough between for the traveling coffers beside them. Discreetly, bits of clothing showed here and there, peeping out from under the coverlets or wedged under the coffers' lids. The cramped quarters would have defeated the tidiest of occupants.

"But other people already live here," Athalie said.

Margot stared at her. "What did you expect, to have your own cell like a nun?" Athalie blanched. "You're lucky not to have ended up in your uncle's closet, or in some hovel in the village. We're always a bit tight here, but goodness, you'd have had to double up almost anywhere."

Suddenly, Athalie felt deflated, as people do when a party ends. Margot laughed. "Cheer up. You'll soon get used to it. And I'll help you, as Mother said. It looks to me like you'll need it. We shall be inseparable, shall we? Come, I permit you to call me 'cousin.'"

"But we aren't cousins," Athalie said. Margot made a face.

"So, you should be honored!"

A knock on the door was followed by the entrance of a woman bearing a large oblong of cloth, which she handed to Athalie with a curtsey, saying, "From Her Majesty, the Queen Mother."

Hastily, the girls opened out the bolt. To protect the fine material, it had been rolled with its rough side out; the inside was amber brocade, so gorgeous that Athalie was struck dumb at the sight of it and simply stared, while Margot rattled on.

"Well, Mother certainly has taken a fancy to you. She doesn't give away things like that every day, I can tell you. My, but it's fine! I guess she saw that you could use it. Not that your dress isn't nice, I mean, the material is beautiful, but — um — it could use a little reworking. And you can't ever have too many dresses, anyway. Trust Mother to think of everything."

Athalie was not offended by Margot's remarks, because she did not hear them. She handled the exquisite brocade as daintily as if it were gossamer, tracing its delicate pattern with her fingers, wonder and gratitude singing through her.

* * *

Gondi was bored. The days since his arrival at Chenonceau had been busy enough, but not in a way that was exciting or fulfilling. There was the problem of setting up a household for Athalie. An elderly nurse might be adequate for small personal matters, but there was no doubt that a somewhat larger staff would be needed in the long run — if there was to be a long run to Athalie's Court existence. For one, a seamstress was clearly a necessity; the Queen Mother had told Gondi more sharply than graciously that Athalie could use the royal seamstresses for now, and eventually, there would have to be horses and equerries and all that paraphernalia. Gondi recognized that it would reflect badly on himself if he did not do right by his niece, particularly as his royal patroness had made it all too plain that she expected no less. Nonetheless, his realism before life's social obligations did not diminish the resentment he felt at each minute of time and each item of expense that was involved in the task of equipping the girl for a life which he hoped she would not lead.

Then there was the question of the King's visit to the vicinity of La Rochelle. This was a matter that occasioned more worry than work, since Gondi did not dare to do anything in the absence of reliable data, or, indeed, of any data at all. Gondi had heard nothing from any agent, except La Renaudie, since the King's departure. Maurice had made his first report, but it contained little enough information and nothing to the point, as Gondi had been quick to note in his response.

La Renaudie's letter was dated May 10, and it ran as follows:

I would not trouble your Lordship with the discomforts of my trip or my difficulties in gaining admittance, but your orders were to report everything, however trivial, and I will begin at the beginning.

I was able to secure a boat from Tours to St. Nazaire, from whence I made my way down the coast to La Rochelle by means of a small fishing craft. I will not speak of the weather, since you also had the misfortune to be afloat on that miserable day. Otherwise, my trip was uneventful and quite rapid. However, I lost all of the time I had gained on my arrival at La Rochelle. It was, alas, obvious to the guards that I had come from an area under Catholic control. Since I arrived on foot and after curfew, their suspicions were redoubled. My fishermen had taken me only as far as La Pallice, being unwilling to enter a Protestant port for fear – although I told them it was groundless – of being commandeered. Such is their distrust of strangers that I spent three days in a most uncomfortable dungeon before I was able to convince anyone of importance of my identity, let alone my bona fides.

I was summoned before a guards' captain the morning of the seventh, and I must say, I spent some very bad moments. They interrogated another prisoner while I waited, a gaunt, tow-headed fellow with a strawberry birthmark on his face. He said his name was Charbonneau and that he was a merchant from Rennes and a true believer. I thought he looked innocent enough, but the guards were convinced he was a Spanish spy, and were all for hanging him then and there. The Captain decided to consult with the Admiral, however, and the man was spared for the time being.

Believe me, I had cause to be terrified when they shoved me forward, but I put a bold face on it. I said I was a Protestant and wanted to join them. The Captain laughed and said he preferred to hang spies at once, rather than be hanged himself for letting one in. I told him I was the son of the renowned La Renaudie, and that at last produced some effect. 'He was a brave man. If you are who you claim to be, you may be all right, but such matters are for the Admiral,' he said.

Several hours later, I was led into the Admiral's presence. He looked at me for several minutes without speaking, rolling his toothpick from one side of his mouth to the other. Finally, he asked very softly, 'Why are you here?' I told him that I had decided I could no longer stomach either the popish nonsense of the Church or the atmosphere at Court. I said I wanted to follow my father and avenge myself on his murderers. He said, 'Good, find a place for him in the guards,' and that was that. I think the conviction I put in my voice was what carried the day.

La Rochelle is an armed camp, and while religious fervor is curiously present everywhere, there are many other currents that will interest you. I doubt that what I have seen of the sincerity of their trust in their ministers and in the leaders in Geneva would be of much use to you, but what I have heard in the guards' mess cannot fail to interest you. The talk is all of plots, revolts, and settling of scores with the Catholics. I heard one captain say that it was too bad Condé had failed to capture the Queen Mother and King Charles back in '67, the King because then he'd have had good advice and could have been kept from those damned Guises, and 'the old witch' (so they said, on my honor), so they could deal with her as a proper witch. His remarks were greeted with general applause, in which you may be sure I joined heartily.

In this same conversation, one of the younger officers said, 'They should all be hanged, every last one of them. I'd rather see the Admiral on the throne than try to get anything but more treachery from that weakling Charlie. Let's hear it for the Old Toothpick.' He wasn't quite able to finish his toast, because one of the senior officers threw his mug at his head. 'Our Admiral stands for justice and not for revolt, you damned fool,' he shouted. 'Talk like that is just what the Catholics want to hear. It would be all they need to crash down on us again. We tried our best last time, but we couldn't quite make it. We have been left alive for now and have had time to rebuild, but not enough. The Admiral knows what he is doing, and he doesn't need your half-baked revolts at a time like this. Just the other day, I heard him say he thought we would have liberty, if everyone would relax. I know it's hard not to see spies and enemies everywhere, but the Admiral is the boss and his way is my way.'

That is the way most people seem to feel, that Coligny runs the show, but that is not to say there are no differences of opinion. The great topic of debate is 'The Enterprise of the Netherlands,' as it is called. Freeing the Dutch from the tyranny of the Inquisition and the brutality of the Duke of Alva is a real Protestant crusade. There is some feeling that the Admiral does not approach this noble cause with quite enough fervor. Indeed, if you believe some of the younger captains, by year's end, the Prince of Navarre will marry Elizabeth of England, and will himself lead English and Huguenot troops into the Low Countries. But I cannot believe that a tyro like Navarre will supplant old Coligny.

Another faction believes that His Majesty the King favors the Dutch adventure and that the King and Coligny will seek to reconcile Catholics and Protestants in this cause. 'Better war with Spain than civil war' is a favorite saying of some at La Rochelle. But others predict a Spanish invasion of France and a Protestant doomsday. In short, each man has his own opinion on the subject.

I could go on, but I am sure you see the general nature of the conversation. It will be an easy task to collect a good deal of seditious material in a short time.

I will continue as your very obedient and most grateful servant.

Maurice de La Renaudie

At first, Gondi had fumed with impotent rage at Maurice's letter. He was acutely conscious of the passage of time. The young King was enjoying his hunting, so the reports and letters from Normandy indicated, but still, he might begin to move toward Brittany and the Atlantic Coast at any time. He was not noted for firmness of purpose, but the young Protestants in his entourage could be counted on to make sure that he did not abandon his dream of bringing the Admiral back into the fold. And, meanwhile, here was Maurice wasting his time with worthless chatter, while his other agent in La Rochelle was incommunicado, if not dead.

He had handled the letter restlessly, letting his anger subside, and thinking out how best to deal with La Renaudie. The young man masked his fears by pretending to be more than he was. Thus, rather than goading him with whips of fear into possibly rash activities, it might be more effective to prick his flanks with spurs of sarcasm.

Gondi had jotted the note down himself:

My dear La Renaudie:

The observations in your letter were helpful, and I congratulate you on not having been hanged, for the present. But you will do no good and will soon come to grief if you persist in failing to see what ought to be obvious. Coligny is one of the great men of our times. He has accepted you provisionally, at best, for your father's sake, but do not delude yourself that you have lulled his suspicions. You will be watched constantly and he will hang you out of hand if you fail to convince him of your sincere conversion to the Protestant faith. You must be completely convincing and consistent in everything you do.

But while keeping you alive is evidently a prerequisite to your continued usefulness, it is scarcely the purpose of your mission. You must get close to Coligny. I don't want to make major decisions on the basis of guardroom gossip, however seditious you may believe it to be. You will have to convince the Admiral that you have something he needs — information about what is going on at Court. I will arrange to send you information from time to time which will first establish your credibility and later will begin to have Coligny believe what we want. It will be dangerous and will require all your wits and subtlety. So do be careful, won't you? I count on you to bring off your mission successfully. I say this though I am aware that your understanding of the consequences of failure will do more to enhance your zeal than any exhortations on my part.

The letter had been sent off posthaste, and in the meantime, there was nothing for Gondi to do but wait. Though he was an impatient man who had schooled himself to patience, intervals of forced inactivity annoyed him. Everything takes so long, he thought miserably. By the time we know what to do, it may be too late to do it.

Chapter VIII

aurice crept back into his darkened sleeping quarters. Pausing just inside the door, he listened to the regular breathing of his companions, visualizing where they lay, and even discerning, or imagining he could discern, their bodies as bulky shapes on the floor that were blacker than the predawn gloom around them. He pushed the door shut; its latch gave out a muffled click that startled him; then, quiet fell again. The quiet and the breathing filled the room. What if I kick one of them on my way to bed? I'll say I needed to relieve myself, I'll say I was sick, anything. He tiptoed by the sleeping forms, and as he passed, one of them rolled over with a sigh. Reaching the far wall, Maurice wrapped his cloak about him, sank down on the pallet that was his, and leaned against the rough stones. The June night was mild, but he felt chilled and shrank gratefully into the heavy folds of the cloak. He longed for sleep, more to escape than to rest, but his taut nerves would never relax in time for him to drift off before dawn called him back to his duties.

His nocturnal sorties terrified Maurice. Dread of them kept him awake as he waited for quiet to fall on the keep; raw nerves reacting to fear banished sleep long after he safely returned. Nothing but an implacable necessity could have driven him from the refuge of his bed, out into the open, out to where light and solitude would enable him to write. Even when he had found a deserted corridor lit by some guttery candle or smoking torch, had taken pen and ink from his satchel, and had crouched on the floor to scratch out his lines, he would still tremble at his task, dreading to hear the tread of the night patrol or the shuffle of some insomniac.

But he had to write. Gondi had told him he had to write. He hated Gondi, who subjected him to the torments of terror, but he bowed to his will. Thus far, Gondi held the whip hand, but someday, Maurice thought, someday, I will get my own back.

As the peaceful room brought him a semblance of calm, Maurice could almost laugh off the cold hand of panic. After all, he told himself, your activities are clandestine whether they are conducted by day or by night. Like a silly child you fear the writing in the dark more than the spying in the light, but you must write in the dark, and there's no harm in it. He had given himself this speech before, and he recognized it for what it was: a way of putting a good face on an evil necessity. Wearily, he examined his life once again to make sure there was no other way. But no, he was trapped and driven to act as he did by the circumstances of his life. During the day the keep of the Gate of Cougnes teemed with soldiers; his every minute was taken up with shared activities, his meals were eaten, his prayers uttered, his instructions received, all in common with his supposed brethren. Even the tour of guard duty, his principal occupation, coupled him with one or another of his fellow officers. To write during the day was out of the question. God knew that even at night, when sleeping bodies, rolled in cloaks or huddled on pallets, jammed the rooms, it was perilous enough. Maurice bared his teeth like a cornered rat, but his mind accepted the inevitable.

The real problem, he thought, is worse than the problem of how to get the letters written. The real problem is that I have nothing to write. He thought back over the letter he had just written, and a sly smile stretched his lips. How he had agonized over that letter! In the hours of waiting, he had composed several letters in his head, and he had even written a few words before the right approach had come to him. He remembered that false start, now, with a cynical amusement that was a far cry from the desperation he had felt at the time. He had written:

Esteemed Sir:

I am all zeal for our cause, but zeal alone is not enough. However hard I work to distinguish myself, no one of significance has favored me with his attention. I can assure you that I would lose no opportunity, but no opportunity has presented itself.

How fatuous, how inadequate, those words had been! They had been a wail from the heart, a protest against fear and frustration, but they had not done what he had wanted them to do. True, he was ever a prey to fear, fear of failure and fear of discovery, the two fears warring and defeating each other. True, a month had gone by, a maddening month, full of chances for self-betrayal, but devoid of opportunities for self-advancement. The days had passed in a monotony of repeated events — guard duty, morning and evening; religious instruction, every day but Sunday; and on Sundays, endless services, preachings, readings and discourses — without his doing anything to break out of the routine. If Maurice had faced the truth, he would have had to admit that his fear of discovery had scuttled every audacious plan his imagination had conjured up long before it could be launched. But he did not want to tell Gondi the truth; he did not want to face it himself. He wanted to impress Gondi with his resourcefulness, with his boldness, with all the qualities he knew he possessed. For he was ingenious and brave. All he needed was an opportunity, and surely, that opportunity would come. He had gone over in his mind the bold strokes, the clever advances that filled his daydreams. None had been carried out, or even attempted by him, but they could have been. By the time Gondi received the letter, he would surely have brought off one of these tremendous feats. Why not satisfy Gondi, now, with a plausible, if fictitious exploit? It was not a lie, merely an anticipation of the truth.

Taking his knife from its sheath, he had carefully cut off the used piece of parchment and had rewritten the letter so that, at last, it created the right impression:

Esteemed Sir:

You will be glad to see that I am still alive and well, and gladder yet to find that I have not wasted my time here. As you know, I was saved from hanging by the Admiral and was assigned to guard duty. I have used that opportunity to make a careful study of the fortifications, which, I should tell you, are elaborate and massive. I will commit these plans to paper and forward them with my next report.

Knowing that you look for material of more immediate utility, and fired by my zeal for your wishes, I immediately sought ways to penetrate the Admiral's inner Council. I saw at once that to disappear into the anonymous ranks of guards would be fatal to my mission; yet, at the outset, I could see no alternative.

I wracked my brains for a ruse, and finally concluded that trusting to my name once again would be best. I pushed my way into Coligny's council chamber and was promptly seized by his bodyguards. They were none too gentle with me. I yelled at the top of my lungs, 'La Renaudie for Coligny.' The Admiral roared at the guards, and they pushed me forward. I threw myself at his feet and laid my sword before him. 'My father died for the holy cause, else he would be with you now. If you will accept the word of La Renaudie, I am your man in any enterprise,' I cried. He looked at me with obvious interest and, I believe, some admiration, and said, 'Your father was a good soldier. If you're half the man he was, I can use you. They tell me you have been at Court?' I assented, and he continued, 'I knew the King as a child, but now he is a man, and that is our hope.' He raised his voice when he said this and was plainly talking to everyone. 'If we show him the way, he will throw off the nefarious influences that have held back his natural goodness. He is our King, and he will give us justice.'

He cracked his famous toothpick, and scowled at some young officers on the other side of the room. I was still kneeling before him, and when he continued, he put his hand on my shoulder.

'I don't know yet how to approach the King,' he said, 'but I know it can be done. I've no doubt my friend here will give me some ideas.'

With that, he thumped me on the back and retired to his dinner.

I am sure that the Admiral will call for me soon.

Of course, success, as you helpfully reminded me, is contingent on my staying alive, so I am confident that you would not wish me to run too many risks. A propos, do you remember the man who was being held as a spy when I arrived? Although they say he revealed nothing on the rack, the authorities were convinced he was a Guise agent. To keep the forms of peace, they trumped up some charge of theft, but everyone knew why he had to die. And so he was hanged.

At this, Maurice had paused in his writing, the happy flow of words stemmed by the brutal memory of that terrible scene. He had seen again the black mass of spectators, somber figures filling the square and every window and balcony overlooking it. It was not the size of the crowd that had appalled him. Any public execution attracts a good turnout. Rather, it was their behavior that had made his skin crawl at the time, and still had the power to raise goose flesh every time he thought of it. No one had thrown mud or vegetables at the condemned man. There had been no laughing or jeering or joking. The mob had stood still and silent, a grim, brooding throng, prematurely in mourning. As the ladder was kicked away, the crowd had broken into song. The square had rung and echoed with the psalmist's baleful words:

I will love thee, O Lord, my strength,
Who has armed my limbs for the battle.
Thou hast subdued those that rose up against me.
Thou hast given me the necks of mine enemies,
That I might destroy them that hate me.
They cried out, but there was none to save them,
Even unto the Lord, but he answered them not.
Then I did beat them as the dust before the wind.
I did cast them out as the dirt in the streets.

So long as the victim had jumped and pirouetted, so long had they sung. Never had the death dance had so frightful an accompaniment. At last, growing impatient, the hangman had cut down the twitching, jerking body and severed its head. The chorus had ceased at that moment; then into the silence, a small boy had booed, and one by one the spectators had begun to hiss and yell in a rising, deafening crescendo.

The scene often haunted Maurice. He could not help but think, They would sing for my torture, they would scream at my death. As he had written the words *"And so he was hanged,"* the picture they conjured up had shattered the fragile optimism that had buoyed up his epistolary efforts, leaving him drained and apathetic, suddenly careless of his task. Scribbling a hasty closing, he had folded the letter, shoved it into his purse, and slipped back to his room.

Even now, many minutes later, the image of the puppet-like body on the rope lingered in the back of his mind, disturbing his reflections.

With a major effort of will, he returned his thoughts to the letter. On the whole, he thought it was a success, though perhaps it should have gone on a bit more. He sniffed in a self-satisfied way, and was alarmed by the noise. Yes, such bravura must impress Gondi, and the words he had attributed to Coligny were no invention; at least, they were consistent with comments he had heard in the officers' mess.

Maurice no longer felt cold, or even nervous. A glow of contentment warmed him, and to his surprise, he even felt quite sleepy. He slid over onto the pallet, tucked his legs up, and drifted into a pleasant reverie, half-dream, half-daydream, that led gently into heavy sleep.

* * *

As Maurice's tour of duty came to a close, he steeled his courage to take his letter across town to the bank courier who would bear it on the first stage of its voyage. Though, at night, when he contemplated his daytime deceptions he considered them facility itself, he found that when the time came for him to carry them out in broad daylight, openly, for anyone to see, he had wished himself back in the solitude of the dark hours.

The banking exchange was located all the way across town, in the corner opposite the Gate of Cougnes, his present home, and he would have to get there and back before the midday meal, if he were to escape notice. It was not the length of the walk in itself that distressed him. Though La Rochelle was a big town, it could be crossed diagonally from the southeast gate of Cougnes to the western line of inner fortifications, which divided the town proper from the port, in fifteen minutes of brisk walking. Rather, it was that his unexplained excursions across town, which he himself made longer by the rambling nonchalance which he forced himself to affect, seemed to him like a conspicuous declaration of unacknowledged, and therefore presumptively improper, conduct. Though he argued to himself that nothing was more natural than for a newcomer to acquaint himself with such a venerable and important burg as La Rochelle, or for so important a person as himself to have numerous banking needs, his own bad conscience made him uneasy.

Thus, it was with elaborate casualness that Maurice issued forth from the Cougnes arch into the meridional glare and hesitated whether to take the axis of the Rue Saint Yon, the most direct route, or to follow the sinuous Grande Rue into the Fisherman's Alley and turn right at the port. Characteristically, he selected the more devious way, and set out at a stroll, weaving back and forth across the central gutter, stopping in pretended admiration of a balustrade supported by caryatids, pausing to drink at the public fountain. The streets were crowded; men-at-arms with emblems of their regiments on their breasts, merchants in long, black gowns, sailors from foreign ports in garb whose vivid colors contrasted with the somber attire of the Rochelais, a handful of disreputables — the poor, the lame, the gypsies — all jostled together, vying for room to walk on the dry cobblestones on each side of the street.

Maurice eyed the crowd warily, lest he discover a familiar face, and with courtesy unusual for the time and especially for himself, ceded the way to nearly all comers, having no desire to attract attention by his normal bluster.

At the carrefour, he passed a tawdry tavern, The Setting Sun, a mariners' hangout which he had once used to explain away an earlier expedition. The dusky wines of Bordeaux graced every table in La Rochelle, but in the dim recesses of the tavern, they were imbibed with more freedom and at considerably cheaper prices than in the better parts of town. On Maurice's only visit to that establishment, one glass had led to another, and what had been a momentary stop for an aperitif had become a lengthy, liquid repast. Maurice recalled little of the occasion, but remembered well enough the reprimand he had received on his late return.

This unpleasant memory alone would have discouraged him from recidivism, but he also had a vague recollection of carousing with the crew of a Spanish merchantman, and found the mere thought of that encounter sobering indeed. Still, such wines were a consolation in times of trouble.

With a sigh, Maurice passed the tavern, and made quick left and right turns into the Fisherman's Alley. Closed in by overhanging buildings, the street reeked of its trapped odors. Maurice's boots squelched through a black muck redolent of low tide and prickly with scales and bones. Though the fish market disgusted him to the point of nausea, Maurice returned to it as often as he could. Never had he seen — or even imagined — such creatures as were peddled there: horny shells dripping with green slime; rubbery, tentacled horrors, black evil-looking glistening enigmas with glassy eyes. The merchants' stalls and tables displayed more captives from the deep than all the beasts, birds, and fish of his childhood bestiary. The very grotesqueness of these fruits of the sea, as they were poetically called, appealed to Maurice in much the same way as spiders fascinate small boys.

The foetid alley led out into an open space, which ran along the inner town walls. Opposite was a sturdy gate, pulled back during the day, which afforded Maurice a skewed glimpse of the harbor. The tide was nearly high; sun sparkled on the lapping waters; a confusion of masts and tackle gleamed against the dark timbers of the port's mouth. Just inside the gate, pyramids of neatly stacked oranges blazed joyously. Unnoticed by the bustling longshoremen, Maurice casually swiped one as he sauntered by. An orange was a delectable luxury, which would taste all the better for being stolen. Peeling the fruit as he walked and dropping its white pulp into the gutter, he sucked the sections with concentrated enjoyment.

A distant, silver-toned bell tinged twelve strokes, and Maurice's pleasure vanished. Startled, he realized that more than half an hour had passed since he had left Cougnes. Dinner back at the mess would soon be on the table; he did not want to miss it, and more importantly, he did not want to be missed. Quite suddenly, his customary fears repossessed him. He rubbed a sticky hand thoughtlessly across his mouth. His carefree gait took on a furtive, hurried look, and with a speed that contrasted strangely with his earlier pace, he completed the few remaining steps of his walk.

The bankers' exchange occupied the ground floor of a wide stone building decorated in the Italian style. High windows made airy spaces between ornate bas-reliefs. The whiteness of the new stone contrasted with the grimy half-timbered façades of the adjoining structures, giving the building an elegant, modern appearance. Inside, dark paneling and marble gave back the light of a necessary fire. The warm glow of wood and cold gleam of stone made it a curious interior, at once cozy and imposing. Finally at his destination, Maurice hesitated, blinking in the sudden semi-obscurity. The room was deserted, except for a red-haired, snub-nosed youth in forest-green livery.

Barely turning toward La Renaudie, the young man said, "I'm just closing up. It's mealtime."

"I'm just making a delivery," Maurice replied. Wondering if his voice sounded unnaturally high-pitched, he continued in a mumble, "It's for banker Pascal in Chinon, and it's important." He drew himself up and projected his parting words in a muted bellow. "See it goes immediately!" The command rang impressively in his ears.

"All right, all right," the other replied. "First thing after grub. Will that suit you?" The youth's freckled face broke into a malicious smile, as he mimed an elaborate bow. Maurice pivoted sharply, banging his scabbard into the counter, and left with as much dignity as he could muster.

This time Maurice did not hesitate to take the most direct route. He hustled across town with none of his earlier ramblings, without even glancing to left or right. Two figures, guardsmen by their emblems, left the shadows of an alley across from the exchange shortly after Maurice emerged into the open and strode in the same direction.

The streets were nearly empty, most Rochelais being indoors for their dinners, and Maurice and the two others made good time, the latter gaining on the former by an occasional sprint. In ten minutes, Maurice reached the great cannon emplacement of the eastern wall and turned right for the short walk to the keep. At the corner, a filthy, footless beggar lay sprawled in the muck. The man grabbed at Maurice's leg as he hurried by and called out in a piercing wail, "Alms, Monsieur, alms!"

Maurice turned and delivered a vicious kick at the prone figure, and looking up, found himself face to face with his pursuers.

The taller of the two, a red-faced man with large square teeth and a loud voice, was the second-in-command of Maurice's regiment. Though they had exchanged few words, Maurice had early on developed an antipathy for his senior officer, irritated by his endless preoccupation with his own virility and implied scorn for the rest of mankind. Maurice sensed that his dislike was reciprocated. His aide, a wiry, brown Southerner, was an old-timer at La Rochelle, and among the more rabid of the religious fanatics of whom the town had more than its share. Although he shared Maurice's quarters, he had remained aloof from the newcomer.

The loud man's voice boomed out, "We must be overfeeding our stalwarts, if they sacrifice their dinners for little strolls around town."

"Well, no, actually, I was just planning on rushing over to the mess. I'm sure there will still be some grub if I hurry." Maurice began to sidle away.

"Not so fast. François here," indicating the Southerner with his thumb, "has been keeping an eye on you, like I told him to, and he's had some intriguing things to report. You must he a very wealthy young man to have such a lot of business with those bankers. Funny thing. One sure wouldn't know it from looking at you, but that's all I can figure. Otherwise, I would have to think that you were up to that old trick of sending clandestine correspondence by bank couriers. But I can't imagine the great La Renaudie doing such a thing!"

"Of course not," Maurice protested. "In fact, if you must know, though I can't see why it's any of your business, it's because I'm hard up that I keep running to the bankers. I'm trying to get them to send me some cash, but it seems my stepfather has been putting pressure on them to keep my money from me. You see, he really hated my coming here." Maurice shrugged pathetically and tried to gauge the other's reaction.

"You know, that's a touching story. The Captain's got a real soft heart, and I think he'd love to hear such an affecting tale. What do you think, François?"

"Sure," said François, whose laconic self-effacement made him the ideal subaltern.

"What's more, I think we might relieve Monsieur of the weight of his sword. What do you think, François?"

The latter carried out his superior's wish without comment, and the two men walked to Cougnes with Maurice between them.

Several hours later, hours spent in a small cache with no amenities save a gutter which ran along the wall to a hole, a very hungry Maurice, together with his captors, stood before the Captain. He was a just man, and he listened attentively first to the story of Maurice's frequent trips to the banking exchange, described with considerable emphasis on Maurice's underhanded manner, and then to Maurice's explanation, but neither account satisfied him. As far as he could see, he explained carefully, the only way to verify La Renaudie's bona fides was to read his letter, but this was not possible since it had already been delivered to the bank. Banking couriers were by common consent inviolate; neither Protestants nor Catholics wanted their finances disrupted. The past was inconclusive, and the future did not seem likely to provide the key to the past. It was after all, too much to expect that La Renaudie would provide the authorities with another opportunity to catch him out.

The Captain shrugged. Looking at Maurice's accusers, he summed up, "Under the circumstances, I mean without anything to show concretely that his behavior was illicit, I see no alternative but to take his word for it, with," he turned to Maurice, "the understanding that he would be wise to submit any further correspondence to my scrutiny before sending it out."

Maurice's sigh of relief was almost audible. He looked triumphantly at the others and thought them impudent in returning his gaze unabashed.

The second-in-command looked the Captain full in the eye. "You say there's nothing to show his behavior was covert. Well, if you could have seen him sneaking around, you wouldn't have much doubt, but there's something else. François here is a light sleeper, and he shares La Renaudie's room, not by accident either. It turns out that the precious letters get written in the dark of night, and if that's honest, then I'm the Pope's confessor." Simultaneously, the three men turned their gaze on La Renaudie.

Terror gripped him at the revelation that his nocturnal activities had been observed, so unexpected after the false sense of security which had possessed him moments before. Where he might otherwise have been able to concoct an explanation for this facet of his behavior, his wits suddenly froze, and he gaped at his accuser with a silence more telling than words.

His eyes still on La Renaudie, the Captain asked his subalterns, "Have you anything more to report?" They shook their heads. "Then you may leave us. Post a guard at the door.

"Well, La Renaudie," he continued, after the others had left. "We gave you a chance, and it seems we made a mistake. It won't save you from getting what you deserve, but I want to know what you've been up to and I want to know fast."

"Sir, it is as I said," Maurice improvised desperately. "It's just I've been so busy, I couldn't find any other time to do my writing. You know I have my religious instruction as well as my guard duties. I'm so far behind everyone else in knowledge of our Faith that, well, it's a real obsession with me to learn and study as much as I can. Money seems so unimportant in comparison. I don't want to waste a single precious minute of daylight. Writing, you see, I can do in the dark, but not my readings. I'm sorry I bothered François." The flow of words trailed off miserably.

"Come, La Renaudie, you don't expect me to believe such rot. Your precious studies didn't stop you from drinking a whole evening away at that hellhole where the foreigners hang out." Since La Renaudie offered no further explanation for his conduct, the Captain shrugged and continued, "I don't personally know if this is a matter for torture, and I'm glad it's not up to me to decide. I can't hang La Renaudie's son out of hand, so I'll let you tell your story to the Admiral, and he can decide whether to believe you, rack you, or simply get rid of you."

Another day passed before La Renaudie had his interview with the Admiral, another day spent in the bare, black cache with no food and barely any water. In his weakened state, the brisk walk to Coligny's headquarters left him breathless and light-headed. A grotesque feeling of emptiness possessed him as he stood before the Admiral; he felt void not just of food, but of ideas, of courage, of resolve.

He stood, and stood, and stood. He wondered if he was weaving on his feet or whether the fear of doing so made his imagination anticipate the reality. The Admiral's piercing blue eyes, which had at first gripped his fascinated gaze, became indistinct and uninteresting. Abruptly, he stopped being afraid. His immediate needs seemed so much more compelling than any new hardships the future might bring.

"Let's start from the beginning," a great voice seemed to boom across a chasm. "Captain Thouars tells me you've been corresponding with an unidentified person by the intermediary of some banker, and that you've been at some pains to keep the nature or even the existence of this correspondence secret. The secrecy of the writing rules out any innocent explanation. Romantic intrigues and monetary needs you could have shared with your comrades. There being no innocent explanation, your conduct reeks of treason. In short, you have been spying on us." Maurice shook his head and ran his tongue across his lips.

"I also understand that you have refused to tell Thouars the identity of your correspondent or what you reported to him. Now that you are before me, I hope you will drop any illusions you have of continued obstructionism. I will have that information by whatever means are necessary."

"No," Maurice mumbled; "No," more loudly; "No!" in a shout that startled his listeners as well as himself.

He stumbled forward and leaned on Coligny's desk.

"I can't tell you. I'm sworn to secrecy, and I am not a man to betray my oath." He grinned wildly.

Coligny and Thouars exchanged puzzled glances.

"Now look here, La Renaudie," Coligny resumed, "you're not doing yourself any good. If the identity of your correspondent requires you to die in torment rather than reveal it, then, don't you see that I have no alternative but to assume the worst, that this person is one of our most terrible enemies. And then, you see, I must hang you. And I assure you I would do so without compunction. But it may be that you are reporting to someone who, though an outsider, has interests at heart which are not inconsistent with our own. Such a person would not hold you to your oath at the cost of your life. And I would not necessarily consider your actions malicious."

Maurice stared blankly at Coligny.

His head seemed steadier. The rhythm of his body had changed, and his earlier weakness had abated. With the return of some clarity of thought, however, came a revival of his terrors; they pulsed through his mind and disrupted his thoughts. As he grasped Coligny's words, the glimmer of an idea came to him, but he could barely keep hold of it for his fear. Coligny strummed his fingers impatiently. "Well?" he asked finally.

Maurice straightened. "You are right. My master's intentions toward you are honorable, indeed benevolent, and he would not wish me to die to keep his name hidden from you."

"Yes?" Thouars and the Admiral spoke together. "Who is it?" Coligny continued.

Putting as much pride in his voice as he could, Maurice replied, "The King."

Stunned silence gripped his listeners for a moment, then both exclaimed, "The King!"

"Yes," La Renaudie resumed haughtily, as would a person of importance who deigns to give explanations to an underling. "His Majesty confided in me before my departure. He said that peace is near and dear to his heart and the estrangement of his subjects from each other and from himself is his greatest sorrow. He would like to bridge the religious gap, but he feels crippled by lack of reliable information. Many people at Court wish to control him and so hide things from him, whereas your own representatives at Court are not necessarily to be trusted, because their job, after all, is propaganda. But he knew he could rely on me."

Maurice spread his hands grandly. "I hope I have not failed him," he concluded with becoming dignity.

"Well, I'll be!" the Admiral said, and stared at La Renaudie with bewilderment tinged with disbelief.

Maurice forged on. "The King was particularly pleased to avail himself of my services, because he planned to meet with you soon in Brittany. He did not use me officially, of course, because he thought it might diminish my effectiveness, meaning no harm."

Coligny seemed to hesitate, then came to a resolve.

"You're well enough informed on the Brittany score. The King's been putting out feelers, very discreetly, I might add. If you know that, you must have some inside information. But is it necessarily the King's, that is the question." Coligny paused, picking at his teeth in a ruminative way.

At last, he resumed, "Well, La Renaudie, I've a mind to increase your so-called effectiveness and check up on your story in one go, and it's this: I'm not thrilled with meeting His Majesty in some wood.

"No insult to His Majesty, but even if he's on the level, the people around him may not be, and I don't suppose he could control them in some godforsaken wilderness. Especially as this is supposed to be a cozy, secret meeting, and I'm not allowed to bring too many of my own people to it. No, I haven't lived this long without wanting to live longer.

"This is important: I'm with His Majesty one hundred percent on pacification, cooperation, and finding ways to enforce the toleration edict to get the papists off our backs, and I would meet him gladly under the right circumstances. Of course, here at La Rochelle would be ideal. I would personally guarantee his safety. He would be received with the same warmth and honor as during his trip here before the last of these terrible wars. These are supposed to be times of peace, after all. He is our sovereign, and we have not forgotten it."

The chasm of fear which had gaped before La Renaudie since yesterday and which had begun to close thanks to his clever ruse now widened terrifyingly before him once again.

"Put these matters to His Majesty," Coligny concluded, rising decisively. "When his response comes, if it bears you out, you will be fully vindicated. In the meantime, we'll have to keep you under lock and key. So you see, I would write His Majesty straightaway if I were you."

* * *

Gondi sat lost in thought. The bare table before him gave no clue as to the cause of his preoccupation. It was not that he was busy; neither personal interests nor state business had demanded much attention in recent weeks. Indeed, it was this apparent calm which worried him. He was a man who liked to exercise control.

The present lack of opportunity for personal involvement did not gull him into thinking that nothing was happening; it merely confirmed his impression that he was not at the scene of the action and therefore not in a position to alter the course of events. Thus, he was pleased and relieved when Julio briskly entered the room, an animated look on his face and a white packet in his hand.

"A courier just arrived with a letter from Pascal," he explained.

"At last!" Gondi exclaimed. "Read it!"

Julio fumbled with the seal under his uncle's irritated glance and perching on a chest, began to read:

16 June 1571

My dear Albert, (Gondi's eyebrows shot up in surprise.)

I was most pleased to be able to provide some small hospitality to you and your niece...

"Blast," Gondi cried. "I thought when you said a letter from Pascal, you meant one from La Renaudie. The last person I want to hear from is Pascal."

"There are several enclosures. Here's a sealed parchment which could be a letter. Let me see, yes, and it's from him. What shall I read first?"

"You may as well finish Pascal's missive. Then we can get on to important matters."

...some small hospitality to you and your niece.

"Why, he doesn't even mention me," Julio interrupted himself in an aggrieved tone.

"He's not interested in you, you little fool. Now, get on with it."

Your niece is as charming as one would expect the offspring of such esteemed forebears to be. My wife and I beg you to transmit to her our warmest regards.

"How he drivels on," said Gondi.

This will confirm that I am pleased to extend the letters of credit which fell due on 15 May and 1 June at the same interest rate as before. I enclose the appropriate documents for signature. You will also find enclosed a letter from the gentleman with whom you put me in communication. Knowing your impatience to receive news from him, I am sending everything by special courier.

It delights me to be of assistance to such an old friend as yourself. I would like to take this opportunity to inquire when it would be convenient for me to call upon you. My son, Aimeri, returns from Paris in two weeks' time, and we would be most pleased to make the journey to Chenonceau to call on you and your niece and to continue our discussions. Please advise me of your wishes.

"Then, there's the usual salutation," Julio concluded, putting the letter down on the edge of the chest. "Damnation," said Gondi. "Read the other letter."

La Rochelle, 14 June 1571
Esteemed Sir,...

Julio's pleasant, even voice read through Maurice's letter: his tours of the fortifications, the gallant offering of his sword to Coligny ("Damn good, if it's true," Gondi commented), and the death of the spy.

"And that's the end of the letter," concluded Julio. "You wouldn't believe it, uncle — all splotches and squiggles." Gondi sat silently, a deep furrow creasing his brow. "Leave me," he said, without looking up. Julio stood, stretched luxuriously, handed his uncle the two letters and the notes, and left the room. Gondi did not hear the door close behind him, so intense was his concentration on the problems presented by Maurice's report. To be able to plunge himself into single-minded, rapt study of a situation for as long as necessary to understand it and to decide on appropriate action was one of Gondi's gifts. His face became hard as he reflected, losing all the warmth and expressiveness it exhibited on social occasions. His hand clenched in an unconsciously aggressive gesture. Gondi reviewed the situation from the beginning. He had employed La Renaudie initially almost as a joke, with no defined purpose other than getting him away from Court without scandal. The realization that La Renaudie was as likely to be killed as to prove useful did not distress him. Maurice's death would have permanently resolved the problems he posed; if, in the meantime, he stayed out of trouble and supplied a few useful insights into the situation at La Rochelle, so much the better.

He had not had any reason to foresee that subsequent circumstances would transform this entertaining gambit into a matter of dire import. He had been shocked when he had learned from La Renaudie himself of the King's decision to seek out Coligny near La Rochelle. Gondi had understood at once that the young monarch's initiative could lead to much more than renewed, direct contact with the Protestant leadership. It could well lead to war in the Netherlands, which meant war with Spain, if the Protestants, not Coligny necessarily, but the younger blades, were allowed to make use of Charles' hotheaded enthusiasm and thirst for glory. La Rochelle had thus become the key to the situation.

Gondi reflected on whether he could be faulted for his reaction to the King's announcement. He thought not. It had never crossed his mind, of course, to leave a delicate and important mission in La Renaudie's hands; he had immediately dispatched one of his most trusted agents, Chabannes, on a long-term mission to La Rochelle and he had been relying on him. By a strange twist of fate, that man had been arrested at the time of Maurice's arrival. He now knew what his fate had been. It was ironic, he thought, that the better man had failed, where the lesser man had so far prevailed. Perhaps Maurice's very inexperience was a safeguard of sorts.

At any rate, as Gondi recognized with a shudder, there was now no getting away from the fact that La Renaudie survived as his only direct contact with the Protestant hierarchy at La Rochelle. The idea was appalling, but, reflected Gondi, as he had often thought in other crises, one must make the best of what one has. He picked up Maurice's letter, noting with disgust the erratic, unruly handwriting. The hand betrays the mind, he thought. This scrawl depicts an undisciplined, unreliable, unstable mentality. Can he be used? His judgment is astigmatic. A warp in his personality magnifies out of all proportion anything which threatens him or which gives him importance, but he is not without intelligence and a certain cunning. Moreover, his name gives him a unique advantage in his efforts to gain access to the Protestant leadership. But can he be controlled? More important, can he be controlled by me?

* * *

The Queen Mother's study was a charming room. Because of its small size and low ceiling, it was welcoming and unpretentious, but its aery fenestration and the intricate carvings of its beams gave it an elegance unparalleled even in much grander rooms. Three windows opposite the door formed an alcove, which looked up the river Cher. In front of the windows was a mahogany table, small in size, but rich in carvings and inlay, and so brightly polished that it shone with jewel-like brilliance. At the table, Catherine sat writing. The study, or library, as it was sometimes called for the collection of rare volumes that it housed, was principally a morning room.

Even now, shortly before noon, warm rays streaming through the windows' intricate filigree of wood and lead created a lacy pattern of light and shadow on the tabletop. The distortions of a hundred panes of glass transformed the geometric regularity of Catherine's formal garden into a kaleidoscopic chaos of vermillion, emerald, and forest green.

As Gondi entered, he admired, as often before, the room's agreeable elegance. It reflected the aesthetic sensibilities of its owner; yet, ironically, her own massive black-robed figure, too heavy for its setting, sounded the only jarring note in the harmonious scene. Catherine sent him a gracious smile. "Be seated, my friend," she said, in their habitual Italian. "I hope you, at least, have been making the most of this lovely day.

"Myself, I am a slave to my epistolary efforts. This correspondence sometimes seems to me as perpetual and relentless as the passage of Time. I wish I felt free to drop everything and hunt and play, as my son does. But..." She made an expansive gesture with both hands, which indicated at once resignation and defiance. How Italian she still is in some ways, Gondi thought. He smiled sympathetically. "Even so, after our dinner, I'm going to abandon all this, and go riding. Will you join me, my dear Alberto? You must."

"If I can, my lady, I will, but sometimes your wonderful repasts put me hors de combat."

"Tsk, you will grow fat." She laughed, more at herself than at him. Noting no responsive gaiety, she dropped her banter and favored him with a sober, calculating look.

"Well?" she asked.

"I must cast a shadow on this sunny day, I fear."

"So I see."

"I have reports from Normandy that the King remains firm in his resolve to meet with Coligny. Indeed, he has turned southwest toward Brittany. Moreover, it appears that every passing day adds fuel to his enthusiasm for the Netherlands Enterprise. My agent in La Rochelle has reported that rescuing the Dutch Protestants is fast becoming a Huguenot Crusade, especially among the younger captains, which confirms my information about those young fanatics whom Charles chooses to associate with."

The Queen Mother sat silent for a moment, then turned to Gondi. "What do you suggest?"

"If we do nothing, there is a chance that Charles will induce Coligny to improvise a meeting near La Rochelle, and a further chance that they will reach an agreement on the Netherlands, which the King could then present to us as a fait accompli. Since we cannot stop the King from going to Brittany, we must try to persuade Coligny not to meet with him."

"No doubt, but how?"

"I believe that my agent in La Rochelle may soon be in a position to gauge the Admiral's own reaction to the King's plans. Indeed, he may be able to influence them. I reason that Coligny and his advisers are suspicious enough of any Catholic initiative to make them most reluctant to leave their place of surety for some 'chance' encounter in the woods. I hope to use my agent to reinforce those suspicions. So far, I think we have a good chance of success.

"But we must look further down the road. We can foil this meeting, but the momentum is there. Unless we block it or channel it, it will someday burst from our control. I propose that we take the initiative out of the King's hands and bring Coligny to Court. Then we will be able to control the King, and... Coligny will be in our hands." Gondi smiled maliciously.

"I agree — reluctantly — but I agree," the Queen Mother responded slowly. "What intrigues me, however, is this: Having persuaded Coligny that it is too dangerous to meet with the King alone, how will you convince him to set his fears aside and take on the entire Catholic nobility?"

"To tell you the honest truth..."

"I hope you always do."

Gondi reddened.

"I have not worked out all of the details and I must perforce leave many of them to my agent. I think that Coligny needs the King. Without the King's support in the Netherlands, he will appear weak to his followers and could lose his leadership to younger men. He will want to meet with the King, never fear. And we must, at all cost, control the circumstances of their meeting."

"Beware, he is no fool," Catherine rejoined.

"I know that," Gondi replied.

The room was now in shadow; gentle, reflected light softened the Queen Mother's features, as she mulled over Gondi's proposal.

"I hope your agent is reliable," she said finally, looking at Gondi. Her eyes twinkled, as she added, "I see you don't take me into your confidence, but no matter, I'm satisfied, as always, to leave such details to your discretion."

"No, no," Gondi's words stumbled over each other in his haste to put the dreaded confession behind him. "I have no secrets from you. It is La Renaudie."

On the instant, the comfortable good humor disappeared from Catherine's face.

"You dare to employ such a man — the half-lunatic son of a traitor — in my affairs and the affairs of my state! I decorated the gates of Amboise with his father's head, and believe me, I would do the same to him, if he gave the slightest pretext. He would be an impoverished beggar, not a courtier, if de Galle hadn't taken it into his head to marry the mother, God knows why. Surely, among the millions of our countrymen, you could have found someone else! Sirrah, this — is — insufferable!" she concluded with emphasis.

"Madame, you would understand if you knew the circumstances."

"I spit on your circumstances."

"Chabannes is dead. I had sent him."

"I'm sorry," she said perfunctorily, refusing to be diverted. "Understand me, I will not have that man in my service."

"We cannot always choose our tools."

"Answer me this, Alberto: How can you rely on him? How will you control him?"

"I assure you, I have ways, Your Majesty."

"I know one must use people, and though I myself trust no one, absolutely no one," — she looked pointedly at Gondi — "I will use people, because I must. But even so, there are limits. I will not have it," she concluded, rising. "Now, we will dine, and speak no more of it."

The meal was spent in unsociable gorging. Catherine found frustration as good a reason for eating as pleasure.

There was no more talk of companionable rides in the woods, and afternoon found Gondi alone in his room, unable to put aside his troubles and enjoy the day, and yet at a loss to discern a way out of the dilemma. The Queen Mother's vehemence had aroused all his powers of self-justification; he now raged inwardly at her unreasonableness, even though her view of Maurice was no different from his own.

A knock interrupted this inner discourse. Julio entered and handed him a tiny, folded, and sealed paper.

Opening it, Gondi read,

Proceed as you wish, but know that you must be to him as your arm is to your hand.

No signature was necessary. All his rage gone, Gondi felt the cold grip of fear. He gestured to Julio. "Take this to La Renaudie:"

It is imperative that you abort any meeting between the two C's. Emphasize the uncertain nature of the proposal and the difficulties of ensuring his safety or the King's under the circumstances. Do not – I repeat, not – reinforce suspicion of the King's motives. An invitation to Court will be forthcoming. He should see it as in his interest to engage in frank discussion with the opposition. Emphasize that he has more friends than he knows, and they will protect him. Talk of the King and de Galle, not of the Queen Mother or myself or Guise. Avoid mentioning anything which would suggest suspicious affiliations, but beware of being too disingenuous.

I am counting on you, and will not forget your service.

He nodded to indicate the epistle was concluded.

"This must go immediately, via Pascal, of course, but with all possible speed. Take a cover letter to Pascal":

My dear Pascal,

I am most grateful for your prompt transmission of the letter from our friend and for your accommodation of our temporary financial needs.

You will find within a response to the letter you forwarded.

It is of the most urgent importance that it reach my friend immediately. I thank you in advance for doing everything necessary to have it delivered as soon as may be.

As for your suggestion that you should visit me here at Chenonceau, delighted though I personally would be, I am afraid it is out of the question.

Gondi paused and reflected. How to be blunt, but not unduly insulting?

The château, as I am sure you know, is small and belongs to Her Majesty, the Queen Mother. Since I am here as a guest in a private home, albeit a royal one, I do not feel it would be proper for me to receive my own visitors without her permission. That might well lead to undesirable inquiries on the part of Her Majesty. I am sure you will understand that so long as I remain here your visit would be untimely.

"With regrets, and my affectionate remembrance to Madame, etc."

"But," Julio piped up, "the Queen doesn't mind your seeing people! You're always conducting business here."

"Julio, the idea that you are a Gondi is quite incredible to me. Any Florentine street peddler would have more subtlety. And will you be so good as to refrain from telling me about the Queen Mother, with whom I was intimate before you were born!"

And what a woman she is, he thought miserably.

Chapter IX

oses and sunshine, sunshine and flowing water. The days slipped by like the Cher's sun-dappled current, gliding beneath the piers of Chenonceau. Much to her surprise, Athalie was happy. She had been resentful at first, but could not sustain the feeling as the perfect summer enveloped her in a warming and nurturing cocoon. She was happy, as she had been as a child, when each day was long and full of implicit and unquestioned meaning, something to be cherished in itself, unthinkingly, without a forward or backward glance.

The days paraded novelties before Athalie's innocent eyes — a picnic, a boat trip, a play by itinerant actors, different musicians nearly every night — but these were not what was important.

They were mere ornamentation on the structure of her new life. Looking back at this summer, Athalie would remember the things that all the days shared, rather than those that distinguished them from each other.

One constant of her new life that both attracted and repelled her was its endless sociability. She shared her room with her young female companions, her meals with the Queen Mother's intimates, her walks with nature lovers, guards, young couples, and others who roamed the gardens for their own ends, as she explored them in search of quiet.

Beyond all this, she was asked to share her life with Margot. Circumstances had thrown Athalie and Margot together during this strange interlude in both their lives, and they had become nearly inseparable companions. Had Court life been in full swing, doubtless Margot would have dropped Athalie within days, but as it was, her new friend filled a gap, a void, a true need — for Margot could never bear solitude, which she found monotonous. Though their relationship was a child of chance, rather than choice, Margot discovered unlooked-for advantages in it. In her own family, she was the little sister and was tormented and scorned in the time-honored way; thus, she relished the rare opportunity of dazzling a true neophyte with her maturity and her savoir faire. With everyone she met, Margot tried to appear witty, knowing, and full of invention; displaying these qualities to one of Athalie's innocence enhanced them in a most satisfying way.

The admiration Margot was sure she inspired in her young companion gave rise to a quite different pleasure from the titillations she had often derived from masculine attentions, but she found she enjoyed it almost as much. Novelty was essential to Margot's happiness, and the mentor's role was a new sensation. As the slow summer wound on, Margot continued to see in Athalie her only defense against the nightmare of boredom. She commanded her presence, demanded her attention, and with a plethora of irrelevancies, implored her affection.

Athalie often found Margot's single-minded occupation of her life stifling and irritating, but seeing no escape and being in a state of mind to accept things as they came, she contented herself with appreciating the benefits that flowed from her friendship and even brought herself to respond with appropriate gratitude. As time passed, she realized that, though she did not really like Margot, she was becoming fond of her. However often she thought Margot vain, obtuse, or malicious, and it was very often, just as often she saw her as kind, amusing, and loyal. Indeed, when the Princess's inflated self-esteem was not involved, Athalie found her capable of considerable shrewdness and some honesty. All in all, her qualities more than made up for her faults.

Roses and sunshine. Athalie and Margot spent long hours amid the great geometric flower beds, magnificent in their manicured ornateness. They played tag in the cool mornings, running among the topiaries, in the shadows of the whimsically shaped bushes, or between the trellises, heavily laden with roses, smelling of sweet musk and humming with bees, or around the mulberry trees or the gnarled trunks of the olive grove, until they collapsed with heaving chests and dry mouths onto benches in vine-shaded arbors. They mocked the shattered privacy of young lovers. They sought out nests in the densely trimmed hedges, only to retreat, with shrill giggles, when the parent birds, shrieking and whirling, protested their invasions. They visited the little enclosure that sheltered the Queen Mother's pet sheep and fondled the lambs that, still suckling rather than grazing for their food, gamboled around their stately, heavy-coated mothers. They hid from the royal guards, ever present, ever watchful, who sternly refused to let them venture beyond the château's protected precincts.

Sometimes, in the afternoon, they would cross the bridge to the far bank and climb up from the river along the brook that ran through the trees until they reached the forest alleys where the hunters rode. Or, less adventurous, they would settle nearer to home, with needlework or cards, for sleepy interludes by the aviary, a tall cage, almost hidden by luxuriant vines, from which emanated the most magical sounds. Those were the hours Athalie loved most.

Sunshine and flowing water. They paddled a rowboat inexpertly across the Cher, slapping the water with their oars, trailing their fingers in the river's brown current, wriggling their bare toes in the growing puddle at their feet. Margot laughed uproariously at the sight of her exquisite garden dress transformed into a sodden weight in the bottom of the boat. Athalie breathed a sigh of relief that she was not yet so snobbish that she felt the need to wear her own best clothes on every occasion. She now had clothes which even the most fashion-conscious lady-in-waiting could have worn with pride, but the dresses were still a marvel to her, not things whose novelty wore off in a day, as they were to Margot. The Queen Mother's bolt of material had been made into a lovely evening gown, and that beginning had been followed by a simpler dinner dress, a riding dress — "but I don't ride," she had said to Margot, who had treated the statement as if it were devoid of meaning — and a lovely, light gown of palest green, her favorite, which Margot said was "for afternoons and whatnot." Athalie had protested the extravagance and wondered who would pay for the materials and the seamstresses.

115

Margot had laughed and asked why Gondi should strut like a peacock, while his ward looked like a sparrow's fledgling. Athalie had protested no more. She still wore the best of her plain country dresses for adventures, which she felt called for sturdy outfits. Margot disapproved, but not as strongly as Athalie frowned on the wanton destruction of finery. On this occasion, Athalie looked down at Margot's ruined skirts with her usual severe gaze, and Margot laughed. Margot was always laughing. Athalie laughed less easily, but her happiness was more profound.

There were many confidences shared during aimless walks through the woods, during quiet afternoons on the riverbanks, during the slow evening hours. To be sure, most of the confidences came from Margot. Her life had a surface glitter which was suitable for display, whereas to understand what made Athalie's life interesting would have required more effort than Margot was willing to expend. Athalie was by nature the better listener. She listened carefully and learned from what she heard.

"My mother wants all of her children to wear a crown. Even me," Margot confided. "Do you know what I'm to be? Queen of Navarre. That's not much, when you think that my sister, Elisabeth, was Queen of Spain, and poor old François was King of France and now Charles is, and Henry is to be King of England, if he can bring himself to marry that witch, Elizabeth, who's old enough to be his mother. Of course, Claude is only Duchess of Lorraine, but she's like a queen there, and anyway, Lorraine is as big as Navarre, or bigger. I don't think Mother's figured out what to do with Hercules. He's so ugly. But she'll find something for him. Anyway, I'm to have Navarre, which isn't really very good, but then, Mother never cared for me. She always preferred the boys. Of course, I can understand that." Margot smiled wickedly. "What annoys me is that she pretends that one shouldn't be interested in men."

"Do you think," Athalie broke in, "that your mother is interested in your brothers because they're men or because they're kings, I mean, because they have power?"

"What difference does it make? That's what it's all about, men have power." At this Margot broke off and aped the arrogant stride which was in style among the young bucks of the Court, crooking her left arm and placing her hand where a sword hilt would be. "That's why women love them, they have that, that, oh, you know..."

Athalie did not know, but did not say so.

"Anyway," Margot resumed, "she never cared for me in particular.

"As girls go, she always preferred Elisabeth, that is, until the meeting in Bayonne. She thought she could get around Elisabeth then, as she always gets around everyone, but it wasn't the same. Elisabeth became a real Spaniard when she became Queen. Mother was furious." Margot's voice hummed with malicious glee.

"I don't want to be a queen," she continued. Athalie cocked an eyebrow but said nothing. "Henri de Navarre is nothing but a boor and a booby, everyone says so. To get a crown at the cost of being unhappy all your life just isn't worth it. I'd rather marry a simple nobleman whom I really loved." Margot sighed theatrically.

Recognizing the signs of an impending confession, Athalie said encouragingly, "Yes?"

"Well, I might as well tell you. You're my friend and you're bound to hear about it." Athalie wondered briefly which reason was the more persuasive. "There's one man who is more than a king to me," Margot rolled her eyes heavenward, "who should have been born a king instead of a mere duke, who..."

"Well, who is it, for heaven's sake?" Athalie asked, suddenly losing patience.

Margot stopped walking, and turning to Athalie, said in a whisper, "Henri de Guise."

She cast a furtive glance up and down the path.

"I'm supposed to have gotten over him. Do you know, Athalie, what they did to me a year ago? Mother and Anjou and Charles tore my clothes and beat me for loving the Duke. Yes, beat me — like a child! Your aunt, the Countess de Retz, brought me to them and your uncle watched the door to keep outsiders out. I've never forgiven them.

"And then Henri married the Princess de Porcien. I'm sure he didn't love her, but they made him. Oh, Athalie, it was so horrible." Margot broke off, and her eyes filled with tears. Seeing that her friend's distress was genuine, Athalie maintained a respectful silence.

Margot snuffled and resumed, "And all that so that I could marry King Sebastian of Portugal, who is a lunatic and would be a pervert if he knew how. He sleeps with a prayer book for a pillow and won't talk to anyone but his monks. Can you imagine? And in the end, he wouldn't have me anyway.

"To think they drove Guise away to preserve my virtue for that man, if you can call him that." She stopped and stared at Athalie, her face working angrily. "Well, my virtue's my own, what there is of it, and I still love Henri de Guise.

"But sometimes I feel so hopeless. He's married and I'm to be stuck with Navarre." Margot's mouth puckered, and for a moment Athalie thought she really might cry, but just as suddenly, the Princess's features smoothed themselves back to normalcy. Her emotional excesses, her pitiful cries of defiance, were not yet something she herself believed in; beneath her turbulent exterior, Margot maintained a firm grasp on the realities of life. She had been brought up to fulfill clearly defined duties to her family and society, and she accepted her role, not merely resignedly, but willingly.

Margot shrugged. "Well, at least, Navarre's normal, but that's about all." An impish glitter came into her eyes. "No, that's not all. He's supposed to be very sexy indeed, but you have to like the rustic approach, you know, behaving like a bull and smelling like a dog, which I don't." Margot ignored Athalie's scandalized stare, but slowly, the mischief faded from her face.

"Mother knows I haven't forgotten Guise," she said quietly. "She watches me like a hawk when he's around, which isn't often, alas!"

Then venom hissed in her voice as she said, "She can't stand him. He's too much of a man for her!"

My mother this, my mother that — Margot's thoughts revolved constantly around the Queen Mother. Margot pretended to hate her, and certainly feared her, but nothing could diminish the power the mother held. Margot was truly "in thrall," bound by an attraction in which fascination was the substitute for affection.

And Margot's not alone, Athalie thought. All this little world revolves around her. We are all drawn to her, whether we will or no. I, too, am puzzled and enthralled.

Athalie thought back over the confused impressions of the last month. As one of many ladies-in-waiting, her duties would normally have been light, and her contacts with the Queen Mother few and superficial, but these lazy summer days made the forbidding Catherine more accessible than was her wont. Moreover, Athalie sensed that the Queen Mother liked her. Athalie was accustomed from her years with the Abbess to dealing with age and authority. She was not afraid of Catherine and found her passionately interesting. Discerning that there was nothing impertinent in the girl's attentiveness, the Queen Mother responded to her with warmth and reciprocated interest. Catherine found in Athalie a likeness to herself when young — partly their shared heritage, half Italian, half French; partly the girl's lean, taut look — Catherine had been thin once, and though motherhood and the passage of time had thickened her figure, it had not made it soft and yielding; partly her separateness — Catherine, too, had been viewed as a bizarre loner, with clothes and manners that were not quite right. These similarities created a bond between them, which was stronger than their short acquaintance would have justified, and Athalie found herself more and more accepted into the Queen Mother's inner circle.

Athalie observed her astutely, sometimes admiring, sometimes shocked, always interested. The older woman was such a mass of contradictions. She could be arrogant, bad-tempered, even rough. Athalie still cringed when she remembered witnessing the Queen Mother humiliate one of the ladies-in-waiting for some clumsy faux pas. "Not even a wench with your modest prospects can get by just on looks," she had said to the flushing, shrinking girl. At times, Catherine's hardness was submerged by a swell of sentimentality. Not infrequently, Athalie had seen tears flowing down her cheeks, as she spoke of her dead children, the young King François and her beloved Elisabeth. Sometimes, the Queen Mother railed wildly against a world of threats and heartaches; at other times, she accepted the same hardships with philosophical resignation. Most surprising, she was capable of great consideration, truly intelligent thoughtfulness. Athalie cherished the gift of a book full of woodcuts of Florence. "It is a fine work, one of the best," the Queen Mother had said, pressing it into Athalie's hands. "It is amazing the strides the printing craft has made in fifty years. And you see, my child, scenes from our Florence. I remember it well, though I was not much older than you when I left it

118

forever. You should know what Florence is like. It is your heritage. It is half of what you are."

The Queen Mother sensed the estrangement between Athalie and her uncle Gondi. At meals, she often placed Gondi beside her and Athalie opposite, and by her talk sought to bring them together.

How charming Gondi was then. Athalie remembered the time the Queen Mother had exclaimed, after a copious meal, that she really should not eat so much at her age and had cast a coquettish glance at Gondi.

Gondi had leaned toward her with merriment in his eyes, and had said, "Madame, everything you eat becomes you." Catherine's look of pleasure and amusement lingered in Athalie's mind. Catherine appeared grateful to Gondi for his attention, as if it showed not mere flattery, but friendship, or even something more than friendship; yet, she was a queen and he a mere nobleman. It was very puzzling.

Toward Athalie, Gondi's attitude changed not a whit, despite the Queen Mother's efforts. Indeed, if anything, their relations grew colder. He seemed to fear that the better she knew him, the more finely tuned her ability to see through him would become, and the more her immunity to his charm would increase. But she saw less of him than she expected, being fully occupied with her duties to the Queen Mother and her frolics with Margot.

One day, Margot asked breathlessly, "Do you know what next Thursday is?"

Athalie shook her head.

"It's Midsummer Day."

"So?"

"Mother is planning a feast. She's like me, you know — she loves parties. I knew she couldn't go much longer without one. My brother, Anjou, is coming — he'll be here tomorrow, they say — and there'll be a hunt and a dinner and a ball, and it will be such fun!"

Athalie felt too many misgivings to agree.

"We'll all have to double up, so the married couples can have rooms. You may sleep with me." Athalie's groan brought a hurt look to Margot's face. "You needn't worry — I'm very quiet. I sleep like a log, when there's nothing better to do." Forgetting her momentary sense of injury, Margot resumed excitedly, "You'll wear your riding dress at last; for all you never want to ride, you can't miss the hunt."

" But I. Don't. Ride," Athalie said, pointedly emphasizing each word.

Margot broke off and stared in amazement. "Nonsense!" she said. "Is that why you never want to come out with me?"

"I told you so, ages ago." Athalie said.

"Nonsense." Margot repeated. "Anyone can ride — now that we have sidesaddles. God knows what women did before, but now, it's easy."

Athalie's pride prevented her from dwelling further on her reluctance, and she resorted to a practical line of resistance. "I don't have a horse, much less a saddle."

119

"Well, my dear, that's no problem. The Captain of the Guard is a friend of mine," how good a friend she did not specify, but Athalie was beginning to be able to guess, "and he is the best horseman in France — except for Henri, of course." Everything was "except for Henri," and Athalie did not need to ask, "Which Henri?"

"So that's settled," Margot said, and twirled round and round, until she collapsed and rolled on the new-scythed grass, thoroughly wetting and staining her skirt. Athalie looked sourly down at Margot, who never guessed that this time her friend's frown had nothing to do with her clothes.

When the dreaded day of the hunt arrived, and Athalie thought back on her discussion with Margot, she wished desperately that she had resisted more adamantly. She sat on her horse — the horse that Margot's Captain had picked for her — and she could have wept that her fear of ridicule had overcome her fear of riding. Well, she thought, you have no one but yourself to blame for ending up in this stupid, horrible predicament.

For Margot's sake, the Captain had chosen well, though he had realized instantly that Athalie would be unable to judge the quality of his choice. He had selected a small horse, a pretty, delicate-boned mare, with a slick, chestnut coat that proclaimed gleamingly her youth and good health. Athalie had been relieved by her modest size, but dismayed by her liveliness. Even now, while the animal stood quietly cropping the turf beside the road, Athalie sat her uneasily, half of her mind still preoccupied with the perils of horsemanship, while the other half grappled with her fear of the lurking menace of the unknown woods around her.

The forest resounded with noise. Low clouds seemed to make an echo chamber of the towering, looming trees. Athalie cocked her head, listening intently to the deep blast of a hunting horn. The instrument bugled a ring in several parts, which was picked up by a strident medley of barking and baying. "Ow, ow, ow, arrhh," the dogs' voices raged, followed by the muffled thunder of hooves and the crash of broken branches.

Athalie pulled nervously at the slack reins. Ignoring the timid gesture, the horse stretched her head to a crisper clump of grass, pulling the reins abruptly from the girl's sticky hands. Mid-summer day heat was oppressive. Athalie perspired without realizing she was hot. She looked anxiously up and down the shadowed road.

She could not judge from the distant din how far the hunt had moved in the short time since she had been left behind. "Left behind" was not really accurate, she admitted to herself. In fact, she had simply refused to follow the perilous mêlée of dogs and horses, when it turned off the wide, straight alley into the forest proper.

Her decision had seemed the only possible one at the time, but it had left her in something of a quandary. Whatever dangers had been presented by the heaving mass of horseflesh, the flashing crops, and the overhanging branches, there had been a certain safety in numbers.

Now, she was alone, alone in the brooding wilderness. Before, she had been one of the hunters; now, she realized uneasily, she herself might be hunted by the very beasts who as prey gave such exciting sport. Boars, she thought fearfully — and wolves, she licked her dry lips — and even bears! She shook her head and took a firm hold on her emotions. After all, a wild animal would not attack a mounted human, surely not!

She looked down at the mare's red-brown neck. The short hairs were slightly mussed where the reins had rubbed them. Occasionally, the skin shuddered to dislodge the perpetual flies. A useful facility, thought Athalie, whose own flesh tickled from tiny bites. If only I had a few more hands, I could hold on, grasp the reins, and chase flies at the same time.

Athalie gripped a handful of mane in her left hand and leaned over to smooth the ruffled hair. The beast, a horse of her very own, inspired in her a curious mixture of feelings, some affection, much awe, and even more fear. Resolutely, Athalie took the reins in both hands and heaved upward. The disgruntled mare gave an abrupt lurch, and Athalie dropped them instantly, grabbing wildly for the saddle's horn. Tears of frustration welled up in her eyes as the mare lowered her head and placidly resumed her interrupted feed. It's no use, Athalie thought. Without the forward momentum of the other horses, this beast will simply graze for the rest of the day.

Athalie sank into gloomy thought. Even if she could make the horse move, she was by no means sure she knew the way home. While the mare continued to munch contentedly, Athalie slumped against the back of the saddle and continued her sorrowful reflections. Each preoccupied with her own interests, neither horse nor rider attended to the muffled noises coming first softly, then more loudly from their right, until the crackling and thudding reached such a volume that it burst into their consciousness. Before Athalie had time to react, her mount skittered sideways, tossed her head back, and half stumbled over a rock. Athalie fell forward on the rough mane, clutching at the muscular neck. A small cloud of dust wafted up to her sweaty face.

As the mare recovered, Athalie pushed herself upright and rubbed her eyes. Looking down the road, she saw a horse and rider poised, motionless, where they had emerged from the forest a hundred meters away.

As they turned and approached her at a brisk canter, Athalie could have laughed with relief. Through the dust clouds, she saw a large bay with a white face, mounted by a big man in the prime of youth, clean-shaven, with ruddy gold curls. The newcomer pulled up next to Athalie and bowed. Together, horse and rider towered over her and the trim, small-boned mare.

For an instant, Athalie thought, the King, it must be the King, though how that could be she could not say, since the King was reported to be in Brittany.

"Pierre de Galle, my Lady," the young man said, "at your service." He glanced around and with a puzzled look, turned back to her.

"Are you all right? Is there some trouble with your horse?"

As she did not answer, Pierre cast a professional eye over the mare, admired unconsciously her graceful proportions and rich coat, and concluded that if anything were wrong, it was nothing serious.

At last, Athalie stopped fumbling with the reins, looked straight into his eyes, and confessed the embarrassing truth.

"No. There's nothing wrong. I just got left behind."

The clear, blue eyes twinkled down on her. Sensing their kind mockery, she continued petulantly, "And what about you, why are you here?"

He explained, pointing as he talked, that as the stag was running east to west, he had thought it would turn south at the creek, so he had taken a direct route, hoping to cut the stag off and beat everyone else out. "But, it was all for nothing," he concluded, "because the stag forded the stream instead of coming down to where I was waiting for it."

Athalie forgot her annoyance, as she tried to understand his maneuver.

"How do you know that," she asked, "since you weren't there?"

"Didn't you hear the horns blowing?" She nodded, still bemused.

"They were blowing the 'beat water,' the signal that a quarry has taken to water. Didn't you hear the notes?"

Shamefaced, she owned up, "The horns don't mean anything to me. I haven't ever hunted before. In fact," she blurted out, "I've never been on a horse before."

Pierre laughed, looking at the slack reins and the small hands clutching fists of mane. "You don't say?"

Athalie could have wept at the blatant amusement in his voice.

"Well, she's a pretty beast," he continued. "Whose is she?"

"She's mine," Athalie replied hotly. "I just got her. The Captain of the Guard found her for me three days ago."

"He has a good eye, that man, but he's a bit of a rogue. He once tried to persuade me to part with a splendid young gelding for half its value by claiming that he could tell from its bone formation that it would be arthritic within months. It was absolute bunk, but very well laid on. If you got her from him, you probably paid twice what she's worth."

"I don't think so. You see, Princess Margot asked him to do it."

"Ah!"

"Anyway," Athalie resumed, "it's my uncle who will pay."

"Who is?"

"Albert de Gondi, Count de Retz. And I am Athalie de la Roque."

Pierre bowed once again. "There is no question," he resumed after a brief silence, "that three days would be a short time in which to learn how to ride."

"I didn't even try. Princess Margot promised to give me some lessons, but she turned flighty — I mean, preoccupied — when all the guests started to arrive, and forgot all about it, and I didn't want to tell anyone else that I didn't know how. So, well, I went to the stables and tried to let her get used to me, you know, make friends with her, but it doesn't seem to have helped."

"If no one else exercised her in the meantime, you're lucky you weren't killed getting this far. You must have figured out by now that you don't have quite the right form."

She nodded sheepishly.

"Look at how you're leaning on the horn of the saddle. It's a wonder it hasn't turned around under you. You must distribute your weight so that you are well balanced on the horse's back. If anything, I lean back rather than forward."

"But my legs drag, and my body seems to follow them."

"You don't have them positioned right and they're too limp. They should be supporting you, not pulling you over."

"Have you ever ridden sidesaddle?" Athalie queried suspiciously.

"No," Pierre admitted, "but I'm sure it's not different in principle from the way men ride. Here," he swung himself lightly to the ground. "I'll try it and see."

Athalie unhooked her leg and timorously slid down the horse's side, while Pierre held both horses' reins.

"You hold Phoebus," he said. Seeing the girl's eyes widen with fear, he laughed. "He looks like a great brute, but he's a true gentleman. He gives no trouble, I assure you."

"Not to you, perhaps."

Pierre looked sternly at her and said, "I shall will him to behave," and chuckled to see the solemnity of her expression. He gave her the reins and moved her hand up to a point under the horse's chin. "Always hold snugly, no matter how well behaved the horse. You should develop good habits."

With a simple, lithe movement, he sprang onto the nervous mare's back and hooked his right leg over the horn. His left leg dangled below the stirrup to the mare's knee, and Athalie giggled at the incongruity. Pierre shifted his weight, and ignoring the stirrup, urged the horse forward with skillful hands and a commanding voice. They cantered a hundred meters down the trail and back again.

"It's as I thought," Pierre said, "only you must compensate for the weight of your legs by sitting slightly to the right of the center of gravity. The stirrup, of course, is to keep you from plummeting over if you lose balance, but you shouldn't rely on it. It's your seat that's important.

"Because she's small and runs like a pony, it's more difficult. If you had a big ark of a beast, like Phoebus, his gait would be slow and long and easy to adjust to. It's the opposite of what you think. Now, come along."

He jumped off and lifted Athalie onto the saddle. As her weight slid automatically toward the horn, he firmly pushed her back. He lengthened the stirrup slightly and carefully positioned her foot in it.

"That will do," he said, with a friendly smile, and turning, mounted Phoebus. "We may as well head back."

"You mustn't feel that you have to accompany me. You should return to the hunt."

Poor, brave girl, Pierre thought to himself. The only way she would get home is by walking, and that's assuming she knows the way.

"I assure you I prefer to return," he said.

"You are very kind," Athalie said stiffly, "but I'm sure you would prefer to join the others."

Half irritated, Pierre explained. "The horn just blew the signal that the stag has broken out into open country and is making a run for it. At this late stage, he will never outstrip the dogs, so this is the beginning of the end. The sound of the horn was very faint, even though the wind is blowing our way, so my guess is that the hunt is a good way away from here, far enough anyway that I would never arrive in time."

Athalie, who had not even heard the signals that Pierre had noted with half an ear and interpreted with expert ease, listened to his description with amazement.

"Besides," Pierre concluded reluctantly, "I don't really like to be in at the kill."

She cocked her head at him. "But you were so eager," she said.

"Well, since I have to hunt, there's no point in being half-hearted about it."

Pierre urged Phoebus forward with an abstracted air. It was true that he abhorred the bloody culmination of a successful hunt, yet it was equally true that he felt driven to excel at the chase. Barring accidents, he was always among the first to overtake the fallen prey and inevitably was in at the death. This curious combination of revulsion and compulsion confused and angered him.

Athalie broke into his reverie. "Why do you have to hunt?"

Pierre subdued an impulse to rudeness and answered gently, "It is expected."

How to explain that he had no choice? It had never occurred to him that he could refuse to join in this favorite activity of his class. Even now that Athalie had suggested the possibility, he knew that her question was a frivolous one. Every able-bodied man, and many women, including the Queen Mother herself, hunted. He would be a laughingstock if he stayed home like a cripple. He could picture the expression of scorn that would cross his father's face at the very idea. No, as he had said, he had to hunt, and since he had to hunt, he had to go all out after the quarry. That was second nature to him, a reflex that had been literally beaten into him as a child. And indeed, he reveled in the glories of the chase, whatever the outcome.

He glanced at Athalie. There was no way to explain such things to someone who did not know them instinctively.

"Look," he said, "I love a flank of venison, well aged and marinated, served with wine and bread. Don't you? The fact that it disgusts me to see the meat gaping raw and gory through the torn hide of a struggling animal doesn't change anything. Yes, it disgusts me, but I can hardly expect to shirk the harvest and still enjoy the fruit."

Though the argument was true, he knew it was beside the point.

He hunted, not to be able to eat venison, but because he would have been ashamed not to. Indeed, he felt abashed even to have such qualms.

Why should he be torn with pity for the beast when no other man, indeed, no woman — thought of anything but adventure and a good supper?

Athalie and Pierre clopped along in silence. Their talk had driven the terrors of horsemanship from her mind. In forgetful relaxation, she had naturally found and held her balance. She looked across at her companion. The sun had emerged hazily from its cover. Pierre's hair glistened in the warm light; his face radiated health and vigor; Athalie thought that she had never seen anything so beautiful. Pheobus, she mused; it is he who should have that name.

Pierre caught her eye and smiled. He saw with pleasure that her seat was steady and she no longer gripped the mane for dear life.

Much encouraged, he said, "Come, you'll learn nothing if we lope all the way to Chenonceau."

They trotted and cantered, stopping for explanations and adjustments, until they reached the magnificent tree-lined approach to the château. Pierre was a good teacher; Athalie was young and supple.

At the last, she made a grand and reckless entrance, traversing the long avenue at a near gallop, flushed, happy, and almost confident.

* * *

The courtiers crowded onto the bridge behind the château. The humid haze of the day was forgotten; it was a clear, sparkling, mild night, a night fit for revels. Lilting strains of music came from the terrace on the left. Below, a hundred barques floated, with torches fore and aft, carrying nymphs and dryads in fantastic, mythical regalia.

A large craft bore Poseidon, a giant of a man with an aquamarine wig and turquoise robes, who held aloft a great trident. The boats slipped beneath the arches; the onlookers hurried across the width of the bridge.

A second orchestra, now on the right, began to play music that was more exuberant than before, almost martial in theme. Both riverbanks flickered and glowed in the light of two tremendous bonfires, the traditional celebration of the midsummer sun. Fireworks burst from behind the bonfire on the right; more fireworks answered from the left; then, from both sides, flaming missiles crossed, making a brilliant arch in the sky.

Athalie gasped and clutched her hands together. She had never seen anything like this soirée — the elegance of the Court, the prodigality of the food, the variety and splendor of the entertainment, and now this! It was the crowning touch. The bursting, dazzling lights seemed like a miracle to Athalie, who had never seen real fireworks, nor even imagined that they were different from the sparklers sold to children on feast days, which she vaguely remembered from years ago.

All evening, she had glowed with well-being. She had danced with sureness and grace, had smiled with gaiety and warmth, had laughed as much and as merrily as Margot. Young men had flocked about her, competing to dance with her, touching her in ways that astonished her, relinquishing her to others with reluctance or anger. She felt lovely tonight, and her sudden popularity did not surprise or ruffle her. She was hardly aware of the bold lewdness of some of her new admirers and had focused not at all on its meaning, yet she brushed their advances aside with the assurance of a practiced courtesan. No one could hold her. She danced, she whirled, she floated on air. Now, as she watched the man-made shooting stars, her wonder was tempered only by her sense that they were a fitting background to this magical time and place. Real shooting stars would have come, if man had not been able to produce imitations.

The last white-gold streak of fire hissed into the water. Athalie realized suddenly that Margot was beside her, pressed against her in the crush. A wave of affection went over her, and she gave Margot's hot hand a squeeze.

"Oh, Athalie," Margot exclaimed breathlessly, "Isn't this exciting? Mother did well, don't you think? And do you know what I heard? We're to leave soon for Fontainebleau. The full Court will assemble there, when Charles returns from hunting. I'm so glad. I've been so bored." Margot's tactlessness was unintentional, and Athalie overlooked it. "Maybe you-know-who will be there. It's so exciting. I'll show you everything, and you'll love it."

Margot drifted away, hiccupping irregularly.

The bridge emptied slowly, but Athalie lingered on. Without the press of warm bodies, she felt chilled — a physical coldness that found an echo deep within her. Things should not end so fast, she thought miserably. Oh, no, indeed they shouldn't!

Chapter X

aurice's newest missive trembled in Gondi's hand. Abandoning all pretense, the frantic young man had scribbled a more straightforward and truthful letter than any he had ever written. It told how he had been arrested, with only a hint of reproach that Gondi's method of communication should have proven faulty, and how he had staved off impending doom by inventing the fantastic story that he was corresponding with King Charles. There was a certain pathos in the very simplicity of the letter. Maurice had bought time with his lie; whether he had also bought his life depended on Gondi. He had feared to increase Gondi's anger by open pleas for mercy, but his words echoed with unspoken cries.

Gondi cared nothing for Maurice's state of mind, nor for the perils he faced, except as they affected him. It was only because the situation seemed inimical to his interests that it gripped his attention; it appalled him the more, the longer he considered it; eventually, it left him feeling more terrified than at any time in recent memory. Controlling his alarm with effort, Gondi tried to analyze the predicament calmly.

What would happen, he asked himself, if he simply ignored the letter? Coligny would soon tire of waiting for a response, would conclude that Maurice had lied to conceal his espionage, and would have him put to death. Nothing would thereby have been lost or compromised. Even if Maurice told the truth under duress, no harm would come of it. It was no secret that Gondi had spies everywhere; so did everyone else. There was, therefore, an easy solution to the dilemma.

It was a pity he had told the Queen Mother about La Renaudie, because now he would have to foretell his demise, and he knew she would hold him responsible for his agent's activities. Still, Maurice had done no permanent harm, and that should temper her wrath.

His first panic ebbed. He could cut his losses without jeopardizing his own position. That being true, he should investigate whether the situation could be turned to his profit before dismissing it from his mind. Though this looked like a disaster, it could prove to be a great opportunity. After all, he thought, as often before, things are rarely as they appear. For example, What makes me think that this letter was not opened by La Renaudie's captors? If so, and they still let it go through and did not execute him out of hand, then I would conclude that they wish to draw me and Her Majesty into the King's silly scheme to meet with Coligny and his advisers. Gondi wondered at himself for not thinking of this before. Given the level of mistrust he believed existed at La Rochelle, he had to assume they had opened the letter, or even obliged La Renaudie to open it and reseal it.

He shook his head suddenly. This is rank speculation, he thought.

The seal was unbroken, and the envelope addressed in that inimitable scrawl, so we must assume that the letter came through intact. What then? It is still safe to conclude that Coligny wants to meet with the King, not under the conditions young Charles first proposed, but under some conditions as yet unspecified. Coligny's invitation to young Charles to come to La Rochelle is, of course, merely an opening gambit, but one that could be put to good use. Gondi smiled a tight little smile. Without a doubt, the situation had sufficient ramifications that it would have to be presented to Catherine. The smile faded; a worry line appeared between his brows.

His conversation with the Queen Mother later that day went much as he had expected. Her initial anger had been like a physical buffeting. The study had seemed too small to contain so violent a force. At the peak of her emotion, she had turned on him, asking in outraged tones, "And how could you, whom I have trusted with everything I value, how could you think to employ such a man, a faithless, unscrupulous, lying rogue, in my service?"

In the pause that followed, Gondi felt an insane impulse to lay before her the shabby truth: that he saw La Renaudie as useful for the very reasons she despised him and that he hoped to control him by the fine art of blackmail. But this was madness. A full confession would disclose Maurice's relationship with Anjou and his own concealment of it. No, total honesty would be fatal. Practical as ever, Gondi opted for a partial truth.

"The fact that he is unscrupulous makes him very useful. After all, he's not stupid, and his lies have gotten Coligny's ear in a very striking way, where better men have failed. However, we can simply ignore him, and he will be killed." He shrugged disinterestedly.

In unconscious imitation, the Queen Mother also shrugged, as if to show that she washed her hands of the entire mess. After a few moments, however, a speculative glint entered her eyes.

"In short," she said, "you think he is still useful."

"Exactly," Gondi broke in eagerly.

"Let me finish. You wish me to believe that he may be more useful than he is dangerous."

"Your Majesty is a brilliant strategist."

"Save your flattery," she said sharply, but flattered in spite of herself, she continued more pleasantly, "The main impediment appears to be that we need Charles to make use of this villain."

"But Your Majesty has always found Charles to be – useful."

"You are impertinent, Sir," she said, smiling in spite of herself. "But Charles is much more 'useful,' not to overuse the word, when he is where he can be controlled, instead of gallivanting around the countryside on his own looking for trouble. I believe you thought that there was no danger that the Admiral would want to indulge my son's fancies of gloriously invading the Netherlands, but now we know that however little Coligny may want a meeting in the woods, he does want a meeting somewhere, very likely to plan for just such an enterprise. You played a more dangerous game than you knew. And the danger is still there. Whatever the Admiral himself may feel about the Netherlands, you've pointed out time and again that he is not entirely his own man. If he is to lead, he must satisfy his followers.

"And I have to satisfy my followers, too."

Gondi watched her intently, knowing better than to interrupt her flow of thought.

At last, she sighed and continued. "The nuisance of it is that my followers include those of the so-called Reformed Religion, whether I want them or not and however much they would hate to hear me say it. If only we had been able to defeat them! Then, it would have been different, simpler.

"Do you know, Alberto, I even sometimes think that, if we can't defeat them, it would be better if they defeated us. Somehow, you and I would bring the ship of state safely through, and at least, it would rid us of the rabid extremists. But nobody wins, nothing is ever resolved. This peace is no more than a badly kept truce — everyone knows it. Look at the petitions all over my desk. Send help here, keep the peace there, rescue this town or that from roving bands of Catholics or Protestants.

"You know my dream, Alberto: to pacify the Protestants, to bring them back into the fold, if I may be permitted an ecclesiastical turn of phrase, by marrying my little Margot to young Navarre. But many of our Faith will fight it tooth and nail.

"So you see, I will need Coligny as a counterweight. Now, I don't want him made suspicious because you sent him a spy, because he discovers that our only direct contact is a lying rogue. That is not to happen, do you understand?"

"Well, Madame," Gondi replied gloomily, "either he already knows and doesn't care, or he doesn't know, and everything is all right."

"If he already knows, fiat, but if he doesn't know, keep it that way."

Gondi meditated silently awhile before speaking. "So we think Coligny wants to see us, or the King rather, because of the Netherlands, and we want to see him because of the Navarre marriage."

"Why so slow today, my friend? It makes me nervous when you belabor things."

"But there are problems with the Navarre marriage that the Admiral can't solve — the Pope for instance. We will need a dispensation for the marriage."

"If need be our bishops will give it — if we promise them peace."

"And Spain, we know what King Philip will say, but who knows what he may do."

"Spain, Spain, you have Spain on the brain! Philip has only himself to blame if Margot marries Navarre. He did nothing to further the Portuguese match. But why bring up all kinds of objections now, when I thought that we at least were agreed on what we want."

"I only bring them up because if we were to have doubts about the Navarre marriage, we wouldn't need Coligny."

"I have no doubts. Do you know what I think, Sirrah? I think you are having 'doubts' because you are afraid that lying, double-crossing scum of yours will scare Coligny off, but I tell you, that had better not come to pass. You know what I want, and you had better see to it that it happens."

Gondi straightened and looked up sharply.

"I will go to the King. I will leave immediately and ride without ceasing. I will make him send the Admiral an invitation that will establish La Renaudie's bona fides and start the ball rolling in the direction we want."

Catherine smiled graciously, as if her tirade of a few moments before were a thing long since forgotten.

"You are so devoted, my dear Albert," she said, and the inconvenience will punish you for your follies, she thought. "But what will you do when you get there? You were only just telling me that you are, at the moment, somewhat out of favor."

"Indeed, but the King's moods do not last. At heart, he is a good boy." They both indulged in sentimental smiles. "At any rate, I have always been able to make him see reason when necessary, by one means or another, though I must say I prefer to cajole than to bully."

A meditative silence fell on them. The late afternoon light filled the room with shades of delicate grey. The Queen Mother looked pensively out of the study window at the overcast landscape.

"In a way, I'm glad for the rain," said the Queen Mother. "After so much sun, the half-tones of a cloudy day seem restful to the eyes."

"This is hardly rain. It's more like misplaced dew."

Catherine stood and moved quietly to the window. Without turning to Gondi, she said, "Peaceful, rainy days make me want to indulge in melancholy musings. I feel calmly realistic until the frenetic pace of life catches me up again and I forget all my philosophy.

"What would my son do without me, Albert? Do I delude myself by thinking that I am his only salvation? Perhaps he would be serious if he had to."

"No, Madame, he still has much to learn from you. He is so young, and responsibility came to him so early. Perhaps he will grow into his responsibilities in time, but for now, only your steady hand can steer us safely through the shoals."

She did not react as she usually did, with a smile, mocking or self-congratulatory, and he saw that her mood had changed again. He had seen rage, determination, and now an infinite world-weariness, all in a short hour.

"In time... but is there time?" She shrugged, but when she spoke again, it was with a firm voice. "Go to him. Make him give up this idea of a bucolic reconciliation with the Admiral. Have him send Coligny a short, mind you, short, letter of invitation to Court. Now that we know Coligny wants to meet with us, an admittedly helpful tip from your protégé, there is no need to make the bait too attractive. If both sides want a meeting, it can be worked out. We should not appear too eager."

Gondi stood and bowed. "Excellent, Your Majesty."

"But understand one thing — and tell your pawn — he is to die rather than lie about such matters again, or I assure you he will die more cruelly at our hands than at theirs." Her voice jarred on his nerves, and he knew her emotions had gone full circle, from anger to anger. He bowed again in humble acquiescence. As he left, he reflected that much as he would like to obey her, he could not communicate her warning to La Renaudie without revealing everything to his captors.

* * *

Gondi drew rein at the top of a ravine, and looked down into its shadowy depths. He had been told that the tracks of the King's party would be easy to follow, and indeed they were. Sunlight on the exposed slope, dry and dusty after a season without rain, revealed pits and ruts left by the rapid passage of an important body of horsemen.

Curbing his horse sharply, Gondi strained to hear noises that would indicate that he was close to his quarry. His escort pulled up behind him with much jangling and creaking, snorting and scuffing; the plaintive whistling of an unseen bird rose above the buzz of the forest; then what passed for silence returned. Gondi dragged his cap off and ran his fingers through his close-cropped hair. He felt dusty, disheveled, and exceedingly weary.

Dismounting, he led the horse slowly down the steep slope to the shrunken rivulet at the bottom. Man and beast drank, and Gondi splashed icy water on his face and ears. Remounting, he continued his course at a brisk trot alongside the stream. The forest here was majestic. Great pines thrust reddish trunks and deep verdant crowns toward a blazing sky. Here and there, massive outcroppings of rock loomed above them, their dull coloring enlivened by the afternoon sun. Shafts of light angled through the trees, throwing streamers of shadow across the carpeted floor.

The going was easy. The clop-clopping of their progress was muffled and cushioned by beds of needles and soft moss. Summer haze shimmered; the thickets throbbed with hidden life; a gentle fragrance of pine and rich soil filled the air. Hungry and tired, Gondi felt pleasantly light-headed.

At last, the tracks turned off into an undergrowth of bushes and bracken, where young trees grew so low and dense that the riders were forced to hunch down over their mounts' necks as they crashed noisily onward. They proceeded with fits and starts through generally difficult terrain, until they emerged into a grove of widely spaced oaks, dark in the lengthening shadows. Gondi pulled up and heard at last the distant echo of the hubbub of a hunt in full cry. Heartened, he put his horse to a gallop, following the scored trail toward the din. Their way ran broad and clear, but no sunlight reached the ground, so high and thick were the ancient trees which blotted out the sky.

The massive shapes were an ominous presence in the semi-obscurity, and Gondi could not tell whether the chill which crept over him came from the growing coolness of the evening or from some obscure sense of danger. He urged his horse along with hands and spurs. The noises they followed grew ever louder; Gondi found the raucous din oddly comforting. At last, they reached a glade, glowing unexpectedly in the last rays of the setting sun, which blinded Gondi momentarily with its glare. He blinked and shaded his eyes with his hand, at first puzzled, then appalled by what he saw. The grass, burnt yellow by the drought, seemed in the strange light to have flaming tips. In this brilliant dream world, a confused mêlée of forms weaved and danced to the accompaniment of a dreadful cacophony of hunters yelling and hounds baying. Presently, Gondi made out some twenty groups of dogs and men, some mounted, some on foot, circling around their victims. For the most part, the fallen stags lay hidden behind the bands of predators, but occasional breaks in the seething ranks afforded Gondi glimpses of the downed beasts, some still struggling, others dead, heads severed and entrails grotesquely displayed. Gore flecked the dogs' gaping mouths and disfigured the tawny hides of their prey. So this is the King's new method of hunting, Gondi thought with mounting disgust — a refinement on what used to be a noble sport.

At first, the approach of Gondi and his men passed unnoticed in the chaos, then a guardsman recognized him and greeted him respectfully, and at last, a thin, dusty figure in crumpled clothes detached itself from a nearby group. Gondi dismounted, doffed his cap, and bowed deeply.

The King's voice rose shrilly, "Ah, de Retz, you've timed your arrival perfectly — as always."

Gondi observed beads of sweat, a heaving chest, wild eyes, and his heart sank.

"I see Your Majesty has had good sport."

"Oh, yes, yes, indeed." The young man laughed, a meaningless cackle.

"But you and your men are not numerous enough to eat all this meat. What do you do with the excess?"

"We leave it. It's not important. The forests are rich in game."

"Many villagers would be glad of the food, but would not dare to take it without your permission."

"Oh, don't prate, man!"

The King stalked away. Gondi watched him jerk one of the trophies, a severed hoof, from the branch where it had been hung to dry, and wave it before his companions with teasing gibes, "Who is the best hunter after myself? I will give him this souvenir!" then scornfully throw it to his favorite dog: "Bellerophon is the best of us all!"

More confusion followed; camp was set up, and meat prepared and cooked. The King's noble sporting mates sprawled around him in the royal pavilion, tearing at the roasted flesh with gusto. Hard riding gives youth a hefty appetite, Gondi reflected. I must be getting on, for it seems that no amount of exercise will permit the gourmand in me to triumph over the gourmet. He wrinkled his nose distastefully.

The venison, un-aged and undercooked, tasted sharp and strong, and he found it slightly repulsive. There were no side dishes, just meat and wine, typical, thought Gondi, of Charles' adulation of the rough life. Or is this miserable meal simply the product of his indifference to the whole subject of food? Charles, he observed, had eaten next to nothing, though he had imbibed a fair quantity of the coarse local vintage. As his companions achieved satiety, sporadic conversation broke out, hunting stories mostly, told with many flourishes to comrades who had already heard them and barely bothered to conceal their boredom. What an empty-headed gaggle of sycophants, Gondi thought, lying back on his elbows and eyeing them scornfully. Not a great name among them. Poor Charles can't bend the mighty to his whims. The real nobility will grasp any opportunity to see to their own interests, whereas this pack have no interests, other than worming their way into the King's affections. Well, that's not entirely true — some of them have other brands in the fire. There's Teligny, the Admiral's nephew, and I can guess what he's up to.

Yawns crossed the faces around the fire. The torpor that had possessed the King since the meal began fell over the group. Slowly, the young men made their excuses to their inattentive monarch, bowed, and withdrew. As the last of them left, Charles gestured wordlessly to his servant. Seeming to understand his master's sign language, the man approached, bent over, and pulled off the King's boots. He placed them carefully in the corner of the tent, and at another sign from the King, slipped out through the flap. The heavy cloth continued to flutter in the breeze after his departure.

The King and Gondi were alone at last. Charles slumped back on his folding camp chair and wiggled his toes in socks that were stiff with perspiration and faintly grey with dust. At his feet, Bellerophon sprawled, an elegant, pearl-white form, sleek, long, and dangerous. Other canine shapes, grey and white, could dimly be seen in the recesses of the tent. The smell of stale sweat blended unpleasantly with the lingering odor of burnt fat and gamey meat and a permanent aroma of dog.

Gondi got up from his reclining position near the brazier and sat on the edge of a camp bed, watching the King alertly. Charles' eyes stared darkly back at him out of an unhealthy pallor.

"I'm sure you didn't come all this way for the pleasure of my company," Charles mumbled at last.

Gondi smiled warmly. "I'm sure that you think I came all this way to scold you on your mother's behalf for running off to meet with the Admiral."

The young man bridled. "I am a King, for God's sake, not a child; I will not be scolded, and I will do as I wish." His sulky voice belied his stout words.

Overlooking the interruption, Gondi continued, "But, as a matter of fact, your mother and I are most impressed with your astuteness and your sense of timing. The meeting is an inspired idea, one which has, perhaps, greater potential than you know. That's really what I want to talk to you about."

Charles sighed wearily. Though the evening was cool, his forehead glittered with perspiration.

"If Your Majesty will forgive me," Gondi's voice rolled smoothly on, "you need Coligny. Let me explain what I mean. The Guises are misbehaving again. They are playing on your brother Anjou's religious convictions, which, though commendable, are sometimes excessive and impractical, shall we say. He continues to oppose marriage with the English Queen, which is most inconvenient. What is worse, he seems to see himself in messianic terms, leading the Catholic forces to victory over the forces of darkness.

"Now, those of the 'Religion' already see themselves as a chosen people languishing in bondage amidst worshippers of idols, and though, from a doctrinal standpoint, their views are unspeakable, they do have a certain poetic appeal. But all of this fanaticism is creating tensions which will lead to another civil war, just when we are trying desperately to nurture the peace. I have explained to Anjou, again and again, that we are one people with you at our head, not factions playing tug-of-war with you in the middle. But he will not listen. He could become difficult, if we do not soon find an occupation for him. He might even make trouble for you."

"Damn him," Charles hissed through clenched teeth.

"So," Gondi took a deep breath, "I strongly urge you to return from your hunts, for with the Guises behind him, there will be no controlling Anjou, unless Your Majesty controls him. I also suggest that a counterweight to the Guises would be of assistance, and that is where Coligny and his forces come in. The Guises think they can get away with murder; perhaps, they will be less rash if they are made to look reality in the face. But to this end, it is necessary to do more than skulk around with Coligny in the woods — indeed, that would do more harm than good, for it would inflame our co-Religionists without frightening them. No, Coligny must be received at Court openly and officially."

Charles' bloodshot eyes flashed with suppressed emotion. Jealousy of his brother, which always smoldered within him, burst under Gondi's deliberate fanning into a burning desire for immediate action, which completely consumed his initial dubious somnolence.

"Yes, yes. I will return at once. I will thrash Anjou. I will..."

"No, Sire, I beg of you. I have said nothing against Monsieur, your brother. His sentiments are not reprehensible, though they need to be watched and controlled. It is the Guises that you must concern yourself with. They are merely using Anjou for their own ends, and behind that ruse is the threat of force. You must meet their threat with another threat."

Charles' enthusiasm burned out as suddenly as it had flamed.

"Whatever you say," he murmured, gazing at his sleeping dog and nudging it with his foot.

He looked up at Gondi. "But how do you know that Coligny wants to come?"

"I have it on good authority from one who is close to the Admiral – Monsieur de La Renaudie."

"Ah, yes," the King smirked, "Anjou's former friend. But even if Coligny wants to come," the King resumed more soberly, "wouldn't it be madness? The Guises have only one thought – to murder Coligny as the old Duke de Guise was murdered. I don't want to have his blood on my head. I believe it's innocent blood, even if the Guises don't."

Gondi racked his brain for an answer. Carefully, he fell back on the pat phrases that, regardless of their logic, always appealed to the youthful monarch. "You are the King," he said. "If his safety and welfare are your special concern, all your subjects must respect that."

Charles gave a shuddering yawn. His bleary eyes looked suddenly young and defenseless.

Gondi continued, "May I suggest that your letter to the Admiral be brief and discreet. There is no point in revealing more of our hand than is necessary."

"You do it, Gondi. I'm so tired. I'll sign whatever you concoct."

Gondi looked at Charles with real concern. "Your Majesty, you shouldn't wear yourself out so." Touched in spite of himself, the King smiled sheepishly; then he straightened and declaimed pompously, "A man must be a man, after all."

"Quite so, Your Majesty, but even a great man must sometimes sleep."

Gondi summoned the King's gentleman, and the King was docile in their hands and went to bed as readily as a child who has been promised a bedtime story. Gondi sat on the camp chair, watching as the man, barely more than a boy, slept, his hands furled together, his emaciated face pillowed against them. What a strange destiny, he thought, would put such responsibilities in such hands at such a time? A terrible destiny, both for him and for France! He reigns and his mother rules. He is weak, and she is doubly weak, having no more power than he, and that at once removed. And I? I have his power twice removed, whereas had I been king, what couldn't I have done? I could have lifted France out of this trough of dissension and placed her at the pinnacle of the world. Even the miserable brat's father could have held things together, though, God knows, Henry was an obtuse man, but with my mind and will, to be king... ah, well!

Gondi rolled himself in his cloak at the foot of the bed and slept.

Chapter XI

ierre and Athalie paused as they entered the Cathedral of St. Gatien. Narrow and tall, the vaulted ceiling arched above them. High on their left, the north windows glowed carmine and blue, and the same hues, softly muted, washed the pillars to their right. Athalie saw how animation warmed Pierre's face, lifting the hint of hardness from his features, bridging his remoteness, and humanizing the statuesqueness of his extraordinary good looks.

"Look how the light slants through the upper windows," Pierre said. "When I was a child, I always thought of forests when I came here. The pillars were stone trees with branches meeting high above the nave. The nave was an avenue between the trees. The light here feels the same as in a forest: divided, yet somehow heightened. Of course, the colors are all wrong, but you see, the feeling is right — magnificent, but... but not oppressive, not threatening, somehow welcoming."

"I don't find forests all that welcoming," she commented ruefully; together, they laughed at their shared memory.

Suddenly hushed, they turned with one mind to contemplate the Cathedral. There was an otherworldliness to the lightness that soared above the semi-obscurity in which they stood: an image of Heaven and earth in human terms, Athalie thought, so obvious, so easily understood, and still so majestic.

"Come," Pierre said. "I'll show you something most people don't see. I'll take you up there." He waved to the heights above them.

"Oh!" she gasped, thrilled to think that she might ascend into the other world of her fantasy.

He touched her elbow to urge her forward. She noticed the touch and noticed that he seemed not to notice.

He paused abruptly and favored her with a dubious look that lingered over her tight bodice and full skirts.

"At least, I will if you're able. It's not an easy climb."

Athalie bridled. "People tell me I should be able to ride in a rig like this. I suppose it won't stop me from climbing."

A gush of resentment extinguished the glow of her happiness. How she longed for the freedom of her simple childhood garb! How she abominated the trussings of fashion: the chest suffocating inside its whalebone prison, the strangulated waist, the burdened hips lumbering beneath the farthingale yoke and its tent-like yards of material.

Even when traveling, the Queen Mother imposed standards of dress that would bolster the dignity of her position. So on this warm afternoon in Tours, where the Court had stopped on its slow passage northward to Fontainebleau, Athalie was clad in a richly decorated gown of heavy brocade, while Pierre wore an embroidered doublet, a slashed velvet broad coat, short padded breeches, long trunk hose, and a feathered cap.

Though less restrictive, his attire was as inappropriate to the weather as hers, but Athalie only envied his freedom of movement and never thought how he, too, had suffered from the heat, as they had languished over the lengthy noonday meal and, afterward had wandered, heavy with food, through the city's stifling, reeking streets. Here, at least, it was cool — that was one of the reasons they had come and her only thought was that his legs were free to leap and run, while hers struggled beneath billowing bolts of brocade.

She burst out angrily, "I hate to be harnessed and weighed down."

"You do?" Pierre cocked his head. "I never thought of it that way."

"I dare say. I'm sure you've never thought of it at all. You don't have to wear the stuff, after all. You just look at it."

He stared at her. She had a naive and unyielding manner, which was utterly at odds with the banal sophistication of her compeers. While it did not attract him, it never failed to catch his interest.

Their occasional encounters since he had rejoined the royal circle two weeks before had always intrigued and amused him. Because of this, and with no awareness of what he was doing, he had begun to seek out her company. The occasions which brought them together, like the present outing, seemed to them both to be the fruit of chance, but were in fact the result of his inclination and her willingness.

"Where do you get such thoughts?" he exclaimed, laughing. "I swear that since Eve first covered her nakedness, every woman has loved finery, whatever the discomfort or cost it entails. Beautiful women wear stylish fripperies to flaunt their looks, plain ones to disguise their ugliness, but either way, your sex is unanimous in loving them. You should remember that, before you tell me I'm thoughtless to think of the attractiveness of feminine dress, rather than its discomforts."

He maintained a bantering tone, but the words led his thoughts from Athalie, who was still ignorant of the time-honored ploys and wiles of womankind, to his wife, Anne, who had never had to learn them, so much did they inhere in the very essence of her character. Athalie's watchful eye saw his expression lose its eagerness and become abstracted and slightly supercilious. Afraid she had unwittingly given offense, she answered him hastily, "I didn't mean to say you were thoughtless. I know there's no reason you should think of such things. They are the way things are at Court."

"And everywhere. And always. How would you have them be?"

Not everywhere, she thought. She, after all, had a point of comparison — the supple, warm, functional robes of a religious were, to her mind, what clothing ought to be and were more beautiful in their severity than the peacock finery of Court dress. She turned to express this thought, and realized that it was an impossible thing to say, inappropriate to the occasion, and probably incomprehensible to her listener.

She became conscious that Pierre's eyes were focused on the translucent linen which rose in gentle folds from the brocade overdress and gathered in soft, open lace about her neck. Just then, she rejoiced not to be wearing monastic garb. She felt her blood rush under her pale skin.

She's a funny one, thought Pierre. She should be grateful for a fashion that lets her look elegant and delicate. Otherwise, everyone would see that her figure is flat and angular, not really pretty at all.

They had been walking as they talked and now came to where the transept crossed the nave and choir. At a sign from Pierre, Athalie gazed left and right at the two rose windows, the north, a circle of brilliant, but delicate hues, framed in a square of stone, the south, a riot of deeper pinks and blues. Seen for the first time, they struck Athalie as more luminous, more rich, and more exquisite than anything she could think of to compare them with — a starry night, an array of precious jewels, light reflecting from a cascade of water. Observing the awe, the exultation, and some emotion that almost resembled fear as they pursued each other across the girl's face, Pierre beamed down at her. Her air of discovery filled him with a spurious pride of creation.

"Come on," he said. Touching her softly on the shoulder, he strode toward the recesses of the north transept. There, hidden in the east wall, was a small but heavy door, which swung back onto the beginning of a narrow, spiral staircase.

"There'll be no light," said Pierre. "I'll go first. Give me your hand, here, and run the other around the inside of the stairway."

Pierre started up, half facing back to hold her hand. She pulled gently away. "No, you see, I must hold my silly skirts." She fussed embarrassedly, catching them up in a bulk over her left arm. Using her right hand as a guide in the dark, she started after him. "I'm all right this way," she said. "It's easier if I have both hands to maneuver with." Though hers was clearly the more practical solution, she felt unaccountably distressed at having refused his offer of help.

They made their way upward in the clammy darkness, Pierre, forgetful, with lithe speed, Athalie, laboriously, and somewhat dizzily. She stopped once and listened as his soft footsteps climbed alone for a while before coming to a halt; then she heard a thud and a muffled exclamation. She giggled, then started, as his knee bumped her from above.

"Damn," Pierre repeated more articulately. "I'm glad you think it's funny that I should practically knock my head off coming back to help you."

"Serves you right for rushing off," she replied, giggling again.

"That's gratitude!" The surly voice, disembodied in the void, sounded more humorous than menacing. Athalie choked back her laughter and took a deep breath.

They continued their climb, round and round, in disconcertingly tight loops. The unseen steps were steep, often slippery, and seemingly innumerable. At length, Athalie no longer heard his steps. As the silent blackness pressed upon her, she felt a sharp thrust of panic, before she circled again and saw light.

They emerged from the dark into a sphere of radiance so powerful as to be nearly overwhelming. The outer wall of the slender gallery on which they stood was a living curtain of stained glass; the inner was a lattice of delicate arches which looked down into the cool dimness of the Cathedral.

"This walkway runs beneath the clerestory windows all the way around the Cathedral," Pierre said. "There's another staircase in the other arm of the transept, and one which leads up from the cloister. One of the canons, Anselm was his name, who had my education for some years, used to bring me up here when I was a boy.

"It was easier climbing for me then, less risk to my head. Stairs like that weren't meant for someone my size." They smiled at each other.

"What a wonderful thing for him to have done," she said, leaning against the stone balustrade and looking around her with awe.

"You mustn't think it was something frivolous he did to skimp on his work. He brought me here for a reason."

He hesitated, recapturing the fugitive memory of those days.

"You see," he continued, "Anselm had some funny ideas about teaching. He liked to take something that interested him and turn it inside out and upside down for my benefit. These windows, for example. We came up here, day after day, and looked at them and talked about how the glass is melted, colored, blown, cut, leaded, cemented — everything.

"But most of all, we talked about why the windows were made. That may seem a silly question, but it isn't really: whether the stories they tell, for each window tells a story, were to teach the faithful, or were for no such functional purpose, but solely to give God praise. Seen from below, you know, you really can't tell much about the subjects of the windows.

"When I was older, he would make me do the same — take something I thought I knew thoroughly and analyze it and see if I really understood what it was and what it was good for. Usually I would find that I didn't understand it half as well as I had thought and had been accepting it myself simply because it was accepted by everyone.

"I remember how we argued about jousts — whether they are essential to hone men's skills for war or whether they accomplish nothing more than flattering knights' vanity and amusing thoughtless, idle folk. He said it was wanton folly to let good men take such risks in sport for the titillation of their ladies and pointed to our late King Henry's death with a lance through his eye. That always stopped me short.

"But still, I wasn't sure he was right. Men will fight no matter what, so my father always says. He believes it's nature's way to keep men keen and fit.

"Anselm and I could never agree about anything having to do with war or fighting. On other subjects, he was very open-minded and would sometimes say I was right and he was wrong. He was the only grown man I ever met who could admit error to a boy. It used to shock me when he did. Although I argued with him passionately, I never wanted him to be wrong. Somehow, the very idea was frightening."

"Do you think," Athalie asked, "you might have been afraid because it was easier to be told what to think than to think for yourself?"

"I don't believe I ever thought of it like that, but now that you mention it, I think Anselm certainly saw it that way." He paused, held by the charm of almost forgotten memories, which, he saw for the first time, were fragile and fleeting, easily lost or warped if neglected or manipulated. In a moment, he chuckled softly.

"I don't think my father ever realized what Anselm was about. He wasn't really interested in that side of my education. Letters were so much less to him than the martial arts and manly sports. I only came two afternoons a week. I would have come daily if permitted, not because the lessons were easy — they weren't, or at least I didn't find them so — but for the fun of grappling with his mind. I always felt he'd taught me a great deal, though I'd be hard put to say exactly what."

"To think, maybe?"

"Well, that there is a need to think, anyway. And he did give me some instruction in the conventional sense as well. After all, I know how to read and write the vernacular," he said, as she smiled at the pride in his voice, "even if my Latin is only rudimentary and my Greek nonexistent."

Pierre looked about with a proprietary gleam in his eye.

"I used to come up here alone after he showed me the way, often. It seemed magical." He glanced at her face to reassure himself that she would not belittle his treasure. "Do you see?" he queried, almost gruffly.

"Of course," she replied gravely.

They walked gingerly along the north transept. Above them, huge staring eyes, looming heads, and vast, distorted bodies stretched away as meaningless planes of color. Coming to the northeast wall, they turned back to see the windows with the benefit of a little distance. Full sunlight blinded them with yellows and reds. The glare, the height, and the narrowness of the walk struck sudden terror into Athalie's heart. She clutched frantically at a slender column. Pierre grabbed and steadied her.

"Don't look down," he said.

"No. It's the light. It's so very bright. It feels like it's burning my brain."

"Close your eyes and relax."

She leaned back against his chest, while he continued to hold her gently but firmly.

After a few moments, she breathed deeply. "It's better now. I'm fine."

She walked slowly forward, moving her hand carefully from column to column, annoyed with herself and embarrassed at her display of weakness.

"It's difficult to climb so high after such a big meal," she blurted out in explanation or excuse. "I still haven't gotten used to all the courses, fish and venison and pasties and sweets. I feel all bloated and constricted." She laid her hands gently on her abdomen. Pierre, who thought Athalie too thin to be pretty, and who could himself eat three times as much as she and still feel hungry, contemplated her with only vague sympathy.

They moved slowly on to the angle of the transept and the choir and stopped. The stone shell of the interior glowed with pale harmonies of filtered light. Above, the choir windows raged in fiery splendor.

"It's an image of Heaven and earth," Athalie said, speaking the thought she had had on seeing the windows from below. "I'm sure that's what they meant it to be, the builders. They had a vision, a holy vision, and they built it in stone and glass.

"I was used to something so different." She tried to describe the massive simplicity of the Abbey Church of Fontevrault, where the stones told of a solid and unswerving faith, severe and courageous, admirable, but primitive and earthbound compared to this house of light, which climbed to impossible heights and sang, in a harmony of color, of God's glory rather than His strength. "Do you think they had a different vision, the builders of Fontevrault?"

"I think it's more a question of what they knew about how to build," Pierre replied. He began to speak of ribbed, groined vaulting, pointed arches, and exterior buttressing. Athalie only half listened, convinced that the things he described were beyond her comprehension.

It amazed her that he should understand such matters, but at the same time, it saddened her that he had not tried to meet her on her own ground. "I'll show you what I mean when we go outside," Pierre concluded, adding as an unnecessary afterthought, "Anselm was fascinated by architecture." Quiet fell on them as their thoughts went their separate ways.

Below, black shapes had clustered in the choir. As the tower bell struck three, they broke into the office of None, their voices rising indistinctly to the listeners above, at first as a slow, breathy chant, then as a haunting, tremulous melody. Athalie's mind sped back to Fontevrault, to the singing of the offices, the life and purpose of the Abbey. She had listened to such singing so often and had pondered the psalms in her heart.

"I would never have seen this, if I had stayed at Fontevrault," she murmured at last.

Pierre glanced at her face, but it was half-averted and shadowed by the strong light from behind, and he could not make out its expression. He noticed how the sun picked out surprising red highlights in the coils of her black hair.

"Of course," he said. "And this is only the beginning. You're going to see all manner of places and things. Churches in the new style, much finer than this. And soon, we'll be in Fontainebleau. I know you've never seen anything like that. I'll wager the château has no parallel in all Europe.

"And then, there's the forest of Fontainebleau. You might care to go hunting again."

She stuck her tongue out at him; they laughed, stared into each other's eyes, and abruptly looked down into the rich gloom below. The office ran its slow course, camouflaging their silence, but at last, it came to an end, and the church was still.

Out of the uncomfortable quiet, Pierre spoke. "I was married there, in the center of the cross, almost exactly two months ago."

The simple statement startled and discomfited Athalie. Again, she turned her head away, humbled and at the same time embittered by the thought that this wonderful afternoon, which she would cherish, would be nothing to Pierre, because he would remember instead other occasions that were more significant to him either because of their innate importance, like the taking of his marriage vows, or because of their repetition, like the formative visits of his youth. There is nothing special in this moment to him, as there is to me, she thought.

"That was the last time that everyone was together," Pierre continued. "Then the King left for Normandy and Court dispersed, and we went to Plessis Gaillard. I'm glad the interlude is over. I never thought I would be, but I am."

Since she made no comment and asked no questions, he did not describe the shame and frustration he felt in admitting that life at Court, empty and even boring as it often seemed to him, was preferable to an existence which was supposed to be that of a normal householder, but was in fact merely a sham of it. The ties that provide the structure for such a life simply aren't there, he thought. My servants are my father's servants, and my wife is... Who or what or whose is she?

They lingered a few moments, but both sensed that something had gone out of the afternoon. At last, with quiet, aimless talk, they made their way down and out, back to the crowd that normally shared their lives.

* * *

The morning sun, tinted by the stained glass which admitted it, fell on Athalie as she huddled in one of the choir stalls the next day, but she was oblivious to its gentle comfort. She shrank between the stall's monstrous carvings, the fanciful beasts and demons, shiny with the patina of age, which arched and grimaced to ward off evil.

Though the seat was hard and awkward, she spared no thought for that. I am unclean, she muttered to herself, unclean, unclean. I have looked with lust on a married man. How can it be that I have such thoughts? I, who was brought up to innocence and purity? I knew nothing of such things, yet I was able to call them up from the vile depths of my own soul.

The man is not to blame. No, no, she thought with desperate shame, he did not transgress by word or deed, or indeed by thought, for all I know. Even now — even now, my thoughts turn to him.

She bowed her head, and a dry sob shook her from her depths.

The words of the day's Gospel echoed in her head:

"Et quodcumque ligaveris super terram, erit ligatum et in coelis."

"And whatsoever thou shalt bind on earth shall be bound in heaven."

142

She had stood among the rustling congregation, her mind a wordless turmoil, and the voice from the pulpit had penetrated the chaos, bringing a message which was for her alone, unlike the meaning which was conveyed to everyone else. She had in an instant understood her situation and its hopelessness. She wanted the man, but as long as the man and his wife shall live, they shall be bound with ties that cannot be loosed.

Of the finality of that dictum, she had no doubt. The desolation she felt now was the result not so much of dashed daydreams as of a profound self-loathing. Nothing outwardly had changed. She had lost nothing that was in any tangible way hers. But inwardly, everything was transformed. For a chimera, she had shattered her integrity. She had sullied herself.

For a while, Athalie sat in a kind of empty stupor. Slowly, calmer thought returned. Was not this self-flagellation simply so much more pride? Was it not another way of turning her back on her ideals, she asked herself with humility and sorrow. She would resolve to put the man from her mind and sin no more in her thoughts. Then, if God would still have her, she would go forward and not let shame hold her back.

The girl felt suddenly weak and tearful. "Our Father," she prayed slowly, "Who art in Heaven, hallowed be Thy name." She rubbed the back of her hand slowly across her eyes. "Thy Kingdom come. Thy will be done, on Earth as it is in Heaven. Give us this day our daily bread, and forgive us our trespasses, as we forgive those who trespass against us, and lead us not into temptation, not into temptation, no, lead us not into temptation, and deliver us from evil."

Chapter XII

A crisp salt tang off the Atlantic refreshed the air in the spacious dining hall of Admiral de Coligny's house in La Rochelle. Small oil lamps, newly lit against the gathering dusk, flickered in the slight draft from the uncovered windows. Two men sat alone amidst the detritus of an ample meal, the Admiral and his old adviser and friend, Antoine de Grève. It was clear from his expression and his restless movements that Coligny was deeply troubled.

The Dutch nobleman Louis of Nassau, William of Orange's younger brother, had been the guest of honor at the dinner, and it was his conversation that had most disturbed Coligny. Nassau had devoted all his talk to describing what he considered a most successful meeting he had had in secret with King Charles at Fontainebleau. Nassau had secured, in the course of the lengthy discussions, the King's promise to participate in The Enterprise, the planned invasion to liberate the Netherlands from Spain and from the brutal Spanish ruler of the Netherlands, the Duke of Alva. Bursting with self-satisfaction, boyish face lit with ardor for the cause, hair wild from excitement, small lean body vibrant with energy, Louis had re-created his exchanges with the King. Ever gullible, Charles had been easily persuaded that The Enterprise would succeed as a matter of course, that by his brutality the ruthless Alva had paved the way to his own downfall, that every town and village would rise at once against the hated Spanish. Louis and the young monarch had hypothesized a partitioning of the Netherlands: Flanders and Artois to France; Holland and Zeeland to England; and the remaining provinces to be placed under protection of the Empire, with Nassau's brother, William, as Elector. Louis's eyes had shone as he moved effortlessly from dream to accomplishment. "Why, Alva has only about 3,000 men," he had proclaimed. "France could field ten times that number, and His Majesty actually said he was willing, if England would join in."

"If England joins in," Coligny had muttered sourly.

Nassau's report had awoken all the latent enthusiasm of the younger members of Coligny's entourage, and had warranted, then and there, a rousing toast to the success of The Enterprise. Coligny had drained his goblet with the others, but his inner misgivings had remained unresolved.

"I don't like it at all," Coligny now said to de Grève. "They are so young, so foolish, and I fear they're going at it all wrong. Invading the Netherlands is a fine idea, in theory. With enough planning and money and support we could do it, and damn it, de Grève, we ought to do it. But these young hotheads could spoil everything by rushing ahead unprepared. Did you hear the 'ifs' in his own report? 'If the Queen of England,' 'If the French,' 'If the Spanish have only 3,000 men...'"

"Well, Admiral, all that is true, but you saw how eager the younger men are to follow him."

"Only too well," Coligny grumbled. "I know it's asking a great deal to make them remain idle, when glory seems just over the horizon. I only wish things were as simple as they seem to think. As it is, much as I like him, Louis has done us no service. It was hard enough before, and now it will be harder still, to keep the younger men here where they belong."

"He seems to have forgotten Charles' part of the agreement."

"Yes, that's interesting, but how far does it go? Charles insists on English help, correctly, I might say, but that isn't going to be easy to get. Elizabeth has her own games to play, and she is always long on promises, very long on negotiation, and damned short on delivery.

"It all puts me in a very difficult position," Coligny continued thoughtfully. "As I see it, the way things stand, I have no choice but to accept the King's invitation to Court. He needs my advice. If I'm there, prodding him and guiding him, perhaps he will enforce the edicts and give some protection to our people. That's what these young fools don't seem to realize: How can we send our strength out of France when we need every man-at-arms right here just to keep hold of what we supposedly gained in the peace last year? Nassau doesn't care about that; he thinks only of his own country crushed under Alva's boot, and I understand him, but we can't forget our own people. No, I think I'll have to go."

"But, my Lord," de Grève replied sharply. "It isn't safe. They will try to kill you."

Evening had deepened. Coligny's restless fingers toyed with the lamp in front of him, and its light wavered and played over his face, shadowing the deep lines between his strong eyebrows, lighting the prominent nose, the heavy jowls, and the stern mouth, which now drooped in dour lines of melancholy, exposing the grizzling beard and thinning hair. Despite the ravaging of age, care, and periodic poor health, Coligny radiated an aura of force. His large, well-built body was tough from years of ceaseless fighting; the eyes that glared fiercely from beneath the bold eyebrows expressed determination, if not optimism. He carried his years with ease, the burdens of his position with more difficulty.

"At first, when our little gambit with La Renaudie produced a King's move, I was elated," Coligny ruminated. "Perhaps, I thought, the time we have hoped for is come at last. The King is his own man and will put aside weak and wicked counsels, and do what is right by his people. If justice for all flowed from his hand, we could beat our swords into plowshares, truly. It could happen, but now, I confess, I am filled with doubt. Louis of Nassau has been there first. There will be so much to do, and so little time."

"If you will permit me," de Grève replied, "We don't know that it really was La Renaudie who brought it about."

"I'll ask the King when I see him. Will that satisfy you?" Coligny retorted testily.

De Grève suppressed a sense of hurt at Coligny's sarcasm and continued impatiently, "We have to consider the question carefully before letting you leave the safety of La Rochelle. This may be no more than another trick to bring you to Court to kill you. Look, it's not only your own safety we have to consider, but that of all of us. You are the real head of our Church. With Condé dead, and only the young princes to lead us if you disappeared, I don't think we could survive for long without you."

"Nonsense. No man is indispensable — for which I thank God daily. We are in the hands of the Lord. If I did not have faith that His will guides us, whether we know it or not, and that His strength is ever our support, I would long since have given over."

De Grève watched Coligny for a few moments before replying.

Coligny's gaunt face, with its craggy features and massive chin, hid anxiety behind an impassive façade. But though de Grève dared not express his fears too openly, they still tormented him, and all the admiration he felt for Coligny's sincerity could not dispel them.

"What you say is true," de Grève replied in considered tones, "but you should keep in mind that, for now, God has given us into your charge, and you should not be reckless with His trust. Anyway, even if we have only your own safety to consider, that's a great enough worry for my part."

"Thank you, old friend, but we cannot consider it. We must do what seems best, regardless, not recklessly, but... but..." Coligny groped for the right word.

"Courageously," de Grève concluded for him. "I know."

Silence fell between the two men. At last, Coligny shook his head. "I don't understand what you mean about a trick, anyway," he said.

"I mean La Renaudie may be working for our enemies."

"Oh, he may well be, though there's a sincerity to his manner that I find quite convincing."

"Yes," de Grève smiled grimly, "but you should remember that you always believe the best of people."

"Me?" Coligny expostulated. "After all these years?"

De Grève emitted a dry laugh. "Whatever it would take to turn you into a cynic hasn't happened yet."

Coligny shrugged indignantly and continued in an annoyed tone. "Look, the letter came from the King. It's not a forgery. Moreover, I don't see what's so surprising about it. His Majesty is growing up, after all."

"Were he as old as Methuselah, do you really think he would have developed enough character to push the old Queen aside?" de Grève queried.

"Of course I don't think so, but unless he's going to die, he'll have to take charge one day. Even she must see that. And even if you are right, she must have had a hand in the letter and must want me herself."

"True, but can you trust her?"

"Trust her? Trust her?" A deep rumble came from Coligny's chest, and he shook with sudden laughter. "Of course, I trust her. I trust her to be completely untrustworthy and completely unscrupulous. She goes after what she wants and plans and schemes until she gets it. But at least I know where I stand with her, and I can be on my guard.

"She's an old friend, after all." His eyes clouded with memories, some bright, some bitter. "I have dealt with her before and I know her tricks. She likes to play both ends against the middle. If I am present and have influence with the King, you can be sure that she will try to use me to weaken someone else, the damned Guises and all the Spanish-loving papists. Spain is not an easy bedfellow. I'm sure she's found that out. So long as I am needed and useful to her, I will not only be safe, but indispensable. That's the way it was the last time I was in favor, and things can't have changed that much."

De Grève stared thoughtfully at the Admiral. He had followed him a long time and knew him well. The love and admiration he felt for him did not disguise from him the weaknesses that were coupled with Coligny's strengths. Coligny's faith, the faith of a true believer, with all the zeal of a convert coupled with the embattled perseverance of the persecuted, was what Coligny himself would have considered his own greatest strength, but de Grève, despite their shared beliefs, feared that the idealistic focus of the Admiral's mind would blind him to the sordid exigencies of political compromise and the baseness of human nature. Coligny had tremendous self-confidence, bolstered by both position and ability. He was one of France's highest magnates; his military successes were legendary; and he had endured and surmounted great hardships, but such self-confidence, however justified, could lead to overconfidence.

De Grève knew that Coligny had often succeeded by sheer force of will and that he would be absolutely certain that he could win over the King. De Grève was not so certain and wondered in any event if the winning would be worth the battle.

"But you are safe here. We can negotiate from here," de Grève tried. "We have been marking time, here, since the last war. I don't see what more I can do, here, and if we give those of our rash, young co-Religionists who have the King's ear — and I include my nephew Teligny in that group — if we give them free rein, there's no telling what they may get us all into. For better or worse, I'm going to have to risk it."

The Admiral looked dreamily off into space. "You know, de Grève, this Netherlands enterprise would be something worth doing, succoring our brothers in Religion while striking a real blow at Spain, and you see, they can't mount an effective campaign without me. With me and enough men, well, we could put France in the front rank again. God, it would be glorious to have our country united again fighting those Spanish dogs."

He turned his fierce, hard eyes on his friend.

"Damn it, de Grève, I'm a Frenchman. I hate hiding here, while the Spanish and the Guises have everything their own way at Court. If the King will protect our people, I'll win him some new provinces in the Netherlands. But I've got to go to Court. It's the only way."

De Grève had looked away from Coligny's burning gaze, but he turned back to him quickly as he paused. "Let's speak of the Guises, then. What of them? You know you will be a target of every attempt they can manage."

Coligny slammed his hand on the table. "Are you saying that I should hide here from them? My family is just as old and just as noble as theirs. Perhaps you forget what honor means to a nobleman. I am clean of old Guise's death, you know that. They have no just quarrel with me, and they know it."

"I don't know if they know it or not," de Grève replied in equally heated tones, "but I do know that they do not love you. And mind you, I'm not talking about some knightly challenge from the Duke. I'm talking about assassins, poison, knives in the dark. God, but you noblemen amaze me sometimes with your sensitivity to honor and your blindness to dishonor and perfidy!"

Coligny smiled a wintry smile at de Grève. "Come, come, old friend, we've been through too many battles together for that kind of talk. You are right, of course. They are dangerous, and when I go, I will take every possible precaution. I'm willing enough to die in a good cause, but certainly agree that to be poisoned or shot by some tool of the Guises is beneath the dignity of my family."

De Grève sighed. Coligny was showing all the signs of having made up his mind: unswerving resolution tempered by a few palliative concessions to bring the opposition into line. If so, there would be no stopping him. However, long experience had taught de Grève that what cannot be stopped can at least be delayed or deflected. He tried a new tack.

"It seems to me that we ought not seem too eager. I don't trust the Guises and I don't trust the Queen Mother. I trust the King only a little more. Let us respond cautiously. Let us see what kind of assurances they will give."

"You are right again, of course," said Coligny. "Assurances have never been much protection against a bullet in the dark, but if they will grant some conditions, we will at least know better what kind of welcome we are going to get. You know, though, that I am going in any case. I've been in too many battles not to have figured out that it's God's will, which some call luck, that plays the decisive part in our affairs, however much we plan and scheme. I believe He sends me to the King to strengthen his youth with my experience, to urge him on to the path of greatness that leads to helping our brothers in the Netherlands. If I am right, and this is His will, I will have all the protection I need.

"But I don't object to your trying to arrange some earthly protection as well. Since La Renaudie claims to have brought about this invitation, why not tell him that we must have the King's assurance, and his mother's, of our safety, and permission for me to bring a couple of troops of horse and men-at-arms in my entourage."

"She'll never agree," de Grève muttered gloomily.

"She will understand my nervousness at leaving this fortified place, de Grève. I tell you, she is far too shrewd to ask me simply to put my head on the block. She has a scheme, probably several, but it won't be anything so crude as simple

148

murder. If she wants me strong, which is my guess, she won't be displeased if I am stronger by a few men-at-arms. They can at least keep the assassins off my back, so I'll be able to get some sleep at night. Have La Renaudie write to his good friend, the King, and we shall see what we shall see."

Fontainebleau

Chapter XIII

wo young men loitered in the welcome shade between the sunny enclaves of the playing grounds of Fontainebleau. Before them spread a golden rectangle of parched grass, enclosed by a dark wall of box-trimmed trees, under whose thick foliage they had taken shelter. Lazily, they watched the brightly clothed figures in front of them, some fencing, some playing ball or tag, some, like themselves, gawking at the sport. From a smaller area behind them came the clacking and thudding of men jousting against a quintain. The sounds punctuated, but did not disrupt, their conversation.

The older and more imposing of the two, Augustin Pascal, was a young man of medium height, very muscular and trim, in whom the blond hair of his family was set off by a well-manicured, reddish beard.

This ornament, whose copper and gold strands made dramatic highlights against the darker hairs, was the young man's pride. To enhance its effect, he generally wore white and contrived to keep his person and clothes immaculate, at considerable inconvenience to himself and cost to his father. On this day, he sparkled in white satin.

Pascal affected a nonchalant pose, resting one hand lightly on his sword hilt and caressing the beard with the other. A scrawny, pale grey puppy slouched against his legs, whimpering and pulling at its leash.

Pascal's companion, Trophime Daudet, a stocky youth with curly, auburn hair and an expressive, good-humored face, leaned against a tree and alternated his gaze between the games and Pascal's face. He wore black, because he was a Protestant and some unspoken rule of that creed required it. Normally, he was proud of this badge of difference, but today he could not stop himself from envying Pascal the relative coolness of his clothing.

The two spent a fair amount of time in each other's company, enough so that, unknown to them, their contrasting garb had provoked considerable ironic comment.

Among the jealousies of Court life, their closeness passed for friendship, even though the relationship owed its survival more to circumstance than affinity. The fact that they appealed to very different types of women and that neither had attracted the attention of anyone important had done much to prevent rivalry from making their companionship inconvenient.

"That's a nice puppy," said Trophime, nudging the beast with his toe.

"I should say so," Augustin responded gloomily. "He cost me two weeks allowance and an extra begging letter to my father."

"He's white like the King's hounds."

"You're so observant! I was assured that he is the progeny of, shall we say, a cadet line to the royal pups. That's why he cost a king's ransom."

"Was that wise?"

"He has his disadvantages, to be sure. He wails if he's not allowed to sleep on my bed, and as he's swarming with fleas, it's absolutely infernal."

The power of suggestion, or his own fleas, made Trophime feel an acute itch near his groin. He turned toward the field and rubbed himself discreetly. Turning back, he continued, "No, I meant getting a dog like the King's, was that wise?"

"I figure he'll be flattered, if he ever notices."

Trophime continued to doubt the wisdom of his friend's move, but knew better than to belabor the point.

The puppy emitted a loud whine, and began to scratch its neck vigorously. "K-, k... quiet," muttered Pascal, jerking the collar viciously.

Trophime glanced tactfully away to let his friend think he had not noticed the stutter. Funny how it changes, he thought to himself. Sometimes poor old Pascal sounds as if he has mail in his mouth, while sometimes, like today, he is almost normal. Trophime had not paid enough attention to Pascal's affliction to recognize that its severity varied in inverse proportion to the ease of his surroundings. His difficulty was always greatest when it was most likely to embarrass him. Pascal felt acutely the shame of his defect, which seemed to him to brand him as an inferior. It was to disguise his secret fear that this mark of Cain reflected some true root of evil in his character that he postured so outrageously and pressed so hard for recognition.

There were times, too, when his inability either to control or to accept his handicap frustrated him to such an extent that his anger burst out in spates of scoffing and cruelty. Because words had often betrayed him, he expressed himself physically, even violently, more than was necessary.

"You seem very out of sorts," Trophime resumed at last.

"My dear, I'm desperate."

"Why?"

"There are so many people at Court, it's simply impossible to get anywhere. The only member of the royal family who even knows who I am is baby brother Hercules! C-can you imagine a minus like that being called Hercules?"

"Oh, he's not all that bad. Anyway, cheer up! I don't think you've done so badly, all things considered."

Pascal tautened, and a dangerous look came into his eyes.

"I meant no offense, my dear friend," the other continued hastily. "I mean that your father bought you a nice property with a respectable title, and he certainly keeps you up very lavishly. You will receive notice in due course."

"If only there'd be a war."

"Heaven forbid," cried Trophime. "Why, we would be pitted against each other."

"It's sure to come to that eventually, and I'd just as soon it did before I die of boredom."

Trophime flushed angrily.

"My father says it's talk like that that makes wars. Our people reproach him for sending me to Court, but he says the King is king to Protestants and Catholics alike, and we must show solidarity to have solidarity."

"Well, that's as it may be," Pascal said, "but you must see my problem. I had hoped before now to do something grand for someone important and become his protégé, but n-nothing's turned up. You either have to do something very good or very bad for anyone to p-pay any attention. I haven't been able to do something splendid, so I'm thinking seriously of doing something very wicked. Notoriety is clearly superior to oblivion."

Daudet looked skeptical and mildly disapproving. Pascal removed his sword from its scabbard, balanced it on its tip, and bending the blade, made it spring back.

"You'll damage it doing that," said his friend.

"Not me," Pascal replied. "Anyway, this is my ornamental sword."

"Looks real enough to me."

"The real one's at home, and what a weapon that is!"

"All right, so what are you planning on doing?"

"I thought I would pick a fight with de Galle."

"My God, you are crazy! If you kill one of the King's most valued councilors, you'll get a lot more notoriety than you bargained for."

"Not Raymond de Galle, you idiot, the stripling de Galle, the blond giant."

Trophime smiled in spite of himself.

"You know perfectly well dueling is prohibited."

"Like everything else, my dear Trophime, it's a matter of style. If it's done with enough panache, everyone secretly admires and openly looks the other way. You know that. I wouldn't kill him unless I had to, and even if I did, no harm would come of it. People recognize that such things happen among gentlemen."

"What makes you think he'd be such easy meat. He's very big."

"Size isn't half of it. Form and brains are what you need to win. He's just an overgrown p-p-pup."

"On what basis could you possibly pick a fight? You don't even know him."

"I thought the conversation might go something like this." Pascal replaced his sword and swaggered past Daudet. "I would greet him so." Pascal executed an exaggerated bow. "My lord," I would say, "I trust you have enjoyed another night in p-paradise." Then since he won't answer, I will continue, "Ah, no? Well, give it time, my lord, give it time. What tricks she learns from others, she will in time teach you. Then your luck may improve."

"Honestly, Augustin!" Trophime burst out. "How can you think of saying such a thing? Why, everyone will think you are a cad."

"Nonsense. If you think that, you are a choir boy in spite of your Protestant upbringing — or maybe because of it!"

Daudet surged forward, and Pascal stepped deftly out of the way. "No, my dear, everyone will roar with laughter, and I can be sure he will have to fight. He is a bit pompous, after all, and will not bear being mocked."

"The Queen Mother will not be amused."

Pascal pursed his thin lips and shrugged. "What do you know of the Queen Mother? Anyway, it is her sons that I aim to impress."

"I think you're likely to end up worse off by far than you are now."

"At least," Pascal burst out laughing, "at least I'll get the attention of that wife of his. She's a fetching baggage, and no mistake, I'd fight six Pierre de Galles for a chance to lay his wife."

"You're disgusting, Pascal. How can you even think to catch a wife's fancy by dueling with her husband? Besides, rumor has it she has her eye on the King, much good may it do her."

"Mm, but from what I hear, she knows to keep in form while she's waiting."

Trophime bit his lip, more vexed than amused.

"Come on, Augustin," he said at last, "say you've been having a good joke on me."

"You don't think I'll do it? I offer you a wager — if I challenge him and he accepts, you will be my second."

"And if you don't? That's more to the point."

"I'll buy a hogshead of wine for us to finish off together."

"Done!" said the other, and they shook on the bargain.

* * *

153

Pierre strolled along the shaded alley thinking of one thing and another, and of nothing in particular. It was a sultry afternoon, and though the overarching elms brought some relief from the sun, the air was close even in the shade. A ribbon of blue ran between the sunlit crests, rich cobalt directly above, fading to muted azure on the horizon. For no reason he could think of, Pierre wondered where Athalie was and why he had seen so little of her since leaving Tours six weeks before.

A young man in dazzling white approached him, followed at a slight distance by a sulky-looking youth. With unthinking courtesy, Pierre moved aside to pass. The white figure bowed deeply.

"My L-Lord," the man said in a slurred mumble. Pierre bowed briefly, and moved forward.

"My Lord!" The voice was clearer now, and held a challenging note.

Pierre stopped and looked the man keenly in the face. "I don't know Monsieur?" he said.

In this simple statement, which Pierre had offered only for confirmation or correction, Pascal was sure he could detect the arrogance of rank. His face flamed above his ruddy beard.

"N-n-no, in-d-deed," he sputtered, "but I n-know M-Monsieur," he sketched a bow, "and M-Monsieur's w-wife." He doubled over in mock reverence. "Everyone knows Monsieur's wife." Pascal smirked, gratified to have spoken the insult without stuttering.

A deep frown creased Pierre's forehead. "Do you intend to give offense?" he asked in a slow, cold voice.

The habit of inquisitiveness had immediately attracted those who were nearby to Pierre and Augustin, and the sight of this small gathering had drawn other eager listeners.

Now that he could play to an audience, Pascal felt less foolish than he had when in tête-à-tête with his reserved and dignified adversary.

"I?" he replied loudly, rolling his eyes at the nearest courtiers, who responded with an appreciative laugh. "M-Monsieur should not take offense at m-me. Unless he wishes to t-take offense at everyone, he should reserve his anger for his better half." A murmur, then a roar of merriment, went up from the group.

Pierre stood motionless as he appraised his adversary and tried to understand his intention. His stillness communicated itself to the others, on whom an expectant hush fell. At last, he spoke, so quietly that the listeners pushed in around the pair the better to hear them.

"Can you fight?"

Enraged, Pascal grasped his sword hilt and pulled the blade a few inches from its scabbard. Struggling for self-control and willing his stutter away, he replied as evenly as he could, "I will show you, g-gladly."

Pierre bowed. "At your convenience," he said. He tapped Pascal lightly on the cheek with the back of his fingers, and turning, elbowed through the crowd.

Pascal looked around him and finding Trophime Daudet, grabbed his arm. "Remember your promise," he muttered. "Go to him immediately. Sword and dagger, of course. They are my forte. Tomorrow, east of the south gate, at dawn." Intentionally raising his voice so as to be audible to all, he repeated, "T-tomorrow at d-dawn, you understand, east of the south g-gate."

* * *

Word spread like a summer fire. Every corridor of the palace, every alley of the park hummed with the news. Those who slept in town made arrangements to be woken early.

Those who slept in the palace made further arrangements to bribe the guards at the postern gate to let them through before dawn. No one wanted to miss the fun.

"Athalie, Athalie," Margot said breathlessly. "Finally, something amusing is going to happen. Of course, it's really shocking, and we should all be angry, and Mother says going to watch merely encourages them, but it is such fun."

"What, for Heaven's sake, what is such fun?"

"There's going to be a duel. Hadn't you heard? It should be pretty good. One of them is a known fighter anyway, and my God, size must count for something."

"Oh, Heavens, Margot. What are you talking about? Who is having a duel and why?"

"Well, it's a duel between de Galle and some fellow, I don't know his name exactly, but he's supposed to be terrible with the sword and dagger, a really famous fighter, though if that's so, I can't think why no one here has heard of him. But you know how these things are. Everyone exaggerates so. As for why, well, you know why."

Athalie had no idea, but in her sudden panic, she did not care to pursue the subject.

"You mean... Pierre de Galle, don't you?"

"Obviously, ninny. Not that Raymond is past it exactly, but I mean, no one would expect him."

"You say Pierre, Pierre de Galle is a fine fighter?"

"No, the other one is supposed to be, but Pierre's had plenty of training and look at the size of him. So it should be a good fight."

"When is it to be?"

"At dawn tomorrow, outside the south gate."

"Dawn!" Athalie gasped, thinking with horror of the hours of anticipation to be lived between now and then, and with even greater horror of the hours that would probably pass after the dawn meeting before she would hear of its outcome. Misery, sharp and dull, pierced and enveloped her.

Oblivious to her friend's distress, Margot asked, "Shall I come for you, or you for me?"

"Come?" asked Athalie, bewildered.

155

"I had better come for you," Margot said. "Wear a cloak with a hood. Everyone goes, but everyone pretends not to go. We'll sneak out of the palace and one of my friends will let us through the south gate."

"Oh, Margot, thank you. You're so kind. You're wonderful." Athalie's eyes filled with tears from the confusion of emotions which surged through her.

"Well, really, dear, I know I am. But so are you, so don't mention it." Taking Athalie's thin face in her two hands, she gave the startled girl a robust kiss and swished away.

* * *

In a simple but opulent room in his mansion in the row of great houses which faced the main gate of the royal palace, Raymond de Galle stalked up and down. The incandescence which often presages a summer storm glowed weirdly through the wide windows. A gentle knock barely penetrated the heavy oak door, but the Duke turned abruptly and bellowed, "Come in!" The door opened, and Pierre walked quietly in.

With no greeting, the two men faced each other, standing close together. Pierre stared into his father's eyes, which were only a finger's width higher than his own. At last, he shifted his gaze and walked toward the window. A transient look of triumph passed over de Galle's face as he turned after his son.

"I hear you've taken to filling your idleness by picking fights with riffraff," he stated to Pierre's averted face. "Well, you're going to become a cropper, I'm afraid. I've had inquiries made about this so-called 'gentleman,' and it appears that he makes up in skill what he lacks in breeding."

Pierre shrugged indifferently. De Galle took his shoulder and roughly pulled him around.

"Well, I say you made a mistake in seeking this quarrel. You are my only son and heir."

"I did not seek any quarrel with that man," Pierre replied in a low voice. "He forced it on me."

"He forced it on you? Since when can vermin bend lords to their will? Tell me how he did it. Recount the nature of the quarrel."

Pierre shook his head.

"You shall!" de Galle roared, and rattled him violently. The two glared at each other, the apoplectic ruddiness of the father reflected by the son's angry flush.

In a voice so soft as to be almost a whisper, Pierre said, "He made an insulting allusion to my wife."

"Allusion! You mean to say he referred to your wife as a bitch in heat whom all the dogs will mount. Tell me, son, do you need me to control your wife? It must be done. I will not have my property pass to the son of a stranger. If you cannot handle this, I assure you I can."

"I can beat women, too, if I wish to, Father."

"And what do you mean by that?"

Pierre made no answer. In the momentary quiet, the two men turned away from each other.

At last, de Galle resumed, "The proper way to deal with such a person is to horsewhip him. My lackeys are waiting to do it when I give the word. When they have done, the man will not be able to walk, much less to fight."

"Please, Father, I will not be shamed."

"And is it not shame to fight with such a man in such a cause? Answer me."

"There was no other way."

"Pierre, that is never an excuse."

The older man sat down on a hard, straight-backed chair. "This morning, I was in Council with the King. Do you know what we spoke of? War. The King wants war with the Spaniard. That's what his position boils down to, however he may season and dress it. I hate the Spaniard, and I have cause. I battled Spanish might in Italy before the King could lift his leg. But I know what war is like. For the King, it is a game.

"And after Council, I come back, and what do I find? My son, too, wants to fight! And what a fight! You, who are destined for greatness, you still play games with street urchins. I hope you don't delude yourself. The fact that such games are dangerous when played by boys in men's bodies doesn't make them honorable."

Pierre sat abruptly on the window seat and stared at the floor. "If you must go through the motions," de Galle resumed, "I will be your second. When he sees me, he will not dare proceed and will make amends."

"Never," Pierre spat out. "You would make me a laughingstock."

"That, it seems, you are already."

Anger surged through Pierre like a lightning bolt. For an instant, he thought to challenge his father, and his hand lifted to reflect the thought. Then it dropped again. By intuition, de Galle knew his son's thought. A rare flash of sympathy took both their minds back to a time, some years before, when in a burst of high spirits, Pierre had challenged his father to tourney and the man and boy had fought, only half in jest, until the boy had dropped defeated. For an instant, then, a gust of exuberant self-confidence had uplifted de Galle; he had laughed at the fallen boy, who was the living proof that manhood at its prime was more than a match for all the advantages of youth. Now, the mirror image of that emotion possessed him. He had never seen such a look on his son's face, and it made him feel suddenly old. It whispered to him that his own flood tide was past, and Pierre could trounce him if he wished.

The silence was broken by a sharp rap on the door, followed by the entrance of Albert de Gondi. Grateful for the interruption, Raymond de Galle rose and gripped him by the arm.

"Ah, my dear fellow," he said, "I'm glad you've come. Much is happening, and not much of it is to my liking."

"Perhaps I interrupt?" Gondi glanced at Pierre, noting with surprise the abruptness of his bow.

"Certainly not," de Galle replied. "I'm troubled by affairs of family, as well as affairs of state, but they need be no secret from you. Indeed, I'm sure you know all about them." He smiled a little maliciously.

"I have heard the gossip."

"Help me make the boy see reason. I've told him a de Galle ought not fight a peddler's son. He should be thrashed instead."

In an even voice, which hid his anger at de Galle's contempt, Gondi said, "He's rather more than a peddler's son. He is the son of a banker, indeed a major creditor of many in high places. It would make no end of trouble if needless offense were given to his family."

"His family! Go on, man! It's as I said. This Pascal is no gentleman; he's a tradesman's son, worse — if what you say is true — a banker's son, a thieving, usurious Jew!"

Gondi's knuckles whitened. Pierre glanced anxiously from Gondi to his father and back. Sensing that the silence of his listeners had become as ominous as the charged pre-storm atmosphere, de Galle hesitated, then added hastily, "Of course, there are bankers and bankers. Look, where you come from, it's possible for a gentleman to be a banker. I can see that, but here, the rules are different. You know that as well as I. Not that we don't all need them at times. You especially — I mean, having to scrounge up money for Their Majesties from the Pascals and the whatnots of the world."

"Yes, from the Gondis in Lyon..." Gondi could not stop himself from mentioning his own family's banking connections, though he knew the irony would be lost on de Galle, who would merely think he had committed a faux pas in bringing up so indelicate a subject.

De Galle ignored the interruption. "No doubt Pascal père is useful, and possibly he is also eminently worthy, but for my son to fight his son simply cannot be allowed. Listen, de Retz, if you know young Pascal, why don't you talk him out of it. I'd be no end obliged."

"I don't know him. I know his father — the tradesman, as you call him. But I have been keeping an eye on the son, and today I did approach him to try to reason with him about this unfortunate situation."

"Well?"

"He was unmovable."

"God's life! I'll have him thrashed. But listen, de Retz, dueling is illegal. You are an officer of the King. You can put an end to it."

"I could, but I wouldn't advise it. How will young Pierre hold up his head, unless he receives satisfaction for this insult Pascal gave him? He's reputed to be a first-rate fighter; if you or I do anything, people will say that the most noble blood in the country has turned cowardly."

"Cowardly!" De Galle roared. "My son a coward?"

"I'm afraid that's what will be whispered, if the fight doesn't come off," Gondi replied smoothly.

De Galle opened and shut his mouth and turned helplessly between Gondi and his son. Lightning whitened the window, pulsing and disappearing into an eerie afterglow. Pierre rose.

"With your leave, Father, I'll go to bed. I must be up early."

"Good luck, Pierre," Gondi said heartily, taking his hand and shaking it vigorously. Hesitantly, de Galle put out his hand; his son did not notice the timid gesture as he strode from the room.

The sound of the door shutting was lost in a distant rumble of thunder. The sky suddenly opened to a noisy deluge of rain. Hastily, de Galle shoved the shutters closed against the drops ricocheting off the stone sill. He fumbled clumsily for the flint, and with much scraping and swearing, lit the wick of the oil lamp on the table. "Drat these summer squalls," he said. "They always catch you unprepared."

Only if you're a fool, Gondi thought. His eyes still smoldered with suppressed emotion. I would be sorry to see Pierre killed, he reflected bitterly, but it would cut this arrogant magnifico down to size if he knew that after his death his lands would go to some cousin, or revert to the Crown.

De Galle faced Gondi, his features nearly invisible above the feeble light. "Now to business. You were at the Council today. Maybe you can tell me what's going on."

"You were there, too."

"I mean what's really going on — behind the scenes. I smell grape, and it worries me. Mind you, I myself would normally have no real objection to Coligny coming to Court. I've no sympathy for those of the Religion, but they're a fact of life, and the Admiral himself is a good man, if misguided. No, I'd be all for his coming to Court if it would clear the air. But the King has got the whole thing mixed up with interfering in the Netherlands. I'm no coward, de Retz, but I'm no fool either. I'd like to know where you stand on all this. You aren't planning on letting that young puppy try to cut his teeth on King Philip's shinbone, are you?"

"That young puppy is King."

"Yes, Albert, I know, but you've held on to his leash pretty well so far." De Galle sat down behind the table. "So if you're letting him have his head — to muddle images a bit — it must be for a reason. I'd like to know what the reason is."

"It's not to further a war with Spain, that I can assure you."

"So I would have thought. Then why bring Coligny to Court? It will only inflame things. It will excite that excitable idiot, who has his Kingly heart set on proving himself in the Netherlands. It will enrage the Guises and let young Anjou use them to make trouble for everyone. Why, man, it'll be a mess."

"Her Majesty wants the Bourbon marriage of her daughter Marguerite with the Protestant Navarre," Gondi explained in a patient tone. "We need Coligny for the marriage. After the marriage, we won't need him any more. He'll go back to being the nuisance he always is."

159

"Bloody dangerous game, if you ask me! The Queen Mother and her marriages, the King and his war! What happens to statecraft in all this confusion?"

Gondi said nothing.

"Listen, de Retz, I'm a plain soldier. I don't have a devious Italian mind. But I do have a say in the government, and I mean to use it when I see fit. To speak my mind plainly, I don't suppose I object to any of your schemes, but I would hate to see the Admiral walk into some kind of trap. I don't believe in that kind of politics."

"Monsieur!" Gondi surged to his feet. De Galle's steady gaze did not waver.

"I don't mean you, necessarily, de Retz. In fact, I'm not sure you're brutal enough for plain murder. But it's no secret that Court is full of people who would like to see him dead. I'm letting it be known that I wouldn't turn a blind eye to an assassination, and I think you should do the same. Otherwise, you see, I would oppose bringing Coligny back to Court."

"I think you've said more than enough to make your point," Gondi answered stiffly.

"Fine, my dear Albert." De Galle stood also, and held out his hand with a genial smile. "I always say, there's no need to belabor the point with a gentleman, eh?"

* * *

The bell tower chimed four strokes. Athalie turned in her bed for the thousandth time, then, with a desperate little sigh, sat up.

Gently pulling back the curtains, she slipped from under the covers and glided toward the window. Dry rushes and herbs murmured beneath her feet; an occasional hint of lavender rose from the crushed matting, evoking the heavy perfume of Provence's sun-scorched hills. Athalie pushed the heavy casement; the thick, distorting panes swung back to reveal a faerie landscape of starlit water and darkly silhouetted trees.

Athalie's chamber looked south over the carp pool, the large body of water which was the centerpiece of Fontainebleau's magnificent gardens and park. The evening storm had swept the skies clean. The velvet darkness of the lake was slashed with ripples, which shimmered beneath an astonishing array of stars. After the absolute blackness of her curtained bed, the panorama beyond her window dazzled Athalie's weary eyes.

Athalie had no precise idea of the hour of dawn, and she doubted that Margot was any better informed. Fool, she thought. You could talk of nothing but the duel from the moment Margot told you of it to the time you went to bed, if not to sleep, and you never thought to ask the crucial question, When is dawn? Pierre's adversary's qualifications — his brilliant swordsmanship, his intensive training, his past successes — she had heard it all, recounted with ghoulish pleasure by those who knew, and repeated in ever more gory detail by those who wished to appear to know. The Court had talked of virtually nothing else that day; the conversation had rarely flagged; whenever it did, she had led it deftly back to her sole interest and concern, Pierre's likely fate at the hands of the villainous Pascal.

Athalie had no doubt that Pascal was villainous. Though all at Court were agreed that Pascal had acted in deplorably bad taste, the cause of the duel was discussed with a certain subdued merriment, which to her was totally baffling. Pascal had grossly insulted the Lady Anne. Pierre would, of course, defend his wife's honor. Pascal's provocation was incomprehensible, but Pierre's response was inevitable.

The man – Pascal – is an animal, she thought, to force a fabricated duel on an inexperienced opponent. If he kills Pierre, it will be murder. If he kills Pierre... tears welled up and trickled from the corners of her eyes down her cheeks. Her tongue ran around her dry lips, tasting the salt from earlier bouts of weeping. She felt like a well gone dry from too much use.

Disgust filled her as she went over the previous day's conversations one more time – how everyone had pretended concern and sympathy for Pierre, while actually relishing the excitement, the little break in the monotony of their existence, which, to them, was well worth the risk of his life. And later they will all be there, like Romans at the circus. How dreadful, she thought, that to all outward appearance, she was one of the thoughtless mob. She had smiled and gabbled with the rest, pushing and probing at her hidden wound.

A slow breeze shushed through the park. From the dressing room next door came a muffled, rhythmic noise, the stertorous breathing of the old nurse, a comforting, familiar echo of childhood. A clear, sweet noise sounded far away, and gradually, but purposefully, the fading darkness was filled with chirping and whistling.

Thought drained away from Athalie's turbulent mind. She was alone, but at peace again, standing in the orchard at Fontevrault; then, as suddenly as it had come, the past fled, though the calm of its momentary visit remained. In this unexpected stillness of being, she faced the implacable truth that the sweet innocence of those days was compromised beyond recall. Rightly or wrongly, jubilantly or furtively, she loved Pierre de Galle, and to pretend otherwise was benighted foolishness. Wherever she went from here, she would never be the same as the child beneath the apple tree.

The bell tower chimed five. Athalie's fears swept back with a vengeance. When would Margot come? If only I knew how to get out of the palace and the grounds in the dead of night, I would leave now, but I cannot. I must rely on Margot. She grimaced. But this is no longer the dead of night! For all I know, dawn may be breaking, though I cannot see it from this window. I am trapped if Margot has forgotten. She cannot have forgotten, she cannot, Athalie incanted to herself with passionate determination.

She turned sharply from the window and with controlled haste began to pull on the clothes she had carefully laid out the night before. Thank God, at least, she thought, that she was staying in the palace, rather than in her uncle Gondi's

161

residence north of the palace walls. She pulled up a stocking and gartered it. How would she have escaped from his house without calling attention to herself? She fastened the other stocking. She would have gone to her uncle and told him she wished to see the duel. Her linen underdress rustled over her head; she shook it out impatiently and pulled its ties tight about her waist. And what would he have thought? She wriggled through the heavy folds of her overdress, a garment she had selected because it required no farthingale or stays, and fumbled with its fastenings. She pictured his piercing eyes staring through her.

Raising her head in an unconscious gesture of pride, she thought, I would have told him the truth, if need be. And what was the truth as you understood it yesterday, you thoughtless, little fool, and how does this "truth," that you are now so proud of, how does it reflect on you? Think, my girl, you are filled with terror and horrified curiosity, because the man you love will engage in mortal combat to protect the honor of his wife. Think on it! Humbled, she felt shame and hopelessness thrust like a knife through her innards. She ran her hand abstractedly over her hair, still braided from the day before.

A muffled knock resonated through the room. Athalie grabbed her cloak and shoes and ran silently to the door. She opened it and stumbled through into the dark corridor, brushing briefly against the cloaked and hooded figure of her friend.

"Oh, Margot!" she exclaimed in an intense whisper, "you finally came."

"Shh," said Margot.

"Why must we be so quiet? From the talk yesterday, it sounded as if everyone was going."

"Not from my mother's apartments, I assure you. You know how she feels about individual combat. It's hardly surprising when you consider that she saw my father killed in that horrible, senseless way, in a joust."

"Yes, of course," said Athalie, "but let's hurry. Oh, Margot! I thought you would never come."

"I was delayed," Margot replied, and the dark hid her impish smile. "But light was only just visible on the horizon when I left my room."

"But then, day is breaking! We'll be too late."

"Nonsense."

As they spoke, they felt their way along the corridor to a corner stairwell and down two flights of stairs to a small doorway.

They pushed, and the door opened easily. Margot said, in an almost normal voice, "Ah, my sweet Captain didn't fail me."

The two put on their shoes, practical suede moccasins for Athalie, dainty, satin slippers for Margot, and Athalie slipped her cloak over her shoulders.

"Here, pull up the hood, silly. If reports go back to my mother that we have been out on this escapade, I promise you we will pay."

The great Courtyard of the Fountain was in shadow as they hurried across it, but to their right, a bright sheen lay on the surface of the carp pond. The light it

162

reflected was no longer the clear brightness of the starry night that Athalie had watched from her room; it was the dim, grey light of dawn. The world was hushed; the birds no longer warbled; the scurrying of their own feet was all that they could hear. They hurried through an archway and turned right into the avenue which led along the edge of the lake to the south gate. Two rows of trees flanked each side of the broad road, ghostly sentinels in the pearly light.

Athalie took Margot's arm; her friend looked at her in surprise. "Hurry!" murmured Athalie, "hurry!"

"I can't go any faster. My heels keep slipping on these infernal pebbles."

"I don't want to miss it, Margot."

"Heavens, dear, how bloodthirsty you are! What has poor Pierre ever done to you? But don't get all fussed. There's a lot of commotion before a duel, bowing and scraping and inspecting weapons, and so on. All very boring. You'll thank me for giving you an extra half hour in bed. I certainly wouldn't give it up to stand in the cold with nothing to watch but a couple of seconds fussing about protocol."

Athalie did not reply, and the two stumbled on in silence. At last, at the head of the avenue, a dark bulk loomed. Another few minutes brought them close enough to see the gables and turrets of the southern entrance to the royal domain. They passed between two columns into an arched hallway, whose coffered ceiling flickered in the torchlight. Rushing through, they found the exterior doors pulled back and hurried out into the open area which separated the palace grounds from the forest of Fontainebleau. On each side of the gate, small groups of guards looked nonchalantly away from them. Margot pulled her hood tight at the neck and giggled.

In a muffled falsetto, one of the men said, "To your right, ladies, to your right, but I would hurry or you'll miss the fun."

Athalie broke away from Margot and ran past the guards, along the palace wall toward the figures in the distance. Tears filled her eyes, as she saw her shadow run before her, black against the sunlit ground. Her hood fell back; one tightly coiled braid began to unwind, jerking looser with every jolting step. Now she could clearly make out the throng ahead and saw that there were two groups, not one, as it had seemed from far away.

To the right, people gathered along the road; to the left, numerous stragglers lurked in the lee of the forest. Between the loose clusters of onlookers stood four men, two in shirtsleeves, two in doublets and capes. As Athalie saw the unmistakable figure of Pierre, she slowed to a walk, pulled her hood over her head and down over her eyes, and clutched the edges of her cloak tightly in front of her. Never taking her eyes from Pierre, Athalie scuttled around the edge of those spectators who had gathered beneath the palace wall and nimbly made her way to a point as close to the duelists as possible. Mutters and protests, to which she paid no heed, followed her progress. She halted in front of a tall, masked and turbaned man, who, well able to see over her shoulder, did not reproach her for taking for herself his front row position.

A mere ten meters away stood the contestants, fair heads gleaming and weapons glinting in the long, golden rays of morning light.

Pierre, in a cream-colored cambric shirt and carmine breeches, stood still and watchful; his adversary, all in white, strutted and preened, as the seconds concluded their deliberations.

"Bad taste, that Pascal, turning up all in white," muttered a nearby man.

"No doubt he doesn't expect to be wounded," came the reply in a woman's voice.

"Show-off!" said the other.

The seconds bowed formally to each other and turned to the contestants. Each man was handed a sword and a long dagger. Blankly, Athalie stared at the weapons, noting mechanically that both swords had elaborate basket hilts and that the handle of each dagger was separated from the blade by a curved crossbar, with a loop which extended beyond the knuckles of its owner's left hand. These common features aside, Pascal's sword and dagger differed considerably from Pierre's, being a matched set, finely ornamented, next to which Pierre's unadorned steel looked drab and commonplace.

At a word from the seconds, the two men bowed and crossed swords.

Athalie stood frozen, petrified eyes staring, hands clenched and white-knuckled. Into the stillness, the whang of swords broke with shocking suddenness as the fighters burst into action. A clash, a whirl, a clash, a whirl — panic-stricken, Athalie attempted to follow the rapid, leaping moves. White and cream and red, colors mingled and separated, a pause, a laugh — whose, oh God! — a whirl, another pause, and a dreadful crash.

Pascal sprang back, a scarlet stain spreading outward from a surface wound on his left upper arm. A host of expressions raced across his face, as pain and shock gave way to a look of naked hatred. Into the pause, the crowd sighed interrogatively, "Ahh!"

Pascal jumped forward; Pierre wheeled on his heel; and a flurry of thrusts and feints followed so rapidly that the onlookers could make nothing out. Pierre yielded suddenly, backing into the ranks of spectators, which broke behind him, and nearly stumbling on the grassy verge of the road. He regained his balance, turned, and half leapt, half ran back to the hard-packed surface of the thoroughfare.

Pascal was after him like a flash, herding and harrying him with lightning cuts and thrusts. The crowd gasped, "Ah!" as Pascal's blade whizzed by Pierre's head. A weal opened on his left cheekbone, bare centimeters below the eye, and blood trickled down the side of his face.

There was no pause in the fighting after Pascal's hit.

Instead, a deadly intensity seemed to radiate from the panting pair, who fought now at close quarters, grappling and shoving, more like wrestlers than swordsmen, until with a great thrust, Pascal seemed to throw Pierre from him. An arc of silver flashed, and Pierre's sword, point down, quivered in the ground. The crowd groaned, expelling in a breath their pent-up emotions, fear and disappointment and relief, all mingled.

"So soon!" a strident female voice rose above the crowd's din. "He must concede," Athalie's neighbor stated.

Through the uproar, a sardonic laugh rang, this time unmistakably Pascal's. Then, the trim, white shape lunged forward, sword, hand, and compact body aimed unerringly for Pierre's chest.

What happened next was the subject of intense debate for weeks to come. Athalie was as well placed as anyone to see, but it seemed as though what her eyes saw, her mind refused to register. The two figures revolved with mindless speed, Pierre to the right and down, Pascal forward, ever faster, first toward Pierre, then almost against Pierre, and finally, with unbroken momentum, over Pierre's crouching figure. In the space of a heartbeat, Pierre had spun on his heel and was upon the prostrate Pascal, his dagger at his throat. His movement coincided with the crowd's belated gasp.

A babble broke out all around Athalie. She heard without listening the exclamations, giggles, shouts, and cheers: "He flipped him, by God, caught the sword point on his dagger and flipped him over by the hilt" — "Pascal stumbled, that's all, he stumbled" — "Oh sure, stumbled right over de Galle's shoulder and landed upside down, some stumble!" The debate was on; even as it raged, the onlookers rushed forward and closed around the fighters. Pascal lay flat on his back, chest heaving and eyes rolling, the point of Pierre's dagger an inch from his jugular.

"Apologize," Pierre said in a clear voice. Pascal gasped for breath.

"Speak so that everyone can hear. You lied, you insulted my wife's honor and my name, and you abase yourself."

"L-let me have my sword," Pascal snarled. "It wasn't fair."

"Don't give me a second reason to kill you. Go on."

"I spoke wildly and f-foolishly," Pascal mumbled.

"Louder," said Pierre.

"May I stand?"

"No."

"I spoke in j-jest," Pascal said in a breathless but audible voice. "I meant no insult to M-Monsieur or his wife. I t-take back my words and apologize for any offense they may have given." Pascal's voice dropped. "Is that enough?"

Pierre sat back on his heel and reflected for a moment, then stood and said in genial tones, "My father will be content that I did not have to dirty my blade with your blood."

Furious, Pascal grabbed up his sword, which lay by his side, and rolled over onto his hands and knees. Before he could throw himself on Pierre, hands grabbed him, and a hubbub of disapproval rose. "Ah, no, Monsieur, that is not done." For a moment, Pierre stared at him; then, without further speech, he joined his second and strode rapidly toward the gate.

He passed so close to Athalie that she could have touched him. She could see the trail of blood, now dark and hard along his face. Her eyes followed him as he emerged from the crowd, covered the open ground to the gate, and disappeared. Her breath, which ever since he had lost his sword had come in tight, painful gasps, became gradually more even and regular. To her surprise, she was conscious not so much of feeling relieved, as of being overcome by a sense of futility. She felt inexplicably forlorn, weary, and befuddled.

A hand grasped her elbow through the thin cloak. Athalie jumped.

Margot's voice was hoarse with excitement.

"What a thing! It was like a conjurer's trick. I couldn't believe my eyes. I'm sure he did it all on purpose, even dropping his sword."

"Nonsense," said a man whom neither Athalie nor Margot knew. "It would be suicide to drop a sword when dueling with an experienced fighter like Pascal. You couldn't count on pulling off a stunt like that to save your skin."

"That's right," said another. "I say it was just luck."

"Luck, man, you're soft in the head," yelled a third. "What you saw was a piece of swordsmanship the like of which hasn't been seen in all Europe since the days of the chevalier Bayard."

"Swordsmanship, yes, but more strength than skill."

"No, it was luck!"

Margot's bell-like laugh rang out.

"Come, cousin. We'll leave these gentlemen to their talk." She and Athalie turned and walked down to the gate. Margot broke stride abruptly. "Look, Athalie," she exclaimed, pointing to the masked and turbaned man who had stood behind Athalie during the duel. "There's my brother."

"Who?"

"The King, silly. Can't you recognize him? His walk is funny. His legs are too short for his height. Oh dear, Mother will be furious."

"How will she know?"

"She always knows. And she'll know I was there, too, because I didn't have the wit to keep quiet. It was so exciting."

"Oh, Margot, you never keep quiet."

"Well, really!" protested Margot.

"No," said Athalie, feeling a little less lost. "I love it. It makes everything seem, somehow, almost normal." Margot squeezed her elbow, laughing.

"You're a funny one," she said.

Margot in the lead, Athalie dawdling and rushing in turn, the two made their way back to the palace and to bed.

* * *

Pierre knocked firmly on the door of his father's study. In answer to a gruff invitation, he pushed it open and went in. Raymond de Galle sat by the open window, full morning sun on his face. As he half turned, the light harshly

166

pinpointed the pouches under his eyes, the veining on his nose, and the deep lines around his eyes and mouth.

Pierre stopped in the middle of the room and said, "I thought you would be interested to know that you still have a son and heir."

Raymond looked briefly at his son, then his gaze returned to the window.

"I knew," he said. "My man was there."

Pierre smiled a tight smile. A "man" of his father's had been present at every significant event of his life. He should have known. He turned to go.

Behind his back, a deep rasp came, "Was it luck?"

Pierre looked back and answered, "No." After a short silence, he continued toward the door.

The voice behind him said quietly, "I didn't think so."

Pierre spun around and faced his father. A stiff smile creased Raymond's face. He got up awkwardly, moved to hold out his hand, but instead waved at a chair.

"Sit, Pierre. I once heard of a man in Italy doing such a thing. He was a great ox of man, as you'll be when you fill out. Even so, it was a seven-day wonder. I've never seen it done. I wish... I wish I'd been there today."

Nonplussed, Pierre groped for a response and finding none, dropped his head and smiled. The two lowered themselves onto their seats. De Galle fumbled in his mind for something appropriate to say.

"Well, all your training wasn't wasted," he broke out at last. "Good thing, too. It would have been damned awkward to lose you. I'll never have another legitimate son, that's pretty sure. And it would have been a shame to see you go at the hands of a nobody.

"Still, you shouldn't have insulted him at the end." Raymond scowled on principle; in fact, he had been much flattered that Pierre had thought of his father at such a time.

"I meant no insult."

De Galle's expression soured. "Either way you're a fool."

The two glared at each other, then the father saw the son's eyes begin to twinkle.

"Well, Father, if you permit, you're a great one to talk. You're lucky not to be out there right now fighting Gondi."

"Me? Gondi?" bellowed de Galle.

"Talk about insults — saying bankers are crooks and no gentlemen, and then excusing Gondi on the ground that he's a foreigner! Phew! I thought he might go for you."

De Galle's blue eyes bulged in his brick red face. "Well, look, it is different! France is built on the land — the peasantry, the nobility, the King, are tiers rising from the foundation of the land. These middlemen and usurers are termites tearing up the structure of society. But Italians are different. There is no Italy really, just a lot of cities, and even the best Italians seem to like trading and swindling. They don't have the same ideas at all."

"But, Father, Gondi thinks he's a gentleman by our standards."

De Galle's face reddened to a yet more choleric shade. "Damn!" he burst out, as a great guffaw suddenly shook him. Pierre sat amazed; laughter slowly bubbled up in his own chest and erupted to join his father's. "Damn," de Galle repeated, wiping his eyes. "We'll have wine and drink to Gondi's health. He's a useful bugger, and no mistake. 'I meant no insult!' Ha! We'll have wine before we dine."

The great man stood and flexed his shoulder muscles, a smile lingering on his mouth. With a sudden return to sobriety, he looked down at Pierre and asked gruffly, "Why didn't you kill him?"

Pierre returned the gaze warily and said nothing. His father turned his back and repeated, "Why didn't you kill him? Too queasy, was that it? Too queasy to do the thing all the way? It would have been your baptism of blood, and about time, too!"

"There was no need," Pierre said, his expression stony, but his voice shaking with emotion. The washed but undressed cut on his face stood out, ugly and raw; his hand moved to go to it, but he forced it down.

De Galle whirled and sent Pierre a narrow, appraising look. "Need? No other man would say that."

"Why should I have taken his life? It would have been a... a gratuitous, a vicious, a murderous act. I had gained my point. I didn't need his death, too."

He thought of Pascal lying on his back beneath the dagger point, his body frozen to immobility, while his features writhed with terror. It was odd, he thought, that what he had felt for him was not pity, but only a kind of revulsion at his helplessness.

De Galle towered over Pierre. "You're wrong on every score. To kill him would have been no loss. He had it coming to him, and he himself did not signify. But there's more: To let a man live under such circumstances is a mistake, the worst possible mistake.

"See here, Pierre. A man is your enemy. You can make it up with him or you can kill him. You decided to fight this fellow. That was your right. You defeated him, so much the better for you. But you did not kill him. It was your right to kill him. I mean, though it is technically illegal, no one would have blamed you or made trouble for you. But you didn't. What's worse, you insulted the man you had just defeated, but not killed. So what has been accomplished? Your humiliated and insulted opponent is alive and well and more implacable in his enmity than ever. Fortunately, he is nothing, but let this be a lesson for the future."

Pierre stood, too, and faced his father. "I did what I had to do throughout, except for what I said at the end, and I meant no harm by that."

They held each other's eyes until at last the older man turned away. "We'll have that wine, then, shall we?"

Chapter XIV

he days flowed on, full summer days, shimmering with heat. So many days of sunshine had followed one another that the summer seemed longer than usual, languid in its pace like a river going dry. And, indeed, the rivers did dry up, the streams disappeared, and in the fields, scrawny heads of wheat drooped on their stalks. Peasants grumbled, while their priests prayed vainly for rain.

The King's Council, unable to govern the weather, grappled with problems which were more properly in its province. Administrative routine was handled piecemeal between great debates on the return of Coligny and the situation in the Netherlands. All opinions were viewed and reviewed, more in the hope of relieving tensions than of affecting the course of events.

While the great men fretted, the less great played. The young blades occupied their idleness with the usual activities — hunting, archery, tennis, and other games and sports; the demoiselles rose late, labored mightily at their toilettes, and sortied for the midday meals, the afternoon promenades, and the evening balls that enabled them to display the fruits of their travail. As August wore on, the worries of those above filtered down to enliven the conversation of those below. The return of Coligny replaced Pierre's achievement at arms as the principal item of gossip. A curious atmosphere of suspense settled on the Court; without seriously disturbing the general feeling of well-being among those not in a position of responsibility, it electrified a summer's end which might otherwise have been too cloudless to be amusing.

Pierre did not share the insouciance of his compeers, though it was not affairs of state that troubled him. If he had had to ascribe a specific cause to his malaise, he would have said it was the duel and its antecedents. The episode had left a bitter taste in his mouth, which his easy victory had not sweetened. Pascal's defeat was not in his eyes a sufficient accomplishment to nullify the humiliation which had preceded it. In general, Pierre felt out of sympathy with his world; the usual activities and the familiar faces bored him; as much as possible, he kept himself to himself, appearing to others even more aloof now than before.

Eleanor d'Avrillac observed Pierre's withdrawal with puzzled dismay.

"What a very long face for such a beautiful day," she chaffed him one morning, as they strolled by the carp pond.

"It's always a beautiful day nowadays, but it isn't human to be cheerful every day."

They walked on in silence under the whispering trees, then turned onto the tree-lined jut of land which stuck out from the shore into the lake. To their left, the waters glinted and sparkled in the morning light. Highlights and blue reflections rippled across the pond's silty depths. Beyond the tongue of water stretched the long, elegant façade of the palace, its deep rose brick startlingly vivid against the brilliant sky. Blue, rose, and blue again, the bands of color vibrated together, while as if to give point to the picture, a swan glided airily into view.

"They are so beautiful one can even forgive them for being so scornful," Elie said.

"Nasty, bad-tempered creatures," Pierre replied.

"Oh, look, Pierre." She nudged him gently. The gleaming white bird floated warily closer, and as they watched, two small cygnets, dark and fuzzy, appeared behind their mother's tightly curled tail. Eleanor fumbled in her pocket and produced a roll of bread.

"I brought it for the carp," she said.

Pierre smiled with adult superiority, as Elie crumbled bread for the cygnets and squatted to watch them dive, fluff their feathers, and jab at each other with frenetic, ungainly movements. At last, the mother drifted away, her offspring paddling after her with palpable reluctance. Elie stood and shook out her skirts. Her gaze met Pierre's amused look; she put her hand through his arm as they continued along the shadowed bank.

"I wonder if you know how proud your father is," she said. Pierre stiffened. "He might not let on to you, but I can tell." She glanced at him to see if this news brought him solace and saw that it did not.

"I'm not proud," he replied at last.

"Why not? The whole Court was filled with admiration."

"More fool they. Anyway, it isn't true. Everyone thought it was luck, not skill."

"No, everyone admires you, because Pascal was an experienced fighter, while you were untried. I was afraid for you for the same reason. You had never been in a duel, and a real fight must be different from mere practice."

"I was once in a duel, not quite a duel, but like it, and I lost. But I knew I would win this time. And you know, all other things being equal, 'mere practice' is what does the trick. The whole point is to repeat every conceivable movement and maneuver so many times that you can do them without thought, and therefore without fear. It works."

"Honestly, though, weren't you just a little afraid?"

He smiled down at her. "Why on earth do you want to know that?"

"I don't know. It's not to gloat or anything nasty like that. I think it's because I will never be in such a position, and I'm curious what it would be like."

"I was not afraid of the duel. I knew I was more than a match for Pascal. The fact that I'm not my father's equal doesn't mean I'm not the equal of everyone else."

"Who says you're not your father's equal?" she asked.

Pierre stopped walking and turned to her. "You dare say that?"

A younger woman would have blushed at his straight gaze. Eleanor drew herself up proudly; her face seemed to glow.

"Yes, Pierre, I do. Remember, I was your mother's friend long before I was your father's."

How lovely she is, thought Pierre. Her looks mirror her goodness. It is easy to see why both my parents loved her. Because of what she is, there is no shame in it. He wished he could say something of the kind to her, but felt tongue-tied; then watching her face, he saw it was not necessary.

He said instead, "Of course, I didn't much relish making a display of myself in front of all those people, but after the beginning, that didn't matter any more. Everything disappears, except what you have to do. It's funny. No, there was only one thing I was afraid of."

"What was that?"

"That I might have to kill him. If he had refused to apologize, I would have had no choice."

"Well, that wouldn't have been so bad, after all."

"You say that, too? Father claims I should have killed him and never mind the apology. But to me, the whole idea seemed... well, sickening. Do you understand at all?"

"I suppose so, except he deserved it, and you know, he would have killed you."

"Yes, I saw that in his eyes. Is that always reason enough? I don't think so," he shrugged.

They reached the end of the promontory. All around them water gleamed, civilized water, captured and controlled by man, with all the beauty of a natural lake but none of its wildness. It was an infinitely satisfying vista. Elie reached into her pocket and brought up the crumbled remains of yet another roll. She tossed a small piece of bread onto the water and watched it disappear with a swish into the seemingly disembodied mouth of a large carp. She laughed and offered her handful of crumbs to Pierre, who hesitated, turning down the corners of his mouth in a wry grimace.

"Heavens, don't be so superior!" she exclaimed, half in amusement, half in genuine annoyance. "Young people are impossible — so busy trying to be grown up, they miss the point completely. Children are much more honest.

"Pierre, do you remember how we used to go down to the river when you were small, you and your mother and I, and feed the ducks. And you would paddle in the water with the village boys. You were very little. Do you remember it at all?"

"Of course," he said, and looked away.

Elie's eyes, gentle and sad, remained on his face. There had been nothing complex, dark, or difficult in that sunny five-year-old. Only years later had she realized that somehow, for some obscure reason, he had become constrained, not simply by the solemnity of adolescence, but by some deeper trouble. She did not know how or even when the change had occurred. Was it his mother's death which had brought it about? Or his father's remarriage? Or simply his father's overbearing and outwardly imperious disposition? She did not know.

Elie sighed. Her playful mood dispelled, she went to toss her handful of crumbs onto the water, when Pierre reached out and cupped her hand in his. Gently, he picked out lumps of bread and dropped them, one by one, into the lake. A plop was followed by a plop-plop, as the fish gathered to gobble the crumbs. The water soon heaved and churned with scaly, ruddy-brown bodies.

"My God, look at that monster!" exclaimed Elie, pointing at a hoary grandfather carp which muscled its way through the teeming multitude.

"Ah, to be like that, what a wonderful thing!" Pierre said, then they both laughed softly. Elie shook her fingers and the remnants fell into the bustle below, which instantly subsided as the last crumb disappeared. The murky water winked placidly at them, no hint of movement disturbing its depths.

Pierre stretched luxuriously. "I think I'll go dig up someone to fence with. It wouldn't do to get out of practice, after all. You can never tell when that sort of thing will come in handy."

"Indeed, but you may have trouble finding anyone willing to cross swords with you."

They grinned at each other and turning, walked back in companionable silence.

When Pierre emerged onto the playing field after half an hour's quick walk past the château and up the tree-lined avenue, he found it almost deserted. The warmth of the morning had quickened, and the closely scythed grass, burnt and dusty, fairly radiated heat. At the edge of the enclosure, a few pairs of young men lolled, shirts open over sweaty chests. One figure alone moved, slowly tocking arrows into a round wooden target.

Pierre watched the archer's careful, clever shooting until the arrows were exhausted, then turned to walk past the target. The youth strolled over to it and began to pull out the arrows. As Pierre approached and their eyes met, a shock of recognition ran through them both. The archer was Pascal's second, Trophime Daudet. They gazed uncomfortably across the short distance between them, unable to ignore, but unwilling to acknowledge, each other. Daudet returned to collecting his arrows, methodically, and with exaggerated concentration. As Pierre made to wander off, he shot a last glance in Daudet's direction and found that the young man was now walking slowly toward him, a fistful of arrows in each hand. Sweat glistening beneath his chestnut curls, his eyes dark with embarrassment and uncertainty, he stood before Pierre in awkward silence and blocked Pierre's escape. Pierre felt a rush of admiration. On an impulse of gratitude for the other's move, he put aside his own awkwardness and said, "I thought I'd see if I could find a fencing partner, but it seems to be a bit too hot..."

"I'd, I'd be honored," Daudet replied and to his amazement, saw Pierre flush furiously. Freed from his own constraint by Pierre's discomfiture, he added with a broad smile, "Archery's no pastime for a gentleman."

Pierre tossed his doublet over a bush and rolled up his sleeves, while Daudet packed the arrows away in their quiver. They bowed, crossed swords, and commenced. Pierre at first moved languidly, limbering up as he appraised his opponent. Daudet's form was nervous and overhasty but not devoid of skill, and his compact body was strong and well coordinated. They circled and parried;

Daudet thrust, Pierre leapt aside; they lunged and withdrew. At last, Pierre moved in, and it seemed to Daudet that he was buffeted by a gale of wind that wrenched his sword from his hand. He gasped and gripped his sore wrist. Pierre looked away awkwardly.

Grinning, Daudet said, "I wouldn't call this practice — not for you, I mean. You'll just get hot and get no benefit from it."

Unable to deny the truth of this, Pierre refrained from comment.

Daudet continued, "I know a little tavern, a dark hole — really rather gloomy — but at least it's cool. Shall we...?"

Though truly a modest establishment, Daudet's tavern was famous — and infamous. It was famous because of its antiquity. Unlike most of the poorer buildings in town, it was built of stone, which permitted it to survive the fires that periodically razed the neighborhood. The massive, rough blocks had come through many such conflagrations blackened but undamaged, except for one corner where the stones had literally melted together. The tavern came by its ill repute, and most of its business, by providing the ladies of the town with their principal place of rendezvous, which would have shocked Daudet had he been aware of it.

Mornings were the slack period; Daudet and Pierre had their choice of the long trestle tables and benches which overfilled the interior. Facing each other, they took places by a wall which ran with condensation. The clammy chill was a delight after a long, hot walk. Scuffling their feet in the matted rushes and herbs which covered the floor, they felt the coldness of stone through the thin leather of their soles. The once fragrant hay had not been changed since midsummer and, when disturbed, gave off an acrid odor.

Their eyes met over their flagons of cellar-cooled cider. Both thought how strange their coming together was; both knew that the other had the same thought.

Finally, Daudet said, "I was close enough to see what you did the other day. Some people thought it was luck, but I know it wasn't, though I could hardly believe my eyes at the time."

"It's not so hard really, if you have the idea and, of course, the weight. I pulled the same trick on my instructor, so I knew it could be done. He was furious."

"I'll bet!" Daudet grinned appreciatively.

Suddenly serious, he ran his fingers through his hair. "You may think it's odd of me to be here — disloyal to Pascal — but you see, though he's my friend, I didn't approve of his putting you up to a duel, and I told him so at the time. I think he got what he deserved."

"I want to put the whole affair behind me and not look back," Pierre said firmly.

"If your admirers will let you forget it." Daudet laughed.

They drank more cider and talked of one thing and another. Soon the formal "Monsieur" was dropped, and it was "Trophime" and "Pierre." They smiled and joked, savoring their newfound camaraderie and attributing too much significance to it, in the way of lonely people.

Their timid intimacy was soon to be put to the test.

"Have you heard Coligny's coming to Court?" Trophime asked.

"It would be hard for me not to have heard. No one talks of anything else."

"Except your prowess."

"Stop it!" said Pierre, laughing in spite of himself.

"For myself, I'm going to be very glad to see him, but still, I think he's crazy to come."

"Why do you say that?" Pierre asked. "It seems to me he should be grateful the King lets bygones be bygones. We should all be thankful. It gives a chance for peace at long last."

"Peace, phah!" Trophime said with disgust.

"By God," Pierre continued, "what everyone says is right: You Huguenots are troublemakers. It's your ill will that breeds war."

"Is that what you think? You think it's our fault? What about the last so-called 'peace'? After the treaty was signed, we of the Religion disarmed and returned home, and what happened? In no time, the Medici woman had her agents out sounding the moat of Condé's fortress at Noyers. Condé and Coligny were forced to flee in secret with their womenfolk and their children. They almost didn't make it to La Rochelle."

"I've heard that story, but I never believed it," Pierre said. "Their Majesties would never do something so dishonorable."

"They would and they did, well, she did, anyway," Trophime insisted. "I'm not saying anything against the King, except that he can't control his mother, or his brother, or the Guises, or any of the Catholic nobility who want to destroy the Reformed Church.

"What's more, I'll say this: I don't think that the few Catholics who would uphold the King's promises have anything to pride themselves on. Even they are willing enough to close their eyes to the truth: War or peace, 'heretics' are always fair game, right? The only difference is that in times of war we can defend ourselves."

"I don't know what you're talking about. You're the ones who go around burning churches and raping and killing nuns and monks."

"Funny how every time a Protestant knocks the head off some statue, it's considered a tragedy and mourned by the whole Court for weeks, whereas no one ever seems to know anything about the double-crossing treachery that we're the victims of."

"Where do you get off yelling treason?" Pierre countered. "For one thing, a King cannot be treasonous. For another, you people have taken up arms against your monarch, and that is treason!"

Trophime half rose, his face suffused with blood. With a visible effort, he mastered himself and slumped back onto the bench.

"I didn't mean to provoke a fight. My father enjoined me strictly to avoid all occasions for religious quarrels." Trophime took a deep breath. "Maybe treachery was too strong a word," he continued with a semblance of calm, "though I don't know — a King can betray his people, I think, and forfeit his right to rule."

Seeing the hostile expression on Pierre's face deepen, he hastened on, "Still, we have no desire to fight our King, but even you must admit that a peace is a peace, and should be kept by all."

"That is true," said Pierre.

"And if one side offers hostilities, the other has a right to defend itself."

"I suppose, but there should never have been a division in the first place."

"So we say, too. We say we are Frenchmen, just like the Catholics, and should have access to the King's ear just the same."

Pierre hunched down, staring at Trophime's still-angry face and hearing his father's oft-repeated condemnation of the Protestants for precipitating civil war and undermining the established order: "They are extremists," de Galle always said, "wanting too much too soon and willing to use any means to get it."

"Why did you come to Court feeling the way you do?" Pierre asked.

"Precisely because we believe that France should be one, united behind its King. My father says we have nothing to be ashamed of, and we should not act as if we were ashamed. I am to make my way at Court, meet my peers, and learn the ways of society and the administration of law, just as he did when he was young. It's difficult, though. I mean, it really isn't the same as when he was young. People are polite to me, mostly, but a lot of them behave as if I have the pox. Pascal has taken up with me because he doesn't have many friends either, but he will drop me when others begin to accept him."

Pierre looked sympathetically at Trophime. He himself had always been something of a loner, but only by his own choice. He had never had cause to wonder what it would be like to be ostracized. He reflected that he would be glad enough to befriend Trophime, if the young Protestant kept his ranting within reasonable bounds.

"I suppose things will be better when Coligny comes," Trophime continued. "He'll be bringing scores of gentlemen of the Religion with him. They're to be received with open arms by all, so we've been told. A new era, that's the byword these days."

"It will be, if everyone approaches it with good will," said Pierre.

"Ah, but will they?" Trophime shook his head sadly. "I can't help but be afraid for him. Still," his face brightened," it will be wonderful, just having him here. He is a great man, Pierre. You will see that for yourself. Do you know what my father says of him? That there is no baseness in him. You can't say that of many people."

"My father says he is a good man." Pierre's reply sounded stiffer than he intended. In fact, Trophime's enthusiasm was infectious, and Pierre found himself looking forward to Coligny's arrival.

"And you'll be glad to have your brother back," Trophime resumed.

Pierre nodded and shrugged, the two gestures eloquent of his ambivalence. "Stepbrother," he corrected mechanically.

"My father writes that La Renaudie is held in great honor at La Rochelle. He has the Admiral's confidence, and that's a wonderful thing."

"Does your father write you often?" Pierre asked, thinking how inconceivable it was that his own father should ever write him.

"Oh yes, quite often, mostly to ask me for news or to give me messages for people." This was uttered with unfeigned innocence. It had never occurred to Trophime Daudet that he was, in a modest way, an agent for his co-Religionists. "I would like to know Monsieur your brother better — the son of the great La Renaudie and one of the Admiral's intimates! Well, I mean, it would be an honor, if you could, if you would."

"Yes, of course," said Pierre, genuinely amused at this novel way of looking at his stepbrother. "And you in turn will bring me in contact with the Admiral, so that I can, as you say, see for myself."

* * *

Early the next day, Pierre retraced the previous morning's stroll. In his pocket was a small loaf and on his face a sheepish smile. He walked out onto the point and stood looking across the lake. The heat was already dispelling the slight haze of morning. There was an intensity to the light that mirrored the fullness of the season and proclaimed yet another glorious day.

A rustle to his right caught Pierre's attention. Turning, he saw a figure in a dark dress crouched by the water's edge. He stepped toward her, dislodging some pebbles which rolled gently toward the water. The girl turned at the noise, and he saw that it was Athalie.

It would have been difficult to say which of the two was the more surprised, and yet, they themselves could not have explained the cause of their astonishment. Athalie stood hastily as Pierre approached. They stood in embarrassed silence, until Athalie noticed that her bread had fallen from her lap into the water.

"Blast," she said heatedly.

Pierre smiled broadly and, as if by sleight of hand, produced his own loaf from his pocket. Athalie exclaimed and laughed, and together they turned to the lake. Pierre broke the bread in two; squatting, they resumed the carps' interrupted meal.

"What brings you out so early, and where have you been all these weeks?" Pierre asked.

"Which question should I answer?"

Pierre looked at her steadily. "The second is the more important — by far."

Athalie dropped her gaze to stare resolutely at the lake's turbulent surface and launched into nervous, voluble speech.

"I always get up early. For years I've risen before dawn every day. I gather, though, that early rising is not the custom here, and in a way, I'm glad. Except on the days when I wait on Her Majesty — she's always an early riser — I could lie abed until midmorning, like all the others. But this way, I get a little time to myself. It's funny, considering how little there is to do, what a luxury free time is.

"I suppose I shouldn't complain — at least here I have a room to myself." She shuddered, remembering Chenonceau's crowded quarters. "I don't think I could bear to do without my own..." She paused, seeking a word that conveyed something more essential than mere sleeping quarters.

"Your own lair?" Pierre said.

"Exactly. However small, it doesn't matter, but I need it, my soul needs it, or something."

"I understand."

"Here come the ducks!" Athalie exclaimed. "And the swan is with them. Do we have any more bread?"

"Enough."

They rose. Athalie made a lap with her skirt, and Pierre crumbled all the remaining bread into it. Holding the skirt with one hand, Athalie threw a few bits at the approaching flotilla. She and Pierre laughed aloud at the chaos that ensued: The ducks rushed forward, the swan bugled and took swipes at the ducks, and the carps seethed amidst the churning webbed feet. Soon the last of the bread was gone, and the two stood breathless in the sudden calm.

"You never answered the more important question," Pierre said. Athalie looked away. How could she tell him that since Tours she had fled him as the rich flee the plague? How could she speak of the turmoil in her emotions which the duel had occasioned? At least, she no longer deceived herself as to how she felt about him, but it would be unpardonable to pour out her love simply because, unsuspecting, he had given her a pretext to do so. Yet she ached for the relief that speaking would have brought.

It was an odd silence that had fallen between them. Uncomfortable, Pierre broke it, saying the first thing that came into his mind. "How does your riding progress?" he asked and then felt foolish for seeming to harp on the comic aspects of their first meeting.

"Oh, much better, thank you. I practice as much as I can. I ride almost every afternoon."

"Soon, you'll be hunting morning, noon, and night, like all the other fanatics."

"Oh, no! Though I shall have to take the plunge one of these days." Her face became grave. "Her Majesty, the Queen Mother, has been after me about it. I'm afraid she's beginning to think I'm a coward, and that annoys her. I suppose I am a coward."

"Perhaps a few pointers would help?"

And so they went riding that very afternoon. Athalie had no will to resist him. Looking back at her earlier efforts at avoiding him, she thought angrily that she had subjected herself to pointless aggravation.

177

They rode for an hour along straight alleys cut through the deep forest. The cool air and the exercise felt good after the hearty noonday meal. Where the road met a stream, they left it and dismounting, let the horses drink.

Athalie dropped down onto a boulder. "I still can't ride for hours on end, as some people can. My behind gets sore."

"I can ride all day and not even notice it."

"You can! I'm not surprised." Leaning over, she splashed water on her face and ears. Its iciness shocked a gasp from her. She scrambled to her feet, and Pierre led the horses back to the road.

"You know," Pierre said, "you can ride in a straight line for two days and still not reach the end of the forest."

"Let's not," she said.

He glanced at her face, which was flushed from exertion and the effects of the cold bath. "Shall we rest a bit?"

"Gladly," she answered, sliding down next to a nearby oak and leaning against its massive trunk. Pierre tethered the horses and sat beside her. Pulling a feathery weed from its green envelope, he sucked the sweet juice from the exposed tip. He pulled up another strand and passed it to Athalie.

To left and right, the alley ran unswerving through lofty trunks.

Pierre gestured down it with his arm. "That's what I meant when I said the Cathedral was like a forest. There's the nave, with the arched roof, and the sun slanting through the upper windows. Only the colors are different — yellows and greens, instead of blues and reds."

"But does it make you feel the same way?" Athalie asked. "I mean, does it inspire you to pray?"

"They both make me feel something otherworldly; it's hard to describe. But it doesn't make me want to pray. I pray the rites, in church. I can't say I do much praying otherwise." He shrugged.

"I used to," she said a little sadly. "Now, it seems as if God is an idea, not a person, so I can't."

She bent abruptly, unfastened her shoes, and slipped them off. She wore pearl-grey silk stockings that caught the sunlight with a shimmer. As she stretched her legs, and laughing, wriggled her toes, Pierre marveled at the daintiness of her feet. He felt a tremendous urge to reach over and grab them, to tickle them, to.... He forced himself to look back down the alley.

Athalie discreetly inspected the hard, red line of Pierre's scar, and thought what a pity it was that it marred the haughty line of his cheekbones.

"You know," she said, "You'll laugh, but when I first saw you, I thought you were the King." Pierre did laugh.

"Now that I've seen him," she continued, "it seems all the more ridiculous." And not, she thought, because you don't look the part, but because he doesn't. She remembered how taken aback she had been when she had first seen the ungainly youth who was Charles IX, and how she had mocked herself for once again fabricating and cherishing an idea that was such a poor likeness of the reality it depicted.

She settled comfortably against the tree, lazily sucking the blade of grass.

"Is it strange or nice to have a surrogate mother?"

Pierre gave her a quick glance. "It depends on the person, of course. Madame d' Avrillac, Tante Elie as I call her, is as affectionate to me as my own mother would have been." Athalie's eyebrows jumped in comic surprise, but Pierre had looked away and continued, unheeding. "Can anyone substitute for another? I suppose not. People are unique, aren't they? So you have with one what you wouldn't have had with another — and you don't have what you would have had."

"I meant, I was referring to Madame de Galle, I mean your stepmother," Athalie stammered.

Pierre's glance was full of amusement and devoid of embarrassment. "Oh!" he said.

Athalie paused, half expecting him to comment on the misunderstanding; his silence made her feel foolish, even though, she argued, it was more his mistake than hers.

"I often wondered when I was a child," she resumed at last, "if I would have been happier if my father had remarried. There would have been no cause to be jealous on my mother's account. I never knew her, so in a funny way, it was as if she never existed. Especially as he never talked of her. She was kind to the servants and very well read; that's about all I know.

"I suppose she must have had charm," she lingered over the word with a touch of bitterness in her voice, "like my uncle Gondi. My uncle never talks about her either," she continued, surprised to notice the fact for the first time. "I wonder if people don't talk about her because they didn't like her or because they loved her. It would be nice to know. It's strange: When people die, if you don't see it, it doesn't seem real somehow. They simply disappear. Did you find that?"

"I saw my mother dead, so... so it wasn't the same." He had been about to say 'so it seemed real enough,' but had it? He remembered how he had turned away after she was lowered into the ground and had not thought about her again for, well, for years. He had even resented it when Elie had spoken of her.

He glanced at Athalie. Why can't I talk about things the way she can? he thought enviously. But nobody talks the way she does; she is naive, but intelligent; honest, yet sensitive.

Athalie thought of all the things she would discuss with Pierre if she dared. She wanted to ask him why he was here, but she sensed that he had not wondered at it and was afraid the question would trouble their peace. She would have liked, also, to talk about the duel.

During that horrible day before the duel, and immediately after it, she had not paused to reflect on why it had happened. She had accepted the situation at face value: Augustin Pascal had insulted Pierre's wife, and Pierre, naturally, had defended her honor. Since that time, the insinuating glances and little laughs which normally accompanied any conversation about the duel had finally penetrated her consciousness, and she had half-guessed the truth.

Now, she wished desperately to know everything, everything about Pierre, everything about his wife; she forced herself to face up to her curiosity, however distasteful; and not only that, but she longed to hear the truth from Pierre's own mouth. But she was afraid.

Suddenly, against her own better judgment, she rushed ahead. "Why did you fight the duel?" she asked in a small, timid voice.

Pierre stared at her. "If you don't know, you are the only one in the world who doesn't know."

"I don't mean the words; I know what he said, I mean. Was it...?"

"Was it what?"

God, why had she started this? she wondered wildly. She looked away and whispered, "Was it true?"

"You have no right to ask me that." The coldness in his tone mortified her.

"I would have thought," he resumed in a warmer voice, a voice heated by undercurrents of anger, "there'd be plenty of people at Court who'd be glad to titillate you with bawdy tales. You should remember, though, there's nothing like firsthand experience. You could get that easily enough, too.

"What do you want from me?" he continued. "Shall I tell you what my wife is like in bed? Or would you rather I gave you the names of some other gentlemen, who could give you more details?"

"Don't. Please, Pierre, don't." She had never before called him "Pierre"; now, the name slipped out unnoticed by either of them.

His anger drained away. He realized he had done her an injustice, but felt too empty and disgusted to wonder how the conversation had started and what, if anything, it signified.

He uncrossed his long legs and got to his feet. Reaching down, he said, "Shall we go back?"

She saw his hand out of the corner of her eye but ignored it, using both her hands to push herself up from the ground.

They rode slowly back the way they had come. At first, Pierre forced himself to prattle with unconvincing cheerfulness about famous hunting exploits he had witnessed, what it would be like when the Court moved to Blois, and other easy topics, but he gave up the attempt at conversation in the face of Athalie's lack of cooperation. Athalie sulked, angrier with herself than with him, though she refused to admit it. As Pierre quickened the pace, she became hot and sore in addition to her other woes. They were both relieved to reach the palace gates.

* * *

During the following days, Athalie avoided occasions for meeting Pierre alone. She gave up her early morning walks and rode out only in the company of other young people. The rest was easy; the busy whirl of Court life made solitary encounters unlikely. She did not, however, deprive herself of all contact with him. To the contrary, she found herself following him around, spying on him whenever he was safely occupied with other people and activities. Though she despised herself for what she was doing, she made no attempt to stop.

She watched him play tennis with the King, noting his efforts to dissemble his superior ability for his monarch's benefit. As he rowed a group of pretty girls around the carp pond, she hid in the shadows of the trees and followed the boat with her eyes. They danced the same dances with different partners. She lived for the moment when they would face each other for a quick bow and curtsey before turning back to their own partners. She was outwardly relieved and inwardly crushed that he never led her out onto the floor. At night, she would lie awake, flushed with the summer heat and the inner boiling of her emotions. Sometimes she cried.

This distressing confusion of mind continued until she happened upon a scene which, she thought at the time, shocked her back to a truer perspective. It was after supper. Athalie had gone alone to the aviary, which, at Fontainebleau, was a remarkable structure, enclosing several large trees, two fountains, and more than a hundred captive songbirds. She stood, her fingers hooked through the grill, her head down, her eyes shut, all her attention held by the evening symphony of the birds and its accompaniment of gurgling, splashing water. Suddenly her ears picked up sounds which seemed alien to this magical world, the muttering of voices and a piercing laugh.

Opening her eyes, she saw a small group emerge from behind the aviary, their figures darkly outlined against the tawny glow. Her gaze immediately focused on Pierre, tall amidst the others, a lute slung over his back. She had momentarily put aside her preoccupation with him; his presence peeved her until she saw his wife and forgot her vexation.

Anne strolled ahead of the others to a stone bench carefully placed to allow nature lovers to feast their eyes and ears in comfort. Stretching away to the front was a panorama of tapestry-like flowerbeds; from behind came the singing of the birds and the murmuring of the fountains. With graceful abandon, Anne cast herself on the low seat and laughed back at her followers.

"Music is what we want," she said in a high, carrying voice.

"We have music." It was Pierre, gesturing, as he spoke, at the giant birdcage. His eyes lighted on Athalie, and he called out, "Come and join us, Mademoiselle."

She came forward with reluctance. Greetings were delivered, then all eyes turned back to Pierre and his wife. Anne's gaze rested lightly on Athalie, then swept away.

"Nonsense," Anne said. "All the little birdies are going to bed. They need a lullaby. Well?" She flashed a radiant smile at the others, who closed in around Pierre, clapping their hands in response to her unspoken request. As Pierre still hesitated, she said, "Why did you agree to bring that thing, if you weren't going to play it?" Her lips puffed out in a pout.

Pierre rested his foot on the edge of the bench and swung the lute into place. He bent, quickly tuning it, then straightened and looked around briefly before launching into a popular chanson by Pierre Certon:

"J'ai le rebours de ce que je souhaite,
J'ai converti en joye contrefaite
Tout le plaisir que perdre craignais tant."

I have the opposite of what I want.
It's gone, the pleasure I feared most to lose,
Transform'd into a mockery of joy.

Pierre's voice was husky, but resonant; it vibrated richly against the lute's deep notes. His listeners picked up and carried the refrain:

"J'ai du mal tant, tant,
Que le coeur me fend,
De voir l'amour défaite."

I have pain, more pain,
Than my heart can bear,
At losing love's pure joy.

Pierre's voice continued alone,

"Plus je connais l' amour sûre et parfait,
Plus me déplait de la voir imparfaite.
Si j'en ai ri, j'en pleure bien autant."

I know that love can sure and perfect be;
Thus I despise the waste and ruin of love.
If I have mocked, I have more often wept.

The group picked up the refrain, coming in over Pierre singing, *"Jai du mal tant, tant..."* Then Pierre went on,

"Ma douleur n'est moins grande que secrete
Mon bien perdu sans espoir je regrette
Qui me soulait l'esprit rendre content."

My sorrow's great, though hidden it must be.
I know what's lost can never be regained.
All's gone, save spirit's discontent and blame.

Everyone sang the refrain, and Pierre repeated it, playing the notes staccato and lilting his voice ironically. As he concluded, he looked down at Anne with hooded eyes.

Athalie slipped down the path around the aviary. Her going was unseen, as she knew it would be. She did not exist for the singers, whose voices, lifted in a new song, followed her hurrying steps. She stopped in a pool of shadow. Had anyone observed her, he would have thought she was watching the light, now more rose than amber, muting the contrasts and the colors of the landscape as it faded. In fact, her staring eyes were unseeing.

So, she thought, whatever that woman does, he still loves her. Even if he hates the pain she causes him, he thinks it's worth it.

And that's how it should be. Isn't it? Part of her protested wildly: He should not feel that way; he should want what is good for him, he should want me. That was it, of course. She was angry, not only with Anne for proving unworthy but with Pierre for accepting it. She realized now that her feelings were wrong, not only because they transgressed everything she had been taught to value, but because the object of them had himself implicitly rejected them.

She recalled bitterly his words of the afternoon of their ride: "You have no right to ask me that."

Muffled sounds of laughter and footsteps told of the departure of her former companions. What seemed like silence followed, until her ears began to hear the small noises of evening: the chirruping of crickets, a gentle soughing in the trees, and the rustling and peeping of the aviary birds. Lullabies, indeed, she thought angrily, yet she couldn't deny that the birds sounded sleepy.

She thought of her tree at Fontevrault. Memory of a place, a time, a state of being that seemed long gone filled her with an aching nostalgia. Things were so simple then. Had they only seemed simple? she wondered. What was true: her perceptions then, or now?

Had the world been different than she had thought, or had she become different? If the latter, then perhaps no permanent damage had been done. Perhaps, just possibly, if she returned, she would rediscover her clarity of purpose. She could at least try. She could, yes, she would, ask her uncle to let her go back. Her heart leapt; Fontevrault is home, she thought.

Chapter XV

imeri Pascal is not a particularly prepossessing youth, Gondi thought, covertly eying him, while mouthing the customary civilities. He saw a tall, angular young man with the pale complexion of the sedentary and wispy, flaxen hair, who bowed clumsily and peered at the world through spectacles with an owlish look of wonder.

Though Aimeri had abandoned his scholar's gown and sported the courtier's ensemble of doublet, puffed breeches, and long hose, the absence of a sword, a slight stoop, and an ungainly walk left little doubt that he was not what he attempted to appear. Gondi could sense his wife's hauteur through the veneer of her hospitality.

One must make exceptions, Gondi thought: His shyness is quite natural. Why, even old Artus is puffing and sputtering. It is understandable, even inevitable, that these people should be overawed by their surroundings. He sent a gratified look around him.

Indeed, the Hotel de Retz at Fontainebleau was an imposing residence. Built in the finest Italian style, with delicate columns separating richly decorated windows, the edifice surrounded, on three sides, a spacious inner courtyard. The fourth side was formed by a high wall bisected by an ornate arch, which was flanked both inside and out by minor classical deities represented in stone as oversized naked humans. With the heavy gates thrown back, it was possible to glimpse through the arch the broad tree-lined avenue which ran along the north wall of the royal palace.

The courtyard itself was divided by graveled paths into four square flowerbeds, precise geometric patterns in reds, pinks, and oranges, set off by hedges of dark box. In the center of the garden stood a charming granite well with a pulley of delicate ironwork. At the corners opposite the arch, trellised, vine-covered enclaves sheltered low stone benches.

Host, hostess, and guests stood on one of the garden walks, making a strange contrast as they faced each other — Gondi's russet velvet and gold filigree and the Countess's mauve satin and pearls were worlds apart from the Pascals' sober black. The conversation, if the stilted exchange of banalities deserved the name, faltered; Gondi took Artus's arm and led him up the walk.

"Come, my friend," he said, "I'll have you and your son shown to your rooms, so you can take a moment to refresh yourselves. Your trunks will already be there. Then, I'd appreciate it if you would come to my study. I'd like to get a few matters out of the way before the meal. If you're not too tired, of course."

"Of course, of course," muttered Pascal.

Very shortly later, having quickly rinsed his hands, splashed his face, and brushed down his slightly crumpled robe, Pascal was sitting in Gondi's study. His composure somewhat restored, he replied affably to Gondi's urbanities, half his mind on their talk, the other half wondering who would bring up the critical subject.

At last, Gondi leaned back in his comfortable armchair and sighed. Pascal sat forward, his eyes fixed expectantly on his host's handsome face. As often before, he was amazed to watch so expressive a face express nothing.

"I have not forgotten the proposal you put forward on your son's behalf," Gondi began. "Indeed, I went so far as to mention it to Her Majesty, the Queen Mother, just to gauge the temperature of the water, so to speak."

Pascal said nothing, but leaned further forward, eagerness written across his visage.

"To continue the image, if I may, the temperature was icy. That august lady allowed that I should know better than to waste her time with something that was out of the question. Her exact words were: 'Allow a banker's son to become Duke de la Roque? It is unthinkable!'"

Pascal bridled. "And yet, my banker's money is good enough for her!"

"It is ever thus."

"I'm no Jew!" Pascal spat out.

"No, no, of course not. Don't take offense, old friend. Royalty will be royalty. Anyway, I did not say all is lost. I have thought of a way that might possibly get us around her objection — if, of course, we think the whole idea of the marriage is appropriate. If, for example, the girl takes a liking to him."

"What difference does that make?" Pascal expostulated.

"It would make a difference to Her Majesty. She's fond of the girl."

"You make her sound almost sentimental."

Gondi chuckled. "You know, at times she is. Every 29th of February, or about that often."

Unamused, Pascal glared at Gondi.

"However," Gondi resumed, "I don't think my niece will care for the idea."

"Leave off, Albert." Pascal broke in. "You're giving me the runaround. I would have thought I was too old a friend for that." Gondi gave a sympathetic cluck.

Pascal continued, "The girl's objections, if she has any, are of no real importance. You know that. If Her Majesty will agree, I mean, if you can overcome her objections, then everything we want will follow easily."

"Mm, yes," said Gondi, picturing Athalie's face with the mulish expression it often wore in his presence. "Yes, of course," he said, somewhat too emphatically.

"So let's talk business, not sentiment," Pascal concluded triumphantly.

Gondi brought his full attention to bear on the discussion. "You are absolutely right, old friend. I only hope you will follow your own excellent advice and not let your judgment be clouded by emotions."

Pascal waited warily.

"Her Majesty's objection is essentially that it is hubris for a young man without name or fame to aspire to the highest rank in the land." He held up his hand. "She would believe this regardless of your son's merits, so there is no point

185

in taking offense. Indeed, if for no other reason than that it would provoke shock and anger amongst the nobility, you can see her point."

Pascal nodded slowly. "So you are saying, as she did, that the marriage is unthinkable."

"No. A dukedom for your son is unthinkable — at least at the present time."

"But the marriage and the dukedom are inseparable. Your niece is the Duchess de la Roque; it follows as the night the day that her husband will be the Duke de la Roque, just as you became Count de Retz by marrying your exquisite wife."

"There is one way out," Gondi said. "As part of the marriage agreement, if we were to go so far, you understand now, we're just talking — my niece could divest herself of the duchy by selling Rocher de la Roque to me. My niece is also a Countess by virtue of at least two other properties and has numerous lesser titles, as the old nobility always does, so your son would become a count, a baron, and lord of a considerable number of minor fiefs. From there, of course, he might move up in the peerage in time, as his merits became known and appreciated at Court, but in that way, he would start off with an honorable, indeed high rank, but one which would not unduly shock Her Majesty or the nobility of France. Thus would Her Majesty's principal objection be circumvented.

"Now, I should add that much as I would like to assist in this project, I have a personal difficulty, which is that my assets, though great as you know, are not liquid enough to permit me to pay cash to take Rocher de la Roque out of my niece's estate. I would, of course, expect suitable financing."

The old fox, thought Pascal. He is to become duke and I am to finance it!

"If everything else worked out satisfactorily, I might be able to persuade Her Majesty to go along with the arrangement as I have described it," Gondi concluded.

Pascal reflected for a moment, then asked, "Are you quite sure that Her Majesty will want you to become Duke de la Roque? After all, you, too, are a mere banker's son."

Gondi averted his eyes, his hands momentarily clenching.

"It's not at all the same. Even you must see that. Anyway, I didn't say I was sure that my suggestion would be accepted, only that it has a chance — provided that the Queen Mother is given other inducements."

"Yes?"

"What I am talking about, of course, is money." He could not stop himself from adding, "There's nothing else you could offer." He took a breath and continued. "The question of the duchy must be arranged, so that the marriage becomes plausible in her eyes, but money is the key. War is in the air, and war is expensive. Easy money on favorable terms — if her need is great, she may not be able to resist. You understand, it is in her hands, hers and the King's. All I can do is advise. She will decide."

"Yes, I understand."

"But I will do my best for you, for us all."

Pascal felt tired and befuddled. The long journey and all this talk and — what else was there? — the pressure of Gondi's presence, all combined to wear down his resistance and confuse his thoughts.

After a moment's pause, he asked diffidently, "Is she present, the Duchess?"

"As lady-in-waiting to Her Majesty, my niece resides in the palace. However, I have arranged for her to be here for the noonday meal and afterward, the two young people can become better acquainted in the garden." He gestured at the flowerbed, visible through the open casement. "Under our supervision, of course, and that of my wife."

* * *

The garden was calm in the afternoon sun. A dense warmth filled the air. Such noises as there were seemed tenuous and sleepy: the low, intermittent humming of hidden insects, the occasional chirping of birds, the slow clop-clopping of travelers passing the front gate. In the shade beneath Gondi's window, his wife walked slowly along the path and turned into an open doorway.

Aimeri and Athalie sheltered from the strong August sun within a trellised arbor. Like the sounds of the garden, their conversation was slow and full of interruptions. They talked first of the weather — gorgeous, then of the harvest — early, but poor, and finally of games that they liked. Too embarrassed to admit to her ignorance of most games, Athalie pretended to greater knowledge than she had.

As the exchange crept along, Athalie puzzled quietly over the oddness of the situation. Why had she been so peremptorily summoned? The day before, her uncle had sought her out and had said, "You will make yourself available, niece, to entertain my guests." Why was it necessary? Her aunt, the Countess de Retz, had returned from postnatal convalescence to resume her role as the best hostess in town. She certainly needed no assistance from her maladroit, tongue-tied niece. Why then was she here? She had known better than to ask, but she could not help wondering.

Hearing the rustle of satin, she turned and saw the mauve of her aunt's dress pass behind the browns and deep greens of their leafy shelter. Aimeri's soft prattle faltered and stumbled to a halt. His eyes followed Athalie's gaze and caught a glimpse of that mauve disappearing into the shadows. He looked back at his companion, an expression of wistful melancholy flitting across his normally self-contained face. It was plain to him that the girl's shyness was even greater than his own, but this realization did not diminish his constraint. He felt helpless and somehow foolish.

As the two sat in uncomfortable silence, the elegant figure of the Countess made its way along the path on the far side of the garden and stopped below Gondi's open window. Gondi leaned out, and he and his wife engaged in a brief exchange, inaudible across the garden. Then, the Countess turned back up the path, casting a quick glance in the direction of their arbor before ostentatiously averting her gaze.

Athalie turned to the young man and burst out, "Why does she keep on circling around us?"

Aimeri gave her a quick look of surprise. "Don't you know? To keep an eye on us."

"Why?..." Athalie began again, then fell silent, continuing the query in her own mind: Why should she keep an eye on us? Why should there be an "us" to keep an eye on? She glanced nervously at Aimeri. With a slender forefinger he pushed his glasses up his nose and thought, she is so young, so delicate, so very lovely — even her gaucheness is charming, since it makes her loveliness completely unaffected.

"Don't you know?..." He broke off suddenly. Seduced by her ingenuousness, he had almost committed the egregious faux pas of mentioning the marriage negotiations before they were concluded.

Athalie saw his embarrassment and felt the intensity of his interest in her, felt it all the more strongly because it was banked down and thus intensified. Suddenly, a glimpse of the truth came to her.

"Is it that you are courting me? Have you been sent by my uncle to court me?"

Her frankness shocked him.

"No, well, not court, exactly," he said. "I mean, nothing has been agreed upon — regarding our marrying."

Athalie stood abruptly, her watered silk skirts falling with a gentle shush into heavy straight lines. She faced him.

"Monsieur, understand me: I will not marry — I will not marry you," she said in a clear, loud voice. The Countess checked her perambulation for a moment, then rushed into the building. Horrified, Aimeri swiveled on the seat, hiding his face from Athalie's gaze.

Though she felt a pang of pity, her expression remained set in obstinate lines.

The young man turned back, but did not raise his eyes to her face. "I know it is presumption," he said in a low voice. "I know I have no right to expect, I am not the right class, not the right rank, but... but..." He turned away again, distracted beyond speech.

"Rank has nothing to do with it," Athalie proclaimed.

As surprise overcame his discomfiture, Aimeri looked at her directly. "How can you say that?"

The evident bitterness in his voice checked her impetuosity. With gentle grace, she resumed her place beside him. As she did so, she reflected that what she had said unthinkingly was nonetheless true. Rank had meant little or nothing to her; she had hardly ever been conscious of its benefits; she had simply taken her position and its privileges for granted.

"No," she repeated, "I don't think disparity of rank would stop me."

Aimeri shook his head and smiled incredulously.

Panic suddenly rose in Athalie's breast. What if he asks the obvious question: If not rank, then what? She looked at him. Could she love him, if...? He has a sensitive face and beautiful, long hands. Marriages are not made for love; I will never marry Pierre.

A slight shiver shook her, despite the warmth of the afternoon. I could tell him that I have vowed myself to God, but would it be true, now?

They sat on in silence, yet both were aware that the silence was less constrained than their earlier attempts at conversation had been.

"Shall I get my lute and play for you?" he asked suddenly. She nodded.

He returned quickly and sitting on the edge of the bench, tuned the instrument with rapid, purposeful movements, unlike his usual diffident and nervous gestures. Then, he began, deep, full notes pouring effortlessly from his fingers in a complex melody, carefully phrased, which, though he played it fast, lost nothing of its intensity or clarity.

By instinct, Athalie knew that she was in the presence of a truly masterful player. With a pang of discomfiture, she compared Aimeri's graceful rendition with Pierre's rougher handling of the same instrument, then she forgot all thought and simply listened. Seeing her rapt expression, her glowing face, Aimeri felt his heart turn over. His hands faltered, and Athalie shook her head slowly, as if waking from a trance.

Aimeri held out the instrument to her. "Will you play?"

She dropped her gaze momentarily, then suddenly confident that he would not think less of her if she spoke the truth, she said, "I have never learned an instrument."

Aimeri had no need to ask her if she wished to learn; her desire was naked on her face. Wordlessly, he slid nearer to her and laying the lute face-up on his lap, slowly began to finger the various chords.

From the window of Gondi's study, Madame de Retz watched them, shaking her head over the whimsicality of youth.

* * *

Margot's bed was warm and frowsty. The damask curtains had been pulled around the short, wide mattress, leaving only a narrow gap to admit the light of a single candle. A cool evening breeze made the flame flicker wildly and blew rivulets of wax over the candle's edge. The gusts of freshness did not penetrate the curtained enclosure, which soon developed a stale odor of sweat and potent perfume.

Supported by a mound of cushions, Margot sat with her knees pulled up under the velvet coverlet. Her bleached and curled hair, freed for the night, stood out wildly from her soft, round face, its artificial blondness looking strange next to her slightly sallow skin. She watched her friend sleepily.

Athalie had been fretful all evening. Knowing she would not be able to sleep, she had come to Margot's bedroom to seek the relief that confiding in a friend always brings. She leaned against a post at the foot of the bed, her legs folded beneath her and her skirts carefully gathered in her lap. Her hands fondled the delicate material as she spoke.

"And so, you see, I finally realized what it was all about."

"I should think so," Margot interjected. "They would never have left you in tête-à-tête with a strange man, even under your aunt's beady eyes, unless there was a question of marriage. You poor love, was he simply awful?"

"No. No, certainly not. I expected the worst, knowing him to be Augustin Pascal's brother, but they couldn't be more different. He is gentle, almost delicate, whereas his brother must be as hard as steel."

"Well, do you want him?"

"What do you mean?"

"Would you marry him?"

"Never."

"That's good. Mother would think it most unsuitable. Of course, I," Margot sighed, "I believe in marriage for love. Love is everything, don't you think, cousin, everything that makes life exciting. But Mother definitely does not believe in love, or marriage for love, or whatever."

She blinked and relaxed her head against the pillows. Her voice sounded half-suffocated as she continued.

"You should be thinking of marrying, Athalie. It would get you out from under your uncle's hand. I wonder what he's up to, anyway: A merchant's son, indeed! Of course, you'd be subject to your husband, but you can at least hope it would be better. You know you can do nothing with your uncle, so I would gamble on an unknown, under the circumstances.

"Really, some men are like melted wax in their wives' hands. I don't know whether I'd like that, though it has its advantages. Yes, it may be the best of all possible worlds, don't you think? A malleable husband and lots of lovers." She stifled a yawn.

Athalie was used to Margot's loose talk. "You don't mean that," she said, "and you know it."

Margot looked up.

"Which would you choose," Athalie asked, "Henri de Navarre and lots of lovers, or Henri de Guise and no lovers?"

"Guise, of course."

"You see. You would prefer to be faithful to a husband you loved."

"Only if he loved me first. Anyway, what are we arguing about? I said I believed in marriage for love."

"Why do you say he must love you first?"

"Oh, look, Athalie, I don't know. It's customary, isn't it?" Margot sighed and focused her wandering thoughts. "I guess what I really mean is, there must be love on both sides. If not, then it's better for there to be no love at all and for both parties to feel free to look for love elsewhere."

Athalie reflected on this for a moment. "You're clearly right," she said. "The worst is if one spouse loves and the other doesn't. Like Pierre de Galle and his wife."

"Mm," said Margot.

"That must be horrible, don't you think?"

Margot wriggled beneath the covers. "I really don't understand it. I find him quite attractive, myself. Don't you? He reminds me a little of Henri." Athalie looked at her sharply.

Margot yawned convulsively.

"But what am I to do if my uncle insists on this marriage?" Athalie resumed after a pause.

"Take it up with Mother. She'll fix his cart for him. It would be a good thing, anyway, to remind her that you're of marrying age."

"Oh, no, Margot, I don't want to do that."

"Why ever not?"

"I will never marry."

Margot gave her a startled look, then laughed. "You say the silliest things. Mother will pick a husband for you before you know it. She'd have done it already, if she weren't so taken up with Anjou's marriage and mine.

"There," she slipped her hand from under the covers and held it out to Athalie.

"Kiss me, cousin. I don't need to stay awake tonight, and my eyes are closing of their own will."

Athalie slid herself up the bed and kissed Margot gently on the forehead. Then she slipped between the curtains and taking the candle, left the room.

* * *

The Pascals stayed three more days. Each noon, a sumptuous dinner was served, meals more notable for their cuisine than their conversation. Indeed, Madame de Retz was careful to include in her menu items that would astonish her bourgeois guests: turkey served in a hot, pepper sauce; melons from Italy, cut open at the table to reveal luscious orange interiors, then liberally sprinkled with black pepper before being served; heron in pastry; fricassee of plover and teal in a heavy, marjoram sauce; sweet tarts made with sugar instead of honey. Never were there fewer than six courses. Each person had his own goblet, which was kept full with sharp, new wine by the young pages, Gondi cousins, who waited at table with many airs and graces. Gondi was urbane as always, but his efforts at affability were somewhat undermined by his wife's pointedly distant courtesy.

That she thought the company below her was something which she could not disguise, however much she approved of her husband's intentions.

The Pascals were impressed and somewhat dismayed. They could think of little to say except to marvel at what was put in front of them. The normally loquacious Artus was rendered tongue-tied by his sense of inadequacy. He was incapable of discussing the arts and could not display his true genius, for the mere mention of money before the Countess was clearly unthinkable. His son could have held his own on most subjects Madame brought up, but he declined to be drawn out. As a result, their hostess was confirmed in her opinion that her guests were boors, too stupid to see through her husband's schemes or too insensitive to be offended if they did. If the Pascals noticed that none of the de Retz friends at Court were invited to dine with them, they did not remark on it.

Athalie was as silent as Aimeri at these meals, but she observed the participants with attention. She felt sure that she was being used by her uncle and aunt, but to what end? She could not tell if the trap was being laid for the Pascals or for herself. Either way, the situation angered and frustrated her. She liked banker Pascal. His plainness and warmth attracted her; she contrasted them favorably with the self-conscious dignity of the Countess and Gondi's ostentatious polish. His awkwardness aroused only sympathy. She had too often subsided into graceless incoherence before her aunt's glittering repartee to judge anyone on a lack of social graces.

Every afternoon, after dinner, the pattern of the first day was repeated. Pascal père and Gondi retired, separately or together, to their affairs. Aimeri and Athalie sat together in the sunny, perfumed courtyard under Madame's discreet surveillance.

The afternoons passed in an orgy of music. Aimeri would play, while Athalie sang in a sweet, timid voice, whose purity made up for its lack of strength. As she lost herself in the music, all their shyness would evaporate, and Aimeri would devour her with his eyes. Then he would pass the instrument to her. She would caress the satin sheen of its surface and set herself to work, fumbling at the strings under Aimeri's critical but affectionate eyes. As the hours passed, her fumblings became more effective, and Aimeri became less critical and even more affectionate.

On their last afternoon, he asked diffidently, "Do I have any hope?"

Athalie started, "What do you... Oh, you mean... No. No, there is no hope. Please forgive me. I'm sorry." Her mumblings trailed away in confusion. "I wish I could explain."

She took hold of herself and spoke more clearly. "I hope you will still be my friend. Believe me, I do," she added, seeing the wounded look on his face. "But as to what you mean, there is no hope at all."

* * *

In the morning, before their departure, Pascal drew Gondi aside.

"My boy says the girl has given him to understand that what we want can never be."

"They are getting ahead of themselves, but no matter. Did she give him a reason?"

"Apparently not. She told him it was not a question of rank."

"Ah. You see, Pascal, as I told you the very first time we discussed this matter, she has ideas of becoming a religious. I believe, though she was too reticent to say so, that this is her reason."

"What is to be done?"

"Don't worry, old friend. I will do my best for you. She must decide, that's all. She simply must decide."

Chapter XVI

t seemed, that September, as if a dam had broken and all the rain, which throughout the summer the skies had held back, came pouring down in relentless torrents. The Court rode south to Blois past sodden fields of broken wheat, parched pastures turned to mud, saturated hayricks rotten from damp. At the best of times, the King's château at Blois was essentially a dreary place, despite the gay veneer of flame-red brick of Louis XII's reconstruction and the frilly modern intricacies of the great François' resplendent addition. Now, it seemed to brood under the banked clouds. Moisture had infiltrated its very joints; foetid smells rose from its gutters; mildew infested its dark corners.

Of course, it rained when the Admiral and his train arrived. Custom demanded that they dismount outside the gates, but even on foot, dark-clad except for gleaming armor, they were a formidable, indeed a somewhat forbidding group. The courtyard was less than full. Many who might have greeted them on a clear day preferred to shelter from the rains; others who did not wish to greet them at all relied on bad weather to excuse their absence. Those courtiers who had braved the downpour made a bright circle around the newcomers as they knelt in homage to the King.

No one could say whether the Huguenots' cheerless countenances reflected their antipathy to the return to Court or merely the physical discomfort of a long, wet journey.

At any rate, all were agreed that the inclement weather was an evil omen.

Not even Noah's deluge could have stopped Athalie from enjoying the garden at Blois. Separated from the cramped enclosure of the château proper by a deep ditch, the garden, like the château, was surrounded by sturdy fortifications. The large area within was divided into several terraced enclaves, walled and distinct, for in truth the Blois garden was many gardens. Even on the wettest days, it was possible to reach the principal quadrangle without being drenched. A covered bridge, decorated with hunting insignia, led from the château to an arbored gallery with elaborate wooden vaults, which, together with a stone structure facing the château, enclosed the area and separated it from the lower and upper gardens. To Athalie, the place seemed a protected haven, a magic island, a man-made Eden. She did not ask herself whether it attracted her because it reminded her of Fontevrault's great cloister or simply because it satisfied some basic need for space and solitude. It was a refuge; she loved it; she came as often as she could.

The spacious parterre within the cloister was divided into square beds of patterned herbs and flowers, set off by manicured borders of box and neat fences. From their midst rose a lovely, timbered pavilion, which covered an octagonal stone basin carved with lion heads and porcupines. To reach this shelter on a rainy day required a sprint through the open. Athalie risked wetness gladly to reach her favorite place in all Blois. Perched on the edge of the basin under the sturdy cupola, she felt protected not only from the stormy weather which buffeted her world from without, but also from the tumult of personalities which raged within.

Against her will, Athalie had been forced to play a role in the many-sided tug of war which was discreetly unfolding beneath the festive façade of Court life. She knew she was expected to provide a binding or linking force in a situation characterized mainly by centrifugal elements, and that knowledge dismayed her.

"Athalie, you would do me a service, wouldn't you?" the Queen Mother had asked during their first afternoon at Blois. To Athalie's surprise at finding herself, in the midst of the confusion of arrival, in a seemingly impromptu tête-à-tête with Her Majesty was added her astonishment at finding her hand grasped and held in Catherine's fleshy but powerful grip. They were alone in the Queen Mother's bedroom, where a jumble of portable furniture lay haphazardly about, filling the room with chaos but no warmth. Their privacy was no accident; Catherine had dismissed her other women just as they were unpacking the bed hangings and tapestries that would begin to transform the room from a bare shell into a sanctum stamped by the Queen Mother's love of ostentation.

"But of course, Madame, I would be delighted," Athalie had replied, without the slightest shadow of doubt to mar her good will. Then she had listened while the Queen Mother, still holding her hand firmly with her right hand and caressing it gently with her left, had explained what she wanted. At first, the discussion had seemed a confused rambling, covering many subjects whose interconnection was obscure, at least to Athalie: Coligny's arrival and its importance, the necessity for women to help each other, the difficulty of finding trustworthy people and, even more, of finding someone who would appear trustworthy to more than one faction.

"There are, of course, practiced courtesans in my entourage," Catherine had continued. "I do not deny it, though I do not admit that they practice all their wiles with my encouragement. Don't think I don't know that they are called, by scurrilous folk, my 'flying squadron.' I'm not deaf or senile, after all. I know what people say."

Athalie had never heard, or at least never understood, that sort of reference to the Queen Mother's celebrated beauties, who, it was said by some, were no better than prostitutes, paid or otherwise rewarded by her for information acquired during the pleasures they conferred; she was now embarrassed both by the rumor and by her ignorance of it.

"But, you see," Catherine said, "the Admiral would never trust such a person. His tastes run to innocent young girls like yourself." As a glimmer of what the Queen Mother intended enlightened her, Athalie protested, "But Madame, he has only just married — "

"Quite — to an innocent young hothead. It proves my point exactly."

The Admiral's second union, to a woman more than twenty years his junior, who, sight unseen, had sought his hand in marriage because it was her great ambition to wed a saint and a hero, had been one of the celebrated events of the year. She had risked all her possessions in Savoy, because the marriage displeased her liege lord, the Duke Emmanuel Philibert, but it was said the lady thought the exchange well worthwhile.

"However," Catherine continued triumphantly, "the Admiral's beloved spouse is in La Rochelle! Now, it may be true that absence makes the heart grow fonder; still, I have never found that an absent wife curbed a husband's apian instincts."

Athalie had remained silent at this, but her eyes had more than adequately conveyed her shock. Dropping her hand, the Queen Mother had said sharply, "My dear, I don't mean that you should do anything improper with him. Heaven forfend! Indeed, I tell you now that I would be most displeased with you if you did. No, I only mean that the Admiral will be lonesome, and he will think he can trust you, and so, he will relax with you. And since I know that I can trust you, well, it will all work out for the best. Do you understand?"

Athalie had not really understood at the time, but now she understood fully. From the moment of Coligny's arrival, she had found herself deliberately thrown in with him, and daily, she had been called on to tell the Queen Mother what she had seen and heard in his presence. It did not bother her much to list the various people who gathered around him, nor even to summarize their talk. With new sophistication, she realized that her Mistress would have other sources for such information.

What she found far more difficult and distasteful was to divulge her own conversations with him, not because there was anything intrinsically secret about them, but because she would normally have considered them private. For the Queen Mother's prediction had been right: The Admiral did like young people and encouraged them to be with him, and he seemed to have taken a special fancy to Athalie.

"What does he say about the marriage?" Catherine would ask almost daily.

"He is in favor of it," Athalie would respond miserably.

"Has he written to Navarre's mother? Nothing can happen without her approval, and she is the kind of person who doesn't approve of much."

"I believe he is in regular contact with both mother and son, for he holds them in high esteem..." There, the catechism would falter. Athalie could not divulge the particulars of this correspondence, because in truth, she was not privy to it.

Once, the Queen Mother had continued, "Does he preach his precious reformed Religion to you, child?"

"Yes, Madame."

"What does he say?"

She had found it hard to cull the essence from her many conversations with him on religious topics and still harder to convey how much they distressed her. The Admiral found her intelligent and opinionated; it amused him to challenge her most deeply felt convictions.

She had lowered her head and blurted out, "He calls Holy Mother the Church the whore of Babylon."

To her surprise, Catherine had smiled. "There is much that the Church has done and left undone that is subject to criticism. But I cannot agree with the methods of the Church's opponents. They claim to be a religion, but they are merely a reform, an attempted reform at that, and one which is doomed to failure, since reform can only be accomplished from within. To the extent that they have an idea which justifies their separate existence, it is that each sinner can find salvation on his own by reading and praying over the Scriptures and listening to the voice within. As to that," she had spread her hands gently, "what I have seen of my fellow creatures does not inspire confidence in their ability to discern the truth in any form."

Athalie had looked both stubborn and unhappy. Seeing this, Catherine had said, "It upsets you, doesn't it?"

"It's not that he says the things he says; it's that he believes them," she had replied.

As she sat in the garden pavilion, listening to the rain patter on the timbered cupola, she mulled it all over, her relationship to the Admiral on the one hand, her relationship to the Queen Mother on the other. Since her arrival at Court in June, the Queen Mother had singled her out for protection and guidance, had taken her interests to heart, and had accorded her tokens of kindness and real affection. Athalie was ashamed that she could not reciprocate by rendering wholehearted, unquestioning service, now, when it was needed, but what the

197

Queen Mother asked went against the girl's grain. Athalie's abhorrence of the task not only made her an unwilling servant for this occasion, it destroyed the very basis of her willingness to serve on any occasion. And Coligny? Athalie could never altogether put out of her mind the Abbess Louise de Bourbon's scathing condemnation of the so-called "new Religion" and its leaders, yet she liked and trusted him, though he represented the enemy in very clear terms.

Liking and trust were two very different sentiments, but in this instance, she felt them both strongly. Though she wondered if she had simply been seduced by his charm, she thought not. Indeed, on reflection, she believed it more likely that she approved of him in spite of his charm, rather than because of it, for her uncle Gondi had taught her to mistrust charm.

She puzzled about that for a while. The two men, Gondi and the Admiral, were more or less of an age, the latter a few years older; both were physically imposing and attractive; in both, she sensed an iron will held in check by manners that were humorous or grave, garrulous or aloof, many things, but always appropriate to the circumstances. Coligny's charm was a natural outcome of these qualities; in Gondi's, however, there was something more, a manipulative ability, which he used and enjoyed. Yes, she thought that was the difference.

She shrugged that puzzle aside, returning to what really troubled her. She knew where her loyalties should lie in the question of Coligny versus the Queen Mother. Indeed, she knew there should not even be a question. But her feelings were directly contrary to what she knew they should be. It seemed as if in every matter of conscience, her thoughts pointed one way, while her feelings pulled violently the other way.

She, who had always thought she understood things so clearly, found her orderly mind reduced to a welter of half-formed, elusive, basically untenable notions. It was mortifying, and even worse, it was terrifying. At times like this, she feared that, by having let herself be polluted by one of the cardinal sins in loving Pierre, she had opened herself to a force which had blinded her to truth, to goodness, to grace. She really did not know what to believe.

Athalie had never spoken to her uncle about returning to Fontevrault. To go back seemed like a choice in itself, and she did not feel clear enough in her mind to make such a choice. Yet, during those moments when she wondered if she were trembling on the brink of perdition, she felt sure she should have tried to return to the source of her beliefs to retrace her progress until she could, once again, see things clearly and simply.

Then, her failure to do anything struck her as one more way that evil had perverted her will. But at other times, when she was calmer, she was confident that she had been right to resist the temptation to run away, and she thought, how brave I am to eschew simplicity and to face difficult questions as they are, as questions still open and deserving of a struggle.

She now shut her mind against its confusion. Resolutely, she took the bundle that lay beside her on the basin's edge and placed it on her lap. She had used her cloak as a wrapping; she unwound it to reveal her newest and most precious possession — a lute. It had arrived just before their departure from Fontainebleau, a gift from Aimeri Pascal. She remembered the stir its provenance had caused in the Hotel de Retz, as her aunt and uncle had debated whether it was proper to accept gifts from a rejected suitor. She herself had simply longed to keep it and had known, anyway, that Aimeri would not misconstrue her acceptance of it, their relationship being too open for that. When her elders had determined it was permissible to give mild encouragement to a suitor who in their view had been discouraged, but not, after all, entirely rejected, she had taken the gift and fled with it, tears of joy and relief in her eyes.

She had often brought the instrument to this garden to fumble at it in private. Now, wrapping her cloak about her, for the damp was chilling, she fondled it as it lay in her lap, stroked its varnished, gleaming surface, and marveled at its softness to her touch.

Shaking off her reverie, she positioned it and began to pick diffidently at the strings, imitating Aimeri Pascal's preliminary tuning. Though she had a good ear, she had no experience; her hesitant plucking and listening were slow work; tuning the lute often left little time for attempts to coax music from it. The process was a discouraging one, but she found it so absorbing that its laboriousness never bothered her.

A voice startled her. "May I interrupt?" it asked, a request which was itself the most effective of interruptions. Her knowledge of the identity of the speaker and her surprise at his sudden appearance momentarily took her words away, but as she turned to face Pierre, she smiled her acquiescence.

Pierre put a foot on the basin's rim and leaning forward, smiled back at her.

"Yesterday," he explained, "I saw you from the upper garden, so today, when I found you weren't in the game room, I thought I'd come and see if you were here."

"You couldn't recognize me from up there, could you? It's too far."

"I might not recognize most people at that distance, but you, I can always recognize."

She smiled rapturously. After a while, she asked, "Is it pretty up there? I've never been..."

"If you like vegetable gardens. It's spacious and empty — of people, I mean. I live up there, in the new building, but of all the people who live there, I seem to be the only one who prefers cabbages to cribbage. And there's a sheltered walk."

"I do like vegetable gardens. I think they're as beautiful as flower gardens, even if they aren't as colorful. They make me think of... of the places where I grew up."

"We'll go there together, if you like. I'll give you a tour of the cabbages."

They laughed, and Pierre sat beside her. The drizzle abated into a pleasing quiet. Pierre eyed the lute questioningly. "I didn't know you played."

"I think you're mocking me. If you listened to what I was doing, you must know I have no skill."

"Then one cannot help but ask, What are you doing with that thing?"

"Someone who gave me a few lessons gave it to me."

"It's a rare master who pays his pupil for the lessons he gives. You should introduce me to him."

"He wasn't a music instructor."

"Ah, I know, an itinerant troubadour who fell in love with you. I could well believe it. Did he write you a song? Could you teach it to me?"

Athalie's hands fussed nervously; the instrument gave a muffled twang as they brushed across the strings. "No, it wasn't like that. It was a young man, it was a gentleman my uncle introduced me to."

"Ah." There followed an ominous silence, then Pierre continued, "So the gift was not entirely a disinterested one. I understand now what he hoped to receive in return."

Athalie looked at him, startled. "No, you don't understand. I had rejected him."

"But then thought better of it and took the gift."

"It wasn't like that at all!"

"May I know who this suitor is? Or should his identity be kept secret 'til there's some kind of announcement?"

"There will never be an announcement, never, and I don't care whether you know his name or not. He's called Pascal, Aimeri Pascal. My uncle knows him through some banking connection."

"Pascal. I know the family well. At least, I know the one I almost killed. His brother, I presume."

As her fondness for Aimeri Pascal had developed, Athalie had pushed out of her mind his connection with the other Pascal, on whom she had lavished such hatred and scorn at the time of the duel.

Now, she was embarrassed by the reminder, which merely added fuel to her annoyance.

"Well, he's not his brother's keeper," she retorted.

"Whatever else he may be, he is surely a nouveau riche parvenu. What can your uncle be thinking of? I didn't think he was so democratic as to feel that everyone should be given the same chances he received. He at least did not start at the bottom of the social ladder and had the decency to climb it more or less rung by rung, but this merchant, it seems, would go from bottom to top in one leap."

"My God!" Athalie burst out angrily. "Why should I have my destiny dictated by such considerations?"

"Ah, well, if you feel that way, anything is possible. Still, most people would think that there weren't any other considerations."

"Well, I don't feel that way. I feel, I think... marriage should be, I mean, the way people feel about each other is important."

Pierre shrugged. The two of them sat in silence, each nursing a sense of having a grievance against the other. At last, Pierre put out a hand toward the lute, saying, "As your tutor cum suitor is not present, perhaps I can replace him. Or perhaps that isn't possible?"

"The only reason that you can't replace him," Athalie blurted out, "is that you don't play as well as he does." She saw Pierre's hand drop as if burned and his face flush a deep, unbecoming red. Why did I have to say that? she thought frantically.

"I didn't mean that," she said. "I mean, it's true, but I don't care, and you shouldn't either. Why must you be best at everything?"

Pierre shook his head and did not reply.

Athalie held out the lute. "Please play. Or at least tune it, so I can try to play."

He took it reluctantly and strummed and adjusted it with exaggerated slowness. At the end, he passed it back without playing any melody. She accepted it, vowed silently to ask him no more favors, and settled herself to play. Though she had, under Aimeri's tutelage, learned a few simple tunes, and though she had practiced them on her own, nerves now made her fingers fumble and stumble over the strings with most unappealing results. Pierre's sullen expression yielded to a look of mingled pain and amusement. Finally, he interrupted, "I don't think much of your tutor's efforts."

Eyes snapping, she rounded on him, but facing his mirth, she met laughter with laughter.

"How can you tell it's not the pupil's fault?" she asked.

"It would be ungallant to say so. Anyway, I could only tell by giving you lessons myself. I could do that, as an experiment, unless, of course, you prefer to abandon the whole enterprise as hopeless."

"No, no," she said, passing him the lute. "I want to learn. But for now, just play."

He picked out the opening bars of the lay she had heard him play at Fontainebleau.

"Not that one," she pleaded. "It makes me sad."

With a quizzical glance, he shifted into a happy, bawdy song, a lovers' dialogue, very popular at Court. They sang the refrain together, then alternated the male and female parts. To hear him again confirmed to her that his fingering was less fine than Aimeri's, but she was more than consoled by the power of his playing and the beauty of his voice.

As they sang the concluding refrain, a new voice joined in faintly. They turned their heads and saw Coligny standing under the vaulted arcade with Trophime Daudet at his side. At the song's end, the newcomers strolled between the parterres to Pierre and Athalie's shelter.

"So," the Admiral said, "you, too, have discovered this refuge from the world." He laughed a little bitterly. "You, at least, can hope to be private here. When I attempt to flee my admirers and my enemies, I bring a whole crowd with me. Look, my guards," he said, gesturing to a small group of Protestants sheltering under the arcade opposite, "and look there," he said, pointing to a figure hanging over the wall of the upper garden, "my spy."

Pierre and Athalie laughed; Trophime scowled.

"I think," Athalie said to Pierre, "that our friend didn't appreciate the song. You should sing a sad song to go with his mood."

"The trouble with Trophime," said the Admiral, "is that I was teasing him about his name, which was unkind, since people are no more responsible for their names than for their relations. Still, it is comic to find an ardent young Protestant named for an imaginary saint who was invented by people who didn't want to give up their local deity when they became Christians. It's the kind of superstitious rubbish that the unenlightened go in for. It fills a kind of void — busy little incantations, instead of real prayer."

Athalie and Pierre looked embarrassed, while Trophime continued to appear truculent.

"And you, Athalie," Coligny continued, "your name has always intrigued me. How came you by it, do you know?"

She shook her head, and her cheeks reddened in a rare blush.

"When I first learned who 'Athalie' was," she replied at last, "the daughter of Ahab and Jezebel," she added, seeing Pierre's puzzled expression, "a murderess, a usurper, an evil woman, stoned to death by her people, I was mortified to be called after someone who was — a kind of witch, a personification of wickedness. I couldn't understand how I could have been given such a name. My father would never have sought a name from antiquity. He was no scholar. And my mother would never have suggested such a name. She was too good a scholar. So I puzzled, and I thought that maybe, when she was dying, my mother suggested a name, a different name, and my father misunderstood."

She looked about at their attentive faces and suffered sudden stage fright, for she had never confided this fantasy to anyone before.

"And what was the name you thought your mother might have given you?" Coligny asked with great gentleness.

"I thought, perhaps 'Aspasie,' and I hoped it was so, for in her world she was as much a personification of good as Athalie was of evil. She was wise and beautiful and erudite, even if she was only the mistress of Pericles and living in what we would consider sin."

"That's interesting," Coligny said. "It's a confusion that could have happened."

"They're both dead now, so I'll never know," Athalie concluded bitterly.

"Never mind," Coligny said briskly. "All those old notions about names, about people being like their namesakes, or whatever, are superstitious nonsense. You are what you are — a good person named 'Athalie.'"

Athalie continued to look miserable. Was she not also evil, in her own way?

She and Coligny broke the silence simultaneously, and he nodded to her to proceed. Hesitantly, she said, "Her Majesty, the Queen Mother, has talked to me about my name. She said she had once been called 'the new Athalie' because she had preserved her children's heritage. She seemed proud of it."

"There are always more ways than one of seeing a thing," the Admiral observed.

Athalie silently recalled how the conversation had continued. The Queen Mother had spoken of the great women of history, rulers, mothers of kings, fighters.

"The matrix of society is in its women," she had said. "That is what the word means. Woman is the mother, the womb, not just of the puling, feeble brats she throws out into the world, but of all the forces that hold society together. And a great woman can shape the future, can protect it and let it take form, sometimes even more than a great man. You will be such a woman.

"You have wealth, beauty, brains, and above all, spirit. You will marry where your gifts will do the most good. A person who has a destiny must live up to its demands, or be accursed."

Athalie remembered now how her words had filled her with a sense of purpose and had aroused in her desires and ambitions which she had never before experienced.

Coligny broke into her recollections. "I knew your father well, both as a friend in the old days and a foe in more recent times. As friend, I loved him; as foe, I admired him. But he was not a gay man after your mother died. It was a great loss."

She nodded, feeling a lump in her throat.

"So, you were brought up by your great-aunt, the Abbess of Fontevrault! She is an admirable woman, a woman of conviction."

At this, remembering what the Abbess had said of Coligny: "He is a traitor to his kind, without the excuse of being stupid enough to have been misled," Athalie bit her lip and looked away.

Coligny laughed. "I can imagine my admiration is not reciprocated. You need not be disturbed on my account."

An awkward silence fell. To break it, Athalie turned to Daudet. "So you see, Trophime, your name isn't so bad. You can cheer up, now that you've heard my sad tale."

"That isn't the point. That isn't what's bothering me at all," Daudet replied.

His fierceness surprised Pierre and Athalie, who glanced first at each other, then at Coligny.

"Trophime is justly offended. He was discoursing on a serious subject, and I was rudely closing my ears."

Trophime turned on Coligny and said, "I don't care about your rudeness. You can be as rude to me as you want, any time you want, as long as you do something about the matter itself."

Athalie and Pierre looked even more bewildered.

"Now we are being rude to you," Coligny said, turning to them.

"You see, my friend Trophime was telling me that he has heard rumors of threats to assassinate me, reliable rumors — if that's not a contradiction in terms —

and he wants me to leave Court, or at the very least, go to the King and ask for more protection. And I have told him that I am a guest in the King's house and my safety is guaranteed by the King's honor. And that is the end of it."

"The King's honor!" Trophime exclaimed.

"Yes, the King's honor." Coligny spoke the words fiercely.

"But the King can't control his brother Anjou, or the Guises. And if they kill you, his honor won't be tarnished."

"Oh, yes, it will. And he knows it, and they know it. Under the circumstances, they will do nothing, fearing his wrath."

"His wrath is a puny thing."

"You're wrong. You're blinded by your perception of the man, so that you lose sight of his position, which makes the man who fills it great. Anyway, you shouldn't say things like that. And finally," he added wearily, "if there is a risk, which I do not concede, it is a risk which must be taken."

A pensive hush fell on the group. The rain, which after the brief respite had returned in strength, rattled on the wooden roof of their shelter; it was a constant noise which no longer penetrated their consciousness.

When a raucous "Halloo!" echoed across the garden, rising above the water's din and piercing their somber thoughts, all four of them jumped. They turned and gazed across to the arcade opposite, where they could see a figure waving at them.

"Ah, it's young La Renaudie," Coligny observed. "I wondered that he hadn't found us sooner." From a pettier man, the words would have had a sarcastic meaning; coming from Coligny, they passed as a simple statement of fact.

As he returned the wave, he continued, "Don't let's say any more on this matter. La Renaudie is so faithful. He is like a shadow already and would cling to me even more if he became convinced my life were in danger."

They heard a muffled roar and Coligny waved again, invitingly.

"You know," he went on, "for all his debonair affectations, he's quite a worrier. That's what makes him such a reliable subordinate."

Of Coligny's auditors, only Athalie seemed unperturbed by Maurice's arrival and Coligny's praise of him. Though Pierre would have preferred to remain alone with Athalie, he did not mind sharing her company with Coligny and Daudet because he liked them, but to accept Maurice's arrival with good grace was more than his sangfroid was capable of. He fidgeted, frowning at his feet to hide his irritation. Daudet's face showed a comic mixture of emotions. Since meeting Maurice, he had developed a hearty dislike for him, but because he feared this antipathy might be nothing more than a disguise for jealousy of Maurice's success with the Admiral, he strove manfully to suppress it, or at least to cover it up with a show of bonhomie.

La Renaudie dashed the forty yards to the sheltered basin and came up to the others, puffing excitedly. He shook himself like a dog, for even his short exposure to the elements had left his hair running with water.

"So here you are, hiding away," he said, creating the impression of an exclusive conversation with the Admiral. "I can understand why. It would be hard to resist the company of the prettiest woman at Court." Without looking at Athalie, he sidled up to her and put his arm around her waist.

Pierre clenched his fists and turned away. If Athalie had noticed, she would have been gratified, but she was too flustered to see beyond her own embarrassment.

For Maurice to take liberties with her was not unusual. He often touched her in apparent playfulness. Even so, it always startled her and left her unable to decide on the spur of the moment whether to be offended or flattered. She gave a nervous, meaningless laugh to cover her discomposure.

"What goes on in the real world?" Coligny asked, unriled by Maurice's teasing.

"The King is fretting about your absence."

"Anything important?"

"Oh, no. He only wants to play horsey with his Papa."

Coligny opened his mouth to reprove Maurice, but before he could speak, the young man continued. "Actually, I think he's bored. Being cooped up like this is getting on everyone's nerves. He was talking of going hunting."

"Ugh!" came spontaneously from everyone's lips.

"So I think we'd better find something else to amuse him."

Coligny stood in quiet thoughtfulness for a moment before speaking. "Come on, then," he said. "If duty calls, we must obey."

Coligny and Maurice hurried through the rain to the cloistered walk and set off more slowly toward the covered bridge. Trophime thought of following, but gave up the idea, shrugging listlessly. Pierre and Athalie glanced sidelong at his unhappy face and looked at each other helplessly.

"Cheer up, Trophime," Athalie said, but without much conviction.

"I'm so worried," he replied. "I don't know what to do. There's nothing I can do, if he won't do anything. When first he came here, he was cautious enough, but now, he's fallen for their ploys with a vengeance. Because the King throws himself at him and calls him 'Father,' and because the persecutions have let up, he thinks the days of strife are over. Unless we watch him all the time, he wanders off alone without a care. Walsingham, Montpensier, everyone has warned him, but he simply repeats that his trust is in God and the King. Do you know his children have left La Rochelle to go home to Châtillon, and he has even sent for his wife to come to Court?"

Oh, God! thought Athalie, do I have to report this conversation to the Queen Mother? And what would she make of it? Would she consider the Protestants seditious to doubt the King's word? Surely not. Perhaps it would be good to warn her, and yet I can't believe there is any threat. Coligny must be right. He is safe under the King's roof. Pierre's voice disturbed her reflections. "Listen, Trophime," he was saying, "I'll talk to my father about this. He'll be able to assess the situation accurately, and do something about it, if anything needs doing."

205

Trophime's face brightened. "Would you, Pierre? That would be the very thing. Your father is one of the few people with any say about what goes on here that we feel we can trust. Without his prestige behind him, I doubt His Majesty could hold the fanatics in check."

"You mean our fanatics. What about your own fanatics?"

"Oh, well. Well, yes — we do have fanatics. At least, I suppose you could look at them that way, though at times, I half believe they're right. But no one would do anything without the Admiral's consent, at least not now that he's doing something instead of just sitting around in La Rochelle, and nobody could call Coligny a fanatic."

"That's true. Well, you'd better tell me all about it. My father will want chapter and verse before he does anything."

"First, I overheard a Guise hanger-on, I don't know which one, and that cousin of de Retz's, Jerome de Gondi, talking about having a mandate from the Pope to assassinate the Admiral and having Spanish money to pay for the work. And then, Augustin Pascal — we're not really friends anymore, but we still talk, sometimes, you know — he was telling me that Coligny's death is considered a sure thing among the Guises."

"How does he know?" Pierre asked. "The Guises aren't even here. They're having some gathering of the clan at Joinville."

"I know. Maybe he was talking to the same Guisard I overheard. He was here on some errand or other."

"Is that all?"

"What do you mean by that? Do you need a corpse to prove that there's danger?"

"No. There's always danger. But rumors don't add or subtract anything to the reality, which any man of sense can see. That's what my father will say. I just know it."

"Christ's blood! Your kind won't ever —"

"Come on, Trophime. I said I'd do it and I will, for whatever good it does. And I like it better when you extol the moderation of my people than when you berate us for blind bigotry."

Trophime gave a feeble laugh.

"Now," Pierre continued, "the Duchess de la Roque and I were about to pay court to the cabbages in the other garden. You're welcome to come."

"Why on earth?"

Athalie broke in, "Because it's too cold to go on sitting here, and we have to do something to pass the time 'til dinner, and anyway, it would be fun."

"No, thanks! I'll carry the lute back, shall I?"

He swung the instrument over his shoulder and went off, following in Coligny's footsteps.

The rain had stopped, and a pale sun had appeared. Puddles between the waterlogged flowerbeds gleamed brightly.

As Pierre and Athalie abandoned their shelter, they squelched into the soft, wet sand of the path, but neither noticed, being too fundamentally happy for the moment to mind minor discomfort.

Gently, Pierre put his hand under Athalie's arm, and led her forward.

Chapter XVII

ondi was taking a bath. Normally, he did not like to bathe except in one of his own houses. It upset the servants, adding the inconvenience of carrying up pots of boiling water from distant kitchens to the other difficulties of maintaining a household away from home. Even though they had no right to be put out, they always were, and their balefulness disturbed his equanimity. And he could not really claim that this bath was a necessity from the point of view of cleanliness; it was just that he longed to feel heat penetrating to the very marrow of his bones, to dispel the chill which seemed endemic to this time and place. After all, he thought, rationalizing his whim, what is the point of carrying around that wooden ark of a tub, if one never uses it?

Whenever Gondi did bathe, he liked to luxuriate in the water until it became quite tepid. Sometimes, he would even prolong his enjoyment by making the servants fetch another steaming cauldron when the water lost its potent warmth. He was not all that interested in washing; what he liked was to relax and let his thoughts flow where they would.

On this occasion, he lolled, his eyes half shut, hoping to feel some cheerful reflection rise to the surface of his consciousness. He was disappointed. Familiar worries nibbled at him like minnows caressing a swimmer's legs.

It was unfair, he thought, for any one individual to be expected to satisfy so many conflicting demands. Despite all his adroitness, he had inevitably become the butt of everyone's hostility: the Protestants, the moderate Catholics who feared he meant to harm the Protestants, and the extreme Catholics who doubted that he ever would. The situation was fraught with possibilities of disaster. He could not satisfy everyone, or even fool everyone into thinking that he was trying to satisfy them. This knowledge tied a knot of anxiety in his innards, which even the soothing waters could not undo. One was so vulnerable, after all.

Out of the vague malaise in which his mind weltered, there emerged the sharp recollection of a nasty incident, which, only recently, had hammered home that very point. The rain having let up one afternoon some days since, he had gone for a stroll through the château's spacious forecourt, not wishing to miss a rare opportunity to stretch his legs without getting soaked. Threatening clouds and a humid chill proclaimed the respite a temporary one, something to be taken advantage of on the spur of the moment or not at all. He had enjoyed wandering along, savoring the smells, the sights, the sounds of the teeming camp of armed men, letting them refresh him, loosening the bonds of the claustrophobic life of the château.

All across the courtyard, soldiers were huddled in groups around small fires, heating kettles of watery stew, from which rose steaming an acrid smell of boiling, rancid meat. He had noted the segregation of the Protestants in their dark clothes from the men who wore the splashy liveries of the various Catholic lords, and he had wondered whether the former were keeping to themselves or were being ostracized by a hostile majority. Whichever it was, he had concluded that the configuration of the men demonstrated the absurdity of the King's dream of reconciliation; the lower orders expressed openly the hostility which their betters hugged to their bosoms.

His aimless rambling had taken him past a little gathering, Protestants by their clothing, which had settled under the eaves of the courtyard wall — not for the first time either, judging by the smoke-blackened beams above the fire. He had stopped to watch them, feeling irritated by those beams. While he sympathized with their need for shelter, it was folly to permit so obvious an incendiary risk. He had determined to speak to the steward about it as a matter of principle, though admittedly the risk was not great in weather like this, and had turned to move on, when he had caught a fragment of the Protestants' conversation.

"This mutton tastes like urine."

"And they say French armies eat well!"

Gondi had smiled. The eternal soldiers' lament — how often had he heard it, how often had he uttered it himself.

"You can't tell me a dish like this can't be improved."

"Marinate it."

"You're an idiot. That's supposed to be done before cooking it."

"Well, it can't hurt."

He had watched the two empty a small wine barrel into the kettle.

At this, the entire band, seemingly aroused by enthusiasm for the experiment, had begun to stoke the fire and to rub their hands in an exaggerated mime of hearty appetite and good cheer. As the wet wood smoked, the men, and he with them, had choked and laughed.

Still chuckling, he had thought to move on, when a small contingent of men-at-arms in the livery of the Duke of Anjou had brushed past him. Its leader had turned suddenly, exclaiming loudly, "Phah! What witches' brew is that?"

One of the Protestants had replied with a coarse gesture, "Altar's blood, you papist pig."

In an instant, the two groups had galvanized into action, cloaks swirling, swords and daggers glinting. An Anjou man had bashed over the kettle, whose contents had poured out, purple-red, on the stones, looking for all the world like blood.

Clapping his hand on his sword hilt, Gondi had rushed forward. Suddenly, from behind, a long blade had appeared, flashing between his torso and forearm. He had leapt aside, sweeping his dagger out of its sheath, and hearing, without registering, the noise of his cloak ripping. Turning he had come face to face with a pale youth in nondescript brown clothing, who had met his gaze with a stare of blank bewilderment.

Thinking back on it, he could barely remember stumbling toward the heaving group, yelling, "Stop! You hooligans! Break it up!"

209

He did recall that the mêlée had continued, until putting all his strength into a bellow which rasped the back of his throat, he had repeated, "Stop! In the name of the King, stop!"

A sudden pause had followed, like an involuntary intake of breath. The combatants had greeted his command with astonished looks. Recognizing the Count de Retz, the liveried captain had lowered his blade and slowly, reluctantly, the others had followed suit.

"You know the King's will. You all know the King's will," he remembered saying. "There is to be none of this fighting. We must have peace."

"Peace!" a swarthy Protestant had exclaimed and spat a wad of tobacco onto the ground.

Gondi had turned on him. "You do that one more time and it'll be the last time."

"You think I chew two wads at once?" the other had jeered, to appreciative snickers from his companions. Gondi had gripped his dagger fiercely and stepped forward on the balls of his feet. Then, thinking better of it, he had mastered his anger and turning to the Anjou officer, had pointed out the brown-clad youth. "Arrest this man and take him to the Captain of the Guard. He's to be held 'til I give orders regarding his fate. Take all your men with you." The Anjou men had looked sullenly, first at him, then at the Protestants.

"Go!" he had said with all the firmness he could muster. At last, they had slowly moved away, the brown youth in their midst.

The Protestants had watched the departing men with an undisguised glee which he had found particularly galling; yet, somehow, he had been unable to gather the strength to rebuke them. Instead, he had turned and walked slowly back toward the château. It was then that the reaction had set in. He had realized with a start that his doublet and hose were soaked with sweat which turned clammy as the heat of the moment wore off. His mind had begun to buzz. Am I so careless, to be knifed in the back? He nearly had me. He should have had me. Inarticulate panic had filled him.

He could still remember vividly how he had felt: The terrible thing had been to suffer a fear so all-encompassing that it evoked no images to be faced and conquered. He had felt as if he were submerged by a black wave; he had seen what it would be like to lose everything he had, everything he had grasped and fought for, everything he enjoyed. There would be nothing, no present, no future. He would never possess the things he coveted.

Even on the rack, his assailant had maintained that he had never intended to attack Gondi but had merely stumbled while running forward to join the fight. Gondi had seen to it that he was hanged. You could not tell the truth of it, and anyway, he felt the need to punish the man for the fright he had sustained.

For that matter, Gondi thought, wiggling his toes in the warm water, he was still frightened. Whether he had survived a real assault or merely escaped the blundering of a fool, he had understood, as never before, how vulnerable he was.

210

He could live surrounded by his guards, as Coligny did, at least at Court, but he shuddered at the thought. And in the end, a determined assassin would have his way.

Look at old Guise, whose death his relatives still blamed on Coligny. A whole company of men had not saved him from being shot down in their midst. No, safety lay in not making enemies. Gondi laughed bitterly. Too late for that, my friend, he thought.

Gondi bellowed for more hot water and attempted to get a grip on his fear. Surely, he was being melodramatic. The present rules of the game required everyone to pretend to be friends. Until the farce was played out, the normal cloak-and-dagger activities would be suspended, at least with regard to the dagger part. But was that true?

After all, it seemed that Coligny's life had been threatened, and his followers, for certain, and maybe others, felt that sauce for the goose was sauce for the gander. For sure, the Admiral kept up the courtesies with him, but his suite's enmity hung over him like a fog.

Yes, any threat to Coligny would be laid at Gondi's door, at least in part, whether he had engineered it or not. Any doubts he might have had on that score had been dispelled by his recent run-in with Raymond de Galle. The Count had stomped into Gondi's study, acting like a bear with a sore head. Gondi had been hard put to grasp the substance of his grievance through all the bluster and the bullying.

The conversation had started off with an incoherent report of some row between de Galle and his son, Pierre.

"He had the nerve," de Galle had thundered, "to claim on the basis of these half-baked rumors that he picked up in the guard hall or on the playing fields or God knows where, that there were plans afoot to assassinate the Admiral. As if I would let such a thing happen, implying that I would turn my back on folly and treason and skullduggery and... by God, I won't! And he ought to know it! He is a thoughtless fool, immature, no judgment. Am I not right, de Retz? I mean, anyone with experience — like yourself, for example, knows that I would never stand by and let the King's name be dishonored and the country plunged into civil war again. No, anyone with brains knows that I am foursquare against fanatics.

"I don't care what their reasons are — revenge or religion, I don't care. I've seen what they can do. And young Charles, too, sees the virtue of balance and moderation. If I can take some credit for his understanding, so much the better, but at the very least, I should think that everyone would realize that there'll be no underhandedness and no letting of blood while I'm around. The King has my full support, and he knows it.

"Anyone who forgets will answer to me."

De Galle had broken off and shot Gondi a sly look, totally out of keeping with his supposed hotheadedness. "I mean the Guises, too, you understand. They are not too grand to be called to order. The whole clan is out at Joinville plotting some mischief, something to do with that lunatic, Anjou, I don't doubt. They'd plunge the whole of France into the cauldron of war to avenge one man's death. Well, de Retz, I won't have it. They should bear in mind, my friend, that if they step out of line, they could end up facing not just the Protestants, but all of us who have any sense, any feeling for the broader perspective. I'm sure they understand that, aren't you, de Retz?" And he had gone off, looking suddenly peaceable and pleased with himself, leaving Gondi feeling persecuted.

The irony of it all, Gondi thought, is that if I hadn't taken the situation in hand, Coligny and his people would never have come to Court. Those who opposed his coming have brains enough to blame me for it, while those who were in favor of it don't give me any credit. They are afraid I brought them here to kill them, that's the truth of it, and the others hope that I did and wonder why I'm taking so long about it.

Why, the young King so doubted Gondi's motives that he had as good as ordered him away from Blois at the beginning of Coligny's stay. Gondi had been able to return only after the Queen Mother had brought her son around with her usual mixture of cajolery and force. The memory rankled. Damn it, he thought, I have no designs on Coligny's life. However I might feel about it if my hands were free, it's clear I couldn't sell the idea to the Queen Mother, not now, anyway. That the King should suspect him, and that de Galle should implicitly accuse him, of plotting something that was in fact beyond his power, however much he might wish for it in the long run, filled him with a sense of grievance.

Nor was de Galle's outburst the only time that day Gondi had found himself the object of unjust criticism. Not half an hour after the Duke's visit, the Spanish Ambassador had called on him.

"Don Francés," Gondi had said wearily, "I wish you wouldn't call on me. Her Majesty holds you in such abhorrence that she views talking with you much as she would communing with the Devil. Forgive me for saying this, but it is better for me to be blunt than to mislead you."

An ambassador must be thick-skinned, and Álava was more so than most. He had waved aside Gondi's comparison and come directly to the point.

"I am King Philip's envoy. You must receive me. Or would your Mistress prefer to receive me herself?"

Shaking his head sadly, Gondi had replied, "We managed fine with your secretary when you did us the favor of absenting yourself. No, I'm sorry. It's just that these are difficult times. You make them more difficult by coming here. That's all."

"These are not difficult times," the Spaniard had broken out, "or if they are, it is because you make them so. These are wonderful times. You have the heretic in your grasp. You have coaxed him out of his stronghold — God knows how, for he is no fool, I'll give him that. But what was the point, if you do not execute him?

"My Master writes to me time and again. What are they waiting for? The man is a heretic and a traitor. He awaits the hand of justice, both God's justice and the

212

King's. The King's majesty and the Faith demand it. Everything demands it. Why do they wait? He asks me again and again. And what's more, hear this, my dear Count, he tells me the Holy Father himself asks the same question. And what is the answer? What am I to say to my Master? I thought you were a man of clear vision and decisive action, but I have misjudged you, perhaps..."

"Oh, for God's sake, Álava, cut out the melodrama, can't you? You know the situation as well as I do. What you suggest is unthinkable. The Admiral came here only because the King and his brothers and the Queen Mother herself guaranteed his safety."

"A trifle!"

"Well, it might be a trifle under some circumstances, but as it is, the reason why the King arranged the guarantees was that he wanted them lived up to."

"A trifle!"

"And the Queen Mother wants it, too! What can I say? Don't be obtuse, man."

"Then, I can only ask: Why did you bring him here?"

"Because... because it was better that way. Look, I don't have to explain myself to you. Now, get out!"

Álava had left, but his question had remained. Well, he had brought Coligny here because the Queen Mother wanted him to be a power, a balance against the Guises. That was it, wasn't it? But was it a mistake? Wasn't her policy of playing one power against another, the Protestants against the Guises, a policy of weakness?

Wasn't the Spaniard right that the country would be better off if the canker of dissension were cut out and destroyed? But the Queen Mother's weakness was not voluntary, after all. Did it leave her any choices? Had he understood what she really wanted? And could he make her want something else?

He ran his hands through his hair, making it stand up in wet points like little spears of grass. He rose abruptly from the water and stepped over the edge of the tub, droplets spraying around him in concentric circles. Two servants rushed forward and wound him around in a downy sheet. When he was thoroughly cocooned, they began to rub him down as they would a horse. He paid them no mind, lost as he was in his perennial struggle to understand the Queen Mother's mind.

He remembered the interview that he had had with her after she had received Coligny on his arrival at Court.

She had been ill and had given audience in bed, propped up against a mound of pillows, in a satin bed jacket of a deep rose color, elaborate with lace and frills. At least, he had thought, she doesn't carry her affectation of black into the bedchamber.

Coligny had left, but Gondi had lingered on, knowing that, despite her fatigue, she wanted company. Her face had looked worn and old, with new lines of irritability, or was it pain, etched across it.

She was quite sick, he had known that, but had felt more fear than sympathy. Her illnesses, which seemed more frequent now than in the past, always terrified him. If she went, where would he be? Even when she was merely incapacitated, he felt like a man adrift, lacking the constant support she gave him in public, however much she upbraided him in private. The chaos that would follow her departure did not bear thinking of. The young King was simply not up to it. He, too, was always sick. In fact, his illnesses seemed to alternate with hers. And Anjou? Perhaps he wasn't prey to the physical frailties that had beset his oldest brother, the late King François, and which were now attacking King Charles, but he suffered from — How should he put it? — maladies of the spirit. His lapses into religious fervor would have embarrassed the most ardent believers, even if they had been fairly constant. No one could watch him roaming the palace wild-eyed from fasting without doubting his sanity, but interspersed as the maladies were with bursts of riotous living and physical excesses of every kind, they made no sense to anyone.

Now, if only young Charles, or Anjou when he succeeded him, would enjoy his hunting or his whoring, or whatever he pleased, and let him, Gondi, assume the responsibilities of rulership, then he could contemplate the Queen Mother's demise with equanimity. But neither of her sons liked or trusted him enough.

He had broken the heavy silence that had followed Coligny's withdrawal from Catherine's bedchamber by voicing to her what was uppermost in his mind. "Your son has packed me off. Not that I mind. I'm just as glad. Sometimes, I feel like Daniel among the lions."

"You've nothing to fear. After all, you did as much as anyone to bring Coligny to Court."

"Yes, but if they'd known, they wouldn't have come."

"Perhaps. Don't underestimate the Admiral. I want you back as soon as possible."

"When I'm invited back."

"Oh, come! You can't stand on ceremony with kings. Anyway, Charles doesn't have the memory of a parakeet."

"So you say."

"And who should know better? You work for me, and you'll do as you're told. I'll fix it." She had sighed, both wearily and petulantly. Silence had fallen again.

At last she had said, "And so the Admiral has come to Court!"

Since Gondi could not think of any intelligent response to this truism, he had remained silent.

"And what has it done for us?" she had resumed more loudly. Her voice had sounded like a rumble of thunder; Gondi had cringed in anticipation of the storm.

"That contract you negotiated with him — you might as well have thrown in the crown jewels. You gave him everything else. He's allowed to go about with a small army, like a prince. Signed promises from every member of the royal family

214

— even me — that we will protect every hair on his head. All the King's troops removed from La Rochelle. My God!"

Her voice had risen and she had spat out the oath quite savagely.

"It was all as Your Majesty agreed," he had pointed out miserably. "What else could I do, after you let things get out of hand?"

That was unfair. It seemed that even she had realized it, for she had continued in a pleasanter tone.

"And now we have the Guises — the whole lot of them — getting together at Joinville and plotting God knows what." Her voice had risen again. "And I can't even blame them."

"Precisely, Madame."

"Precisely, what?"

"We needed Coligny, because of the Guises, and he wouldn't come without the contract. Or do you wish to be governed by the Cardinal of Lorraine and his strongman nephew?"

"I'll be governed by no one," she had said, but her defiant words had sounded tired and sad. "The Admiral must play his part. I know we need him, but he must help us."

"Speak to him."

"Ye Gods! Didn't you see what he was like just now? Full of courteous words, but underneath, like a brick wall that I must batter my head against. He doesn't trust me — nor I him. But I will speak to him again — again and again, if necessary. I will have the marriage, and the marriage will bring us peace."

That was it, of course. That was what she wanted. But could she get it? Could she have the marriage? And would the marriage bring peace? Not if anyone else had any say about it.

He shook his head. It was time to dress for the final interview between the Admiral and the Queen Mother, for today, the Protestants were leaving. Would she be able to bring it off at the last minute?

His valet held out a doublet of deep blue-green, sober and suitable. Gondi laughed suddenly.

"No, Armand. No sad clothes. I'll have the russet with the orange sashings. By God, it will do me proud to be a peacock among the crows!"

* * *

The Queen Mother still looks ill, Gondi thought, but she would die rather than let an adversary know that she feels weakness or suffers pain. She sits forward on her chair deliberately, keeping her back ramrod straight without support from behind, as if it will prove that she still has the resilience of youth. And Coligny? Maturity sits well on him. His face shows the wisdom that comes with years, but his body has not fallen into the flabbiness that usually accompanies it.

Has he outlasted her? She is ten years older, after all. But no, she is not finished yet. She may be a madam now, instead of a whore, but it would be a mistake to think she has retired. They are old adversaries; the balance between them goes back and forth, one up, one down, one down, one up, undulating like a wave. But what is she up to? She can't believe the pap she is feeding him, surely. Well, she made it clear enough that she is calling the shots. I need do nothing but sit back and be all smiles.

"The marriage is the thing," Catherine was saying. "There are two ways to conduct the affairs of state — by wars and by marriages — and marriages are by far the preferred way. They are always less costly and their gains tend to be more lasting. The heritage of the great Hapsburg, the Emperor Charles, shows us that. Why did his dominions span the world? Because his grandparents made felicitous marriages — 'Bella gerant alii, tu, felix Austria, nube,' as the saying went."

Gondi groaned inwardly. Coligny forced a forbearing smile.

"But we don't have to look to foreigners for our models. France is what it is, more because of the marriages than the wars of our ancestors."

Our ancestors, that's rich, thought Gondi.

"Madame," said Coligny, "in simpler times, simpler methods may have been effective. In difficult times such as these..."

She waved a hand and interrupted airily, "All times are difficult, my dear friend. People always think their own times are more difficult than what went before. That's human nature.

"Now, I grant you, by the marriage of the Princess Marguerite to Henri de Navarre, we are trying to accomplish something a little different from mere territorial aggrandizement. Indeed, since Navarre will remain unassimilated, there will be no territorial gain. But, if the marriage accomplishes what I hope, the gain will be infinitely greater and more valuable than mere material enrichment.

"You know, my dear Admiral, how I have sought for years to bring about a compromise between those of your — er — Religion and those of our Faith. How I pinned my hopes on the Colloquy at Poissy ten years ago exactly, do you realize? It failed, but I have never given up hope of a reconciliation. We will bring all factions together, and we will crown the union by the one lasting and unmistakable symbol of two entities becoming one — marriage!"

"Madame, there are underlying differences, which will not disappear by uttering an incantation over them. We must have protection; the toleration edict must be enforced; and the freedoms that were promised us must be ensured."

"Yes, yes, of course..."

"No, Madame, don't wave your hands, as if the matter were settled and can be lightly brushed aside. Ten years of antagonism — of bloodshed and undying hatred — cannot be so easily overlooked. I regret it as much as you, but violence breeds violence, a momentum builds up which must be channeled, rather than ignored. You cannot summon mortal foes to a combat and at the last minute ask them to sit down to a banquet. They will cut each other's throats with the cutlery. No, it is necessary to replace the enmity of Frenchmen against Frenchmen with a common foe that all Frenchmen can hate, the Spanish. Your son, the King, sees that."

"You have persuaded him of it. You have filled his poor little head with dreams of easy glory, as if he could play David to Philip's Goliath. I am trying to persuade you, now, that your view is shortsighted. We do not have the means to defeat Spain."

"Not in Spain perhaps, but in the Netherlands."

"The Netherlands are Spain. Philip will never let the Netherlands go."

"Madame, hear me out. I believe The Enterprise is feasible. The Netherlands are not Spain. We can strike fast and brutally. I agree with you, the outcome is not sure. It never is. But..." he waved her to silence, "but my hands are tied. That is what you must understand. The Dutch are being persecuted for their Religion far more viciously than even we have been. You talked of symbols before. Well, to my people, the Dutch are a symbol of religious intolerance, and the only symbol of peace that they would understand would be a united front of Frenchmen, of all beliefs, against the Spaniard."

"Come, you don't feel that way. What are the Dutch to you?"

Coligny's face reddened. "I do feel that way. You do me an injustice. But what I am trying to make you understand, Madame, is that it doesn't matter how I feel. There are those in my party who will not give up The Enterprise, and I must represent them if I am to hold my people together. You see that I am being frank with you."

"Nonsense. My dear Admiral, you are their leader. Indeed, you are the only conceivable leader that they have. Young Navarre can't hold a candle to your experience. They must follow you and do as you say."

"Your Majesty, we are both getting old. Young blood will have its way. Your sons, Navarre, Condé, my hotheads — all their youth and vigor is what fights wars and what wins them. We cannot hold them back. If we try to dam up their energy, they will overwhelm us."

"War, war, war, all you think of is war. It always seems that men want to make war. But I am in control here. You will see. And you must be guided by me."

"Madame, I cannot do the impossible. The course of history — ten years of fighting — cannot be dammed up. It can be deflected, perhaps, as I have suggested, but it cannot be held back, not without flooding the countryside."

"I could call that statement treason."

"You can call it anything you like. I have been branded a traitor before. Names have never changed anything. I do what I must do. That is all.

"If you want the marriage of the princess, your darling daughter, and young Navarre to symbolize a union, the union itself must exist. I have shown you how I think unity of purpose can be achieved. If you can give support to the Netherlands Enterprise, I would be able to support the marriage with all my heart."

"You would barter with me, as if I were a fishmonger's wife," she retorted angrily. Coligny stared into space, an implacable look in his eyes.

A silence fell over the group. At last, Catherine sighed and looked beseechingly at Gondi. Taking his cue, Gondi intervened for the first time.

217

"Admiral, it is not that we are against your Enterprise as a matter of principle. You have spoken as a practical man. But we, too, must be practical; we, too, have our constraints. One of these is that there can be no successful invasion of the Netherlands without the backing of Elizabeth of England. Her active backing, I mean, mind you, not pretty words and fair promises. Then, we could see our way to proceeding with a fair chance of success."

"It would help, certainly," Coligny assented.

"We are in agreement, you see. Now, we must push forward with diplomatic overtures to England and diplomatic overtures to Navarre, so that the two matters can go forward hand in hand."

Coligny nodded reluctantly.

"Well, you must go to His Majesty and take your leave of him. We will accompany you, will we not, Madame?" Gondi stood and offered his arm gallantly to assist the Queen Mother in rising.

Coligny's face expressed reserved pleasure. He would have preferred to dispense with their company, but etiquette required that he appear gratified by their courtesy.

* * *

"I wish to God you weren't leaving," the young King repeated. He looked up suspiciously. "You aren't leaving because you feel threatened, are you? I have summoned the Guises, and they've agreed to come with no more than the usual retinue. They know my will. I want the hatchet buried between your House and theirs. You are willing, I know, and they will be, too, or face my wrath. But I wish you wouldn't leave."

"Your Majesty, I must go to Châtillon. You know how my home was ruined in the last war. Now that you have given me the chance, I must try to put it in order."

"Oh, I understand. It's just that I don't feel we've accomplished anything."

"On the contrary, Your Majesty," Gondi broke in smoothly, hastening to preclude Coligny from giving his version of the preceding conversation. "It's all agreed. We will work wholeheartedly toward the marriage of Madame your sister and young Navarre and toward putting together a feasible expedition into the Netherlands — one which has the backing of England. Isn't that right, Admiral?" Coligny nodded.

"Well, yes, that's excellent," Charles said, "but we were all agreed on that before, I thought." Gondi and the Queen Mother exchanged worried glances. "What I meant was, I wanted to get the Guise question all settled."

"Your Majesty," Coligny replied, "if all goes as it should, I will be back soon. I won't be gone for long." The Admiral bowed low, his cap in his hand.

Charles hurried forward and held the older man by the shoulders. With a voice that trembled slightly, he said, "I hope so. Promise you'll come when I summon you."

218

"I am your faithful servant, never doubt it." Coligny bowed again, then bent to Catherine, nodded to Gondi, and strode from the room. Charles collapsed onto a chair, looking disconsolate. Standing on each side, the Queen Mother and Gondi talked to each other over his head.

"Well, that went as well as could be expected," said the Queen Mother.

"I thought your discourse on marriage as the alpha and the omega was well — a bit much, perhaps."

"Nothing ventured, nothing gained. I thought I might be able to distract him from his fixation."

"All you achieved was to make me afraid that you'd started believing in easy solutions."

She shrugged. "No, naivete is not my forte. I don't know where my sons get it from."

Between them, Charles gave a start, stood up, and faced his mother, turning his back on Gondi. "The Admiral is right about the Netherlands. You'd see it, if you weren't a woman. This is a kingdom, not a shop. We can pull off a coup in the Netherlands that will make me famous." He turned away, and his lower lip trembled. Gondi wondered for an instant if he would cry, but he continued, "God, I'll miss him. He didn't treat me like a child. He spoke to me as a man speaks to a man, as a general advises a King." His voice trailed away miserably at the end.

Gondi could see the anger in Catherine's face and was surprised by the studied calm of her voice. "No one is saying you can't be the savior of the Netherlands. But you will, of course, have thought about it a lot and have realized what a major project it is. You aren't planning a little skirmish, after all, but something that will have lasting effects.

"You will need a great army, with strong backing by the fleet, and allies, most important, allies. But you'll have thought of all this and talked it over with everyone — not just the Admiral and his henchmen, but your brother, who is the Lieutenant-General of the Kingdom, after all, and the English Ambassador, and the envoys of the various German princes."

Charles sat back down and cradled his head in his hand.

"Well," she concluded, "we'll have to keep working on putting the whole thing together. But you must not forget, my son, that you can't declare war without the consent of the Lieutenant-General and the Council. You can't do it, and it would be folly in any event."

Charles said nothing.

"Promise me that you will take no steps that might lead to war without my consent."

Silence.

"Promise," she said harshly.

"All right," he replied at last and stood up again with an irritable gesture.

"You need my help, you know," she continued, "all of our help."

He looked at her hopelessly and mumbled, "I promised some of the men I'd go hunting with them. Never let the courtiers get bored, that's what you always say." He sneered at her unpleasantly.

She overlooked his hostility and said with real anxiety, "How can you ride out in the pouring rain? You'll catch your death of cold!"

"I don't need your consent to go hunting, do I?" Without waiting for an answer, he turned on his heel and left the room.

Catherine sent Gondi a look that was a strange combination of desperation and resignation. "He's hopeless," she said at last.

She walked over to the window and looked down into the courtyard. "God, will it never stop raining?"

Chapter XVIII

rom the outset, the evening was bizarre, and that may explain what happened later. When a hundred or so of the ladies and gentlemen of the Court approached the supper table that night, they made, as always, the rapid calculations about seating that protocol required, which any experienced courtier could do instinctively, noting at a glance who was absent and who was present, and the exact order of precedence of the latter. In the same moment, they discovered an astonishing fact: None of the royal family's most prominent members was present. This was as odd, and almost as disorienting, as if the laws of gravity had been suspended for a few hours. The royal family was the sun to the Court's solar system: without it, every courtier knew, his life would have neither purpose nor order.

Charles was, after all, king. His whim was law, his love was the ultimate prize. The Duke of Anjou eventually would be king, so everyone believed, though no one dared to speak the thought out loud; the farsighted valued Anjou's favor, even over that of the King. Behind them both was the Queen Mother, whose preference was harder to come by and in some ways more problematical than that of any of her children. Yet even those who despaired of or were indifferent to her good opinion were subject to her will, for she imposed her manners as law. It was the royalty who gave coherence and a certain decorum to a society which would otherwise have been essentially chaotic, being governed for the most part by the ambitions of its members rather than by any moral code.

Like the ancients with their gods, the ambitious among the nobility of France aimed both to placate and to exploit the King and his relatives. To obtain a foothold in the affections of any member of the royal family was a courtier's first goal; to progress from the ambit of its lesser to its greater members, without offense to either, was his long-term ambition; to ogle at the successes and laugh at the failures of others as they clambered up the same treacherous slope to social prominence provided the greatest and most constant amusement of his life. But tonight, the social athletes found that the game had been suspended. The Queen Mother was ill; the King was hunting; the Duke of Anjou was fasting. They could not even console themselves with lesser royal luminaries. Princess Margot was sulking, while Charles' young Austrian Queen refused to appear in solitary splendor, whether because of shyness or a sense of superiority, no one knew.

Thus, the table was presided over by the youngest of the Valois royals, Monsieur the King's brother, Hercule-François, Duke d'Alençon. Though he was plainly thrilled to be, for once, the center of attention, his presence counted for little to those in the know, who had long since concluded that however easily they could scramble into his good grace, it would not be worth the effort. Indeed, the true cognoscenti had known that this night the supper would not merit their attention and had found better uses for their time elsewhere.

The absence of the Court dignitaries created an unusual atmosphere at table. The unexpected truce in the struggle for advancement took the edge off the evening's amusements, but it also lifted the restrictions that protocol and fear of giving offense normally imposed. A kind of juvenile hilarity slowly took possession of the group, which, as the meal progressed, took on a reckless cast. The Queen Mother frowned on unmannerly drunkenness; in her absence, some of the young blades took the liberty of letting their wine go to their heads. Their raucous mirth gradually infected the others, with the result that the meal was noisier and more ribald than any in recent memory. Everyone seemed eager to throw off the anxious sobriety of the Admiral's recent visit and fill the drafty gloom of the dining hall with mirth.

Divided by a row of pillars into halves, each covered by a wooden, barreled ceiling, the hall was magnificently suited to pompous occasions but inappropriately vast for supper served on a smaller scale. The table ran along one side in front of a fireplace with a high, sloping chimney supported by columns, which, notwithstanding its pretensions, gave out, disappointingly, only a modest heat, since the better part of its warmth was dissipated and lost, fanning out undirected and rising to the heights of the ceiling. The blaze cast a circle of brightness around the diners while the rest of the hall lay in obscurity; the wall torches, flickering and smoking, seemed to throw more shadows than light. The bright, slow evenings of summer were long gone.

At the center of the table, his back to the fire, sat young Alençon. His knobby, pockmarked face radiated impish glee. Athalie occupied the place of honor but found it more intimidating than edifying. Pierre faced Alençon, while his wife graced the prince's left.

Rather than permitting envy of Athalie to corrode her gratification at being so near the table's center, Anne consoled herself by occupying the royal youth's attentions as fully as she could. No game was too petty to be worthy of her snares. Hercule-François was more than happy to attend to her, for he found Athalie poor company. Anne was vivacious and frankly titillating; in contrast, Athalie, in her shyness, seemed quiet and demure.

Hercule-François, Duke d'Alençon, did not object to girls being quiet, but at this time in his life, the high point of his adolescent prurience, he found demureness insufferable. Ignoring Athalie, he talked to Anne, and past Anne to his friend Brantôme, seated further down across the table to his left.

Pierre de Bourdeille, Abbé and Seigneur de Brantôme, a man nearly twice the Prince's age, was a sardonic sycophant. He spiced the cloying platitudes of adulation with bittersweet sarcasm, so that his fawning was at least amusing and sometimes almost convincing.

Brantôme was a man with the gift of being in the right place at the right time. Rome had received him at the election and coronation of Pius IV. He had attended Charles' crowning in '61 as a matter of course. As one who escorted Mary Stuart, the exiled Queen, to her Scottish homeland, he had stood by her side as the ship left French shores and listened to her bewail the loss of her beloved France.

He had witnessed the assassination of the late Duke de Guise, Henri's father. Spain, Morocco, Portugal, Malta, he had seen them all, and like every knight of renown, had wielded arms in the major conflicts of his times, but the reputation his prowess on the field had merited was as nothing beside that gained by his prowess in bed.

In short, Brantôme knew everyone, had been everywhere, had done everything — or so he asked his listeners to believe. Hercule-François did believe it. He camouflaged his desire to ape his friend's every act by teasing him unmercifully; nonetheless, the desire was there.

"Eh, Brantôme," the Prince said, his mouth full of food, "there's nothing like wine to liven a party, is there? We should have tried its effects on Monsieur the Admiral's cohorts. A good spree might have loosened things up. But no," he drew himself up to exaggerated erectness, "we all had to be good boys. Navarre's sour dam is to be made to believe that the Court of France is a safe place for children. Well, I warrant it won't work. Madame my sister will be married, if and when they get what they want — every last item — and not before. So, wine was the only hope. It might have made them forget things. Wine makes me forget a lot."

He leaned toward Anne more than was necessary. "Silly, really, worrying about a boy. A girl, maybe, but what can a boy learn that isn't useful?"

Belatedly addressing the first topic, Brantôme commented, "Wine, my Prince, is a funny commodity. It makes a gathering seem livelier, but to my mind, wit is the life of a party, and wine is the enemy of wit. I'll wager no one here will remember tomorrow anything that was said tonight. That being so, what's the point of saying anything?"

"Ah, Brantôme, my dear friend, never fear. Your gems will not go unappreciated. Tomorrow, the swine will wear pearls." Alençon gave a guttural laugh and reached for a pig's hock from the central platter.

"Anyway," Alençon continued, "you should consider it a challenge. You're a gladiator who must keep Caesar amused while fighting a poor opponent, or Caesar will be angry. Come on, Brantôme, give us a story. Tales which even the besotted will remember."

Brantôme scowled. The near-empty platter with its congealed grease was replaced with another, heavy with roasted shanks of game.

The meats were hot in spices, though tepid in temperature. It was a long way from spit to trencher, but this was a common problem. The guests would have been more startled than pleased to be served food that sizzled or steamed. Brantôme helped himself and gnawed busily to conceal his annoyance.

"Speaking of wine," Alençon continued, "I bought a goblet the other day, the likes of which I'll wager even you haven't seen, Brantôme. Solid gold — that merely added to the price, not the interest — all covered, the cup, the base, the stem, with figures, and guess what the figures were doing?"

223

He looked around expectantly. Every eye was fixed on him. Listening intently from his distant seat, Maurice ran his tongue around his lips, and withdrawing it, remained with his lips half-parted.

Brantôme, who disliked having anyone steal his thunder, cleaned his bone with care before replying. "Knowing you, my Prince, I would guess that it depicted that activity by which a cock puts a chick in the egg, or a goat puts the horns on a nanny's billy, or..."

"You have it, and in every posture known to man. I think it even has a few that the industrious and resourceful Arétin overlooked."

Alençon turned a malicious look on Athalie. "Your uncle has a fine example of Arétin's book. You must have seen it among his Italian works."

Athalie shook her head.

"No? And yet, you look like a reader to me."

"Yes, Monsieur," she replied gravely, "reading is a great pleasure, but there's little time for it."

"Mm. I find little time for it, too. But Arétin is an easy book — all pictures. You ask your uncle for it. I know he took the Countess his wife through it, picture by picture."

The rumble of merriment which had echoed the exchange burst into a clap of laughter. Pierre's chuckle ended in a smile directed at Athalie. He wondered if she could possibly be ignorant of that encyclopedia of lewdness which had been the rage of the season. He doubted that the puzzled innocence of manner with which she nodded to the Prince could be feigned. He glanced at his wife, who was still laughing, her open mouth showing small sharp teeth. She had been given a copy by an admirer who, he was confident, had hoped to try out some of its poses with her. The giver had no doubt thought she would hide the book, but she had not bothered. Briefly, Pierre laughed aloud. He was glad she had left it lying about, for he had found it both enjoyable and instructive.

Anne stopped laughing and sent Pierre a look that was both challenging and inviting. Abruptly, he felt angry, and irrationally, directed the anger at Athalie. She is, he thought, ridiculously out of touch, excessively wrapped up in her own ideas, obstinately naive.

"Now, I've an idea about my goblet," Alençon was saying. "I'll invite all the prettiest demoiselles to sup with me, and there'll be wonderful things to eat — asparagus and morels, truffles and artichokes, pumpkin pasties, the crests of chanticleers and their privy parts, chard, and the hot little milk thistles that donkeys eat, all the things my friend Brantôme tells me are good to whet the appetite — but for drinking wine, there'll be nothing but my goblet. The dainty advocates of modesty will have to go thirsty or renounce their principles, but those who love life and live love will drink to their hearts' content.

"You'll drink nectar from my cup, won't you, Madame?"

Anne dimpled with a smile that skillfully blended sophisticated appreciation with an appearance of coyness.

"And you, Mademoiselle?" he asked Athalie, hardly caring whether she would understand and be insulted, or would once again play stooge to his barbs.

She looked at him steadily as she replied. "I would come, for your wish is almost a command. And yes, I would drink. Your cup, if it does not leak, will serve wine as well as another. Its images will not defile the drinker."

Brantôme stopped sucking his fingers for a moment and looked at Athalie with sudden interest. "But do you not think, Mademoiselle, that knowledge defiles, some knowledge, in some cases?" he asked.

She paused. "No. I don't think knowledge defiles. What is, is, and it must be better to know it than not."

"I think you are wrong," he replied. "Indeed, I know you are wrong, but it is right that you should think as you do, for youth should seek knowledge everywhere."

"Even at the risk of being defiled?" she asked.

"Oh, yes. I never said purity was the highest value."

"But, Brantôme," the Prince burst in, "you said yourself the other day that a husband should think twice before teaching his wife Arétin's poses, for once she learns them she will want to show off her skills to others. By your own argument, then, knowledge is an evil in such a case."

"For the husband, surely, but not for the wife, nor necessarily for society." His eyes twinkled. "If all the wives were kept pure by their husbands, what would we unmarried men do?"

"Agreed," Hercule-François laughed, "but not everyone feels that way. There are those who say that the man who puts horns on a husband deserves death — aye, and the wife, too."

"Those who speak such rubbish are all husbands, Sir," Brantôme replied, "and even the husbands are not unanimous. There are many who are happy to give and take, to poach on another's preserves while others poach on his."

"But the law will not punish those husbands who take vengeance on adulterers, so to that extent, society agrees with angry cuckolds."

"How can society condemn what is so common? Not that there are no women who hold themselves for one man, but..." Brantôme spread his fingers in a leveling gesture, "...female nature is such that, given its way, matrons would prefer to be mounted by more than one rider. Not just matrons either. Maidens, unless they are curbed, will accept a cavalier or two."

Athalie watched Brantôme's face, fascinated in spite of herself. It was flushed and animated and bore the marks of a certain conflict of emotions. It was as if part of the man went out to his audience, caressing them, leading them, and reveling in their appreciation, while part of him took his knowledge of their foibles and cherished it in secret, laughing at them.

It was a face well worth watching and a safe place on which to direct her gaze. She dared not look at Pierre or Anne. They had introduced her to this perilous world of lust and love, Anne who was what Brantôme described and Pierre who had shown her what she herself could be. She felt that if she looked at either of them, her own face would attract all eyes, and she would have to mold it into a form of hypocritical sternness to keep it from revealing her confused longings. Instead, she studied Brantôme, schooling her face to an air of reserved interest.

"And so," Brantôme was continuing, "a husband can be cuckolded by the same wife twice."

"Surely more than twice," Hercule-François said. "There is no limit to the horns a man can be made to wear when his wife gallops away from him. What's the song?" He hummed loudly and not well, then warbled, "Five horns shall he wear, who thinks his wife is true, though fair." The Prince hummed again, thrumming his fingers impatiently. "One horn has he..." he groped for the words.

Brantôme interrupted the attempt at song. "I meant that a man can be cuckolded in two ways, in the bud and in the flower, once by marrying a maiden who is no virgin, and again, when the maiden, now wedded, proves faithless."

Anne reached a delicate hand across the table toward Brantôme. "Madame?" he said ironically.

"That's merely silly, Sir. I was married twice. Is my second lord thereby cuckolded?"

"Thereby... thereby," Brantôme repeated, exchanging a delighted glance with the Prince. Turning again to Anne, he replied, "Some would say so, Madame, though most would agree that he need bear no shame from that."

"Tush, man," Alençon said, in tones of mock reproof, "you are not gallant. Discretion better fits the occasion than valor." He glanced knowingly from Anne to Brantôme, before looking pointedly at Pierre. Pierre's stillness and his flared nostrils were his only signs of wrath. It had been some months since he had stopped blushing like a boy.

There was a distinctly uncomfortable pause, and even the Prince, whose status protected him from challenge, decided that truly discretion would be the wiser course.

"But surely, Madame," Alençon said, facing Anne, and deftly, but circumspectly, dropping his hand to her thigh, "that was not my friend's gist. A case more in point would be," he turned now to Athalie and grasped her hand where it lay on the table, "if someone serviced this dear demoiselle, then, when she married later, her husband would be well and truly cuckolded."

Her hand squirmed in his, but he held it tightly. A hot flush spread across her face, so that even her eyes appeared bloodshot.

"But perhaps her husband would not be the worse off, for innocence is not always amusing," the Prince added. "What say you?" he asked, staring directly at Pierre.

Pierre glanced at Athalie, whose face, still flushed, bore an expression of intense misery. Her eyes did not meet his, and he was glad of it.

"Those with lecherous tastes," he replied slowly, "sow their oats in well-worn ruts. The Duchess is an unplowed field. Whatever gallant wins her hand will be rewarded by virtue instead of skill, for the skills you talk of are not learned in convents."

"What a reward!" Anne said, and someone snickered.

"You disappoint me, Monsieur," said the Prince. "I rather fancied you had taken the lady's education in hand. We see you often together, and the usual explanation sprang to mind."

Pierre looked startled, then leaned back and laughed. "Our interests are musical. For the rest, I don't need to take my pleasures from an untutored maiden, when Venus's cornucopia is handy to my reach."

A veritable cachinnation greeted this response. Athalie did not see the look of vindictive triumph that Hercule-François sent her. Her hand still lay under his, an extension of her frozen immobility; irritated by its passivity, the Prince let it go, and turned his back on her.

A buzz of general conversation broke out. Athalie did not attempt to follow it. Sometime later, she could not have said how long, she realized her neighbors were rising, and a desperate feeling of relief flooded her. Escape, she thought, now I can escape.

A group of avid youths rushed up from the table's end to surround the Prince, and soon there was talk of cards. There would be no dancing tonight. A general exodus headed for the stairs. The musicians picked up their instruments and trailed after their audience. Athalie slowly followed behind.

She could not go to her room. The servants would not yet have lit the lamp or warmed the bed, and it would be dark and bitter cold. The doors to the garden were barred for the night. Numb and indecisive, she wandered after the stragglers, up the zigzagging stairs. She emerged into the spacious first floor game room, as the musicians were setting up their instruments. She saw without noticing that they looked bored. The Prince and his admirers were already huddled over their cards, surrounded by a group of onlookers.

She could not make out what they were playing. Pierre and a bearded, flamboyant youth were playing pinochle. She observed that Pierre, too, looked bored.

The room was bright and seemed warm after the chill of the hall. A hearty fire burned at each end; oil lamps on stands lit the tapestries with a wavering light. Athalie hesitated a moment on the threshold, watching the chattering groups, while a bitter blankness possessed her. Then, she made up her mind and walked past the blazing fire to her right.

In the far wall of the game room, there was a balcony enclosed with wooden shutters, looking out over the moat which separated the château from its gardens. During the day, the shutters were pulled back. When it was warm enough, chess or card players set up their games in the recess, sitting on the stone seats on each side. To insulate the room from the cold night winds, a heavily embroidered curtain was pulled across the opening after dark, hiding the recess behind it. It was to this refuge that Athalie fled.

As the tapestry swished at her back, her first impression was of pitch-blackness. The shutters had been closed for the night; she pulled back one of the wooden screens and gradually shapes emerged: the obdurate darkness of the ditch, the palely lit windows of the gallery, and in the distance, obscure shapes picked out from the garden by an errant moon.

Alone at last, Athalie could listen to the turmoil within her.

She felt bruised and buffeted, shamed and angry. Different strands of emotion unraveled in her consciousness, each producing a new sensation of distaste and dismay. She had faced and accepted her passions, only to be scoffed at as a tyro in life and love. She had acknowledged to herself her love for Pierre, had bade her conscience to give off wailing, had cast aside her peace of mind, and now Pierre rewarded her by joining the ranks of her mockers. Take her, the Prince had said, and Pierre had laughed. They were wrong, all of them, to scorn her for the reason they did, but though mistaken in the reason, their contempt was merited and could not exceed her own self-disdain. And yet, she cried to herself, to bear their contempt and my own self-hate is too much punishment for a sin committed only in thought.

She had been unhappy for some time, she thought, but only now did her misery, recognized, stand before her stark and uncompromising, demanding help. She did not fit in. Her nature and her upbringing had not made her an easy companion. Yet she longed for acceptance as much as anyone. Proud independence could disguise her discomfort, but could not make it go away.

The curtain rustled behind her; a shaft of light came and went; a dark shape loomed beside her. Not him, she thought, please not him, but her breath quickened imperceptibly.

"Hiding, little Duchess? Or waiting for someone?"

She sighed. It was not Pierre.

A sword scraped against the wall as the newcomer turned toward her in the small space. Their situation seemed unreal to her; it was so like a tryst, but her companion was a strange man, not an eagerly awaited lover. What would they all think, if they knew? She laughed nervously.

The man's mass was close enough to feel.

"They made a sport of you, and you were hurt," the voice came again, and this time she knew it.

"Monsieur de la Renaudie?" she whispered.

"Himself."

"What are you doing here?"

"Talking to you."

She thought she heard a rumble of laughter and felt her hand being grasped and held.

"It hurt you, didn't it, to be the butt of their joke?" he continued.

She should push him away and leave, she thought, but the situation itself seemed to hold her, its dreamlike quality feeding on her exhaustion.

228

"I could tell. I've often been the victim of tormenters. But you shouldn't have let it bother you. They were wrong; men of discernment could see that. You're no cold vestal virgin, are you?"

He pressed closer, pushing her against the shutters. "I can see that. So can Brantôme. Only those who are immature, like our young Prince, or foolish, like my stepbrother, can't see behind the façade. But you shouldn't mind. You will have the best of both worlds — be able to pick the ones you want and fool the ones you don't."

Silence fell, total silence: even the music from within was silent. In it, she could hear his breathing. It sounded strange to her, labored and intense.

"You would like that, wouldn't you?" he asked.

He was right, of course. He had seen through her. The thought that he knew her soul terrified her and yet made her passive to his advances. She had realized that all this was a prelude, but though the idea of what was to come appalled her, she felt powerless to resist.

His hand moved to her shoulder, then to her neck, then to her hair. Suddenly, it was behind her head, pushing it forward. She gasped.

The curtain swung wide. A golden light traversed the enclosure, revealing her staring eyes and shocked expression. Maurice turned sharply. Pierre leaned against the heavy folds of tapestry, crushing them against the wall.

"So here you are, Maurice," he said. "Brantôme's looking for you to play chess."

"Leave the curtain, man," La Renaudie mumbled hoarsely. "Have you no care for a maiden's reputation?"

Pierre straightened. "Oh, get out, Maurice," he said irritably. La Renaudie hesitated, then pushed past Pierre into the room.

As Pierre stepped into Athalie's shelter, the curtain swung to, rustling past the end of his sword. Maurice stood outside for a moment, a pensive look in his eyes. Behind the curtain, the two stood in the darkness, feeling each other's presence and groping for something to say.

"Maybe he's right," Pierre said at last. "Have I saved your virtue, but sacrificed your reputation? I don't think anyone else saw Maurice, but God knows who saw me." She made no comment.

He felt the blood coursing through his veins; he had reached the point where inebriation exhilarates; he wished he could wrestle with someone or take a horse out and gallop it very fast over open country. When finally she addressed him, her voice was tight and small. Its dissonance with his mood annoyed him.

"I don't care about my reputation," she said.

"Clearly not, or you wouldn't have come here. This is a notorious lovers' nest. I'm surprised you found it empty."

"I didn't know."

He turned to go, then laughing, turned back. "Granted, you don't care about your reputation, what about your virtue, do you care about that?" God, what a question to ask the poor girl, he thought, smiling this time at his own tipsy high spirits. He ran his hands through his hair and reached for the curtain, when a noise arrested him. It was a very small sound, but unmistakable at such close quarters: a sob.

His gaiety dropped away; a kind of baffled irritation replaced it. He had known, of course, that she was upset. He had known that she was upset with him. But while knowing these things on some level, he had staunchly refused to give cognizance to the knowledge, to accept it, and to proceed to the whys and wherefores of it.

To the extent that he had allowed it to penetrate his consciousness, he had told himself that, though he was sorry for her, for he liked her, her distress was nothing to him. And after all, what had happened? They had laughed at her. But they laughed at everyone at one time or another. It was a matter of no great moment.

Yet underneath it all, he knew there was more to it than that, and he knew that it did concern him, or could, if he let it. Should he grapple with it now, meeting her halfway? Or should he leave her to it? If he took the easy way, she would suffer for it in the short run, but in the long, wouldn't she be better off? He knew that if this thing were brought out between them and made real, there would no longer be an easy way out. He turned to go.

From the blind darkness, her voice followed him, answering at last his silly question. "What difference does it make?" she cried. It was a thin wail, pathetic and desperate, and it seemed to release a flow of hidden grief. "If it were true virtue, I would cherish it, but this, this mime and show of virtue, what good is it? I despise it, knowing it false, and the world despises it, thinking it real. Ah-h," she ended, in a sob that was pronouncedly audible.

He did not understand her, but he knew the moment for leaving had passed. He went to her and asked huskily, "What do you mean, false virtue? You are good, and they envy you your goodness. No, not just that, you are good in thought as well as act. That's why they mock you, to hide their jealousy. Because, you see, even if they pretended to be models of virtue and decorum, they would still know what they were resisting, and do in their minds what they eschewed in action.

"Don't you see, an innocent way of looking at things, once lost, can never be regained? That's what Brantôme meant by knowledge defiling. I know. I was innocent once."

She lifted her face to his, searching its expression in the dimness. Her cheeks were still wet, but she was no longer crying. Her voice was steady when she spoke. "You call me innocent. You say I am innocent, and you are not. Have you no eyes? Or do you really despise me? I'm unformed clay, not even worth the effort of modeling."

Her anger died away before his silence.

"I'm sorry," she said. "I don't know what I want, and God knows, I don't know why I want it."

She hooked her fingers in the latticework of the shutters and rested her forehead wearily on them.

"Come, sit by me," he said gently, taking her shoulders and steering her to the bench. "I didn't know, not really. At least, I didn't know it mattered so much. I'm a fool."

"Your brother said so," she laughed jerkily. "He is not always wrong."

Her hands were very cold. He stroked them as they lay in her lap, then picked them up and rubbed them between his, then separated them and kissed each palm. She smelt of herbs, or forest leaves, different from other women. He could not see her hair, but he could picture the glossy braided coils twined rope-like about her head. He realized that he had often wanted to stroke them and now he did. He knew her ear was small and delicate and very white against the black tresses. He could just see the dark line of her hair. Pulling her forward, he kissed her ear and then her mouth. Athalie settled against him, as he enveloped her in his long, strong grasp and kissed her again.

* * *

"Don Francés de Álava."

Julio introduced the Spanish Ambassador with a flourish. To Gondi, his young cousin's manner seemed to grow more courtly with every passing day: to say it verged on the pompous would have been an understatement. The Count, whose own style was always just on the right side of the line which separates elegance from stuffiness, rose, bowed, and gestured toward a seat, all in one fluid motion.

The old man settled awkwardly, his knobby knees pointing gracelessly at his host.

"Some wine, Don Francés?" Gondi asked, seating himself again behind his wide table.

The Spaniard shook his head vehemently.

"Come, Don Francés, a little hot mulled wine. It's just what you need on a raw November day."

"Give over. I am not so easily distracted," the other replied harshly.

God, he never changes, thought Gondi. He had seen Álava only once since his recent return to Court after an absence of three months brought about by the French crown's repeated complaints against him for uncompromising bigotry and a willingness to resort to subterfuge and double-dealing which exceeded even that of his ambassadorial colleagues. That the last and most effective of the royal protests had been carried personally to King Philip by Gondi's own cousin lay between the two men, unmentioned but not forgotten; that their sole encounter since his return had been brief and unfriendly added a rawness to the rough edge of their relations.

"You'll have heard of the great victory of our Holy League in the Bay of Lepanto," the Spaniard launched in.

"Ours?"

"Not yours, certainly. It is a crying shame, a crime against Christendom, that the Holy League should have come together to smite the infidel dog, and France, instead of joining it, stood by, mocking. Worse. You always opposed it. Dax, that wolf in sheep's clothing, that prince of Satan's church — for he is no true bishop, and you know it — why, he was in Venice not a month before our victory, cajoling the Venetians away from their duty and pushing them into bed with the infidel dog."

"That's a nice image, if a bit mixed: France the pimp, Venice the whore, the Holy League the cuckold, and Turkey, what is Turkey?"

"Will you be serious, man! You did not believe that the League would accomplish anything, but now you have seen what it can do. God be praised! Spain at least saw its duty and was rewarded for it by the greatest victory since, since..."

"Since Charles Martel repulsed the Infidel from the land of the Franks, sending him back into what is now Spain?" Álava glared at Gondi, who continued, "But surely you mistake the matter: Are Spain and the League interchangeable, so that victory for the League is all to Spain's glory? Surely, the Holy See and Venice, Mother of the Seas, can claim some credit?"

"Aye, but we carried the brunt of the thing. If we had not done what was needful, nothing would have been accomplished."

"Mm," Gondi ruminated. "Venice would have made peace with the Sublime Porte, and everyone else would have muddled along as usual. And what duty did Spain see? Wasn't it rather the opportunity to bolster up its possessions in North Africa and Italy that caught your master's eye?"

"You dare impugn my Master's motives! He, whose gaze never wavers from the lodestar of his Faith..."

"Peace, Don Francés, we are reasonable men, exchanging views. There's no need to be so quick to anger. As I was saying, lastly, what has in fact been accomplished? Monsieur the Bishop of Dax — he is the Ambassador of my sovereign and I will have you use him with respect — reports that the forces of Don John of Austria lost 10 galleys, 8,000 men killed, 21,000 wounded, and not an inch of ground gained. My word, we should be tolling the knell, not ringing a joyful clarion."

"Your Bishop is a fool as well as a knave."

"Come, Don Francés, you know Dax is no fool."

"He should have reported the Turkish losses."

"Oh, he did, but shall we weigh an infidel against a Christian, one on one? You are becoming broad-minded, Don Francés."

"Don't you see what we have done?" The Ambassador burst out, his anger aggravated beyond control. "In Lepanto's waters 30,000 Turkish swine drowned, but even better, we took 3,000 prisoners and freed 15,000 galley slaves. How will they man their boats, hereafter? Will the Sultan himself take an oar? No, he must sit home and wait for our coming, eh?"

"Eh?"

"Yes, in the spring, there will be a crusade, as in olden times, and the Christian world will strike down the infidel. The cross will stand over Istanbul, over Jerusalem, over Mecca itself."

Gondi laughed out loud, heaving and guffawing until tears filled his eyes. At last, he gasped out, "Well, that's good news, by Christ!" He gasped again.

"I should say so," Álava said angrily.

"Yes, good news. You'll be busy enough to mind your own business; we'll be safe from your meddling at last."

Silence fell, as Gondi wiped his eyes. He glanced warily at the Spaniard's frozen figure, half-regretting his unconsidered outbreak, and in truth, when Álava spoke, his coldness seemed more deadly than his choler.

"I took you for a reasonable man, de Retz, and came to talk with you, for your benefit more than my own. Now, I'll palaver no longer, but only state my say, so you may know my Master's will: Your Queen traffics with heretics. She gives them comfort and promises them succor. In the Netherlands, sedition spreads, while Ludovic of Nassau is received like a brother in both La Rochelle and in Fontainebleau. Your Admiral's privateers make common cause with the Sea Beggars to harry our American shipping. These are acts of war, but your Mistress, her mind filled to capacity with her infernal marriages, turns a blind eye, while the heretics take the upper hand and threaten the well-being of the realm. I told her long ago that there is no remedy for the Kingdom's sickness but that it should pluck out the eye that offends. Unless they are radically extirpated, the weeds will grow again. And she agreed with me. This was in '69. Aye, she told me then that she'd offered good money — 50,000 écus — for the Admiral's hide, back in '62. She knows what's right..."

"Things change," said Gondi.

"Some things should not change. What you are is on the wrong side of everything. Your Mistress is a weathervane — puff, and she turns, puff, and she turns again! We have been patient, but we will wait no longer. Pay attention now, and get this straight: The young King must give up the notion of reconciling the House of Châtillon and the House of Guise; he must sound the death knell for the heretics, and Guise will be at his right hand; and it goes without saying that there must be no further meddling in the Netherlands."

"Or?"

"Young Charles should remember that he has a brother."

"Not one, but two, and what of it?"

"There are those who favor the Duke of Anjou for king, the Guises among them. True, he dabbled in heresy during that misguided Colloquy of Poissy, but they all did, and he was only a child. True, his longing for the crown of England tempted him to consider marriage with the bitch, its Queen, but I had little trouble persuading him that he would be better off taking England by the sword than bedding a barren heretic. He is staunch enough in his Faith, now. His fasting and praying will earn him pardon for the impetuosity of his youth. His heart is in the right place, and he has gained the loyalty of the pure and true elements of this rotten Kingdom."

"What are you saying, Don Francés?"

"Must I spell it out? You are so afraid of civil war that you refuse to do what is right. Well, you can have civil war with those of the pretended Reformed Religion, and have Spanish money to fight it. Or you can have civil war between brother and brother, and young Anjou will have the money."

Gondi stood slowly. "What you have said, Monsieur, is enough to have you banished from this realm."

Álava cackled dryly. "I thought we were just reasonable men, exchanging views. Why so hasty?" He stood, too, and spoke gravely. "Do not give further offense to my Master. I advise against it — most strongly."

"Leave me," Gondi replied, his controlled tone belied by his blazing eyes.

Álava half bowed with a smirk and turned away.

* * *

Anjou lobbed the ball gently into the air, and Maurice rammed it across the court. Brantôme, Anjou's partner, tried desperately to retrieve it, but the best he could manage under the circumstances was a wild toss, which sent the ball directly to Maurice's partner, Alençon. Alençon put it away, and that was that. On the stands, the women clapped.

Anjou's shoulders sagged. If he trembled slightly, like a sweated horse, it was more from emotion than exertion. What galled was the knowledge that he should have won. Brantôme was a strong player, and he himself was far better than his twit of a brother, or even Maurice for that matter. He remembered matches he had played with Maurice in the days of their friendship, when his extra energy and verve had more than compensated for Maurice's solid strength. In those days, Maurice would run up to him at game's end and congratulate him on his victory, admiration written all over his face. But this was a new Maurice.

Anjou would never have played with Maurice, for his policy now was to cut him dead, but Brantôme and Alençon had insisted. He might still have refused, but when his pretty mistress, Renée de Rieux, Mademoiselle de Châteauneuf, had joined her voice to theirs, there was no resisting, for her word was law at the moment.

They swarmed around him now as he drew near the stands and picked up his cloak, Renée smiling a sweet sad smile, Maurice clapping his back, Anne de Revillars de Galle batting her eyelashes, though she ought to have known better in this company, and on the fringes, Brantôme and Alençon exchanging knowing smiles and, yes, winks. However much Anjou averted his eyes, he could not escape La Renaudie's sarcastic sympathy or ignore Alençon's self-satisfaction.

Maurice left off his pounding, but his hand lingered on Anjou's back. The Prince flinched away, flung his cloak about his shoulders, and turned to go. As La

Renaudie hugged Anjou's right and Anne hovered to his left, Renée, whose comfort was all he sought, fell behind, chatting with Brantôme and Alençon.

"You'll forgive me, my Prince," Maurice was saying, "but it seems to me that your Highness is not in form. I say it not to offend, but from concern. Honesty has, after all, always been the rule between us."

Anjou glared at Maurice. It was true, of course. Having Maurice and Renée around him at the same time made him nervous, and nerves made him inattentive.

Anne addressed La Renaudie with a lofty air. "You let a lucky win go to your head, my dear Maurice. You made a few good hits and the wind was right for you, but you should not mistake these chances for a good game. Monsieur the Duke's game is far beyond yours, and you, of course, have had little opportunity to acquaint yourself with it."

"Madame, I thank you," Anjou said coldly. "I thank you both." He sped his steps in an attempt to outpace them.

"Madame," Maurice said, speaking across Anjou's back, "the Prince and I were playing tennis while you were still mucking out sties, or should I say, different sties from the ones you wallow in now." A leap brought him even with Anjou as they reached the exit. "Really, my Prince, you should have a care. To ruin your health, fasting and flagellating yourself, would be a wicked waste. You were not cut out to be a mystic; there are many here who would bear witness to that."

Anjou wrenched open the door before the liveried doorkeeper could pull it back; he and Maurice issued together into the walled avenue beyond. Finding himself for an instant alone with his tormenter, Anjou hissed, "Go to hell, Maurice. Go to my brother, he likes your kind."

"Nowhere near as much as you do, as far as I've been able to tell."

"Heretics. I mean heretics," Anjou spat, and nearly ran up the avenue.

As Anne scurried through the door, she found Maurice sauntering in front of it. "Your prey has escaped, my dear stepsister. Allow me to provide alternate entertainment." He slipped an arm quickly around her narrow waist. She looked into his face, blurted a strangled "Phah!" and wriggling from his grasp, ran after the Prince, nearly knocking down a small page who hesitated by the door.

Grabbing the instant that Maurice was out of everyone's earshot, the lad pressed to his side and whispered urgently, "Monsieur the Count de Retz requests your presence immediately." Maurice looked speculatively at the innocent upturned face, flipped the boy a copper, and strolled along the avenue toward the château.

The little page scurried alongside. They passed beneath the turreted arch of the Porte des Champs, around the wide, curving corridor, and through the second guarded archway into the courtyard in front of the château. As they reached open space, a brisk gust of wind slapped their faces. Maurice made for the château's entrance, the arch of white stone, resplendent in the brick façade, over which, disdainful but benevolent, rode Louis XII's equestrian figure. The boy pulled

Maurice's cloak, which slipped off his shoulder. Maurice glared down at the child, who mumbled, "No, no, Monsieur, this way."

Now the boy led, scrambling across the forecourt, while Maurice followed at a dignified lope. They skirted the well, always a center of activity, hurried past the buttresses of the Church of the Savior, and came at last, slightly breathless, to the enclave which sheltered the kennels.

The trees, which in summer provided shade for the dogs, were now nearly bare. Underneath one of them had been placed a heavy oak chair, throne-like in form, whose presence in the forecourt Maurice could not begin to explain. On it sat Gondi.

Puzzled and irritated by his puzzlement as Maurice was, he could not help but admire the scene. Gondi looked magnificent. A leather jacket, fur-lined and with a broad fur collar, nearly covered his doublet of deep blue-green — the color the Italians called Veronese. Its openings gave full value to the snowy lace of the ruff and cuffs and the diamond buttons that winked down his chest.

The tree, the throne, the fine clothes, the splendid figure of the man himself, all evoked to perfection the aura of the lord of the manor dispensing justice to his tenants. Maurice did not doubt that Gondi had set the scene, as a playwright sets his actors in place before his pageant opens, but its effectiveness was such that a touch of dread chilled his desire to laugh.

Gondi raised a hand in slow summons. Maurice approached, and resisting the urge to go down on one knee, bowed. The wind dropped; into the lull, Gondi's voice carried cold and haughty.

"My cousin tells me that you approached him to buy one of my animals."

Maurice checked and caught a glimpse of Julio hovering behind the tree. What madness is this? he thought.

"It is not well to despoil a lord of his possessions behind his back. The faithless servant who would sell what does not belong to him and the buyer who thinks thereby to get a bargain are both to be punished. In this instance, I find no fault with Julio, for he was honest with me, but what of you, Monsieur?"

"I... I..." Maurice thought frantically. "I meant no harm, my Lord. I believed your cousin to be an honest servant and thought he had authority in such matters. I did not think to trouble your Lordship. Who would dare distract you from your great concerns with such a trifle?"

"Why do you think my dogs are the finest, second only to His Majesty's?" Gondi replied. "Because I concern myself with them. It is with dogs, as with horses, as with men, as with everything: Only constant attention will get you what you want. Come, Julio, get Monsieur a seat, and we will display our wares."

Julio dragged forward a truncated log, which gave Maurice a low and uncomfortable perch next to Gondi's throne, and smiled maliciously as Maurice reluctantly lowered himself onto it. A handler in Gondi's livery led out a big-boned, brindled dog, whose new-grown winter coat gleamed like silk in the pale light.

His broad, wedge-shaped head, large upright ears, and bright eyes turned toward Maurice. Though he had no love for dogs, Maurice suffered a sudden longing to possess the creature. The brute's singular nobility qualified it as an unquestionable mark of prestige. The thought that his own meager eminence would be enhanced merely by owning such an animal, and that it was for now hopelessly beyond his means, angered him, and left him tingling with jealousy both of Gondi, who had more badges of significance than he needed, and of the dog itself, whom nature had made perfect. The handler pulled on the short lead attached to the beast's wide, jeweled collar, and it turned away.

"You did well," Gondi said in a low voice, "but you should train yourself never to show such surprise, even for an instant."

Maurice scowled.

"I will tell you quickly what you need to know, but you must go through the motions of interest. With the next dog, check his teeth, and run your hands over his points."

"What about him?" Maurice gestured at the handler approaching with an elegant, pearl-grey hunter, whose long, feathery tail curled jauntily over its back.

"He is deaf and dumb."

Startled, Maurice glanced at Gondi's face. "How....?"

"He trains them with hand signals and a whistle. I have my whistle, too." He reached into a pocket and pulled out a thin, carved reed.

The dog posed motionless, his head at La Renaudie's shoulder. Hesitantly, Maurice slipped his fingers beneath the soft lips and pried the muzzle open. At the sight of the gleaming rows of ivory, he dropped his hands brusquely and nodded as if satisfied. The handler's dark eyes mocked him as he turned away.

"You're not accomplishing much here, right at the moment," Gondi said.

La Renaudie drew himself up, offended; his log lurched beneath him. "On the contrary, I am the eyes and ears of the Admiral and his liaison with the King. He said so."

"Yes, well, it's useful to have a conduit to pass stories to the Admiral, but I'd like you to take a more active role."

Gondi's slighting view of Maurice's achievements came as a vicious blow to Maurice's pride; he yearned for the courage to get up and walk away.

There was a delay in bringing out the third dog. Gondi leaned forward, ostensibly to rest his elbows on his knees, but really to be better heard by Maurice.

"The Spanish Ambassador is a thorn in my side, in all of our sides. We had thought to be rid of him last summer, but here he is again. Her Majesty wishes to see the last of him."

"But, the Spanish are..."

"Never mind what you think the Spanish are. Here's what you will do: When Álava sends his next report to his Master, you will waylay the dispatch rider. Not here. He must be well away from Court, so that nothing trickles back to Álava. He is to be the last to know.

237

"In the dispatches, you will find one which will detail schemes against Coligny, Condé, Navarre, all the leaders of the Religion; in addition, a plot with Guise backing, to assassinate the English Queen and put Mary of Scotland on the throne, something good enough to promise to erase Ridolfi's failure; and well, finally, a hint that Anjou is to be preferred to the King."

"Something for everyone." Maurice grinned. "Quite. But what if there is no such dispatch?"

"There will be. You will bring the report back and put it before His Majesty, taking full credit for the venture, both to the King and in your reports to the Admiral. It would raise awkward questions if I were perceived to have had a hand in the maneuver. You will say you acted on your own initiative after being told by one of the Ambassador's servants that the report was being sent. It will redound greatly to your favor among your many friends and admirers."

Maurice ignored the irony and lapsed into pleased contemplation of the coup and the fame it would bring him. The third dog, a bay brute, whose skin was curiously spotted with dark specks, arrived unnoticed, nudged Maurice's leg, and solemnly proffered his paw for shaking. Maurice shook it irritably and caught the unmistakable gleam of amusement in the handler's eyes.

La Renaudie roused himself and commented gruffly, "Well, it sounds easy enough."

"You think so? You must understand. The point is, Álava must have no warning. I want him to take the full blast of young Charles' petulance before he gets the boot in the rear.

"Now," he said loudly, "you have seen my three best, but of course, I will not part with them. Jehan will now show you the one he has picked out for you. Julio tells me you offered 200 pounds for the one I call 'Il Gattopardo,' and truly you chose well, for he obviously has a fondness for you. Nonetheless, I cannot part with him. Fortunately for you, however, the leopard has sired a cub. His training is only rudimentary, but he has more years before him. I think I could bring myself to part with him for the price you offered for the sire."

The handler brought out a thin-chested, big-footed miniature of the last dog he had seen. The pup squirmed in the man's hands, rolling his eyes and yelping ungraciously.

God in Heaven! thought La Renaudie. He's actually going to make me buy one of his blasted dogs. Doesn't he realize I don't have that kind of household? He imagined his own livery on Jehan, but the exercise only made him more angry.

Maurice sniffed disgustedly. "Monsieur's too kind, but I fear I must decline," he said. "Now that I have seen him, I would not settle for any but the first of your dogs."

"Is that so?" Gondi slapped his hand on his thigh and made a short crowing noise. "Well, by God, you shall have him! You shall have him for 500 pounds, and your renown will be made at Court, for you will own the finest of dogs and will have paid the highest of prices for him."

Gondi stood abruptly, as if the matter were settled. At the small, gurgling noise from his companion, he turned and said quietly, "He will be yours, La Renaudie, if you bring this off perfectly. In the world's eyes, he will be a spectacular purchase, but between us, we will know that you earned him otherwise. But if you fail in any particular, then you must buy and pay full money for him. That's how we'll play it."

Gondi smiled briefly and strode away, followed at a respectful distance by Julio. The handler and the dog had disappeared inside the kennel. Maurice wished he could see the bold, brave, brindled dog again. By God, he thought, a dog like that is worthy of a king, and I will own him.

* * *

The room was cold, and the blankets lay heavy on them. Pierre was sorry, for he liked to see Athalie, not only to touch her. Her face was pressed against his chest, snuggled in the hollow beneath his collarbone; below the piles of gleaming black hair, he could see skin stretched tight over a thin shoulder blade, white skin that had never seen the sun, glossy like well polished parchment. It was not white as other skins are white, white suffused with pink or tainted with yellow; its whiteness gleamed like the shining surface of dark water. He extricated an arm from the covers and hugged the shoulder to him, crushing it and Athalie against his ribs.

She sighed. He knew that she had not been asleep, but only resting, resting in the most complete sense of the word, peaceful, rich, and full. When they lay together, he always knew what she felt, her joys, her sorrows, her wants, her satisfactions. Athalie, who had never had another lover, did not know her fortune. It was a side of Pierre his wife would never know, for however much he hungered for Anne, that affinity was never there, almost as if the urgency of his desire dulled his sensitivity, whereas with Athalie, he had found a balance between her needs and his own.

They came here often, to Athalie's room. Her rank and her desperate pleas had obtained for her, on her arrival at Blois, the privilege of a room alone. It was not much of a room, but to have it at all was a rare honor for an unmarried girl at Court. How they would have managed without it he could not imagine. At first, they had come to it seldom and cautiously, but every occasion that brought them together loosened the bonds of convention. When they lay together, caution seemed a paltry thing, almost shameful, whereas their love seemed blameless and brave. But the luck which had given her this room, and had placed it in a secluded area of the château, held good for them. He did not think that their secret life was common property, yet.

He looked around the bare cell, denuded of belongings save a wardrobe, the bed, and its covers. He thought of Athalie's reflections on the apparel of the Queen Mother's suite, the tapestries, the curios, the manuscripts — pillows, coins, gems, silver, pewter, faience — the harvest of a lifetime's interest in costly and beautiful objects. Athalie took such childish pleasure in them but did not covet them. Poor little rich girl, with such wealth, and so little to show for it! But after all, he mused, possessions were not an unmixed blessing. For some, like his father, they were a burden, or at least a duty; for others, like his wife, they were an obsession. Perhaps it was better to be free of them, even if the freedom was, in Athalie's case, a little artificial.

The narrow window glowed in the darkening room. Athalie sat up, and the coils heaped at the nape of her neck tumbled over her breasts. She looked a little dazed, like someone roused from a dream.

"Is it time to go?" she asked softly.

"No, dearest, they just rang nones."

"Just? It was a while ago. I must be at vespers or I will be missed."

"I know." He caught a knot of hair and pulled her down beside him. She relaxed, then murmured, "How short the days are!"

He knew she meant not only that night came early, but that time was rushing by.

"I know," he said. "One always thinks of love in the spring — new life, new beginnings. I thought that way when I was married. One doesn't think of love like this — in the lengthening shadows, a way to keep warm as the days grow cold." A way to keep alive when everything is dead, he continued the thought to himself. Yet, now is the fallow time, the time for dreams, the time for plans. But what plans? he asked himself bitterly. What plans could he make in such a bind?

"I sometimes think the mind is more active in winter," she said.

"But is love of the mind or of the body?" Pierre toyed with his own question. Funny, he mused, he would have said that for him it was more of the mind, whereas for Athalie it was more of the body, but he did not dare say so aloud, knowing it would offend her.

"When I think of spring, I always think of Islette," she said.

"It was lovely then — all green and gold. In winter, you could see it was a massive, old dungeon, but when the ivy crept along its base and the new leaves unfurled and blurred its outlines, it looked to me like an enchanted place."

She sat up. "You know, Pierre, the other day, my uncle told me he was going to sell Islette. He said it was isolated and poorly maintained and not worth the trouble to modernize. I was appalled. I... I didn't know what to say. Somehow, I had to stop him, and I could think of nothing, but finally, I blurted out that I loved it, that it was my childhood home."

"And what did he say?"

"He said it didn't fit in with his scheme of things, that he wanted to consolidate my possessions as much as possible and be rid of unprofitable bits of land. I thought all was lost, until he added that good management must sometimes give way before sentiment. He said that was what money was for, to let you have things that it didn't make sense to have, but that you wanted."

"You see, you wrong him."

"Oh, I don't know. I think he just didn't want me to make a scene."

"Do you make scenes, Lie-lie?"

"Well, no, not scenes exactly, but we throw ourselves against each other in funny ways, and he doesn't like it. I sometimes think he's afraid."

"Afraid? I doubt that."

"I mean, he likes to control people. Well, I don't know. But he knows I can always go to Her Majesty."

"So can he."

"Yes, but there are some things she can't do for him, that her principles won't permit."

"But, surely, she would never interfere with his administration of your estates. You know, he's very good at it. My father relies on him a great deal, for advice in financial matters, I mean."

"I'm sure he encourages him to."

"Oh, Lie-lie, you're unfair."

"It gives him power."

It was an old argument, and they dropped it. After a while, Pierre said, "Speaking of your uncle, wasn't it funny the way my stepbrother suddenly bought that dog of his? He spent a fortune on it and looked very glum about it, too. I couldn't understand. You know, Maurice isn't fond of animals, and he's very tight with his money. He doesn't have very much."

Athalie sat up, her eyes alive with interest. "You don't know the latest. You weren't there this morning, but I saw it. We were all in the game room, and Monsieur the Duke d'Anjou was playing chess with Brantôme — and losing, I think — when the door was thrown open, you couldn't see by whom, and the dog came in. All by himself.

"I thought at first he'd gotten loose by mistake; he seemed to amble aimlessly from one person to the next. When he came near Monsieur, however, he stopped wandering and made directly for him and 'pointed' — you know, with his nose out, and his tail all straight..."

"Yes, I know," said Pierre dryly.

"Oh, all right," she said. "He looked glorious, anyway. Attached to his collar was a cylinder in which there was a parchment scroll. I heard later that all it said was, 'Avenir. I will follow you.' Once Monsieur slipped the parchment out, the dog sat and put his paw on his knee. Monsieur looked puzzled, then thrilled. It was very pretty. But what, in Heaven's name, do you make of it?"

Pierre leaned his head back, his eyes half-closed. "The dog's name is 'Avenir' — 'to come' as in 'future,' and also, I suppose, as in 'to follow.' That's very good! But why Maurice should send Anjou a gift and such a promise at this time..."

"I would have thought they would be mortal enemies."

"You wouldn't know, it was before you came, but Anjou and my stepbrother used to be as thick as thieves. It's only since Maurice's 'reformation,' if I may say, that they've been enemies.

241

"But, of course, they need him, I mean those of the Religion need Anjou for their Netherlands Enterprise. He is, after all, the Lieutenant-General, and it would be essential that he not oppose it. So, if a little flattery can win him around, it's very clever."

"Oh, he was thrilled. And no wonder. The dog followed Anjou from the room, his head high, prancing, his coat all burnished. You should have seen him. But how did the dog know?"

"Good, solid training. And they must have borrowed something of Anjou's to give him the smell. Very clever."

It was really very clever, Pierre thought, with a pang of jealousy. Perhaps, the Admiral had paid for the dog after all. Then a thought occurred to him, and he said it aloud. "But it will hardly do Maurice any good to cozy up with Anjou, if he thereby wins the King's enmity."

"But, he didn't, at least I don't think so. I saw His Majesty, and Monsieur, and the dog, all walking together quite peacefully before I came up here. I was surprised because everyone says they've been at each other's throats for weeks."

"For once, what everyone says is true. They came to blows a few days ago. Indeed, the King pulled a knife on his brother."

"Really?"

"Well, it's not supposed to be common knowledge. My father told me. But if Maurice's crazy ploy brought about a thaw, then he must have cleared his gift to Anjou with the King first. Shew! Who can fathom the workings of his mind?"

* * *

Maurice watched from the arcade as the King and his brother strolled in the garden followed by the dog. His beautiful dog. It was worth it, he thought. How many people could have brought about the scene he was now observing? He had told the King that he would give Anjou a gift to sweeten him toward the precious Enterprise, and the King had agreed. And when Anjou had summoned Maurice to accept his gift, with a tormented wariness that had thawed into fulsome graciousness, Maurice had suggested to the Prince, with infinite tact, that the dog's message would lose none of its meaning if it were passed along. The dog, Maurice had said, would always symbolize his own loyalty to Anjou, who was the star of the future, but he had brazenly pointed out in the short run, the future would be brighter for them all if the King's hatred for Anjou abated. And everyone knew the way to the King's heart was through his dogs.

So the King now owned the dog; King and Prince each believed Maurice was loyal only to himself; each thought Maurice had done him a great service; Coligny would pay for the dog; and best of all, Gondi would be balked. Bitterness at Gondi seethed in Maurice's heart. Gondi had tricked him.

Maurice had done his best; Álava had been caught with the goods — and such goods — and it was not Maurice's fault that Álava had been warned. Maurice had no idea how the Spaniard had learned of his danger, but when the furiously irate

242

King had commanded his presence, Álava had been nowhere to be found. His Majesty's rage had given way to hysterical derision when he had learned that the old fox had slipped across to Flanders dressed as a nun. Gondi should have been satisfied. To accuse Maurice of failure was absurd, unjust, and to exact his ridiculous price for the dog, to which Maurice had never agreed, was outrageous. Who did Gondi think he was? How could he forget what Maurice was? Gondi thought Maurice was a nonentity, but Maurice had obtained recognition and influence, and all through his own wit. Look at what he had accomplished!

Of course, it wouldn't last. Thanks to the Spaniard's dispatch — genuine or forged, Maurice didn't know or care — the Guises were out of favor, and young Anjou had been scared back into apparent docility that would, for now, neutralize his opposition to the Netherlands invasion. But nothing had changed, not the Guises' hatred for the Châtillons, nor their dreaded strength at arms. In the last month, the Guises had raised an army, which, mustering all the forces they could, the Protestants could barely match. At a word from the Guises, Paris had been torn by riots. In all the hundreds of towns where their influence reached, those of the Religion walked in fear of their lives.

No, the Guises would have their way with Coligny in the end, and Anjou would throw in with them again, and Charles would hate him for it. Nothing fundamental had changed. The only important thing that had happened was that today had marked the beginning of Maurice's return to Anjou's side, though Anjou himself did not fully understand it. Maurice thought, Charles will die, and Anjou will be king: King Henri, the third of that name, and long may he live! On that day, he thought, I will be where Gondi is, and then, ware to my enemies!

THE END OF PART I

Part II

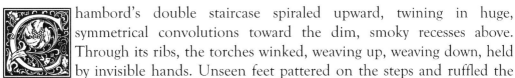

Chapter XIX

hambord's double staircase spiraled upward, twining in huge, symmetrical convolutions toward the dim, smoky recesses above. Through its ribs, the torches winked, weaving up, weaving down, held by invisible hands. Unseen feet pattered on the steps and ruffled the edges of Anne's consciousness like the disquieting sound of midnight rain. Silence broke the irritating cadence, as the web of stone erupted into a pillar of fire, whose tongues of flame blazed briefly before branching into the emerald leaves of a sinuous vine that undulated, dew-laden and sparkling, between the naked bodies of Pierre and Anne: gleaming, smooth skin, dappled with sunlight; a riot of flowers in their hair, Adam and Eve in their Eden days, young and unsullied. The flowers, she saw, were crowns, Epiphany crowns.

Anne awoke to jabbing, needle-like pains in her calves. She flexed her cold toes and revolved her feet outward, then inward, with excruciating slowness. How absurd dreams are, she thought, and how... how distasteful! The brilliant green, the green of full spring burgeoning into summer, still vibrated in her mind, but otherwise the image had faded, leaving nothing but the sad, sour sense of exclusion.

Anne shuddered. Drink was what did it, she thought. Awake, we act like fools, and we are punished when the foolery returns to plague our sleep.

That was the trouble: The fortnight of Christmas had been an endless feast, where one meal's sweet played reluctant host to the next meal's fish. No man, and hardly any woman, could get through it, except borne on the current of ciders, ales, meads, and wines. The days were divided between churching and feasting. The saint and the fool danced round and round 'til they fell on the floor in each other's arms. She smiled sleepily.

Still, Pierre was a fool. Making Athalie his Epiphany queen was such an obvious joke, whereas picking his own wife would have called for genuine inspiration. How Alençon would have laughed then! True, the laugh would have been somewhat at Pierre's expense, but Pierre should have selected Anne for Epiphany queen anyway. It would have been one of her great moments, and in fairness, she would have let him share it. The others could have laughed as they wished, but they would have recognized what a woman she was, a woman who could collect men like jewels to keep or to give away. She would have gloried in Pierre's tribute, and in her splendor, he, too, would have shone.

But he had not done it. She made a moue in the dark and shivered slightly. She could never remember a colder January, and it was a bitter enough month even at its best. Her ill humor disappeared as she recalled Brantôme's story of the man who had boasted to a lady how often he could perform in one night, but who had been so cold on reaching her chamber for a demonstration that all he could do was tremble as with an ague, much to the lady's derision and that of her coterie.

She snuggled, back to back, against Pierre. He is always warm, she thought enviously, then passed with only unfocused wonder over the odd fact that he had taken to sleeping naked again just as the cold had set in. Good for me, anyway, for it makes his warmth more available. She nestled her icy feet against the back of his legs, and smiled to herself at the gentle stirring her action provoked. She felt no guilt at disturbing him. It seemed only right that she should derive some advantage from his presence.

Not that he was much of an inconvenience, she admitted. Like all the idle youths, he had taken to gaming and hunting, and so he came to bed ever later and left ever earlier. Almost always he arrived in the middle of the night to find her feigning virtuous sleep. On the rare occasions when she had come in after him, he had accepted her playful lies with placid unconcern. She supposed it was one of the advantages of marrying the very young: They were so easy to train. Still, in her own household, she would insist on separate quarters, and when Pierre became Duke de Galle, their rank would enable them to demand space and privacy even at Court. Then, things would be more convenient. She would not always have to leave the locale of her assignations to the whim of chance — to the availability of her lover's bedroom, or of one or another dark recess, tawdry from overuse, or, worst of all, in summer, of the grassy hiding places in the shrubbery, so beloved of romantic youths, but so hideously uncomfortable and dirty. Though she managed well enough, she longed for the ease which greater privacy would bring.

She saw herself suddenly as a spider in the middle of its web, and the image shocked her more than she wanted to admit. The trouble lay, she continued hastily, in the paradox that while reputation for desirability and generosity in affairs of the heart was the sine qua non of a woman's success, yet if matters were not handled carefully, a specific liaison, or its fruit, could prove her undoing. There was only one exception to that rule. The mistress of a king could be as blatant as she wished, or rather as he wished, even to the point of bearing his bastard. Bastardy under royal auspices was an honor, not a reproach, and not for the child only, but for its mother. There was a great tradition: Madame d'Étampes, the great François' mistress; Diane de Poitiers, Henri II's truest love; why not Anne de Galle? The vision warmed her innards, and the idea of actual relations with young Charles did not intrude on it, but at last, reality cast a pall in a different way.

You are getting ahead of yourself, my girl, she sternly admonished the dreamer within. Marie Touchet must be deposed before you can take your place as the Court's most radiant star. The King is so infatuated with her, it is pathetic. Anne drained the dregs of envy, and all her happy fantasies washed away.

Pushing closer to Pierre, she willed sleep to return. How she hated these nighttime reveries, when the mind ran and ran, like a stag leaping in full course through forest undergrowth. Inexorably, thought followed thought. To bear someone else's bastard, her mind ran on, that was a different matter. God forbid that it should happen to her, and yet, if it did, she reassured herself, no one need ever know. With elementary precautions, such misfortunes could be guarded from knowledge, if not from speculation.

A flaccid dullness began to pervade her mind. She savored it, murmuring, Sleep is coming! Sleep is coming! in her mind. Funny, she mused fuzzily: Pierre, who for so long oscillated frantically between the extremes of thwarted passion — all fire one moment, all ice the next — subsided at some point into reserved and courteous calm. The short nights he devotes to our bed are, in fact, spent in sleep. He does not merely sleep, he sleeps with all the disinterest of a child or of a man greatly fatigued. There was a juxtaposition of ideas which hovered uncomfortably just beyond her awareness. She wriggled her shoulders in the semblance of a shrug. She had no desire or need for his attentions, she reminded herself firmly, beyond the fundamental safeguard that occasional marital relations provided. When was the last time, she wondered? Blois, surely. No, not Blois, Fontainebleau. But Fontainebleau was months ago; with a thrust, this realization broke through the blanket of somnolence.

Cursed fool that I am! Complacent, thoughtless wretch! She fought her panic, straightening her body into a rigid expression of control. Nothing is compromised yet, nothing is lost, she told herself. She moved her limbs gently beneath the heavy covers. Tucking up her feet, she rubbed them vigorously for warmth. Then, she turned over and softly pushed her breasts against Pierre's back, insinuating an arm around his chest.

Pierre snapped, with motionless but acute awareness, out of deep sleep into total wakefulness. As his mind identified his surroundings, he relaxed back into the reposeful calm that lay on the borders of oblivion. He felt Anne's hand creeping across his chest, and he thought of the golden hair, of the pert mouth, of the pear-like breasts, molded and luscious. Then, he thought of Athalie: ivory, not pink; firm, but not hard; vibrant, generous, and loving. A glow of satisfaction filled him; the two images mingled as he slept.

* * *

Athalie slipped off the bed, ragged the heavy quilted coverlet around her, and padded to the window. Pierre had long since gone, but she was still awake, still suspended in that state of tranquil excitement that lingered after many of their encounters. Life alternated between peaks of near ecstasy and periods of sick apathy and depletion.

She pulled at the shutters with numb fingers. Bound by frost, they resisted at first, but yielded finally and swung back to reveal a landscape brilliant with moonlight.

The blinding cocoon of snow and sleet which had enveloped the château all the day long had blown by, and the weather's work stood revealed. The decorative moat was a white carpet of snow on ice; the open reaches of the gardens swept away in harmonies of white, silver-grey, and black; the distant trees were feathered and gemmed with icicles and lacy frost. The surprising beauty before Athalie's eyes seemed to liberate her and throw her into the clear atmosphere like a hawk soaring above the ground. The moment held her, innocent of thought and oblivious of bodily discomfort. After a while, the tingling of her chilled feet recalled her to herself, and she pushed the shutters together and returned to her bed.

As she lay tunneled within the layers of blankets, she wondered at her wakefulness. It was nearly forty-eight hours since she had slept, for Twelfth Night had disgorged its revelers straight into the Mass of the Kings. Twelfth Night! The memory of it was better than any dream. Pierre the King — she saw him seated on Charles' throne, so regal that even the absurd crown of paper flowers and ribbons stuck in a cap of straw detracted nothing from his splendor. She had mistaken him for the King once, for an instant, and now he was King, if only for a night. It struck her as bizarre that fantasy should echo fantasy, and stranger still that it should mock reality. There was no mistaking it: The true King had sulked to see his seat filled in jest better than he himself could fill it.

To placate the dethroned monarch, Pierre had done the obvious thing: He had appointed Charles his Master of the Hunt and ordered him to bugle for the dogs, which Charles had done, to his own delight and the confusion and dismay of the guests. In response to his summons, out from under the tables, from the corners of the great hall, from the foot of the double staircase, the beasts had streamed to mill among and rummage around the wide skirts and between the stockinged legs, jumping, yelping, and wagging their tails. Charles had shrieked with laughter.

That had been the first of Pierre's whimsies. A spate of farcical commands had followed. Pierre had appointed Maurice to be Duke de Galle and had forced from him an oath of fealty. Seeing Raymond's apoplectic face, Athalie had wondered at Pierre's audacity, but the trick had succeeded well enough, since the old Duke's temper had improved as his substitute's had worsened. Pierre had commanded young Alençon to bring his mother a drink in his famous new cup.

The Prince had declined, claiming the cup was still at Blois, a lie, Athalie felt sure, and one which no one had believed. As punishment, Alençon had been made the King's fool. To his protest that fools are born not made, his mother had replied, "Precisely so," which had merely confirmed what everyone suspected, that the joke had been entirely on Alençon, and not at all on the Queen Mother. To the young Prince's credit, he had given in with good will, stealing the dwarf's bicolored hat, enveloping himself in a scarlet cloak, and buffooning ceaselessly for the duration of the night.

So, Pierre had continued, picking out his family, his officeholders, and his servants, the grand and menial alike: Anjou, the torchbearer; Brantôme, the King's confessor; Margot, not queen, as everyone had thought, but mother of the King.

"And I, my liege, have you nothing for me?" the real Queen Mother had asked, and in the pause that followed, everyone had speculated that he would make her queen. But instead he had replied, "I would know you anywhere for the darling of my eye, my baby sister, Margot."

"Then, I will carry you off to my bedchamber," Catherine had continued, to hearty laughter and applause and furious blushes from her daughter.

"I regret, Madame, but only my bride and queen can do that," Pierre had replied.

An expectant hush had fallen, and Athalie's great moment had come upon her, unexpected, terrifying, and wonderful.

"The Duchess de la Roque shall be my bride and queen."

In a daze, she had gone to sit beside him. He had crowned her with flowers and had kissed her hand. Only then had he called for wine and drunk the ceremonial toast. "The King drinks! The King drinks!" the crowd had roared. "The King drinks." The room reverberated with the noise.

Rising, Pierre had led Athalie forward, and behind them the whole Court had formed into lines, in all their heavy finery, marching in time to the melody of the branle. The musicians, caroling, had led the dancers around the massive base of the staircase, about whose base the torchbearers had clustered, while other torches were borne around the hall's circumference. Between the rows of light, the stately procession moved until the two ends joined and the circle was complete.

The men had stepped toward the center and bowed, and the dance proper had begun. And there had been more dances, and more after that, and a pageant, complete with courtiers dressed as camels, of the Magi offering their gifts to a small page who played the infant Jesus. Pierre – Athalie saw him still – had been chief among the kings, and had knelt first, gold-headed, gold-clad, holding out a massive golden centerpiece, shaped like a ship, as if its weight were nothing. Torchlight chased up and down the staircase, along the drafty corridors, and through the echoing chambers, to the sounds of music, ringing tauntingly from alcoves and balconies, and more toasts, this time with steaming tankards of spiced wine. "The King drinks," they had cried again. At last, shutters and curtains pulled back to show the fire and ice of dawn on snow, they had trooped into the chapel and sung and prayed that all the people of the earth should honor their true King.

The images blazed through Athalie's dulled mind. How had Pierre dared to make her his queen? She had marveled over it again and again, not really seeking an answer, but enjoying the question. He had been drunk, it had seemed – not with wine, of that she was sure, but with a sense of power, of soaring high into a world that included earthbound creatures and made them insignificant. His confidence had freed her from fear and shyness, letting her live for a moment the act itself without its consequences. But now, the triumph was over, and what was left of it? A memory that she would cherish and nothing else. After the soaring comes the crash, she thought, without bitterness or reproach. After the act come its consequences.

At last, an exhausted sleep overcame her. She woke to a queasiness that obliterated all other feeling. She lay, immobile, within the curtained darkness of her bed, conscious of nothing but the unique and seemingly insupportable misery which is the essence of an unsatisfied desire to vomit. As the peak of nausea passed, she remembered hearing the familiar noises of morning: the creaking and bumping of shutters pulled back and fastened; the scratch of a waxed screen pushed into place; the striking of flint and the hissing of kindling taking flame.

"Nou-nou," she called out weakly, "what time it it?"

"Nigh on to sext," she heard the old woman's voice grate through the muffling draperies, "and what the Queen Mother will think of it, I couldn't say." The curtains at the foot of the bed jerked apart to reveal a stocky frame lit from behind by the now crackling fire. Athalie shrank from the violence and the sudden light.

"Missing the rising, missing Mass, looking to skip the noonday meal no doubt," the nurse rumbled on, glaring at Athalie's livid face.

"I think," Athalie began timidly, propping herself up on one elbow, "I think I'm sick."

The nurse laughed. It was a harsh, unpleasant sound, which made Athalie pull back and sink into the mound of cushions. With sharp, noisy movements, the nurse circled the bed, opening the other draperies and rustling them into place. All the while, she muttered, "Sick. That's good, it is. Sick, very sick. Such an illness…" Athalie's eyes followed her fearfully. At last, she stopped, and turned on her young mistress.

252

"You know," she cried out, "I'm not a fool. I wash for you, don't I? And care for you? I've seen this sickness before. I know its name full well, and what's more, you do, too. If you were too innocent to know it, you'd have been too innocent to get it."

All the fear that Athalie had been holding back by main force, lest it ruin her happiness, flooded through her, bringing in its wake a misery that made simple physical discomfort seem a mere bagatelle. Her eyes swam with tears. The old nurse sat abruptly on the bed, and watched her own hands twisting. "What's to be done," she said at last, "God only knows. It'll be the ruin of you."

There seemed nothing further for either of them to say. After a while, the old nurse sat up and said, "I'll fetch you an infusion. It'll settle your stomach."

"Oh, no," Athalie protested.

"Yes, it will. And you'll drink it."

Athalie was still in bed when Margot came, though the bitter brew the old woman had forced on her — or the passage of time — had in fact dispelled her queasiness. She simply felt she could not face the world and shrank even from Margot, whose breezily cheerful manner buffeted the shell of Athalie's moroseness.

The Princess plunked herself on the edge of the mattress, laying out her furred sleeves on her lap before plunging her hands into the cuffs.

"My poor angel! You're positively green. I told Mother you were sick. She missed you right away, and you know how she hates people not to be where she expects them to be. But I pointed out that you were ever the model of fidelity, and so, you must be sick, and she agreed. She'll be sending to inquire — or perhaps she'll come herself.

"She knows I'm here, of course. She told me to be sure to fetch a doctor, if you needed one. As if I needed telling! Of course, I shall, and nothing but the best will do for my poor little cousin."

"Oh, no," Athalie wailed.

Margot took a hand out from the fur and waved it imperiously. "Ambroise Paré. My brother swears by him, ever since he made him able to flex his arm again. Charles will gladly lend him to you."

"I've never been examined by a doctor, and I shan't be now. Why... why, it's not decent!"

Margot laughed, "My dear, you're so provincial! Utterly charming! But this is a serious matter, and you're not to worry about anything. That's the nice thing about illness. One can simply resign from the human race and let everyone else handle everything. You just let me take care of you. Relax, and let what comes, come."

"No!"

"Do you hate Paré so much? He's a gruff old man, I'll give you that, but I've always found him goodhearted. After all, surgery is hardly a profession for a person of delicate sensibilities, so you really can't expect..."

"No, it's not that." And indeed, though Paré's conversation was often sprinkled with anecdotes of a robust gruesomeness which Athalie found unappetizing, still, on the few occasions she had observed him, she had detected an unaffected kindliness which had greatly pleased her. "It's not that," she repeated, and tears began to trickle down her face.

"There, there." Margot patted her leg heartily. "You're very weak. Paré will give you some ghastly concoction that will pep you right up. You must remember: The worse it tastes, the better it is for you." She rose and swept out before Athalie could say another word.

Though in his sixties, Ambroise Paré was still a strong, muscular man, and there was about him the vitality that comes from health and physical prowess. Even more important to his effect on others, however, was the force of his personality. As he strode into Athalie's chamber, it seemed to fill the room; she felt almost as if it pressed her back against her pillows. He stopped at the foot of the bed, subjected her to a shrewd glance, then turned on the old nurse.

"Stoke up that fire, will you? It's a brutal day, and no mistake."

The old woman gave him the baleful look of one who questions another's standing to give orders, before turning to obey. As she rattled about her work, he put up an arm and leaned casually against the bedpost, keeping his eyes on Athalie's tense face while he talked. "It puts me in mind of a winter I spent in Paris when I was young. I was training at the Hôtel Dieu, and we were suffering through a winter which makes the like of this look mild. I was going my rounds one day, and I came to a bed that stood in a particularly exposed part of the hospital, and it turned out that all four of the patients in the bed had gotten frozen noses. So there was nothing for it: I operated on them, one after the other."

Athalie stared at him hypnotically.

"Well, don't you want to know what happened?" She nodded.

"Two died and two survived." He laughed brusquely. "I learned young what to expect from my profession."

Still watching her humorless face, he shrugged. "I ought to know better than to talk about it, though. The old get garrulous. Well, we'll get on with it, shall we?"

Athalie said nothing and could barely stop herself from cowering as he approached her.

"We'll have your woman stay, if you've no objection," he said. "It's not necessary, of course, but it's customary." It was the old nurse who replied, "I should say so, and you'll not get me out!" He looked from her to Athalie and nodded.

He examined her, quickly but gently. Athalie was more conscious of the cold of skin exposed to open air than of his probing fingers. At the end, he tucked the blankets around her shoulders and moved to the bottom of the bed, where he sat, leaning against a post.

"Well, Mademoiselle," he spoke at last, "you know what you have."

She nodded, and he nodded, too, like a thoughtful echo. "There is nothing I can do, of course, but keep your secret. That I must do: It is a law of my profession, and one that I believe in. Perhaps your guardian could claim a right to know, but," he held up a hand as Athalie started, "you are not a child and I believe in privacy. It will all be for nothing in the end, however; that is what you must give thought to. I'm too old and experienced, and you will not be offended if I speak to you frankly.

"For today, I will give you all the excuses you need. Even our eager young Princess will believe you have a flux. I will give you a potion, just an herbal brew, something strengthening — and everyone will marvel at the speed of the old quack's cures. Yes. For you see, tomorrow you must get up, and the next day, and the next, however you feel, or people will talk. There is nothing I could do or say that would prevent it.

"You, there," he turned to the nurse, "be careful how you do her waist. Concealment is good, yes, but not discomfort. And warmth: She must dress warmly. You understand? And food, of course, food for two."

"She's not the first," the old woman answered and turned away.

Paré laughed. "Indeed not."

He focused again on Athalie. "In a month, maybe two, it will be no secret. So I tell you this: You must go away. As soon as you can develop a plausible reason, you must leave. People may guess, but guessing isn't knowing. You've a demure look that could give the lie to the nastiest mind."

He patted her on the head, and she reached out an arm and caught his hand. "Thank you," she whispered.

"It is nothing," he said, and left briskly.

* * *

Time seemed as immobile as a stagnant pool. At first Athalie lingered on in her room, not thinking about what was happening to her and what it might mean for the future, but simply existing in an abyss of fear. Then, a wild restlessness possessed her. Mindful of what people might surmise about an illness that came in the morning and left in the afternoon, she rose and dressed with care, selecting a robe of figured damask, deep red on purple, and brushing her hair back into a stylish cap of purple with a carmine band and feather. She inspected herself as best she could in the round polished metal of her mirror and went down to take her place among the ladies of the Court.

The King and his men were hunting, Pierre among them, and, thank the Lord, Athalie thought, Gondi, too. None of the women had accompanied them; it was not the season for casual sports. The women had gathered around the fire in one of the rooms off the great hall, sewing, embroidering, chattering. Athalie joined them and resumed her needlepoint. From time to time, she clutched with white-knuckled fingers the wooden frame that held her work, as spasms of panic came and went. Margot read verses of Ronsard, then a moral tale by an unidentified author — herself? Athalie wondered without interest. One of the ladies took a lute and trebled out the song of the dying rose. Ronsard's melancholy words echoed Athalie's thoughts:

"For Nature's nature is unkind,
That such a flower cannot last,
Mere dawn to dusk, and it is past.

My lovely, listen, hear the truth:
Anow's your time for budding life,
With glowing greenness, lush and rife,

Oh gather, gather up your youth,
For even like this flower's blush
Old age your bloom will surely crush."

Margot pulled a stool over to Athalie's chair; Athalie forced a smile to her face and gracious words of thanks from her lips. One moment filled her mind: Pierre's return.

Dusk came and went; night came; and still the hunters did not come. The Queen Mother ate alone, anger written across her face. Athalie went to wait on her but was dismissed. Margot supped with the women, giggling like a truant. An artificial jollity took hold, though only briefly; the evening games were quick and dull; the music seemed insipid. Margot beat Athalie thrice at backgammon, then, in a high temper, left her to call for jugglers and acrobats. An acrobat fell on a dagger and was removed. One of the jugglers began to teach Margot his tricks, and soon, the whole group was clustered around her, cheering her on and roaring at her mistakes. So much noise did they make that no one, not even Athalie, heard when the men arrived at last.

Chapter XX

aymond de Galle rode the woodland trail in a tranquil frame of mind. The rising sun, a fierce ball that barely cleared the horizon beyond the naked trees, striped the snow with pink and cobalt blue. It was a still, clear morning, surprising after the vicious bluster of the preceding day. However often he greeted the day in his saddle, invigorated by the lingering cold of night and the thrill with which any intelligent man contemplated the prospect of dangerous sport, it never palled on him. He let the chill air clear his head, enjoyed the familiar pull of reins between his fingers, and eyed his companions with a curious blend of complacency and enthusiasm. White blinked through the dark tree trunks: the dull white of wool jerkins, the shiny, bulky white of padded satin doublets, to the fluffy white of rabbit-fur-lined collars and cuffs. Even some of the hounds wore white quilted coats strapped around their bodies, though their coverings were not so much for warmth or even camouflage as for protection.

Hunting boar was a brutal sport, the last of the great sports now that bears were almost gone and wolf numbers were dwindling. He saw the dog, Avenir, gold-studded collar around its neck and a heavy white coat on its back, but even the reminder it brought of his stepson did not deflect his enjoyment. White, the color some wore for mourning — Raymond shrugged. The black-and-white panorama before him hid more color than the banal greenery of an overblown summer day. It was beautiful to his eyes. He thought that he had never before so appreciated the simple pleasure of looking.

Not that, for all its beauty, he would necessarily have picked this day for hunting. The sunny peace was deceptive and kept the mind from thinking of the hazardous conditions which no sane man would have overlooked had winter shown its teeth.

Successive frosts and thaws had built hard and perilous layers of ice which lay just beneath the carpet of snow. Raymond heard the noise of clicking hooves and knew what it meant, but even he had no desire to pay heed to common sense on such a glorious morning. Still less would the King trouble his mind with any obstacle to his ruling passion. Raymond watched him riding ahead, white satin and gold fleur-de-lis glistening, ermine at neck and wrist, gleaming ostrich feather in his cap, laughing and chattering with the gleeful abandon that he reserved for his beloved hunts.

De Galle glanced at Pierre riding by his side. White suits him, he thought, wondering what lay behind the still, expressionless face. Nothing, probably. Thank God that I have reached the age when I need not see a feast through to its end. When the Queen Mother leaves, I leave. But Pierre and that band of hellions he hangs around with probably haven't slept two hours out of the last forty-eight.

A smile creased the old Duke's cold cheeks as he thought about Pierre's whimsical appointments as Epiphany King. "You've got guts, I'll say that, even if your manners lack something," he broke out with a muffled chuckle. Pierre looked at him, startled. "Appointing that swine, Maurice, as Duke de Galle — over my dead body, I thought, even in jest! But when I saw how he took it, why, first, he was thrilled, you could see it, but when he had to put his hands between yours and swear fealty, it nearly killed him. It's worth it, I thought, just to see him squirm." De Galle laughed out loud, coughing a billow of mist into the air. Pierre smiled back at him.

"The young Duchess, she's a pretty girl," de Galle continued after a pause. "It's funny, I never noticed her much until you picked her out, and then she seemed to grow into the part. Her mother now, who was de Retz's sister, she was a beauty, and her father cut a fine figure, but I always thought the child was a mousy type."

Pierre's failure to reply neither discouraged nor offended his father. "Glad you picked her. More fun that way, and maybe it will take your Anne down a peg or two."

Pierre's horse stumbled on a hidden rock, and he bent to pat its neck. The two men rode on in companionable silence. Encouraged by it, Raymond broached a subject which he suspected of being a sore spot between them.

"You see, that business with the Admiral all came to nothing, as I told you it would at the time. His life was not in danger, with the Guises out of the way and the King having given his word. Still, you were right to bring it up to me, completely right, and I should not have... have repulsed you." To Pierre's astounded ears, the words rang as close to an apology as any he had heard his father utter.

"The latent danger is always there," de Galle continued, "and one should never overlook signs that it is pushing toward the surface. We all know what they want, the Guises, Anjou, de Retz, and it is up to us to stop them from getting it. By us, I mean the moderates of course, and God knows there are few enough of us."

De Galle caught his son's attentive look before continuing ruminatively. "Do you know why? It takes strength to stay in the center and hold the extremes in balance. It leaves one vulnerable to accusations of cynicism and cowardice — the two least edifying qualities of humankind — and one must meet the accusations without the support of a whole passel of myths and hatreds. The Queen Mother, now, she has the force of character for such a role, but it's not enough. You need muscle, too. That's why she needs us."

They reached the gathering place, an open glade ringed with low trees so bent under their weight of ice and snow as to look more like an encircling fence than freestanding trees. Everyone dismounted and milled around the fires the grooms had lit.

All but the King were more interested in enjoying a ladleful of bouillon than in listening to the tracker's report. Charles waved away the groom who, bowing, held out his bowl with stiff-armed obsequiousness; he kept all his attention for the tracker. Raymond de Galle bore his cup over to his monarch's side and listened to the report.

There were tracks, well enough, splayed marks of different sizes, showing that several boars had passed through, one very large, the tracker estimated, gesticulating freely to make his point. He waved his arms toward the branches he had broken to mark the trails. Charles looked with passionate interest in the direction indicated; Raymond stared, too, and concluded that only a wizard could distinguish the branches broken by man from those that Nature had blasted. Shrewdly, he watched the animated groom enthuse upon the good sport they were to have, and rightly judged that the man's volubility was a cover for his dog's failure to pick up a scent. Since the hounds were of the King's pack, no one but Charles would dare complain. De Galle stamped his feet, his good humor dissipating like mist in the air.

They set out, anyway, following the prints in the snow, the tracker, his assistants and his hounds in the lead; the King next, with his nobles in a compact knot behind; the grooms, white coats covering their varied liveries; with the hunting dogs, tightly leashed, bringing up the rear. In the end, it was an Alençon man, who had wormed his way to the front with his dog, who bugled a triumphant call: The scent was fresh, the hunt was on.

Straining on their leads and whimpering, the boarhounds were brought to the fore; the riders fanned out for freer movement; the horn blew again. Released, the dogs led off, all their earlier excitement transformed into professional deadliness. With mastiff strength and greyhound litheness, they were a beautiful and fearful sight. Grey, brown, tan, white, they streamed across the barren landscape, baying in full voice.

It was heavy going for the horses. Banks of straw hid treacherous undergrowth. Bare rock sheeted with ice capped windswept hilltops. Trees brushed in passing dislodged minor avalanches onto mount and rider alike. The orderly phalanx of hunters soon disintegrated into stumbling, crashing twosomes and threesomes. Pierre held his course on track by sight rather than sound, following closely behind the King instead of striking out on his own. On much the same principle, Raymond de Galle wallowed along behind his son and the King, sparing his horse the effort of cutting a fresh path. On one hillock, father and son drew abreast and exchanged smiles of complicity by which each told the other that he knew what the other was doing and why.

The day wore painfully on. The scent was lost, then found again. The pause was a blessing in disguise for it enabled the scattered band of hunters to gather in its stragglers and regroup.

When they started out again, it was with some semblance of order to their ranks, but the illusion of organization was short-lived. There had been some confusion during the halt whether they were chasing one beast or several, de Galle recalled with a grim smile; he would not be surprised if the group were to splinter and lose various parts altogether. He would never have hunted boar so far into the winter, he told himself again, with a sense of superior judgment that was small recompense for his physical discomfort. At least, the cold stops the wet from penetrating boots and hose, he thought, but that is no consolation for frozen toes. There was no gainsaying it; his extremities were more sensitive now than in his youth, and the hand that had been frostbitten once, years ago, was a source of agony at times like this. He flexed the cramped fingers in the stiff glove, feeling needles of pain jab the numbed flesh. He looked ahead at Pierre, rock-like atop the heaving mound of muscle that plowed through the snow, and a twinge of envy tormented him. It passed, for he did not indulge it.

Cunningly, Pierre and he had resumed, after the stop, the same positions they had held previously. They now spread out in a thin line linked by burrowed snow — Charles, Pierre, and Raymond. To the left and right, muffled crashes signaled the presence of their companions. Clouds tarnished the gleam of the day. The afternoon sun became a dully glowing globe suspended against a backdrop of grey. The landscape assumed the look of a poor quality tapestry which years of use had faded. Raymond began to weary of the endless, fruitless chase; his fatigue brought on an attack of irritability tinged with self-reproach. Even the King's manic enthusiasm subsided at last into sullen resentment, broken only by occasional thrusts of petulance. Pierre alone was unperturbed by the apparent futility of their quest. His mind attained the rhythmic emptiness which physical activity sometimes brought him and which enabled him to achieve an effortless perfection of motion, like that of a flowing stream.

The three, Charles and Pierre, with Raymond close behind, emerged in midafternoon into an open glade, a platform of bedrock coated with snow-covered ice and surrounded by a gloomy wall of pine. An angry wind soughed through the needled boughs, masking the rumble of the hunt. The King pulled up with a jerk so vicious that his mount stumbled and nearly fell. He shouted something back at his companions, but the words were swept away.

Charles swung from the saddle, and tossing his reins and spear to Pierre, stumped past Raymond to the clearing's edge and discreetly turned his back. De Galle shook his head disapprovingly before settling back in his saddle with a feeling of relief. Pierre's mood was broken; he felt his stiff muscles ache while they had moved uncomplainingly; a huge yawn painfully stretched his cheek muscles.

Undiscerned, a nearby rumble merged with the crashings and thunderings of the riders traversing the pine grove. A new noise came to the three, unnoticed at first: low gruntings punctuated by strange, shrill sounds of uncontrolled rage. At the same time the unconscious listeners became aware of it, their eyes identified its source. The King looked over his shoulder, de Galle glowered from beneath bristling eyebrows, Pierre's wandering eyes were arrested: All were frozen in a moment of horror.

Their quarry had found them. Its dark wet hide almost invisible against the blackened trunks, heavy-shouldered, head lowered, white tusks gleaming, the boar paused, caught and held for an instant on the edge of their vision as of their awareness, but only for an instant. It plunged on, eyes rolling and glinting with demented light, past the two riders, along the row of trees whose snow-laden boughs brushed its back, toward the immobile King.

Dropping the reins of Charles' horse, Pierre drove his own forward with his knees, a spear in each hand. Clutching at his reins with his left hand, clumsy from the burden of the King's spear, Pierre pulled Phoebus parallel to the boar and hurled his spear with all his might. His aim was true, but alas, his target was no neophyte. It was an animal that had reached a maturity where cunning and strength were matched. The boar swerved; the spear notched the bristles on his back and imbedded itself, quivering, in a bank of snow. Barely slowed, the boar continued its ferocious attack. As Pierre maneuvered, Raymond de Galle swung from the saddle, his stiffened joints protesting the suddenness of his movement.

Hurtling forward, he came to a spot halfway between the King and the surging beast, and threw himself to his knees, lowering his spear and bracing it against the ground. The point gleamed wickedly above the crossbar that was designed to stop a transfixed boar from continuing his murderous assault. Many times had de Galle stood or knelt waiting for the attack of such a beast — but never alone. Where were the hunting dogs trained to slow the boar, each gripping one ear? Where were the companions whose thrusts could deflect the animal's single-minded charge? Time stood still, but de Galle was not afraid. He had never failed. The boar burst through the illusion of timelessness and drove itself, unswerving, on the point. The base of the spear ground and wrenched against the rock until it hit ice and gave way. Spear point embedded in its chest, the boar pushed against the crossbar and lowering its head, thrust its tusks into de Galle.

Pierre, too, had been gripped in an instant of timelessness which seemed to drive thought and even horror from his mind. As in one motion, he shifted the King's spear from left to right, gripped spear and reins, and kicked forward. Leaning over, he thrust the spear down with the full weight of his chest and shoulders, drove its point through the ridge of the boar's back, and severed its spinal cord. With an unearthly shriek, the animal keeled over beside de Galle's prone figure. Its death scream was echoed by hysterical cries as Charles laughed and sobbed, blowing gusts of steam from his mouth.

Onto this scene, Gondi rode. A huntsman, with a horn slung across his back, followed close behind. Gondi's glance took in the shuddering monarch, the prone figures of the boar and the Duke, and Pierre's kneeling form at his father's side. Paling, he gestured to his companion to signal the hunt's halt and swung from his horse. Kneeling next to Pierre, he looked down at the ghastly wound in the Duke's abdomen. From there, his eyes wandered slowly to the fallen man's averted face: The eyes screwed tight, the brow creased, the teeth grinding, all spoke of unendurable pain.

Full of wonder and sorrow, Gondi allowed his gaze to roam from the man's agonized face to his clenched fists, until slowly, he bent his look on Pierre. His attention went unremarked by its subject, whose eyes were for his father alone.

Gondi shook Pierre by the shoulder; the drawn face turned; a blank look met his; and Pierre turned back to the fallen man.

Gondi stumbled to his feet, and going over to the King, yelled, "Stop it! Your Majesty, stop!" The gibbering ceased. The young King flushed and walked over to Pierre and his father. Next to de Galle, the hulk of the boar sprawled, its small eyes no longer wild, but motionless and dull. Across the rough pelt, a bare spot sported a hideous scar. Charles knelt and ran his hand over the tusks, the straight and the curved, then timidly touched the scar. Standing abruptly, he addressed Gondi in a high-pitched tone. "A good size beast, don't you think? He'll make a fine trophy." Shocked, Gondi looked at Pierre, who, unnoticing, gazed at his father.

The clearing filled slowly. Little by little, as small groups answered the horn's summons, the work of the hunt was replaced by the restless clopping of hoofs, the jangle of bits, the swishing of tails, and over all, the shocked murmurs of the crowd. A litter was made up for the wounded man, as Gondi threw his cloak over the Duke, and Pierre, aroused at last, followed suit. Slowly, the group began the long trek home, riders in the lead, followed by the Duke's litter, Pierre walking by its side, and in the rear, two grooms bearing the boar swinging by its heels from a stave. The initial whispers of shock and grief gave place to bursts of conversation, as the King told the tale of the boar's attack, creating for himself a bold role which, though it had never occurred, lived bravely in his imagination. His listeners, who had seen nothing, passed the story up and down the ranks of noblemen with splendid additions of their own. Only two men remained silent throughout the tedious scramble across the frozen countryside: Pierre, who walked by his father's litter, his eyes ever on his face, and the Duke, whose mindless agony passed into coma and at last into death.

* * *

It was a silent procession that rode out of the forest onto the open plain around the château. The intense discomfort of the return had stilled the talk of even the most ardent gossips. They were tough men, these hunters — the lords no less than their servants — but still, the cold seemed past enduring. Hands and feet were bone-chilled through their leathers; frost sprouted like moss on beards and mustaches; limb bones ached beneath numbed exteriors. To most, the sight of the château, a distant beacon of wavering light, brought no comfort; they were beyond the point where hope could warm them.

The avenue, broad and straight, led to the King's Gate. Between the torches winking on the snow, all save the King dismounted. Charles rode over the moat, across the Court of Honor, up to the grand entrance, and dismounted. The litter of the dead Duke was borne behind him, and slowly the courtyard filled with the lords, their retainers, the huntsmen, the archers, the grooms, and the footmen. Like a flood of water channeled by a dam, they collected around the main entrance and began to trickle into the guard hall behind the King and the Duke's body. The incoming flow met the wash of ladies pouring down the spiral stairs into the huge hall.

Like ripples, the news of the hunt's return and its tragic harvest spread through the château, and streams of people flowed down staircases and through corridors into the hall. As wave upon wave arrived, the subdued shushing of the arriving hunters was submerged in a gabble of horrified protest and comment. Above the din, the King's voice rang out, "Summon Paré! Bring Ambroise Paré!"

The heavy oak which barred the entrance to the Queen Mother's apartments was pulled back. Silence, commanded by her mere presence, quelled the near-hysteria. A heavy robe covering her nightdress, Catherine's squat, but massive figure dominated the crowd, which parted to let her approach the bearers and their burden. She looked down at the still face of Raymond de Galle, from which death had wiped all signs of agony. When she spoke, it was quietly, but the sound of her voice carried down the three arms of the guard hall. "Let Paré sleep. His ministrations are no longer needed."

The ranks of watchers rustled apart to permit two women to pass through: Tall and dark, fully dressed, for she had been awaiting her Duke's return, his wife approached his body, with Anne close by her side. She glanced down, gave a piercing scream, and throwing her hands to her head, crumpled against her daughter-in-law. The Queen Mother stared at her, sternly, but with pity, and turned to speak to Anne. "Madame la Duchess," she said in ringing tones, "accompany the Dowager Duchess to her rooms."

"But..." Anne began to protest.

"She is not herself," Catherine cut in. "She can do nothing here." And the cold eyes that held Anne's face seemed to add, "nor can you." Anne attempted a curtsey before turning and supporting the half-fainting woman through the crowd.

The Queen Mother's eyes sought Gondi among the hunters.

"Monsieur de Retz," she said, "you will see to it that all is done that is fitting to the rank of this great lord, who was beloved of our heart." He nodded gravely. "In times gone by, white was worn for mourning, though today's customs require black. Those who take the first vigil tonight will remain in white. So will a hunter's death be mourned. You, my son," she gestured to Hercule-François, "will bear witness to our grief, and you," she held out her hand to Pierre, "will wish to honor your father." Allowing his hand to be taken, Pierre looked again at the dead Duke, his eyes reddening with unshed tears. "Let others be chosen to watch with these two, and more to relieve the watchers throughout the night.

"In the morning, there will be a Mass for the Dead. Then, Your Majesty," she turned to the King, "we will leave for Blois. It is too late to leave tonight; we must go on the morrow as soon as may be, for it is not seemly for you to share lodgings with the dead.

"And now, bear the body to the chapel."

A small torchlight procession made its way back into the courtyard and around the keep to the chapel. It took time to set up a raised bier, covered with black satin, to locate and hang black draperies on the walls, to clothe the body in rich, black garments, placing the ducal coronet on its brow. When all was as it should be, the watchers took their places, forming a candlelit nucleus in the brooding darkness of the chapel.

Throughout the château, agitated groups came together and broke up, as they chewed over the news of de Galle's demise, digested it, and assimilated it into the solid flesh of accepted reality. Slowly their frenzy gave way to calmer and more purposeful activities. Chambord's residents set in motion the preparations necessary for an early departure. As the courtiers and ladies and their servants disappeared into the warren-like recesses of the huge building, Athalie slipped down the corridor which skirted the King's apartments and made for the chapel. Its great doors were pulled back, revealing a lighted island in a sea of obscurity. Breathing quickly, more from emotion than exertion, Athalie pressed herself against the back wall and waited for Pierre to be relieved. When the new mourners arrived and, bending their knees, took their places around the bier, Athalie relied on the darkness to hide her as she watched those they replaced leave the candlelight and make for the dimly lit vestibule. On the threshold, the group stopped, the young men pressing around Pierre to squeeze an arm or shoulder, before leaving him lingering alone, looking back, dazed, at the arc of light around his father's body. Athalie slipped from the shadows and took his arm. Pierre looked at her with a blank, uncomprehending stare.

"Come," she whispered, and led him by the hand into the vestibule and up the narrow stairs to the tribune which overlooked the chapel's interior. He stumbled once in the dark, and Athalie's thoughts went back to St. Gatien's and the stairs they climbed when the darkness had wielded no power over their carefree hearts. The balcony was unlit; its only illumination rose from the candles far below. Athalie led Pierre to a wooden bench and pulled him down beside her. For a while, neither spoke. Athalie stroked him, his face, his hair, his hands, his arms, his thighs. Then, at last, Pierre began to speak.

"I failed him. My God, Lie-lie. I failed him the only time he ever needed me. He's dead, because of me."

"Hush, Pierre, you mustn't reproach yourself."

"He gave me the best training a man could have. Everything. He made me! And I rewarded him by this."

"You did all you could. I wasn't there, but I know it. I know you."

"All I could — my God!"

"You mustn't judge your actions by what came of them. Events are not in man's control. There is God's will."

"I can't see why I was made, if what I do, even... even when I want to do right, try so hard, produces the opposite of what I strive for. There is no point, no point to anything."

"Pierre, you blaspheme. Dearest, you must not talk like that." Feeling the wet on her own cheeks, she searched for his face, and though it was dry, wiped it with her hand. "Perhaps," she continued, "perhaps the doing, the trying, is all that counts, regardless of the consequences." She thought of what she, what they, had done and the consequences of the doing. She longed fiercely to speak of her terrifying secret, to share it with Pierre as she had planned and waited for, counting the minutes until his return. But now, his greater trouble dwarfed the burden that she had thought was too heavy for her to bear alone. Some other time, they would talk of it, though when, she could not imagine, since a family in mourning would leave Court immediately. She wished he could hear her thoughts, and she knew the wish to be selfish and unworthy of her, fruitless, too, for she doubted he even heard her words.

"I never knew him," he cried out. "And he never knew me."

"Fathers cannot know their sons. You are becoming something else, because of his death. He could hardly live to see it. And anyway, maybe he does see you, maybe he will watch you continuing to become whatever God means you to be."

She could feel the protest that raged unspoken through him, as if it were a physical tremor. "I wish I had died instead of him," he said.

"Think what you are saying, Pierre. Your father would scorn such words, he who believed in the family, in the heritage of his ancestors, for which he was only a vessel. As you are."

He sat silently for a few moments, then sighed and stood. "I will go to my stepmother. She and Elie will need comforting."

They parted in the dark with no more than a brief handclasp.

It was dawn when Athalie went to her uncle's chambers. She had not slept. On leaving Pierre, she had returned to her room and had prayed, kneeling, for the dead Duke; for Pierre, that his grief would bring strength rather than despair, strength to bear his new responsibilities; and finally, for herself, and the great responsibility that she must shoulder, that was partly Pierre's, but so much more her own. The brief night had passed. She had changed into a plain dress of charcoal grey, one of the few relics of her pre-Court days and the only garb she owned that could pass for mourning. As the servants began to bang back the shutters to let in the ghastly first light of an overcast, drab day, she went to seek out Gondi in his tower suite, whose two large rooms with an antechamber and dressing room bore witness to his elevated station.

He was up and dressed, as she had expected, but a hint of reproach in his look suggested nonetheless that her arrival had inconvenienced him. The Countess, his wife, was seated on a low stool before a maidservant who was energetically brushing her gleaming auburn tresses. She gave Athalie a quick glance, then turned back to allow the grooming to continue.

"Uncle, I must speak to you." Athalie said. "Speak," Gondi replied with a shrug.

"When the Court leaves for Blois this morning, I... I do not wish to accompany it."

Gondi, startled, bent his full attention on her. "How is that, niece?"

"I wish to go to Fontevrault, I believe, I hope, to rest." Her words stumbled hopelessly, and she averted her gaze from his.

The Countess gestured impatiently for her maid to stop and turned to watch.

"I'm afraid I don't understand," Gondi said.

"I'm sick," Athalie burst out.

"Sick?" Gondi looked her over with a kind of wary disbelief, noting her drawn face and shadowed eyes.

"Sick at soul," Athalie said, her hands moving in a plea for understanding. "I've lost my..." She sought desperately for words that would convey something she herself did not fully understand. What had she lost? Her vision of the Universe? Her inner drive and the understanding that had fueled it? Or simply her innocence?

"I've lost my peace of mind," she said at last, conscious that the platitude was inadequate to the point of mendacity, but caring only that her uncle and aunt should let her have her way, regardless of their own knowledge or understanding.

"You mean," Gondi said, "because you turned away from your calling?"

"Perhaps. Perhaps I am being punished," Athalie replied, with intentional ambiguity.

The Countess raised her eyebrows expressively, and Gondi relaxed imperceptibly.

"I have no objection," he said at last, "but you must, of course, seek the Queen Mother's permission."

"Uncle, I don't wish to return to Blois. There will be delays which could be avoided if I left right away. I have a need which is urgent. There will never be time to talk to Her Majesty between the Mass and the departure. You could make it right with her." Athalie's dread of facing the Queen Mother's piercing scrutiny gave her pleas a persuasiveness that words themselves did not express.

"I wish I could explain," she mumbled not quite truthfully. "Her Majesty will be angry, and rightly so."

Gondi was unable to keep complacency from his voice. After a pause, he added, "I will do what I can for you, Athalie. I will explain matters in the best light to our Mistress. Be prepared to leave after the service. I will have an escort ready."

"Thank you, uncle," Athalie said with a genuine warmth which surprised him. "I bid you both farewell." She curtseyed graciously and left.

She rushed to her room to make sure the packing was well under way, then, taking refuge, with a writing board and paper, pen, and ink, in the nurse's now-bare cubbyhole, she began the most important task of the morning. At first, as she sat on the window seat, she rubbed her forehead as if to exorcise the blankness of her mind. When words came, it was in a flow, which she penned, almost without thought, into her letter.

When, a short while later, she reached the chapel doors, letter in hand, the big room was already full of black-garbed courtiers and ladies. Death had made its ominous presence felt with a vengeance. The narrow aisle between the moving masses of black — the shushing velvets, the rustling damasks, the gently frothing silks — showed Raymond de Galle's raised bier, its flowing satin coverings embroidered with gold thread holding gleaming pieces of agate, his shield and weapons arrayed at his feet. In front, Pierre stood tall and motionless, as much beyond her reach as his dead father.

Confused and desperate, Athalie hesitated on the chapel's threshold. A hand placed on her shoulder, with a suggestion of pressure and then removed, made her start and turn. Maurice de la Renaudie smiled and bowed.

La Renaudie's habitual black garb had obviated the necessity of a hypocritical change of dress. For that he was grateful. To make feigned grief an effort would have been distasteful, though he had no wish to provoke censure by overtly inappropriate behavior. His dallying before the requiem Mass, which had brought him to the chapel doors after most of the mourners had already passed through, was not intentional, though it did reflect his repugnance for the event. The idea of begging off attending because of his Protestant convictions had tempted him, but he had thought better of it. He had come, ostensibly to mourn, but his face gave the lie to his action.

Athalie greeted his unexpected presence with relief. "Monsieur, I have a letter for your stepbrother. It contains some... some news I know he would wish to have. But I am afraid that I won't be able to greet him before he leaves. After the Mass they will bear the Duke's body, I mean, the defunct Duke's body, in procession from the chapel, and will begin the journey to his home. Isn't that how it will be?"

"Yes, Mademoiselle."

"So there will be no chance to give him this, and I thought..."

"But, of course, my dear Duchess. You entrust your missive to uncle Maurice." Though she had not said the letter was hers, he had guessed that it was, and her failure to deny it made him sure of it. He took the sealed packet and stuffed it into the front of his doublet.

She found his smile odd, but thought no more of it after they had passed together through the chapel doors.

Chapter XXI

ierre rested his elbows on the table and his head on his hands. All around him books of account lay amidst rolls and piles of loose paper and parchment. Sturdy and stable though his working place appeared, Pierre wondered that the trestles did not buckle beneath the documents' weight, as he himself felt crushed by their contents. It came to him, then, alone in the tower room, with his sole companions these papers which could have communicated a world of knowledge but were as incomprehensible to him as a rabble of foreigners, that the predominant emotion that he had felt since his father's death was loneliness. This perception surprised him, for he had not expected that out of the welter of feelings which had succeeded one another since the accident, a terrible feeling of solitude would be the only one to prove enduring.

As was normal, the numbed shock of the first hours of Pierre's grief had soon given way to confusion. Beset by a host of demands and hindered by the latent conflicts and inadequacies within his own household, Pierre, once he had come to feel anything, had felt bewildered and overwhelmed. The dead Duke's widow had collapsed like a puppet abandoned by its puppeteer. To Pierre's relief and his wife's chagrin, Elie had replaced her as the one who infused life and love into the rituals that protocol demanded. Pierre had been grateful beyond expression, but Anne, who had thought that as the new Duchess she and she alone should be the power behind Pierre, had taken umbrage. Eleanor, however, would not relinquish what she saw as her last duty to her Duke, that of seeing him to rest with pomp and affection, and Pierre had supported her in every way he could, and thus, Anne had been forced to accept a subsidiary role. This she had done with poor grace, firmly resolved that her setback would be only temporary.

The old Duke had been borne home by a procession of mourning monks and grieving knights, had lain in state in the great hall of Plessis Gaillard at last in the marble sepulchre that he himself had ordered, a monument that was both simple and grand, as the man himself had been. Receiving the emblems of his rank on the eve of his father's entombment, Pierre had felt no elation, only relief that the elaborate ceremonies of death would soon be concluded. When the gathered mourners, turning from the old lord to the new, one by one, had knelt, placed their hands between Pierre's and sworn fealty to him, the moment had been like intoxication by a heady wine, but the aftermath had been as disappointing. Life went on, and it seemed that its hours of grueling labor and worry engulfed its minutes of glory.

Since then, Pierre's main preoccupation had been to attempt to grasp the nature and extent of the family assets: Plessis Gaillard and its domain, farms in Touraine and Picardy, two grist mills, a salt mine, a naval galley with its full complement of slaves, crew, and soldiers, and the properties that had constituted

Anne's dowry — Villandry on the Cher and its extensive grounds, more farms north of Chinon, and vineyards near Bourgeuil. The task of mentally subjecting these varied lands and their appendages to his rule was herculean, and yet was only preliminary to his real work: that of understanding what obligations went with his new position and, most important, how he would meet them. As Pierre slowly unraveled the web of privileges and duties which now centered on himself, he found that despite his far-flung holdings, there did not seem to be enough money to make ends meet — to support his private household, to maintain his men at arms, to keep his lands fallow and fruitful and his buildings in good repair, and to pay the interest on the loans.

The loans! The chief steward, on whom Pierre had confidently expected to rely, had proven disappointingly unhelpful. He was a rotund elder, full of his own importance, whose outward subservience barely marked his arrogant contempt for his new master and whose reassurances rang less and less true with every item of information that Pierre, unassisted, uncovered for himself. To Pierre's queries, he would prevaricate: "My Lord your father did things thus and so"; "Your Lordship need not concern himself with that"; "Your esteemed father left such matters to me." Whether the man could not or would not cooperate, Pierre was unable to determine. It was nonetheless evident that his assistance would not support Pierre as he had hoped. Finally, this afternoon, Pierre had sent him away while he tackled the ledgers and papers alone. They lay around him now, deeds, notes, reports, accounts, some mysterious to him, others evidently requiring action, but what action? There was the watermill whose wheel had been damaged by ice. There was the tenant farmer who claimed his Lord should bear the cost of repairing a stable roof crushed by a falling branch. There were this farmer and that who had fallen behind in their contributions because the harvest had been bad. And there was the interest on the loans — and no money to pay it.

Pierre rubbed his temples. He felt as if there were a lump in his head. His new responsibilities weighed on him, terrified him, and beneath the stormy turbulence of his mind's surface lay a great depth of loneliness, loneliness and anger. He missed his father, who had provided the structure and confines of his life, always taken for granted, often resented, but ever a source of strength. Even more, he missed Athalie. It was unavoidable that his father's death should have separated them for the short run. He knew that. It was also true that there was no long run for them, that their relationship would die, like the flowers in spring, as the poems and songs of love predicted with banal, but accurate wisdom. He knew the truth of those melancholy phrases, though he scarcely ever admitted it to himself. What he could not understand was why Athalie should suddenly have disappeared without a word, adding the burden of her silence to the double loss of her absence and his father's death. At first, he had waited with unquestioning trust, confident that his beloved would not fail him in his hour of need, but the passage of time had disillusioned him and anger had supplanted trust, adding its peculiar sting to his many-faceted malaise.

He pressed his palms against his temples, as if to crush the source of his pain. His mind felt dull and slow, as he forced it back to the problem at hand. Surely, a brilliant solution to his financial woes would be evident to a man of experience, though it eluded a dolt like himself. Well, he thought grimly, a dolt must behave as a dolt and take a simple approach. With a sigh, he took paper and pen and began to write in an awkward, unpracticed hand. The request he penned was indeed a simple one, coupling a wish for guidance in the matter of the loans with an offer of hospitality and of an opportunity to peruse the accounts. The message's humility was out of keeping, Pierre thought, with the grandness of the signature: "Pierre de Galle, Duke of Touraine."

With a sadly incredulous smile, he looked at his own title, then folded and sealed the paper and addressed it to Artus Pascal, banker of Chinon. That done, Pierre sat on in the gloaming, wondering what he had overlooked, feeling useless, but oddly reluctant to move on to another employment. The darkness of an early dusk and the oppressive threat of snow mirrored the deadening pall that seemed to lie over the landscape of his mind. In the room, the light and heat from a bravely blazing fire fought the inhospitable gloom of the chamber's recesses. The near side of Pierre's body tingled, half-scorched through his clothes, while the far side ached from cold.

A knock on the door passed for preamble to its opening, no word of welcome or acquiescence apparently being required by the newcomer. A rustle of clothes identified Pierre's visitor to his ears before the door swung to behind her. The firelight picked out Anne's white face pinnacled above a mound of mourning clothes: skirts and underskirts, outer sleeves and inner sleeves, jacket, shawl, high collar, close-fitting cap — the clothing cocooned Anne's slim form, obscuring its elegant lines. Out of the blackness, shadowed eyes stared with a balefulness that her brittle smile failed to mask. A mere glance at her face set Pierre's teeth on edge. Why, he wondered, must she vent her humors on me at such a time? Were I to show emotion, there would be some reason for it, but what has she to cry about? She has no real troubles, but like a spoiled child, she mourns, not for my father's death, but for the loss of her playmates. She cannot bear a life of seclusion and finds my company but meager consolation. Instead of assisting me, she demands that I sacrifice my energies to her pleasure. He watched her approach with sullen resentfulness. Anne had at first faltered on the threshold, as if uncertain of her purpose; her eyes had scanned the littered table and rested on Pierre's morose face, before she had swept across the room and taken the vacant chair opposite his that the steward usually occupied. The silence that lay between them was not the comfortable silence of easy companionship, but the taut silence of unbridged misunderstandings. At last, Anne said, "I'm so cold!"

Pierre shrugged and agreed without interest. "It's been a very cold winter."

"Cold winter, indeed!" she burst out angrily. "I'll warrant in May we'll still be shivering. This... this place... would make a fine shelter for livestock, but it's no human abode. Rooms like dens! How can one help but freeze? The windows are not suited for glass, but it's no matter since I doubt your ancestors ever heard of it."

"No one's ancestors ever heard of it. Shutters and screens have done well enough for hundreds of years and would do fine now if the winter weren't exceptionally harsh."

"Ah! And haven't you seen how the modern châteaux are built? People who live as we should live have buildings that are graceful and functional. Or hadn't you noticed? I grant you that in years gone by, places like this were the best people had, but this is 1572, after all. Must we live in the past, we of all people, who have means and taste and a rank to uphold?"

Startled out of his listlessness, Pierre rejoined hotly, "Plessis was good enough for my father and mother; it is good enough for the dowager Duchess and Aunt Eleanor and me; and it damn well is going to be good enough for you. I see no reason to offend either the living or the memory of the dead to satisfy your thirst for display. You can't change buildings like dresses. Do you want our home to look like Blois — a new wing for every duke and each one in a different style?"

"You could do worse. The royal family has a fine sense of where things are going. And as for giving offense, who has the right to be offended? Are we not the master and mistress of our own house?

"I'm glad, by the way," she continued less passionately, but no less stubbornly, "I'm very glad you brought that up. I've been meaning to speak to you about that very subject. It's high time we took charge of our household; we can't limp along in the old way forever. It isn't fitting. The dowager Duchess must have a household of her own, some farm or property with a suitable abode. She'll feel much better when she's no longer surrounded by so many reminders of your father, and with her out of the way, it is possible, just barely possible, that our slovenly servants will learn how a household ought to be run. Where there are two mistresses in a house, the result is always chaos.

"As things are now," her voice rose to shrill heights, "there are not two, but three mistresses! That, at least, you will surely agree, cannot continue. Eleanor d'Avrillac — your aunt Elie, as you so touchingly, if somewhat misleadingly, call her — must return to her own home. She has a home, somewhere, I assume?" Her eyebrow lifted in a well-practiced manner.

At his stone-like irresponsiveness, she resumed petulantly, "Well, really. It was bad enough for your father to keep a resident mistress, but it's out of the question for you to keep your father's mistress. I mean, it's not as if she's too old..."

"That's enough!" Pierre cut in.

Anne stopped abruptly, the change in Pierre having shocked her into silence without her really being conscious of it. A tiny voice in the recesses of her mind murmured caution, but she disregarded it.

"Pierre, I am your wife. You owe it to me to put my well-being ahead of everyone else's. I can't live in a rude, rough place. I didn't marry you for that; it isn't right that you should expect it of me."

With a burst of irritation, Pierre swept the rolls of paper in front of him to one side. "Whatever the merits of your sentiments," he said after a pause, "your timing is atrocious. My world has been stood on its head, and all you can think of is that we should start to dismember my home stone by stone. Well, it's not going to happen. Even if I had no one but you to think of, I wouldn't do it, at least not now. But I don't have just you. There is a whole household of family, servants, soldiers, tenants, whose welfare depends on me. By rights, you should be helping me, but if you can't, you should at least stay out of the way."

"You took me too literally," she said. "We don't have to do anything to your precious Plessis Gaillard. I doubt it would be worth the effort, now that I think about it. No, what we should do is take Villandry and expand it, as the Queen Mother is expanding Chenonceau." A vision of her gracious home filled her mind. She saw it in full summer, white stone reflecting the sun, a perfection of gleaming symmetry, surrounded by decorative moats, dominating an expanse of brilliant gardens.

A wave of longing rushed over her. "That," she concluded, "is the kind of place I want to live in, when we're not at Court. Of course, we would still come here to hold court as your functions required, but..."

"Would we!" Pierre rose and towered over her.

"Yes, but..." Anne's talk ceased, as something in the huge dark silhouette edged with reflected light struck an ominous note.

Pierre spoke quickly. "You may go to Villandry at your whim. You may go now, if you wish. Don't feel that I'm detaining you."

"What do you mean?"

"I mean very simply, that you have my permission, indeed my encouragement, to leave for Villandry. If I could force you to be what a wife should be, then I would force you to stay by my side where you belong. It seems, however, that I can't. In these times of trouble, when it might be expected that your better nature would show forth, you've done nothing but indulge your whimsies — and nasty, peevish whimsies they've been. You've driven my stepmother into seclusion, you've persecuted Elie, you've baited me, you've driven the servants to distraction, and offended my oldest retainers.

"Now, I grant you," he continued, "you've alternated your spates of bad humor with unwonted displays of affection to me — yes, I did notice — but I ascribe that to nothing more than a hankering for variety. In short, we would all be better off without you. You can't return to Court without me, but you need not stay here. You say being here is affecting your health. Perhaps it is, though I know of no condition that would explain it. Since you will indulge your whims no matter what, you may as well indulge your desire to be at Villandry. Go."

Anne stood and hurried around the table to Pierre. At first, she hesitated in front of him, then she reached out and took one of his fists in her hands. "Pierre, I didn't mean, I never meant, that I wanted to leave you." A note of panic rose in her voice. He looked at her quizzically. "I meant that we should go there together, live there together. We would walk in the gardens and pick new grounds for parterres and what we would grow in them. We would agree on how to expand the building, what new wings could be added, without ruining the balance, the beautiful symmetry of the place. I have a lot of ideas. I would describe them so you would see what the work would be like before the builders built it. We would make it a place we could be proud of, a gem, a place the Queen Mother herself would envy. That's what I meant. I don't want to go there alone. Don't send me away."

Pierre pulled his hand gently away, stood back, and looked at his wife's face. Entreaty and enthusiasm mingled and touched him in spite of himself. "It's a wonderful idea, except that we have no money."

"No money!" she cried. "How can that be?"

"If you really want to know, you'd have to plow through all this," he gestured largely across the table, "as I've been doing."

She bit back a desire to lash out at him and said, "But your father was one of the richest men in the kingdom. That's what we were told when I contracted to marry you."

"And so he was, and so I am. But being rich is not as simple a matter as I thought." Anne leaned back against the edge of the table, turning Pierre's surprising revelation over in her mind. She found to her amazement that it did not shock or chagrin her as much as she would have expected. Though lack of ready assets would make her plans more difficult to execute, the added challenge would add spice to her ventures and make her achievements more valuable in her own eyes.

"Well," she said finally, "we mustn't be discouraged, or lack of heart will be a greater obstacle than lack of money."

"True," said Pierre, relieved if surprised at her philosophical approach. "But we must get on with things. That much is clear."

"What do you mean?"

"As soon as we can decently come out of mourning, we must return to Court."

"Yes, and you must push yourself forward. Your father was a great man, but he didn't make the most of his greatness. For example, he had a commission for a naval galley. Well, the Count de Retz has two, or even three, and you must have four. Why should de Retz be Gentleman of the King's Bedchamber, instead of you? I pick de Retz as an example because he is such a good model. Look where he began and what he has already achieved. What would he have accomplished, if he'd started where you are! Why, a man like you should aspire to the stars. You should be an admiral, governor of provinces, a marshal of France, the King's first minister and right-hand man. You must fight to obtain the rank you deserve. And when that happens, we'll not lack for money. Does de Retz ever pinch his pennies? Money comes to him as the Nile comes to Egypt." Her dazzled gaze darted to his face, and caught the scorn that twisted his features.

"Why look at me that way?" she asked angrily. "I'm looking out for you."

"Save yourself the trouble, Madame." He turned and walked away, talking to her over his shoulder. "You have, I am afraid, missed the point. One who starts, as you say, where I am does not need to scramble for the heights. I am a de Galle. There have been de Galles for all the time there have been Valois, and then longer still. It was my good fortune, merited or not, to have been born on a summit. Thus, I need not scramble like a banker's boy. If you don't understand that, you know nothing of the rank to which I was born, and into which you married."

"But...!"

"I will gladly serve the King in whatever capacity I can, and he may reward me as he sees fit, but I will never be lackey to anyone, not even a king."

"But to be great isn't incompatible with advancement!"

He looked back over his shoulder. "What is there to advance to, my dear?"

"Everything I said!"

He turned slowly on the balls of his feet and bore down on her. Stopping just short of her, he said, "You understood nothing. What a good thing that you don't have to understand." Her eyes blazed, and she opened her mouth to reply, when a sharp knock startled them both. At Pierre's curt reply, a page entered and announced, "My Lord, the Count de Retz is below, and begs leave to call on you." Catching his wife's eye, Pierre laughed heartily; Anne, reluctantly, joined in; even the page giggled, though without knowing why.

* * *

The formalities of the meal ground on, to Pierre's intense frustration. The second course was served with only slightly less pomp than the first. The server and the carver fussed about the meats and the wines, their officiousness interfering with conversation even more than the distance between Pierre's great chair and the seats of his companions. Until now, Pierre had not objected to the enforced solitude of state meals, where everything was designed to isolate and elevate the lord of the household. His recent moroseness had tended to make him taciturn. Ceremony had obviated the need for any pretense at conviviality, and the novelty of being the object of everyone's attentions still supplied a modicum of interest.

But today, he felt different about it. He wanted desperately to speak with Gondi and resented every obstacle to that end. Gondi had gladly accepted Pierre's offer of hospitality. Indeed, it had been obvious that he had intended to break his journey at Plessis Gaillard and that his arrival was not quite the casual stop that his unaffected manner had implied.

Gondi's gratification at the arrangement had been as nothing, however, compared with Pierre's. Gondi's coming had filled Pierre with more than relief, indeed with intense joy and hope. Here, he had thought, is someone who can tell me what I most want to know: What has become of Athalie and how can I contrive to see her? Only now did Pierre realize that what he wanted would not prove easy to come by.

274

Gondi's formal welcoming passed, leaving Pierre's questions where they had been at the onset — on the tip of his tongue. Pierre had vowed that Athalie would be the first subject of dinner conversation, but when he had made his official entry into the great chamber and had seen Gondi standing at the table, he had received an inkling of the futility of his hopes. Though Gondi, as befitted a high-ranking guest, was seated closest to Pierre, even so, the distance between them made casual conversation impossible, and Pierre could hardly boom his queries across the yards between them. Later, he knew, there would be reading and music, and in the morning, Gondi would be gone. Pierre's mouth went dry at the thought that this apparently god-sent opportunity would prove to be no opportunity at all. He simply had to find a natural occasion for engaging Gondi in the kind of quiet conversation in which polite, but extensive, inquiries about his niece would lose themselves in a plethora of other material.

A solution so fitting that it seemed made to order sprang suddenly to mind: He would take Gondi aside to consult him about his money. What could be more natural than a neophyte like himself seeking advice from a man who was known throughout France as a financial wizard? Raymond de Galle himself had not scrupled to make use of Gondi's many talents. Pierre had once heard his father say to an impecunious and importunate nobleman: "If you want a horseshoe, you go to a farrier; if you want a loan, go to a banker. Try Gondi." And for advice, if not for money, the old Duke had not scrupled to go to Gondi himself.

Indeed, thought Pierre, one of the benefits of using money as a pretext for a tête-à-tête was that Gondi would almost certainly show him a way out of his dilemmas. Whereas before Pierre had lingered, fretting and inattentive, over his food, now, wishing to hasten the meal to a close, he shoveled the food into his mouth. The sweet was at last served and cleared, and the ceremony of concluding the meal had begun. The lesser guests left the ends of the table and ranged themselves along the wall. Gondi, as the guest of honor, rose and took his place in front of them. The tablecloth was removed and the table and trestles carried out.

Pierre rose from where he sat in solitary splendor, dipped his fingers into a bowl held up by a kneeling gentleman, and clapped his hands to signify that the postprandial activities should commence. Normally, this would have been the time for dancing and gaming, but the proprieties of mourning forbade such levity. The subdued guests arranged themselves on benches and chairs for an evening of religious readings, versifying, and song. Pierre knew that these edifying, but less than thrilling, activities would not hold the group for long.

Losing no time, he strode over to Gondi and touched his arm. "A word with you, if you will."

"Gladly."

Passing the bowing remnant of the dinner crowd, they withdrew into the adjoining chamber, Pierre's sleeping quarters, and sat beside the fire. Now that the moment was upon him, Pierre felt suddenly tongue-tied, and found Gondi's sympathetic, but mildly inquisitive, smile more irritating than encouraging. He would have preferred, he realized now, to find his own way through the thicket of his responsibilities than to reveal his ignorance, and hence his weakness, to an outsider.

But Gondi, he reassured himself, is a friend, and anyway, there's no alternative. In quiet, dignified tones, Pierre described his plight: the chaotic disarray he believed he detected in the books of account, the difficulties with the steward, the lack of readily available cash needed for a host of obligations, and the Pascal loans and their interest, which soon would be past due.

Gondi nodded sagely. "Your father was a man who mistrusted indebtedness. He thought a man should buy what he could pay for, and no more. A limiting view, I always thought: too inflexible for our times, when opportunities often present themselves out of season, so to speak. We did not see eye to eye on that, as you can imagine." Pierre could, and smiled agreement.

"However," Gondi continued, "even your father could not keep himself secure from the vicissitudes of fortune. Last year, the drought killed the crops and the bad harvest killed the revenues. Your father was not the only one to suffer from it — far from it. Those of us who were, well, more versatile with our money were less affected. But that's neither here nor there. At any rate, your father came to me for advice. I was honored that he would turn to me in his time of need. I suggested Pascal, the banker in Chinon."

"I saw his name. I could not help but wonder if he were related to... Augustin?"

"Yes, he and your erstwhile opponent are father and son. Your father was outraged for that very reason, but I overcame his objections quite simply. I believed, you see, that you had more than gotten your own back with young Augustin, and the matter need concern you and your family no further. The father is a good man, and a good banker, which was more important under the circumstances. That's how it came about. But since he is a good man, he will, I'm confident, bend over backward to be of assistance. It happens I'm on my way to see him and will add my own good word to any letter you wish to give me."

"You're more than kind." Pierre bowed from the waist.

"Anything that I can do." Gondi returned the bow. "In the matter of your steward, it sounds greatly as if replacing the man is called for. If you wish, I will put my mind to it. It may be that I can find you a man with more experience than those of your household would likely possess."

"If you would..." Pierre mumbled. His mind had left the matters of his household, as fear gripped him lest the conversation end without reaching what was — to him — its point. He heard himself blurting out, in falsely jovial tones, "And how is Madame your wife?"

"Poorly." Gondi shook his head sadly. "The cold weather does not agree with her. Some are tougher than others. I myself, while I don't like it, am not handicapped by it, and my niece..."

"Yes, your niece?"

"Well, as I was going to say, my niece seems to have no objection to winter travel."

There was a pause, as Pierre gathered his courage. "Well," he said, "she has to travel, when the Court travels."

"True," Gondi said, "if she had stayed at Court. What I meant was the trip from Chambord to Blois is nothing, but Fontevrault is a bit of a trek. Ah, but of course, you didn't know. Secluded as you are in your grief, you aren't troubled with the world's trivia."

Pierre's mouth opened slightly; he looked rather than spoke his bewilderment.

"Yes, my niece has returned to Fontevrault. It was best: I could not gainsay it. You know, she wasn't happy at Court, not really, so her aunt's experiment failed."

"I don't understand," Pierre began.

"No, of course not, and I don't know why I'm boring you with it. You see, my niece has a vocation. Quite clearly. But her great-aunt, the Abbess, felt that she should be sent out into the world, subjected to its temptations, oh, you know the kind of talk — and so, the young Duchess came to Court."

Pierre stared dumbstruck.

"But now she has returned to Fontevrault. I myself, thinking of the poor child's interests, am delighted, though, speaking frankly, Her Majesty the Queen Mother was not much pleased. As I saw it, the girl must go where she is suited. We're not all made alike."

Perturbed by Pierre's silence, Gondi added hurriedly, "Don't misunderstand: Everyone at Court was most kind to her, from the Queen Mother herself on down. Why, you yourself took great pains with her. We noticed, my wife and I, and were most grateful."

Silence fell again. The stirring refrains of a ballad sifted, muted, into their room, barely audible above the crackling of the fire.

"So," Pierre said stupidly, "she won't be at Court, when I, my wife and I, return."

"No, indeed," Gondi replied cheerfully.

"I wish, I wish I could have said goodbye."

"I'll tell her when I write, shall I? It's kind of you to think of it." Gondi glanced from Pierre to the door; Pierre rose slowly.

"We'll return, then," he said, and led the way back.

In the great chamber, a cheerful attitude was penetrating the fog of decorum. The ballad, ribald at times in the best military tradition, was suitable, but only just, to the occasion, and the younger of Pierre's retainers were making the most of it. Pierre resumed his place in the great chair and let his eyes wander over the group.

There, he saw, is Boisel, a weak leader and poor administrator. He will stay in my household unless I send him home: Where would he do the most mischief? And there is the cheeky devil who arrived only after the funeral. Is he tainted with heresy, as they say, or is he merely rebellious by temperament? Pierre's thoughts numbly ran along the course they had followed other nights, while below the surface of his mind, a great anguish welled.

How could she go away with no word, no warning, no explanation? Of course, he knew she had dreamed once of vowing herself to God, and he suspected that at times she pined for the death of that dream. But how could she go back now, after what they had found together? Even though their love was hopeless, surely, if it were the force it seemed, it could not yield without warning in so incompatible a choice. He could understand better, indeed, he knew he would one day have to accept, that she should love another man, but this abandonment he could not understand. Did it not say that their love was nothing? Or was this her desperate protest against the trap of futile human love? Or could it be guilt that drove her? Surely not guilt. It would be a crime to cut off that spring of warmth, of love, of humanity, for guilt. Anything would be better.

In the silence that followed the ballad's conclusion, which Pierre had never noticed, all eyes were fixed on him for guidance. With him in the room, they had to defer to his wishes. He suddenly became aware of the anxious lull. The trappings of power overlaid his real powerlessness. The juxtaposition angered him, and in a moment of rebellion, he stood and left the room without a word. His puzzled entourage stumbled to their feet, bowed or curtseyed, and scurried from his path, while the gentlemen of his bedchamber grabbed torches and rushed to light him to his bed. Anne hesitated, then fled precipitously after her husband.

Later, Anne and Pierre lay silent in the master bed, separated by a lonely expanse of mattress which humped between the valleys made by their bodies. Neither slept, and while Pierre was oblivious to Anne's wakefulness, she was acutely aware of his. For the first time, she was glad that her wish for separate quarters had not been gratified. How would she have overcome the gulf between herself and Pierre, a gulf which was of his making and, therefore, unacceptable, if their nights did not bring them together, or at least offer the possibility, as yet unrealized, of their coming together?

She spoke in the silence. "My Lord, you left so abruptly. Your guests were all startled."

After a pause, his voice replied, "I was tired. I am tired."

She inched across the mattress, searching all the while for something more to say. "About what we spoke of this afternoon," she said, "you know I meant no offense, my Lord. We must not become estranged, my Lord. We have so much, and could have so much more." She reached his side of the bed. Her knees brushed his thighs. "I don't mean money or worldly goods. I mean what is between us two, as man and woman."

He swung his legs out of the bed, and sitting up, thrust back the curtains, letting in the dim glow of the dying fire. On a low table a nighttime meal of cheese and bread and wine had been laid out, according to the custom. He reached for the wine and poured himself a large tumblerful. Anne subsided against the cushions. Glancing around, he caught her dark gaze on him with pinpoints of reflected light blazing, but whether from anger or something else, he could not tell.

"I want to give you a child," she resumed finally. "A son. Then, I will be fulfilled."

Pierre swallowed the wine in two gulps, then emptied the carafe into the tumbler. "This is new talk," he said. "I thought all you wanted was rank and money." He sipped the wine more slowly, feeling it warm his innards despite the ambient cold of the room.

"I wish your father could have lived to see the son we will make. What is the use of rank if we are alone?"

A great sadness filled Pierre. She was right, of course. Duty, and more than that, need, a fundamental need, supported her demands. He felt alone, cut off, with neither father nor son to anchor him. He looked at Anne again. Was she his harbor? His future? She made demands as of right, for he recognized instinctively the urgency behind her words. On what basis could he refuse her? Why should he?

He jerked the curtain to, and rolled back onto the mattress, pulling the covers around them both. For a while, he played with her, played at arousing her, as she had done him so many times in the past. In the end, as always before, it was he who was the more aroused. He had forgotten how much pleasure her niggardly passion could permit, and was surprised to rediscover it. For her, the relief in accomplishing her purpose at last simulated joy with sufficient closeness that they were both deceived by it. When they turned their thoughts to sleep, both viewed their future together with a modicum of hope.

* * *

Past the antechamber, in the dead of night, Maurice crept, unheard by the guards who slept rolled in their cloaks, on benches or in the straw that matted the floor. When he reached the state bedroom reserved for prestigious guests, he scratched gently against the grain of the door, and Gondi, who had been on the qui vive, admitted him without delay. He pushed the door silently closed behind his visitor and retreated into the room.

"Why all the cloak and dagger?" Maurice muttered, as he padded after Gondi.

"Don't be boring," Gondi replied. "I'm done in, and there's another early departure looking me in the face." Maurice shrugged indifferently.

"This is what I came here to Plessis Gaillard to tell you," Gondi said. "The Protestants are mobilizing. All over France, they're gathering and arming themselves. Between these walls, I'll say I don't blame them. The Guises are setting themselves up as a kingdom within the Kingdom. The Protestants are terrified. They know the King cannot protect them. Remember the riots about the Cross of Gâtines? Of course, that was Paris, but Paris isn't the only place where heretics are considered fair game."

Gondi paused, reflecting to himself — yes, they're terrified.

"Actually," he laughed softly, "They're torn between fear and hope, and that's what gives us our chance. They hope for a union of all Frenchmen to be symbolized by the marriage of Princess Marguerite with Navarre and to culminate in an expedition against the Spanish in the Netherlands. Meanwhile, they fear that they will be massacred in their beds by the Guises. Hence, the mobilization and their general refractories. Now, the two emotions are as incompatible as — as Comedy and Tragedy. Their fear stands in the way of what their hope should lead them to: the marriage, which we, of course, want even more than they do. So, our job must be to allay their fears. We can promise them anything which will make them lay down their arms and support the marriage. After the marriage, we can find that circumstances have changed and prevent us from living up to our promises."

Maurice grinned appreciatively.

"How does this affect you?" Gondi asked rhetorically. "First, it's obvious that you must return to La Rochelle. They perceive this as a period of crisis, and your absence even for a good cause will provoke unfavorable comment certainly, and probably, if it were prolonged, cast doubts on your sincerity. You must return, and of course, make the most of the fact that you cut short your period of mourning to be at Coligny's side. 'You have found a new father in the Admiral': That sort of thing."

Maurice snickered. "I'll say this for the Admiral: I may not love him, but at least, I don't hate him as I hated the defunct Duke."

Gondi waved a hand impatiently. "Be that as it may, I don't want you to love the Admiral; just pretend to. When you're there, I'll want what I always want: useful, reliable information at all times, and on special occasions, that you should influence their actions in whatever way I indicate. Your present eminence should put you more or less above suspicion, which shall make communication between us a great deal easier."

"That's right," Maurice said with a ring of pride, and no thanks to you, he added to himself. "Well, that's all," Gondi concluded, and without further ado, Maurice found himself ushered from the room.

Back in his own quarters, La Renaudie found that sleep eluded him. He felt a certain excitement at the thought of returning to action, enhanced by the idea that his departure would shock his stepfamily. Still, the predominant emotion that troubled his rest was not a pleasant one. Gondi had treated him like a churl again and he resented it. It was that which seethed in his mind and kept him brooding over the embers of his fire. Gondi, he thought, treats me as a pawn, even though what I have achieved I have achieved on my own, in spite of him, and even though he has no real hold on me. That's true! he thought delightedly. After the extensive use he has made of me, he cannot afford to discredit me. And so, why should I continue to obey him? Because, he answered himself, even though the stick is no longer there, the carrot is. How better can I advance myself than in Gondi's service?

He could see no real alternative but to throw in his lot with the Protestants. Here, if he did, would Gondi dare reveal that Maurice had been his agent throughout, simply to destroy him? No, it would cast doubt on the sincerity of the King's reconciliation with Coligny, and unless circumstances changed, Gondi would not do that. Maurice thought for a moment that he had perceived a real choice, and he felt a spurt of elation, but it subsided quickly. How could he pick the Protestants as long as they remained a losing cause?

Chapter XXII

thalie's journey from Chambord to Fontevrault proved to be arduous in the extreme. Passage by water was impossible; ice floes blocked the river at many points. Travel over land was only barely manageable. The snow had simply obliterated all but the main roads, and Athalie's party often seemed to struggle over a treacherous, chartless desert. There was also the fear of attack by the bands of starving and homeless who marauded like wolves on the outskirts of civilization. Athalie's escort was numerous enough to make such an attack unwise, but the winter's harshness had made many people desperate.

Though her companions rejoiced at their arrival as they would have greeted the Second Coming, Athalie could not join in their relief. Indeed, she would gladly have suffered further hardships to postpone the inevitable moment of confrontation with the Abbess. It was less than a year since they had parted, but more had happened than the passage of mere months. The influence of time is greatest at the extremes of human life; in youth and age, a year is more than a year, whereas in middle life, it may seem like less. Athalie knew how she herself had changed, and there was a fine-drawn quality about the austerity of her great-aunt's face that had not been so evident before and that struck a pang even in her overwrought heart.

Knowing nothing of the turmoil in Athalie's mind, the Abbess welcomed her with unalloyed joy. They sat in the guest suite, basking in the glow from the newly lit fire. Both needed the heat. In the conventual part of the Abbey, there were no fires, except in the kitchens and laundry, so for the old woman, sitting with her beloved niece before the crackling blaze was a double treat; for Athalie, tired and cold to the marrow of her bones from the bitter ride, it brought a sense of renewal and with it a revival of fears that in her numbed state, she had been able to ignore. She now rallied her energies to meet the buffeting of the Abbess's questions; her strained gaiety of manner passed unnoticed by her aunt in the excitement of the moment. The health of the royal family had to be disposed of, member by member.

And how, Louise de Bourbon asked with a shrewd regard, did Athalie find the Queen Mother? And had she liked the Admiral? Yes, but his very reasonableness made him the greater sinner, and how could His Majesty have received him with open arms and called him "Father"? Athalie did not argue, and the expostulations died out. In a quiet voice, the Abbess asked about Raymond de Galle's death, the news of which had reached their gate only the day before, and listened attentively to Athalie's listless description of its circumstances. An hour elapsed. The tolling of the Church bell confirmed its passage to Athalie's anxious ears. The moment she dreaded could not be far off.

"It is a bad time to be on the road, but I bless whatever brought you," the Abbess was saying. "My eyes have seen nothing that gladdened them as much as the sight of you. Where are you headed, and how long will you be able to stay with us?"

Athalie looked away from the old woman's bird-like gaze. "As long as you wish, or will have me," she replied in a low voice.

Louise de Bourbon cocked her head as if to hear better. "You may stay as long as you wish, child, certainly until the weather breaks, if that suits your plans. But where are you headed, and for what purpose?"

"I'm not going anywhere. I came to see you."

"I see," said the Abbess, who thought she did, but could not have been farther from the mark. "And was it, perchance, your uncle Gondi who sent you back?"

"No, Mother, he knows nothing of why I left Court, though I've no doubt he was delighted. I came..." At the last minute, her courage failed her and she literally hung her head in shamefaced silence. Her great-aunt watched, bewildered. "Mother, I'm in the family way," Athalie blurted. "There was no place else I could go."

Louise de Bourbon's silence endured. Even the faint puzzlement remained frozen on her features during the few moments she needed to assimilate her niece's meaning and experience her own disbelief. At last, she said, "What do you know of such things. You must be mistaken. It takes more than pinching and kissing, you know, and if you're late, it means nothing. Winter weakens folk, no vegetables, these things can happen, especially at your age. You're not full grown, yet."

"Mother," Athalie interrupted, "those who have not done what is necessary may not know it, but those who have can be in no doubt. How can I say it to you? What I have seen the farmyard animals do, I have done."

"I see. And who was your bull, if I may ask?"

"Nothing would be served by telling you that."

At this, the Abbess rose in an eruption of anger. "You're mad. Am I to understand that he is so ignoble that you cannot marry him?"

"He is not ignoble, but he cannot marry me."

"Ah. Aha. So, let me understand you fully. We are talking of two grievous sins, not one: not fornication only, but fornication and adultery." She retreated to the far corner of the room, distancing herself both from her niece and the fire whose heat she no longer needed, since her own passions had brought sweat to her brow.

Turning and glaring back, she said, "I'm glad we took such care over your upbringing. What might you have become without it?" Athalie felt her throat tighten and her lips begin to tremble. I will not cry, she vowed in silent desperation. She will not make me cry.

"And when is it to be, the happy event?" The harsh voice rasped against her sensibilities.

"I don't know," she replied inaudibly. The Abbess strode back to her side, and grasping her shoulder in a painful vise, viciously shook her thin frame. "I don't know," Athalie gasped, "but it's been three months." The Abbess released her, and began to count on her fingers. Athalie spoke through a fog of tears that she seemed to feel more in her throat and nose than in her eyes, "It could be July or perhaps August."

"And you intend to stay here until then? And bring your bastard into the world within these walls? How can I, in my position, let you do it? If you were a milkmaid, it would be considered a charity and no one would care, but with one such as you, it is a scandal. And you are my niece."

"I know," she wailed.

"The nuns will see you, and while they may not talk to the outside world, they write."

Athalie's sobs broke from her in ugly, painful gasps. "I had..." she coughed, "I had no place else to go." She took a huge sniff and continued in more normal tones, "You are my family, and you love me. I know you do. You should not treat me worse than you would a milkmaid."

The Abbess looked down at her bent head, and reflected a moment. "I don't know what to say," she replied. "I must think this through and see what's best." She dropped her hand again to Athalie's shoulder, but this time, her grip was brief and gentle. Then, she turned and left the room.

* * *

Throughout the days that followed, Louise de Bourbon gnawed at the edges of the problem and harried Athalie with questions and suggestions. Athalie, like a caged animal, was forced to endure her importunities. Effectively, she was trapped. The bitter cold and short, brooding, sunless days made her existence a claustrophobic nightmare. The deep drifts that filled the Abbey's gardens and meadows made outdoor walking impossible. Having no desire to wander through the Abbey proper resuming commerce with her former companions, she confined herself to her rooms in the guesthouse and meekly obeyed the strictures imposed by the old nurse.

Wrapped in her furs and blankets, Athalie would sit before the fire, hour after hour, embroidery in her lap. Seldom, however, did her handiwork advance. The enforced idleness of her days left her vulnerable above all else to every fear and sorrow her own mind could conjure up. The tormenting twists and turns of her thoughts — remorse and self-pity and endless forebodings — seemed to occupy her entire life, leaving no energy or desire for even the modest demands of her needlework.

The baby, as she thought of it during these melancholy musings, came more and more to epitomize the wages of sin. Because of Pierre, there was the baby; because of Pierre and the baby, she would never be a bride, not the Bride of Christ, as she had once desired, not anyone's bride. The baby was to be her punishment, but by some unfair necessity, the baby too would be punished. The baby's life, she thought, would be harder than her own had been. She, at least, had been legitimate, even if her parents had given her little in the way of guidance. Inescapably, her thoughts turned back to the glimpse of family life that the Pascal household had given her almost a year before. The image of human warmth that she had seen in their kitchen that day had often returned to tantalize her. As she had grown more sophisticated, she had come to laugh at the naivete of the Pascals' motivations, but something within her recognized that their kitchen meant something, even if their ideas did not; someone within her wept to belong to such a place, such a milieu, such a home. She had never had a nest for her tender youth. No one had nurtured her, molded her, pushed her to her limits, encouraged her to be — what? A member of the society that she was, even now, pushing away from her.

Here, self-pity broke on the rack of inner truth: Guided or not, she had willed the desire of her heart, knowing full well the issues involved, and she would not now deny it. And was it so wrong? She tortured herself with the question, day in and day out. It seemed as if either she could no longer take hold of her ideas or perhaps that her ideas did not grasp the realities of her life. As time passed, her doubts simply blossomed and bore fruit. Perhaps, she told herself, the apparent wrongness of her actions was no more than the simple truth.

She did not recognize that the seeds from which these fears grew were her increasing misgivings about Pierre. Deep within, the question that was her true torment was, Could she have been wrong about Pierre? She had expected so little; she had not cast him in the role of savior; the little she looked for, however, was the sine qua non, the absence of which shook her to the very depths of her being. That he should be silent and offer no comfort at such a time was gratuitous cruelty, an affront to decency, much less to the love which was between them. If she could have been so mistaken about his character, she could rely on nothing, least of all her own impressions.

Into this turmoil, the Abbess injected her part of frenzy. Was Athalie refusing to name the father because she did not know his identity? She wanted to know. Having come to wonder to what lengths her niece might have gone, she greeted Athalie's quiet denial with unwarranted relief. Was there truly no hope of marriage? None at all? At least then, the Abbess reasoned, there was no need to heed the father; he could be ignored completely, and that was a blessing in a way. Mutely, Athalie received this wisdom, but her heart cried out against it. Pierre could do nothing for her, that she knew, but she longed for a word from him that would give meaning to what she would do.

As Athalie dozed one day, exhausted by the inner strife that was so much more wearing than physical labor, the Abbess burst in upon her. "I have reached a decision," she proclaimed. Athalie struggled upright and focused her dulled mind on her great-aunt. Louise de Bourbon sat, but the rigidity of her body spoke of compressed energy, as of a taut bowstring, rather than of slackness.

"You were right, of course, to come here," the Abbess declared. "It places me in a terrible position, but —"

"I'm..."

"Hush." The Abbess waved imperiously and continued, "but there was really no alternative, things being what they were. At least here we have some small hope of containing the scandal. You will remain 'til the birth. We have few guests in times like this, and while this house is empty, you may stay here. If visitors of rank seek our hospitality, we will move you, and in the spring, that will surely be necessary. We will install you in rooms well away from the novices' quarters. That some of my older nuns will know you are here, and will eventually know why, cannot be helped. I will swear them to secrecy, and some of them will keep their oath.

"Of course, anyone with any sense will know what happened, but that can't be helped. You will say nothing, and after the child is born, you will resume your life as if nothing had happened. We may have to be open with Her Majesty the Queen Mother. It would be a great mistake to add the error of attempted deception to the original offense. We'll have to see."

She paused and looked at Athalie's pinched face. "At any rate, child, you must not worry. The important thing is to take care of yourself. I'll take care of everything else." The Abbess's words had neither reassured nor troubled Athalie. She did not know if there was a solution to her problem. It did not strike her as the kind of problem that had a solution. Indeed, she was not sure that it was right to think of the situation in those terms. Was life itself a "problem"? In any event, she was becoming increasingly convinced that it was she and she alone who was called upon to determine upon which stars she would orient her course.

In the twilight the Abbess returned. As she settled on a stool near Athalie, she no longer emanated potent energy. It was one of the facets of her life now that her fire burned out before her day was done. The whisper of old age was a sound she rarely heard and even less often acknowledged, and she had not yet learned, and perhaps never would learn, to let gentleness do the work which all her life sheer will had performed. Her hooded eyes seemed to disappear into their sockets as she contemplated her niece. The firelight picked out the blue veining of the lids and faintly tinged with pink the almost translucent shroud of skin tightly molded over the ridge of her cheekbones.

She rallied her faltering forces and spoke in a voice low with fatigue. "I suppose, child, by now you've accepted that you are not made for a life of religion."

As Athalie remained silent, she continued, "It's not that you couldn't become a postulant after the birth. Many have come to us that way. But they had vocations.

"You have to have a vocation," she repeated quietly, "and that is not the common thing. I should think that this unfortunate episode demonstrates that in your case, as in most others, your true vocation is marriage and motherhood. You must start again, of course. But that's where your heart is, I suppose?"

Reluctantly, Athalie murmured, "I don't know, Mother. Nothing is clear to me."

Louise de Bourbon straightened and put her hands on her knees. "Well," she said, "even if you're confused, you should return to Court."

Something of her old verve returned to the girl and prompted her to reply with heavy sarcasm, "With the baby?" Her great-aunt looked startled, but not alarmed.

Like a tutor repeating a lesson, she replied with asperity. "Of course not. You'll give the baby up. That was understood. You needn't worry. I told you I would see to it. It's too early to look for a suitable home, but when the time comes, we'll have no trouble." She stood and smiled. "It's a shame, really, that we can't keep it here, but I fear it would cause too great a scandal."

Later, in the safe haven of her bed, Athalie confronted the full implications of her great-aunt's words. For the first time she admitted to herself that the same idea had lurked in the recesses of her own mind: She could give the baby away. That was what people in her circumstances did. She recalled how, when she had first heard the news, a great sorrow had filled her, not for the trouble which had engulfed her, not for what she had lost or stood to love, but for the wonderful world that could never be. She had felt instinctively the joy that would have been hers if she could have borne his child openly, as his wife, in honor and security.

Thinking things through, she now realized that it was unfair, no worse, untrue, to make the unborn infant the crux of her difficulties. It was not because of the child that she was alone in the world. She did not wish to marry anyone but Pierre, baby or no baby. Blinking back tears that were the strange offspring of relief, not desperation — she tore a gem of hope from the murk of despond. She had not been able to remain true to an ideal — God, she realized now, had never been more than that to her — but she could keep faith with a person. Now, in the harshness of winter as in the easy days of summer, her love would be a stout, enduring plant. The child would be its flower, not its sacrificial victim.

Chapter XXIII

atherine's eyes lingered broodily on the intent faces of her two listeners. "However you look at it, the situation is a mess," she said. Gondi, who sensed that the storm of the Queen Mother's frustration would soon break over his head, sent a nervous glance in his wife's direction. "Let me recapitulate," Catherine continued, "so that we may try to draw some sense from it.

"Henri Navarre's doting Mamá, bristling with Protestant principles, will soon be upon us. I must receive her here, in my own home, because the papal legate — riding post haste — has outdistanced the Queen of Navarre and he, Alessandrino, must be received at Court by my son, who cannot be caught dallying with the Protestants at the same time.

"Together with the Queen of Navarre, and almost as embarrassing, we must receive Henri's uncle, Louis de Nassau, Prince of Condé, who has attached himself to her lest we forget that the marriage is merely a gauge for our commitment to war in the Netherlands." Catherine's distress raised the timbre of her voice.

"We also are plagued by the English ambassadors who buzz like bees about the honey pot, although they, it seems, do not want war in the Netherlands. What do they want, I wonder. I would have thought that Anjou's really outrageous behavior in the question of his marriage to their Queen would at least have discouraged them.

"Meanwhile, the papal legate, His Holiness's dear nephew, the little Alexander, cloaked in whey-faced and mushy diffuseness, but sharp as unsheathed steel underneath, brandishes promises with one hand and threats with the other. Spanish troops he offers us, 4,000 of them, if we will give the Protestants the boot. The nerve of the man." Catherine looked at Gondi.

"And so, the outsiders close in on us. And we, of course, have a strong, united front with which to meet them," she added sarcastically. "Take my sons, ever a source of support: Charles. Now, Charles tells the Admiral, his beloved surrogate father, his newest idol, to stay home for his own safety. I like that: for the Admiral's safety. This the Admiral happily does — and raises 20,000 foot and 7,000 horse to make sure of things.

"Meanwhile, because the Guises will not yield before my clever boy's demands that they be reconciled with Coligny, he sends them from him like rejected playmates, leaving them free to take off for Paris where they can plot against him in secret. So much for Charles' machinations."

"Now, Anjou, my little Henri, my true gem, has become, for our bedevilment, more Catholic than the Guises. But why? Because the whirligig of his religious mania has momentarily brought the Holy Roman Church to the forefront of his busy brain? Because he is in love with Mademoiselle de Châteauneuf, and therefore had to destroy all chance of an English marriage? Or because he hopes that the Guises will support him in an adventure against his brother the King? Whatever the reason, you may be sure that mischief will come of it." She sighed, her expression grim.

"And Alençon, last in line, but ever first in impetuosity: If Henri will play Catholic, he will play Protestant. He will welcome all who flee his brother's fanaticism. He will put his heart, his will, and his mind such as it is into obtaining the throne of England for himself. I don't know what else he will do, but knowing him, I am confident that making up as ever in ingenuity what he lacks in substance, he will find other ways to plague us."

Her voice wound down into its lowest register like a clock running out. Gondi and his wife listened with concern; both knew her, and her moods, but rarely had they detected such bitterness in her. Catherine took a deep breath.

"So," she said, "where do we go from here? I confess, in the face of all our difficulties, I sometimes lose sight of what we would accomplish if we could. Can you keep it all in mind?" she asked, turning to Gondi.

"Yes," he replied, though it was not entirely true.

"Good. Well, don't enlighten me. The way I feel today, I can deal with only one thing at a time, and the most imminent of our problems, of my problems at any rate, is the Queen of Navarre's arrival."

"Yes," Gondi broke in, "but it may not be as bad as you seem to expect. She, too, has cause to be discouraged. She will be tired. She will know that the papal legate will have arrived before her. She cannot offer us wholehearted Protestant support, and she knows that without it we cannot face down the Guises. She..."

"How very encouraging," Catherine drawled. "However, why go over it all again? Discouragement counts for nothing with a person like that. She is constitutionally incapable of compromise. Her husband, the dead King, was a jelly and she is a ramrod. What the son will be like," she added as an aside, "I cannot imagine. But the mother, at least, we know, and I for one cannot stomach her. As you both know, I hate doctrinaire people and especially, doctrinaire women."

"But surely, Madame," the Countess interjected, "she does have some excuse. When Navarre died, she found herself forced to defend an isolated kingdom and a helpless son, as best she could. Though I have no sympathy for her beliefs, I cannot help but feel for her position."

"Harrumph, her position, indeed. There's nothing there to excuse her behavior, or make you lose your sense of perspective," the Queen Mother replied. "After all, look at what I've had to face."

Hastening to cut off this fruitless exchange, Gondi interjected, "I myself am by no means sure that her fanaticism is not at least in part a negotiating strategy. How better to extort a lot of concessions than by taking a stand on principles which are claimed to be beyond dispute?"

"I don't believe it. Such zeal cannot be faked, not over a lifetime, anyway. In any event, from the point of view of dealing with her, it makes no odds."

Catherine slumped against the hard chair back and attempted to rally her thoughts.

"Ah," she added, sitting up abruptly. "I've forgotten one of my brood, the most important of them in this context. I gather that my lovely Margot is brooding. She doesn't dare sulk to my face, but I know her whims and moods so well I don't need to see them to sense them. Well, I'll not have it. She will not only play her part, that goes without saying, but she'll do it with a good heart. I look to you," she turned to the Countess, "to see to it."

Madame de Retz coughed nervously. "I will do my best, Madame."

"As to that, I couldn't care less. You must succeed."

"With all due respect, a word from you would accomplish in a trice what I could occasion only with great grief. You know the authority you have over your children." The blatant inconsistency of this piece of flattery with everything that had gone before passed entirely unnoticed by the Queen Mother, as the Countess had known it would.

"Hmm," Catherine said. "That may well be. Summon her. We need lose no more time."

Shortly, Margot arrived. Her normally sallow complexion had grown pasty in part because the harsh weather had confined her indoors and in part because, as her mother suspected, she had been indulging her humors to the detriment of her appetite. She hesitated inside the door, glancing warily from her mother, whom she feared, to the Gondis, whom she distrusted. The tight control she exercised over her facial expressions robbed them of their natural good nature and gave them an unbecoming surly cast. Catherine appraised her daughter's mood covertly and did not bid her sit.

"Daughter," she said, "to date, your life has been of small consequence, but your moment of glory is at hand. To you is given the fortune of binding the wounds of our poor torn country. Your marriage will be a healing salve. You and your intended by your union will, rightly guided, bring unity from division, order from chaos. You know my meaning? You understand?"

"Mother, I have ever bowed to your will. In the question of my marriage, above all else, I have been your willing tool. All I have asked is that you remember I am a true Catholic."

"Well done, daughter, well said. Even though you and Anjou squabble like puppies, you are not above aping his style. Why not? But let us be consistent. Did your devoutness fire your ardor for a marriage with that most Catholic of princes, Sebastian of Portugal?"

"But Mother, he was..."

"He was... not to your fancy. And Henri of Navarre is not to your fancy. Well, a pox on your fancy. You will marry an ape, if France will be the better for it. As for your Catholicism, console yourself with this: You will be the means of bringing young Navarre, and with him his followers, back into the fold. Not right away, perhaps, but if you play your part, and are ably assisted, it may come to pass that our most cherished hope will be fulfilled. Now that is a destiny few girls can aspire to. You will not merely be a bearer of sons. You yourself will act on history. Come, Margot," she gestured the girl forward and took her hand in a warm grasp, "you would not shirk greatness for a mere foible?" She swung the Princess's arm back and forth to emphasize her point.

Margot swallowed back tears and stared bleakly ahead for a moment before meeting her mother's gaze. "No, Madame," she replied softly.

"There's my good girl."

* * *

21 April 1572

My dear cousin,

I would have written sooner, but so much has happened that I can hardly gather my thoughts. Usually, winter is the boring time, but not even the worst of weather, it seems, can hold back two women like my mother and my mother-in-law-to-be. It is, of course, the continuing saga of my proposed marriage to Navarre that has kept us turning like tops. You were here for the first part. You know that she, the dreaded She, the She-wolf, the She-Devil, was expected in December, but she did not rush. There was, after all, talk of war, and then the apple of her eye was incapacitated, and so finally, it was February before she reached us.

Well, in the meantime that will teach her not to make us wait on her pleasure, the Forces of Heaven were not idle. Cardinal Alessandrino arrived, as papal legate, with Salviati playing valet, and together they raised a tremendous fuss. Once we had gratefully declined their offer of Spanish troops to put the heretics to the sword, we had to listen to them shout that under no circumstances would His Holiness grant a dispensation for the marriage. Mother tried the old argument that young Henri would, like his dear departed father, return to the fold in due time, but since the defunct King changed sides more often than either side likes to remember, that did not go down particularly well. So we had to fall back on the Gallican Church – 'we can do it all ourselves' approach – and there was muttering of schism and excommunication and things that are usually not mentioned even under one's breath. By the end of the month, Rome retreated, proclaiming fire and brimstone like a newly discovered alchemy. That left us free to regroup in the greater pomp of Blois, and to resume our bouts with Herself.

There was, needless to say, much private wrangling behind the public displays of amity. Nassau and the English were very much to the fore, so much so that I sometimes wonder on whose altar I am to be sacrificed. Naturally, I am supposed to be too stupid to think of these things. Mother invariably underestimates her children. At any rate, I was not to be involved in anything of substance. My role was to display myself to my poor best advantage. You will hardly credit it, my dear Athalie, but she was deceived despite my reputation, of which she could hardly have been ignorant. My blinking and smirking convinced her that I was the very epitome of an innocent young thing. That did not save me from her lecture on all the worldly sins which surround me, but it earned me her praise for my fortitude in turning my back on temptation. What will you: Willpower and shrewdness are not inseparable, though Mother's example might make one think otherwise.

No sign of the Princeling. The excuse given was that he injured himself falling from a horse. Falling out of bed is more likely. The best I have heard of my intended is that he is as lascivious as the best of men. Speaking of that...

There followed a stream of gossip which Athalie skimmed until an item caught her eye:

Pierre and Anne de Galle were here last week. They are gradually resuming an active life. I think I can guess, however, what they have been doing to keep amused in their retirement, for I could have sworn that she was pregnant. You know what a good instinct I have for these things.

Athalie stared, riveted, at her friend's gaudy script, before at last forcing her eyes to move on.

But what has become of you, cousin? There is no end of rumors. You can imagine the kind. I look knowing, even though you've told me nothing. If you were in trouble, you would surely have confided in me. I cannot believe that you are considering a life of Religion. Write me at once. There is no greater torment than unsatisfied curiosity for one such as myself. Please put me out of my misery. Jest aside, I must know how you are and what you plan, for I will not let you do some folly to your detriment.
I remain your dear friend and sister in affection,
Margot

Athalie sat on a bench placed on the rise overlooking the orchard. There was a new warmth in the air, but like watered eau de vie, it lacked potency and promised more fire than it gave. Athalie had found recently that her extremities suffered most from the cold and now tucked her feet inside her heavy skirts and shoved her hands deep into her pockets. In the right pocket, her fingers encountered the fine vellum of Margot's letter. She rolled the square of folded paper into a tube, and grasped it tightly like a baton. The letter was like a talisman to her: It seemed to promise that she would make the right decision in this crisis and turning point in her life. It symbolized the world she had left, for surely Margot was the epitome of that little cosmos of grace, style, learning, and elegance which gravitated around the throne of France. It was a link with Pierre, Pierre who had stayed in that world, Pierre who by breeding an heir had done his duty to that world. It also stated, through Margot's acceptance of her marriage, that all women — all humans? — must bow to their fate and can find the strength to do what is right.

She, Athalie, had made her decision; she only hoped that it was right. Knowing Pierre's wife to be pregnant, she had known that the decision of what to do with her own child was hers alone. This was not a rational realization. Anne's condition made no difference to her own, and certainly in Athalie's eyes, did not excuse Pierre's silence. But it had brought home to her, as nothing else, her exclusion from the mainstream of human intercourse. She felt cut off even to the extent that no one could understand her isolation. To the Abbess's practical mind, for example, her predicament was nothing more than a detour on the road; her sin was a peccadillo, common in nature, whose consequences, properly handled, need not be far-reaching.

So reconciled had her great-aunt become to the situation that she was able to find humor in it. Athalie recalled a recent exchange when Louise de Bourbon had spoken of a letter she had received from Gondi. "He says, Athalie," she had told her, "that he assumes from your silence that you are leading the contemplative life of a postulant. He says he's told the Queen Mother you felt the need to retire and pray about the future. It seems she was angry at your hasty departure, but now is more concerned than angry. According to your uncle, she wants to know what you've decided, and he needs to know because she is always bothering him about it. But tell me, child, did you tell the poor man nothing?" Athalie had shaken her head. The Abbess had laughed out loud. "That someone so well-informed should suspect nothing. How people are gulled by their hopes."

But now, Athalie thought, now that she knew her own mind, there was no reason why she should not satisfy the curiosity of her uncle, of Margot, of the Queen Mother, of all the world that mattered. By no amount of rationalization, however, could she justify doing anything so radical, so determinative of her future, as the step she contemplated, without first informing her great-aunt, and that was a process which she dreaded. She lingered, therefore, in the garden, drinking in the new light and letting it slowly, gently, warm her innards. Athalie did not feel, as she had felt the year before, that she was part of the burgeoning of life that was clearly under way around her. The sticky mud clinging to her boots and skirts, the blushing of the fruit trees, the manic chatter of the birds, the daubs of green on sunlit slopes, everything testified that the desolation around her was besieged and near defeat by the forces of life. Throughout, she seemed to hold herself aloof from the battle. She had no extra strength. It was as if the new life she was carrying, whose tiny movements she at times believed she could feel, had consumed all of her vitality.

Stringing her thoughts together like petals on a daisy chain, she turned her mind again to Pierre. Should she write him? Should he not be told, even if he did not wish to know? Sadly, she shook her head. Why should she step back into his life at the very moment when he was remaking it? Whatever wrong she had done before, that would merely compound it. However desperately she desired the contrary, the fact remained that she had nothing to offer him.

* * *

"And so, Mother," Athalie told the Abbess later that day, "when the child is born, I will take it with me to Islette. Since such a thing can hardly be kept secret, there seems no reason to keep it secret now." The old woman listened in stunned silence. Athalie found this more disturbing than the outburst she had been expecting. "You see..." she began again, but the Abbess cut her off.

"You dare to come to me with your troubles, and when I show you the way out, to plunge willfully into deeper water. You are not merely weak and unfortunate as I thought, but wrong-headed, wrong-willed, wicked."

The two stared at each other. The Abbess resumed more quietly. "Athalie, it is full noon, but you are blind as a bat. Why is that? Why can't you see what everyone else sees?"

"What should I see?" Athalie asked reluctantly. "I am merely..."

"You should see your duty to society, is what you should see. You've compromised your place in life badly enough, but now you must accept the consequences of your actions and forge ahead. It will be hard, I know that. Though I've never been a mother, I'm not blind to the fact that God has put an instinct in all creatures to cleave to their young. But human beings also have higher motivations."

"But the baby..."

"The baby is not important. The world is full of babies. They are grass before the reaper. What you are is important. You did not ask to be born into your station in life, nor is it your position to question it. You must take it as it is and not run away from it. The fact that you have stupidly made it more difficult for yourself is neither here nor there."

"Mother," Athalie burst out in a wave of intense frustration, "It's you who doesn't understand. Whatever might have been before, can no longer be. I am faced with several responsibilities, not one, and I have to choose between them. I think it's more important to accept the responsibility that my own actions brought about than passively to follow the course of social obligation. That's how I see it. I'm sorry."

"You will see it differently. You must," the Abbess stated flatly. "In the meantime, you'll do nothing to make your present situation fully irrevocable. Do you hear me? Nothing. You will write to no one concerning this matter until I give you leave. You put yourself in my hands. By God, you'll do as I say."

Unhappily, Athalie nodded.

Chapter XXIV

ierre smiled down at the letter. Even in his excitement, Trophime Daudet's handwriting was tight and well formed, the product of years of discipline. To Pierre, it seemed to symbolize his friend's most salient characteristic: impetuosity held in check. But he had cause for excitement, no doubt of that: The city of Brill, the northern key to the Netherlands, left ungarrisoned by the Spanish, had fallen into the hands of a roving band of pirates, and Spain's dominion over the Low Countries was now under attack from within. Daudet's script ran on:

Pierre, I write in haste to let you know my news. You will have heard how La Monck and his Sea Beggars took Brill from the Spanish. I must be sure that you understand what this means. The Enterprise is launched. The first blow has been struck. The whole of the Netherlands will rise in revolt. Victory is assured.

I was in La Rochelle when ships arrived from England to join the many vessels already arming to intercept the Spanish fleet. You will have heard of their victory. All La Rochelle rang with joy when that news reached us, but our rejoicing was multiplied a hundredfold when we learned of Brill's fall on April 1. While before we were timid and patient, laying our schemes, now the clarion call is sounded. William, Lord of Orange, has declared his present intention to deliver the Netherlands from foreign tyranny. The time of waiting is over. It was thought that nothing would come to pass until the union of our Prince Henri and the Princess Marguerite, and to many, the delays in its accomplishment seemed interminable, but now that happy event, which cannot be long in coming, will be the crown, not the cause, of our achievements.

Pierre, you must not think that this is a sectarian fight. Our King, who at last stands at the head of Protestants and Catholics alike, is fired more than ever with ardor for The Enterprise. A company of men is already on its way to Dieppe for embarkation for Flanders and letters patent have gone out ordering the strongholds and frontier towns to lay in stores. Men will be siphoned off from them and made free to partake in The Enterprise. At La Rochelle, a great fleet is assembling, soon to sail for the Low Countries.

My Lord of Nassau is already on his way by land, armed with His Majesty's blessing and promises of further aid. I have been honored with the Admiral's trust and counsel, and have been privy to much of the above. He has sent me hither and thither between himself and his nephew of Teligny and my Lord of Nassau. Thus, I have seen with my own eyes how the King's affection for the Admiral waxes and does not wane. You can believe what I tell you.

My friend, you must take your rightful place in this brave Enterprise. I see you leading a company of men to fame and glory. Nothing else will do. You must not wait: Every town and village will rise against the oppressor, who cannot long hold out. We have everything on our side. Might and Right are one. Do not hesitate, or your chance for greatness will pass you by.

I missed you at Blois, and now that the King hunts again, I am leaving for La Rochelle. Write me, or better still, summon up your vassals and your men-at-arms and join me there. We can always find space in the ships for bold men.

Yours, ever in friendship,

Trophime

Pierre stood, and approaching the narrow aperture in the thick wall that served for a window in his tower fastness, looked out over the greening landscape. All the restlessness that had recently been his torment, his confusion of longings and misgivings, his impatience at the shackles of duty, his spring verve — seemed to reach a climax, brought about by his friend's naive enthusiasm. Here, thought Pierre, was an outlet worthy of a man in his position. But more frankly, though his mind merely skirted around the issue rather than dealing with it honestly, here was an avenue of escape which he could take without laying himself open to the least reproach.

If his King was engaged in this business, how could anyone — not Anne, not banker Pascal, whose arrival that very day Pierre was awaiting with dread, deny that Pierre had the right, indeed the duty, to throw himself into The Enterprise with all the might, personal and inherent in his rank, that was at his disposal. Here, at last, was something worthy of the exercise of the powers his undoubted prowess and his long training had given him. Here, at last, was something that would transform the burdens of his position into the assets they were intended to be. He would call up his men and ride at their head to join the army of the Netherlands.

In the midst of Pierre's excitement, a page announced Pascal's arrival. With the new perspective on his affairs that his forthcoming adventures gave him, Pierre received the banker with greater brusqueness than he would have otherwise; he was prepared to give the matter of his financial situation shorter shrift than the hours of worry leading up to Pascal's invitation would have seemed to justify.

The interview, however, progressed according to Pascal's plans, rather than Pierre's. With the fortitude of an experienced negotiator, the banker settled down with patience, almost with relish, to the tedious business of inspecting the books of account. The perusal was in fact twofold: The accounts themselves were scrutinized with care, and so was the young new Duke. As to the latter, Pascal liked what he saw. He deemed Pierre's impatience with figures and his evident passion to throw everything aside and be off in quest of glory as only natural in a man of his age.

These and other follies Pascal was confident he could control, to the extent that they concerned him, and beneath, behind, or beyond the imperfections of youth, he thought he detected a germ of statesmanship that time would surely nourish.

Thus, Pascal was confirmed in the belief to which he had leaned, that the benefits of assisting Pierre would, in the long run, vastly outweigh any advantage that he could derive from embarrassing him in the matter of the outstanding loans.

The indebtedness, however, gave Pascal the curb he needed to check any outbursts of unwise impetuosity. Thus, whenever Pierre attempted to divert the discussion into the all-engrossing subject of raising a company of men for The Enterprise, Pascal would cluck sadly and murmur how even the greatest gallantry must be paid for. It was a hard world, no doubt about it. The hours wore on, leaving Pascal as sprightly as a sparrow in spring, while Pierre subsided into chastened, if somewhat surly, acquiescence. As to the accounts themselves, Pascal's most important discovery was clear proof that the steward had falsified them to cover his own peculations. The banker shed his restraining mode and became all positive practicality. The offender's arrest and punishment were decided on with dispatch. Pascal overwhelmed Pierre with offers to find an honest and capable replacement and suggestions on putting the estate's revenue collections and accounting on a regular basis. All of these, Pierre accepted. The matter of deferring interest payments was then graciously agreed to, and the business of the day was over.

Pierre would gladly have been quit of Pascal's presence, but there was no polite way of refusing to entertain him for the evening. The supper, served in the relative privacy of the great bedchamber, began, as Pierre had expected, as an awkward and tiresome affair. Predictably, Anne was unhelpful: She viewed sitting down with the banker much as she would have dining with the groom, and Pierre's explanation of why it would be politic, not to say polite, to humor the man had merely aggravated her bad humor. Pascal himself made the situation worse by fawning on Anne with an abjectness which merely intensified her scorn and added to Pierre's acute discomfort. Pleading a headache, Anne retired early to the new, separate quarters which she had demanded of Pierre by virtue of her delicate condition.

At this point, Pierre would dispose to join his household for the evening revels, except that he detected in his guest a desire to linger over the meal, which, as he thought, would cost him nothing to humor. The banker had fallen into a reflective mood, which seemed to free him to lay down his burden of numbers and expand about the issues that gave the numbers their raison d'être.

"These are difficult times all around," Pascal was saying. "With all due respect to your friend, whoever he is, this Brill business spells trouble for everyone."

Bored, but unwilling to let such provocation pass unnoticed, Pierre replied, "How can you say that? Why, Brill is just the first step in The Enterprise which everyone has cherished for months. I'm out of touch, perhaps, but even back in the fall, I could see it was so."

"Some have cherished the idea of some kind of Netherlands adventure, no doubt about that. But that's not to say there aren't many who wouldn't go along with it, even if wild horses were dragging them."

"Well, the Guises, maybe."

"And Her Majesty, the Queen Mother. Not exactly nobody. And for another thing, this Brill episode is just an accident, a mistake. The English Queen threw the pirates out and they had to put into port somewhere and Brill was where they landed. They themselves didn't expect anything to come of it. I've heard tell Louis of Nassau was horrified and the King all in a tither. Fact is, no one was prepared."

"Forgive me, Monsieur, but you're absolutely wrong. The Sea Beggars attack was part of an overall plan. My friend is absolutely clear on that."

"With all respect, my Lord, your friend, whoever he is, may be as clear as he wants, but there's a lot of wishful thinking always, and a lot of wishful talking when things go wrong. Of course, now that the matter's blown off half-cocked, my Lords of Orange and Nassau must make declarations to suit the occasion. But I can assure you, they don't tell anything about what went before."

No longer bored, but instead frankly annoyed, Pierre interjected hastily, "Go wrong? Nothing's gone wrong. Brill is a triumph."

Pascal burped and wiped his mouth discreetly with his hand. "Brill's a mess. Take my word for it. I've reason to know. We bankers keep in touch."

Pierre leaned back with a smile. "I can see how hostilities might be considered disturbing to business, though I should think you'd benefit in the end. You always do." Pascal cocked an ironic eyebrow and watched his host attentively.

"Still," Pierre continued, "I don't think you should let your interests warp your view of the facts. Even if one were to accept your view of what went before Brill, which I don't, you've only to look at what came after to grasp its true significance. Right after Brill was captured, the terms of the Navarre marriage contract were agreed to, and at last, the English signed a treaty with us."

"Much of nothing, my Lord: The Navarre marriage is connected with the Dutch adventure only in the minds of those who wish them to be connected. And the English treaty was merely defensive. Anyway, not much could be expected from that quarter, for the English Queen has been grievously ill, so they say, and so has her minister, that Berg, Bourg, Burgh — whatever his name is. Near death, he is, by all reports. I've colleagues in London, too, you know."

"Oh?" said Pierre, nettled. "Well, never mind the English. We don't need them. We've enough Frenchmen, and more."

"Enough Frenchmen for war with Spain? I doubt it — especially if half of them stay home to fight Protestants."

"But that's exactly the point: The Enterprise unites us all."

"Guises, too? I thought we'd agreed they at least remained disaffected."

"The King just reaffirmed the Admiral's innocence in the matter of the late Duke de Guise's death and I know he has sent embassies to him begging him to be reconciled with Guise."

"Yes, but it's Guise who has to be reconciled, isn't it?"

"You'll see, he will be."

"I may see it, but I won't believe it. Ah, well," Pascal yawned abruptly, "I wonder what the Duke your Father would have said."

Pierre paused. He knew quite well what his father would have thought: just what Pascal apparently thought. So would Gondi. So would, as Pascal had pointed out, the Queen Mother. Who was he, Pierre, to think he knew better?

"I've enjoyed my time with you," Pascal continued. "It was a pleasure, too, to meet your lovely wife," a twinkle came into his eye, "and to see that she is how shall I say — doing her duty by you. Forgive my mentioning it. I only wished to express my happiness." Pierre, who thought Anne's condition was still indiscernible, looked slightly shocked. "You know," said Pascal, "I once heard our mutual friend, Monsieur de Retz, mention that there'd been talk of coupling yourself with that sweet young ward of his, the Duchess de la Roque. That would have been a fine match, but it seems to me that you've done well for yourself as it is."

At Pierre's silence, Artus stood and spoke gruffly, "Forgive my presumption. Such matters are not my province. Now, if you'll excuse me, I'm mortally tired."

Pierre sat on after his guest had departed. Could there be anything in what Pascal had said? He had never heard of such a match. That did not necessarily mean anything. His father had not been in the habit of consulting him, even on things that concerned him intimately. By the time he had married, Blaise de la Roque had been dead and Gondi had become Athalie's guardian. But Gondi had acted as go-between in his marriage to Anne, and could surely have arranged a union with his niece instead. It would have been a most appropriate match. A fountain of anger spurted within him. What strange fate had ruined things for everyone? The question aggravated and rendered acute the dull sorrow he carried around within him.

He would write to her, he thought; by God, he would! She should not simply slip from his life, as meaningless as a spring snow. He took a deep breath and squeezed his eyes tightly shut. But what was the point of it? If she had found peace at Fontevrault, found the peace of spirit she had had before meeting him, why should he thunder through it again, when there still was nothing he could offer her but grief?

Chapter XXV

he bed dominated the room, both because of its size and because of the intensely palpable presence of its occupant. Its four posters thrust toward the low ceiling, seeming to crush the baldachin, with its somewhat superfluous feathers, against the exposed beams. The shortness of the mattress emphasized the squareness and massiveness that were its principal attributes.

In the middle of the square sat the Admiral de Coligny. Unlike other, lesser men, he was not disadvantaged by a recumbent position. His large torso rose trunk-like from a discreet hill of brocade, the whiteness of his linen standing out against the dark hanging behind the bed. He had fallen ill with stomach trouble shortly after his return to Court in mid-July. He was improving, but still felt weak and nauseated.

When the King burst into the room straight from his morning tennis game and rushed impetuously toward the bed, no one in the room would have been surprised to see the stripling monarch bow to the Admiral, rather than the reverse. Nonetheless, ponderously, the older man moved to rise, but Charles stopped him, perching on the bed and pushing Coligny back against the pillows with a gesture at once familiar and respectful.

The young men of the Admiral's entourage bowed and murmured around the two until the King waved them away, less with grace than indifference. They withdrew to the far side of the room and gathered self-consciously about a heavy deal table where the liquid remains of a not very luxurious dinner still lingered. Clearing a space, they settled to cards, trying to look as if they were not snooping on the conversation of their betters.

Maurice, who had accompanied the King, did not withdraw, and the young men at the table threw him covert glances full of envy and distaste. Noticing him, the Admiral said, "Fetch de Grève."

I should send the others away, Coligny thought. The King should have the wit to do it himself, but his eagerness pushes aside caution. For myself, it is a choice: The advantage of having witnesses must be weighed against the chance that one of them is a betrayer. I believe they are all loyal, he told himself firmly, stifling the bubble of fear that rose in his innards whenever he felt ill. Could it be poison? the twinges in his gut whispered to him. But ordinary men fell sick, too, he answered that tiny inner voice.

De Grève appeared and bowed; Maurice hovered at his elbow; Coligny decisively turned his attention to the King. "Father, I was much chagrined to hear you were not well," Charles was saying. "We have fruit for you. It will be coming soon. They say it helps. Paris is a sickly town, yet I must be here, and my joy to have you again, at last, at my side is such that I cannot bear to let you go. Yet, to make you sick..."

"Think nothing of it, my Liege," Coligny replied. "It is nothing. I don't think Paris has anything to do with it." He hesitated and knew that he and the King meant different things when they thought of the dangers of Paris. It was not the city's marshes and refuse that frightened Coligny, but his vulnerability to his enemies. "You do me great honor," the Admiral continued. "More than my House can bear."

"Never that!" the King laughed. "The great Houses of France can never have their fill of honor. Between you and the Guises, I've had a time of it."

"And I am sorry for it, Your Majesty. But it was not I... "

"Never mind. I know. I was only teasing." Charles waved his hands. "It was not your honor that brought me here, but mine own." He continued, drawing himself up. "So much is going on. We must talk. We must plan. Unless, of course, you are too weak."

Coligny shook his head. Longing for silence and a darkened room, he forced himself to focus on his Monarch's words.

"Everything you said, Father, is coming true," the King cried. "The Sea Beggars are holding firm, the towns in the Netherlands are rising, the Spanish have not been able to reassert themselves. If we throw ourselves behind the Dutch, great Spain will have to bow at last. Yes, Philip will bow to me. The world will see what I am made of. I will have done something at last, something that will be remembered.

"You, of course, will be my right arm," said Charles.

"What of Anjou?" the Admiral inquired.

"He won't want to fight, and I want no half-hearts."

"This is a cause all good Frenchmen should want to join."

"I know that," the King replied, "but just to spite me he will oppose it. He is not interested in my glory, only his own."

Coligny and de Grève exchanged uncomfortable glances, and the Admiral caught sight of Maurice's looming figure behind de Grève.

"La Renaudie," Coligny asked, "what of your stepbrother, the new Duke? It is too soon to suppose he could pull men together as did his father, but his name would help. Will he follow or stay away?"

Maurice shrugged scornfully.

"He's just like his father, always seeing problems and looking on the dark side of things. He can't really be relied on." Maurice swelled his chest to convey his own solidity.

"Well, there are different temperaments, of course," Coligny mused, "but a position of responsibility also breeds respect for circumstances."

"What do you say?" the King queried, taking the Admiral's remark as if it had been directed at him, and wondering if a reproach had been intended.

"Nothing, Your Majesty. We were just speculating whether we could count on Pierre de Galle to throw himself altogether behind you. It would help. But La Renaudie says he's not very wholehearted."

"Womanly timorousness!" the King shouted. "He probably got it from his mother. She was English, after all. Look at what they're like, look at that Queen of theirs — nothing but devious double-tracking. Words, words, but no action!" His outburst brought on a fit of coughing. When it cleared, he continued, "But young Pierre will do as he's told."

"Of course," Coligny agreed. "But if his heart isn't in it, he'll think of all kinds of reasons to hold back men and materials, unless, of course, he's too innocent to have learned that game yet."

"No matter," the King said. "We have your men."

The same thought went through Coligny's and de Grève's minds: Yes, we have men, but who will defend those of the Religion at home, while our men are fighting in the Netherlands?

"We must be sure..." Coligny began, but he was never able to finish his plea for enforcement of the Edicts, for the King burst out in bitter tones, "And we have time to get more men, for one thing's sure: Neither of us can leave before my sister's wedding. Her Majesty, my Mother, would never stand for it."

"Who is King?" La Renaudie interrupted impertinently. The King sent him a baleful look, and Coligny and de Grève stared at him coldly.

"De Retz is always telling me I would be nothing without my Mother and Anjou," Charles said, turning back to the Admiral as if to address only him, but his words were in fact an answer to La Renaudie. Maurice suppressed a smile. Coligny squirmed. The making of the statement alone is proof of its truth, he thought inwardly.

Unabashed, Maurice spoke again, and unwillingly the others turned to him. "There seems to be a dilemma. Action now seems imperative, and yet The Enterprise's natural leaders cannot act now. Surely, some temporary leader should be sent forth with enough troops to hold the status quo at least." La Renaudie's eyes gleamed. What if they chose me? he thought. Gondi would be appalled, but what of it.

"Yes, my lord, Your Majesty," de Grève broke in. "That's what I've been saying, and I think we have the man — Genlis. We can raise 3,000, maybe 4,000, men and send them across the border under his command. They will keep the Spanish busy, stop them from counterattacking, until we can bring up the full extent of our forces and begin a real offensive."

So, Genlis! thought Maurice. And I will get to stay home and play nursemaid to the Admiral. Well, we'll see. The babble of excited murmurs surged around him and broke at last into ultimate agreement. He contributed nothing more, but listened with spite in his heart.

* * *

Don Diego Zúñiga smiled graciously with the practiced ease of an experienced courtier. It was one of those summer evenings that only Paris can produce and Zúñiga felt relaxed as Albert de Gondi finished the formalities of greeting him outside the Hôtel de Perron, Gondi's Paris residence. If he felt a trifle bored, it was only because this was the fifth such reception in as many days since, as King Philip's new ambassador, he had made his formal entry and been accredited. If he was more than a trifle wary beneath his handsome smile, it was because King Philip had warned him about Gondi.

"Silk," they had agreed to call him in dispatches, for even Spanish dispatches were opened and read from time to time. And an appropriate name, too, Zúñiga thought, as he took Gondi's measure at home, as it were.

Philip had given Zúñiga not just one, but many, briefings, and the importance of his mission had been made very clear. Simply stated, it was to keep France out of the Netherlands by whatever means were necessary. Indeed, he had been told in no uncertain terms to get hold of a situation which from Spain's point of view was slipping badly. They had agreed that Gondi would be an important factor in their objective, but Philip had warned Zúñiga to beware of him: Gondi knows too much about the Protestants.

Spain's network of spies and informers was second to none in Europe, the American silver being more and more abundant in the Spanish coffers, and the number and quality of such agents being largely a question of money. Still, they had not penetrated the French Protestants. Yet somehow, it had been reported in Madrid that Gondi seemed to know a lot about their plans. It was entirely possible, Philip had cautioned, that Gondi had ties to the Protestants and even possible that his mistress, Catherine de Medici, had the same thing in mind.

"You cannot trust the French in matters of religion," Philip had asserted. "In 1562 Catherine was prepared to have a French church with the heretics in it. It was a divine miracle — all present had crossed themselves reverently — that they couldn't agree on the form of worship. But it may well be that they have been preparing a welcome for themselves if the wind should change in the Protestants' favor. Why, look at Coligny, strutting about their Court as if he owned it, instead of kicking at the end of a rope as he deserves. Be careful, Zúñiga, remember your predecessor."

Zúñiga smiled inwardly at the memory of the irascible de Álava escaping over the border to the Netherlands at night. Dressed as a woman, they had said. Well, he would not disgrace centuries of Castilian nobility by any such antics.

Gondi's welcoming speech was drawing into its peroration. Elegantly done, thought Zúñiga, and how well "Silk" fits him. Gondi had outdone even his customary sartorial splendor for this occasion. His tunic and hose were of deep blue silk and his short cloak, which he had negligently thrown back on his shoulders, was of the same hue intricately crested with gold thread bearing his arms, lined with a contrasting color of dazzling orange silk that would have been too much if it had been a shade more brilliant. "Exquisite taste," Philip had said. I suppose that is what it really means, Zúñiga thought, to be able to go right up to the edge, but never over it. It must take practice as well as instinct.

Gondi was surrounded by a small entourage, his wife the Countess, whose firm hand the Ambassador had kissed with a bow, and Jerome Gondi, often seen in Spain, whom he knew already. A useful fellow, but so openly allied with Spain that he might as well be a Spaniard. "These merchants," King Philip had sniffed, "follow trade wherever it goes. The borders of our realms mean nothing to them. He is here because money is here."

"If my lord would accompany me," Gondi said, taking the Ambassador's arm, and, followed by his little court, they entered the great hall. Zúñiga was too experienced to show anything but amused appreciation, but inwardly his jaw dropped. A mere count living like this? Gondi's taste did not stop at clothes. His new residence incorporated the very latest Italian architecture and decoration. Gondi's hotel was about a quarter of a mile along the road to the faubourg Saint Antoine to the north of the Queen Mother's garden at the Tuileries, and rather in the country. Zúñiga had expressed a bit of surprise that Gondi had chosen to build so far away from the center of Paris.

"Well, of course, we have apartments at the Louvre, but Paris is getting so crowded and one wants more space for entertaining. It is no secret, my lord Ambassador, that I am expected to entertain His Majesty and my royal Mistress, his Mother, rather frequently. They like nice things, she especially, and I am only trying to show my gratitude for their favors by maintaining a place where they can feel comfortable."

Thinking back to the dark and cramped Louvre where he had been received by the King, Zúñiga wondered whether Gondi wasn't going a bit too far. But then Queen Catherine herself was building the Tuileries, which when completed, would be a truly royal residence. Its gardens were already the talk of Europe, and he looked forward to a supper there, al fresco, for which Catherine de Medici was famous. Gondi's all too obvious pride in his new dwelling was becoming somewhat annoying. He escorted Zúñiga into one lovely chamber after another, each exquisitely crafted in the latest fashion, and tastefully decorated with furniture that was obviously new and expensive. There seemed no point of style too small for Gondi to fail to point it out to his guest. The ensemble of rooms had about it the same air as Gondi himself. Perfect, just perfect, and just on the right side of the line between elegance and ostentation.

With a flourish the entourage entered the dining hall, a beautifully proportioned room of two storeys on the west side of the house, still brilliantly lit by the westering sun. The silver and crystal on the heavy tablecloths gave back a golden glow. A consort of viols and recorders in the gallery above struck up a popular Spanish dance, and Zúñiga bowed slightly to acknowledge the courtesy. The dinner, Zúñiga reflected, was of a piece with the mansion; that is to say, it was flawless. Its perfection was marred, if that was not too strong a word, only by Gondi's care in pointing out to the Ambassador the finer points of his cuisine. Not long past the roast quail, Gondi raised his goblet and observed that Zúñiga's arrival was thought by many to herald a new and, it was hoped, more cordial era in relations between France and Spain than had been represented by his predecessor. Gondi's toast to better times was warmly seconded by all.

The mention of de Álava had brought a titter of laughter from the right end of the long table where some of Gondi's younger relations, or so Zúñiga presumed them to be, were grouped. De Álava was a damn fool, thought Zúñiga, but Spanish ambassadors are not to be made the butt of japes by such as those. His frosty glance to the right instantly silenced the laughter.

His gesture was not lost on Gondi. "Your predecessor was a worthy man and I had many dealings with him. He was getting a bit old, though, and was not always the easiest of men. We are looking forward to some fresh ideas."

"Worthy he was, indeed," Zúñiga replied smoothly, "But an ambassador must be able to speak and be listened to in the Court to which he is accredited. My master believes that unworthy though I am, my office as his spokesman will suffice to get me an attentive hearing."

"We are all ears for your messages, my lord," Gondi replied. Then just as smoothly but in a lower voice, "My mistress, Queen Catherine, has suggested specifically that I open discussions with you of the utmost frankness." Has she now, thought Zúñiga. A guest in a house such as this would do well to follow his host's lead.

"If you are not pressed," Zúñiga replied, "we could speak more privately later."

"As you wish."

Zúñiga sat back and allowed himself to be pampered by the seemingly unending procession of liveried servants bearing first one dainty, then another.

"Your King seems determined to proceed with the marriage of his own sister to the Protestant King of Navarre," Zúñiga said as he sampled the sweet being proferred. "My master wonders how so loyal a member of the Church as yourself can fail to use what influence you have to make the King see that such a marriage would be a most grievous mistake."

"Ah, Ambassador, you touch on a delicate subject, one that is all too dear to the heart of Queen Catherine."

"But it is deplorable, Count, really it is, almost to legitimize their scandalous heresy. King Philip is much alarmed, and I may say angered, by the prospect."

"My dear Zúñiga, when you have been among us a little longer, you will learn what is simple, black-and-white in your land, where you have only the true faith, is here complex and fraught with difficulties. It goes without saying that I share your horror at the so-called Reformed Religion, but I have had to become reconciled to the inevitable.

"We have fought three wars in ten years to stamp it out, and still it flourishes. Queen Catherine believes it must at least be domesticated instead of running wild about the countryside. She hopes, as do I, that when young Henri of Navarre is safely a member of the royal family, he can be brought back into the Church with many of his followers as well."

Gondi wiped his mouth on a monogrammed napkin. "Will you not join me in my study?"

The dinner, having progressed by ever more sumptuous stages through its sugary finale, was followed by more lively music and dancing. Gondi and Zúñiga had no difficulty in leaving the festivities behind, and the silence when Gondi closed the door to his private study was complete.

"I would not say it openly," Gondi began, "but I was much distressed at the difficulties Don Francés, your predecessor, encountered. There was much that needed to be discussed, and his personality caused much friction. I rejoice that your master has sent you, as my cousin, Jerome, speaks highly of your honor and good sense."

"We have heard much of you as well, my lord," Zúñiga replied. "Your welcome has been most impressive." Zúñiga, relaxed and self-confident, realized it would be a grave error to underestimate Gondi, despite his pretensions. Beneath his magnificent clothes his body appeared lithe and strong, and Zúñiga was aware that Gondi had earned a reputation for strength and courage as well as shrewdness.

"If we might continue our discussion," Zúñiga said evenly, "have you no fear that once the Protestants are brought into the royal family they will be unstoppable? How will you curb their ambitions?"

"My dear Zúñiga, you will soon see for yourself, and I am sure you have already heard, that the Protestants are not the only power in France. Nor is the crown the only power to control them. It has been all the King can do to keep his brother Anjou and the Guises from making trouble for them."

"And a good thing if he would let them!" the Ambassador cried as he struck the table. "I cannot tell you how we rejoiced at the death of Jeanne d'Albret. It was poison, I presume?" He arched an eyebrow at Gondi. Gondi sat down in a gilded armchair and negligently crossed his leg over the arm.

"Jeanne d'Albret was the guest of Their Majesties, Ambassador. I myself had to entertain her at Queen Catherine's request. I don't mind saying that she did not seem nearly as appreciative of my hospitality as you. As to her sudden demise, well, she had left Court and was returning to Navarre when she, er, was taken ill. I know nothing whatever of foul play. Rumors abound, of course, but where is the proof?"

"Between us, Albert, I may call you Albert?" Zúñiga leaned forward eagerly, "I had rather hoped you would know more about it. She was a devil! Her death brought real pleasure in Madrid. My master does not forget those who do good for the Faith, and ridding the world of her was a very good thing."

Zúñiga's eyes never left Gondi's, but the latter betrayed nothing. Either he really knows nothing, thought Zúñiga, or he is very good at his game. The two courtiers were well matched, better than Zúñiga had thought earlier in the evening. Zúñiga might strut a bit, but he was no fool. Gondi for his part seemed affable and at ease, if a bit eager to be noticed and to please. The conversation circled around various inconsequential subjects before Zúñiga again attempted to sound Gondi out.

"Still," the Ambassador observed, "a marriage would bring a lot of Protestants, indeed all of the important ones, to Paris. In a loyal Catholic city it might be possible to accomplish what all your wars have failed to do."

"Really, sir," Gondi stiffened, "I doubt greatly that Queen Catherine would think that a festive way to celebrate her daughter's wedding. You must try to understand our difficulties. Coligny and his followers are loyal Frenchmen."

"But Albert, King Philip does not think it is a festive occasion. And why are they armed? Don't they trust their King to protect them?"

Gondi shrugged. "It is only too clear that they do not. That is why Catherine is so anxious to cement a lasting peace. But Diego, I may, I take it, call you Diego, since we are to be friends. I cannot help wondering at your apparent concern about one marriage. Surely Spain has its own problems. The Netherlands are scarcely a peaceful garden. I am told things have gone badly indeed for your great General of Alva."

"The Dutch rebels will be crushed and their leaders hanged," Zúñiga snarled. "Listen, Albert, we will brook no interference there. None. I may as well tell you straight out — we fear your Protestants may try to march north to aid their fellow heretics. Indeed, it is no secret that Coligny has ideas of doing just that. My master would consider that an act of war by France. We look to you to at least control that rabble, if you won't take my advice and rid yourselves of them, once and for all."

Now it was Gondi's turn to bristle. "'An act of war!' Those are strong words, Ambassador. Not that we have any intention of meddling there. The Queen Mother has never stopped opposing any such adventure. I admit that it has not always been possible to control every hothead on the edge of society, but really, I should use those words carefully, even among friends."

"Believe me, Albert, I can show my friendship for you in no better a way than to see that your eyes are open to your danger. My master will have that revolt crushed. If he thinks France is trying to exploit what you must see is a temporary weakness, he will have to act. And he can act. Don John of Austria has not yet set forth for the summer campaign against the Turks. King Philip believes, as should all Christians, that the crusade against the infidel Turks is a holy duty, but this summer he has decided to let the Turks wait. You know that he would not do that unless he was even more concerned about France. Those galleys could be on your south coast in days. We would strike at the heart of the Protestant stronghold. France and Spain would once again be united in a single, unbroken faith. Please, Albert," he concluded earnestly, "believe me, it is not a fantasy."

Gondi was silent for some moments. He knew that he had just heard spoken the Queen Mother's worst nightmare. The Spanish army could tumble her carefully balanced house of cards into ruins. It would reduce France to a Spanish satrapy. He knew she would do anything to avoid it.

"I see, Albert," the Ambassador continued smoothly, "that what I have said has made an impression on you. I am glad you are intelligent enough to see our position, but when I said I come in friendship, I did not mean merely my own poor friendship, but that of my royal master as well. He has a long memory and is most generous to those who serve him well. A man in your position could do much to get others to see that an adventure into the Netherlands would be very much against France's interests. Such a man could be sure of King Philip's gratitude."

"I can only do my duty," Gondi said, without looking at Zúñiga.

"Come, come, Albert, of course you are going to do your duty. As I see it, your duty and your own advancement go hand in hand. Why, I must tell you that there are those in Madrid who have wondered why a man of your ability and proven service is still a Count. Surely it is time you were a Maréchal, perhaps even a Duke. I can see at a glance at this house that elevation to the highest levels would suit you well. My master's gratitude is often tangible and that might be of some assistance to you."

"How do I know I can trust you?" Gondi said in a low voice.

"That is easy," Zúñiga replied. "Ask your cousin, Jerome. His contacts can verify everything I say. The question, if I may be indelicate, Albert, is, can we trust you? I, having met you, can tell you at once that I personally could never doubt you, but there are those at home who have asked questions."

"Questions about what?"

"About your religion."

"You can't be serious," Gondi protested. "I am a friend of the Duke of Anjou. There is not a more loyal Catholic in France than I. On what possible basis can my religion be questioned?"

"It is said, Albert, that you know a great deal, more than any outsider could, about the Protestant plans and intentions. We have the best sources, but have always found the Protestants opaque to our designs. Yet you seem to know things. You can see how questions might arise."

Gondi's tenseness, which he had been trying to mask, vanished at once, and he roared with laughter so genuine that it more than anything convinced Zúñiga.

"Ah, Diego," he chortled, "indeed I do know a thing or two about the Protestants. To know things, c'est mon metier. It is why I have been able to earn and keep Their Majesties' confidence. Yes, I know things about them, and I am not surprised that your master has had difficulties. But really, my friend, speaking as one professional to another, just because I have succeeded where he has failed should not make my religion suspect."

"I am satisfied, Albert," Zúñiga laughed. "I take it that it will be useless for me to ask how you do it. But to satisfy King Philip I need something to send him, some tidbit that will show him Gondi is no Protestant. I leave it to you to devise something suitable."

"I will give you something 'suitable' right now," said Gondi evenly. "A band of adventurers led by the Count de Genlis has slipped out toward Mos. They are perhaps as many as a couple of thousand. They plan to join forces with the Duke of Nassau. It should be no great trick to intercept them with this intelligence. They are wholly unofficial, you understand. The King knows nothing of their scheme."

"Excellent, Albert," Zúñiga replied, his handsome face beaming. "I think our friendship is off to a splendid start. I had not counted on something like this tonight. I assure you again His Catholic Majesty will be most grateful. But King Charles will have to disavow those rascals when we have caught them. You can see to it, can't you?"

"I believe I can," said Gondi. "I will take thought on the rest of our conversation. But let us join the others. People will think I have been boring you with my art collection."

Later, as he made his way home, Don Diego de Zúñiga reflected to himself on the amazing predictability of human nature. Could it have been so easy? All he wants is status and all he needs is more money. So long as we can provide, we will have a useful friend at Court. He was already composing his dispatch as he reached his residence. It began: "'Silk' can be had at a price."

Chapter XXVI

grin suffused Pierre's face as he stood at the bow of Gondi's great gilded barge moving with the rhythmic thump of oars down the Seine. His grin reflected sheer delight at the early morning sun glittering now on the river, now on the gold carvings around him. Mostly he was pleased because he was eighteen, the Duke de Galle, and being escorted to a private audience with the Queen Mother by her trusted confidant and his great friend, Albert de Gondi. Pierre looked like some kind of divinity who had elected to act as a ship's figurehead. He was dressed in the grey silk of half mourning, his doublet slashed with grey and black embroidered with the silver stag of de Galle. His tawny curls rippled in the breeze, which felt better than it smelled, as the Seine was lower than normal and its sorry burden of the great city's refuse all too obvious.

"Ugh," he exclaimed to Gondi. "A brisk trot would have been warm, but at least we would have been spared this."

"It will be better downstream," Gondi replied. "It was vital that we speak. This meeting will be difficult and you could do yourself harm if you are not prepared."

Oh, no, here he goes again, thought Pierre. More politics. But he was pleased enough with the situation that even the prospect of a lecture did not disturb him.

Pierre had grown up a lot in the months since his father's death, especially in his own estimation. The new steward sent by banker Pascal had rapidly taken charge of the baffling minutiae of the operation of his large properties. Credits from Pascal materialized like magic.

Always there was the witty, urbane, helpful, and never patronizing presence of Gondi himself, who had proved himself, thought Pierre, a man one could really count on. The sadness, the loss, the emptiness he had felt as winter ebbed, turned, as spring had ripened into summer, to profound gratitude that his father had done so well, and had left him so well provided for, not just in wealth, but in friends like Gondi, and connections. While he did not yet consider himself the man his father had been, he was becoming more and more sure that in time he would fill that role very well indeed.

Even Athalie's inexplicable silence, which he had at first thought would drive him mad, had begun to prey on his mind less and less. He had even commenced believing that in time he would forget her; that wonderful, mysterious, and deep as she had been, she had been only an experience of his youth, to which in time neither he nor anyone else would attach any great importance. He knew well enough that for others of his rank, hopping in and out of one bed after another was hardly more than a game. It really hadn't been at all like that with Athalie. Their lovemaking had been wonderful, of course; but being with her, falling in love with her, had been like waking up after having been dreaming, like a clear sunny morning after weeks of clouds and dampness. Pierre could not pretend, and did not try to, that something profound had not happened. He had a nagging sense of incompleteness now, in stark contrast to the feeling of wholeness and completion when they had come together.

But Pierre had tried to put Athalie out of his mind, had tried to concentrate on Anne, which had proved far less burdensome than he had feared. At first at Plessis Gaillard it was perhaps the lack of other interests; later, in June when they joined the Court in Paris, it was perhaps that Pierre was after all the Duke, sought after and deferred to. Whatever the reason, Anne had given generously of her amorous best. Pierre looked and felt replete, even if his relations with her continued to be otherwise difficult.

The situation seemed far from terrible; indeed, he found it hard to think of the shame, awkwardness, and loneliness Anne had made him feel the year before. He did not trust her, but then, he didn't need to trust her as her advancing pregnancy presumably reduced her interest to others. Pierre found he was almost accustomed to not trusting her, and it was so much more pleasant when she was a bit affectionate.

Pierre had never been fond of Paris. His early memories of the capital were formed more of being deprived of the woods and fields of his beloved Touraine, than of actually disliking the bustle and commotion of the loud, boisterous, crowded old town Paris then was. Fortunately, so he had thought, it was not often necessary for his father, and as a consequence for the whole family and entourage, to take up residence at the Hôtel de Galle, a somber pile of stone crowded against the south side of the former royal palace of the Îsle de la Cité. Their royal masters had long since removed to the Right Bank, and their palace, the Louvre, had itself become old fashioned and badly in need of the renovations that were slowly transferring it from fortress to villa. Still, de Galle, with typical lack of interest in change or fashion, had continued to reside in what was no longer a fashionable area.

Pierre had dreaded Anne's barbed comments about his old hotel when they had rejoined the Court. Even more, he had feared the endless whining for a "suitable palace," perhaps north of the garden of the Tuileries. But whether it was on account of her advancing pregnancy, or the stifling breathless heat that had been enveloping Paris for weeks, Anne had been subdued even on an issue as close to her heart as the style of her residence. Combined with his duties at Court, mostly ceremonial, but some real, all this had transformed Paris for Pierre into a garden of delights.

"Whatever are you talking about, Albert? My father was one of Their Majesties' most trusted counselors, and I have always been treated most kindly by them. It is only right that they should wish to have me present."

"Pierre," Gondi cried with exasperation, "Pierre, are you listening?"

"Yes, Albert," he replied, "whatever you say."

"Pierre," Gondi sighed, "you are simply too young to understand the importance of these things. The country, that is to say, the Queen Mother, is in a perilous and baffling situation. A wrong move would spell disaster, and that in my experience never improves Madame's temper."

"Albert, Albert," Pierre replied, grinning, "how you do fret. The King will decide, and it is clear that he is going to choose war in the Netherlands. We have all been talking about it, and it seems to me that it would be jolly sport. My father used to tell me about those grand battles you and he had with the Spanish in Italy, and you must know that I am really looking forward to trying my hand at it."

"Pierre, listen to me," Gondi said, placing his hand on Pierre's arm. "I have tried to help you since your father died. I like you and I want to see you prosper. Believe me, there are some things you must understand. War with Spain now would be a catastrophe. Not just for France but for you, too. When I heard that you were thinking of going off with Genlis on his raid two weeks ago, I advised against it. I know you were annoyed but I think you will thank me."

"You are as bad as my father was!" Pierre said petulantly. "Why must it always be no? Genlis will have all the fun and adventure and come back covered with glory. He is a mere baron. I must do something soon worthy of my name!"

They passed the Louvre and the city walls, and the musical cacophony of the street vendors' cries faded away. They passed into the countryside past the Abbey of Saint Germain des Prés. The noises of the city were replaced by the bells of oxen and the cooing of waterfowl. As Gondi had promised, the smell improved. As the barge turned south with the Seine past the fields of the prés au clercs, the shadows of the awning darkened Gondi's face. Gondi was sweating freely and his eyes were drawn and anxious. He is afraid, thought Pierre. That Gondi's life had been several times threatened by the Protestants, Pierre well knew; indeed another attempt had miscarried only a week before. He placed a huge hand on Gondi's arm.

"Don't be afraid, Albert. We have enough men on the boat to keep off any chance encounters, and no one will harm you at close quarters while I can still use my sword."

In spite of himself Gondi was touched by Pierre's sincerity. How simple these nobles are, he thought. Pierre de Galle would throw away on an adventure more than he, Gondi, dared to dream of, and yet he would risk his life to save Gondi's without a second thought. "You are a good friend, Pierre, and your father's son," he murmured, "but it is not an ambush that concerns me just now. I fear this meeting."

Pierre regarded Gondi with interest. Curiosity finally overcame his disdain for the kind of politics Gondi seemed always to be talking about.

"Well, Albert, you'd better get on with it. I'll try to keep it all straight."

"This meeting will have to do with the Netherlands," Gondi began, slowly. "I do not know exactly what has happened but I suspect Genlis has gotten into trouble."

Gondi noted with some satisfaction that he suddenly had Pierre's complete attention.

"We will be asked for our advice. I advise you most strongly, follow my lead. Do not say anything rash. This meeting is likely to be stormy."

"I still don't understand why we can't just go in and take them," said Pierre.

"Because of Spain." Gondi smote the side of the barge with his fist. "Spain is too much for us. Her galleys have been poised to strike our southern coast. Philip wants to help us cleanse the land of the heretics, but Catherine fears Spain's embrace, perhaps too much, but nevertheless greatly. To counter Spain she has tried to keep some sort of peace in the country, siding first with the Catholics then with the Protestants, always using one against the other. She has tried to domesticate the Protestants by the forthcoming marriage of Henri of Navarre and her daughter, Margot. She is trying desperately to get Queen Elizabeth of England into an alliance. She almost had her married to Anjou last year, but that fell apart because of his violent Catholicism. She is now trying to get the Queen to accept Alençon."

"But what has all that got to do with the Netherlands?"

"Everything," Gondi hissed. "Catherine believes that only if England joined us wholeheartedly, with ships, men and above all, money, could we perhaps contemplate a joint conquest of the Netherlands. Lacking that, Spain still threatens us, while England watches her great adversaries at each other's throat."

"I don't imagine King Philip would relish a marriage between Alençon and Elizabeth."

"Hardly. For that matter he is doing everything he can in Rome to block the papal dispensation Margot needs to marry Navarre, because they are cousins, after all. France's disunity is Spain's strength and King Philip never forgets it."

"But doesn't Elizabeth favor our Protestants?" Pierre asked. "I have heard she sends them money."

"That is still another reason for Catherine's haste to get Navarre into her family," Gondi replied. "The Protestants have for some time had their own foreign policy. Queen Catherine sees only too well how weak it makes France to have an often disloyal and practically separate state within our bosom. That is why the marriage with Navarre is so vital to her. At least on paper it will unify France and force Elizabeth to deal with only one France instead of two."

Pierre wiped his brow and looked blankly at Gondi. "But you said the meeting was about the Netherlands."

"The Netherlands is the abyss into which all these plans can fall. Our Protestants have been clamoring to get France to fight there. They know well enough the fate their fellows in the Netherlands can expect if Spain crushes the revolt."

"That is what I thought we should do all along," Pierre responded, baffled. "The King agrees. I told..."

"No, no, don't you see?" Gondi interrupted. "He is just being drawn in by Coligny. Invasion in the Netherlands would give the Protestants control of France!

"Look, Pierre," he went on earnestly. "If our Catholic armies march off to the Netherlands, the Protestants here would be stronger than ever. If they send a strong force north and Charles won with their help, they would be the leading party in France. We'd all soon enough be saying our prayers in French instead of Latin. Protestant domination would be bad enough, but Spain would never tolerate it. Spain would invade France and we would end up under Spanish domination. Queen Catherine does not want to be dominated by either the Protestants or the Spanish. Nor," he smiled wryly, "by the Catholics. In a way I admire her balancing act, as such it has been brilliant. But I fear the other side of the coin is the inherent instability. These mighty forces are held in check only by each other."

Pierre gazed into the distance. The barge had passed the fields and hills west of the city and had begun to turn north with the river along the west side of the Bois de Boulogne. Although it was still early, the shade was welcome.

"You are right, Albert," he said heavily. "I wish I had my father's experience."

Soon Pierre found himself following Gondi off the barge at the landing in the Bois. They were met by three lackeys in the Queen Mother's livery, whose bowings were brief because of her obvious instructions that no time should be wasted in conducting Pierre and Gondi to her presence. Catherine de Medici was impressive at any time, but as Pierre met her flashing eyes in the little garden west of the château, he inwardly blessed Gondi for his warnings.

"So you are here at last, Messieurs. We have a bad business here, a very bad business. Genlis has been captured. He had letters from my son, Charles. Under torture his men have said Charles had promised them all the help in the world. King Philip is having apoplexy. Albert, I won't have this! Do you hear? Charles has got to stop playing with fire or he will burn down our whole kingdom. You, Monsieur de Galle, I asked you here to help convince him. Albert, Albert," she sighed and looked heavenward, "what are we going to do? This is all the pretext the Spanish have ever needed!"

"My lady," Gondi began. Pierre could see that even Gondi, not often at a loss for words, was shocked at the news and what it meant. "Genlis must be disowned. The letters are forgeries. His men are liars. What else can we say?"

"Will Philip believe it?"

"Who can say, Madame. Perhaps he will find it convenient to believe it, if we give him no more provocation."

"Let us confront my son," she snapped, and without another word strode into the château, her ladies scurrying behind her, servants darting out of her path, Pierre and Gondi bringing up the rear.

The château, built by François I forty years earlier, was a charming hunting lodge, rather like a miniature Fontainebleau. The Florentine frescoes that adorned the entrance hall brought a stab of memory to Pierre's mind of conversations with Athalie at Fontainebleau about the similar gods and goddesses who populated the walls there.

Pierre was not given much time for reverie.

"I think, Pierre," Gondi whispered as they hurried along, "you are going to see some parental guidance administered. Never breathe a word of this to anyone."

With a final thunderous crash, Catherine herself threw open the door of Charles' study.

The most Christian King of France, Charles IX, was sprawled on the floor removing a tick from his favorite hunting dog. The look that crossed his face of one about to ward off a blow spoke eloquently of his feelings.

"My son," the Queen Mother exploded, "Genlis has been captured and the Spanish have proof of your involvement! Charles, your recklessness is going to ruin us! We may be at war with Spain right now!"

The King rose to his feet. He blinked unsteadily, his mouth working, but his reply was cut off by his mother's continuing tirade. "I have told you a thousand times the Netherlands and those young fools are a deadly mixture. You did this behind my back! You did it behind your Council's back!"

"Genlis must have been betrayed," the King mumbled weakly. "There are traitors around us."

He glared without love in Gondi's direction.

"Traitors, indeed!" his mother shot back. "Then you admit you were behind this foolish idea. If you don't hatch stupid plots, then you won't have to worry about traitors betraying them. You must disown these fools at once. Let the Spanish do what they wish. You will say the papers are lies and these men were on their own. Thank God, they are Protestants."

"I can never do that," the King replied, his voice gathering strength. "The Admiral assured me this plan would work. Genlis is my friend and a brave man. We must rescue him."

"Rescue him! Are you out of your mind!" she shrieked.

"Madame, I am the King," he replied sternly, striking what would have been a regal pose if he had had his boots on. "Please do not use a loud voice in my presence."

"I shall do better," she replied theatrically. "I shall take my loud voice and my advice and my poor self directly back to Florence. You can try to teach King Philip how loud to speak. At any rate, I shall be at peace. If my counsel is not wanted, so be it."

"Mother, please," he pleaded, suddenly contrite, "it's just that it is so unmanly not to do anything."

"No, Charles," she said, noble resignation in her voice. "I must go. I am just a poor old woman. All I have is love for you and your brothers. If you find me an obstacle to your manly whims, you must send me away."

"Mother, please be reasonable," he begged. "You must stay. You know I can't manage without you."

"You can surely rely on the Admiral, your 'father' as you call him!" she said, with a note of genuine bitterness.

"No, no, Mother," the King stammered, "please tell me what I must do. I'll do it. You'll see."

"You must deny everything," she replied briskly, suddenly all business. "Perhaps you will be believed, at least long enough for us to get Henri married to Margot. Call a Council meeting for tomorrow so we can deal with Coligny."

"He will want an invasion at once," the King replied. "The Protestants will be wild when they hear about poor Genlis."

"He shall not have an invasion!" Catherine shouted. "You are the King. The country will support you, not him. Isn't that right, Monsieur de Galle?"

Pierre, bemused by the spectacle, was tongue-tied until he realized that he was required to say only, "Of course, Madame."

"Albert," she said, turning to Gondi, "will you see to the denials and arrangements for the meeting? My son and I are most pleased with the prompt attendance and invaluable counsel you have given us. You may withdraw."

With muttered good mornings to the King, who seemed oblivious of their presence, Pierre and Gondi backed out. As the door closed, they could see Catherine de Medici massaging Charles' temples and cooing softly to him.

As the barge moved slowly upstream to the city under a hazy sun, Pierre regarded Gondi, who seemed absorbed in thought. He looked like one who has just seen lightning strike someone else. It seemed to Pierre that the bolt had been rather too close for comfort.

* * *

The noon sun the next day blazed down on the Pont au Change as Pierre and his men-at-arms crossed to the Right Bank. Pierre had thought to have a pleasant stroll to the Louvre to attend the King's Council, but his brief journey had already been marred by several fights, one of them an ugly one, that his men had had to break up.

The Parisian street people were not about to attack a nobleman of Pierre's stature surrounded by a well-armed company. But they were in a bellicose mood and found each other fair game.

A wheezing, elderly man in black with a thin gold chain around his neck bowed before Pierre.

"Please, my lord, could your men help me? There's another riot on the next street and I haven't men enough to disperse the crowd. They say the Protestant shopkeeper cheated a customer. Any pretext is enough for them in this weather, my lord."

Pierre followed the little man into a dark, narrow street filled with the sounds of fighting. The stench was all but overpowering. "Disperse, people, go back to your homes!" he shouted. When that didn't work, he ordered his men to break up the fighting, which they did, none too gently.

"Let us at them, you damned Calvinist!" shouted a scrawny, disheveled man as he picked up something unnamable to hurl at Pierre.

He was stopped by Marcel, Pierre's sergeant, who threw him flat at Pierre's feet.

"Now, that's no way to talk to his lordship. What shall I do with him, my lord, throw him in the Seine?"

"Let him rise, Marcel. Get up, fellow. I am no Protestant. You must stop this rioting."

"Oh, we were just trying to stop their stealing from us, my lord, I'm sure. There are thousands of them come to town, eating the bread of honest Catholics. They threw rocks at our procession, when we were thanking God for the defeat of that robber baron, Genlis. We're only getting back our own, my lord. I'm sure we didn't recognize you. Please, my lord, don't hurt us," the man whined.

"Be off at once," shouted Pierre. More cowed by his men than his words, the mob dispersed. The provost of merchants assistant thanked Pierre profusely. "We do our best, my lord, but we don't have enough men. It was bad enough before the Protestants came to town. With them and the weather, this place is like a powder keg. If you could mention to the King that we could use a few of his archers until the weather cools, I'd be greatly obliged."

"I will mention it, of course," said Pierre, as he resumed his way toward the Louvre.

After two hours of argument, Pierre felt as if he were going to suffocate. The King's council chamber at the Louvre had been built for simpler times and cooler weather. The debate had been long and inconclusive. Everyone but Admiral Coligny seemed to be against any action now in the Netherlands, but it was far from clear, despite several pointed reminders from the Queen Mother, that King Charles was persuaded.

"You see, dash it all," he finally interjected, "I want to lead an army into the Netherlands, an army all good Frenchmen could be proud to be part of. And the great victories will give me a chance to write my name on these times!"

The passion with which the King spoke, then broke off in a fit of coughing, was touching even to those who most disagreed. Looks were exchanged; it was thought that Charles would not have a very long reign.

The Duke of Anjou, who was sitting next to Pierre, had been particularly unpleasant.

"I have looked into the military situation, my dear brother, and I am absolutely persuaded of two things. First, we should be on the side of Spain in crushing the heretic revolt, and second, that we had better look out for our own heretics. They have been gathering a rather large force of late. Do you dare deny it, my lord Admiral?"

Coligny had bristled and straightened his great body. That he had no love for Anjou was well known, but his reply was even and directed to the King.

"Your Majesty, let me recapitulate a bit. I'm afraid my lord Anjou has left out a good deal. My first objective, one we all, I thought, shared was to put this divided kingdom back together. It is toward this end that I have willingly assisted

Madame, your Mother, in her efforts to marry Princess Margot to our leader, Henri of Navarre. But even more important, I thought to channel the energies of those who have done so much fighting here at home toward the north where it can be dissipated, at the same time winning glory for France and freeing the people of the low countries from Spain's brutal oppression.

"I have to admit," Coligny continued, looking down at the table, "the military situation has taken a turn for the worse. I further admit that Genlis did not follow his orders, but more important," he said, raising his voice and looking pointedly at Anjou, "he was betrayed. His desperate plight has made me bold to say that my people are clamoring for war now. Why, I can raise 20,000 foot and 10,000 horse at once," he said turning to the King, "and I will offer these if Your Majesty sees fit to use them as an instrument of your own greatness."

"You dare!" Anjou burst out. "You dare to offer the King of France his own Frenchmen as if they were yours as a potentate to give or withhold?"

"I beg you, Sire," Coligny continued, without any notice. "Time is running out."

"Indeed it is," hissed Anjou to Pierre.

"I really think the Admiral has said it all," said the King.

"Charles, please listen to me." The Queen Mother's throaty voice seemed to slide around Charles to envelope him as if in a soft embrace, slowly, to turn him around.

"Charles, my son," she said softly, "no one is more jealous of your glory than I. But you must not forget how fragile is the base of this so-called Enterprise. You must remember that the first thing is to get your sister married to Henri. We really can't think of launching wars until that is done. Why, you can't be away for the wedding, can you?

"Then," she continued patiently, "you must steer an even course until then. Starting on an adventure now would only invite a Spanish invasion, and we don't want that, do we?" She paused for breath. There was dead silence in the room.

"The most telling point to my mind is England," she continued, turning slowly toward Admiral Coligny. "We have said over and over we needed their help in the Netherlands. Why, the Admiral even said he could get it for us. If we had that, why, it would greatly improve your chances for glory. You did say English help could be obtained, didn't you, my lord Admiral?"

"I did, Madame," Coligny rumbled, "but you know the English, it is hard to get them actually to put money on the table and men in the field."

"Exactly, my dear Admiral," her voice flowed on sweetly, "we understand each other. I suggest we table the invasion of the Netherlands and try our best, with your help of course, Admiral, to get Queen Elizabeth to join us. Charles, why don't you ask for a show of hands?"

Everyone agreed with the Queen Mother except Coligny. "I want to hear what the King says," said Coligny. Charles squirmed and looked miserable. "I will abide by the wishes of the Council," he finally said.

"I am sorry for the vote of your Council, Sire," Coligny said quietly. "If you won't have a war in the Netherlands, I pray you will not have one in France, whether you wish it or no."

"Surely, that statement is not meant to be treasonous, my lord," purred the Queen Mother.

"Certainly not, Your Majesty," he replied with dignity. "I am only trying to be realistic. There are forces that none of us may be able to control. If William of Orange is driven from the Netherlands, he might attack France, and bring the Spanish in after him. Then you would have the Spanish anyway."

There was an uneasy silence. It was plain that several members of the Council did not believe that was what the Admiral had meant. King Charles finally rose, breaking the tension, and the members filed out of the room.

As the Council left the stuffy room for the relatively fresh air of the courtyard, Coligny found himself next to the King. "I have not given in," the King whispered. "I will get word to you."

A little later, Pierre himself encountered the Admiral in the courtyard.

"Ah, Pierre," he said, clapping Pierre on the shoulder, "it was good to see you in your father's seat at Council. He was a great man and my friend. You have some mighty footsteps to follow. Tell me, how do you think he would have regarded this morning's debate, and what did you make of it?"

Pierre hesitated, then answered slowly. "I don't know; there are so many crosscurrents I think he would have found it hard to judge, as do I."

"In a difficult place, a man must look to those principles he believes in," the Admiral said.

"Yes, I know that," Pierre said, "but sometimes that oracle does not speak as clearly as one would wish. I know that my father was in favor of French victories at Spanish expense, but I think he felt it more important that we have internal peace. I know he made it clear to the Guises and even to Anjou that they would have to deal with him if they went against you. But I'm not sure he wouldn't have said the same thing to you, my lord, if you were going against them."

"You are your father's son, and no mistake." Coligny gazed into Pierre's grey eyes. "He would have said just that, and I don't mind telling you, last fall he came to see me, and did say it, about that bluntly, too. He was not much of a one for honey coatings."

"Then, you see my problem," Pierre responded. "I can see the glory in a short war in the Netherlands. But I was disturbed by the large force you said you have. I know emotion colors what Anjou says about it, but I think his fears are not all unfounded."

"Pierre," Coligny said, lowering his voice, "that is just why we must strike soon. You know I have hotheads, too, men just as rabid as Anjou. I must get them north and fighting Spaniards while I can still control them. The marriage of Henri and Margot will do some good, but it must be more than show. The King understands this, but I fear his mother does not."

"But don't you fear the Spanish?" Pierre asked.

"I fear all evils!" Coligny replied bleakly, "but in a difficult pass a man must choose. I deem the Spanish the lesser evil and a risk I must run."

"You have a hard choice."

"Not just me, Pierre, all of us, you included. Well," Coligny continued after a pause, "I did not prevail today. But I must not lose heart. I will explain the matter to my own council, but I must, I must be allowed to move north! If not today, then soon."

Coligny looked suddenly old, but he smiled as he took his leave of Pierre.

Chapter XXVII

ondi glanced at the short note bidding him join the Queen Mother in the Tuileries garden at once, and wearily shoved aside the pile of accounts on his desk. The hot, tiresome work had taken most of the sultry mid-August afternoon, and as he suspected, had revealed more than the usual dishonesty on the part of a marble supplier for the King's new château near Lyons. Worse, it would mean a trip south in the torrid weather, and he dared not leave Court at this juncture. The note which dashed his plans of a quiet evening at home with music and poetry was, he thought, the last straw. As he rose to obey, he was plunged into a brief spasm of self-pity. He thrust it down as he had risen, as he knew only too well he survived by giving prompt, faithful service whenever his Mistress demanded it.

What now, he wondered, as he walked with his bodyguard out of the Louvre, along the bank of the Seine to clear his head, through the rampart and thence past the multicolored marble shell of the palace of the Tuileries, magnificent even incomplete.

So far, at least, the interests of his two clients, as he thought of them, Queen Catherine and Don Diego Zúñiga, coincided. So far he had run only the usual risk of her wrath at his failure or failure in general. Beyond that he did not like to think.

As he entered the great garden itself, he found himself resenting the spectacle of order and beauty it presented. To his right, two of the Queen's gardeners were carefully trimming the ornate border of one of the parterres that divided the great, enclosed space into so many rooms, as if it were a palace open to the sky. He suppressed a wave of envy. Why can't I live in peace as those men do? Why can't I have even a single day to sit without cares and watch the flowers grow? He supposed that the Queen Mother had in mind another short, uncomfortable trip to England for him to urge one more time a marriage for Alençon or money for the Netherlands. Well, *a chaque jour suffit sa peine* — unto each day, the evil thereof.

Gondi found his royal mistress as she had directed, in the pavilion enclosing her nearly completed grotto. An airy peristyle led into an elegant open structure which enclosed a veritable world of its own. The centerpiece was a miniature mountain, covered with greenery and flowers, populated by animals, birds, and demi-gods, gushing, gurgling, and flowing with water in streams, jets, and little lakes. The Queen Mother was talking to the chief engineer, who was taking notes of her suggestions for improvement. Gondi had not seen the water in operation and was amazed.

"Madame, this is truly wonderful. I have never seen anything like it."

"That's certainly true, Alberto," she replied, flattered, "for there is nothing like it. It is pleasant to hear the water on such a hot day. No?"

"Indeed it is," he replied. "I came as soon as I received your summons." The engineer withdrew at a glance from the Queen Mother.

"It seems that I cannot be absent even for a few days, even to visit my poor sick daughter, without some new mischief by my son," she said sadly, wringing her hands. "Those men-at-arms that Alva claims to have seen in the Netherlands, what have you found out?"

"I spoke to the King this morning, Madame," Gondi replied quickly. "He first feigned ignorance. Then he said they had 'escaped' against his will. He knew I didn't believe him, and he didn't seem to care. It's plain to me that he simply disregarded the Council's vote, and more important, your own advice."

"Albert, he cannot be controlled any longer."

"Apparently, he can be, Madame, by Admiral Coligny."

"Oh, Albert, how I love these gardens." She turned back toward the fountain. "Ah, the beauty one can create out of wasteland. How I long to be free of the burdens of the realm, to devote myself wholly to beauty. Perhaps I should leave the King to it." She shrugged. "Perhaps I should leave all these heavy cares and return to my beautiful Florence."

"Madame, please!" Gondi said with concern.

"Perhaps Charles and his new adviser will force me to retire!" She continued vehemently, "To Florence, to an abbey, any place where I can die without troubling further, with my old woman's counsels, these bold captains of the ship of state!"

"Please, my lady, do not lose your head."

"I had not thought of that possibility," she smiled wryly.

"He has not dared to defy you openly," Gondi continued. "And what has happened may not yet be irreparable."

"But, Albert, my friend, realistically, how much longer can we keep the King out of the Netherlands?"

Gondi stiffened. There were few worse signs than when Catherine de Medici called someone "my friend."

"You know that as well as I, my lady," he replied cautiously.

"Indeed. Can we keep him quiet until the wedding? Albert, we must have that wedding." The catch in her voice showing real emotion was a hopeful sign.

"Of course, Your Majesty. But when is the wedding going to take place? We still have no papal dispensation. The Admiral will not be idle. He intends an adventure sooner or later, and I would be failing in my duty if I told you he can be held back forever. He is under pressure, too."

"Listen, Albert. We know that my son is going to send more men and money to Flanders. How will the Spanish like that?"

"I am sure they won't like it at all," Gondi said reflectively. "But if you mean will they fight us over a few men infiltrating over the border, I think not."

"Albert," she said with passion, "we must have the marriage and we must have it soon. I will not have all I have worked for destroyed by a mad adventurer.

322

Perhaps we can buy time by letting Charles think he is deceiving us with these games, throwing enough to Coligny to let him seem to be doing something and so keep him quiet for a while?"

"That will work, Madame, if at all, only briefly," Gondi replied. "Coligny will settle only for a real war in the Netherlands. Spain will fight tooth and nail to keep its province. In the end there has to be an explosion."

"Albert," the Queen whispered, "I have had a thought. Oh, what I have to bear for my son's safety. What mother ever had such burdens, such sorrows! Albert, Coligny perhaps ought to be removed from the board. We need him until the marriage, but as soon as the marriage is behind us, perhaps... Without him, I think there would be no invasion."

The gentle splash of water coursing down the little sculptured park was almost louder than the sound of her words.

Gondi hesitated, not knowing what to say. Does she want me to talk her out of it, or agree, or sympathize? He decided to temporize.

"Certainly that would be one way out, Madame."

"Come, my friend," she hissed. "Tell me another way if you know it. Do you think I say this lightly, I, who would have to bear this sin? What else can we do, short of killing all of them, as your friend, King Philip, counsels — no, don't try to hide it. I suspect you are, shall we say, on a bit of a retainer from him. I am not afraid of you, Gondino. I made you and I can make you greater. I can also un-make you. A small wage from Philip saves me a little current expense, and makes it easier for you to lend me funds when I need them. You are too shrewd to jeopardize all you have worked for. No, in this, Philip and I are strangely allied, although I do what I do to keep him away. He would not be displeased with such a course?"

"That at least I am sure of," Gondi said stiffly. "But Madame, the Protestants are here in force. They would not take this lightly."

"Without their leader they would be much less dangerous, Albert," she said calmly. "If we struck their 'king,' who would they have? A boy of nineteen, Henri Navarre, who will be my son-in-law. Why, we could even help the Protestants get justice if their anger has the proper focus."

"What do you mean, my lady?" Gondi asked weakly, unable to hide his alarm. "I will be suspected. They will hunt me down! They have already made three attempts."

"No, no, Alberto," she soothed. "This would be too big for you to take the blame. You are supposed to be creative in these affairs! You might involve the Guises, or let it seem so. Heaven knows they have talked enough about their precious vendetta against the Admiral. Let them take the blame. It wouldn't do for them to become too powerful.

"Coligny at least has been a valuable counterweight to their ambitions. If some Protestant revenges his lord at the expense of the Duke de Guise..." She shrugged. Her pale face was very close to his. She placed a delicate hand on his arm. "Albert, you would have to act with stealth. If anyone suspected you, they might suspect me. You understand, I think?" She paused and turned back toward the fountain. There was for a minute or two no sound but the splashing water.

"Then, caro Gondi," she continued briskly, facing him, "You know my thinking. You might think about it. It would have to be a clean, quick cut, perfectly executed, but I know I could leave that sort of detail to you, could I not?"

"Of course," Gondi stammered, "but I don't know."

"Don't trouble me with details, Albert. The wedding will be a week from now, on the eighteenth, and my mind is all full of the arrangements."

"The eighteenth? Has the pope's dispatch arrived at last?"

"Well, not exactly," she smiled coyly. "His Holiness is apparently still feeling too much pressure from King Philip. Our last word was that it was all in order but for a technicality. I will suggest to the King that he tell the Archbishop that he has enough authorization. I have already written to the frontier that all post riders from Italy be stopped at the border in case they bear any contrary message. Once the marriage is accomplished, it will take a hundred years to undo if it can be done at all. I will write to the pope afterward, and tell him we had no choice." She turned away and sat down on a bench.

"Oh, another point, Alberto. I wish you would hint to the King that I wouldn't oppose an invasion of the Netherlands, if it were led by the Admiral a week or so after the wedding."

"A week!" he cried. "That is only two weeks from now, Your Majesty. How can preparations for an invasion be completed in such a short... Oh, I see." A thin smile crossed Gondi's face. "It doesn't give me much time."

"I am gambling a lot on you, Alberto." Her voice was mellow with assurance of Gondi's loyalty and ability. "It will not be possible to pull back from failure. So don't fail me."

Surrounded once again by his bodyguard, Gondi left the garden through the north wall and headed west on the rue Saint Honoré toward his hotel. He was as oblivious of the garden's manicured charms, luridly distorted by the distant lightning, as he was of the sky itself that looked like the end of the world. He decided that what he needed more than music and poetry was a great deal of wine.

Even if I know what she wants, he thought petulantly, shall I do it? How to avoid being caught? How to avoid failure? She did not want to discuss the details. I can take care of the details.

Gondi ground his teeth in frustration. He could also get himself killed by the Protestants, or be blamed by her for the invasion if he couldn't get the job done. If he tried and failed, King Philip could conclude that he had been a Protestant sympathizer all along.

He quickened his pace homeward, not because of the apprehensive looks his men were casting at the awful sky, but because he really needed that wine.

* * *

324

On the eighteenth of August, the great parvis of Notre Dame Cathedral was packed since before dawn with the high and low of Paris, come to see the King of Navarre wed Princess Margot. As was customary, the bride-to-be had spent the night in the Archbishop's palace next to the Cathedral. Little else but the splendor, however, was normal, and the huge crowd, restless and irritable from the heat, seemed more like the throng at an execution than at a spectacle of royal pomp.

An ugly feeling drifted upward with the overpowering smell of several thousand sweaty bodies. There had already been several incidents of violence dealt with more or less promptly by the King's archers who were as surly as the crowd. Paris didn't want to miss the show, but Paris did not like the marriage.

With a deafening peal of trumpets, answered by the sonorous clang of the Cathedral's great bells, the procession, like players on a stage, began slowly to move along a raised platform built across the parvis and extending into the church itself. Preceded by men-at-arms in the royal blue-and-white livery, the King himself, in gold and ermine, escorted his sister. Over a heavy gown of silver, Margot wore the ermine-fringed blue velvet mantle of a daughter of France, its long train borne by three princesses.

Just behind, the Queen Mother, in black velvet, was escorted by Admiral Coligny and the Duke of Anjou. Henri Navarre had put off the mourning garb he had been wearing for his mother, Jeanne d'Albret, and resplendent in red and gold, the crown of his little kingdom on his head, he looked confident and content.

Maurice de la Renaudie was thoroughly enjoying himself in spite of the heat. He could forgive the snub of being placed well to the rear of the nobility in the procession as his escort was the Duke de Guise. The icy venom be felt from his violently Catholic partner was one of the ironies that made the splendid scene, for him, almost comic. A brief but vital conversation with Gondi four days earlier had augured a great change in his life and made the Duke de Guise's malice toward the Protestants seem trivial. A feeling of elation welled up in him. He was almost finished with the Protestant masquerade, almost back to Court, almost back to Anjou. And for such a small service. No, my lad, he thought to himself, when the good Admiral is with the angels, you'll have it made. But gently, gently, we mustn't spoil it now.

Looking down the dais, he could see Coligny and the Queen Mother smile at each other as he assisted her to her seat. They look, he thought, like two peasants on market day buying and selling cattle, each imagining that he has bested the other. A wedding for an invasion — not a bad bargain, unless you aren't going to live to enjoy it.

As Maurice looked on, the bridal party was greeted at the door of the Cathedral by the Cardinal de Bourbon, Henri Navarre's uncle. Because Henri was a Protestant, the marriage itself could not be held inside, so the glorious pair had to be wed on the platform outside.

The Archbishop, Maurice thought, looked none too pleased, as the papal dispensation long promised by the royal family had never arrived. And hadn't that vixen, Margot, cast one longing glance at her former lover, Henri de Guise, at his side?

Maurice doubted that he was the only one who felt the rejoicing somewhat forced. But if the people had come to see a grand show, they were not disappointed. He had to admit that the King from a distance looked almost healthy in his gold brocade. And Margot, not the most beautiful woman at close quarters, was positively radiant. After more fanfares, the Cardinal raised his hand in benediction and the marriage was done.

It had been a relief when the procession had left the noise and heat for the relative coolness and sudden darkness of the Cathedral as they escorted Margot and the Catholics in for Mass. Maurice reflected that his tour of duty as a Protestant had at least opened his eyes to the blind insensitivity the rulers of his country betrayed at every turn, even here when they were supposedly trying to cement peace. He could well imagine how Admiral Coligny must have winced to see, among the flags of vanquished enemies of France decorating the nave, his own flag and those of his dear dead friends, captured at Jarnac and Moncontour. He thought of his golden stepbrother, carrying Navarre's sword, the disdain of his late stepfather, and yes, he could feel like a Protestant when exposed to their blind, superior, self-confident contempt.

The trumpets and drums had given way to the chanting of the midday office while the royal procession moved slowly down the nave. At the tribune, the steps down from the platform divided ahead to the choir and to the left into the transept and out of the church. It was, of course, out of the question that the Catholics would forgo the most elaborate Mass, accompanied by new music composed by de Lassus, the Queen Mother's favorite musician, and equally out of the question that the Protestants would participate in the barbarous rites. Protestants to the left, Catholics straight ahead. The crudity again struck Maurice as wildly comic.

The heat and light crashed down on the Protestants as they emerged from the Cathedral. Even more ominous was the rumbling of the huge crowd, now bored and with no prospect of distraction until the interminable service ended. A guard roughly warned Maurice to stay behind the archers. "Not meaning any disrespect, Monsieur," he said. "But the people don't hold with your kind, and if anything happened, we'd catch that from the captain, and no mistake. So if you would, sir, stay behind me."

As a gesture of politeness, several members of the Catholic nobility had been requested to keep the Protestants company, among them the Duke of Anjou, who very pointedly snubbed Maurice, and Pierre de Galle, who to Maurice's even greater annoyance was getting on famously with Henri of Navarre.

Maurice did not like Henri of Navarre for the simple and sufficient reason that Navarre had made it plain that he did not want Maurice within a mile of him. Only the Admiral's good offices had kept the situation tolerable. But there he was chatting away with Pierre about women (he beamed respectfully and appreciatively at Pierre, apropos of Anne's charms), horses (he had never seen a finer horse than Pierre's great stallion), fighting (by God, he wished he'd seen that duel, did you really flip him? Pierre preferred not to talk about it). Navarre promised to make his own investigation of Pierre's prowess the day of the mock battle. Pierre clapped him on the back and invited him to try. Henri growled. Damned if he couldn't use some ale. How did they expect a man to stand around for hours in this heat while a bunch of papists sang their damn long Mass! "Pardon me, Pierre, thoughtless of me," he added.

Enjoy yourselves, little boys, thought Maurice. Enjoy your camaraderie. I have man's work to do, and you both would wet your pants if you were in my position.

It was just then that a dark form hurtled through the cordon of archers and came to a sprawl among the Protestant lords.

"Save me, for God's sake," the man cried, a Protestant judging from his dark gown, but so badly beaten that his face was not recognizable. "The Catholics, right over there, I was trying to get a look, they pulled me down and beat me."

There had been an audible clank as dozens of hands had found their sword belts.

"Peace!" shouted the Admiral. "There will be no blood shed by us on my lord's wedding day. If these dogs fight, we must turn the other cheek. See to this man's wounds, someone. He is only beaten. This mob won't attack the King's archers. Relax, everyone."

* * *

The tournament took place two days later on what all were saying was the hottest day of the torrid summer. And, Maurice reflected, its bad taste made the Protestant battle flags decorating the Cathedral look trivial. There was to be, for the Court's amusement, a battle of the angels and devils before the gates of the Garden of Eden.

The devils were, of course, to be the Protestants with Henri of Navarre at their head, and the angels were the flower of the Catholic nobility led by his well-loved stepbrother in the guise of St. Michael, the Archangel. Maurice had been sure the Protestants would refuse when told of the insulting arrangements, but Henri of Navarre had guffawed and said he'd fight dressed as a toad if he could have a passage or two with Pierre de Galle. Although it was not strictly proper, the judicious clinking of gold testified that a good deal was being wagered on the battle, good taste or no.

Maurice had excused himself from the tourney, ostensibly because of a bit of colic. He had managed to accompany Coligny, who himself was sitting in the royal box overlooking the rue Saint Antoine, where the games were to take place. He did not envy the contestants, fifty on each side. Protestants were suited in black armor from head to toe, with red flame-like feathers on their helms. Henri

Navarre had a gilded band down his back and chest, and a crown gilded his helm. The Catholics were similarly armed, in silvered armor with white wings affixed to their backs.

Pierre's armor was entirely gilded as if his great stature were not enough to distinguish him. They were a gorgeous sight, but as Maurice mused, ventilation is never good in armor, and in this heat we'll have more than a few steamed to death.

His prediction proved accurate, and within a few minutes the ranks on both sides were sadly depleted. The prostrate hulks made an unintended obstacle course for the survivors, and many more joined their prostrate brothers as they tripped and fell. In the center of what was left of the mêlée, Pierre and Henri whacked away at each other, without any apparent advantage. A moment later Navarre stepped back and held his sword hilt up, which was correctly interpreted as a request for a time out. He and Pierre conferred briefly as the crowd buzzed. They both stepped back and removed their helmets.

Gasping in the fresh air, sweat streaming from their faces, they grinned at each other. With a horrible yell, Henri attacked. Pierre parried and the battle began anew.

Pierre had the advantage in height and weight, but it was soon apparent that Navarre compensated by endurance and an unshakable determination to win. He charged, and again Pierre parried and with a deft twist to the left went in under Navarre's guard.

"De Galle is as good as his father," the King observed to Coligny.

"He is better, Your Majesty," the Admiral replied. "He has all his father's strength with more grace and, if I may say it without disrespect to the late Duke, more brains. He is a fine man. You should give him all your trust and confidence."

The object of this accolade parried again and with a twist disarmed Navarre. A cheer went up from the crowd that turned into a gasp. Navarre, crooking a leg behind Pierre's, toppled him onto his back, then none too gently, plopped astride his chest.

"Not as elegant as your trick, my friend, but just as effective," Navarre chuckled. "Yield!"

Pinned as he was, Pierre had little choice, much to the crowd's very evident displeasure, as much for the bets lost as for the bad theology of the outcome. Grinning broadly, Navarre helped Pierre up and they left the field arm in arm.

"I should think my stepbrother threw that contest," Maurice said to the Admiral.

"Do you really think so?" asked the King, who had overheard.

"Oh, yes," Maurice sneered. "He never loses at games."

"Well, I don't mind telling you, I lost a lot on that one," said the King. "And I doubt I was the only one. Mother will have a fit, to say nothing of the Archbishop."

The festivities that evening, the fourth and final night of celebration, outdid everything that had gone before. There had been a procession of tableaux vivants on wheels, moving slowly through the great hall of the Louvre, showing allegories of the expected civil peace; there had been a fountain flowing with wine and a ballet reminiscent of the Elysian Fields populated with nymphs, dryads, and demigods.

But four nights of feasting had taken their toll even on experienced courtiers, and much of the extravagance went unappreciated, if not unnoticed.

For Anne de Galle, this last evening was a definite trial, although she was too practiced to show it. Fortunately, her advancing pregnancy had allowed her the status of mother-to-be, which, combined with her rank of Duchess, exempted her from everything she did not really want to do. Her radiant beauty made her, without effort or movement, the center of considerable attention. Pleased with herself, petted by others, she was content if bored with the seemingly endless celebration of Margot's marriage.

Pierre, who had been chatting with a group of lords around Henri of Navarre, strolled over to his wife's side and placed a hand on her silken shoulder, something he would have found impossibly difficult the year before.

"Pierre, darling," she said, looking up at him, "couldn't we make our excuses soon? I think I'll scream if I see another dryad. We can say I'm feeling indisposed."

"As you wish," he replied. "I have certainly had enough wine and there is a Council meeting tomorrow morning."

"Anything new?"

"Not really," he said absently. "They say Coligny has been given some sort of assurance about being allowed to leave soon with an army. I'm not sure of that, but that is the word. As I see it, such a move would require Council approval, as I doubt even the King would risk authorizing anything like that on his own."

"Please, dear," Anne yawned. "I know you enjoy it, but politics bores me to tears. Incidentally," she continued, as Pierre helped her to rise, "you remember that little Duchess de la Roque, Athalie, the one you gave riding lessons to? I heard the stupidest story from the Countess de Tournelle. She says she heard that Athalie left Court not for any religious reasons, but because she was pregnant! I told her I never heard such rubbish in my life! Why, I scarcely talked to Athalie myself, but one look at that bookish expression of hers would send a real man fleeing even if she has such a great fortune, which I doubt. And what's more she has too much breeding and looks too much the nun to do it with one of the grooms.

"I told Madame de Tournelle I thought it disgraceful for a mere countess to spread rumors about a duchess. Athalie is a stick and may have made a fool of herself for all I know, but I am not about to tolerate that sort of gossip from someone of so much lower rank than ours. I had half a mind to tell the Queen

Mother about that woman's cheek. She'd box that silly ass's ears. Pierre, are you listening?"

Pierre had heard nothing after the first words. In a daze, he said good night to the King and Queen Mother. It couldn't be true! Or could it? If it were, Athalie would surely have told him. They had been so close, it wasn't possible that she could be silent about it. But how could such a rumor have been started? He had to admit that what Anne had said about Athalie was probably the general view, false as he knew that monochrome picture of Athalie to be. God, if I could only see her, if I could only talk to her for half an hour.

Pierre had had this conversation with himself before and recognized it. He knew he was supposed to pacify himself with the notion that Athalie had given herself to God, and he must not tempt her from her vocation. Damn! But if she was having a baby, his baby, she would need him, she would want him. There would be no vocation to tempt her from. There would be just Athalie, Athalie! But why, oh why then, was she silent? Pierre thought he would go mad.

As they reached the Hôtel de Galle, Pierre realized that Anne had been chattering about the ball for some time, and that he had heard nothing of what she had said. Pierre mumbled something about needing sleep. Anne with an amused peck dismissed him, clucking cheerfully about the folly of too much wine after so much exercise in the hot sun. As soon as he was alone, he threw himself into a chair and buried his head in his hands.

Athalie was not bound to Fontevrault. He had been a fool. But if a fool, had she not fooled him, wasn't it that she, recognizing the impossibility of their love, had chosen a decisive break?

Unbidden, the image of her slender, taut body flooded his mind, an image he had struggled to repress, but now, why repress it? I can have her again, he thought, oh God, again!

But if she were pregnant, the baby would be born soon. He counted on his fingers. She had left Court on Epiphany, January 6. Tomorrow was August 22, two days from St. Bartholomew's Day. Almost nine months since he had seen her. If the story were true, the child might be born already.

He was surprised at how certain he was about what he was going to do. He would go at once to Fontevrault. Perhaps she would send him away without a word, but he could not believe she would. She would need help, he would provide it. He found he was suddenly desperate to see the baby. His baby. What would Athalie do with it?

Duchesses didn't have babies, at least not unmarried duchesses. Pierre was suddenly submerged with remorse. What had they done, what had he done? What would he, what could they, do now? He imagined himself putting his wealth at her disposal, building her a château, caring for her forever. He smiled bitterly. She was far better able than he, he supposed, to build a château. Her fortune was supposed to be huge to begin with and had been managed by Gondi, not squandered as his had been by his father. Damn it all, his father had kept a resident mistress for years, why couldn't he? The answer came back, mocking, Athalie is a duchess, not someone to be kept as a pet.

Pierre ground his knuckles into his temples. He mastered himself with difficulty, finally deciding that he must take first things first. He would set out the next morning. He suddenly remembered the Council meeting, and that he was the Duke de Galle. He could not just vanish from Court, he had to have the King's permission. He would say he needed to see to something on his estates, his vineyard at Bourgeuil. For that matter, he thought, even Anne would believe it. The icy hand of panic seized his heart. The invasion, the Netherlands, the Protestants had all been talking about it. It was going to be allowed and soon. He knew he would have to take part, and it might be months, or years, or never before he could talk to Athalie! A few weeks ago it had seemed like a great adventure; now he saw it only as a nuisance, an obstacle. But if the King was going to get his way, if Coligny had persuaded him, Pierre would never be allowed to leave Court.

Sleep finally silenced the inconclusive debate in his thoughts.

Chapter XXVIII

ierre fidgeted nervously in his seat, praying that the Council meeting the morning of August 22 would be like the others, rambling, inconclusive, and above all, soon over. As he sat in the hot, stuffy room that had become all too familiar to him, he thought suddenly of how many times in the past weeks he had longed that a speaker would keep to his point, and that a point could be made once, not a dozen times. Today, the more confusion, the better. Please, God, don't let us vote to invade the Netherlands, not today. People had whispered as the meeting started that the Queen Mother, after long opposition, was at last giving way, and was prepared to agree to an enterprise of sorts.

However, as the familiar arguments and oppositions were repeated for what seemed the hundredth time, as inconclusively as ever, Pierre realized that all he wanted was for the meeting to end. The Queen Mother was silent, and her silence after Coligny finished another speech in favor of invasion could be taken as a softening of her opposition. The Count de Retz seemed to be saying that all things considered, a bold action might force the English to join in or be left out, and Coligny, from his expression, seemed highly pleased with the apparent change of position. Pierre's own dreams of glory in the Netherlands seemed to him as remote as another world. Please, please, not the Netherlands, not now, not today. Let me go, let me go, was all he could think of.

An elderly Protestant lord from Auvergne was adding his weight, if any, to what Coligny had just said, and indeed, had said in every previous Council meeting Pierre had attended. That he was contributing nothing new did not seem to occur to the old gentleman, nor did it serve to shorten his oration. Pierre half noticed, with only the slightest curiosity, that no one was interrupting his interminable rehearsal of the self-evident benefit of all good Frenchmen fighting Spanish tyranny in the low countries. Speakers like this one were usually cut off by some sarcastic quip by Anjou. The ritual called for someone to say, "But that means war with Spain and we don't want that, do we?"

Almost in panic, Pierre thought, maybe the rumors are right. There has been a bargain struck. Coligny has given Henri's marriage to Margot, the Queen Mother has given Coligny his invasion. But Pierre couldn't go, not then, he had to get to see Athalie — distance, Abbeys, vows, invasions be damned. He had to see her, see about his child, see about everything, see about her silence. Oh, God, would they never finish.

"And so, my lords, Your Majesty," Pierre realized with a start that the Queen Mother herself was speaking, "it is clear there is a real sentiment among us to do something in the Netherlands. While I am not prepared to back a foolhardy adventure, a strong blow properly administered might be as prudent a move as we could make at this difficult juncture. For never is the course of great states plain and obvious. Always there are mists and shoals to be avoided if the voyage is to prosper. Then have we need of a great Captain to steer us on to victory." She nodded in Coligny's direction, and he acknowledged her compliment.

"I propose," she continued, "that if Your Majesty approves, Admiral Coligny present us two days hence a specific plan — what can be done and how he proposes to do it. If it is feasible, I may well be able to give it my blessing."

Pierre was so relieved to hear "two days" that he quite overlooked the fact that it was the Queen Mother who had seemingly endorsed action against Spain. A few moments later, the session rose, and he made his way to the King's side.

"If Your Majesty please," he began hurriedly.

"Ah, Monsieur de Galle, good morning to you," the King replied.

"Please, Sire, I have an emergency on one of my estates near Bourgeuil. It appears the steward has absconded. I must beg your leave to be excused from Court for a few days to go and see to it."

"Well, of course, I suppose, if you must," replied the King, "but we may need you soon for the Netherlands. Coligny has almost brought my Mamá around. You may leave tomorrow, but you must return at once."

"Of course, Sire," he mumbled, bowing.

Pierre had dreaded a cross examination from Gondi who knew almost as much about Bourgeuil as he did. Fortunately, Gondi, who had plainly heard the exchange, was talking quietly with the Queen Mother. He gave Pierre a quizzical look, as did she, but was unable to follow Pierre as he bade the King farewell and hurried from the room. He ducked through the chaos of men-at-arms, servants, and workmen in the courtyard outside, barely pausing to call his escort in his haste to return to his hotel to prepare for his departure.

His stepbrother's rapid passage through the courtyard would have piqued the curiosity of Maurice de la Renaudie if he had not been entirely preoccupied with his own business. He had feigned idleness in the relatively cool shade of the old southeast tower as he had waited with mounting impatience for the seemingly interminable session to adjourn.

The bright morning sun had moved toward noon and illuminated the sculpted goddesses on the west side of the Louvre's massive courtyard. The serene marble deities contrasted grotesquely with the tumult of activity below as workmen removed the staging and scenery of last night's fête, and other servants groaned under the heavy baskets of leftover dainties that were being readied for the noonday distribution to the poor. The harsh sun beat down on the carpenters and porters as they dismantled the fantasy world the Court had occupied for the last four days.

Maurice, pressing his back against the relatively cool stone, fidgeted again as he waited impatiently. He had accompanied the Admiral's party two hours before to the Louvre from their headquarters in the Hôtel of the Count de Ponthieu. Admiral Coligny had been in a good humor, in marked contrast to the gloom which had deepened about him in the preceding days of feasting.

"I don't mind telling you," Coligny said as they walked along the street past the Abbey of St. Germaine l'Auxerois, "I'm glad to have that revelry behind us. I don't begrudge honor to my lord Henri, and Queen Catherine has a rare gift for spectacles, but enough is enough. Our duty lies north fighting Spaniards, not dancing and drinking here at our ease. Oh, how I long to be away! The King gave me his word I could leave on Monday the 25th. Pray God my enemies in the Council have not turned him around again."

In a few minutes, Maurice reflected, he would have to approach the Admiral and set in motion a train of events that could bring Maurice back to Court in glory, or be his undoing. "Nothing simpler," Gondi had told him. "All you have to do is get him separated from his guard as he returns to his residence." When Maurice had asked what came next, Gondi had shrugged and told him that there was no need for him to know more. Indeed, in certain unfortunate circumstances which he, Gondi, was sure need not be mentioned, it would be better if Maurice knew as little as possible. Better for whom? Maurice thought nervously. He choked back a wave of hatred for Gondi, for the way he took for granted that he could risk Maurice's neck. That wave was succeeded by one of jealousy for Pierre, who seemed to have prospered and grown since his father's death. Pierre was even now sitting with the great lords of the realm, pondering the fate of the Kingdom, while he, Maurice, waited to do Gondi's dirty work. The focus of his venom moved to the Admiral, who had so readily taken to Pierre in the last few weeks. The Admiral tolerates me because I'm useful, thought Maurice. His followers scarcely tolerate me at all. He realized that he would have to calm himself. It had to seem natural, something any loyal friend would do. God, won't they ever finish? he thought.

The Swiss guards, lounging around the entrance to the King's apartments at the far end of the south wing, had suddenly snapped to attention. A door had opened and the counselors began to emerge in twos and threes, the Catholic lords resplendent in their customary finery, the Protestants once again in their habitual black. After Pierre had emerged with the Chancellor and hurried away, he had been followed by the Duke of Anjou. Gondi had passed through the courtyard and left.

Finally the Admiral stepped out into the bright sunlight. He stretched as he gratefully savored the release from the closeness of the chamber within.

Maurice practically ran, dodging baskets and workmen, and was out of breath when he reached Coligny's side. He seized Coligny's arm and whispered hoarsely, "My lord, I've just been told they are going to kill you. A group of archers..."

"Why, La Renaudie!" the Admiral rumbled, "Get hold of yourself, man. This won't be the first time I've heard those words. Now what is this all about?"

"I have learned," Maurice began again, more coherently, "that a group of archers is positioned in houses all along your route back to the Hôtel de Ponthieu."

"Who told you?"

Maurice hesitated. "Er, my stepbrother — he said he had it from the Guises. He is an honorable man. He said he would not see you come to harm."

"This may be serious." Coligny nodded thoughtfully. "I am grateful to you, but I will be safe with my men about me."

"No, Admiral! You must listen to me!" Maurice had once again seized Coligny's arm. "You must not run this terrible risk. I have a plan: you will wait here, out of view. Instruct your guardsmen to proceed as usual. I will take your cloak and cap and walk in their midst and give you mine for camouflage. When we are gone, you can follow us quietly to your lodgings. We will walk on a little further and return to give you more time."

"La Renaudie, you are a brave and resourceful young man! I always thought so." Coligny gripped Maurice's arm in an impulse of gratitude. "But why should I allow you to risk your young life for mine? No, I will go myself, but we will take a different route."

"Please, my lord," Maurice cried, and the emotion in his voice was no artifice, "they must have prepared for that and have men watching and in readiness in case you change your plans. The only safety is in my ruse. I will be in no danger, for I will throw off the cloak and cap as soon as we are away from the Louvre. By then it will be too late for them to track you. I only say this to reassure and persuade you. Even if there were danger to me, I would gladly and rightly suffer it for your sake. You are everything to us."

Coligny, much moved, averted his eyes. "Fiat." He handed Maurice his cloak and cap of austere black velvet and donned, with some distaste, Maurice's cloak of black satin lined in gleaming white and his cap which sported an exaggeratedly large, white plume.

"There," said Maurice. "I may pass for Admiral Coligny at a distance, but no one will ever take you for him now, my lord. No one has ever seen our Admiral in such gaudy togs."

"In my youth, they did," he replied with a sudden smile. "You will pass, I think, if you keep your head down. All that is needed is a tall figure at the center of the men. Go now, and send Daudet to accompany me. God be with you."

The Admiral and Daudet watched the large group of Protestant gentlemen march out. At the center walked a tall figure with eyes downcast as if in thought. The Admiral explained the situation to Daudet.

"The villains!" Daudet exclaimed. "After all their fine words and promises! How can we ever trust them?"

"It is ever thus, young Trophime," said Coligny, thoughtfully. "I have long lived in fear of death. It is true fear, although I would not admit it to most men. Yet, I thank the Lord that He has let me see that death is as truly my constant shadow as He is my constant sun. Thus I know He keeps my spirit trim and fit, like a warrior girded for battle. This is the true Christian state. The bridegroom cometh, but we know not when. For, Trophime, if life were fat and slack, how would we keep ready?" Coligny stopped, then continued quietly.

335

"My enemies have never let me forget their hatred, and I thank them and pity them. They are cursed by it and I will be saved by it. Their fair words do not deceive me. Indeed, I sometimes think they were not meant to."

He shrugged, looked at Trophime's solemn, worried face and put a hand on his shoulder reassuringly. "Come, how do I look in a young cock's plumage?" he asked, smiling. Daudet shook his head angrily.

"Shall I crow for you?" Coligny inquired, cocking his hat at a jaunty angle. Daudet laughed, the laugh catching in his throat. He rubbed his hands across his eyes. Looking up, he smiled weakly and replied, "La Renaudie's finery passes for sobriety in this Court."

"True, enough. Come, let's go."

They passed out through the heavy medieval arch, across the moat and then north along the moat toward Coligny's lodgings in rue Bethizy, a brisk ten minutes' walk. Maurice and the bodyguard were by then some way ahead, having passed along the street without incident. Coligny and Daudet had nearly arrived when the Admiral slowed and bent to tie his shoelace.

Suddenly, a shot rang out. Daudet struggled to catch the Admiral as he fell, then laid him gently on the ground and quickly examined him for wounds. Coligny's left arm had been pierced by a bullet and his right hand was bleeding profusely.

"It's all right. It's all right," Coligny gasped. "I'll be all right."

Coligny's ashen color belied his words. Daudet was trying to help him to his feet when he was surrounded by the Admiral's bodyguard led by Maurice.

"My God, what has happened?" Maurice shouted. He gasped and looked about wildly.

"There was a shot," Daudet said. "I think it came from that house."

"I have been fooled," Maurice cried. "The devils! The limbs of Satan!" He threw himself on his knees beside the Admiral rocking back and forth, moaning. Daudet regarded Maurice with suspicion and disgust as a group of the guard, with a roar, broke down the door of the home Daudet had indicated.

Daudet shouted to the rest, "Help me get him home. It is not safe here in the street!"

Maurice moved to help Coligny up. "No, not you," Daudet cried, warding him away with a sweeping gesture. "You," he said, indicating a group of young men. Struggling with the Admiral's bulk, they followed Daudet's orders.

"I shall inform the King! I shall get his own doctor, Ambroise Paré," Maurice cried over the tumult.

"Be careful," someone shouted. "There may be danger. They may be planning to kill us all."

"I care nothing for danger," cried Maurice as he ran back toward the Louvre. "Our leader must be saved!"

* * *

"Something must be done," the Queen Mother was saying. "Something must be done, although how we can save the situation God only knows. Here I am confined to this little turnip patch. 'Don't go into the Tuileries,' you tell me, Albert, 'It's not safe,' you tell me. The Protestants are wild because some fool has shot their leader, and we, as a result, are no better than prisoners!"

It was Saturday, the day after the attempt on Coligny's life, and golden light of evening softened the Queen Mother's face, but could scarcely hide the concern that pursed her mouth.

She had now made the circuit around the old garden between the Louvre and the Seine four times trying to get control of the situation, accompanied by Gondi and by Anjou, whose single-minded interest in wiping out heretics had finally provoked a curt "Oh, shut up, Henri," from his mother.

The heat of the day had abated slightly, but the air was still unpleasantly warm and humid. As Catherine de Medici continued the forced march along the north wall of the enclosed garden, their shadows stretched out before them dark on the golden path. The air of grave impassivity the Queen had maintained since the day before, when she heard of the shooting of the Admiral, was beginning to take its toll. Anjou's continual interruptions had not helped her mood.

Suddenly she cried out, "Oh, God, why did this terrible thing have to happen? Here we are in this roasting powder keg of a city, and some lunatic throws not a match but a bomb into it!"

"But Madame," Gondi replied in his most thoughtful and sober manner, "this 'terrible thing' as you call it — if it had come off, if the lion had been killed, not just wounded, it would have been a godsend, surely. With Coligny gone, the Netherlands Enterprise would have collapsed, and with it, our fears of Spain. Moreover, we could have prevented the Protestants from taking reprisals, for we could have used the two princes, Henri Navarre and Condé, as hostages for their good behavior. Even if there had been violence as a result, it would have been the Admiral's House of Châtillon against the House of Guise, and a little even-handed bloodletting would only have left you stronger."

Catherine stopped, looked at Gondi with profound suspicion, opened her mouth to ask a question, then shut it again.

"You're absolutely right," Anjou interjected. "It was, and still is, a brilliant idea."

The Queen Mother said finally, "Whatever it might have been as a success, as a failure it is a disaster. An unmitigated disaster, you understand, Albert."

"Yes, indeed — I do understand," Gondi agreed submissively. "Ambroise Paré had to take off one of his fingers, but he is strong as an ox. The Admiral will be after the Guises, or worse, all too soon, I fear."

"Well," she continued, "when the court of inquiry the King set up this morning decides that Guise was behind it, we can still direct the wrath of the Protestants against Guise and his retainers." Her face brightened a bit, then clouded again. "But all Paris will fight for Guise. No, it will be a bloodbath."

"Madame," Gondi said quietly, "though it will increase your worries, which I hate to do, I must warn you of one thing: the court of inquiry may not find Guise to blame."

"How do you mean, Sirrah?" she demanded, halting and facing Gondi. "Everything points to him: the house from which the shot was fired belongs to Guise's former preceptor, the man who took the assassin to the house is Guise's uncle's maître d'hôtel, and the horse he escaped on came from Guise's stables. And the assassin, they say it was Maurevert himself, was a page of the Guises. It's only too obvious."

"Quite." Gondi avoided her look. "If the attempt had succeeded, no one would have looked beyond the obvious, but as it is..." He spread his hands. "You see, when Maurevert assassinated the Admiral's first Lieutenant, Mouy de Saint-Phal back in '69 and tried to kill the Admiral himself, everyone assumed that he was working for His Majesty, which is to say for us, and the fact that he was awarded the Order of Saint-Michel merely served to confirm that. So I fear now everyone may think the same. I, myself, Madame, think it appears that he was acting on his own, hoping, of course, for a similar reward, which in my opinion he ought to receive, in due course."

"Right!" Anjou interjected.

Catherine pressed both hands to her temples for a moment.

Gondi continued, "You have heard what the Protestants have been shouting outside the gates of the palace all day — 'We will strike, we will kill, we will have justice.'"

"But they must be harassing Guise and his uncle in the same way," Catherine said anxiously. "Mind you, they're made to do it, milling around and shouting and flaunting their arms. They will rouse the mob, and there will be rioting and... and..."

"Good," said Anjou.

"Shut your mouth. You're a fool sometimes, Henri." She turned back to Gondi. "Why didn't they leave? Coligny should send them away."

"To fight in the Netherlands?" he asked.

Catherine rubbed a hand across her face. "I cannot help respecting his courage, though I hate his obsession with the Netherlands. To think that Coligny, lying in bed, just having been shot at, had the nerve to tell my son that he must immediately make open war against Spain in the Netherlands. Today, before my very eyes!

"And we had done him the honor of visiting him," she continued, "the entire royal family! This is how we are repaid. Charles calling him 'Father.' My God! Charles is absolutely besotted with ideas of glory in the Netherlands."

"The Admiral has always said he wishes to avoid a civil war, Madame. Perhaps he really does wish it."

"And so do I, Albert, so do I! But there must be another way. And yet, I see nothing, nothing."

"Why is everyone so afraid of civil war?" Anjou asked. "'Civil war,' everyone always says and quakes as he says it, but what does it mean? Nothing more than war against the heretics, and that is not something to turn away from. Indeed, it is our bounden duty as true Christians."

"Madame," Gondi interposed, as Catherine turned savagely to silence Anjou, "It is not like you to be so pessimistic. Can we not say that having the Protestants here in Paris is a golden opportunity, as shooting Coligny was a golden opportunity, unfortunately missed?"

"What are you saying, Albert?" she snapped. "That we should turn the Guises and mobs and... and my son here, and his brigands, against the Protestants, who are, after all, guests at my daughter's wedding and under the protection of the King of France. You are as mad as he is, Albert! To kill Coligny perhaps — his death, though I, of course, did not will it, might have saved many others, but what are you suggesting now?"

"I am not talking about murdering your guests, Your Majesty. I am talking of executing traitors," Gondi said firmly.

"It's a little late to rake up the sins of the past," she snapped.

"Has it never occurred to you, Madame," said Gondi in a low voice, "that the Protestants may mean the things that they yell at you?"

"They are hotheads, angry, who can blame them?" she demurred.

"What are you saying, exactly, my lord de Retz?" Anjou asked sharply.

"I am waiting for a report from my agent which will confirm or refute my suspicions," Gondi replied. "My guts tell me that the Protestants will strike first unless we stop them."

"Well, where is your agent? Who is he?" Anjou asked.

"I told him to join me here. Ah," Gondi gestured dramatically, "here he is."

Maurice de la Renaudie stepped out of the lengthening shadows. Both the Queen Mother and Anjou appeared startled.

"Tell me what you have learned, La Renaudie," Gondi barked. "Quickly! If I am right, time is of the essence."

"It is worse than you feared, Your Majesty, my lords," Maurice replied. "They all met..."

"Who?" the Queen Mother demanded.

"Navarre, Condé, Teligny, La Noue, Briquemault, Piles, de Grève, Monino, young Daudet — everyone — 20 or 30 of them around Coligny's bed."

"And what?"

"It was agreed they would move as soon as possible," Maurice's words came out in a rush, "against the Louvre, the King, and all the royal family. They want to save the King if possible; they think he is basically on their side; but as for you, Madame...." He nodded solemnly at his listeners and shrugged. "They are sending messengers out to bring up a contingent of cavalry. Then their forces will number 4,000. They expect to be ready by Tuesday, the 26th."

"Can this be true?" Catherine turned to Gondi.

"Madame," Maurice replied. "I was there, I heard it all."

Anjou broke out of his stupor. "The damned traitors! And you, why are you here?"

Maurice looked toward Gondi and thought back to the panic he had seen in Gondi's eyes when he had received his final instructions last night, so different from his calm assurance now. You owe, me, you bastard, Maurice said to himself. Gondi placed his hand on Maurice's shoulder. "Monsieur de La Renaudie has been acting as my most confidential agent since he left Court last year. Indeed, it was to serve me that he left."

Anjou laughed, with a gasp almost like a sob. "And you couldn't have told me?" he continued to address Maurice.

Gondi again replied. "Absolutely no one was to know."

"Not even my Mamá?" Anjou's eyes moved slowly from Maurice to Gondi to his mother. Catherine stared for a moment at Gondi, then broke out, "What does this matter? We must do something. We have barely two days!"

"Nay, Madame," said Gondi. "It may be that they now plan to wait until Tuesday, but emotions are high and may break out at any time. They are a constant and imminent threat. Act now, or we may all regret it."

"This is not a decision I can make alone, Albert. You know that."

"The others, Nevers, Birague, Tavannes, will be in favor. They ask nothing better than to go against the Protestants, if you give them the lead. They said as much this afternoon."

"Yes, but what of de Galle? He asked for permission to leave Court at once. Something about his estates. Does he know something, Albert?"

"He has, I am afraid, been very thick with the Admiral of late," Maurice interrupted. "I should not count on him in this fight."

"Your Majesty," Gondi responded. "I think I know Pierre de Galle as well as anyone at Court, even better than you, Maurice. He is absolutely loyal and I can tell you his estates do need watching."

"Very well, Albert," she replied, "but keep your own eye on him. Things may not be as they seem with Monsieur the Duke."

"What of Guise and his cousin, Aumale?" the Queen asked.

"Ah, that is more complicated," Gondi replied.

"Surely not," said Anjou.

"But yes, Monsieur," Gondi answered. "Of course, they want Coligny's blood. They always have, and that of his followers, too. 'Put all the Protestants to the sword' — that's almost their motto. But you cannot expect Guise to bear the responsibility for something on this scale. He is smart enough to see the danger. Indeed, he left Court and went off to his hotel precisely for that reason — to protest the fact that His Majesty prematurely blamed him for the attempt on Coligny's life."

"You are right, of course," Catherine agreed. "This must be a legal execution, done under the King's authority. But, will the King agree?"

"Madame, if we are agreed, I will see to it that he agrees."

"You?"

"Yes, Madame. I can always make him see reason in times of necessity."

Anjou glared at Gondi with resentment. "He should listen to me, I'm his Lieutenant-General."

"And I, his Mother," Catherine muttered.

"Why should he listen to you," Anjou continued, "just because you were once his tutor?"

"No, he listens to me because I'm right," Gondi asserted.

"Might makes right in character as in politics, is that it?" Anjou laughed sarcastically.

Gondi shrugged.

"Listen, Albert," Catherine broke in, almost in tears. "I'm afraid. Paris is a desperate city. The people are hungry. There's no wheat. And for the wretches who are starving and who have watched the heretics, whom they despise, living like princes in the bosom of the Court — there is such hatred, such anger, Albert... How do we hope to control the city? Paris is a monster. How can we...?"

"No, no, Your Majesty. It will be all right," Gondi assured her. "The provost of merchants and the militia will control the city. The bourgeois shopkeepers don't want riots any more than we do."

"But there are always riots — remember the Cross of the Gâtines last December?"

"Precisely, Madame," Gondi said smoothly, "there are always riots and they come to nothing. Well, are we agreed?"

Catherine nodded. "One last thing," said Catherine after a long pause, "Henri Navarre and Condé must be spared."

"Of course," Gondi replied. "It would not do to leave the House of Guise with no enemies."

They smiled suddenly at each other.

"Fine," said Gondi. "Then I will go to His Majesty, and we shall have a full Council meeting anon."

"Excuse me, Your Majesty, my lords," Maurice interjected, "what are your orders for me? It will no longer be possible for me to remain among the Protestants."

"You may join my guard for now," Gondi replied.

"Why not," Catherine shrugged. "Albert, I want a word with you privately." Taking Gondi's arm, she walked down the graveled path to an arbor.

"You are sure you know what you are doing, Albert?" He cocked his head quizzically. "This must be done right and for the right reasons. I am taking that man's word because his word is your word. I must trust you."

"Madame, be at peace. What must be, must be. There is no other way. When people years from now look back on tomorrow, Saint Bartholomew's Day, they will know that you did what you had to do — with malice toward none."

A little later Gondi hurried through the great hall of the Louvre, now silent and dark, the marble caryatids supporting the musicians' balcony ghostly in the gathering dusk. He passed quickly through the doubled guard as First Lord of the Bedchamber and entered the King's private apartments. Charles IX was alone, seated at a table. The nearly empty carafe of wine revealed his most recent occupation.

"Oh, it's you, Gondi," he said dully.

"Sire, I must speak to you. It is urgent."

"The only urgent thing is to bring Henri de Guise to justice. We can do more than behead him, can't we? It was lèse-majesté, and he deserves worse. Damn him!" the King swore and rising unsteadily, knocked over his goblet.

"Please, Sire, you must listen..."

"No, you listen to me! They are all going to listen to me!" The King strode unsteadily back and forth; beads of sweat in the thin black hair of his chest could be seen through his open singlet.

"I tell you, Gondi, Henri de Guise is to blame for this mess and I'll have his head for it and then some. God, when I think how he made peace with the Admiral, gave him his hands and kissed him on both cheeks, and now this! He broke his word to me, and I'll have him drawn and quartered. My court of inquiry will get to the bottom of it, and justice will be done, however high and mighty the offender. The Protestants demand justice, and they shall have it."

"Your Majesty, it isn't that simple."

"Oh, God – here we go. Lecture by my sage preceptor."

"What the court of inquiry finds is one thing, what really happened is another – but neither of those things is important. What counts is what the Protestants think."

"And I suppose you know that!" the King snapped.

"I do."

"I suppose they came running to confide in little Papá Gondi – even though they know you wish them in Hell!"

Gondi wiped his brow and continued evenly, "I have my methods, and they are reliable. I know the following for a fact – and you would do well to sit down and listen carefully. The Admiral and his followers believe that the Queen, your Mother, and your brother Anjou are responsible for the attempt on his life. Not only that, but they think that you gave your consent and will reward Maurevert, who is said to be the assassin, as you rewarded him after he shot down Mouy de St. Phal."

"They can't think that!"

"They do, Sire. And they will have their revenge. They met today around Coligny's bed and agreed to attack the Louvre and take you and all your family captive. If they can take the Guises, too, so much the better, but it is not crucial to their plans. They believe if they have you, they have the Kingdom. And make no mistake, it is death for your Mother and your brother – and perhaps for you."

Charles stared at Gondi; his eyes, bloodshot, seemed about to pop from his head. "Coligny would not be King," he stammered.

"No, Sire, but why not Navarre? Or even your brother Alençon, little Hercules — he has shown favor to those of the Religion."

The strain of the last day showed in the King's sallow face and the dark circles under his eyes. Furious, he swept goblet, carafe, and papers in a crash from the table.

"Gondi, you have made this up!" he shrieked. "I cannot believe it!"

"Your Majesty, I speak only the truth."

"How can you possibly know?"

"La Renaudie, who has the Admiral's confidence, is a true Catholic; he has been acting for us..."

"Spying."

"It is no shame for a man to spy for his lord, the King, Sire. He is a true and loyal gentleman, he serves only you. Coligny is a traitor. La Renaudie heard everything — the plot and the threats. It is as I say."

The King sat down, silent, his eyes dark wells of sorrow in the shadows, his lips trembling.

"We must strike first, Your Majesty. They have deserved death, and for your own safety, there can be no forgiving."

The King continued to stare blankly.

"Do you understand me, Sire? You must summon the Council and give the order."

The King remained silent, motionless. He seemed in shock.

"Your Majesty... you must..." Gondi tried again.

Slowly, as if he were swimming up from great depths of the sea, the King rose to his feet.

"Do it," he said softly.

"Yes, Sire, I will organize everything, but you, Your Majesty, you must give the order."

"I said do it!" the King cried, as a note of hysteria began to rise in his voice. "But, Gondi," he rasped, seizing Gondi's doublet, "if they must be killed, let none of them survive! Let not one return to reproach me!

"Do you understand?" he shrieked, "None of them!" He crumpled back onto his seat, his head in his hands. "How could they do this," he moaned. "How could they make me do this? How could he whom I trusted..."

"Thank you, Sire," Gondi said soothingly as he disengaged himself. "I understand perfectly. Your Majesty's will shall be accomplished."

Gondi bowed and retired, closing the door gently behind him. Only then did he begin to run.

Chapter XXIX

It was late that same evening when the royal messengers delivered to Pierre a summons to attend immediately a special Council meeting at the Louvre. Reluctantly, he put aside his preparations for an early morning departure for Fontevrault, and even more reluctantly, his thoughts of Athalie. He hurried quickly through the deserted streets and then through the dark passages of the Louvre. His eyes blinked as he entered the King's chamber, now brightly lit and humming with excited talk. He looked quickly around, taking in the great lords standing around the seated King and Queen Mother: Guise, his cousin Aumale, Anjou, and the others. He noticed suddenly that there were no Protestants. He was even more surprised to see his stepbrother, Maurice, not only present but sporting the livery of the Count de Retz. He was about to ask what this meant, when at a sign from the Queen Mother, Gondi stepped forward and a hush fell on the room.

"Your Majesties, my lords," Gondi began. "You have been summoned here tonight because we must deal at once with the basest treason and revolt in our midst. Coligny and the Protestant lords are even now planning a coup d'etat. They plan to seize the King, kill his family and doubtless most of us as well. Our lord, the King, believes we must forestall their wicked scheme by striking first. That you may know the truth of this peril, I will ask Monsieur de la Renaudie, who for the last year has acted as our agent in their midst, to report to you all what they conspired to do this very evening."

Maurice repeated his story, embellishing the bare facts he had given earlier, with vivid oaths and bloodcurdling descriptions of what the Protestants had in store. Nervousness, as ever, brought out the worst in Maurice.

"I tell you," he paused for dramatic effect, "I heard them cry, 'Death is too good for the Italian witch and her familiars. Slow strangulation is what we need to revenge her poisoning of the Queen of Navarre! Anjou and Guise are to be crucified to reward them for their ardent religious beliefs!'" As he warmed to his subject, his voice rose, his gestures became even more theatrical.

Pierre watched his stepbrother's posturing with growing distaste, aware that he was not the only one to feel repugnance, though his contempt was the sharper for the greater familiarity which it reflected.

The Queen Mother arched an eyebrow at Gondi, who, stepping forward, said, "Thank you, I think we understand enough." Whatever the listeners thought of the teller, the tale itself was more than sufficient to arouse anger and dismay at the Protestants and protestations of loyalty to the King. Maurice, cut off in mid-flight, retired in some confusion as Gondi continued.

"His Majesty has wisely determined that this evil must be pulled out root and branch. All of the Protestant leaders from Coligny down must die this very night. Only then will the kingdom be safe." A buzz of approval filled the room.

Pierre was troubled and uneasy, but felt entirely isolated in his doubts. He struggled with himself and, at last, though he was not in the habit of questioning his elders, gestured timidly for leave to speak.

"If Your Majesty please," he said, "why is it necessary to execute them? Why cannot they be arrested and given an opportunity to answer these accusations?"

The room buzzed again, this time with a more sour note. The King, who had sat apathetic throughout the meeting, swiveled his eyes toward Pierre, then looked away.

Gondi bowed in the direction of the King before answering. "It is only because this is an emergency, my lord de Galle. They are too numerous and too well armed for us to take the risks which your suggestion entails."

"I see," Pierre paused, unconvinced, then continued. "But why is it necessary to kill all of the Protestant lords, even those who did not attend the meeting?"

There was now no mistaking the hostility in the room. The young King roused himself. "They are all traitors, traitors... every one!"

"Traitors and heretics," cried Anjou, eying Pierre with dislike.

"Yes," Gondi picked up, "every person on our list owes loyalty to the Admiral and will obey his orders, and not our liege lord's orders. They are, therefore, traitors. This is an act of justice. And I would add, it is also a political act, which will also have military consequences. Purely as a military matter, we must take advantage of the enemy's surprise to gain the most thoroughgoing victory possible. The more we kill today, the fewer we will fight tomorrow. Indeed, if we are thorough tonight, there will be no fighting tomorrow."

"God willing!" exclaimed the Queen Mother; she crossed herself and the others followed.

Pierre nodded slowly, aware that not a few quizzical eyes were on him.

The meeting continued briskly: charges were handed out, men assigned to leaders, the responsibility for individual executions allocated to each of those present. The King's steward was summoned to tell where each of the condemned had been assigned lodgings.

"But of course," Gondi added, "if you encounter someone who is on the list but is not your responsibility, don't hesitate to dispatch him. The important thing is that no one escape the King's justice."

Pierre wished desperately that he could talk to someone, but he was deeply relieved that his list did not contain anyone he knew well. He felt Gondi squeeze his arm. "I know you won't like this, Pierre, but it has to be done. It's always hardest at first. Think of it as a battle — you'll do just fine. Actually, the men you will lead will do all the dirty work. Good luck to you."

Two municipal magistrates, Claude Marcel and the provost of merchants, Le Charron, were summoned and told of the Protestant plot and the King's orders. They were told to arrange for the city gates to be closed and locked, to have the ferries chained up to prevent escapes across the Seine, to arm the bourgeois and the militia, and to prepare the cannon to defend the Hôtel de Ville. The King's

Swiss Guards were roused and armed to carry out the executions within the Louvre itself. All were stationed in readiness for the signal to be given — the chiming of the bells of the Palace of Justice.

Small groups of men waited in the courtyard of the Louvre. No torches were permitted for fear of rousing those Protestants who were actually residing in the palace. The men were restless and keyed up, with the strained, somewhat artificial vitality that comes to people who are active in the small hours of the morning.

Gondi sought out Maurice and took him aside.

"When I spoke to His Majesty, he said 'Let none of them return,'" Gondi whispered. "Now, he was a little hysterical, not really choosing his words with care. Certainly, however, we have been given no reason to doubt that is how he feels. Indeed, that is how he feels tonight. So we must act on those orders and emphasize to the others that those are the King's express wishes. Of course, I need hardly point out to you how important it is that no one returns or survives to contradict your version of their meeting. Everyone who was at that meeting must die — expeditiously."

Maurice licked his lips feverishly and nodded several times with emphasis.

"Go," Gondi murmured, pushing him gently. "This is a good time to talk to the men, arouse their fervor. Go."

Maurice drifted away in the gloom. Gondi expelled his breath sharply, partly to relieve his inner tension and partly to express his intense satisfaction.

* * *

At three, the bells of St. Germain l'Auxerrois just outside the Louvre suddenly rang out. Bands of nervous waiting men taking this for the agreed signal hurried out of the courtyard toward their destinations. The narrow and twisted maze of streets near the Louvre was dark under the overcast night sky. The attempt to move quietly, so as not to alarm the quarry, soon broke down into noisy confusion with armed men stumbling into each other, challenging each other, shouting and running. The entire quarter was soon roused, torches were lit, explanations were demanded and sometimes given.

When Pierre arrived at the lodgings of the first man on his list, a Protestant lord from the South with whom he had only a nodding acquaintance, he found the house in commotion, its Catholic owners alarmed and angry, and the Protestant gone. A debate followed as to whether he escaped by the door or the roof. Pierre's group split and set off in pursuit. In the pandemonium of the chase, Pierre's men scattered, and Pierre found himself on a dark street, a leader without followers. He set off alone for the lodgings of the second Protestant assigned to him.

Pierre had developed some knowledge of the twisted streets of Paris during his stay in the city, but he was really only able to navigate them with concentration in broad daylight. Under the present circumstances, though he knew where he was, he was baffled as to how to get to where he wanted to go. A group of men with drawn swords and torches held high stormed past him. He called out to them but they ran on without turning. He drew his own sword and took a torch from a wall bracket and trotted up the street. Coming to an archway, he turned underneath it and strode up the narrow way, his guttering torch the only light in the blackness. Suddenly, reaching a wall, he realized that he was in a cul-de-sac. He turned back with a muttered curse. As he did so, he saw a door open and a man slip into the street. Nervously, he thrust his torch forward; the flame revealed the face of Trophime Daudet.

Daudet was fumbling with his sword-belt buckle; he looked up, raised a hand against the glare and asked, "Who's that?"

Pierre lowered the torch.

Daudet's worried face brightened. "Oh, Pierre," he said, "I heard the tocsin and then a lot of noise in the streets. The others are still asleep. I came out to see what was going on. Normally I wouldn't have bothered — this city is pretty raucous; but the tocsin — I couldn't account for that. What's going on?" He shifted and looked down at the buckle he was still fumbling with. "Hold the torch close for a second, Pierre."

"Drop the sword," Pierre said.

Trophime looked up, amazed, raising both hands in the gesture of surrender.

"I would do nothing against you with my sword, as you well know, Pierre, but why should you think I would try?"

Pierre's throat constricted and his words came out sounding harsh. "The King has charged you, and many others — all Protestants — with treason against his person. The executions are to be carried out tonight. I would do anything to be excused from this, but this is my duty, to kill you though you were once my friend. It can't be helped now. What you and your friends did made this inevitable."

Trophime stared at Pierre, aghast. "So it has come to this — I was right when I first spoke to you of the Religion. As long as we're outnumbered, we'll be tracked and killed like animals." His face was white under his tan; though his expression was stern, he eyes showed his fear. Pierre looked away, thinking to himself, this is unbelievable — this moment, this situation, is impossible.

"But Pierre," Trophime continued, raising his head and staring Pierre in the eyes, "I am luckier than you — I can die proudly, but you, how will you live?"

In a burst of rage, Pierre cried out, "My conscience will be clear. You talk as if you were some holy martyr, but you're a traitor, like all the rest."

"Tell me," Daudet said quietly, "you owe me this much, pray, What is my supposed treason?"

Pierre repeated the story of the meeting, the planned invasion of the Louvre, the intended kidnapping of the King and butchering of his family, while Trophime listened with growing wonder.

"But Pierre," Daudet cried, "that is all a lie. Yes, there was a meeting, but everything else is a stinking lie. Only one person at the meeting argued for violence, and that person was your stepbrother, La Renaudie. He was shrieking

347

about how he personally would dispatch the Queen Mother. It was his right, he said, to avenge his father's death.

"A few people might — I say, might — have felt the same, but they never had a chance. The Admiral quashed the idea immediately and with such firmness that no one dared to mention it again. Then there was some discussion about whether we should flee Paris en masse, but Navarre and Condé argued against it, saying the King would not abandon his friends. Coligny said he himself could not leave because his work here was not completed, but that anyone who had no stomach for a fight could leave with his blessing. And that was how it was left.

"I swear to you on my word of honor," he concluded earnestly, "no, on my Religion, which is more sacred to me than anything — that what I have said is the truth."

Pierre had gradually lowered his sword point as Trophime spoke. He thought of Maurice's recital in the Council and looked into his friend's face. He knew there could be no doubt which version was the truth. Suddenly, he rushed forward and sheathing his sword with a deft movement, pulled Daudet to him in a hug.

"Thank God, I ran into you. It's pure chance, you know. You weren't on my list of... of victims, and when I think how grateful I was not to be assigned to kill you and how my heart sank when I saw you..."

"But come," he said, grabbing Daudet's arm and pulling him toward the arch, "all over Paris people are dying because of this, this story."

Daudet stopped short and turned to him. "Wait," he said. "Before I go with you, let me know who told this 'story,' as you call it."

"La Renaudie," Pierre replied, "of course."

They stared into each other's eyes, then turning, rushed through the arch and up the street.

They were barely able to force their way through the narrow, winding streets for the carnage and confusion that they met. There were mangled corpses heaped and strewn in doorways and across culverts. The gutters, always slimy, were slippery with a noisome brew of mud and gore. Armed bands muscled by, climbing around and over the bodies, waving smoking torches and bloodied weapons.

They found a crossroads completely blocked with the dead and the dying. Trophime staggered and propped himself against a wall, choking back his vomit. Pierre steered Trophime back up the street, around a corner, and down another thoroughfare to the Louvre.

The courtyard of the Palace more than matched the city streets for horror. At one end, bodies were heaped in a small mountain, a mountain that moved and groaned. In the middle stood rows of Swiss Guards with halberds lowered while others shoved forward small groups of victims. Some were in nightclothes, some naked and clutching in shame at their privy parts, some sobbing, some calm, as they were pushed against the lowered points of the Guards' weapons.

A bonfire lit up the far end of the courtyard, its flickering glare giving a grotesque illusion of movement to the serene marble goddesses above. The heat near the fire was overwhelming. Pierre saw Gondi standing away from the fire, silhouetted against it, aloof from the massacre, but watching it with a fixed, fascinated stare. Pierre ran up to him pulling Trophime along behind. Gondi snapped out of his trance and looked at Pierre.

"Monsieur," Pierre burst out, "I must speak to His Majesty the King and his Mother the Queen. This is all a horrible mistake. It must be stopped. My friend here — I will vouch for his word, as my own — he was at that meeting. He has told me everything. There was no treason there, except that of my stepbrother. He alone should die for this, not all these innocents."

Gondi took his arm gently. "Pierre, you're upset. This youngster would tell you anything he could think of to save his skin. It's only natural, but you should not be swayed by his fibs — or by your friendship. You know the King's orders, and you know your duty — or you should."

Pierre drew himself up, towering over Gondi. "Monsieur, what I do know is my stepbrother, and so I believe must you, if he was your agent as you say. I know whom to believe. His Majesty the King should also be given the choice of whom to believe. We have two versions and two people. Let them face each other and then let the King decide."

"Well, Pierre, you may have something there. I will see what I can arrange."

"Hurry!"

"Oh, I shall. Wait over there, beyond the bonfire."

Gondi disappeared into the crowd; Pierre and Daudet moved to one side. Shortly, Gondi reappeared with eight Guards, two of whom roughly pulled Daudet forward and disappeared with him around the bonfire, while the others surrounded Pierre with their weapons drawn.

"You will wait here, Monsieur de Galle," Gondi said. "People have suspected your loyalty more than once this evening. I had to vouch for you myself, but this rashness of yours makes things very difficult. I will do what I can to save you, but I can't promise anything."

"My loyalty?" Pierre shouted. "What are you...?"

"You know your orders," Gondi said to the Guards' Captain, as he turned away. Pierre moved to follow but found six swords pointing at his chest. He could see the two other guards reappear beyond the fire, dragging and pushing Daudet toward the executioners. Daudet looked back for a brief moment before falling beneath the executioners' blows. Pierre surged forward, pulling at his sword, to find the points of the Guards' swords only inches from his neck. "We have orders to kill you if you move, my lord," the Captain said. Pierre hesitated, his eyes flashing wildly in the firelight, then fell back against the wall, still grasping his sword hilt. The knuckles of his hand showed white through the skin.

Thus constrained, Pierre fixed his eyes on the other side of the courtyard — on the milling mob eerily lit up by the flickering light of the great fire, the last of the

Protestants being dragged from the palace, bands of men-at-arms, some uniformed, others not, some returning from the streets of Paris with arms full of loot, some hustling prisoners toward the executioners. He could see his stepbrother enter through the gate followed by men in the colors of the Duke of Anjou; he watched Gondi take him quickly aside and saw Maurice look furtively in his direction, then detach himself from Gondi and make his way across the courtyard. In mid-course, La Renaudie turned, looked straight at Pierre, and half bowed with a mocking smile. Pierre's guards glanced continuously over their shoulders and were muttering among themselves, resentful at being kept from the main action.

In Maurice's smirk, Pierre suddenly found something horrible as the pieces came together. Maurice knew all about it, Pierre said to himself. Gondi knew all about it, and now he is going to kill me as well to save his own skin. He is really going to do it.

Pierre felt rising within him, gradually but inexorably, a tremendous rage. It felt as if something was about to burst in his head, blinding him and transforming him into an avenging storm. That this should be happening, that he should be made to watch it happen, that Gondi should be letting it happen — no, making it happen — the situation was unbearable. Suddenly, Pierre felt as if he had split in two — a rational human part watching an inhuman force — and at the same moment he felt himself wrench out his sword and bound forward.

His guards, taken by surprise and momentarily terrified by his strength, fell back. Pierre slashed left and right. Two of the men fell in their tracks as Pierre rushed past. He dodged and leaped, thrusting obstructions aside, hacking blindly but effectively at opponents, real or imagined, until he reached the gate. With a final whirlwind thrust, he burst through a small group of guards gathered in the gateway and found himself in the comparative darkness of the street. He paused for a moment, then started off at a run down a street chosen at random.

At first, he ran wildly and thoughtlessly, sliding in the gutters, weaving through half-discerned piles of bodies and debris, crashing up against doorways. The streets were nearly deserted by the living, although scores of the dead remained. Dawn was breaking, casting a grey, hideous pallor across the darkness, lighting up the bloody horror in the streets which, as it became ever more visible, seemed to Pierre less and less real. He slowed to a shambling trot, staring about him with a stupid, blank gaze. There were women among the bodies, he could see that now, women. But how can there be women? he asked himself, concentrating slowly and intensely on something that seemed impossible. There were no women on the list. This was to be a legal execution. He stumbled around a corner, his foot catching on a small obstacle. He looked down and saw that it was the swaddled body of an infant, its throat slit, its bonnet half fallen from its head. It's a baby, he said to himself, blinking moronically. A baby, he repeated inaudibly, resting his shoulder against the wall. In what seemed to him like an eternity, he swiveled slowly, bent over, and retched his innards out. He squatted and retched again, swaying and supporting himself with his hands. He retched still again, but no more came.

For a few moments, Pierre remained where he was. He swayed slowly back and forth on his haunches. He tasted the vile sourness in his mouth, savoring it with a perverse pleasure, his eyes tightly closed against the world. At last, he stood up. His hands felt strange; he held them up and peered down at them in the weird, distorting half-light. The left hand was thoroughly caked with mud, the right still clutched his sword. He shifted the sword to his other hand and gazed abstractedly at the deep impression of the hilt on the grey palm of his right hand. Still staring at his hand as if he were trying to remember something important, he turned and walked up the street.

He stopped abruptly. He sheathed his sword and, taking out a handkerchief, he carefully wiped the sweat from his face and then cleaned his hands as best he could. As he performed these menial tasks, taking comfort from their banality, he lectured himself sternly.

This is all very well, my boy, he told himself, but somehow or other you have to extricate yourself... remove yourself from... get out of this awful mess, this inferno. These bodies, he felt his bile rising dangerously once again, no, listen to me, they're horrible, but... if you're not careful, you'll end up one of them.

He started to walk slowly along. Why that should be, I don't really know, he continued to himself, but it is. So... the first thing to do is to get home. And the second is to get out of Paris... somehow.

He paused at an intersection to get his bearings. The streets were filling up again with ordinary Parisians who were wandering around, some looking dazed, some excited. A few straggling bands of courtiers and men-at-arms were still about, making their way toward the Louvre.

Suddenly, Pierre felt so overcome with fatigue — both physically exhausted and emotionally drained — that he could hardly put one foot in front of another. It was a good thirty minutes' walk to the Hôtel de Galle on the Îsle de la Cité at the best of times; Pierre realized desperately it would take all morning to get there the way things were going now. Indeed, the streets were really filling up, clogged with excited, irascible Parisians. Pierre forced himself to continue. When I get to a wider street, the rue St. Honoré, the going will be easier, he thought.

Unbidden, the image of Trophime Daudet falling to the ground flashed into his mind, and Pierre, mortified, realized that for the last hour his mind had been a blank to the past, even so recent a past as the moment of Trophime's death, so completely had it been filled with the emotions of each instant. Images of the courtyard, the bodies, the fire, flooded back. A sorrow beyond tears gripped him, the sorrow and despair that come from an irrevocable deed, an irreplaceable loss. Momentarily, Pierre faltered in his stride, immobilized by a sense that there was no point going on. There was nothing to be done, he repeated to himself, over and over, nothing to be done. He was buffeted by the jostling crowd and was dimly aware of being cursed. He shook his head vigorously and by a conscious act

351

of will reasserted control over himself. If there is nothing to be done, he thought, there still was no point in standing there like a fool. He set off again at a brisker pace.

Emerging into the rue St. Honoré, he was shocked again at what he saw. The street was a seething cauldron of violence — every shop smashed and plundered, doors burst open, furniture and clothing trampled underfoot, and above all, bodies — live bodies gesticulating like monstrous puppets, dead and wounded bodies sprawled in doorways, hanging over window sills, spread-eagled in gutters, many of them dismembered, most naked, or covered only with shredded remnants of clothing.

A new energy, a new anger surged through Pierre, not like the wild fury which seized him at the Louvre, but a cold anger, more akin to hatred than to rage. Pierre was galvanized and forced his way through the crowd, clearing the struggling and fighting vandals from his path. He saw a small group of militiamen huddled in an archway, watching the street with sullen expressions. Under the arm of one of them was a shiny pewter urn. Pierre strode up and bellowed, "So this is how you do your duty! Look at this — riot and murder — and you, officers of the law, stand around like fat Romans at the Circus!"

Their leader cowered, "What can we do against so many?"

Pierre's eye caught the glint of pewter. Grabbing the urn, he slammed it into the officer's face; the man gasped and clutched at his crushed nose. Furious, Pierre stalked away. I must get away from this madness, this Hell, he muttered to himself. He charged up the rue St. Honoré; frightened people jumped out of his way. He turned south on the rue St. Denis heading for the Grand Pont. The stretch of street before him was, by some chance, clearer than the one he had just left; the relative peace seemed like the lull in a storm; the buzzing in his ears ceased. He slowed down and took several deep breaths. The air was hot and vile, but Pierre paid it no mind.

In a doorway, Pierre saw two bodies, a man's almost hiding that of a girl beneath, his arm across her face, pushing her head back and down. Clinically, Pierre observed the girl's stockinged legs splayed out and the man's rhythmic motion. Bitter saliva flooded his mouth and with the same detachment, he realized that he had just tasted the flavor of his own fury made tangible. In one bound, he covered the distance to the pair and with another swift movement left the man sprawled on his back in the gutter a yard away. The man moved to get up, but Pierre was upon him. The force of his first kick broke the man's neck, the second drove his head into the mud. Pierre regarded him for a moment, not really taking in what he had accomplished. Then he turned back to the girl. For a moment, he thought that she was dead. She looked like a broken doll, her black dress torn and crumpled, her neck still twisted, her eyes staring glassily at nothing. He knelt, put a hand before her mouth, felt moist breath, and taking her by the shoulders, dragged her back into the shadows of the doorway. He propped her, half-sitting, against the doorjamb, thinking, she really is like a doll.

"Are you all right?" he asked, feeling the question to be foolish, but somehow necessary. Her eyes swiveled to meet his, but their expression was still blank.

"Where are you from? Where can I take you?" She made no answer.

"Come, if I am to help you, you must give me some guidance."

She stared at him as if seeing him for the first time, then waved vaguely toward the house's interior.

"This is where you live?"

She shook her head, then nodded, and closed her eyes. When she opened them again, her blank look had returned.

Pierre rose and, bending down, picked her up and carried her into the house. She was little and light, but to his surprise she struggled slightly. The ground floor room which they entered was a chaos of broken furniture and scattered pots.

On the floor near the hearth lay an old man in a long, black robe, clearly dead. Against the overturned kitchen table was the body of a boy in a black doublet torn open, with blood showing through a gash in his singlet. The boy's staring eyes seemed to be fixed on Pierre and the girl in the doorway.

Pierre looked down at the girl's face. Her cheeks were wet, and he saw that she was still crying.

"These were your people?" he asked and was almost surprised to hear her voice.

"My father. My brother." Pierre turned to go.

A little louder, she said, "Leave me here."

"No," Pierre replied, "that wouldn't do."

She struggled suddenly; he shifted her in his arms, throwing her gently over his shoulder, gripping her thighs and skirts in a strong hold. After a few kicks, she was quiet. He left the house and continued toward the Grand Pont.

At the entrance to the bridge, he looked about for the toll collector and noted his absence with wry amusement. It takes a real crisis to draw away a money collector, he thought. The bridge was crowded, and a glance sufficed to tell him why — the jewelry and bullion shops and the moneychangers had all been broken into and ransacked. He noticed, here and there, foot soldiers in the livery of the Duke of Anjou. A few stared at him curiously; he tightened his grip on the girl with his left arm, freeing his right arm in case of need.

A rough, burly fellow stopped his passage, staring belligerently into Pierre's eyes. Then suddenly he laughed a braying laugh and turned to his companions.

"Here's a real gentleman for you," he called out, "taking a pretty heretic home to fuck in his bed."

Pierre twisted his mouth into a caricature of a laugh, and, avoiding the man, continued. It was with considerable relief that he stepped off the bridge onto the Île de la Cité. He turned right into a narrow back street and found his way blocked once again. A mob of vagabonds, street urchins, and beggars was gathered around and across from a doorway in which Pierre could barely see the figures of two men.

353

The older of the two, thin in his long black robe, stood in the back of the doorway, a dazed expression on his face, blood trickling from a cut on his forehead. The younger man, in singlet and hose, half-sheltered the older, standing forward in the doorway. He was clutching his right arm just below the shoulder with his left hand. Pierre could see blood running through the fingers from a deep wound in the arm. The young man was still holding his sword and waving it uselessly in front of him.

Pierre glanced up and down the street, then dropped the girl gently on her feet and propped her against the wall. "Stay here, you understand?" Pulling his sword, he leapt into the mob giving an inarticulate, but ferocious yell. Several of the ruffians stumbled and fell from the collision. A beggar turned on him, waving his dummy crutch as a weapon. Pierre cleaved his skull with a neat downward stroke. He pushed forward, holding his long weapon with both hands and swinging it in a vicious, whistling curve. Several of the mob were hit, but the awful sword did not slow in its motions. Suddenly, panic struck the crowd, which split into two uneven groups, one rushing back toward the bridge, the other stampeding down an alley toward the river.

Pierre wiped his blade on the rags of one of his victims and slipped it back into its sheath, calling out in the meantime to the two men, "Can you walk?"

"Oh, yes!" they replied.

"Come on then; my house is nearby."

He strode back to the girl who remained rooted to the spot where he left her, and pulling her along at a half-run, he and his companions hurried up the street. At a door in a low wall, Pierre stopped, tried the door, and finding it locked, rattled it and knocked urgently. A head with grizzled white hair above a livid face appeared for a moment above the wall, then disappeared. The door opened immediately.

An old man in the family colors stood aside. "My lord, you've returned, thank God. What is happening out there?"

"Has anyone come looking for me?"

"No."

"Monsieur de la Renaudie?"

"No, sir."

"Fine. Take these three to the top floor, the old nursery, and send one of Madame's ladies to assist them. I will want to see Marcel, Étienne, Pascal, and Raoul in the main hall immediately, and you yourself are to return there as soon as may be."

Chapter XXX

nne de Galle, after a sleepless night, finally tired of her chamber and nervously descended the spiral steps to the great hall below. She was not in good humor. Pierre's curt announcement the preceding evening that he must leave Court at once to see to some tiresome business about the vineyards at Bourgeuil was ridiculous, and she had told him so. That he should think of taking himself off after she had gone to so much trouble, not to say scheming, to put together an intimate evening with the Duke of Anjou, was preposterous. Then he had marched off in the middle of the night with an armed escort without a word of explanation. "Council business," was all he had said, leaving her alone while riots were going on outside, something about getting even with the Protestants, one of her servants had said. She had actually been grateful, for the first time to be sure, for the massive stone walls that had plainly been built to keep out more than an unruly mob. She rehearsed again the good piece of her mind she was going to give Pierre when he returned.

Pierre simply must remain in Paris, as she really couldn't explain to the Duke of Anjou that her soirée was canceled because of some vineyard. Really, it was all too stupid.

Anne heard the gates unbarred, the sound of men's voices, short, as if orders were being given, then the tall, oak door swung open and Pierre entered. Anne leapt at once into the fray.

"Pierre, what on earth is going on?" she cried, her voice shrill, almost strident with impatience. "Where have you been? I must speak to you right now about your plans! Our evening with Anjou is just too important for us!"

She paused, as approaching in the dim light, she saw him sway slightly with fatigue. "Pierre, what has happened to your doublet? My God! It is covered with blood!"

"My dear," he replied heavily, "I was summoned to the Palace, as you know. All the lords, except those of the Religion, were summoned, for the King's advisers had determined to execute the Admiral and all his chief men." He paused. There seemed absolutely no point to saying anything more. "No, it's really too complicated."

He went on, "I'll explain later. There's rioting in Paris — rioting, and pillage, and out-and-out murder. Anne, we must all leave Paris at once. Get ready. I've brought three Protestants — arrange for them to discard their black clothes and wear my colors. There is a girl. She can go as your lady-in-waiting. See to it."

Pierre turned away. Anne stood for a moment as if she had been struck. She rallied and resumed her attack.

"Leave? Leave Paris? Leave Court? For what? You are no Protestant. This business has nothing to do with us. Pierre, you are mad!"

"Anne," Pierre sighed wearily, "do as I say. We have very little time."

"I shall certainly not do anything of the sort," she snapped back. "If there is danger, we can go over to the Louvre."

"That will not be possible — anyway, we'd never get there. The streets are jammed with madmen and criminals. I only hope the Left Bank is calm enough so we can pass through and out the South gate."

"I can't travel," Anne whined, clutching her protruding belly.

"Damn it, Anne!" Pierre rose and stepped toward her. "You traveled well enough a month ago to get here. It was worth it for the balls and feasting, wasn't it? Well, it will be worth it, too, to save four lives."

"Four lives?" she asked.

"My three Protestant refugees and my own, you little fool!" he snapped.

"Fool?" she cried, her cheeks white with rage. "Who is a fool? Pierre, what have you done?"

"In a word, I tried to stop the executions," he replied tonelessly. "I had to defy the King's orders. I had to confront Albert de Gondi with the truth. I suppose I have rebelled. It really seemed that all of them, the King, Gondi and the rest, had rebelled against me. Now, I suppose, I am being hunted by Gondi and his 'agent,' my dear stepbrother. Anne, I have had enough of words with you. Go!"

His icy and implacable gaze told Anne further discussion would be futile and might be dangerous. Troubled, hurt, and bitterly disappointed at the turn of events, she walked slowly from the room.

Waiting for her ladies to see to the Protestant girl and assemble a traveling kit, she reflected sourly that Pierre's words were so bizarre as to be incomprehensible. Gondi had been Pierre's mentor at Court, endlessly charming and helpful. Anne liked Gondi and was sure the feeling was reciprocated. What could have gone wrong?

Protestants were boring and occasionally nasty. If the King decided a few of them should be executed, what difference could it make to her husband, Pierre? But here they were, mixed up with three of them. Admittedly, executing Protestants was not something nobles were asked to do every day; presumably there were people who handled executions and similar matters, without troubling dukes and duchesses about it.

But Pierre had not acted as if his dignity had been slighted. No, there was something deeper. He had rebelled. He had refused the King. Anne was quite sure that one did not do that sort of thing.

It was bound to be most disagreeable. Apparently, its first consequence was a precipitous journey away from everything she loved into she knew not what. And rebelling could not be good for Pierre's career. The idea that she would have to give thought to controlling Pierre's impetuosity crossed her mind. But he hadn't been impetuous before. Really, she used to wish he had a little more spark. He was actually rather dull and hardly the sort to bolt into rebellion.

It was really bad of him; if one was dull, one was supposed to be safe. A man who was both dull and dangerous — well, that was insufferable. Anne concluded an agreement with herself that she had been wronged and would have to use every opportunity to take matters into her own hands.

Pierre watched Anne disappear up the great staircase, and in spite of himself a wave of self-pity rose up within him. He knew he had to get her out of Paris as well as himself, but then what? More than ever he longed to see Athalie, beg Athalie to help him make sense of this mad nightmare from which he could not seem to wake. Well, he thought, unless we can get away from here soon, it will all be moot.

With determination, he turned to the four large men in the chartreuse and russet colors of de Galle, who entered the hall with the steward and bowed to Pierre.

"I expect my brother, the Sieur de la Renaudie," Pierre said, "to arrive shortly, accompanied by some men-at-arms, not too many, I hope, but I really don't know. Olivier, here," he indicated the old man, "will pull in the great door — you four will be behind it with your weapons drawn. As they come in, you will spring on them from behind and disarm them. I will be in the doorway back there and will advance to handle my stepbrother and however many of the others as may be necessary. We are few and have not time for anything more elaborate. I want to capture La Renaudie, but we must kill them all if we have to. Understood?"

The men nodded.

Not long after, Maurice arrived with six men in the livery of the Count of Retz. The trap was sprung and in a few violent seconds four of the men were disarmed and Maurice found himself with Pierre's sword at his throat. He dropped his own sword and the others followed suit. Maurice's little troop was taken off to confinement in the cellar, with somewhat ironic apologies from Pierre, while Pierre escorted Maurice to the window embrasure in the large back room.

Maurice perched on the stone seat, while Pierre stood facing him.

The glint of humor Pierre had shown in the great hall was gone; his face wore a cold, rigid expression. There were shadows under his eyes, and harsh lines of fatigue ran from the sides of his nose to his mouth. Maurice stared back at Pierre. His dilated pupils made his eyes look black in his pasty face. Sweat beaded his forehead. A muscle jumped under his left eye.

"Well, you put your foot in it, Blondel," Maurice sneered. "Treason, they're calling it back at Court. You'll never get away with this little ruse. You can't hold out against the King's troops, and I assure you, they are going to come after you."

"I don't wish to bandy words with you, Maurice," Pierre replied. "I gambled that you would come here more or less alone, and I was right. The authorities have too much on their hands to worry about my fate, or yours — or even Albert de Gondi's. Paris is out of control." He gestured vaguely beyond the window and shuddered. "I saw that and so did you. So, you are on your own for the time being, which was what I assumed. Whatever Gondi could do in normal times, he can't do much today. The poor beggars in my cellar were all he could spare, am I not right?"

357

Maurice stared at Pierre without vouchsafing a reply. Pierre took a deep breath.

"So, now, if ever, is the time to get away," he continued. "I'll stick with my first assessment of the odds. There is no hue and cry after me yet. If we all saddle up and ride south, no one will try to stop us. Am I right, Maurice?"

Maurice's mouth twisted in a hideous grin. "I'll never tell, Blondel, Blondel."

"You're mad, Maurice, and, what's worse, you're a fool," Pierre replied through clenched teeth. "Listen, and listen well. I'm going to do what I just described; I'm going to take you with me. And, Maurice, if there is the slightest sign of danger to me or my people, I'm going to cut you in two." He paused. "So, if you think my plan won't work, now is the time to say so."

* * *

Shortly after nones had rung, Pierre watched his little cavalcade clatter out of the courtyard. There was an eerie stillness in the street instead of the usual press of traffic. The narrow street that led to the bridge was littered with broken glass, furniture, and wood where shutters had been torn from houses and shops. The deserted rooms, unlit, stared back at the street like eyeless sockets. Black smoke rose vertical in the still air from several points. In the distance, a great roaring, as of some huge beast worrying its prey, could be heard, intermittently punctuated by the sliver of a scream.

"It is still going on," Pierre said, turning toward Anne. "We must hurry." Anne clutched the side of her palfrey, her eyes glassy with horror. Following her gaze, Pierre saw the body of a woman, at least he supposed it was a woman, so mutilated it was hard to be sure. "We must hurry," Pierre repeated.

Pierre had counted on the long summer day to allow them to make a good start out of the city, but he realized with deep apprehension that they would make but slow progress with a pregnant woman and a wounded man in their midst. Some of his retainers had straggled in during the afternoon, exhausted from the night's work, on which he had led them so few hours — but it seemed a lifetime — ago. Pierre had done his best to prepare for all eventualities, taking nearly all his retainers, leaving the old steward of the Paris house with only a skeleton staff to protect their furnishings which, much to Anne's annoyance, had to be left behind.

His men, while few, were heavily armed and well trained. In case of pursuit, he had instructed them to defend their mistress and bring her safely to Plessis Gaillard, leaving him and his Protestant wards to fend for themselves. He shuddered at the thought of flight with a girl, a wounded youth, an old man — and Maurice. What should he do with Maurice? Pierre watched him riding ahead, his horse held by lead straps in the hands of two stalwart cavaliers.

Pierre had discussed all this, before they left, with the Protestant girl. She was called Meraude, Meraude de la Somme, he had ascertained, in the course of advising her to stay with his wife in case of pursuit. Though she appeared passive, even lifeless, about everything, at this suggestion she had protested wildly. She had said she must at all costs stay with her co-Religionists and go with them to La Rochelle, if God would permit. Pierre glanced at her, and the thought sprang unbidden to his mind that she was a little like Athalie, dark, lithe, and pretty. There the superficial resemblance ended. Unlike Athalie, Meraude was small in stature, her face drawn and washed out. Pierre tried to visualize Athalie's face; it had become almost a game he played with himself, a way to torment himself, like a bully taunting a weakling. A hundred times he had tried to call up an image, but he could see only her expression, never her features.

He returned to more practical thoughts. Pursuit might not be very likely, but ambush would always be a possibility. Well, then, he thought, we will stand and fight, all together, as anyone would. These were the risks travelers always ran. Twenty-five armed men, not counting the two Protestants — or himself, he should count himself; indeed, if he were not so tired, he could count himself for two — they should, he reasoned, be able to scare off most bands of marauders and hold out against all but the most determined. The breastplates of his men shimmered in the afternoon glare, a long line in front and back, rising and falling to the rhythm of the horses. His own armor, half-armor only for he had left off the leg guards, seemed intolerably heavy, a metal prison, stifling, suffocating. His clothing under the metal was wringing wet. He had stripped and splashed himself all over with water and donned a fresh singlet before leaving. It had helped at the time; he had felt a little more alert and resilient; but now his body seemed to sag beneath him and time seemed to have lost its pace and its meaning.

They reached the bridge to the Left Bank. The toll collector was on duty. Watching his man dismount and haggle with him, Pierre shook his head regretfully. It cost a pretty sum to pass thirty people and a baggage train. They were hardly an inconspicuous group, he thought with some misgiving, but being impressive had its advantages as well, at least he hoped it would. The bridge itself was deserted, all its houses closed and shuttered. Pierre stared ahead up the rue St. Michel to the Petit Châtelet, the defensive bastion of the Left Bank. His throat constricted nervously and he squinted against the glare. Was the gate open? Yes, the gate was open, but the portcullis was down and guarded.

Pierre spurred his horse and rode closer to Maurice. "Remember what I said," he rasped.

Reining up before the massive archway, Pierre drew himself up to his full height and stared down at the corporal of the guards. The officer looked sidelong at the armed retinue then back to Pierre.

"I must ask your business, sir," he asked timidly.

"You know me, corporal," Pierre replied.

"I see your colors, sir."

"I have the King's permission to escort my lady wife to safety. I also bring the King's orders to the provincial governors of Beauce and Touraine."

"If I could see the letters, sir. Just the King's seal, I mean," the corporal persisted.

"Sirrah, do you take me for a mere courier?" Pierre shouted. "A letter carrier? You have misunderstood me. I myself carry the King's word. I am his mouthpiece!"

"Forgive me, sir. I meant no offense. I'll ask the captain." The corporal hurried into the fortress. Time seemed to stand still. Maurice smiled sardonically at Pierre. The watch at the gate stood nervously around, their halberds catching the westering sun. As the minutes dragged on, Anne realized she was very much afraid. Pierre was just deciding that he had about an even chance of dispatching Maurice and fighting it out with the guards, when the corporal returned.

"Me and the Captain talked it over, sir," the corporal said. "Our orders were to let no one pass. But we figure that was for last night and was for the Protestants." He spat reflectively.

"The captain, he says the Duke d'Anjou is going south to give the scum the same medicine they're getting here, and about time it is, too." He spat again. "So we decided the orders didn't apply to your grace, and all. So, I'll pass you, and Godspeed to you, my lord."

Pierre said nothing but lifted a hand in acknowledgment. The corporal whose guttural French had become more heavily accented as he became nervous, seemed to find relief in resorting to the patois of his native province as he barked out commands. A flurry of movement and a dull crashing and grinding accompanied the lifting of the heavy iron grille. Out of the corner of his eye Pierre saw Maurice's face twist and his mouth open to speak. Instantly, Pierre leaned sideways and slapped Maurice's horse heavily on the rump, shouting, "Onward!" They cantered across the paving stones and onto the dusty road beyond.

As soon as they had cleared the outskirts of Paris, Pierre halted his little cavalcade. The first order of business was to bind Maurice's arms behind him. His protests were cut off by Pierre's curt observation that their pace would only be as rapid as Anne's litter, a trot at best, which should pose little more than inconvenience to so accomplished a horseman as Maurice.

Pierre turned to Marcel, the leader of his small band of men-at-arms, whose worried expression showed that he had little liking for this expedition. "The best I can think of for today is to get as far south toward Orléans as possible. After I've had some sleep, I may be able to think of a more elaborate plan. Ultimately, we have to get the women and these Protestants to safety beyond the Loire."

"Well, my lord," Marcel replied, "how are we going to get across the Loire? And what are we going to do for shelter. Shall we try to get to Montlhéry tonight? There is a decent inn there, as I recall."

"No, Marcel, we cannot risk a town yet. We'll try to get as far as we can, but I am afraid we'll have to sleep along the road. While we are on the road, I hope we will be taken for what we look like, a group on the King's business escorting the Duchess and her ladies. I don't want to be questioned too closely, and I don't want our movements to be more obvious than need be. I'm counting on a few days while the butchery back there runs its course and is stopped. By then I hope to have thought of something; for now, let's get moving. Let two of your lads ride beside the Sieur la Renaudie. Kill him if he tries anything," he concluded, raising his voice at the end for Maurice's benefit.

The paved road south was usually well traveled and thanks to the drought was in far better condition than usual. They made surprisingly good progress, despite the infirmities of the wounded man and Anne. A little before sundown, Pierre called a halt and they bivouacked passably, if without comfort, under some trees near the road. A guard was mounted, horses were tethered, a meal of sorts was prepared, and Pierre, finally exhausted, put his troubles out of his mind, and rolling himself in his cloak, fell instantly asleep.

Chapter XXXI

he following day the company made a late start as Pierre was forced to dispatch Marcel and two others to ride ahead and secure provisions at Montlhéry, which they reckoned would be the next town. Marcel returned at about 11 o'clock with a supply of victuals, but ashen-faced at the horrors he had found. "There's been trouble in the villages, too, my lord," he said. "Just like Paris, but somehow it was worse, seeing just one or two cut up like that." Realizing he would have to be prepared for trouble, Pierre had the Protestants ride with Anne in the center of the group. He rode with Maurice to ensure his silence, although the prospect of hours in Maurice's company under these circumstances was scarcely appealing.

The day's ride proved that Marcel had not exaggerated. Marks of savagery were fresh in nearly every town they passed. The remains of a house smoking at Montlhéry, a shop pillaged at Arpajon, a makeshift gibbet outside Étampes, on it a man in a torn black robe, turning slowly in the warm breeze. A nasty mob gathered in Étampes itself, and only a determined show of force at last opened the way without the bloodshed Pierre had begun to fear. He became increasingly fearful for his Protestant charges as Meraude repeatedly gave way to bursts of tears at the sight of the mutilated bodies, grotesque in the August sunshine, that they passed throughout the day.

That night they took shelter outside, in a wooded area that seemed free of habitation. Pierre decided that as secrecy was not possible, they ought to try to appear as a military escort and perhaps by bluff escape attack. On his instructions his men built a large fire to keep off animals and human marauders.

Later, around the fire, they talked among themselves of the massacre and its grisly aftermath in the countryside — nothing else seemed important. At first, Pierre found conversation with the Protestants difficult, feeling the constraint one feels with the recently bereaved. What was there to say — they had all suffered such terrible loss, and had been exposed over and over that day to ghastly reminders of how near and continuing was the savagery.

The situation for Pierre, as much a pariah as these Protestants, did not make things easier, for he was not accustomed to think of himself as a fellow outcast; no, he wanted to imagine himself a knight errant righting wrongs and acting chivalrously. Meraude looked at Pierre with a mixture of curiosity and pity that made him feel uncomfortable. Damn it, he thought, one did what one had to do; he wanted no one's pity.

Talk around the fireside stumbled and faltered. Anne had maintained a sullen pout since they arrived. Pierre glanced at her profile glowing in the firelight. How beautiful she is, he thought. It amazed him, not for the first time, that without apparent effort even in these wild surroundings, she contrived to look perfect, her blonde hair elegant, her gown arranged gracefully around her figure. A feeling of sadness swept over him. Sadness for Anne, sadness for himself, sadness for the kingdom.

The old Protestant broke the silence first, mumbling to himself, then raising his voice until he was fairly shouting of his losses and the cruelty of fate.

"I've left all my sons behind in Paris — all three, dead!" he wailed. "There is no future. My line is dead! I have nothing left, nothing, nothing! That's what your people have done to me," he cried, turning and pointing a bony finger at Pierre.

Curiously, the old man's volubility loosened other tongues as he continued his keening lament, "Cruel, bloody papists! Worse than the Romans who slaughtered our ancestors, you are." The young Protestant, whom Pierre had taken for the old man's son, began to reprove him with the greatest respect.

"Please, my lord," the young man said to Pierre. "All he has said is true and I fear it has unhinged his mind a bit. He came to us with his sons from Geneva only two months ago. He is one of Théodore de Bèze's closest friends, and he worked with Calvin himself in developing and regularizing our religion in Geneva. The Admiral," and here tears welled up in his eyes, "the Admiral himself asked him to come to Paris. He had hoped for so much with the King's protection. Now the Admiral is dead, and our church is dead. Please don't blame him, my lord. We all owe you our lives, and he knows that, too."

"I am not offended, Monsieur," Pierre replied. "I do not begin to understand what happened. I don't think any of us do. I cannot really believe there can be such violence in so many people."

"You don't understand, you say." The old man's eyes glowed like coals. "Well, I'll explain it to you. These are the last days and we are the saints, and the demons of Babylon are set upon us to cut the sheep from the goats! Horribly the saints must suffer, but for a time only. Then I say to you, the Lord himself shall come, with fire unquenchable and you and all your brood with the whore of Babylon shall perish forever in the lake of everlasting fire!" He broke off in a fit of what might have been coughing or weeping.

Pierre found the old man's ranting unpleasant, and he did not like the mutterings he could hear among his men. He shuddered at the thought of a mutiny and his own people joining in the carnage.

"Peace, old man," Pierre said firmly. "Not all of our faith wish you ill. If there were only some way we could live together in peace."

"There can never be peace or compromise," the young Protestant shouted. "If any jot or tittle of the truth is sacrificed, the whole becomes false!"

"I don't understand how you can say that," Pierre remonstrated. "Your own people don't all believe the same things — which one then is the Truth? If you say there can be no compromise because you cannot trust us — that I would understand after what has happened. But to say no compromise as a matter of principle is madness."

"Madness, is it?" The young man's cheeks reddened. "It is written in the Scripture, 'What does it profit a man if he gain the whole world and lose his own soul,' and again, 'If the eye offend thee, pluck it out, for it is better to enter into life blind than be thrown into Hell with two eyes.' There is no compromise in Scripture, my lord. 'Who is not with me is against me,' saith the Lord. We cannot talk of compromise in the face of such clear direction from Scripture. You, my lord, must join us if you are to be saved; you must not delude yourself with the idea of compromise," he concluded earnestly.

Pierre kicked a log with his foot. It was a fine night and if it were not for his cares and the danger, Pierre would have enjoyed it. His pause was so long that the young Protestant, thinking that he had been offensive, added hurriedly, "It's not that we don't recognize your kindness, my lord. Indeed, it is just because I believe you are a good man that I want to show you the error of your ways."

Pierre resisted the impulse of saying "young man" in reply, as the fellow was certainly at least as old as he.

"Listen," Pierre said, "I have heard all of this before. Trophime Daudet was my friend..." and here it was Pierre's eyes that filled with tears as the awful vision of Trophime falling beneath the blows in the Louvre flashed across his mind. "He was my friend. We talked often about your so-called Reformed Religion and he never convinced me of anything but his own sincerity. I have two cousins who are archbishops and an uncle in Rome who is a cardinal, and might have been Pope last spring, if it weren't for the Spanish. There have been many bishops in my family. And saints, too, we have had our share. I have no patience with your black clothes and ban on amusements. I myself have seen the statues broken, the lovely glass smashed, and churches that had been beautiful for centuries destroyed because you say they are 'idols.' I do not and cannot hold with it."

"You talk of statues, my lord. Your kind smash women and little children!"

"My friend," Pierre replied wearily, "I am not exactly part of a 'kind.' I am, after all, here with you. But even if what they did was a brutal outrage, it does not make your religion true. I will not see you harmed, but I will never hold with you."

Anne suddenly burst out in a torrent of abuse. "Then I do not know, my lord, who is the bigger fool, you or this fellow," indicating the young man with a wave of disgust. "Their boring cant sickens me, but you! You have got us into God knows what danger and for what?

"Rescuing three of these common dogs and you don't even sympathize with what they are striving for! Damn you, Pierre! These vermin have brought misery and war not only on themselves but on all of France! They have only themselves to blame. They deserved to be..." As she spoke the word "killed" into the horrified silence, Maurice sniggered in the darkness. Anne broke down into a spate of convulsive weeping.

Pierre helped her to her tent, then strode back into the firelight. "Now listen to me, all of you," he shouted, "We are on our own and in great danger. I will not have strife among us, about religion or about anything else. Anyone who starts dissension will have me to deal with, and that goes for you, too," he said to the young Protestant. There was dead silence. "Now, get some sleep, all of you. Marcel, mount a guard as we did last night. Call me if there is anything amiss."

As Pierre returned to his tent, Maurice, bound securely to a tree, made himself as comfortable as possible. He reflected to himself that all was not well in the ducal family, oh no, indeed, and he had a suspicion of the reason. With the skill of a practiced artist he thought of the amazing combinations of mischief that could flow from the several facts he knew, and no one else knew, nor knew that he knew. Indeed, as he fell into as deep a sleep as the tree root would permit, he thought to himself that he was in an enviable position, if it were not that he was bound hand and foot in the power of his hated stepbrother who was probably going to kill him.

* * *

By dint of an early start and few stops for rest they skirted Pithiviers and reached the northern edge of the forest of Orléans by late afternoon. Pierre, who had ridden silently for the better part of the day, now called a halt. He rode up to Marcel.

"I have to deal with him," he whispered, gesturing toward Maurice. "When I am out of sight with him, move off westward. I'll catch up."

He cantered up to Maurice and said, "This is as far as you are going, Maurice. Get off your horse. Unbind his arms, someone. Now, my dear brother, you and I are going into the forest for a little private discussion. Now! Run!"

Maurice stumbled and ran into the great forest, followed closely by Pierre trotting behind on Phoebus.

Pierre had planned for the moment all afternoon, but now that it had arrived, he was unsure of himself. There was every reason to dispatch his wretched stepbrother and get on with it. His responsibility for the horrors in Paris, now spreading throughout the land like some evil miasma was clear. Or was it? Had even Maurice any idea of the extent of the destruction he had set in motion? Pierre doubted it. The peasants in the last village had never heard of Maurice nor he of them. Yet they had hanged the Protestant blacksmith quickly enough and burned his smithy to the ground. Was Maurice responsible for that? In a way he was. In a way he wasn't. On a more practical level, it was plain that Maurice would try to kill him as soon as he was able to and it would be only prudent for Pierre to rid himself of that danger. And then again, his sniggering at the corpses, his utter lack of sorrow, made him odious in Pierre's eyes. Odious as he had always been, breaking, stealing, hurting, when Pierre was a child. He called to Maurice to stop. They were deep among the great oaks of the forest. The westering sun dappled the ground between them.

Maurice turned and looked up at Pierre. The look of panic in his eyes and his pasty color showed what he feared. He expects what he would surely do to me, if our places were reversed, Pierre thought. He regarded Maurice for a moment of silent contempt.

365

He thought of the almost reflexive ease with which he had killed in Paris. A great longing to rid his sight of Maurice rose black within him. With an effort he forced the feeling down.

I cannot kill him, not like this; the thought became a certainty.

He leapt down from his horse and stood facing Maurice, his sword inches from his breast.

Terror overcame Maurice, who fell to his knees, whimpering, "Don't murder me, Blondel! You haven't even asked me how it all came about. Let me explain..."

"What is there to explain," Pierre snapped. "You pretended to resume your father's religion. You palmed yourself off as a hero's son. You played the Judas goat and led your people to the slaughter. I don't know what de Retz promised you, or threatened you with, and if I didn't know you so well, I might be curious. But you see, I do know you, Maurice. I know... Oh, hell!" he cried out, "What's the use? What's the use of saying anything to you!" The image of Trophime Daudet flashed again before his eyes and his knuckles whitened as he gripped his sword.

"You can't kill me, Blondel." The statement was meant to be fact, but it contained far more hope than Maurice had intended.

"Even though you have the blood of hundreds, no thousands, on your hands? Friends of mine, and yours, too, supposedly." Pierre smiled sardonically. "Can't I now? I am the avenging angel!" he shouted and brandished the sword.

Maurice's eyes widened in panic, but he hissed, "Vengeance is mine, saith the Lord. Are you pure enough to be His sword?"

"Were you?" Pierre replied bitterly. He shrugged and lowered the sword. "Throw me your purse and take off your clothes."

Maurice, relieved, giggled nervously, but made no move to obey.

"Damn you, move!" Pierre exploded, striking Maurice on the buttocks with the flat of his sword. "Perhaps I won't kill you in cold blood, but so help me God, if you raise my wrath, I will!"

Maurice chucked over his purse and fumbled with the lacings of his doublet. Pierre examined the purse, removing the few gold pieces, and smoothed out the folded parchment he found at the bottom. Wryly, he read the warrant for his own arrest drafted by Gondi and signed by the King, or at least in his name. He put it in his pouch and continued inspecting Maurice's belongings for weapons. He examined the boot heels and put the boots in his saddlebag. Panic had again returned to Maurice's eyes.

"Blondel! Don't take my boots!" he whimpered. "If you leave me here with no weapons, no money, and no boots, you might as well kill me. It will be murder just the same."

"Here," said Pierre contemptuously, throwing the boots at Maurice's feet. "Don't ask for anything else. Whatever I leave you with will be used against me. We both know that." He sprang to his saddle, wheeled his horse, and cantered away without another word.

"Well, my lordling," Maurice said to himself as he pulled on his boots. "Old Noiret is still alive and has a few things in store for you. I can't do much until I get back to Paris, but then we'll see. Oh, yes, indeed. We'll see."

* * *

At a full gallop, Pierre soon overtook his party. Marcel dropped back beside Pierre and reported that they had proceeded without incident. He cocked his head quizzically in the direction of the forest and drew his finger across his throat. "No," said Pierre quietly, "I didn't."

"Well, you know best, my lord, I'm sure." Marcel answered. "But that one is a snake if I ever saw one. You are in danger so long as he breathes."

"Perhaps. No, well, Marcel, of course you are right. But he can't do us any harm until he can hobble back to Paris, and that will take him some days, maybe even two weeks. Time enough for me to get to a safe place. I couldn't kill him in cold blood. That was all there was to it."

"Well, I know what the Duke, your father, would have done."

"Damn it, man," Pierre roared. "I am the Duke now, and don't you forget it!" He passed his hand wearily across his eyes. "I'm sorry, Marcel, I didn't mean to shout at you."

"Beg pardon, my lord, I meant no offense. It's just that I've been in service to your family for a long time. I've never liked that stinker and it sticks in my throat to see him go against you after your father practically rescued him and his mother."

Pierre gripped Marcel's arm affectionately as they rode along together.

"Excuse me, my lord, you said a place of safety. I've been wondering where we were headed."

"So have I, Marcel, old friend. I had thought of crossing the Loire at Orléans, but entering a city like that was out of the question with my stepbrother. And I don't dare expose our Protestant guests to more than we can handle in the villages. Still, they are going to have to cross the Loire to get to La Rochelle. The best plan I have been able to think of is to head southwest and pass south of Châteaudun.

"The Beauce plateau is mostly flat grainfields, and we can make as good time on the back roads as on the main ones. We'll hope this madness hasn't reached as far east as Tours. Somewhere between Blois and Tours we ought to be able to cross. What do you think?"

"I agree on the direction, my lord," Marcel replied thoughtfully, "but can you risk this company taking a boat? When we get closer, I and a couple of the lads can reconnoiter one of the bridges. It wouldn't be a problem, but for the Protestants." He sighed, and it was plain he wished he could leave them behind.

"Protestants, Marcel?" Pierre smiled ruefully. "You are forgetting you are escorting a fugitive and a traitor, that's what it says in the warrant La Renaudie was carrying."

"Traitor! God's Blood!" spluttered Marcel. "My poor lord! The swine! The filthy, lying swine!"

"Calm yourself, Marcel. I will not be caught. But we cannot, I cannot, risk a major bridge crossing. Messengers from Paris may well have been there before us. But come what may, Marcel, I, at least, must cross the Loire."

"Then I don't know, my lord. I really don't know."

They rode on in silence, and rode on again the next day and the next. The countryside, pleasant at first with its golden brown color under the soft, blue sky, began to become irksome, as each day brought more of the same flat farmland punctuated by the darker smudges of villages on the horizon with their low houses and squat church towers.

They made good progress west and south and the uneventful days began to make even Pierre feel more secure. This sort of trip did not seem much different from others they had made, albeit with more pomp and comfort, across France's granary.

But closer contact proved that the first impressions of health and serenity were deceptive. Too many fields were fallow because of lack of seed; the peasants they saw in the fields had the preoccupied, withdrawn look of people who are not yet desperate, but are full of foreboding. The sadness of the land began to affect the travelers' spirits, subtly transferring their individual emotions of shock and rage into a more universal sense of helplessness before the menace of nature. They began to talk of farming, the weather, of food and famine, of subjects that would have seemed trivial a week before, but which seemed to emerge as a basic bond underlying their own differences and uniting them to the peasants they passed.

It was in the forest of Marchenoir, on the fourth day, when they had forgotten to be afraid, that what Pierre had dreaded finally happened. The road, dark in the shadow of the ageless oaks and cool, blissfully cool — rounded the outcropping of a jut of rock, and they were ambushed.

Flight was out of the question; Pierre gathered his men in an elipse facing outward protecting the women, the old Protestant, and his wounded companion. Pierre peered into the gloom. He guessed their foes numbered at least thirty and maybe as many as fifty. As they slowly materialized from behind the trees and rocks, they appeared a motley crew as to both armor and weapons. Some, who seemed to be German mercenaries, wore colorful capes under their shoulder guards and feathers in their helmets. The others were less easy to place, having nothing distinctive about their armor. Their weapons included pistols and several arquebuses, as well as swords and lances. Their faces were invisible behind their lowered visors. They made little sound as they moved to encircle the party.

A voice boomed from Pierre's left; he could not be sure which was the speaker, but judged from the accent that the man was French and from the south.

"A prettier pack of papists I've never seen — rich looking, too."

"Sirs," Pierre called out, "we are traveling light — there is little to be had from our baggage but food. If you are hungry, we will share it with you."

"Break bread with you papist swine? Not on your life," the helmeted figure retorted, "which I'll add isn't worth much since I have my pistol pointed at your head! We'll eat your food all right but we'll dispense with your company."

A harsh laugh rippled around the circle at their leader's pleasantry.

Pierre had by then identified the speaker, near and looking straight at him, and said, "Sir, we have women in our midst..."

"There were women killed and children, too, by all accounts, in Paris, Orléans, and La Charité and... everywhere. Why are your women sacred while ours are of no account?"

The young Protestant urged his horse forward, "Monsieur," he said to Pierre, "perhaps you are too proud to point out our situation to these good people, but..." He broke off, then shouted to the southerner, "This man is indeed a papist, but not like the others of his faith. He saved me — and that old man and that girl — at the risk of his own life. He smuggled us out of Paris in his retinue — and we three are Protestants!"

"So you say," the man rumbled.

"For God's love, man. I come from Montauban and by your voice I'd say you are from Toulouse. We are countrymen of the same county and followers of the same religion. Would I say this if it weren't true?"

"To save your skin you might."

"And this," the young man shouted, pointing at the sling holding his broken arm, "where did I get this, fighting reiters?"

"Maybe," the man replied, but there was a good-humored, if sardonic ring to his muffled voice. The man lifted his visor, revealing a hooked nose and a thick, curly beard. "I believe you, young sir, and for your sake and our Religion's sake, I will pay your debt to this Catholic lord — his life for yours."

There was a disappointed rumble from the surrounding cavaliers. At this, the leader added, "But we'll take up your offer of food."

They roasted a stag, shot by Pierre's men earlier that morning, and while they waited, shared big, round cheeses, bowls of salted herring, and flacons of strong Burgundian wine. The meal, and perhaps especially the wine, brought out an unexpected conviviality in the group. Even Anne forgot her petulance, the wine perhaps having gone to her head. With much giggling and many exaggerated gestures, she flirted with the hirsute Protestant leader, comparing him to Henri of Navarre to flatter him. This amused Pierre, as at Paris Anne had made it no secret that she despised the Protestant prince whom she considered an uncouth and callow youngster.

It was soon apparent that the Protestant band was making its way southwest across France with all possible speed, heading for the haven and rallying point of La Rochelle. Pierre consulted the three Protestants, then begged the bearded leader to allow the trio to join the trek to the Coast. At first, his request met with considerable reluctance, but the old man, grown garrulous again in his cups, broke down all resistance with his pleas.

Thus, the next morning, after the Protestant band departed, Pierre and Anne found themselves alone with their retinue on the road to the Loire. At midmorning, they had come to the end of Marchenoir forest, and there, at the forest's edge, in the lee of the outer trees facing the sunny plain, they stopped for a rest.

"Anne," Pierre said, "here I am going to leave you."

She looked up startled, and, to Pierre's surprise, afraid. "You must see," he continued, "that it would be madness for me to go on with you to Plessis Gaillard. If I am pursued, and I am almost sure that I will be, that is the first place they will look for me. You must go there, however. You will be safe enough, they have no reason to touch you, and you will be able to act for me in the management of my property, assuming that I am left with my property, that the King's wrath does not run to confiscation. Thank God, you have some familiarity with what needs to be done. You can rely on the steward for the details. He seems honest and faithful."

"But Pierre, where will you go? Where will you be?"

"I don't know."

Anne put one hand on her belly and reached out the other to clutch at him in a pathetic gesture. "And the baby, must I be alone when it comes?"

In spite of himself, Pierre was touched by her fear and her forlorn expression. The irony struck him that he should be leaving her the first time she seemed to need him.

"I will let you know how you can reach me," he said. "When it is your time, and if you see that it is safe, then summon me and I'll come as quickly as I can."

Anne shrugged, infusing the resignation of the gesture with a touch of her normal petulance. "Can I not go to Villandry, my own place? Plessis Gaillard is so... so depressing."

"But Villandry is farther and less secure," he protested.

"I must have pretty surroundings — it's important to me," she demanded. "You never wanted to understand!"

"Well, you must do as you wish," Pierre replied. "You will have to depend on your own charms for security in any event. The walls of Plessis Gaillard won't be any more help than your gardens at Villandry unless you can persuade my pursuers that you had no part in this."

Anne bristled. "So it's to be up to me! And none too easy a task you have set me. So far as I can see you have ruined everything by insulting Gondi, flouting the King, harboring his enemies, and even mistreating your own stepbrother." Anne was warming to the fight, her voice rising shrill. "At least he knows enough to be on the right side! At least he was obeying the King, not fleeing across France like some bandit chief!"

"Anne," Pierre interjected. "Anne, you do not understand, and whatever you do, beware of La Renaudie. He will stick at nothing to finish me, that I know for sure. Now you must go."

"Then go I shall, my dear Duke, if you still are one, that is!"

370

Anne would have flounced off dramatically but her position, reclining on a litter, made that gesture impossible. She compensated by turning her face away. Her golden hair, as the sunlight struck it, was dazzling.

Pierre summoned Marcel and explained the situation to him. "Go west 'til you're past Vendôme and then go south toward Tours, that would be my choice, but you'll have to see how the land lies as you go. You should have no difficulty without me, and I, well, I at least can cross the Loire in a boat without too much suspicion being roused."

Marcel nodded and turning aside, passed his sleeve across his eyes. "God go with you, my lord. I'll see your lady safely home. And I'll come when you want to lead a rising or something, just send word." He broke off again to wipe his eyes.

"No, Marcel, old friend, I do not see that in the future. I have a task to do, then try to get reinstated. But I have to stay alive to do that, don't I?" Pierre gripped Marcel's arm, then released him.

Pierre watched Anne borne away by his men, then he turned south. Soon he stopped again, for no reason except to savor the beauty of the country and the new joy in his heart. The road sloped gently down from the plateau, and in the blue haze of the horizon, Pierre's eye was caught by a shiny ribbon of water, the Loire at last. This is my country, he thought, and I am free, free as the wind. Now I can make speed, make speed to Fontevrault, to Athalie.

Chapter XXXII

The July morning was clear and hot. Even in the Abbess's garden, shaded by lime trees and perfumed by roses, Athalie was uncomfortably warm. She had cut short her late morning stroll and seated herself on a stone bench with her back against the wall of the great church. She looked and felt clumsy, heavy, and huge. Overdue, old Mathilde, her nurse, had said. "That happens with the first," she had added uncomfortingly. "Your mother was overdue with you, too." And she died, thought Athalie, without saying the words.

The air was heavy with the rich summer smells of flowers and earth. Through the open window of the church the psalms of the morning office rose and fell like gentle breathing on the warm current of the breeze. In the silence between the verses, the bees droned an accompaniment. Athalie was peaceful, replete. If this moment could only be prolonged, but it would not last. Her time was almost come and then what? Then she would have to put her mad plan into action, leave the comfort and security of her aunt's love, and go into what?

Athalie glanced idly at the flowers now drooping a little in the heat, but still profuse. How her aunt had beamed with pleasure at the bouquets Athalie had taken to arranging for her guest table. Flowers and gardens were a passion she had not realized she had, until the Abbess's enthusiasm had kindled her own. Since summer they had spent much of the Abbess's all-too-brief leisure time in the garden or discussing plants, their history, care, and uses. She had intended to make another bouquet, but it was too hot, and she felt weary of her size and ungainly appearance.

She thought back to the morning in May when she had realized with certainty that come what might, she would never abandon her baby. May, June, and July had passed peacefully enough except for the too frequent confrontations with her aunt on the subject of her future. The lazy months had seen a true contest of wills between the young woman and the Abbess, and often Athalie emerged feeling as though she had been beaten with rods.

"You must, you must think of your position!" the Abbess had stormed.

"Does a woman forget the babe at her breast, or a mother the child of her womb?" murmured Athalie, quoting Isaiah.

"You dare quote scripture to me, young lady?"

"It is scripture, nonetheless," Athalie whispered, her eyes downcast.

"We will speak more of it later," said the Abbess, turning her back and marching off.

And so it had gone. First silent, sometimes placid, sometimes surly or cowed, Athalie mulishly refused to budge from her resolve.

"Your father came here with your mother the year before you were born," the Abbess said one evening. "It was the first time I saw her. I was not the only one in the family who raised an eyebrow at your father's choice for a wife. But he was a masterful man. He always got his way, usually by reason of his charm, though he could use force if he had to, and did. He was a handsome man, too. You have his eyes, child, though most of the rest of you favors your mother.

"Ah, me," the Abbess sighed. "I braced myself to receive her in charity. I lectured myself on not judging others, but the family is the family." Her old face softened as she recalled the meeting.

"It was an evening in May when they arrived. The apple and pear trees were in flower and it was warm. Your father helped her, lifted her practically from her litter, and she approached to kiss my ring. You will smile, Athalie, but I never believed in love at first sight. After that, I did. There was no more talk about family, and to be just, her connections were every bit as illustrious as ours, even if they were Italian. But her charm, her wit, her gentleness. I have never met a more tranquil person. Peace descended on any room she entered, yes, and a kind of joy, too. She put everyone at ease, she brought out wit and charm in everyone else. She never paraded her learning, but her scholarship was awesome. Yet in conversation she always managed to make her partner appear to be the clever one. Ah, it was a pity God called her from us. And how like her to have left behind so much of herself in you, my child. Athalie, Athalie, you must see reason. You are too good to just drop out of the world."

That had been the worst time.

The psalm ended. Like a graceful arabesque in the warm air, the antiphon for the next psalm hung suspended, so sweet, so slow. She should be inside singing with them, Athalie thought. A year ago she would have been. A year ago she would have remained after the office for a half hour of silent prayer. Lately she had become irregular about the offices that were not absolutely mandatory. And when she attended, she found her mind wandering into the most unlikely places. She found that unnerving, not just because her devotions were not supposed to be like that, so she had always been told, but also because she did not like her mind to wander. She was used to her mind being a careful, quiet, orderly place where facts and opinions were weighed and judgments judged, fairly and correctly. During High Mass, which she still attended regularly to avoid offending the Abbess, her mind had taken to darting off anywhere. She had thought of her father, of Pierre's father, of Margot, of Aimeri Pascal, dear sweet man, how she would love to talk to him. Her mind had even had fantasies of a frankly and very realistically intimate sort about Pierre. It was these particularly that she felt were inappropriate, and so she had stopped going.

She had long since resigned herself to Pierre's silence. "Shattered by his father's death," and "took it hard, very hard," her uncle had written last spring. "Occupied by his estates," "much to look after," "bright future at Court," "his wife, Anne, with child," "early fall he would guess," and so on, and so on. Athalie didn't know much about estates, but she did know about the death of fathers. She remembered her own bereavement. Had it been like that for Pierre? Had he felt the tremendous emptiness where so much had been? It had been sudden; he, too, had had no time to prepare. She had loved her father. Had he loved his father? She supposed he had, in his way, but she doubted that he had ever said so. Why were men so reticent about what was so important, and for that matter, so obvious?

Athalie wondered about God. She had sinned, she knew that, and so she supposed she had been punished. But she didn't feel punished.

She felt happy. Not to have Pierre at her side, in her arms, was that punishment? It seemed an odd sort of God who would act like that, it was too petty and too far from the essence of the matter. She had had Pierre's love, and she had loved him. She had really loved him, which meant that she would always love him. Death itself would not end such love, she thought, so how much less a matter was this mere separation, even if it were always? Her beloved was happy, "he has a bright future at Court," she said the words over again to herself. If he is happy, how can I grudge him anything? How can that be punishment? And the child, surely that was a joy beyond hope and beyond price. Surely it would be blasphemous to think of the child as punishment. The child was more a reward than a punishment. But how could a thing be both a reward and a punishment? What kind of God would order things like that?

Many people, her Aunt Louise for one, would consider the blow to her social position a punishment. But that wasn't really right, either. That would be how her uncle Albert would see it, the loss of something he desperately wanted to have. No, in her aunt's eyes, Athalie's conduct was more a dereliction of duty, a failure to hold up her end, an act almost of disloyalty. It was not so much a punishment as a continuing sin.

Athalie vaguely felt that Catherine de Medici would see it similarly, but more opportunistically, that Athalie had failed to take advantage of a good situation, and worse, put herself out of the running for the glittering prizes there were to be won. The Queen Mother would suffer disappointment that one with promise should be unfulfilled, pique, and maybe anger that a pawn she could have moved on the board to her own advantage had been taken out of her hands. How strange, Athalie thought, leaning for a moment against the cool wall, that everyone sees or would see my trouble so differently. And none of them see it as I see it. She thought again of the baby and again she felt joy and gratitude. Here was love made flesh. Here was her own love, for her to nourish and care for. Beside this love, this tremendous thing, her duchy, her wealth, the crown that was perhaps hoped for her, indeed all the duchies and wealth and crowns in the world, were so much wind. She had not asked for them and had not wanted them and did not mourn their loss. She checked herself, for she had had this conversation far too many times with her aunt.

She respected the old Abbess more than the others because she knew Louise de Bourbon was entirely selfless in her implacable position. Athalie simply was her family. The family was all-important. Therefore, Athalie must act for the good of the family. It was a simple argument and it was one, furthermore, that she knew Pierre would understand, as his family was if anything older than her own. But if there was a God, if He still existed for her, if He might ever again hear her prayers, she was sure His name was not de la Roque. Whatever God might be, he was not the family. Yet wasn't she being asked to sacrifice to a god named "family"? Indeed, to sacrifice her infant child to that god? She shuddered, thinking of the worship of Baal so strongly condemned by the prophets. No, that could not be right. Life and love were the stars she sailed by. She could do nothing else.

She rose and strolled under the lime trees. With a start she realized that the chanting had stopped. The bell for the noon meal was ringing. She realized she had been a long time in the garden. She sighed with contentment. She knew she had decided something important, that life might be hard, dangerous, and painful from now on, but that nothing would swerve her from her path.

It grieved her aunt; it would anger the Queen Mother; it would frustrate Albert Gondi. They would all make a great deal of noise and might cause her much pain. They might, and probably would, strip her of her wealth and titles. She might be sent into exile. She might be reduced to the life of a peasant. She smiled in the sunshine. She was seventeen and her duty, as a shining road, lay plain before her. These other things did not terrify her.

* * *

That afternoon, as she was about to take her siesta, her pains began. "Nou-nou," she cried to her nurse, "what is happening?"

"It's your time, that's all," the nurse curtly replied.

Athalie burst into a fit of uncontrolled tears, clutching the old nurse's bony arm. "Nou-nou, I'm so afraid. My mother died, Nou-nou. I don't want to die."

"There, there, you'll be fine. It'll be a while yet, as this is your first. Rest and I'll tell the Reverend Mother."

The pains came and came and went and came again throughout the evening and into the following morning. Athalie, drained, cried out before noon, "Nou-nou, I can't, I can't." Then suddenly, the little girl was born.

It was very hot in Athalie's room on the second floor of the Abbess's palace; the bedclothes and Athalie's shift were wringing wet, and Athalie herself was lying back on the bed, exhausted, her white face smudged with fatigue, her hair dark with perspiration.

The old nurse bustled around, swabbing Athalie clean, changing the bed linen, lifting the girl up to pull off her shift and slip on a clean one. At last, she settled the pillows comfortably behind Athalie's head and covered her tidily with a fresh, cool sheet.

"There," she said, "good as new."

Athalie sighed. "It was so hard, Nou-nou."

"That's all right, dear. Now, it's over."

Tears filled Athalie's eyes and slowly ran down her cheeks. "I was afraid."

"Afraid?" the old nurse replied with a pretense of outrage. "Afraid? There was no need. Yours isn't the first I've delivered, you know. You may not remember, but I delivered you."

"And my mother died," Athalie whimpered.

"Such things are in the hands of God. You'll do well enough if you do as you're told, and right now what you need is sleep."

"Where's my baby?" Athalie demanded with surprising force.

A lay sister, a former farmhand who had assisted the nurse in her work, passed the baby to the old woman, who tucked it gently under the sheet in a crook in Athalie's arm.

The baby was a tightly swaddled white bundle, above which appeared a strangely elongated head with puckered, angry red skin.

"Why does she look so strange, Nou-nou?" Athalie asked in an anxious voice.

"Strange? Why, she's a beautiful baby."

The door opened softly, and the Abbess entered.

Athalie grinned lopsidedly. "I did it, Mother. You see?"

The old nurse harrumphed disgustedly. "The girl's fey — crying and laughing. And, Reverend Mother, complaining about the baby! Tell her she's a lovely little girl, so the silly wench can give over this blather and go to sleep."

"I cannot claim any expertise on the newborn," the Abbess replied, "but if it's healthy, that's all that counts."

"Daughter," she said to Athalie.

Athalie blinked sleepily.

"Today is the feast of St. Anne. Anne would be a fitting name."

The girl's eyes widened. "No," she said in a clear, loud voice. After a pause, she looked down at the baby and murmured, "I have decided to call her 'Gabrielle.'"

* * *

The next day, Athalie was attempting to give milk to the baby while the old nurse poured out a steady commentary, a mixture of instructions and reproofs. Without warning, the Abbess entered.

"What is going on here?" she demanded.

The old nurse replied volubly, "Reverend Mother, the girl's unreasonable. If I take the baby to change her clothing, she becomes hysterical. She has the vapors, I say. It's not unusual. Now, she is insisting on nursing the baby. I couldn't stop her, and if the baby's not nursed by someone, she'll starve. The poor thing was crying her head off!"

Athalie looked up with her eyes flashing. "And I told you, 'No.' I will not give my baby away."

"But child," the Abbess continued gently, "you must see by now a gentlewoman does not suckle her young like a cow. Even if the child were legitimate, and you could raise her as your own, you would have a wet nurse."

"No," Athalie cried out. "You're trying to trick me. You know I must keep the baby now, if I'm to keep her later. I can't stay here with Gabrielle. I must return to my estates. I must travel. Someone must be able to give her milk. Unless you have a traveling wet nurse, it must be me, if I'm to have her with me.

"Now, go away. Please. It's hard enough.

"I don't understand, Nou-nou," she said, turning to the old nurse, "there's so little milk and it hurts so much."

The nurse looked furtively at the Abbess, then moved to the head of the bed. Stroking Athalie's hair tenderly, she said, "It will come, little one. It will come."

* * *

On the Feast of the Assumption, Athalie bade her great-aunt farewell. The old woman was sullen and resentful, almost childishly so. Accustomed as she was to mastery over the people around her, she found her powerlessness in the face of Athalie's resistance baffling and frustrating.

She gestured to Athalie to be seated.

"You're a fool, girl, to travel so soon. It's been only three weeks."

"Farm girls deliver in the fields and get up to finish the reaping, or so I've heard it told," said Athalie, a little too pugnaciously.

"You aren't a farm girl, Athalie, for God's sake," the Abbess replied, her voice rising unsteadily, "for all you try to behave like one! I cannot, I cannot understand you!"

"I'm sorry, Mother," Athalie said simply. "I wish you could understand. It grieves me to hurt you, I would do anything else on earth to make it different, but I cannot give way on something so important."

"It's because it is important that your behavior hurts me," the old woman said peevishly. "I'm not a person to fret over trivia."

"I know." Athalie looked miserable. She felt torn between genuine affection and gratitude, and an overpowering desire never to have this conversation again.

"Well," the Abbess continued, "I've had the Queen Mother's letter asking for news of you two months now. What should I say to her?"

"As you wish."

"Shall I tell her the truth?"

"I don't see what good lying would do, what purpose it would serve, but I leave it to you," Athalie replied softly.

"You don't think your uncle Gondi will leave you in peace, in your precious Islette, do you?" the Abbess demanded sharply.

"Oh, it's all so impossible! If you were a man, you could abdicate your duchy, which would be foolish, but at least possible. Now, all that can happen is for Gondi as your guardian to take your place. I would rather bear your disgrace than see him as duke! That parvenu as head of the family — it is unthinkable! But he has, unfortunately, full power over your affairs. You have considered that, I suppose?"

"Please, Mother, we have been over this a hundred times. Anyway, what can he do?" Athalie straightened with proud defiance. "He can hardly marry me off or send me to a nunnery while I have my baby."

"He keeps your property 'til he does marry you off."

"Then he should be satisfied," Athalie retorted. "I will not ask much for my little household."

"You are a fool!" The Abbess's tones rang with bitterness. "And you, at your age, planning to live out your life like a hermit, but a hermit without religion, an outcast with an outcast daughter. What will become of her, do you think? We can only hope that God will free you both by gathering the child to Himself."

"How can you... Mother!" Athalie rose abruptly and turned to leave, but seeing the old woman crumpled within herself and defeated, pity penetrated and dissolved her anger. She knelt, kissed the Abbess's ring, and stroking the old hand, murmured farewell.

Chapter XXXIII

he little parish church at Luré was packed that morning, the Feast of Saint Bartholomew; all of the countryside it seemed wanted to get a glimpse of the Duchess who had come, it was said, to live among them. Athalie found she was gradually shedding her amazement at the mixture of curiosity, awe, affection, and respect she had felt as she entered the nave, preceded by Jean Paul, the old bailiff, and his wife, Louisette, both bursting with pride and obviously the envy of all their neighbors. Thus escorted, Athalie took her seat apart from the congregation under the old and rather faded canopy on the left side of the choir.

Poor Père Bernard, she thought. He had come out to Islette le château at her summons yesterday, and while delighted to welcome her at Sunday Mass, seemed discomfited by her request, indeed insistence, on a solemn *Te Deum* in thanksgiving. Pressed, he revealed his principal difficulty was the music, as she did not have, and he coughed apologetically, "the retinue your father, the Duke, who was," at which he crossed himself piously, "used to bring on his visits here." There had always been, he pointed out, musicians and a goodly group of singers, so that the ducal services had had a modicum of pomp and circumstance. It was said in the village, although as he had been here for only ten years, he couldn't vouch for

379

it, that the Duke, no musician himself, had continued the music established by his late wife, her ladyship's mother, and here he crossed himself again with equal piety. So he was sure her ladyship would see that her request was not practical, with only the village people, who could not read, let alone read music. Moreover, the service would already be longer than usual as it was the holy day of Saint Bartholomew.

Athalie, who had been sitting on the small terrace overlooking the millrace, all dappled with sun and shadow, burst out laughing. "Oh, Father," she finally said, "that is all past. I wish we had a great choir and a concert of musicians, but we don't and what is more, I doubt we ever will." She laughed again, and the priest began to look uncomfortable. "But the fact we are few, and the church is small, is no reason we cannot have the prayers sung. Why, you shall simply sing the whole *Te Deum* yourself. I'm sure God won't mind at all."

"The village people won't mind either, as they won't understand it."

"But I want it, Father. I have so much to be thankful for."

And now, as Père Bernard's not unmusical voice concluded the final prayers of the High Mass, Athalie stood as the priest began the ancient Prayer of Thanksgiving.

"*Te Deum laudamus*," he sang, his voice rising with surprising strength and beauty. "*We acknowledge you as Lord. All the earth venerates you, Eternal Father.*"

Tears came unbidden to Athalie's eyes as she looked down the nave at the crowd of faces, old, young, pretty, gnarled with age, as they were. My people, she said to herself, oh, my dear people. She had hardly known what possessed her to ask for the special service, at a time when all worship had become so difficult. Yet it had seemed so obvious, so right, once the idea had crossed her mind. Here I am in this tiny place, and most people I know would think I had lost everything worth having, but I feel so content, so certain, so at peace. And, she thought, God cannot very well refuse my thanks, whatever He may think of me and my prayers.

"*The glorious chorus of Apostles praises you, The company of the prophets, The white-clad army of martyrs.*"

As the priest's voice continued, she thought again how wonderful, how happy a chance that she had come here. The château — so it was called, but it was fancy or hope rather than fact — was smaller and much shabbier than she remembered. She had been twelve the last time she came here with her father, and it had been August, about this time of the year. Islette was far from being one of his principal estates, and its economic unimportance matched its unprepossessing dwelling. It was also the newest acquisition of the duchy, having been purchased a year before Athalie's birth from the impoverished remnant of the local nobility because her mother had liked the site. She had come to have great plans for it, but only the barest beginnings of her designs had been realized when her death stopped all further work.

All of the old buildings remained with their squat, round turrets and slit windows redolent of older times. Springing out of the west side, accenting its shabbiness, was an elegant row of marble arches, the framework of a new wing that was to have run along the Indre river. Vividly the memory returned of her father standing by the river, his hand on one of the marble columns, weeping. It had been the only time she had ever seen him in tears, and it had greatly disturbed her. He had not seen her lithe form withdraw behind an outbuilding, and they had never spoken of the incident.

The evening after her arrival at Islette, she had walked down to the Indre, and stood beside the unfinished wing. The slow green flow of the river seemed to echo the stately procession of the marble curves, overgrown though the bases of the pillars were. She tried to remember where her father had stood that day. She walked forward and put her hand on the marble. Mother? she thought. But Mother was not really a person she could summon up. She thought again of her father, how mention of her mother had always softened the gruff, old warrior. How happy she must have made him. Why hadn't he finished this wing? Why hadn't he finished all of her work? The idea burst upon her that she, heir of both of them, she would accomplish it. She would make an edifice here on the Indre as fine as Chenonceau. She would find the plans, or the builder, and.... She laughed at herself, standing alone in the weeds, alone in the world.

Islette was not just old, but small. It was soon clear that they had barely enough food for the winter. Its gardens had all run to weeds. The peasants looked none too prosperous, and although fresh fruit and vegetables were plentiful now, she wondered what next spring would be like. No, indeed, palaces cost a great deal and long before her mother's dream was made reality, the mill wheel would have to be improved, the roof over the hall repaired, and fuel for the winter secured. With what? she wondered. Jean Paul and Louisette lived comfortably enough in a small apartment in the château. Their son and his seemingly endless family lived in the mill, the château's principal industry, on a little island just downstream from the main property.

In theory all the grain in the surrounding area had to be ground there, but as Jean Paul had told her, with much wringing of his knobbled hands, the peasants were crafty and took their grain elsewhere. He was too old to ride herd on them, though God knew he had done what he could. Moreover, the harvest had been bad two years running; this year was the worst of all, he sighed, one of the worst he could remember.

Athalie smiled happily. There was so much to do, yet the prospect of doing it pleased her immensely. Indeed, she found the practical problems of establishing a household wonderfully occupying her mind. Strangely, she found herself explaining to Pierre how she was going to make the hall more habitable, or how the sweeping view down to the river was going to be as lovely as she remembered it, once the brush was cleared away next spring.

Gabrielle seemed strong, healthy, and growing. Athalie had again had to refuse Louisette's offer to get a wet nurse. It was apparently as much out of the question for old Louisette as it had been for her aunt the Abbess that she should nurse the child herself. Dear me, she thought, I am such a trial to them all, and she smiled again because she was seventeen and happy, and these things didn't seem to matter.

Have mercy on us, Lord, have mercy,
Let your mercy fall on us who have hoped in Thee.
In you, O Lord, I have hoped
I shall not be confounded in eternity.

The priest concluded the long chant, his voice, unaccustomed to so much exercise, a bit hoarse toward the end. He blessed the congregation, then turned and gave a special blessing to Athalie as she knelt at her elaborately carved, and so she thought, very uncomfortable prie-dieu.

Then Athalie resumed her seat on the ducal throne as the priest knelt before her and kissed her hands. They rose, and making a little procession, left the church, the villagers kneeling as Athalie passed. This ritual made her feel less odd than she had feared it would. She reflected that if she had not felt their love, she could not have gone through with the ceremony.

But from the day of her arrival from Fontevrault, when children, dogs, men, and women had clogged the road as she approached Islette so that it was hard to get into the courtyard, when the little girls had come forward presenting flowers, when the peasants had bowed with their baskets of fruits and produce, it had come to seem natural for her to accept their love and return it with gratitude and thanksgiving.

* * *

The next day Athalie was overjoyed to receive an entirely unlooked-for visit from Aimeri Pascal. Athalie made no pretense of hiding her pleasure as she bade him rise from his deep bow.

"A friend at last! Someone to talk to! But how did you know I was here? Where did you come from?"

"Which question do you want me to answer first?" he said, laughing. "It is all very simple. My main property is up the Indre across from Montbazon. The news of the arrival of the Duchess de la Roque has spread all over the region. I heard it only this morning from my bailiff, and, well, I came at once. It is only about a day's ride, nothing really," he concluded lamely.

"I am so glad to see you," Athalie said, elated. "You and your men must stay the night. I'm afraid the duchess's château is not very grand. But come, I must show you my little domain before it gets dark."

Taking his arm, Athalie led Pascal through the cleared area down to the river. The river, green and tawny, reflected the westering sun obliquely and provided Athalie with a backdrop for the rich images into which she transformed her tawdry gardens by her flow of words.

382

"You'll see," she said as they returned and entered the house, "what I shall accomplish. It won't take me long at all, but, as for now, I'm sure my hall is less grand than yours."

Aimeri glanced with embarrassment first at the plain red tile floor, then at the large bare room whose only decorations were an imposing but plain fireplace, some painted beams, and a few wooden armchairs. He coughed politely and admitted that he did have somewhat more furniture.

"You'll see," Athalie was repeating with the same enthusiasm, when following his gaze she saw that he was watching Mathilde emerging from the stairs carrying Gabrielle in her arms. Aimeri shuffled awkwardly and seemed at a loss for words.

Athalie put her hand on Aimeri's arm. "Now, old friend, you will meet the most important person here." She took the baby, still a tiny white bundle, but one whose face was now rounded and smooth, pink and endearing. The little girl crowed toothlessly. Aimeri looked bewildered from the mother to the daughter.

"Yes," Athalie said, "she is mine."

The dinner, though plain, was abundant. Their conversation roamed happily, if a bit awkwardly, through farming, gardens, peasants, the weather. Athalie, hostess in her own house for the first time, was flushed with excitement and pleasure.

Despite his awkwardness, Aimeri's face radiated love, and never more than when he tuned his lute after the meal and began slowly a lay of Ronsard:

"Comme on voit sur le branche au mois du mai la rose
En sa belle jeunesse, en sa première fleur
Rendre le ciel jaloux de sa vive couleur
Quand l'Aube de ses pleurs, au point du jour l'arosse;"

As appears as on leafy branch in May, the rose
In its shining youth, its early budding
Making heaven jealous of its vivid hues
When dawn's dewy tears at daybreak make it gleam.

Grace, within its blooms, and Love repose
Filling the trees and garden with its sweet perfume;
But, beaten down by rain, or too much heat,
Languishing, it dies, its petals falling one by one away.

Thus in your first young flowering
When heaven and earth were your beauty singing
By Fate you were slain; in ashes you repose.

For requiem take my weeping and my tears in showers
This vase of milk, this basket full of flowers

383

So that living or dead your form be naught but roses.

"Pour obsèques reçois mes larmes et mes pleurs
Ce vase plein de lait, ce panier plein de fleurs
Afin que vif, et mort, ton corps ne soit que roses."

As the last chord died away, Athalie, her eyes downcast, murmured, "So lovely and so very sad." She looked up and brushed her eyes. "He must have loved her very much. No one who has lost someone he loved could hear those verses without tears." She sighed and fell silent.

Aimeri moved closer to her and tentatively placed his arm around her shoulder.

"But Aimeri, the music, too, was wonderful. I'm sure I never heard that tune before. You must teach it to me, though I'm sure I couldn't do the runs you put in it. Where did you get it?"

"I made it myself, Athalie," he replied hoarsely. "I, I made it for you. Athalie, the baby makes no difference to me."

"Well," Athalie replied softly, "she makes a big difference to me."

"No, I'm sorry," he stammered, "I'm so clumsy. I mean, I would marry you gladly, and be a father... try to be a father... I mean, unless the father..."

"No," Athalie said sadly, "there is no question of my marrying the father."

"Is he dead?" he asked.

"No! no! Not dead!" she cried.

"Well, but you are free, you almost have a duty..."

"Aimeri," Athalie stopped him, putting her slender hand on his arm, "you are very kind and your kindness, no, your... your affection, means a great deal to me. But please, don't push me.

"You are so very dear to me," she said, rising and turning toward the fire. "Your goodness has warmed me ever since we met. But Aimeri, I just can't, I can't love you that way. Not yet anyway. Maybe never. Oh, I don't know. I don't know. But to know that I have a friend, not too far away — it's a help for me just to know it."

"Help!" he cried eagerly. "Of course, I will gladly help in any way I can. At least I can do that!"

"There really isn't anything I need," she said, "but I'm glad to know you're there."

"What do you mean there isn't anything," he protested. "I've been a gentleman farmer for a year now. I'm no expert, but compared with you, I'm an old hand. I can tell you, you need a couple of goats to keep the field cropped, you need one or two milk cows and at least ten chickens; you should be slaughtering a pig for salting, and you don't even have a pig; you need seed grain, manure... Athalie, unless you're planning on eating horsemeat, you need just about everything.

"It's not too late to get something into your barns," he went on briskly, now all business, "though most of the work must await the new year. I couldn't help noticing that your bailiff must have been ready for pasture in King Francis' time. Oh, Athalie, you must let me help you." He seized her hand and gazed imploringly at her.

Her half-hearted protests were brushed aside by Aimeri's eagerness, and warming to his subject, he went on into the night with methods and projects. Athalie found the mundane practicality soothing, although she understood little of the technical side.

Aimeri Pascal reappeared a week later. On the morning of the feast of St. Stephen the King, Athalie's astonished gaze fell on a small procession as it came to a dusty halt in front of the great door. There were two cows, small but fat and glossy; two oxen "for winter clearing," Aimeri said; a family of goats "if you don't need them all, you can always eat a couple of them"; and a wagon groaning under its load — slatted cages full of poultry; "The ducks will do wonderfully here and the rooster is a marvel — he crows so loud, he'll wake the miller down the stream"; a pig, already slaughtered and cured; two casks of new wine, "they grow it near Montbazon"; ropes of onions and garlic; and three platters of cheeses swaddled in wet cloths.

Athalie, choked with gratitude, was speechless and almost tearful.

Aimeri positively swelled with pride. "And that's not all," he said.

He motioned to a sturdy peasant in his entourage of men-at-arms to step forward.

"This is Étienne. He's my bailiff's son. He says he's hankering for a man's responsibilities, and I know he couldn't be better trained.

"Forgive my presumption, but couldn't you use an experienced man around the place? Your miller's boys seem willing, but somewhat simple..."

Athalie gulped and nodded.

"All that's for the work. Now for something that's part pleasure and part work." He reached into the wagon and brought out a large crate. He lifted out a puppy and handed it to Athalie. The puppy squirmed energetically, licking at Athalie's face. Athalie squealed and held the fuzzy body tighter.

"Put her down, or there may be an accident," Aimeri said, hastily. "She's older than your little one, eight weeks old at least. Now, she's nothing fancy — honest farm stock, but her mother's a hard worker and earns her meat, and if you've got flocks, you need dogs."

Athalie watched the round, fluffy, wobbly, floppy-eared, large-footed, multicolored mongrel trotting busily across the drive and suddenly began to laugh. Aimeri joined in and they rocked back and forth, laughing 'til the tears ran down their faces.

"You know," Athalie gasped, "Oh, Aimeri, you'll hate me, but with her tubby midriff and her important walk and her tan and silver fluff — oh dear! She reminds me of your mother."

Aimeri choked and laughed again. "You're so right and she's got a very sincere look, direct and kind, like my Mamá's. If you call her 'Amelie,' I promise I won't tell her namesake. I'm afraid she wouldn't appreciate the honor."

Athalie looked into his eyes. "You'll stay a while?" she asked.

"No, thank you. I cannot." Aimeri looked away, quickly. "We stopped the night at the farm of the tenant I told you about. He'd short-changed me, so to speak. It's hard for them in a year like this, but if you let them get away with it once, there'll be no stopping it. If we leave now, we'll reach home by nightfall."

Long after Aimeri's departure, the household bustled with excitement over the new acquisitions. Athalie scurried between the kitchens, the stables, and the chicken run, supervising, encouraging, and sometimes simply admiring.

At last, she stopped, breathless, on her way back to the house, and gazed over the lawn to the river. A new confidence welled up, deep inside her, adding a joyful vitality to what up to then had been simply a kind of dogged determination. Perhaps my life, this new life, will work out after all, she thought wonderingly.

Chapter XXXIV

The Queen Mother held the Abbess's letter in a hand which trembled slightly from the intensity of her emotions. She was filled with rage — a very catholic and universal rage which encompassed Athalie: "careless, thoughtless, little fool — and a hypocrite, too — oh yes! a hypocrite, and who would have thought it?"; the Abbess: "old schemer — she would have hidden everything from me if the situation had not gotten beyond her control"; and finally, ultimately, Gondi, *caro Gondino*, she mouthed the words to herself, as she laid the letter on the table. This last, this utter treachery, added to the other grievances with which in secret she taxed him, brought her silent, sullen resentment to the boiling point. He shall feel my wrath, this very day, this very morning, she said to herself.

She rang a small brass bell on the table and a lady-in-waiting appeared. "Send word to the Count de Retz to come immediately. I shall receive him in my gardens."

Early September had brought rain and a welcome breath of autumn chill to Paris, calm with a convalescent exhaustion after its frenzy on Saint Bartholomew's Day. Paris had seen horrors before and would see them again. But now, under cloudy skies, Paris was picking up its pieces, its irrepressible life flowing into the voids left by its orgy of destruction. Paris had long ago lost its innocence. But who, having seen its bestial ferocity, could ever feel wholly safe within its walls?

Certainly not Catherine de Medici, as she walked slowly westward along the Seine from the Louvre to the Tuileries. She savored the sense of release at finding a focal point for her blind, suppressed resentment of Gondi: for her suspicion that her confidence had been abused, for her fear of the consequences of what he had done, or rather of what he had made her do. The morning breeze tasted of autumn; it was refreshing and cooling; she felt the heat of her anger subside, to be replaced by an implacable, cold determination to reassert her mastery over her trusted minister. She was glad of it, knowing that she would be more effective if she were in complete control of herself.

Gondi could not be found in the Louvre and such was the congestion in the Paris streets that it was nearly an hour before he arrived at the gate to the Tuileries gardens. The delay did not improve the Queen Mother's humor. Gondi entered and walked toward the cool, shadowy bower which was his Royal Mistress's favorite haunt. He felt taut with inner tension. What could she want? he asked himself. What is new? What couldn't wait until this afternoon? As he approached, he appraised her discreetly, looking for indications of her mood. She smiled a stiff, pro forma smile, and gestured him toward a bench. He sat, adopting a rigid position, wary, and expectant.

"What news from abroad, my dear Albert?" she asked evenly.

"I thought we were to discuss that this afternoon, Your Majesty."

"What is the matter with now?" she snapped.

"Nothing, Your Majesty." He drew himself up. "Well, the German princes are — how shall I put it — unhappy, certainly, and suspicious. I have the impression they believe we have not been candid with them about the killings, and that somehow they think the troubles were too convenient not to have been planned."

"You will have to go to them."

"Yes, Your Majesty, it would be best. I shall leave as soon as I can get away. As for England, well — great distress, Coligny was very popular there, but more diplomatically expressed than I dared to hope. I believe when we explain to Elizabeth that the Protestants were planning an assault on the royal family, we will give her something that she can understand — the putting down of sedition is not, after all, a religious stance."

"Albert, what happened must not be allowed to affect our chances for Alençon's marriage alliance with Elizabeth."

"No," he replied smoothly, "I think it will all die down. The revolt in the Netherlands has petered out, as I supposed it would, without strong intervention by our French Protestants. Spain and the Holy Father, are, of course, delighted — they have congratulated us on taking hold of a promising situation and turning it to our advantage, indeed, for all Christendom. It was, of course, necessary to tell them every single death was intended, as it wouldn't do to have the Spanish realize we were powerless to control the mobs in Paris. I must say, my lady, it wouldn't do at all to have them believe that the Catholic party is stronger than the Crown."

"So," she said stiffly, "the Spanish have what they always wanted, don't they, my dear Gondi?"

He nodded complacently. "And so, my lady — those who are happy are very happy, and the others will get over it."

"How delightful," she replied, idly examining the roses at the border. "Delightful for them, I mean. But what about us? What about France?

"What happened here, Alberto, is bad enough. I will never forget it — like prisoners in the Louvre, no, like shipwrecked people on a raft in stormy seas. Do you remember how it felt, my dear Albert? The noise, the stench, the bodies in the Seine. I don't think my poor boy will ever get over it. You know, Charles is so very sensitive and — and, well, not strong.

"And now, it is spreading like some contagious infection, all over France, the same violence, the same carnage, the same pillaging. Everything we have fought for is lost." She slumped on a bench and covered her face with her hands.

"No, Madame, you take too bleak a view," he protested.

"Quiet," she barked. "I'm not through. The provincial governors cannot be relied on to quell the mischief. Each one suits himself according to his own predilections. Everyone is out for himself, isn't that the rule?"

"It is sure, Madame, that we must be prepared to take action ourselves. The Duke of Anjou has stressed the need for military preparedness, and I agree with him wholeheartedly. I have been investigating the financial possibilities for raising a large army, and am happy to report favorably."

"Indeed? And have you come into money lately, my dear Albert? Somehow, I feel very sure that you have. You look like a man upon whom Fortune smiles — for now." There could be no mistaking the menace in her tones and a quiver of apprehension passed over Gondi's face.

"Madame, I don't know what you're talking about. I meant a concerted effort between the bankers of Lyons and the Florentines, with loans possible from Savoy and the Holy See."

"More debt and more taxes — the usual solution, in short."

"But," Gondi continued earnestly, "on very good terms, I have been assured."

"Why such unexpected generosity? No matter — the terms can be as good as you want, but unless the money is a gift, we cannot afford it."

"We must afford it."

"Oh, yes, my dear Count. I know that. There is no going forward and no going back, and yet we must go forward. Whether we want it or not, civil war is upon us again. As usual, it seems my hands are tied. Go on back, tell England we did it for politics, and Spain that we did it for religion. My dreams are dead. Make whatever plans you wish with my sons. What you have started you must finish."

She looked away, her eyes hooded to hide her smoldering resentment. Gondi started to rise.

"And what of your protégé, the Duke de Galle. Where is he, my learned councilor?"

"I'm afraid I have no further word on him, Your Majesty. Now that order has been restored here, we can spare the men to track him down. He failed us all. He is disloyal and dangerous."

"It must be a blow to you, Albert. It did not escape my notice that you were helpful to him, no doubt expecting some return on the generous gift of your experience. What do you propose to do when your men find him?"

"He is dangerous, Madame. He ran through Paris killing people and he captured La Renaudie. Heaven knows what has become of that poor wretch in the hands of a madman like de Galle. I fear, Madame, that he may be too dangerous to capture. I shall suggest that my men dispose of him without undue risk to themselves."

"Do you not think it odd, Albert, that he bolted?"

"Why, no, Your Majesty. I admit finding it hard to fathom the old nobility, but Pierre's case is plain enough. He was obviously a Protestant sympathizer all along. You saw yourself how well Coligny liked him."

"Well, oh master of intrigue, no doubt a person like you would find it hard to understand a true nobleman, and I tell you, I think his running off very odd indeed. Coligny liked him for the same reason he liked his father. And as for being Protestant, he is too much the noble to embrace it for reasons of conscience, and I can't believe he would throw in with them for political reasons.

He had everything to lose and nothing to gain by such a move. No, Albert, I fear you have not riddled Monsieur de Galle rightly. You shall not have him killed. Capture him and bring him here. I shall hear his reasons from his own mouth. And do not tell me that your men had to do it as he was trying to escape. Why so pale, Alberto?"

"I beg your pardon, my lady," Gondi stammered. "It's just that it will not be easy to do as you command."

"But it is my command. I trust I make myself understood?"

"Yes, Your Majesty," he replied weakly. His mind was racing. *Why is she doing this? What has happened?*

"One more thing, old friend," she said, turning toward him, stretching her mouth into the semblance of a smile. "I have today received most interesting news of a different kind. If I tell you that it came by a letter from the Abbess of Fontevrault, would you know what the news was?"

"Yes, Madame, I..."

She held up a hand. "Do you know why I received this information? Because I myself wrote to the Abbess Louise asking for news, asking to be kept informed, because you see, my dear Gondi, I'm not the old fool you take me for! I knew I could not rely on you for honest information about your own ward, and how right I was!"

"But Madame, let me..."

"I know your dreams and your hopes, my dear Albert. You have coveted her property and her title since her father's death. Oh, what a plum — what a feather in your cap! Well, I had dreams, too. She is a little fool, but she is quality. I could have arranged a diplomatic marriage of importance to our state. And now? Your hopes and mine are equally dashed. She will be neither a nun nor a princess."

"But, Madame, she can still marry. Do you remember the son of banker Pascal, he was interested. He would still be interested."

"Oh, no doubt he would, Sirrah! and how convenient for you. *Il Gondino* becomes duke, and everyone lives happily ever after! Well, I tell you, my dear friend, I think that happy solution would be a mistake. It would reward you for dereliction of duty, and that offends me. You see, I hold you responsible for this — entirely responsible. She was your ward. Now she is disgraced, and flaunting the fruits of her sin."

"Madame," Gondi attempted weakly, "no one knows of it. You would not let me explain, but I myself learned of it only this week. I have spies everywhere, but none in the nunnery." He smiled timidly at his little joke; she smiled not at all.

"They were discretion itself at Fontevrault. My first report came after she returned to one of her estates. I... when she went to Fontevrault... I hoped, I assumed, it was her vocation that had called her back — for she told me herself she had a vocation."

The Queen Mother listened to the bitterness in Gondi's voice and was half-convinced of his sincerity. "I would not have believed that you could be ignorant of such a thing, but no matter. You are to blame, as much for your ignorance, as for your inaction." She turned away and gazed into the distance.

"But if what you say is true," she continued slowly, "then perhaps all is not lost. She can be made to put away the baby and return to Court. People will suspect — that cannot be helped — but her position is such that if it does not put her above suspicion, at least it makes suspicion almost irrelevant."

She faced him and shouted, "Gondi, I will give you one last chance. See to it that the situation is set right with all possible speed, and we will start anew. Otherwise, I will revoke the wardship. The Duchesse de la Roque will become a ward of the crown. Her income will go to the King — who needs it more than you — and you will have nothing further to say about her future."

"Madame, I will do my best, but..."

"Do as you will. I've told you what I will do.

"And Albert," she continued, her voice now mellow with sarcasm, "I would not dream of a dukedom too soon. Such things must be worked for, they must be deserved, by a long career of good service...."

"Madame, already I have served you long, as best I could."

"...good service. If I were well served, my life would not be the trial, the burden that it is."

"Madame..."

"Go. I'm tired."

* * *

Gondi fairly ran out of the Gardens to the street and boarded his litter unceremoniously. All the long way back to the Hôtel de Retz, he gnawed and worried at this new addition to the myriad problems which were already oppressing him.

He should have known, he thought, known that the silly wench had gotten herself into trouble, but with whom? He had never suspected because he had never seen anything to suspect — ah! she's a deep one, and no mistake; that the old... old... well, never mind, in Fontevrault would not lose the opportunity of getting in ahead of him with the Queen Mother, that the old, yes, God dammit, the old bitch, his Mistress, would have found out somehow, some way, and would make him pay for it.

An undifferentiated anger at everyone involved boiled through him and was gone, leaving only the unbearable certainty that he had been duped. If he had focused only on the matter of Athalie, it would never have gotten out of control, but there had been so many other things, and, yes! he must admit it, it had been as if he had had a blind spot. It was his hope that had blinded him and nurtured his inaction through the long months when he had been busy elsewhere. I have only myself to blame, he thought.

But all is not lost, he comforted himself. I will do everything the Queen Mother wants, but instead of freeing the girl to further her own silly schemes, she will be my pawn once again. If she will not be a nun, she will marry whom I choose and when I choose, and the Queen Mother will accept my choice and my terms. I will set it up so that she has no alternative.

A bitter surge of resentment possessed him momentarily. How dare she mock me and reproach me? I, who have served her well — better than she knows. And why should I not have my reward? and my revenge! I will be even with them all. The emotion ebbed, leaving him drained.

He turned back to the practicalities of the situation. Whom should he send? Which of his agents could be trusted with the admittedly unpleasant task of getting rid of the baby and bringing the girl back, presumably against her will. Gondi smiled a tight smile thinking how the choice would normally be obvious. But where was La Renaudie?

Gondi recognized with grim fatigue that his train of thought had come full circle. There were so many problems — whether to restrain the provincial governors from bloody excesses against the Protestants, as he had been ordered by the King, or to urge them on and please the Spanish; whether to open negotiations in La Rochelle in an attempt to head off the next civil war; how to get his hands on young de Galle and close his mouth before he did irreversible harm; how to do that in the face of the Queen Mother's command to speak to him herself. He clenched his teeth. That interview, at least, must never take place.

Just when I need him most, he thought, that idiot of a La Renaudie has to get himself abducted by the very man he was sent to capture. And God alone knew what Maurice might not do or say under stress, Gondi reflected, remembering, with distaste, La Renaudie's wild, indecent elation, his ardor, his — lust, was frankly the word — lust for blood, during that awful night. Gondi shuddered. He did not shirk from blood when it was necessary, but he did not relish it. The thought that Maurice was even more dangerous than Pierre struggled toward recognition and was ruthlessly suppressed. I must get him back, I must see what state he is in and use him if I can. I need all the help I can get.

The slow, bumping pace of the litter provided a momentary focus for his anger. He thrust his head through the curtains and let out a raucous yell at the bearers, who continued their slow, weaving jog with massive indifference. At last, they drew up before the imposing entrance to Gondi's hotel.

Gondi walked thoughtfully through the courtyard, through the great hall, oblivious to its treasures, to his study. As he reached the door, he was met by a flustered Julio.

"Sir," the youth blurted, "I knew how much you wanted to see him, so I took him straight into your study. He was so awfully foul-tempered. Swore. Said he wouldn't wait anywhere else. So I thought..."

"For Christ's sake, man," Gondi broke in angrily, "can't you be a little coherent. Who are you talking about?"

"Why, Maurice, sir, La Renaudie. I thought..." He tried to continue, but Gondi thrust past him, pushed the door open, and strode into the study.

Maurice was sitting at Gondi's table, which was clear of all papers, Gondi having long since learned to lock everything in a coffer to which he alone had the key.

The young man's black clothes were rumpled and stained, his boots were caked with mud, his hair needed cutting, and his nose was peeling from sunburn. Gondi stopped in the middle of the room and stared at him appraisingly. How like him, he thought, to rush in to see me without taking the time to wash himself or brush the dirt off his clothes. How melodramatic! Still, he has lost that mad, exalted look he had when last I saw him. Now he looks merely tired and frightened, quite subdued really. Gondi nodded to himself complacently.

Indeed, Maurice did feel subdued. Behind him was an arduous and humiliating trip surviving on stolen food, several days on foot, the rest on a horse borrowed from a local seigneur whose heart was softened by Maurice's story of having been attacked by robbers.

Maurice was tired, and even worse, he was afraid; afraid of Gondi's wrath at his setback, afraid of the danger Pierre posed, afraid of his own powerlessness. Gondi's silent attention intensified his nervousness. He shifted and moved to get up from Gondi's chair.

"No, no, my dear boy," Gondi raised his hand. "Stay where you are, if it makes you feel better. I will sit over here by the window."

An awkward silence fell. Maurice ran his tongue around his parched lips.

"Well, well," said Gondi, beaming benevolently. "I hardly thought to see you again. Young Pierre has shown a regrettable lack of brains or character, or both, in letting you make your way back to your uncle Gondi. Now, we can turn your good fortune into his misfortune and teach him the folly of pusillanimity. Still, however much of a fool he was, he certainly made a bigger fool out of you, didn't he?"

Maurice seemed to settle into himself as his slouch deepened.

"Funny, when you stop to think," Gondi continued. "Pierre seems to have a real penchant for getting his enemies at his mercy, and then letting them go. Like that episode with Augustin Pascal. He could have killed him, and no one would have blamed him. By the by, I've taken Pascal into my service. He's not without ability. And of course, anyone in his right mind in Pierre's situation would have killed you out of hand. Luckily for you, Pierre's not like his father. No ruthlessness. Old de Galle was tougher."

Gondi fell silent, puzzling over the character of Pierre, considering him in a novel light, as someone to be reckoned with — as an adversary instead of someone inconsequential — the fledging son of a friend.

"Still," Gondi went on, "he's his father's son. The problem with people like that is that they're incorruptible. Well, no," Gondi interrupted himself with a wry laugh, "no one is that, but still, they can't be bought directly, as most people can. That's because they perceive themselves as having everything that's important — land and position — and having it as a matter of right, because of some quirk of history that no one is allowed to question.

"That's why Pierre de Galle is so dangerous. He can't be controlled the way..." Gondi broke off just before saying "the way you can," and concluded lamely, "...other people can. That's why he has to be exterminated.

"It's too bad," he said gazing thoughtfully out to his spacious garden, "because I'm fond of Pierre." Gondi mouthed the platitude unthinking, or, rather, thinking only that it was at least possible to be fond of Pierre, whereas having a warm sentiment for Maurice was beyond his power. He caught himself up, admitting to himself that any gentle or affectionate emotion he might feel toward Pierre was overshadowed, consumed by the jealousy he felt for him, with the hatred for someone who had come out on the top of the heap without effort, without merit of character, for no reason other than blind luck, and who emphasized his contempt for everyone else by throwing it all away as if it meant nothing to him. How dare he make himself a threat to me? Gondi thought. He felt a sudden sympathy for Maurice; if I suffer from jealousy of Pierre, how much more must he suffer!

He turned back toward Maurice. "Getting back to the situation at hand, having let him get away from you..."

"If you'd given me enough men..." Maurice interjected.

"I did my best for you," said Gondi with a dismissive wave of his hand. "The situation called for brains rather than brawn. I would have thought you had the brains and Pierre had the brawn, but I suppose you weren't using your head that day and he was." He shrugged. "But, as I was saying, having let him get away, you must do everything to get him back again. Do you still have the King's warrant?"

"No," Maurice replied. "He took it. He took my money, my horse, my sword, everything. I told him it was as bad as killing me. He doesn't have the guts to kill someone outright. He's... he's a weakling."

"It wasn't the same as killing you, though, was it? As for his being a weakling, I'm not sure I understand all of it, but it's certainly more complicated than that."

Gondi at last asked the question Maurice has been dreading, "Well, how do you plan to proceed?"

Maurice shifted, and a succession of emotions flitted across his face — anguish, fear, belligerency. "I'll go down to the Loire and track him from there."

"He's not stupid enough simply to go home and wait for you to come."

Maurice straightened abruptly and declaimed loudly, "I know where to find him."

Gondi's instinct was too good for him to be deceived by this piece of bravado. He was profoundly troubled. If Maurice did not know how to catch up with Pierre, no one else did either, Gondi reasoned. After all, Maurice was the logical person to set on Pierre's trail since he was in the most danger from Pierre running loose.

Gondi leaned forward, resting his elbows on his knees. What about this other business? he thought. Would he be capable of handling it? Eighteen months ago he would never have thought so, but hadn't Maurice proven his worth beyond

Gondi's wildest imaginings, at least with Coligny. Even if he were capable of carrying out so delicate a mission, which he probably was, did he dare to confide such a secret to him?

And yet, it was imperative that he know the ramifications of the situation if he were to handle it intelligently.

"I came back to Paris..." La Renaudie broke into Gondi's reverie.

"Shut up, I'm thinking."

With a mixture of malice and heightened anxiety, Maurice realized that things must be hopelessly bad to stump the most quick-witted man in France.

Abruptly, Gondi straightened and resumed the conversation in his normal decisive tones.

"I have another mission which I wish you to combine if possible with your search for de Galle. It is a delicate one. I am putting it in your hands because, in spite of this recent setback, I am impressed with your ingenuity and your discretion."

Maurice's face contorted, expressing a curious combination of skepticism and gratification. He rubbed his hair back from his forehead.

"It concerns my niece, Athalie," Gondi said slowly. "She has had the misfortune of becoming involved with some man who, apparently, took advantage of her and... well, briefly, she has had a baby.

"Now, get this through your head, La Renaudie, no one at Court knows this other than myself and the Queen Mother except you. If there is any gossip about the Duchess's misfortune, I shall know the source of it, and I'm sure you can imagine how the Queen Mother will react."

Half-amused, half-intimidated, Maurice digested Gondi's threat and wondered what the disclosure was leading up to. Finally, he asked, "Do I take it that the Duchess is still at Fontevrault?"

"No," Gondi replied. "She has left Fontevrault for a small property on the Indre called Islette."

With a flash of inspiration, Maurice realized that Gondi had unwittingly provided him with the solution to the problem of finding Pierre. He gasped with relief, opened his mouth, and closed it again.

Shall I tell him what I know? Never! Maurice laughed a short and unpleasant laugh.

Gondi watched him worriedly. After a pause, he continued, "Obviously, this situation can't be allowed to continue. What I want you to do is to go to Islette, dispose of the baby discreetly, and bring the Duchess back to Court. Do you think you can combine that with taking young de Galle into custody?"

"Oh, yes!" Maurice laughed again. "Oh, yes, I can handle them both easily."

Gondi recognized from his tone and manner that La Renaudie believed what he had just undertaken. He was bewildered by the transformation from timid defeatism to brash self-confidence, which had taken place before his very eyes.

"Your services will not go unrewarded, I need hardly add."

"So you always say," Maurice burst out, "but I haven't seen much from you yet."

Suddenly enraged, Gondi turned on him. "You were nothing when I picked you up, you had no reason to think you'd ever be anything. Look at you now: very grand is the young lord! That's reward enough."

"That was no gift from you," Maurice snarled. "I got where I am because I earned it. I earned the King's friendship myself, no thanks to you, and now that I have it, you'd better not think I'm nothing. I'm not going to be stopped. I want a good marriage — property, a grand title — that's the reward I'm looking for. If I'm to do your dirty work for you, and never fear, I'll do it all right, well, my lord de Retz, you'd better be thinking how you are going to make it worth my while."

"Oh, I shall, my young friend, never fear," Gondi said in a quiet way. "You just keep your mind on the job."

Maurice rose, and puffing out his chest, looked down at Gondi. "I shall need men — enough men this time, and money, of course."

"Of course," Gondi murmured.

"That's what I came back to Paris for. Otherwise, I'd already be hard on the bastard's heels."

"Quite." Gondi also rose. "I will arrange for a new order for de Galle's arrest. One complication. The Queen Mother wants him captured alive and brought back for personal interrogation. I can see by your dismay that you realize the danger that poses for us both. Now listen, I cannot openly flout her orders as it is plain she suspects something. But if de Galle were to confess to his treason, with some persuasion if necessary, before she talks to him, well, I doubt he would pose much of a problem."

Maurice licked his lips and a glow started in his eyes.

"No, Maurice, not on the trail. This must be official, duly witnessed, with a proper transcript, so it can't be challenged. Bring him safe to a nice cell in the conciergerie and we'll get a story quickly enough. I'll even let you supervise, shall I?" Gondi looked away from the burning coals Maurice's eyes had become. He continued briskly, "Well, tell Julio what you need and I'll see to it that you have it. I'll even give you Augustin Pascal as a second in command. He's a good swordsman and the chase should amuse you both."

Gondi slapped Maurice on the shoulder, and suppressing his distaste at the slight mist of dust which rose from Maurice's clothes, said heartily, "Good luck!"

Chapter XXXV

he September evening was breathless, still, and cool, noisy with the songs of hundreds of invisible birds, and entirely peaceful. The golden bars of sunlight on the sluggish, glowing surface of the Indre alternated with deepening shadows. Athalie, as she strolled along the bank following a path half overgrown with weeds, was peaceful in the same way, she thought, as this gentle autumn: a tentative peace, aware, yet defiant of insecurity, as this summer warmth lingers in the face of the coming winter.

Gabrielle, well fed, slept noiselessly in Athalie's arms; she stirred, blinked, and slept again as Athalie sang softly to her.

"Quand la rose..." she continued softly, her voice not strong, but silvery, musical, rising and falling with the tune she had been working on in odd moments. It was a slow, deep melody that caught, she thought, the sadness and sense of loss that made the verses so poignant. Aimeri, dear, dear man, she thought fondly. How simple and uncomplicated was his goodness, how effortless and pleasant his company. She gazed over the clear surface of the water; the line of poplars on the opposite bank reflected as in a glass, and puffy clouds seemed to move through the water. The sun dazzled her eyes, while the suggestion of a breeze ruffled the water and broke the poplars and clouds into myriad patches of changing color. The distant sound of the gate banging shut and a horse neighing startled her from her reverie.

Looking back she could see against the golden haze a horseman approach the main steps of the house and speak briefly with the old nurse sitting on the top step sunning herself. Aimeri? Athalie wondered. But surely not alone. A messenger? A chill of foreboding gripped her heart.

The old woman scrambled awkwardly to her feet, curtseyed stiffly, and gestured vaguely toward the river in Athalie's direction. The rider turned and strode across the roughly scythed grass. By his walk Athalie knew him. She stood transfixed for a moment, as tears of joy filled her eyes, then clutching Gabrielle, she ran forward. Pierre had wondered about his reception, but seeing the startled happiness in her face he swooped down on her, wrapping her and the baby in a great embrace.

Suddenly they were laughing together, swaying back and forth, Pierre planting kisses on her hair and forehead and mouth. Then just as suddenly they were silent, filled with a kind of awe.

Athalie shook herself from her reverie and held Gabrielle out to Pierre. "This is your daughter," she said. "I called her Gabrielle, not knowing..." She stopped, hoping he would not notice the touch of reproach that came unbidden in her voice. Indeed, Pierre did not notice it, as he was entirely engrossed in the child. Awkwardly he put his hand against the baby's face, and they laughed together, struck by the incongruity of tininess and hugeness.

"Will you hold her?" Athalie slid the baby from her shoulder, and cradling her in her arms, held her out to Pierre. He took her clumsily, fumbling to position his hand under her head and shoulders. Startled by the sudden movement, the sleepy infant wriggled and opened her eyes very wide. "She has blue eyes!" he cried.

"Why not?" said Athalie, smiling, "but they may change. Nou-nou says all babies' eyes are blue in the beginning."

"I hope they will," Pierre replied. "I pictured the baby — a girl, I don't know why — looking like you, not pink and fuzzy and blue-eyed."

"When did you find out," Athalie asked anxiously, "and how?"

"I didn't really know 'til I came to Fontevrault. Before that I had only heard a rumor. It was the night before the..." He stopped speaking as a look of anguish passed over his face. He had come here to help her. He could not, he must not, inflict his horrors on her. With a grimace that was almost a shudder, he went on quickly, "I came as quickly as I could, but your Abbess was not very forthcoming. I realized later that she derived a pleasure — almost sadistic — in knowing I was a father without letting me know I had a daughter. And she teased me with her silences and her hints, trying to make me say what business I had with you. I didn't know what to say, what you had told her..."

"I told her nothing, about you," Athalie said slowly, her eyes downcast. "But of course, on seeing you, she would have guessed the truth."

"Take her, take Gabrielle," Pierre said hoarsely. "It frightens me to hold her."

"Silly — you could hold her in two fingers and not drop her."

"I know," Pierre grinned foolishly, "but she feels — breakable."

The evening was drawing on, and Athalie gathered Gabrielle into her arms and shivered slightly.

"You are what I want to hold, Lie-lie." Pierre threw his cloak around Athalie and hugged her close. They began to walk toward the house.

Athalie looked up into Pierre's face. "Perhaps you thought it was a girl because you were afraid, well, that you didn't want your firstborn son to be a bastard."

"I could have thought about that," he replied without looking at her, "but I didn't. I just pictured a new little creature made in your image. However, it would be best if no one knew I had come here."

"Of course," Athalie replied. "But, Pierre," Athalie stopped suddenly, "when you arrived, did anyone hear you say who you were?"

"There was only your Nou-nou and she knows who I am."

"We must make her keep quiet. Hurry!"

"No — wait. Athalie — what should — we — I — do?"

"Oh, Pierre!" Entreaty flooded Athalie's face. "Please, stay with me — as long as you can. We'll make Nou-nou keep quiet; we'll call you 'Monsieur Pierre.'"

"But there must be others who would know me."

"No," she went on desperately, "I sent all the Court people back when I arrived at Fontevrault. My great-aunt insisted then that we try to maintain secrecy. All my people are from here or newly hired."

"But, Lie-lie, what will they think of you? I can't think only of myself."

"They will think no worse than they already do. You know, no one believes my little Gaby was conceived without sin." She laughed. "Come," she said, pulling at his arm and hurrying him along.

"These people," she continued as they walked, "the old steward and his wife, they were like parents to me. I used to come here to play with their children. They love me, and they don't question me. It is not their place. The new steward is my man — and he's nice. He'll always be loyal to me first."

A black figure scuttled up out of the dusk. "I brought a shawl," the old nurse grumbled, "but now I see you don't need it." She turned to go.

"Nou-nou, wait," Athalie called out. "Have you told anyone who is come?"

"No!" she spat the word out. "I'd be ashamed. I'm hoping he'll leave."

"No one must know who this is."

"What difference does it make," she hissed. "This is all madness."

"Nou-nou, no one must know."

"I don't care. There's nothing I can do. It doesn't make any difference."

"Promise, Nou-nou."

"I promise! I promise! You should be ashamed..." Pierre and Athalie heard her mumbling as she shuffled away across the grass.

Athalie sighed softly. Pierre was silent, not knowing what to say.

"Come," Athalie resumed. "We'll sup now. We always sup at nightfall, and then go to bed and rise at dawn."

"The little Duchess becomes a farm girl — will wonders never cease!" Pierre chortled.

"Oh, yes!" she said earnestly. "Tomorrow, I'll show you everything. We have chickens and ducks, cows, goats — and there's Amelie, who will be frantic by now. She followed me into the kitchen before I came out, and I left her there with Louisette by a trick — otherwise I could never be rid of her."

"Who is Amelie? Who is Louisette?" Pierre looked baffled.

"Louisette is the wife of old Jean Paul, the bailiff, and our cook. Funny to be old and still be called little Louise! You will meet them all."

They reached the steps and pushed open the heavy front door and entered the hall, large and plain. The huge fireplace was dark and the heavy trestle table was empty.

"I'm sorry it's not very elegant."

Pierre laughed out loud. "Lie-lie, you have never been to Plessis Gaillard. This place is positively modern! But where does the Duchess take her meals?"

"We don't eat here. It seems so huge and gloomy. I always eat in the kitchen with Michel and Louisette, Nou-nou, and young Étienne — except when there's company, of course, but today, they didn't know. Can you bear it, love? And then you can rest. You must be tired."

"What I really want is a bath," he said. "You know, I never in all my life thought that I would ever long for a bath as I do now. I feel as if I have never been clean, since Paris."

Pierre reached out in the dark of the room and clutched Athalie's shoulder.

The kitchen was a blaze of light and warmth. The old nurse took the baby and laid her in the cradle near the fire. After the puppy's frantic greetings had subsided, Athalie was able to introduce "Monsieur Pierre, a friend, who has just come from Fontevrault." They ate all together at the long table, cold pork pie and thick slices of bread, washed down with wine from Montbazon. Pierre's initial constraint, which communicated itself to the others, wore off as the wine jug passed around the table. Even the old nurse, prevailed upon to drink her share, became quite giddy, so that Athalie began to fear that her newly loosened tongue might become indiscreet. But all passed off well, and Pierre, as the recognition of safety, joy, and contentment began to melt away his cares, positively beamed with pleasure.

After dinner, Jean Paul and Étienne carried the old wooden tub and then several buckets of boiling water up the narrow, winding stairs, followed by Louisette with huge rough towels, lye soap, and a brush, Nou-nou with the baby, and Amelie, racing about seemingly under as many feet as possible. When all save the puppy had been sent off about their business and Pierre had ensconced himself in the steaming tub, knees drawn up, head leaning against the edge, he laughed and said, "I thought for a while they were all going to stay and watch. It was such a procession."

"Pierre, dear, I wish I could make this a palace for you, but everything here is so plain. Can you bear it, Monsieur le Duc?"

"Athalie, I'm used to it."

"But at Court..."

"I've told you, I didn't grow up at Court. If you think my father believed in luxury and fine food, you're dreaming. He didn't much believe in baths, either. Athalie, come in with me."

"Oh, Pierre!"

"Why not?"

"There isn't room."

"There's always room."

Athalie turned away, undressing shyly as if it were the first time, as indeed in a way it was. All thought of washing forgotten, Pierre watched her bare shoulders emerge from her shift, her petticoats fall from her slender hips, her long, slim legs lift gracefully from the pile of clothing.

As Athalie stepped over the edge into the water, Amelie woke abruptly from her sleep and rushed toward the tub barking raucously.

"Damn that dog!" Pierre growled.

Athalie slid down into the water, squeezing herself tightly between his legs.

"We could have her in the tub, too," Athalie remarked, giggling maliciously.

"Damn you, too. There is no room for that dog — not in this tub and not in our bed. Do you understand?"

Athalie merely giggled.

Pierre stretched out a huge hand and, forcing her head forward, dunked her face, sputtering, into the water.

Later that night, much later, they lay quietly, Athalie nestled in the crook of Pierre's arm. The chill breeze through the narrow window made the heavy blankets welcome. "I never thought to see you again," she whispered.

"Hush, little love."

"It's almost a year, since we first..."

Pierre rolled toward her and kissed her cheek. "So much time wasted," he said.

"How could I have done otherwise? How can we...?"

"Hush, little love."

* * *

The next day was sunny and mild once the heavy morning mist burned away, leaving only a soft haze above the river. Pierre gratefully accepted Athalie's amusingly eager offer for a tour of her little estate. He knew he had to tell her everything. Indeed, he wanted advice, but how to broach it, the horror, the stink of it, her uncle Gondi by the bonfire, and that he had to flee, soon, for his life.

Hand in hand they inspected the livestock, the poultry, the garden remnants, the yellowing fields, the shady riverbank. Pierre quickly joined her happy chatter, happy that the conversation was diverted for a moment from his plans.

"My father loved this place," Athalie reminisced. "I could only guess why. It is so humble compared with Rocher de la Roque. I used to think it odd that someone so grand should be satisfied, when he came here, with so little. I loved it, of course, but that was different. Then one day he told me how my mother had got him to buy Islette, how she wanted to live here and make it beautiful, to add a new wing in the Italian style and fine gardens, an aviary, a pond.

"None of it happened after she died, but my father still came here, and I suppose, dreamed of it. It was well kept up in those days, not like now. I have been thinking that I would try to do what she wanted. Do you know it was almost the only time he spoke to me of her."

"But you have plenty of money," Pierre replied, gazing at the unfinished arches appraisingly.

"My uncle Gondi has the money. God knows how long he will leave me here in peace!" She shivered slightly.

It was a pleasant day and they avoided the subjects that would cast a shadow on their happiness. Pierre reflected sourly that he had to tell her of Paris, but he dreaded facing it again as much as he feared making her face it. In addition, unspoken, the resentment each harbored against the other for the long silence after Athalie left Court hung in the air. Instinctively each groped to annihilate that resentment by bringing it out into the open. But both dreaded the pain of doing so. Athalie, finally, shrank from asking when Pierre would leave and return to his wife. So they spent the day quietly, talking of what they saw and what they remembered, avoiding revelations and confrontations. Unexpectedly, one moment of trouble came between them.

"If everything was so rundown when you came," Pierre observed at the end of his tour, "you've worked wonders. In a few weeks, you've made as much of a beginning as would be possible at this time of year."

"Well, I had help," Athalie replied and looked away.

Pierre, surprised, regarded her quizzically.

"Aimeri Pascal, my uncle's friend's son, the banker's son, you remember I told you about him?" She stumbled over her words, embarrassed, and angry at being embarrassed.

"The one who wanted to marry you," he replied, arching an eyebrow. "Oh, yes, I remember very well. You said you turned him down."

"I did — a year ago, more. I'd almost forgotten him, but he came one day, and then he came back with lots of things, animals, seed, grain, wine." She hesitated, but honesty compelled her to go on, "Amelie."

"I wondered who had visited you when you mentioned visitors last night," he said. "Well, does he still want to marry you?"

"Yes," she said softly. "He said I should for Gabrielle's sake. I told him..."

"He's absolutely right," Pierre shouted. Athalie turned and stared at Pierre's face, flushed an angry, ugly red.

"Oh, Pierre," she said miserably, "I am not your wife."

"Quite!" he snapped, his lips pressed tightly together.

"No," she said clutching his arm, "I meant I'm not like your wife. I have never been unfaithful to you, never for an instant, not by a single thought. I have done the child a great wrong, but I will not make it better by doing you a wrong."

"More fool you," he replied bitterly.

"How dare you say that to me?" Tears of rage stang Athalie's eyes.

Pierre was suddenly contrite, indeed mortified. "I'm sorry, I'm so sorry," he murmured, gently kissing the top of her head. They held each other, silent for a few moments, then continued their walk, dropping the distressing subject.

That evening, beside the Indre, Athalie, wrapped in a thick woolen shawl, rested her head against Pierre's shoulder. Gabrielle, tightly bundled, slept between her parents as Amelie reclined on her back, balanced against Pierre's leg, her overlarge feet flapping over her fuzzy belly.

"You see," Athalie pointed at the dog, "she has spots on her tummy. That's what I love best."

"If you keep mooning about that dog, I'll get jealous." Pierre spoke sternly, and Athalie shifted her eyes nervously. "Could anyone be so fond of something so unprepossessing," Pierre continued thoughtfully, "if she didn't love the giver of it?" Athalie darted a look at Pierre, and seeing him laugh, broke into a thin smile.

"The funny thing," she said, "is that Amelie seems to have taken a great liking to you. Aimeri would be so angry if he knew."

"Vixen!" he chuckled. "We could shorten her name to 'Lie-lie' then when I called, you could both come running."

Athalie gave Pierre a hard shove. He rolled to his knees, letting the puppy collapse on her side, and crawled to Athalie's other side. "The trouble is, that all these creatures get in the way." Pierre put his arm around her and held her tight; they sat so for a long while, in quiet communion with each other.

At last Athalie broke the silence timidly. "When will your child be born, Anne's child?"

"She says mid-October."

"Tomorrow is the feast of the Nativity of Our Lady. Saint Anne gave birth that day. We'll go and pray for your Anne."

"You wish that?" Pierre's puzzled expression was half hidden in the gathering dusk. "Yes, well, we shall go. I am perhaps capable of praying for that. I don't know," his voice trailed off.

"Pierre, what is wrong? Surely you can ask God for a safe birth for your child."

"Yes, of course," he replied heavily. "It's not that. It's — Athalie, sweet love, I don't want to talk about it, not now anyway. Perhaps later. Oh, hold me Athalie, please hold me!"

* * *

Pierre glanced curiously around the church at Luré the next day. Its massive walls of thick stones were dark with age, the paintings on the walls faded and discolored, to seemingly darken the interior with images which were mysterious in the semi-obscurity. The congregation, rapidly augmented when word of their Lady's attendance spread through the valley, plain folk of the neighboring farms, made no secret of their greater interest in Pierre and Athalie than in the service mumbled by the Père Bernard. Athalie was resplendent in a silk gown the color of cornflowers and a tight-fitting cap of deep mauve velvet laced with gold filigree and studded with pearls. Men and women alike gaped at her, though for different reasons, and all gazed awestruck at Pierre who stood head and shoulders above the tallest of the men.

"If I had the money," Athalie said as they rode back to Islette, "I would tear that old church down and build a new one, high and airy and delicate."

"I wonder if they would like it," he replied. "They seemed all of a piece, your people, the curé and the old stones, like things that have grown together out of the soil. Why not build a chapel at Islette?"

"Yes. There was one, you know. I found its ruins in the woods a little way from the château. God knows how old it is or when it was last used. No one around here seems to know anything about it. Strange to think of it outlasting its own history. We'll go to see it later. It's a pretty place."

That afternoon, after a particularly festive noonday meal, while the house subsided into postprandial somnolence, Pierre and Athalie left by a side door and entered the woods. They passed easily among the large trees through the large

403

ferns that covered the ground, now turning with the season, ochre and burnt umber, and lying in disarray along their path. They came to a clearing in the trees, a place of pale sunlight in the lowering dark of the grove.

In the middle was a mossy knoll of ancient stone, the ruins of a squat building. Parts of the walls remained half collapsed, open to the sky. Crude heads of beasts on the columned doorway peered down at Pierre and Athalie, through and around a tracery of vines and leaves. Hands linked, they walked slowly through the arch.

Within, on the broken paving stones, they felt as if gripped by a brooding presence, but whether emanating from the encroaching forest or from the place itself they could not say. They walked slowly to a collapsed wall and sat tight together on the masonry. Athalie gripped Pierre's hand tightly.

"You know," she mused, "I can stand in church, like this morning, and I can still pray, though I'm... though I'm not in grace. Does that seem odd?"

"I..." Pierre fumbled for his words, "I cannot pray. I could not pray this morning. I stand there and the liturgy seems to roll on around me and I don't seem to hear it. It's as if my mind is occupied by evil spirits, full of confusion and images of violence."

"Because of us?" Athalie asked, bewildered.

"No," he croaked harshly. And then Pierre began to describe the dawn of St. Bartholomew's Day in Paris, haltingly at first, then in a torrent of words — the torches, the bodies, the streets, the bonfire at the Louvre, Trophime Daudet, and then his own bloody passage across demented Paris. He covered his face with his hands. His voice, muffled, droned out the burning, rape, and death.

Athalie listened, shaken and withdrawn. She could not take hold of the enormity of the horror in the instant of telling. It settled deep inside her while the surface of her consciousness was wholly occupied with concern for Pierre.

He stumbled in his narrative, clenching his hands together and averting his head. "And so, you see, I bashed his head in with my feet, like an animal." Pierre saw again the man's crumpled bulk, his face buried in the mud; try as he would, he could not see Meraude, the girl he saved, he could not hide from his remorse behind her image. He lurched to the side and buried his face in Athalie's lap.

"My poor, lovely Pierre," she whispered, stroking his head. "But what you did was right. Look what he had done, the man you killed. He raped her and would have killed her. Probably he had killed others."

"Oh, he had," Pierre said bleakly and described the scene in the house, the dead father and brother.

"So you see," said Athalie. "Why do you blame yourself?"

Pierre grimaced and said through clenched teeth, "It's that I've always been afraid of the violence in me, strength and violence, what it could do. Athalie, it was so easy to kill!" He raised his head and looked at her with eyes filled with sorrow. "It was just as easy as I always feared. I felt as though I had fallen into a cesspool. I stink of death. And I know I would do it again, and I almost surely will do it again. Perhaps it is I who should enter religion!" He laughed a harsh, bitter laugh.

Tears filled Athalie's eyes as she drew his head to her bosom, holding him, rocking him, soothing him. "Darling Pierre," she murmured. "It is all right, you are all right, but why must the world make someone as lovely as you do such awful things. Oh, Pierre, how very much I love you, not just because you are brave, but because you have the courage to endure this sorrow for doing what you had to do. Because you are so vulnerable, yet so strong. Pierre, take my love's blessing and know that I am sure your heart is pure, however much your hands are red with blood. See here, I kiss them, and I wash them with my tears."

Pierre lifted his head and looked at Athalie with eyes shining with tears. "I knew, I knew you would see and understand. I knew I would find sanity and peace in your arms. Athalie, I have nothing in the world but your love, and I feel like the lord of creation."

Athalie kissed his cheeks again and said in a low voice, "Now go on. Tell me the rest. I can bear it."

He took a deep breath and continued his tale, through the rescue of the two Protestants to the escape from Paris. Again he raised his head.

Athalie pulled his head against her breast and whispered softly, "Pierre, what you did was... heroic. Don't ever reproach yourself." Again and again she stroked his head. "You must remember, you saved people's lives."

"I killed as many as I saved," he said tonelessly, pulling away.

"But look who you killed and who you saved," she protested.

"Does it make a difference?" He looked at her with haunted eyes. "Lives are lives."

"No, Pierre, please, it does make a difference. Of course it does. You're too upset to see it." Athalie forced a wan smile. "Was she pretty?"

"What? Oh. Yes, I suppose. She was like a washed-out version of you."

"Anyone would be washed out, wrung out, under the circumstances."

"The problem is," Pierre finally said after a long silence, "what to do now? I'm accused and have been convicted, for all I know, as a traitor. Maurice was carrying a warrant for my arrest." He fumbled in his belt purse. "Here, look at it."

She took it, unfolded it, and smoothed it with hands that trembled slightly. "Oh, Pierre," she whispered, dropping the page as the written words brought home the enormity of the message.

"He'll have another one by now," Pierre said. "He must come after me. He knows that I know what he did. And behind Maurice is de Retz."

Athalie looked down at her hands. "Can you be sure," she asked softly, "about my uncle, I mean?"

"I can think of no explanation of what he did other than that he knew of my stepbrother's lies. If de Retz knew of them, then he almost certainly put Maurice up to them. He's never been anybody's dupe. You know that."

She nodded slowly.

"I'm sorry, Lie-lie, but your uncle had Trophime killed and me arrested, all because... well, simply because we knew the truth. Also, I don't think Maurice could have obtained an order for my arrest so quickly without help. I don't know, but I don't think he could have."

"Pierre, if my uncle was part of this monstrous deception, might there have been others?"

"Yes," he replied. "I've thought about it a lot, but I don't know how we can know."

"The Queen Mother? The Duke of Anjou?"

"All possible."

"What would they do if they caught you?" Athalie asked quietly.

"I think we have to assume that, well, they would have me executed. And you know, even if I can successfully escape, they may well order that my lands be forfeit to the crown. Perhaps they'll bestow them on Maurice to reward him for his service to the King and the true Faith." Pierre laughed a harsh, mirthless laugh.

"Oh, no," Athalie whispered, her face white with fear.

"Why not?" he asked, rising and turning away from her. "It makes sense. I mean, in the context of this insanity, it makes sense."

"Why not write to the King or the Queen Mother and explain?"

"I know," he said turning back. "I've thought it over a hundred times. Yes, that's a possibility, but Athalie, listen to the arguments against it. First, who can say that they weren't part of the scheme? Second, de Retz opens all the King's mail and much of the Queen Mother's before they even see it. Third, even if they weren't in on the game and even if they received the letter, they would hardly be convinced by a letter alone. Indeed, I don't suppose they would believe me if I pleaded with them face to face. Fifth... fourth, or whatever, I cannot write without giving them some way of getting in touch with me, which is as good as giving myself up. So you see, I think that's hopeless." He spread his hands in a gesture of helplessness.

Athalie turned Pierre's predicament over and over in her mind, feeling the wave of desperation rising in her.

"I could write," she said finally. "I could write to the Queen Mother."

"What earthly pretext could you give to explain your involvement in this mess?"

"I don't know," she said simply. "None, perhaps. I would describe the situation and say I could get in touch with you, and that you would come in person if the King gave you safe conduct."

"That's clever, Lie-lie, very clever, but I don't think it would work. As an aside, by getting involved, you would of course reveal everything about us; even if you said nothing, the Queen Mother would know, which may be fine, but bears thinking about. And Kings don't normally bargain with traitors. Moreover, you would have put yourself in the position of aiding and abetting a traitor, and, for all I know, they could confiscate your lands, yes, or threaten to do so, to blackmail you into giving me up. No, it won't do."

"All right, then, what will?"

"The only thing I have been able to think of, really, is to lie low until it all blows over. You know how, at the end of every one of these outbursts, there seems to be an amnesty as part of the peace. It's been that way since 1560, my father used to say. I simply have to hope that I can claim the benefit of the next one."

"And, in the meantime, you'll go to La Rochelle? Yes, that would work."

"No. I didn't mean that," he replied. "I don't want to go to La Rochelle. I have nothing in common with the adherents of the so-called Reformed Religion. The fact that a lot of Catholics killed a lot of Protestants doesn't make the Protestants right."

"Yes, Pierre, you do have something in common with them. You believe innocent people shouldn't be killed indiscriminately, and so that puts you on their side against the King, under the circumstances."

"No, it doesn't. That is just what your uncle will accuse me of. I won't see people massacred for a crime they didn't commit. If it's all politics, then I think it should be fair and open politics. But I don't necessarily believe that they should be free to say or believe anything they choose. One faith is part of the order of things. If His Majesty wanted to execute every last Protestant as a heretic, and if he could do it, I'm not sure he wouldn't be within his rights. It was the underhandedness of it all, inviting them to a wedding, then trying to kill their leader, then slandering them and butchering them — that's what got to me. It was disgusting." Pierre spat the words out.

"At first," he went on, "what had happened, what I'd seen in Paris, it was as if I had been turned inside out. I couldn't think about anything rationally for a while. But as we rode south, things in my head seemed to calm down somewhat. I could think again. In fact, I not only could think, but I had to think, as I've never thought before. And it came to me that fundamentally nothing was changed. What was right before was still right, what was wrong, wrong. It was possible to face the fact that so many people had died, and that my whole life had been shattered, and really, on a larger scale, the whole thing doesn't mean anything." Pierre shrugged hopelessly.

"So you see," he resumed, "I can't go to La Rochelle, at least not with a view to taking up arms against the King. I've no reason to declare myself against the order, the faith, everything I was taught to believe in."

"Even if the King ordered all those people killed knowing them to be innocent?" Athalie asked.

"Even so," Pierre replied slowly. "As an individual, he would be a heinous criminal, but his position makes him more than what he is. Anyway, somehow I don't think he knew. At any rate, I'm not going to assume he did."

"What then?" Athalie sighed. The color seemed to have gone out of the day. Her pretty, bucolic dream seemed silly and pointless, a flimsy painted scene exposed to a gale. "What will you do? You can remain here. I'll hide you, but there will always be a risk."

"No." He reached out, took her hand and kissed it. "How I would love to stay with you! But it wouldn't be safe in the long run. No, I thought I would go to England, to my mother's family, and basically abide events."

"Isn't that as bad as La Rochelle?"

"No. Our Protestants are declared enemies, in open warfare with the King, whereas the English are neutral, in theory at least. Indeed, an English marriage is the Queen Mother's dream — first, she tried Anjou, now Hercule-François — whomever Elizabeth of England will have!" They both laughed.

"In fact," Pierre continued, "I'll have to go to La Rochelle to get a ship to England, but I won't linger. And then we'll see. Things don't seem to be in my control, and though it angers me, I don't know how I can change that." Pierre spoke quietly, but Athalie, looking at his face and hearing the timbre of his voice, guessed at the intensity of his anger.

"When will you go?" she asked, in a voice made low by fear.

"I don't want to go too far until Anne's child is born. I owe her that, at least, to be nearby at such a time."

Athalie suddenly wanted to cry out, "Yet, you didn't owe me anything," but she bit back the words.

At last, mastering her bitterness, she said, "You can stay here until then. No one will think to find you here, except the Abbess, and she is not looking for you, nor would anyone think to ask her about you."

"She might accidentally give me away by, say, writing to the Queen Mother about us."

"She might, but I don't think she will. Since you're married, she would not see you as the solution to her great concern, what to do with me."

"The problem of what to do with you," Pierre said musingly. He stroked her hand gently. "Oh, Lie-lie, at least, we have this time together. We can't complain, as long as we have that." He took her in his arms and kissed her, at first gently and then passionately.

* * *

The rain came that evening on a chill wind out of the west that later, as Pierre and Athalie lay warm in bed, buffeted the old tower and slapped sheets of rain against the papered windows. The conversation had been desultory as they lay close, drained, dulled, by the day's emotions. Exhausted, Athalie found the courage — or carelessness — to ask the question which had been tormenting her.

"Pierre, I must ask you. Why did you never answer my letter?"

Pierre stirred, rousing himself from his somnolence. More by instinct than by any intellectual act, he recognized that the crucial subject was upon them, and so with wariness he answered her question with a question.

"What letter?"

Athalie thought back over the months, seeing, in the blackness of the night, that frozen January morning when her life was turned upside down.

"That day at Chambord when you went hunting," she whispered haltingly, "when your father was killed, that was the morning I first realized I was pregnant. I waited all day to tell you. I thought I would die from waiting. But you didn't come back until so very late and then I couldn't speak to you about it; I could not add to your troubles at such a time. You left the next day, and all I could think to do was write to you, telling you about everything and that I was going to Fontevrault and would await your word as what I should do. Oh, Pierre, darling Pierre, it was so long and I was so alone. Why, Pierre?"

"I got no letter," Pierre said.

"You'd left before I could give you my letter," she went on, reflectively, "so I gave it to one of your people to give to you. And then I left and waited month after month. I never doubted our love, but I heard from my uncle that you were a great man at Court and that Anne was with child. I thought you'd abandoned me. I couldn't blame you for deciding that we must each live our own lives, but it seemed cruel to leave me without a word. Finally, I gave you up for lost, no, that isn't right, not lost, but in your own way, lost to me, I mean. I faced the decision by myself of how I would live, what life I would try to make for myself. Ultimately, I came here."

Pierre considered repeating the denial, "I got no letter," but he was stopped by his realization that it was not an answer, not a complete excuse. He remembered the months of frustration, anger, and hurt pride, and suddenly he was filled with shame.

"What a mess I've made of things, Athalie," he said hoarsely. "I thought only that you'd gone without a word or a farewell. I thought your qualms of conscience and religion had overcome you. I even thought you might have seen my father's death as some sort of punishment. I thought it was possible that you'd left me without comfort just when my life seemed to come down around my ears."

"I would never have done such a thing!" Athalie said, scandalized.

"Not from malice, I never thought that, but because you felt you had to," Pierre continued. "I don't know. I wasn't thinking very clearly. Your silence seemed incomprehensible. I had no idea that you... Oh, dammit! I wanted you to write. I imagined you singing psalms with all the time in the world to write to me, and then when weeks went by, I was angry, too angry to go after you, to admit to you how desperately I needed you. Then I put you out of my mind. Or I tried to. I tried to love Anne. Then I heard that you were pregnant. I didn't know if it was true, but I was going to set out the next day. Then all that killing happened, and, oh God, Athalie, what have we done to each other? What have I done to you?"

Propped up on the bank of cushions, they faced each other. A long silence settled between them, broken at last by Pierre.

"It's my fault," he said quietly. "You made an effort, I made none. It wasn't because I didn't care, but... forgive me, love."

She reached out, feeling for his face, and finding it, laid her hand on his cheek. He covered it with his own and, groping in the dark, threw his arm around her and pulled her to him.

* * *

The next morning Pierre woke filled with exuberance, despite the cold grey mist that shrouded the château. He felt liberated from worries and emotions which had oppressed him for months. We have been granted a respite, he thought, let us enjoy it to the full. The vacant covers on the other side of the bed indicated that Athalie had already risen to feed the baby. Pierre dressed in haste and tumbled down the stairs. Beaming with happiness, he found Athalie in the kitchen with the servants, and picking up the bowl of bread porridge which was waiting for him, he pulled her toward the door.

"No," she said. "It's too cold and wet."

"Take a shawl," he insisted, and drawing a heavy knitted wrap from a peg, she followed him out. They sat on the steps, sheltered under a portico, while Pierre gobbled his breakfast like a famished man. As he finished, he noticed for the first time that Athalie's face wore an expression that was troubled, withdrawn, almost sullen. He felt a flash of anger and self-pity that his own gaiety should be so vulnerable.

"Pierre," Athalie said quietly, "I've remembered who it was that I gave my letter to. I gave it to Maurice." The name rattled in the stillness like a dagger dropped on the floor.

"I was so upset," she went on hurriedly, "I thought nothing of it. There was nothing to think — at the time."

Pierre weighed her statement carefully; slowly his rage built up within him. Suddenly, he stood and hurled his bowl against the wall. It shattered, leaving a sticky imprint that began to ooze slowly down. His face contorted with fury, he burst out, "That bastard! He put us through Hell. For nothing! What had he to gain from it? God blast him! In everything he does he is a — a swine."

"No, but Pierre," she interrupted, her face drawn with fear, "don't you see, if he didn't give it to you, he must have opened it, so he knows about you and me. So he knows everything."

"Obviously!" Pierre spat. "It never occurred to me that he wouldn't have opened it."

"But, darling, if he knows, then this is where he'll come to look for you. He'll go to Fontevrault and ask for me, or doubtless my uncle Gondi knows I'm here by now. He has servants everywhere. Anyway, sooner or later, Maurice will come here.

"My God, Pierre, it's already the 9th of September. You left him more than a week ago, ten days it must be. He could be here any time."

"I should have killed him. By God, I should have killed him! I'm a fool."

"No, Pierre, don't think like that."

410

"I thought you approved of killing villains!"

"Not in cold blood. I don't think I could admit that."

"He would do it to me, gladly, I assure you."

"Pierre," Athalie said after a long pause, "I know you will hate this but I've been thinking, desperately, ever since I remembered about Maurice. You must leave here at once, and I've figured out a place where you can be safe until you see your wife and can leave for England."

He looked at her interrogatively.

"Aimeri Pascal. He has a large estate near Montbazon. He would find a place for you among his retainers, discreetly of course, anonymously. No one would ever think of looking for you there, and if I ask him, I know he can be trusted." Pierre's eyes blazed fiercely.

"No one would think of it, because the very idea is unthinkable! Marquis, you said he calls himself? My horse is more a marquis than he is! It's repugnant, degrading..."

"He would gladly do it."

"I don't doubt it for a moment. Indeed, that proves my point exactly."

"Pierre," she pleaded, "do it, please. Show me that you trust me. Oh, never mind that — save yourself. Do it for my sake." Athalie sank down on the step and buried her head in her hands.

Pierre gulped a deep breath and stared at Athalie silently, solemnly. She groped for his hand and squeezed it.

"Please."

Pierre agreed at last, swallowing his humiliation miserably.

Later in the morning, Pierre once again bade Athalie farewell. He stood beside Athalie's mare, his own great mount tied behind, on the pretext that he had been found lame. His bags were stuffed with old, worn clothes that he would put on as soon as he was outside the village, whose people would see the blonde lord ride off, but would never know of his transformation into a poor man-at-arms seeking a position of the wealthy new lord at Montbazon.

Athalie drew him close, her eyes glistening with tears. "God be with you, my love. Write me from England. You can use Pascal. Pierre, my only consolation at losing you will be knowing you are safe."

"I will, Lie-lie, but you, too, beware of my stepbrother. He is altogether base."

"I do not fear him, Pierre. I must have some value to my uncle Gondi; I doubt he will trouble me much. It is for you I fear. Go now, dearest love," Athalie cried suddenly, "while there is a little sun. I don't want to remember you riding off in the rain."

THE END OF PART II

411

Part III

Chapter XXXVI

he rain came and went and came again during the days after Pierre's departure. The ground was soggy, the sky dark, and Athalie's mood not better than the weather. Her tears came and went like the rain, tears of sadness at the pain that tore at her when she recalled her last glimpse of Pierre's golden head as he rounded the turn toward Luré. Tears, too, of rage and frustration at the evil fates that raised her up to a pinnacle of joy only to dash her on the rocks of despair. Suddenly Islette, lovely Islette, and all her pretty plans seemed empty, stupid, pointless. Ten days ago, she had been her own mistress; now she knew that she was bound forever by ties she could not break, nor even wish to. Bound to a man who was everything to her, but who, even if he escaped the mortal danger that threatened him, would never, never be hers. It only remained to be seen, she reflected sadly, how her heart would be broken. Would she hear of his death? Or would she see him restored to favor seated beside Anne on the ducal throne?

Throwing down the needlework which she had been pretending to work on, she paced up and down in the uncomfortable hall. She must check these thoughts and get a grip on herself, she thought. I cannot and I will not wish his death, I will wish his happiness, anything less would be a betrayal of my love. I have had his love, I have its fruit. If I never have anything else, I will count myself blest. Oh, Holy Mother of God, she prayed, protect him.

She grimaced wryly as she thought of Anne, and how she had almost had to urge Pierre to go to his wife. Athalie's attitudes toward Anne were highly ambiguous. Beneath a certain smugness at having bested an expert at her own game, Athalie genuinely admired Anne's effortless grace with men, the ease with which she captivated them, and the obvious pleasure she gave simply by entering a room.

Anne, while patronizing in the extreme at what she considered Athalie's inexperience, nevertheless had treated her rank and her friendship with Margot with respect, and her person with not a little rough kindness.

Athalie had the humility to realize that her relations with Pierre would be inconceivable to Anne and had needed no more dissimulation on her part than acting normal. Until Athalie had left Court, she and Anne, while not close, were on good terms.

On the other hand, Athalie deplored Anne's treatment of Pierre, however much that callous disregard of his feelings had benefited herself. Athalie had no doubt that Pierre's love was the best thing in the universe, and Anne, fool that she was, had, so to speak, left it by the roadside. Athalie reproached Anne for having made a terrible mistake, an unnecessary and irretrievable mistake, rather than for the hurt that Pierre had suffered at her hands. Then, too, there was her jealousy — oh, yes, she admitted to herself, she was jealous — of Pierre's all-too-obvious fascination with Anne's wealth of experience in bed. Pierre had even clumsily tried to pass on to his innocent mistress some of the simpler exercises in Anne's seemingly inexhaustible repertoire. Pierre had been so earnest about it, but Athalie had found it more cerebral than pleasurable, and being self-conscious, realized with a pang that she was mildly disappointing to Pierre, when she wanted to give him only joy.

Just as she abruptly halted this line of thought, resolutely forcing herself to concentrate on the garden nearest the Indre, which desperately needed work, if only the rain would stop, the memory of Maurice's imminent arrival opened like a black chasm at her feet. An icicle of fear pierced her heart. She shivered slightly at the thought of him. What would he say? What would he do? She shuddered again at the memory of his hands always seeming to be touching her, his full red lips. She was afraid for Pierre, afraid for herself, afraid for Gabrielle. Revulsion shook her at the idea of Maurice with Gabrielle. He shall not touch her, she swore to herself.

The next morning, warm and clear, found Athalie in the courtyard discussing landscaping with Étienne, who was enthusiastically agreeing with her ideas. A commotion at the gate revealed a peasant from the village, his cap in his hand, gesturing wildly to the gatekeeper. Étienne motioned him forward, saying to Athalie, "He is one of the blacksmith's people, my lady."

The man approached and bowed low to Athalie, then addressed Étienne.

"Please sir, there is a great troop of men-at-arms in the village. The master told me to cut over here sharp and say they was lookin' for a tall blond lord, same as accompanied my lady, the duchess, to church the other day. The master told 'em he'd been gone these three days now, but they're still nosing around the village."

Athalie's heart had stopped at the first mention of troops. Maurice. It had to be Maurice, and it was plain he meant business. She mastered her fear and turned to the peasant.

"Your master did well to send word, good man. Return to the village and say that I have given no leave for these men to vex the villagers. Let their leader appear here and state his business."

The peasant was mumbling his when with very little noise, quickly and very efficiently, fifty men passed through the gates, encircled the courtyard, and came to a stop with their weapons drawn. The only sound was the clink of harness. Maurice and Augustin Pascal rode slowly in, both resplendent in the livery of the Comte de Retz in spite of the stains left by a rapid journey.

Maurice dismounted gracefully and, doffing his plumed hat, bowed mockingly before Athalie. He regarded her silently for two full minutes, confident that the precision of the envelopment would speak eloquently to her that flight, resistance, and hope were out of the question. He gave a sidelong glance at the peasant, who had been unable to leave. He turned to Augustin and drawled, "That man is from the village. He was, I think, interfering with the King's business. Take care of him."

At a nod from Augustin, two men seized the peasant, lifting him boldly off the ground as he tried to throw himself at Athalie's feet. One of them drew a finger across his own throat as he looked up interrogatively at Augustin.

"No!" Maurice said, "A good beating will suffice. That way he can live to tell the rest of the rabble that we will not be trifled with. Time presses. See to it."

The two men hurried the peasant off, and as his screams began, Maurice turned smoothly to Athalie.

"Well, my dear Duchess, I'm sure you know why I'm here. Let us have my brother at once and you will be left here in peace. Although, I confess, I cannot imagine why so lovely a flower as you would wish to hide itself in this backwater."

He moved a step closer, his cloak thrown nonchalantly back on his shoulders, and licked his lips. Athalie, very straight and very pale, gazed unblinking at him, and his easy smirk slowly faded.

"I have nothing to say to you, Monsieur de La Renaudie, and I wish to say nothing to you but that your treatment of that innocent man was exactly what I would expect of you."

"Then, Duchess," he hissed, "you will recognize the futility of bandying words with me. Where is he?"

"I do not know anything about your brother," she lied. "I only wish he were here to deal with you as you deserve."

"Duchess," Maurice began again, "my stepbrother is a felon and a traitor to our lord the King. I have the royal warrant to seize him and to command assistance from all persons. I demand that you tell me where he is."

"And I do not accept 'demands' from the likes of you," she replied with dignity. "Or will you flog me as you did that poor wretch? With fifty men-at-arms you certainly have enough force to subdue a handful of men and two women. But I see that you are wearing the livery of my dear uncle Gondi. Somehow, I don't believe your orders include hurting me. I do not fear you, sirrah, but I do despise you!"

Athalie turned and walked slowly through the ring of men into the château. She knew she was not deceiving Maurice, but hoped that she could hold him at bay by the force of her will. Maurice winked broadly at Augustin and motioned to him to have the men stand down.

"An intimate conversation with my lady Athalie, I feel, would be a more fruitful course at this juncture," he said, sauntering into the house after her.

Inside the hall, he confronted her again.

"Now listen, Athalie, it is common knowledge in that pigsty of a village that a tall blonde cavalier has been staying at Islette. It strains credulity to suppose there are two such gentlemen. Pierre was here. Where is he now?"

"I have nothing, as I said before, to say to you. Please go."

"Athalie, Athalie," he replied gently. "I know all this must have been a shock to you, but you really must help me. I may as well say right now, I have other orders from your uncle. I am to deal with a child that rumor has it you have here with you." He noted with satisfaction that Athalie's hand flew to her mouth, as the color drained from her face.

"There, I thought that would get your interest," he said, sprawling on a chair. "I can, of course, interpret my instructions any way I choose. What I want is Pierre de Galle. Help me and I will see to it that nothing happens to the child."

Panic seized Athalie, paralyzing her very thoughts.

"If I tell you where he is," she whispered at last, "will you leave me and the child in peace?"

Maurice nodded. "Absolutely. You have my word as a gentleman."

"He went to Plessis to be with his wife."

With a snarl, Maurice bounded from the chair. "Do you expect me to believe that rubbish," he shouted. "I tell you for the last time, I will not put up with more of your lies, Duchess. How can you suppose I'd believe that he would go to his own château when he knows that is the first place his pursuers would seek him. That he would leave you," he sneered, "for a wife who cuckolded him a hundred times?"

"I expect you to believe it," she replied icily, "because I would not invent so stupid a tale if it were not true. Of course, I can see that it would be hard for you to understand, that he might do something kind, something honorable, at the risk of his life, for a woman who has not always been kind or honorable to him." In spite of herself, Athalie's face twisted a little in pain.

Maurice watched her with hooded eyes. There is truth there, he thought, though what it is, I am not sure. Still, there is some truth, for it hurts her to speak of it. He gazed at her for some moments in silence.

Maurice smiled at last, not a pretty smile.

"I don't believe you, quite," he said, "but I will follow your lead as far as it takes me. In the meantime, you will stay here with the child. Whatever happens, my dear Athalie, I'll come back for you. I rather like that part of my instructions." He grinned again at her.

"I will need most of my men, but I can spare a handful to protect you. And I will leave my lieutenant as well. He is also a friend of my stepbrother. I'm sure you know him as well — Augustin Pascal? He has flawless manners, and I'm sure you will enjoy his company. Au revoir, Madame."

After a brief conversation with Augustin Pascal, Maurice rode off with the bulk of his men, reflecting that he would have to revise a part of the plan that had been troubling him — Athalie's certain knowledge of what Pierre had seen in Paris. Having seen her again, proud, disdainful, cold, yet knowing for certain that she was not cold, sent an exquisite thrill through his body. The shape of a scheme moved heavily through the depths of his mind.

* * *

For Athalie, the days following Maurice's departure seemed to reveal themselves slowly, sadly, and endlessly; they dawned, dark and hidden, to clear by full afternoon, but only half-heartedly, leaving breathless haze through which the sun glowed without warmth or cheer. In the mornings, she lay listless in her bed, postponing the inevitable confrontations that filled her with dread. Once she was up and about, it seemed she was never alone. If she walked in the garden, if she sat by the kitchen fire, if she rode out to the village church, she was always followed and watched by one of Maurice's men.

Though the men themselves were quiet and distant, their constant presence destroyed the freedom that had been her joy. She longed to hide from them in the refuge of her bedroom, but to meet Gabrielle's demands, and also to maintain her own self-respect, she forced herself to continue the routine of her life.

Though the underlings did not intrude more than was necessary, their chief was not so reticent. It amused Augustin Pascal to assume the attitude of a guest, rather than a jailer. To maintain this pretense, he took dinner and supper with Athalie, insulting her, she thought, by the affectation of exquisite courtesy and debonair conversation.

She felt that she hated him more than anyone she had ever known, perhaps because the very first time she had taken cognizance of his existence, it had been as an avowed enemy of Pierre, perhaps because he seemed to mock as well as threaten her.

In her imagination, she saw Maurice as a hideous toad, whose repulsive evil was displayed with an extenuating honesty, whereas this — fop — was handsome, virile, graceful, and yet behind his trappings, was as treacherous and black-hearted as Maurice. Only his stammer marred his outward perfection, and Athalie came to anticipate and appreciate it. Once, indeed, she laughed out loud as he spoke, she who would normally have found it shameful to mock a cripple. She knew by instinct that Pascal wanted to strike her for laughing, but instead of fear, she felt exultation, and her defiance stopped him in his tracks.

How could two brothers be so different, she often wondered. Then, she would comfort herself with the bitter irony that while Augustin held her prisoner, Aimeri was ensuring Pierre's freedom.

Her thoughts seemed to circle in a pattern of relentless, unrelieved gloom. If she shook off the hold of one form of dread, it would only be to fall headlong into yet another pit of despond.

First and foremost, the fate of her baby occupied her mind. She would wake in a vise of panic; the same fear would grip her as she drifted off to sleep. She turned over in her mind a hundred times the same solutions that were no solutions — send the baby away, but how? and with whom? and to whom? Her nurse could be trusted, but she was too old, and how would she evade the watchful eyes all around them?

Or perhaps she herself could escape at night, but the drop from her window was a sheer fifty feet, and a man slept across her door. Exhausted, she would push the problem from her mind, only to find the void filled with an inchoate dread concerning Pierre, Pierre and herself, Pierre and his wife, Pierre....

If, at last, she tried to suppress all personal preoccupations, she found increasingly that the very state of the world seemed to urge her to despair. More and more, she was haunted by images of brutality and faithlessness and intolerance.

She dreamed one morning that she was at Court, in bed with Pierre and happy, oh, so happy. She awoke in the misty October gloom with a panic-stricken sense that she had lost him forever. "My God," she whispered, "I am well punished for usurping the right to love you, by the horror the thought of losing you inspires in me."

Chapter XXXVII

he days of autumn seemed tiresome and dismal to Anne. Her time was near — of that she was certain, though how near, she could not say for sure. Her body felt like an ark, clumsy and heavy. Each activity required more effort than it should, more effort often than it was worth. Normally vibrant with activity, she found the enforced idleness, with its time for unwanted reflection, added restlessness to her discomfort.

Even the graceful charms of Villandry failed to arouse her interest, although she found them soothing and pleasant. She strolled with her ladies in the celebrated gardens, although the hot, dry summer had not left them at their best. They attempted a picnic on the banks of the Cher, but the hazy sunshine had faded and a chilly, damp breeze had forced the party indoors. They had sung madrigals, played draughts, and read poetry. None of it helped much. Anne was bored, bored, bored!

At least, she thought sourly, I am here rather than in that great prison, Plessis Gaillard. She shuddered as she remembered its cheerless damp last spring, relieved by the stiff and old-fashioned protocol of meals which seemed all of a piece with its ancient stonework. This line of thought led, as it often did, to Pierre, whom she contemplated with a mixture of emotions in which bitterness and pique predominated. She brooded often on his plight, which threatened her position as much as his own.

He had told her little enough of his activities in Paris, but from snippets of conversation she had formed a bleak view of his prospects. His present situation in hiding somewhere, resulting in her own exile from Court and civilization, was not only unendurable, it was frightening. If his lands were confiscated, where would that leave her and her child? Perhaps it would blow over and he would be pardoned, but he must have made some powerful enemies. Perhaps he would be captured, perhaps the King would be satisfied with his head and would allow the family properties to pass to her child. She would manage the property and raise the child; both things she would do well. In time, she would remarry, perhaps even better than before, although a traitor's widow might encounter difficulties on that score. But a wealthy traitor's widow? All things could be accomplished by someone who was adroit and energetic.

Anne thought about these alternatives quite cold-bloodedly, as was her wont. She was not sentimental about things that mattered. And yet, she felt a certain regret tinge her reflections. Pierre's brusque decisiveness in Paris and his ironfisted control of their march south had presented an intriguing novelty, had attracted her, in fact. There were, she realized, sides to his character that she had overlooked. It seemed a waste that she should be deprived of the opportunity of knowing him through and through, and waste was something she abhorred. Sitting by her window in the chilly sunlight, the rectangles and arabesques of the gardens spread out below her, she found herself dreaming of Pierre, pardoned and reinstated, and herself, the leading lord and lady of the land. When she caught herself at these fantasies, she never failed to be amazed at herself. She attributed the daydreams to the monotony of her existence.

Above all things, Anne was a social creature. She found her seclusion and the lack of news, gossip, and conversation almost unbearable. So it was that when a servant announced Maurice's arrival, her heart surged with unreasonable delight. It was not that she had any special fondness for him. Indeed, she had never accounted him significant enough to warrant attention. Still, he was company and at Court he had always been amusing enough. She did experience a momentary qualm remembering the circumstances of their departure from Paris, but, she thought, that embarrassment was nothing to her at the time and could be put behind them.

Maurice had the long ride from Plessis Gaillard north of the Loire to Villandry to plan his approach to Anne. He had not really been surprised to find Pierre's fortress deserted, and he doubted that Pierre would be found at Villandry, either. However, he suspected that Anne was the key, odd as that might have seemed. He chuckled to himself, that what was even odder was that it should seem bizarre: to suppose a man would want to be near his own wife.

His reflections typically included a calculation of how he could use the events fate put before him, first of all for his own benefit. As his troop trotted over the plateau between the Loire and the Cher, he concluded that the situation presented a number of promising possibilities, particularly as he was removed by many days and miles from Gondi's supervision. He had already made sure of Athalie. She was under control and, at worst, he would simply carry out his orders, bringing her, sans child, to seclusion in Burgundy.

It remained to be seen whether a more amusing and potentially more profitable use could be found for the lovely and disdainful duchess. That use, he recognized, would require some hard bargaining with Gondi. Maurice smirked as he considered that having Pierre in his power, he would have rather a lot to bargain with.

That brought his thoughts to Anne, Anne the golden, mischievous, brilliant darling of every unattached, and many married, men at Court. She had always been polite to him, and he did not remember giving her offense. She had seemed in a daze on their trip south. It was clear from her outburst that she had no part in Pierre's exploits in Paris, indeed seemed to deplore them. She was beautiful, and was, it was to be hoped, soon to be a widow.

But would she be a wealthy widow? By herself, she was only another charming woman, but if she had the title, or her child did, if she had the wardship — if, he chuckled, he should have it — well, that would be worth looking into. He chuckled again as he thought how sweet it would be to be lord where that old bastard, the late Duke, had so humiliated him. And for his most excellent service, what would be a more fitting reward?

He decided that Anne was potentially a friend and was most definitely needed as an ally. Despite the long ride, he was in excellent spirits when they arrived at Villandry. He elected to gamble that Pierre was not at home and left his men outside the walls, so he could more readily approach his dear sister-in-law as the friend he hoped to become.

Maurice found Anne seated in an armchair padded with red brocade, her feet on a matching stool. She had draped the heavy folds of her skirt as decoratively as possible over her protruding belly. Despite the damp chill in the air, she looked hot. In spite of himself, Maurice found the inevitable words, how lovely she is, forming in his mind.

Anne stretched out her hand, and he bent down and kissed it, then sprawled on an armchair facing her.

"And how do I find Madame la Duchesse?" he asked with exaggerated solicitude.

"As well as can be expected." She smiled, waving her hand gracefully over her belly. "This, too, will pass, my friend."

She lowered her head and shot a coy glance at him through her lashes. "I don't know what brings you here," she continued, her voice low and melodious, "but for my part, your arrival is most welcome. I hope you will not hurry away. Can you not make this your home for a while?"

Maurice contrasted her coquettish manner and swollen physique and decided that she was repulsive.

"That depends," he replied brusquely.

"I never knew exactly what passed between my husband and you," she continued, innocently raising her eyes, "but surely it need not preclude our friendship in the future. Families should stick together, don't you think?"

Maurice was momentarily nonplussed. Dissembling bitch, he thought, what is she after? And what kind of fool does she take me for?

"Ah, yes, your husband, my stepbrother," Maurice replied, suddenly all business. "That brings me to the point of my visit." He paused and thought, if she wants to play the game of sweet innocence, perhaps it will serve my purpose. "There was, as you say, a misunderstanding, an unfortunate misunderstanding, between Blondel and myself. I would like to set things right. Where is he, if I may ask?"

"Pierre is — is — how shall I say it? Keeping himself safe in concealment. He believes he is in danger, but I suppose you know all about that."

"I need to see him."

"I would like to see him, too. Of course," she replied sweetly.

"I would reassure him."

"How?" she asked, genuinely interested. Perhaps things were going to turn out for the best....

Maurice tapped his purse. "I have a pardon for him."

A flash of unfeigned joy crossed Anne's face, followed by a cloud of worry. "I would like to see it."

"Madame," Maurice replied stiffly, "it is for your husband, not for you."

She reflected for a moment, then said quietly, "The last time you bore the King's writ to my husband, it was for his arrest. He showed it to me. I must see this new paper."

"Madame, the King's business is no concern of yours."

"If it concerns my husband, it concerns me," she retorted more sharply than she had intended.

"How noble!" Maurice's lip curled sarcastically.

"At any rate," she continued with a gentle shrug, "I don't know where he is."

She looked at him curiously.

"What brought you here, Maurice, in the first place?"

"In the first place?" Maurice laughed, then continued in a serious tone. "Why, Madame, I was and I am confident that the wife of Pierre knows Pierre's whereabouts."

"You are mistaken."

Maurice cocked his head and looked at her, disbelieving.

"He told me it was safer thus," she added almost apologetically.

Maurice stood abruptly, towering over her. "Don't toy with me. Because of that," he jabbed a finger at her belly, "he would not leave you. Whatever you may be, you bear the heir to the de Galle estates. And so, I know he would stay in touch."

She shrugged, looking up at him with an expression of pride and defiance.

"You know how to find him," Maurice said, "and you will do it for me."

"You're mad, Maurice. Please sit down. Looking up at you is giving me a crick in the neck."

He lowered himself obediently into the armchair and contemplated her in silence. She smiled triumphantly at his apparent meekness.

"Do you want to know," Maurice said at last, "why you will do it for me?"

She rolled her eyes heavenward, then stared at him coldly. "You will tell me, whatever I say, so let's get it over with."

"You believe you carry the heir to the de Galle estates," he said quietly, "or rather, you wish the world to believe it."

Anne rose up in anger. "You dare!"

"Never mind," he said placatingly. "That's beside the point. The point is, when Pierre gets through with his foolishness, will there be any estates to be heir to?"

"So," she hissed, "your pardon was a lie!"

"You played with me; I played with you." Maurice shrugged and helped himself to the wine in a carafe at Anne's side.

"I don't see how delivering him into your hands, assuming I could do it, would help matters," Anne asked.

"Bear with me." He smiled unpleasantly. "There is a second problem with the inheritance — and this, I believe you do not know. That," he pointed again at her belly, "had better be a boy."

"It is to be wished, certainly."

"From your point of view, Madame, it is essential," Maurice paused theatrically. "Because," he lied, "your husband already has a son."

Anne's face drained white, taking on a blank and stupid expression from the shock of his revelation.

"He has a son by the Duchess de la Roque," Maurice continued. "I've seen the baby with my own eyes, a fine, healthy child. You asked me before why I came here, and I mouthed some tale of conjugal piety. I will tell you the truth. Athalie herself told me Pierre had gone to be with you at Plessis Gaillard. Now, I knew she was lying. Indeed, you were not at Plessis Gaillard, but here at Villandry and Pierre is not with you. And yet, I also knew there was a grain of truth in it. I knew Pierre had arranged for you to summon him when the baby was born. And do you know how I know that?"

He paused. Anne stared at him numbly. "Do you?" he insisted.

Forced to react, she shook her head.

"Because she — his mistress — told me that if your baby was a girl, Pierre intended to recognize the bastard, her child, as his heir. You see, Anne, he will never return to you. If you produce a legitimate heir, all well and good, but otherwise Athalie's son will be heir — heir to whatever there is to inherit when Pierre dies. But in either event, he won't come back to you. You might as well be a widow."

"You're lying," Anne hissed. "You are a devil, Maurice, a devil. I won't listen to you." Her voice rose in pitch as she spoke, and she covered her ears with her palms.

"It's true that he told you how to summon him," he barked, "isn't it?" Her hands still at her head, the fingers splayed, Anne turned her face away.

"Now you know why. You didn't really think it was affection for you." Maurice's voice was harsh. "In honesty, how could he feel love for you? or for that?" he said, indicating Anne's swollen middle. Maurice then slipped around her footstool and knelt by her chair, leaning on the arm. "Be honest," he said softly. "You're a realist and I respect that."

She dropped her hands into her lap but kept her eyes averted.

"Listen," Maurice went on gently. "You're upset, but the solution is obvious. Let me help you. Summon him. Your time is nearly come, isn't it?"

She nodded. "October. Any time now," she whispered.

"It's not too late," he said. "Summon him."

"What good will that do?" Anne asked wearily, "and if you take him, what of it? My child is at least legitimate, and anyway, Pierre's land will be forfeit. He has made a mess of everything, and how can you help matters?" She eyed him appraisingly.

"Don't count on forfeiture," Maurice replied. "He is, after all, a member of the club." There was no dissimulation of the bitterness in his voice. "All the great nobles, his father's friends, will pester the King on his behalf. He'll die all right, but with a purple cloth on the scaffold and everyone in Paris weeping. He'll be allowed to leave his lands as he pleases, and I tell you it will be to Athalie's son. Believe me, I know how these things work. They won't let a rich wardship be forfeited. It will go to Albert de Gondi, Athalie's uncle, most likely. Athalie's son will be duke, and you will be put out to pasture.

"Even if you have a son," he paused for breath, "Pierre can complicate matters endlessly, leaving your son an older brother with a good claim and powerful friends. Anne, I simply can't let the fool do this to someone like you."

Anne stared silently into the distance. Finally she said, "I still don't see how you can help, or why you would want to. You are Albert de Gondi's man, after all."

"I am my own man," Maurice bristled. "I wear these colors for the time being, but I tell you that in a little while Albert de Gondi will be glad to call himself my friend. For you, Anne, for both of us," he added huskily, ignoring her raised eyebrow, "all you have to do is this: Summon him. I will carry out the King's order and place him under arrest. Thereafter, I am sure he will try to escape, and it will be necessary... I'm sure you understand.

"It won't be difficult, you see, Pierre is basically a coward," Maurice assured her earnestly.

"Well, he certainly had you bested the last time we met," she said, breaking her resolve not to speak of their last encounter.

"No, but I knew he'd never have the guts to hurt me. That was the only thing the old Duke and I ever agreed on," he laughed harshly.

"I don't mind telling you," he continued, "I warned Gondi more than once that he could never count on my stepbrother. All Gondi ever wanted was to push him forward; now I'm sure you can see Pierre has put Gondi in a very difficult position. I, of course, have proven my loyalty in the most difficult possible assignment. But you must see that Pierre has completely blotted his copybook."

"Oh, I see that all right, it's just what I said to him myself!" Anne cried bitterly.

"If you do as I say," Maurice chattered on, "he will never have time to arrange matters with his mistress. The other child will be nothing — an unknown, unclaimed bastard. For your service to the King, which I will vouch for, I can guarantee there will be no confiscation. I promise it. You and your child will come into your own, into what is yours by right. If you wait, it will be too late. Once the child is born, if it's a girl, he won't come. We'll both be thwarted then."

Anne turned away. "Athalie," she whispered slowly, "the little nun, it isn't possible, he wouldn't. It is humiliating. Athalie?"

Anne's eyes filled with tears. She brushed them away impatiently, dropping her hand again into her lap. Maurice covered her two small hands with his large one.

"Let me help you," he whispered earnestly. "Let us help each other. You said," a half laugh rumbled in his throat, "you said families should stay together. Let me be your family. Pierre doesn't want you, but I? You've done nothing to me. I admire you. Together we can save things, yes, make something wonderful!"

She turned and stared into his intense, brown eyes, only inches from her own. She shuddered. "I'll tell you where he said to write. Then you can go... and do what you will."

"No." Maurice squatted back on his haunches. "A troop like mine is noticed. He might be warned of our coming and slip away. Here, we can lie low, and he'll walk into the trap all unsuspecting."

"I don't want him here, not after..."

"Be brave," he gripped her hands. "I know you are brave. My dear Anne, permit me. I understand you. Pierre never did. You are magnificent. Your reward will be great..."

She suppressed a hysterical desire to laugh, but nodded. "All right," she murmured, "all right."

"I knew I could count on your good sense," Maurice beamed warmly. And, he thought, with Pierre available when I wish, I can spare a few days to cement things with my dear sister-in-law. I shall be so much better able to comfort her if we become better acquainted.

"Yes," he said to Anne. "I will accept your offer of hospitality."

The next days revealed to Anne that Maurice had a fund of Court gossip which, much to her surprise, made even her blush, as well as less interesting, to

427

her, tales of his days with the Protestants. It began to seem that in all of his stories, vivid and amusing as they were, it was Maurice who was the hero, the center around which generals, ladies, dukes, kings, and clergymen revolved like so many puppets.

A few days were enough to convince her that if he was not altogether mad, he was certainly both odd and unpleasant. She realized that he was in his own grotesque way courting her.

She felt a horror slowly rising within her, a horror at where this was heading even if Maurice were able to fulfill half what he promised. Her feelings soon turned, as they often did, to rage at Pierre, whose criminal disregard of his rank and prospects had placed her in this dreadful position.

She began to make her own plans. Let Maurice work his will on Pierre. Pierre had reneged on his bargain with her, so best have him out of the way. As for Maurice, she coolly decided she would be his match in intrigue. She, at least, was not mad, and after the birth of her child, she would be as desirable as ever. She, too, had had the King's ear more than once. Giving full flight to her fancy, she imagined the royal interview, the tears, the protestation of loyalty, the embrace, and then the wardship. No, she concluded, she could deal with Monsieur de La Renaudie.

Afterward, everyone agreed that it had been an accident. Anne had returned from a stroll with Maurice in early October, a stroll she had decided on to profit from the suddenly fine weather, but which had too soon tired her. Perhaps, they said, it was because of her fatigue that she tripped on the stairs to her chamber and fell heavily into the hall below.

She was not hurt badly, she said. Her right arm was twisted, that was all, she would be all right. Her ladies fluttered and scolded, and soon she was put to bed. But then the pains came, and more quickly than anyone expected, a male child appeared among the bedclothes. The midwife, summoned late, looked grim, advised heat then cold, then looked even more grim.

Weak and wanting only sleep, Anne ground her teeth with pride and determination. "Write at once," she said to one of her ladies. "Write at once to Artus Pascal in Chinon, say I need a large loan. Send it today. Get someone to ride today."

Frightened by her lady's intensity, the maid complied, although she wondered if her mistress were not delirious.

Chapter XXXVIII

The warmth of Aimeri Pascal's greeting completely disarmed Pierre. Aimeri had politely refused his thanks or indeed any conversation until Pierre had bathed after his journey and rested. Pierre found that he had a comfortable room overlooking the town and the River Indre below. His host and employer had provided suitable attire, and rather sheepishly dressed in the strange blue-green livery, trying to still keep his inveterate chip on his shoulder, Pierre joined Aimeri two hours later in his study.

"Monsieur de Galle," Aimeri began, with what Pierre found surprising directness, "you are going to be my guest here for some days, and I thought it best if I should be frank with you from the start. I hope you will excuse my bluntness, but my father has taught me that it is often best to deal with awkward matters first. Here it is: I love Athalie with all my heart. I have asked her to marry me and have been refused. I know now that is because her heart is entirely yours. I respect that. I will love her for the rest of my life, but I know that she is yours, not mine. It is for the sake of her love that I will harbor you and help you as if you were she."

"I scarcely know how to reply, Monsieur de..."

"Please," Aimeri interjected, "call me Aimeri. I know how you old families feel about someone in my position. I'm sure I would feel as you do if our places were reversed. But it seems to be the way of things, and believe me, I know as well as you that it may take a few generations before someone like me could feel comfortable with a sword. I prefer books, myself. Some more wine? My father sent it over from Chinon. But forgive me, you were saying?"

Pierre smiled. "I was saying I don't know how to begin. I confess I was uncomfortable on two points, and you have just eliminated both of them! I love Athalie," Pierre said slowly, suddenly realizing for the first time that he was with someone to whom he could speak of his love. "I love her, Aimeri; it feels so dumbfounding to be loved by her, that is the thing. I say, you don't mind my going on about her, do you?"

"Mind," Aimeri cried, "I should like nothing better! She is so educated, so knowledgeable about the Latin poets, and is a very good musician, although she needs practice, and the taste she shows in what she plans for Islette! Ah, what a woman!"

"Is she those things?" Pierre replied slowly. "I suppose she is. You are right, she did mention something to me about Islette, funny little place, she seems to have fond memories about it. Look, I'm no scholar and I'm not much with Latin poets. For me it was so simple, I find it hard to put it in words. It's like when instruments are finally put in perfect tune, like the way you feel on a clear morning and your horse's canter has just the right rhythm..." Pierre stopped, blushing, realizing that his choice of image was not in the best taste.

"No, look here, Aimeri, it is just the rightness of it all, when I am with her everything that is important is right, there is something almost magical about her, about the way she touches things and they are right — sort of the way I remember my mother setting us right when we had messed things up in the nursery." He fell silent, his eyes downcast. "Ah, it was hard to leave her."

Aimeri regarded him with pity and affection. "I can do this for you," he said. "I will help her and protect her as much as I can. My father, whom I know you have consulted, is not without friends in high places. Not to put too fine a point on it, but certain people are rather dependent on his good will." He shrugged and smiled in self-mockery. "No doubt you would consider such tactics base, but I assure you they have been remarkably effective in the past."

"Do what you will and what you can," Pierre replied. "'Base' has depths I never believed possible. The baseness of money is nothing to the baseness of brutality I have seen."

"It must have been terrible," Aimeri said softly, "and it has not stopped. My father has told me of massacres in all the great cities, Lyons, Rouen, Tours. The south is in full rebellion. La Rochelle is the only Protestant stronghold left. It will soon be under siege.

"I suppose you know that the Netherlands Enterprise business fizzled out? No? Well, after St. Bartholomew's Day, the Dutch Protestants knew they could get no help from France. William of Orange has had to flee to Germany. My father is as worried about him as he is about you."

"About me, what do you mean?" Pierre looked up, surprised.

"Oh, my, yes." Aimeri said with a smile. "He was most distressed when so valued a client was attainted with insurrection, rebellion, treason, and lèse-majesté against the King's own specific orders. But my father takes a long view of things. He knows that if you can escape, you will probably be pardoned eventually. In the meantime, his credits are a bit shaky. Fortunately, those who will seize your lands also owe him money, so he won't be entirely unprotected. I say, I hope I'm not being too callous about it. My father likes you and was very glad I could help you."

Pierre rose and walked over to the window embrasure.

"Oh, I don't mind, Aimeri. Or rather, I do mind; it is, or should be, humiliating to be discussed as if I were a farm or a herd of prize cattle. But really, I have lost so much more that it doesn't seem important. Do you know what I feel most? I feel free! I have one duty to perform, to see my new heir, then I'm off for England. I'll be free. Perhaps I shall stay there. It's very beautiful, you know, great castles on rolling green hills. My mother used to talk to me about it. It would be so good never to see Paris again. Do you think they can ever wash the blood from her streets?"

"Well, you will be comfortable and safe here for a while," Aimeri replied. "I have put it about that you are a German mercenary I have hired as a bodyguard. It will be natural for you to accompany me, and it will provide an explanation for your sudden appearance. I am not exactly on the noble circuit, in fact I have been rather snubbed by your sort. I doubt I will have any visitors who would recognize you.

"Let's go in to dinner," he added, brightly, "shall we? I prefer to dine early to allow time for reading while there is still light. You say you don't know the Latin poets? You must allow me to introduce you. Now, Ovid, take the divine Ovid..."

Pierre allowed himself to be borne along, his misgivings, for the moment, put aside.

* * *

In the middle of October a courier unexpectedly brought the letter from Aimeri's father about family affairs, containing the lines:

By the way, Madame de Galle has written asking for a substantial loan. In view of her lord's situation I am inclined to turn her down, but I would value your thoughts.

The signal was given, and Pierre, with hasty but sincere farewells, set off that afternoon for Villandry.

He rode slowly along the poor roads between the villages on the plateau between the Indre and the Cher. It was the feast day of Luke the Evangelist, the 18th of October, and as is often the case, the autumn weather cleared and lightened into an apologetic echo of summer. Pierre made slow progress. Prudence had dictated leaving Phoebus, his great stallion, with Aimeri Pascal, and he was mounted uncomfortably on a wiry runt borrowed from Aimeri Pascal's stables. The steed was unremarkable enough, Pierre reflected, unless people had the wit to laugh at the sight of his great limbs hanging below the horse's knees.

He whistled softly through his teeth. "*J'ai du mal, tant, tant, Que le cœur me fend,*" the words of the old refrain returned to him. The poets always sang of love as a source of sorrow. His heart rebelled at the idea, and yet, in his brief time, had not the pain outweighed the joy? Anne, Athalie — what I have I don't want, what I want I can't have: a hopeless muddle, in short, but is it worth it? Yes, truly, it has been worth it.

Pierre clucked loudly and urged the horse forward with a gentle pressure of his legs toward the crossroad, then north to Tours, west toward La Roque. He would take the west road, but not as far as La Roque, only to Villandry, halfway to La Roque. He noticed with wry amusement the unwitting symbolism of the journey — his wife's domain was halfway to Athalie's, and now it would seem to be his final destination.

Ten miles to the crossroad, ten more to Villandry — he would never make the trip during daylight on this unwilling nag. How silly to have been forced to choose between anonymity and speed. Oh, well, why hurry? Pierre realized that he was happier at this instant than he had been for a long time, rejoicing in his freedom, even glad for being alone. A pang of guilt tweaked his conscience. Surely, he should feel something for his wife and the soon-to-be-born child — or is it already born? — but here on the lonely road, he felt complete, isolated, indifferent to their claims, to their very existence. And what is this pilgrimage intended to accomplish? Pierre asked himself. Oh, yes, you pretend to a sense of duty, but surely it is not that simple.

He recognized that the question that had softly nagged him for months was what bothered him. Is the child even your own? he asked himself. Surely you can't expect a great moment of truth. But Anne will not say anything, and if she did, you could not believe it. And the baby's face? It will show you nothing; it will not bear some visible stamp of its father's identity.

What is the point then? Do you want to punish her, see her helpless and in pain, and then leave her? Surely not, and yet... he knew how he cherished the thought of escaping to freedom, however perilous, how he hungered for the simplicity of danger that would be so much easier to handle than the entanglements of emotional demands. La Rochelle, the high seas, England — they were not merely an escape that circumstances had forced upon him, but a choice that he now made freely, with his whole heart.

He inhaled slowly, savoring a momentary exhilaration, before a nagging doubt took aim at the bubble of his exultation. Would these alluring vistas call him with such passion if he could have what he wanted? If his life were not a muddle, but straightforward, the way he knew it should be? He breathed deeply again, wishing his thoughts and feelings were as clear as the pure, crisp air of this lovely day.

The next day dawned as beautiful as its predecessor. Pierre had bivouacked in a copse by the River Cher, not far from Villandry, on a pile of leaves that some autumn storm had blown against a rocky ledge and left for the sun to dry. Pierre scrambled down the slope to the river's edge and stopped, crouching on the bank, to listen to the tumble of the water and the cry — pee-wit! pee-wit! — of an invisible bird. All around him stretched a brown world of bare trunks, denuded slopes, and sandy, silty banks, and yet, his surroundings did not appear barren or sad; the rosy light of dawn clove the darkness as a roaring fire gives a warm center to a draughty room. Pierre splashed water on his face and was shocked by its coldness, so completely had he fallen under the illusion that water which reflects the sun in pink and flame must of necessity be warm. He drank, filled his flask, and climbed quickly back up the bank.

A sudden impatience possessed him to have done with the getting there, to arrive. He cut a thick slice of cheese and crammed it into his mouth. Still chewing, he packed away the remainder in his saddlebag, collected the saddle blanket and the cloak which had served as coverings in the night, and throwing the one over the horse's back, the other over his own, completed the saddling with economical, practical movements.

A narrow, rutted path ran through the trees beside the Cher; he followed it. The horse's gait rattled unevenly against his legs; Pierre dismounted and led the beast, making better time on foot than riding. At last, the bank widened and opened out; the narrow forest gave way to a broad swath of flat, grassy land. In the

432

distance, he could see the outfall of the canal which enclosed the gardens of Villandry. He remounted and urged the little gelding to a canter.

Pierre rode across the plank bridge which spanned the outer canal, through the meadow to the moat, and across the small drawbridge into the courtyard of the silent château. Only then did he realize what was happening to him. From the shadowed arches that surrounded the courtyard, a score of men-at-arms surged toward him. They were ready for me, he thought, and wondered briefly if the melodious birdcall that he had cherished had been the warning of a sentinel. He heard the grinding of the drawbridge being raised and without further thought, pulled the horse around and drove it toward the tilting planks of wood. It would have been a tricky feat for the best of mounts to run up the slanting bridge and leap for the other side. There was no chance with this one. The little gelding swerved, stumbled, and shuddered to a halt. Pierre used the swerve to slide over the horse's side, and shielding himself with its body, pulled a thick, heavy dagger from his belt and faced his enemies. They came at him in a circle, slowly, cautiously, like men who know that the game is won and have no need to take a risk. Pierre glanced behind him — in the black opening, the moat ran to the left and right. It was narrow, but not narrow enough to jump. Turning forward, he saw Maurice.

For a moment, Pierre hesitated, then he threw down his weapon and ambled around the horse, his arms half raised, talking as he walked.

"Don't delude yourself, my dear Maurice. It's not your physical prowess that so impresses me. It's only that I've no desire to give you the pretext of killing me while resisting arrest. I could have enjoyed a fair fight with your stalwart friends — it would have been fair, if a little uneven — but your arrival changed the rules of the game."

"Go get him, you fools," Maurice hissed. "What are you waiting for?" The men looked up, startled, as if Pierre's banter had half-hypnotized them. Sheepishly, they trooped over to Pierre and surrounded him.

"Stepbrother of mine, tell me at least whether the reason for my summons has come to pass. Has my devoted wife given birth?"

One of Pierre's guards, a fresh-faced youth who had watched Pierre's every move with growing admiration, blurted out,

"It is a boy, Monsieur."

Maurice shot the young man a venomous look and remained silent.

Pierre continued to address him. "Do I get to admire the little brat and pay my compliments to his mother?"

"No!" Maurice spat out.

"Surely..." Pierre's eyes appealed to the soldiers, "that is heartless and unnatural." They looked away embarrassed, and all were silent as they entered the château.

When Pierre was alone, locked in what he imagined was an empty storeroom, a ground floor room with a high, barred window and a heavy door, he wondered at himself. Why had he asked to see her? To strangle the bitch? She had deserved it well enough, but anger and violence seemed futile in the face of a disaster, which, having already occurred, was immutable. He found, not without surprise, that he did not want to hate her.

He puzzled over that for a while, then thought of other things, inconsequential things in the present context. How would he ever now be able to repay Aimeri Pascal? That was indeed trivial, at any rate he realized that Pascal himself would think it so, but it bothered him. He could guess at the passage of time from the angle of light slanting through the window. As the day wore on, his preoccupations took on a more physical nature: thirst, hunger, the need to relieve himself. It was the lack of the basic necessities, rather than the overall situation, that began to rouse him to anger. In a way, he was glad — his own calm, his emptiness of emotion, had seemed unnatural.

It was dusk when at last the key rasped, jarring unpleasantly on his nerves, and the door swung open. Maurice entered, leaving four men with drawn swords in the doorway. His face bore a look Pierre had never seen before, a mixture of disappointment and resignation.

"It seems," he said, "that your wife now shares your desire for a tender reunion. Indeed, she has insisted on it. She had, it appears, a difficult delivery. These things happen, I believe. In any event, it struck me that it would be unfitting to obstruct what promises to be a unique event, so I've agreed.

"Take him," Maurice snapped to the four men. Maurice watched them go, wishing he could listen invisibly to Pierre's interview with Anne.

Two in front, two in back, the escort guided Pierre up a back staircase, through a great hall, up a main staircase and along a corridor. Pierre had spent little time in this, Anne's favorite house, but was familiar enough with its layout to know that they had reached one of the two massive towers high above the moat which were joined by the main part of the building.

The leading guard opened the door and stepped back, letting Pierre through, and shutting it behind him.

"He'll be safe enough in there," the leader said. "It's sixty feet down to the moat."

"But," one of the others protested, "he said to go in, and listen, and report what they say."

"I didn't hear it," snarled the leader, then he muttered half under his breath, "It's disgusting," or perhaps he said, "He's disgusting," the others couldn't be sure.

Anne's bedroom was a pretty room, almost as large as the tower itself, with big windows looking over the moat to the gardens, its walls covered with tapestries of cream and pale grey, with embroidery of gold and primary reds and blues. It was normally a light, airy room, reflecting well the elegant, fastidious tastes of its owner, but today it seemed to Pierre that an evil transformation had come over it. The closed shutters let in only an oppressive half-light, the fire gave off more heat than the stuffy room could absorb, and there was, yes, that was it — it was the

434

smell, pungent and noisome, of stale wine or boiled herbs or rank blood, he could not say. He approached the canopied bed.

Anne lay almost flat, a small mountain of discarded pillows piled beside the bed. Pierre looked down at her in silence, looked at her pinched, white face, her sunken eyes, the dots of fever on her cheeks, the beads of sweat — he looked and knew the truth. Pity and tenderness rose in his breast, pushing out every other emotion. She was only asleep; he could hear her breathe; she was still sleeping.

Anne opened her eyes. Without addressing him, she turned them toward a woman whom Pierre had not noticed, seated on the other side of the bed.

"Leave," Anne said.

The pretty, buxom attendant shrugged, rose, and left the room. Pierre watched her go, as if mesmerized by her reassuring ordinariness; he heard her laughter and that of the guards; and he wished that he, too, could escape into the trivia of life. He walked around the bed and sat down, staring at his hands.

"I know," Anne whispered, "what your face shows I already know. They wouldn't tell me anything, but I'm not a fool. I'm bleeding. They've tried everything — slanting my body up, packing poultices between my legs, even ice — they brought ice from God knows where — but nothing works. And then, this morning, the priest came. They still lied, but I wasn't fooled."

She swallowed and continued. "So many women die this way. Why should I be different?"

Pierre raised his eyes. Now that he no longer needed to fear that she would discover the truth in his eyes, he watched her face intently.

"I feel so weak." He could hardly hear her. "My life is draining away."

Her eyes filled with tears, blurring her vision of the things around her, of the gold brocade coverlet, the embroidered silk screen, the gleaming marble fireplace, pink with veins of white. So many beautiful things. She had loved them so much, and for what? The tears spilled gently over. She looked back at Pierre.

"I cry because I'm weak. It's not that I'm afraid. I don't think I'm afraid. It's just..." Suddenly, her voice rose with surprising force, "It's just that it's a shame!"

"I understand," Pierre mumbled, a constriction in his throat making the words indistinct. But did he understand? He could not bear to think of it. "Can I get you something?"

"No, nothing. What would you do for me?"

Pierre sent a befuddled glance around the room. "The baby...?"

"Is fine," she said. "A boy, Pierre, your heir."

He did not understand the intensity in her voice, but he murmured reassuringly, "Of course."

"I would like him to be named 'Gatien,' to remember our wedding."

"Fine." He gave his answer absently; he did not care, his mind was altogether elsewhere.

"Was the baby..." he began, "is the baby...?" He stopped. He would ask her. She would tell him whether the child was his. At such a time, there would be no more lies. There would be a moment of truth, as he had dreamed. But he could not ask it. Looking into her face, he knew it was impossible. He reached out and took her hand in his. It lay between his palms, limp, soft, unresisting. The gesture seemed to call her back.

"There were so many things I wanted to say to you," she began again, "but I can't.... They aren't important."

She sucked in a deep breath with difficulty.

"In the corner of this room there is a staircase. In each tower, there's a corner staircase. Behind the screen. Over there."

He nodded, wondering if she was delirious, then said, "Yes," for her eyes were closed. There was a long pause. He thought she must be sleeping. She opened her eyes suddenly.

"It goes all the way down, right down into the foundations. There are vaults, stone arches. I saw them when I was a child. We had wine..."

"Yes." He stroked her hand gently.

"This is the tower near the river."

"Yes."

She raised her head and seemed to focus her thoughts with an effort. "I told you, do you remember, Pierre, about a tunnel that runs from Villandry all the way to Tours?"

"I remember."

"It goes under the Cher and all the way across Tours to St. Gatien Cathedral."

"It sounded incredible. I remember your telling me."

"It's true, Pierre. The entrance is opposite the foot of this staircase, the staircase of the tower near the river. It's true, and it's your only chance."

"I see." He thought for a while, then added, "Thank you." He meant no irony; understanding it as he meant it, she smiled as she closed her eyes.

The room was dark now, except for the flickering firelight. The attendant stuck her head around the door, and as abruptly, withdrew. He heard her laughter again, and her heavy footsteps. Then he concentrated on trying to catch the sound of Anne's breathing between the crackling and sputtering of the fire. From time to time, he stroked her hand.

She opened her eyes once. She wanted to tell him to leave, but she could not. After a while, he saw that her eyes were still open, but he knew they were unseeing. He put a hand over her face, closing them, and got up heavily. There was a candle on a table near the window. He took it, lit it at the fire, and made his way around the screen to the staircase door.

Chapter XXXIX

he stairway was circular, wide enough for Pierre to pass with ease, well-swept and well-maintained. At the ground floor level, the muffled voices of Maurice's men arguing over dice came through a heavy door. But the stair, narrowing, went on down; the curve of stone was a tight fit for Pierre's broad shoulders, and he could hear the rough surface of the wall rub against his sleeve. A moist draft wafted upward to greet him, making the candle's flame gyrate wildly.

At the bottom, the stairs led directly out into a wide space. Pierre could make out a row of massive columns dividing the hall in two, and shadows of vaults around as much of the walls as he could see. To his left, the light touched column upon column before fading into darkness.

It was not possible to discern how far this subterranean edifice ran; it must run the length of the château, Pierre surmised. The vaulted hall was an imposing structure, with solid masonry and well formed arches, fitting for something grander than a storage place — a cathedral crypt, perhaps. Indeed, the smell reminded him of crypts he had visited on some short pilgrimages made in his boyhood.

It was not unpleasant, despite its unappetizing components — dust, desiccated rodent carcasses, mold. The reek evoked an agelessness beyond decay; as a child, he had thought that, caught up in devotions he did not understand, it was what was meant by the "odor of sanctity."

But how big this place was! For a moment, fear gripped him. What if the dying woman had been confused as to the location of the entrance to the tunnel? His candle would burn out long before he could explore this man-made cavern. But no, she had said it was opposite the stairway of the tower near the river, and that made sense since, by all accounts, the tunnel ran along the river. He had to assume that pursuit could not be far behind. He forced himself to think, not to hurry. He had no time for false moves.

The silence was absolute. He could not tell whether the thick stone muffled sound or whether the guards were still unaware of his escape.

Holding the candle out, stiff-armed, he walked around the column opposite the stairs and approached the nearest vault. If Anne was right, surely the door would be here. His eyes met only stone, stained black from some unseen leak, but otherwise blank. He swung around on his heel. He could see the column and the arch that rose from it, and, past the arch, the outline of the stairs and to his left more recesses in the wall. What he could not see was a door, anywhere.

He fought to control his panic and walked toward the row of columns. If he traversed the center of the chamber, he thought he would be able to see into the wall recesses, enough at least to make out if there was a door. He started out; at the first long stride, his foot hit a metal ring in the floor.

The entrance was cleverly made, a stone slab neatly fitted into the floor, hidden by the pillar from view from the stairs. Pierre's toe suffered a momentary wrench of pain, but he greeted the twinge with joy. He could have gone to his death, because, in nervous haste, he had overlooked a ring in the floor. A stubbed toe was little enough punishment for such folly.

Pierre braced his legs, grabbed the ring with his free hand, and pulled up. The slab moved, slowly at first, then with a sudden release which sent him sprawling against the pillar. The candle went out. Cursing, Pierre fumbled in the leather purse at his waist and brought out a flint and steel. He rubbed them together impatiently and at last produced a spark.

He knelt and held the newly-lit candle down into the abyss revealed by the lifted slab. There were steps, he saw, a flight of steep, wooden steps, discolored with age, that dropped three toises, three body-lengths, at least, at the bottom of which he imagined he could see ground. He swung his legs over the edge of the hole and hesitated, mistrusting the look of the planks. With a sigh, he nipped out his precious light, stuffed the candle down the front of his doublet, and bracing himself with his arms, lowered himself onto a step below. An ominous noise greeted his descent — not a sharp report from the cracking of sturdy wood, but a shush of yielding rot. Still bracing himself, he dropped his legs another step. It groaned at half his weight, and he did not dare test it further. His arm muscles screaming from the effort, he lowered his feet another step, spreading them apart to balance on the edges of the step. The wood held. He dropped one hand to the top step and leaned his body against it. The top of his chest just cleared the hole through which he had dropped. He reached out and felt along the cover slab in the dark. The ring on the top of the slab now flat against the floor was matched by one on the other side. His groping hand found it. Pierre gave a mighty heave and pulled the stone toward him and down over his head. It felt to him as if the entire staircase moaned and swayed beneath him, and sweat beaded his brow. Distributing his weight over as many steps as possible, he lowered himself gradually, in fits and starts, down the steps to the ground.

When, at last, his feet met rough stone, Pierre pushed himself from the hated stairs and dropped to the ground. He felt giddy. He remembered now that hunk of cheese so carelessly gobbled twelve hours before, and his stomach gave a convulsion like a sack being flattened and kneaded. How long had it taken him to reach this point, and how soon would Maurice and the others discover the stairs? Would they find the tunnel? He had no true sense of time. It seemed a miracle they had not followed him yet; he felt a movement of gratitude toward the fates, until a nasty thought struck him. He swiveled his eyes upward, though he could not see the stairs in the dark. Should he ever want to leave by the way he had come, it would be impossible. There would be no way to get enough leverage on those rotten planks to push up the heavy stone. The thought of being trapped in a sarcophagus, black, dank, with a monumental, immovable cover, flashed uninvited through his mind and brought on a spasm of queasiness. He forced himself to shrug. Why would he ever want to return to his captors? Fumbling nervously, he struck a spark and lit the candle.

The dim light reflected dully off the rough stone surfaces. He was surprised at the yellowness of the rock. Limestone, he thought; he vaguely remembered talk of quarries, and that they made soap up the road. It all came back to him slowly.

It was a great relief to see that the tunnel was high enough to clear his head; he had had visions of crawling on hands and knees all the way to Tours. How far was it, anyway? He stopped and thought — ten miles, maybe twelve. His heart sank at the prospect.

One thing was certain: this candle, a third burned away already, would not last for more than a tiny fraction of the way. He would use it to get the feel of things, then it would have to be put away and saved for unforeseen difficulties. He set out, running his hand along the wall, not out of need, but to get the hang of it for when he would be in darkness. The ground was occasionally wet, and where it was wet, it was slippery. What was worse, it was studded, here and there, with sharp points of accumulated calcium: This he discovered by walking on them, rather than noticing them, but a short while later, he did observe that each needle in the floor had a corresponding icicle of stone hanging from the ceiling directly above. Every few minutes he found a stalagmite that was tall enough to trip over; each such obstruction was matched by a stalactite that was long enough to hit his forehead as he passed beneath it. They boded ill for blind navigation, he thought with dismay.

The air was cool, but not uncomfortable. He was reminded of the nether regions of Plessis Gaillard, which he had explored as a boy. The cells and storerooms, the well chamber and the abandoned caves — he had thought of them as caves, though they were the work of art, not nature — had been sure refuges from the full heat of summer, yet in the winter they had been warmer than the draughty living quarters above.

The memory of his boyhood explorations comforted him; this was not so different, he told himself. With this illusion, he found the courage to blow out the candle.

It was curious how different the place felt in the dark; odd, too, that he had become accustomed to it, lit, in the short time he had spent walking by candlelight. Now, all its strangeness was renewed. He groped along, feeling himself hunch down from instinct and stumble from fear of obstacles, rather than from actually encountering them.

He felt colder, too, in the dark. That is certainly irrational, he chided himself — that poor little flame could hardly warm a moth. He put a brave face on it, straightened, and walked as steadily as he could. By following the wall with one hand to have some sense of his bearings, and holding the other in front and above his head, he made fair progress, avoiding for the most part bumps on the head and at the same time being forewarned of and sidestepping the more prominent stalagmites. It helped to alternate hands before the shoulder muscles of the raised arm protested too sorely. Yet even with all these precautions, the soles of his feet became painful, as the uneven, abrasive surface took its toll.

To forget his discomforts, Pierre thought about Anne, turning over the multiple facets of their relationship like a gem: she had betrayed him, she had saved him; he had hated her, and, yes, he had loved her. He wondered if Athalie would be glad at her demise, or whether she would feel troubled, bewildered, and a little sad, as he did. She had lost nothing by Anne's death, after all, yet he knew he would think it abject if she rejoiced in it.

As this train of thought proved more disturbing than comforting, he let the clamor of his physical wants overwhelm his psyche: fatigue had almost numbed his hunger, but nothing could disguise his thirst. Once, when he hand encountered moisture, he put a wet fingertip in his mouth. It left a harsh and bitter taste. Time passed slowly, he thought, but in truth, all sense of time was lost in the mind-numbing blackness. He had no notion whether he had been struggling along for an hour or for half the night. At last, a kind of dullness overcame him, such that he felt and fumbled along with hardly a thought.

He did not notice for a few seconds that the hand which had been following the wall shot out into emptiness and it took him a few more seconds to make his mind revive itself enough to focus on the fact. Now that his ceaseless onward motion had stopped, his legs felt wobbly. He let himself drop to the ground, grateful for the interruption, regardless of what it might betoken. Striking a spark seemed more difficult than he remembered; he realized after several attempts that the trouble was in the trembling of his fingers. At last, he made a spark and lit the candle hastily.

The sudden light, though little and dim, nonetheless made Pierre blink. As his eyes became accustomed to it, he saw that he was in a large cave, too large for him to discern its dimensions. He pushed himself to his feet and held the light up. It was an eerie place, filled with jagged stone shapes growing from ceiling and floor, some of them meeting completely like a half-drawn curtain.

Indeed, to Pierre's left the columns stood in a row, bulbous at top and bottom. Pierre peered around the last of these and what he saw made him think his eyes were deceiving him. There, beautiful and glistening in the light, was a shallow pool of clear water. Though it was very still, Pierre supposed that it must be fed by some kind of underground river, though he could not make out an entrance or exit in the shadows. He had heard of such things, and, indeed, knew of a place near Plessis Gaillard where such a river emerged into the open. He had even heard that water, flowing mysteriously under the earth, carved out caves and passages, and he wondered for a moment whether all these subterranean workings might have been architected by mindless water, but no, the tunnels were human work, sure enough.

He knelt down, and propping the candle in a crevice, splashed his face. Though hardly colder than the air, the water invigorated him. Cautiously, he took a sip from his cupped hand. The drink left a brackish aftertaste, but the simple sensation of liquid in his mouth brought such joy that he threw caution to the wind and gulped handfuls of water until he lost count of them. He felt like a new man, light-headed but full of energy. On the spur of the moment, he took off his supple, thin-soled boots, stripped away his stockings, and plunged his feet into the pool. Madness, he thought, laughing to himself, but though his body was cold, the irritated soles of his feet burned, and the tingling and prickling from the icy bath drowned their discomfort. He could not bear the sensation for long. After a few seconds, he lifted his legs and kicked them vigorously in the air in an attempt to dry them, then with difficulty he pulled his stockings onto his still-wet feet and slipped on his boots. He sat still for a moment, listening. No sounds of running feet or cries broke the silence. Pursuit, at least, was still far behind.

Pierre wondered whether there might not be a way out of this cavern into the open. He let his eye wander around until the light of the candle caught it and he saw with shock how fast it was burning down. There was no time for exploration. He must take the sure path, the tunnel, to the end.

He found the opening to the continuation of the tunnel easily enough and blew out the candle as soon as he reached it, but the merest glimpse of the dark, narrow corridor stretching away ahead of him was enough to give him a claustrophobic feeling akin to panic. He resumed his careful forward progress, but his mind raced. If he could find a way out of this rat warren, he would take it as soon as he could, regardless where it left him on the surface. The more he thought of it, the less he liked the idea of going all the way to Tours. Indeed, for him to go to Tours at all was folly, since it was, of all the places in the world, the one where he was most likely to be recognized. No, the obvious course was to go south from the Cher back to Montbazon, back to Aimeri Pascal's, and beg help again, much as it irked him even to consider it. Pierre's face burned. He had hated to accept protection because another man loved Athalie, and now he would be going back uninvited, of his own accord. It seemed loathsome to him, particularly as he felt certain Pascal would welcome him with open arms. Yet, he could see no other option. He could not go to Athalie, he could not go home, and he could not set out for England without help, with no money, no horse, no sword.

Pierre was so lost in thought that at first he did not realize that the tunnel had begun to descend gently. When at last he noticed the incline, he was puzzled. Could he have already reached the passage under the Cher? He was certain he had not gone so far, and surely, if he had, he would have noticed the northward turn. He continued more cautiously. The walls seemed wetter here and occasionally his feet slipped on patches of damp, smooth stone. He longed to light the stub of candle, but forced himself to resist the temptation. He heard a slap as his foot came down on a real puddle of water. He slowed his advance even more, putting one foot in front of the other with deliberate care. He felt water seep through the leather of his soles, then he realized his ankles were wet, finally he imagined that there was water up to his calves, and bending over, he plunged a hand into water six inches below his knees. He could not believe what he felt. He turned back, climbing the gentle slope to dry rock. There he lit the precious stub and looked ahead.

The tunnel, roof and floor, fell gently away, but straight ahead was an expanse of water, no puddle, but rather a small lake. He could not see whether the farther end of the tunnel was fully submerged; he thought he could see a small, dark gap between the water and the stone roof, but he could not tell for sure.

He blew out the candle and squatted down. Panic clutched at his throat, destroying momentarily his ability to think clearly. After the fear, and mingled with it, came rage — rage at Anne who had brought him to this pass. Could she, pretending to save him, have actually sent him to his death? And what a death, he thought shuddering — to drown or to starve seemed to be his choice. He fell back into a seated position on the slimy rock, feeling cold to the very marrow of his bones, and tried to think. Had she known there was no egress from this tunnel? He thought not. He saw her dying face in his mind's eye, and he could not believe that hatred had filled her in that moment of peace and gentleness. And anyway, how would she have known? Her people had not used this refuge in recent years. No, she had told him the truth as she knew it — that there was a tunnel which ran from Villandry along and then under the Cher to Tours. This then was an accident of nature, a crack in the stone walls or rise in the groundwater, he could not say. He felt a momentary relief, before admitting to himself that his predicament was likely to be fatal regardless of its cause and regardless of whether Anne knew about it or not. Despair filled him.

He could go back, but what good would it do? Even if there was an exit from the cavern, he could never find it in the dark, and if he returned all the way to the château, he could never get back through the trap door. The road back led to starvation; he would rather drown. Suddenly, a wild hope filled him: Perhaps even now, Maurice and his men were tracking him through the tunnel. The thought of the torches they would carry, the food they would give him, the simple human companionship their presence would provide, brought him a momentary elation until the craziness of the idea struck him, and he shook his head. No, it was madness to see his captors as saviors.

There was nothing for it but to take the plunge. He put the candle carefully away in his leather purse, with the flint and steel, then stood and slowly walked forward. The water rose by inches up his calves, up his thighs. He gasped as the icy flood hit his groin and forced himself to end the agony of slow immersion by thrusting himself into the water and kicking off.

There was a nightmarish quality to this bone-chilling blackness, this terrifying thrust into nothingness, but he had never had a dream which was as intensely frightening as this reality. He swam with long, slow strokes, bumping into one side of the wall of the tunnel, then swimming freely for a while, then bumping into the other wall. At last, he reached the point where the roof of the tunnel came down to the water's edge. He could feel the stone right above his head, slanting higher behind him and lower ahead. He treaded water with big scissor-like movements and felt along the stone in front to where it met, or almost met, the water line. Yes, there was a gap, barely the width of his hand, but what did it signify? How far back did it go? He wished desperately for light. Perhaps the tunnel dipped here, then began to rise out of the water. If so, he might dive through and come out safely. But perhaps this was merely an unevenness in the ceiling of a tunnel which continued to run downhill, filled with water all the way. Then, if he dove, it would be to a watery grave. He pounded against the rock face in a sudden paroxysm of fury. The force of his own violence drove his body down, filling his mouth and nose with water. He came up snorting, his emotions cooled to a hard resolution. There was no other way. He had to take a chance and take it now, before he was worn out utterly by the cold.

Pierre felt with his hands to be sure of the direction, sucked in a deep breath and dove. He kicked firmly forward — one toise of distance, two, three. His shoulder bumped against the side of the tunnel. Four toises, five. His body was rising. He felt his head hit the stone arch above; deciding to take a chance, he flipped over to see if there was a gap of oxygen above. Water gushed through his nostrils and down the back of his throat. He coughed reflexively, covering his mouth with his hand, trying to hold in the air — a little longer, and then what? He kicked hard, again, six toises, seven. He wondered if he would know if he blacked out in the total darkness. Would the water in his mouth, in his lungs, wake him up or would he go, oblivious, to his death? He knew the ultimate moment was upon him and forced himself to kick again and again. Ten toises, had he gone even ten toises? He revolved slowly onto his back and opened his mouth. His lungs were bursting within him. Air rushed out, water poured in; he sputtered, gasped, coughed, and breathed air.

Pierre floated on his back, half-conscious, breathing frantically at first, then regularly. As his waterlogged clothes dragged him down, he paddled gently to stay afloat. Minutes passed before he lifted his arm and felt above his head. The roof was there, a foot or two away. He kicked languidly, again and again. He had no sense of urgency. The cold had frozen his fear, numbed him into thoughtlessness. At last, a kick brought his head against the stone of the floor. He turned over and crawled out of the water.

How long he lay facedown on the stone, Pierre could not have said. He had, in fact, quite given up caring. Finally, it was his own discomfort more than any more important consideration that made him move. The stone was hard, rough, irregular, and cold — everything was cold. Pierre gathered his knees in a tight embrace, and as if that physical act was a spur, he began also to collect his thoughts. Against all odds, a miracle had occurred. He was still alive. But if he did not use the chance he had been given soon, it would be wasted, for he knew that he had reached the point where he could fall into the sleep of death simply by relinquishing his will. He would lie down, huddled in on himself, and death would come. He thought, even, that it would be a painless death, the simple ebbing of life, and the idea tempted him. After all, he thought, why struggle on?

There will be another dip of the tunnel into water and he would not make it through the next one. He wouldn't even try.

As he became more conscious of his state, he realized that his teeth were chattering violently and that his whole body shuddered convulsively with chills. On the whole, he thought slowly, he did not want to sit here shaking and chattering. It was not... "dignified," and something tiny inside of him laughed at the word. He struggled to his feet and staggered forward. He did not even have the curiosity to think of lighting the candle.

Slowly, movement made his blood circulate and warmed him slightly. To be warm or even to think of being warm was inconceivable, but he noticed that he shuddered less and was no longer acutely conscious of the cold, but rather was simply numbed by it. And so, he made his way forward, not knowing how far he had gone, not even thinking about it. He forgot the cold, forgot the hunger; in spite of everything, he somehow had the strength to go forward, on and on.

When the northward turn came, he plunged forward, his left hand groping in emptiness, until he crashed into the wall opposite. The jar of impact shook him back to attentiveness. He leaned against the wall and tried to think. After a long, dull pause, he remembered the stub of candle, formerly so precious, recently completely forgotten. He fumbled in his wallet and pulled out the candle, flint, and steel. They were still wet, but he worked slowly, patiently, at making light, and at last succeeded.

He found himself facing back toward the tunnel; to his right, steps fell away — surely, he thought, that is the underpass to Tours, and just as surely, it must be underwater, unless the lake which was nearly my death was a pocket of water caused by an isolated leak. Anxiously, he turned left, praying but hardly daring to hope for an exit to the surface. His heart leaped. There was a narrow outlet, smaller than the tunnel, like some animal's hole, but just big enough for a human animal. He went toward it; it bent sharply as stone gave way to surface of packed clay. Pierre had to crawl. The walls were uneven; where they bulged, he had to wriggle to get his shoulders through. The candle was an inch-long stub, which he grasped tightly, holding it in front until, at last, he saw what he expected to see: a stone slab blocking his way. Please God, he thought, let it not be jammed too tightly, for I've precious little strength for pushing. He collected himself against the slab and pushed up and out. It gave readily, so that he half fell into the thick underbrush which masked the slab on the outside. He lay sprawled for a few moments, then crawled into the open and looked about. It was still night, but there was a suggestion of light in the bits of sky which he could see through the treetops above. Dawn, he thought, dawn of what day? He did not care. He rubbed his eyes. Ten more miles to Pascal's. Darkness, he would need darkness. His thoughts lumbered through his head; he could not seem to grasp them. He fell forward onto all fours, crawled into the brush, and slept.

Chapter XL

aurice de La Renaudie entered the library, closed the door, and walked slowly to the ornate table. There, mocking him, was the letter he had been writing to Gondi the evening before, after sending Pierre in to see Anne. Now what to say, he thought, as he sat heavily in the seat he had occupied the evening before. He had been engrossed in the problems of presenting his successes and laying the groundwork for the rewards he so richly deserved. He read it again:

Monsieur de Retz

I have the honor to report complete success in the matters you placed in my hands. Your niece is safely under guard, her embarrassment is dealt with, and my esteemed half brother is well and truly captured..."

Maurice remembered how he had heard the sounds, strange, — well, not strange but wrong, so inappropriate that the sounds did not at first register. Then, slowly he realized something wasn't right. What he heard was a woman's laugh, not just a laugh but giggling, playful laughter. That was what was wrong, laughter where all should have been solemnity for the deathwatch above.

With a bound he had left the room. Now the laughter was unmistakable, tinkling merrily down the dark stairway. He had run up the steps two at a time and then down the long passage to Anne's chamber and as he turned the corner, he saw the serving maids in the arms of his guards — the guards who should never have taken their eyes off Pierre de Galle — sprawled on the bench. Furious, he kicked one of the guards as he passed and burst into the chamber.

The room within was dark, silent, the only light the dying fire and the only sound the gentle hiss of burning logs. Suddenly cautious, Maurice backed quickly out of the room, slammed the door, and bawled for torches.

A few moments later Anne's lovely room, garish in the torchlight, smiled innocently at him. A glance at Anne's complete stillness told him that she was no longer among the living. Of Pierre there was no trace. Slowly, with weapons drawn, they looked under the bed, behind the drapery, in an armoire. So certain was Maurice that Pierre was waiting his chance to spring that a good five minutes passed before Maurice's eyes lit upon the tower door, and an icy claw of panic grasped his heart.

"There," he shouted, "search there! Call out the guards, he won't have gone far!" With a bound and a clatter, they leapt down the stairs and burst out onto the surprised dice players in the guardroom below.

These, interrogated, said they had heard and seen nothing. Maurice told a squad to cover the outside and plunged with the rest back onto the stairway and down.

The great vaulted cellar soon echoed with the trackers' shouts, and the great stone columns seemed to move and flicker in the torchlight like oaks in some ancient forest. The great space gaped, empty of any trace of Pierre.

A shout near the stairs indicated that the trapdoor had been found. It was unceremoniously opened and the dungeon-like pit beneath examined.

"You there," Maurice cried to one of the unlucky romantics at Anne's doorway. "Down you go, and tell us what it is. It looks like an oubliette to me."

Grasping his torch, the man started briskly down the ladder, then vanished with a shriek amid the sounds of cracking wood. His torch below illuminated his form, his neck crooked at an angle no living man could assume. Maurice swore softly under his breath, then straightening up, said aloud, "De Galle is a big man. He could never have used that rotten ladder. There must be another exit."

The searchers abandoned the hole and their fallen comrade and set off again to look for an exit from the vast hall. They found three, and all three were strongly bolted from the inside. Decades of undisturbed dust argued strongly that Pierre had not escaped by that route. Panic like icy liquid seemed to seep up from Maurice's groin. He resolutely forced himself to remain calm and gave orders that the hall was to be searched carefully by quarters. It was nearly an hour before he concluded that it was certain Pierre was not there and probably never had been.

Maurice walked slowly back to the stairs and sat down. Pierre had not jumped out the window. He had to have come down these stairs. He could not have gone through the doors and then re-barred them from the other side. He walked back to the hole opposite the stairs. He knelt, and shielding his eyes from his torch, tried to see how large the space was. He straightened up and barked an order, "Get rope, fast!" Pierre had gone down those rotten steps because he couldn't have done anything else. Certain that he was on the right track, Maurice fumed over the delay as men ascended to the guard room and came back with rope.

It was quickly put round a column and two men with torches were sent below.

"It goes on, sir," came the shout. "Looks like a tunnel."

With a cry between a snarl and a roar, Maurice slid down the rope.

"After him," he shouted. He cursed bitterly that more than an hour had been wasted. Pierre could have emerged from some exit and be miles away! Furiously he lashed his men along, and only after nearly two hours of trotting did he stop to ponder the amazing length the tunnel seemed to have. He was beginning to wonder where it led when they found the chamber on the right where Pierre had stopped to drink. There in the torchlight, unmistakable, were his footprints in the mud and the depression where he had stooped to drink.

Prudence told Maurice to search the cavern for an exit, but instinct urged him onward, and soon the squad was running, dodging rock formations as they thundered along the tunnel. "Hurry!" shouted Maurice at his flagging men as he saw Pierre's footprints again in the mud.

Suddenly they stopped, the glare of torches clear on the still, black surface of water across the whole tunnel.

"The prints lead in but not out, sir," one of the men observed.

"Where he went, we can follow. In you go, fellow," Maurice ordered.

"I'm afraid, sir. It is so black."

"Nonsense, it must be just a dip. Swim through and investigate. Here, stop your moaning. You shall have a rope and we'll pull you back if you get into trouble."

Timidly the guard waded into the icy water, a rope around his waist being played out slowly by his comrades. At last he kicked off and disappeared under the shelf of rock. Seconds passed, then a minute. Then there was a feeble tug at the rope. Quickly the rope was pulled in and the guard's form soon appeared face down, unmoving.

"Pull him in," shouted Maurice.

Hauled out onto the mud, the man lay unconscious, a bad gash on his head where he had struck a rock. Slapping and shaking him, his comrades brought him around until he moaned.

"Well?" demanded Maurice.

"Please, sir," the man mumbled. "It don't come up. I found nothing but water. He must be down there."

Maurice gnawed his fingernails in frustration. He sent one, then another to search the bottom for a body, and after half an hour, gave up. "He must have gone in, and he must be there still. He probably dove in out of fear when he heard us," said the sergeant.

"Perhaps. Leave two men. They are to search until they find something. His body, a boot, a belt, anything. We'll go back. I must find out what is known about this tunnel."

Several footsore hours later Maurice and the rest of his men, chilled to the bone, reached the rope and hauled themselves up to the great cave beneath the château. Dawn was nearly breaking as Maurice's men tumbled servants out of their beds without gentleness and herded them into the great hall.

"Which of you scum can tell me anything about the tunnel," Maurice snarled, looking balefully at the cowering group. Silence.

"Answer me!" he shouted. There was no answer.

"How's this, then?" he held up a gold ducat; it glittered in the torchlight.

An ancient crone, a cook by the look of her, sidled forward and made a semblance of a curtsey.

"If you please, Monsieur, I heard tell of a tunnel when I was a lass. Sieur de Revillars' father used to use it to escape his bankers," she cackled and wheezed. "They used to say it went under the Cher all the way to Tours, but that can't be true. No one has used it in years, not in my time anyway. Can I have the coin, Monsieur?" she crooned, looking at him with slanted, crafty eyes.

"Not so fast. Did your mistress know of it?"

"She may have done, the old master used to go all over the house with her talkin' of the ornaments and all. But you can bet her ladyship wouldn't go down underground. And now she's going to be put there forever!" she cried, bursting into tears.

Maurice idly handed her the coin, which seemed to provide considerable solace.

Maurice walked abstractedly to the window embrasure. Dawn was turning the trees golden pink. Is he dead? How did he find the tunnel? Did she know? Did she send him to his death? If he was dead, all was not lost. But if he had somehow escaped... Maurice shuddered. It was then that the men he had left behind lurched into the room, staggering with cold and weariness.

Revived a bit with wine, shivering by the fire, they reported that they had searched the pool as far back as light would shine through the clear water. Of Pierre they had found no trace except for two or three small blobs of wax. They conjectured that they were from his candle.

"Could the tunnel not go on, beyond the pool?" speculated Maurice.

"Aye, it probably does," said the sergeant. "But it must be worse flooded when it gets near the Cher. Even if it does come up, and even if he got through, there would only be an island with black water before and behind. He's a goner, sir, you can bank on it."

Maurice gnawed his knuckles. He wanted desperately to believe the sergeant. But he wasn't totally sure.

"You are right," he said at last. "You must be right, but I want to make sure. Take a troop to Tours. Look along the riverbank. He is not exactly inconspicuous."

"Now, sir? The men have been up all night."

"Yes, now! You damned idiot! Your men let him out of their sight. Suppose he did get out, he could be in England while your slugs have their breakfast! Go, now!"

Muttering, the men followed the sergeant out of the hall. Maurice sat down in the window seat and called for porridge.

* * *

It was afternoon when his men returned and the sergeant, his eyes red with lack of sleep, made his report. Not only were there no signs of Pierre, but they had even followed the tunnel back from the Cathedral. The retired dean, roused from contemplation in the cloister, remembered its existence and even knew where to find the key to the door in the crypt. They had followed a passage similar to the one near the château for some distance. About when they judged they were approaching the Cher, they found the way again submerged. There had been no trace of recent use, and the door in the Cathedral had been locked and bolted for many years.

Maurice smiled, then laughed and clapped the sergeant on the back. "Well, well, well, gone at last is Monsieur de Galle. See your men get some wine, tell them they have done well so far."

448

Slowly he nibbled at the pen as he took stock of the situation. A good deal of his success remained – Athalie and the baby. Pierre dead was not what he had been ordered to achieve, but thinking back to his last conversation with Gondi, he felt sure that Gondi would not be at all displeased. He would have some explaining to do to the Queen Mother to be sure, but if Maurice could provide an explanation, wasn't that the best of all possible results? After all, the important thing was that Pierre's mouth be shut; and, he reflected, what he had said to Anne about Pierre's ability to rally the flower of the nobility to the de Galle cause was not just talk. No, in many ways this was a heaven-sent outcome, if only he could get around the nasty point that his men had let de Galle escape in the first place.

Slowly the plan began to emerge. His men hadn't done anything wrong. Pierre was meant to escape, or think he could escape, into what was really a watery grave. He shuddered at the memory of that water, absolutely still and dark. But how did it happen, how did he find it? Anne! That was it. Anne was the key! Anne had sent him to his death. And happily, she was no longer available to say otherwise.

He sat back in the chair and smiled. Well, if Anne was the loyal servant of the Crown, she would have to have a fitting funeral. He would muster his men the next morning and do it right. He would take the young de Galle heir back with Athalie. The irony made him giggle. All would be well.

Suddenly, as when a cloud on a sunny day obscures the sun, the colors drain from the landscape, and the air is suddenly chill, the thought hit him: perhaps Pierre had escaped, after all. He reviewed in his mind every one of the reasons why that was impossible, yet something in him nagged that it just might be possible. Almost as if Pierre had escaped to spite him, to ruin everything for Maurice one more time. Yes, he thought, and ground his teeth, he would do it just to get me. And too, he thought, it would be well to make sure before claiming victory.

Reluctantly putting aside the golden visions of rewards, he forced himself to think of what Pierre would do if he had escaped. The Loire was the obvious answer. Pierre had to get to England. He had to get to the coast. In a boat, disguised, he could do it. Maurice decided then and there that as soon as Anne was buried, he would set out, make a thorough job of it, inquiring at the ports. If that turned up nothing, it would be as certain as anything could be, short of having his carcass, that Pierre, the Duke de Galle, had gone to join his ancestors. Then he would complete his report to Monsieur de Retz and be certain of its warm reception.

Chapter XLI

arly in November, Aimeri Pascal arrived at Islette with a small entourage. He joked pleasantly with his brother Augustin and made a remark about Augustin and Athalie that made the younger man's stutter obliterate his reply altogether. Aimeri, in fact, treated Augustin as one might a good-spirited but badly trained dog.

When Augustin tried to prevent his brother from speaking alone to Athalie, Aimeri simply dismissed him, and like a dog that has misbehaved, Augustin slunk away, plainly uncomfortable about his orders but unable to keep his older brother from having his way.

Holding Aimeri's arm as they strolled toward the Indre, Athalie giggled.

"However do you master the mighty swordsman? I have stopped him once or twice by laughing at him, but I haven't wanted to press my luck."

"Laughing at him would be dangerous," Aimeri replied, suddenly serious. "He is very good with his weapons and has a very thin skin. But he is used to being my little brother and even though he could beat me with one arm, it is in his head that he feels smaller."

The lazy morning sun was pleasant, but it was too cold and damp to sit. They walked up and down followed unceremoniously by Aimelie, the fuzzy, gangly sheepdog.

"My brother is keeping his distance, but I won't hold him off forever," Aimeri said. "First, Pierre is on his way — safely, I hope — to La Rochelle."

"La Rochelle?"

"Yes," he replied. "We decided it was the only way for him to have even a hope of getting to England. Rather than crossing the channel, we figured he could slip down the Loire by boat, then hire a fishing craft for the short distance to La Rochelle. He isn't someone who can easily pass unnoticed. We thought it would be better than trying to cross two-thirds of France to the channel. Once at La Rochelle, he should be able to get on a merchantman bound for England."

Aimeri paused, frowning slightly.

"Even so, I'm worried. There are rumors of war, and if there is war, the first place to be affected will be La Rochelle. And the English, though they be Protestants, are businessmen first; at the first musket shot, every English commercial vessel will flee the French coast like the plague, and there'll be no ships for England unless their Queen sends the navy. And why would she do that? Why shouldn't foreigners rejoice to see Frenchmen kill Frenchmen?

"Anyway, the King's forces could close the port, blockade it somehow. These things can be done, I suppose, even at La Rochelle. Still, it was his best hope."

"Unless the city falls," Athalie said. "Can the King's forces take La Rochelle?"

"I don't think so," he mused. "I've never been there, but I've heard tell it's a fabulous place — massive towers and walls surrounded by canals and swamps.

Everyone always says that it's impregnable. Still, I suppose it would be possible to starve the city into submission."

He shrugged. "There's no point in our debating such things," he added. "We don't know enough."

They walked for a little while in silence, through the long weeds wet with dew. At last, Athalie asked in a stifled voice, "Did he see his wife?"

"Oh, yes," Aimeri replied in a voice, half-mocking, half-sad. "He saw her all right. I'll tell you all about it." Briefly he described Maurice's trap, Anne's death, Pierre's flight through the tunnel. Athalie watched his face, her eyes wide with wonder.

"You should have seen what he looked like when he arrived," he laughed.

Athalie could see the lines around his eyes crinkling behind his thick glasses. She laughed out loud for the first time since his arrival. "Why, Aimeri, you're unkind to mock a man in such a state."

"Am I?" he said, holding her hand. "Yes, I suppose I am. I laugh at him when he is down, because when he is himself, I am consumed with envy. I suppose it is base of me."

Athalie put a hand gently on his arm. "Base! Dear Aimeri, baseness is the farthest thing from your character."

He flushed and turned his face away.

"But I wish you wouldn't... envy him," she continued.

He looked back at her. "How can I help it? I wish I looked the way he looks. I try to remember him all undone, but it doesn't help.

"Even more, I wish I could be like him. My God, to do the things he's done — what he did in Paris, and then this! The endurance! Pierre means rock, and he is a rock.

"You know," he continued earnestly, "my dear love, for I will call you that, and to Hell with it! But what I wanted to say was I don't envy him in the sense that I think he has received something that he doesn't deserve. It's just that I wish I could be like him, so I could deserve — you."

"Oh, Aimeri!" Athalie cried out in distress.

Aimeri took a deep breath and resumed more calmly, "Excuse me. There's no point carrying on like that, upsetting you." He stopped, then went on, "I don't just admire him. I like him, you know. Although he is... odd, complicated, I don't know."

"So are you," she said softly.

"Me? Perhaps. But not in the same way.

"I made him stay two weeks, though it was hard to sacrifice the time, because La Renaudie was roaring up and down the Cher like a madman. A hunter who thundered around like that would never catch his prey. We figured he must never have discovered the trap door and the tunnel. Pierre thought if he had, he would have come to the flooded part and probably have assumed Pierre was dead. That's what we hoped had happened. As he told it, no one would have had the guts to

451

dive and see if the body was there. Apparently La Renaudie never had a clue to what had happened.

"We finally had word that he had set off down the Loire, checking port by port for news of Pierre. So Pierre set out after him."

"Then Maurice will be here soon." Athalie trembled, and her words stumbled out haltingly. "He frightens me so much. He is just a little mad, I think, and so very evil. And he will be angry, anyway, I mean."

"Why are you afraid of him?" Aimeri stopped, looking at her. "And why should he come here again? He must know Pierre can't come back here. And why, for that matter, is my oaf of a brother camping out here and throwing his weight around?"

"Because La Renaudie works for my uncle Gondi," she hissed sharply, "and your brother does, too, or works for La Renaudie or something. Anyway, they are here with a commission from my uncle to... to get rid of my baby and bring me back to Court." Athalie stopped walking, turned her face away, and stood thus, stock still, as tears filled her eyes and ran slowly down her cheeks. Aimeri resisted the temptation to gather her in his arms and tried to think about her situation.

"Well," he said after a while, "I don't know that I can kidnap you and carry you away under their very eyes, so to speak, but I might be able to do something about the child. I don't know what they mean by 'get rid of'..."

"I don't either," Athalie sobbed.

"... but I don't suppose they really have murder in mind."

Athalie sniffled loudly and tried to dry her face with the back of her hand.

"I suppose they want to farm her out to some peasant family," he continued. "If so, I might be able to persuade Augustin to indulge the whim of his senile, older brother – for a small consideration. Augustin has always had his price – and it isn't very high."

Athalie picked up a corner of her shawl and rubbed her face with it, then looked at him with shining eyes.

"That's another reason why I've always had the upper hand of him, for all that he's a fierce warrior and I'm merely a feeble scholar. But that's neither here nor there.

"I think he may well make the condition that you are not to know of it, of where the baby's going I mean, so there'll be a whole pretense of my leaving and a day or two later his men will simply come and take little Gabrielle. If that happens, you must pretend to be very upset."

"It would be no pretense," she cried. "I don't know if I could do it."

"Even if Gabrielle were coming to me?"

"But I won't know for sure." Athalie's voice was tight and strained. "Maybe they'll take her and throw her down a well." Her tears started up again.

"I will let you know somehow, though it will be hard. I promise, dearest." He squeezed her hand tightly. "The only alternative is to do nothing, which is to let them have their way entirely."

"They're beasts, animals," she spat out viciously, then stopped. "I'm sorry. He's your brother."

He shrugged. "Yes, he is my brother. And, Athalie, as long as it's up to my brother, I don't think you have to worry."

"Aimeri, I hate to say this, but I loathe your brother. I fear him almost as much as La Renaudie."

"In that, Athalie, you misjudge him. He is a fool and has fallen into evil company. But he is not wicked in his heart. When he was little, he was generous to a fault and he cannot have wholly lost that trait. But I fear for him. Your uncle does not pick up someone like my brother without having some hold on him. And sending him out on this sort of a maneuver with La Renaudie... well, I fear for him."

"But why can't he be like you?" Athalie asked. "He is everything you are not, an arrogant bully!"

"Was it so hard for me to be good?" he replied slowly. "Did it pain me to be my father's favorite, always praised, always given responsibility, always taught that one day I would be the head of my family? Whereas he always had to take second place, always got into trouble, always, it seemed, deserved the trouble he got himself into. No, dearest, you must see, things are more complicated."

"Well, you can scarcely blame me for my feelings toward him," she snapped. "I first saw him trying to kill Pierre, now he is my jailer and may murder my child! I don't care what may have made him do it. To me he is a deadly enemy!"

A look of pain and sadness crossed Aimeri's face. Slowly he tried again.

"Please, listen, I am responsible for him. My father has set me up so I can really become the head of a family. My children..." he stopped, paused and looked away. "My children will be real nobles, with land, retainers, and skill at arms. They will be men the King can count on. That is what I must prepare. But Athalie, for him, all my father could do was to buy him a little title and hope his skill at arms would earn him some notice or military position. Instead he has made a fool of himself. It nearly broke my father's heart when he heard about that duel."

"Aimeri," Athalie said, grasping his arm. "Forgive me. You are so much better than I am! At least, if you can do what you say with him, you can keep him from..." she trembled, "from that terrible sin."

"And I shall try. Better Augustin should be dependent on me than on La Renaudie anyway. Here he comes, creeping closer. We'd best return. And if we want to do business with him, we shouldn't anger him needlessly. Come." He took her arm, and turned back toward the château. "Oh, see that red rock by the path?"

"Yes, I see it. Why?"

"Remember it. I'm going to tie my shoe and slip something for you under it. Come back for it after I've gone. Pierre loves you very much," he said softly.

As they walked back, she asked, "One last thing. Pierre's baby — Anne's — was it all right?"

"Yes. A boy. Pierre said his wife wanted him to be called Gatien."

Athalie nodded slowly, thinking of the Cathedral of St. Gatien, where she and Pierre had stood, looking down at the spot where they, Pierre and Anne, had been married. She nodded again, with great sadness and then walked on.

"W-w-w-well, esteemed older b-brother," Augustin bowed gracefully, "come t-t-take some refreshment. You must need it after being snubbed again by her chilly ladyship!" He laughed harshly and took Aimeri's arm as they entered the hall.

"It caused quite a titter at Court last summer, you know," he continued. "You with those spectacles and her with her convent eyes. Now you know that she w-w-would have c-c-cuckolded you. I'm ashamed of your manhood to see you here. But then," he drawled, heaving a red leg over the arm of his chair, "you wouldn't know much more about manhood than what you can read in b-b-b-books."

"Have you quite finished?" Aimeri snapped. "Because if you have, I wish to discuss getting you out of the mess you are in."

"What are you t-t-talking about? I have the honor to serve the Count de Retz, who is in high favor, and to work with his most trusted agent, Sieur la-la-La Renaudie."

"Spare me, Augustin, I know all that. The question is why you are in that enviable position. I know it must be trouble, and I only hope it is something that money can buy you out of."

"T-t-t-trouble?" Augustin gasped, turning pale. "How can you know that?"

"The Count de Retz is nobody's fool. He takes on people he can use in unpleasant matters such as this one because he has some hold on them. You'd better tell me about it."

"Well, I sort of got in over my h-h-head in a d-d-dice game," he smiled, all of his bravado gone.

"Dice? You mean you couldn't pay a gambling debt? To whom, may I ask?"

"The King," he murmured.

"The King!" Aimeri shouted. "You damned fool, you cheated the King?"

"Well, I didn't exactly cheat. We were playing after hunting one day in August. It was right after that mess in Paris, you remember, when that Protestant plot was revealed. Well, after that, the King was a demon for hunting. We went out two, and once three, times in the same day."

"What's that got to do with it?"

"Well, one night we were all sitting around, d-d-d-drinking and I had a l-l-lot and so had the K-K-King.

"We got to playing dice and he kept raising the stakes. Soon, I was the only one left. He put his arm around me and said I was his only friend. You should have seen the looks of envy they all gave me. Then I rolled and lost. In the morning, his squire came for the money."

"How much?"

"Ten thousand."

"Ten thousand what, livres?"

454

"Ten thousand gold ducats," he whispered.

Aimeri Pascal sat down and passed his hand over his eyes. "Oh, Augustin, Augustin, how could you have done such a thing? That's enough money to launch a small war. The King must have figured the family would come up with it. Oh, God, what did father say?"

"I couldn't t-t-tell him, could I? I told the squire I'd have to send for it. When we got back from the hunt, Gondi called me in. He said I'd made a fool of myself; I was in disgrace, b-b-but he would f-f-fix it and would t-t-take me on. I didn't know what to do. Then he sent me off with La Renaudie, and now I have this on my hands." He buried his head in his hands.

"What is it you have to do?" Aimeri asked gently.

"I have to kill that baby," he cried bitterly. "I'd fight anyone for him, I'm n-n-not afraid to die, but I haven't been able to d-d-do that." He looked up at Aimeri, his eyes dark with sorrow.

"Well, well, well," Aimeri rose and warmed his hands by the fire. "I think I can help you. What is more important, I will help you. The family will help you, and that is most important of all." He walked over to Augustin and put his hand on his brother's shoulder.

"First the baby. I will arrange to take the baby away. I'll send some of my people over tomorrow saying they are gypsies. They'll tell you they need a little girl for some purpose or other. You will seize the child and give her to them. The Duchess will not know what is happening and I'm sure her hysterics will pass muster when your people report them to La Renaudie. The gypsies are an invention that will amuse him and remove you from suspicion."

Augustin nodded dumbly.

"As for the money. It is a large sum. More than I can raise and one that even father won't find easy. But I promise you it will be done. But how to handle it?" At last he turned and smiled. "Augustin, I have it! Here is what you are to do."

* * *

A few days later, on a morning suddenly clear after some days of chilly drizzle, Maurice de La Renaudie arrived at Islette. His arrival was subdued, businesslike. Ten days down the Loire and up again had, as he hoped and feared, turned up no trace of Pierre.

It seemed safe to announce Pierre's death, but the close brush with disaster had taken the bloom from his enthusiasm. It was with mild annoyance that he accepted Augustin Pascal's elegant welcome, as if he were lord here.

"All is quiet here, Monsieur," he said. "The Duchess has passed a tranquil time occupied chiefly by those dreary little gardens by the Indre. The other resident problem has, er, b-b-been attended to." Maurice arched an eyebrow at him.

"Has it, now? That is good work, Pascal. Sometimes a man has a difficult job to perform, a job that takes real courage. I know it can't have been easy. I'll mention your work to our employer. This kind of loyalty should not go unnoticed."

"Th-th-thank you, Monsieur," he stammered. "Will you see Madame the Duchess now? I'm sure she is d-d-dying to receive you." His wink underscored his heavy sarcasm.

Maurice entered and ensconced himself in the most comfortable corner of the hall and helped himself to the wine and cake that had been placed on the table. The fire was welcome, for the day, though bright and clear, had turned sharply colder, and the autumn damp clung to the stones inside.

Athalie entered alone. She wore a dark blue velvet overskirt whose severe lines emphasized her height. Her dark hair was pulled back and held in place by a band covered with seed pearls. Maurice realized for the first time that she was a good inch taller than he was. She stood rigidly erect, an expression of disdain and contempt on her face. The slight flush on her cheeks was the only visible sign of her emotion.

Maurice regarded her in silence for a moment. "I trust Monsieur Pascal has entertained you suitably, Duchess? No, well at least he has followed his orders. Your, eh, child, will be no further nuisance. Your uncle Gondi has ordered your safe delivery to Ancy le Franc in Burgundy. It is the magnificent château of his wife, your noble aunt, I believe. I'm told it is most pleasant at this time of the year."

"If you were a man," Athalie said slowly, "you would be the most despicable man on earth!"

Maurice stirred uneasily. Her haughty contempt pricked him, and in spite of himself, he decided to cut her down to size now rather than later.

"Indeed," he said. "Well, I have more news for you. Anne de Galle died in childbirth. She produced a healthy son."

Athalie crossed herself and lowered her eyes.

"I'm afraid that your pleasure at the news must be somewhat diminished when I tell you that before she died, she sent Pierre to a watery grave. I regret to have to burden you at once with the loss of both your child and its father."

Athalie stiffened, her eyes flashing defiance. "I praise God that both Pierre and my little Gabrielle are beyond your evil power!" she snapped.

Athalie's reaction was not what Maurice expected. Puzzled, he shrugged.

"Your views are of very little interest to me or anyone else, Duchess. My orders are to bring you back to Burgundy where you can be kept out of mischief. Your airs won't count for much when your uncle marries you off to some Baltic lordling, if one can be found to have you. Alternatively, of course, I might consider taking damaged goods off his hands...

"We'll leave tomorrow," he concluded with a mocking half bow.

Athalie turned and left the room.

Maurice stared for a long time at the door as it closed behind her. Something like lust surged within him — not lust for her body but lust to dominate her, to break her proud spirit. He found he actually enjoyed her scorn and abuse, the feeling of power that emanated from her slender person. Rather than enraging him, it attracted him. He wanted to know it, in all its aspects, feel its masterful sway, and then bend it to his own will. He counted on the slow trip to Burgundy as time for beginning an acquaintance with this sharp-edged bitch.

In the stairwell outside the hall, Athalie, alone, felt for the worn piece of parchment hidden in her sleeve. Cautiously she drew it out, kissed it, then opened it carefully. Slowly and lovingly, her eyes traced the strong, well-formed letters that were her joy.

Dearest,

I write in haste to assure you of my constant love and to beg your prayers for Anne who gave to you the gift of my life. I will not rest until I have brought you safe to England to be mine forever. Do not keep this letter, it could put us both in grave danger.

P

Chapter XLII

ierre woke, brushed the moldy straw from his travel-stained doublet, and clapped his hands to try to warm up a bit. The small window high in the wall showed a patch of dull grey sky. It was day at any rate. He tried to think how many days it had been — two, or was it three? It seemed always to be dull overcast sky or night. Night or day, the narrow cell received only a glimmer of light. The day before, or was it the day before that, he had leaped up and succeeded in getting a glimpse out of the window. But for all his effort, all he could see was a rectangle of grey sky where the wall of the tower was pierced. He had not bothered to make a second attempt.

He sat down on the narrow bunk and pulled the straw around him for warmth. Nothing seemed to be able to keep out the chilly salt wind that blew in the slit from the Atlantic. In a slow despairing way, he turned over in his mind the elements of his situation since his arrival in La Rochelle, however many days ago it was.

Though he had no fight with the Crown, men armed with the King's authority were tracking him like a beast across France; and though the reason for this mortal pursuit was that he once defended the right of loyal Protestants to live, Protestants had thrown him in jail the moment they clapped their eyes on him. When he had been slammed into the wretched cell, he was not beyond seeing the humor of the situation, but he was now past being amused by the ironies of life.

He glanced longingly at the empty breadbasket. His jug held a mouthful of fishy-tasting water. So far, he mused, sourly, his plan of getting to England had not advanced very far. Aimeri Pascal had found a loyal waterman with a small fishing craft to take him down the Loire to Nantes on the Atlantic coast. But the trip had been agonizingly slow, as they had to travel by night, tying up by day to avoid the hue and cry of La Renaudie. Nantes itself Pierre judged too dangerous, close as it was to Gondi's home base, the county of Retz, and he determined to reach La Rochelle, seventy miles to the south, on foot. Again traveling mostly at night, he had made but slow progress, and November was nearly past when he arrived. The weather, rainy and cold, had cleared and warmed as he approached the massive outer fortifications. The frantic work of strengthening and rebuilding was everywhere evident as the citizens of La Rochelle profited from the momentarily fine weather. The bristling walls gave the city a forbidding appearance despite the morning sunshine, and Pierre was just giving thanks that his sojourn within the walls would be brief when he was seized and unceremoniously locked up in this dismal chamber. He was not afraid, but he was bored, frustrated, and hungry, damned hungry.

With a harsh scream of its lock, the door of the cell clanged open, and a dark young man, stern of expression, but full of vitality, strode in. So transformed was he by good health and an aura of authority that at first Pierre did not recognize the wounded young Protestant he had brought out of Paris three months before. Michel de Brossan looked trim and spry in black velour and shining breastplate; beside him, Pierre felt scruffy and clumsy. Michel grasped Pierre's whole forearm in his two hands and pumped it up and down.

"Monsieur," he said, "I came as soon as I heard you were here. This is a disgrace, but I hope you will understand. We are attacked from all sides, so distrust is a sign of the times.

"I have told our leaders who you are and what you did for us. But now you must come and explain what brings you here. I'm sorry, 'explain' is perhaps a bad word, I mean, I don't myself think that we have a right to demand explanations of someone like you, but the leaders..."

"I've already explained what brought me here to anyone who would listen," Pierre replied with weary impatience, "but I will be glad to explain again to your leaders, who I am confident don't share your diffidence in the matter of demanding explanations."

"Well, no," Michel looked embarrassed. "You'll want to wash up. I'll take you first to my room. Come, I am authorized to conduct you." Pierre, cold and hungry, did not have to be invited twice to leave his unpleasant lodging. He followed his liberator down out of the tower, around the docks, and into and up the tower on the other side.

That de Brossan was a person of some rank was indicated by the fact that he did, in fact, have a room of his own, a small cubbyhole which faced west over the moat and the mudflats beyond. As Pierre splashed himself with water and brushed down his clothes, de Brossan cut a large hunk of black bread and passed Pierre a goblet of wine. As Pierre ate ravenously, his host attempted the delicate task of explaining the situation at La Rochelle in a way which would warn Pierre of the pitfalls he should avoid in his coming interrogation, without either offending his visitor or appearing disloyal to his own masters.

"You see, the reverend ministers have taken charge of the city. The noble lords of our faith are all, well, either dead or absent. Some are absent under circumstances which, I must say, we find deplorable," he said bitterly. "I am referring to our princes, Navarre and Condé. They recanted and embraced the Catholic faith to save their lives during the August massacre. They kissed the hands red with the blood of so many of our brothers and sisters."

"'He who fights and runs away, lives to fight another day.'" Pierre mumbled the quotation through the folds of the singlet which he was pulling over his head.

"Yes," Michel said, "I know, but one doesn't like to think of people like that, not people one admires, or used to admire."

Pierre's head popped through the top of his shirt. "Don't you understand it?" he asked. "They're young, like you and me. They want to live."

"Yes, I understand it, but there are those here who won't. Even I, in my head, think it's wrong to put survival in front of everything. There are things worth dying for."

"I can't think of anything," Pierre snapped.

"You!" Michel exclaimed. "You nearly died for us in Paris..."

"That was different. There were people involved. And besides, I didn't die. I killed people myself. And..."

"There are always people involved," Michel broke in. "Martyrs who die for their beliefs do it for the people they leave behind."

"Do they? Well," Pierre said with a humility born of his inner confusion, "you must know better than I. You've surely thought about it a lot more."

Michel continued after a pause. "Well, we digress. I was trying to give you an idea of what goes on here.

"As I was saying," he continued, and observing Pierre's gaze drift toward the loaf of bread, he smiled and cut him another slice, "the ministers have assumed their rightful place as leaders of the City. They are the shepherds who must save the flock, as the Gospel says. We are all members of the Church here, and though there are many churches, and many ministers, we are really one big congregation. There are fifty-four ministers, and each has a say, a vote, in the government of the city, but of course, there are elders among the ministers, men of experience and authority. They are listened to. For example, there is de Grève, who was Admiral Coligny's right-hand man."

"But de Grève was in Paris..."

"He escaped by a most fortuitous accident. He had been sent to confer with Montgomery and the other lords who were lodged across the river in the Faubourg St. Germain, and he escaped with them. But he is very bitter over the death of the Admiral, even more than the rest of us. He was his closest friend, and..."

"I understand," Pierre broke in, almost rudely. "I understand his bitterness and anger, but what has it to do with me? I've nothing against you. I've certainly done nothing against you."

"No, no," the other mumbled, "to the contrary. It's just, you must understand, if they seem suspicious or unwelcoming, it's the fear and the bitterness speaking; more, it is their wrath. It is just and right that they should feel anger. They are the vessels of God, as we all are, but they especially, and they express His wrath."

"Look, that's fine, but..."

"Well, it's just that they will feel that anyone who is not with us is against us. Regardless of the past, they will want to know where you stand now, today."

Pierre shrugged. "All this is beside the point. I don't want to help the ministers or to hinder them. I only want to get on the next boat to England and be done with it."

"Yes, but you can't."

"Why not?" Pierre cried, "Why on earth would your people want to keep an unwilling, unhelpful, uninvolved outsider, like myself, hanging around?"

"It's not that," Michel said softly, "it's that — there aren't any boats to England."

Half an hour later, Pierre found himself standing before a group of severely clad, stern-faced men, seated around him in a circle. No one asked him to be seated, so he remained standing. As an effort at intimidation, as it may have been, this ruse was not a success, for Pierre towered above them, looking down from his great height with a natural, unconscious arrogance, which reminded each one in his audience of his own inferiority of birth and rank. Unfortunately for Pierre, this merely added hostility to the suspicion which he faced. A Protestant Inquisition, Pierre thought to himself, wryly amused.

An elderly man with sparse, grey hair and sunken, burning eyes opened the proceedings. De Grève, Pierre came to realize.

"We have been told by young de Brossan of your feats in Paris, Monsieur. Are we to understand that you have now come to join us in a more permanent way?"

"Not at all, Monsieur. My life is not safe. I am being pursued by the King's men, or men who claim to be acting with the King's authority, the Sieur La Renaudie, in fact, whom I suppose some of you have reason to know."

An angry buzz filled the room. It was being pointed out that Pierre was connected to La Renaudie — half brother or stepbrother. Repelled by that distasteful relationship, Pierre continued undaunted. "Therefore, I conceived the plan to go to my family in England, my mother's family; and there was no safe way for me to make the crossing but through this port. That is what brought me here. I had no wish to impose on your — hospitality — for a moment longer than necessary. I supposed that I could at least ask for the slight assistance of a safe passage through your city."

"You will now have heard that your plan is impossible," the old man replied tonelessly. "Every merchant vessel, English or other, fled days ago. You see, the Count de Retz's Italians prepared a rather nasty surprise for us, which, even though it didn't come off, scared away all the outsiders. Perhaps you know of this?" De Grève's hooded eyes watched Pierre shrewdly.

"Nothing."

"Fiesque, captain of one of de Retz's galleys, brought his ship into our port, supposedly to discuss with us, again, whether we would open our gates to the King's governor, but really he was reconnoitering. We caught him at his spying, his galley and another of de Retz's galleys. Between the first and second guard, we sent out three sloops and captured Fiesque's galley. De Retz's galley got away, though, so the evil is done. Are you sure you know nothing of this?"

"Nothing at all."

"It's just we thought it a bit odd, your turning up right after this incident. To put it plainly, some of my colleagues have wondered if you weren't a spy."

"For God's sake!" Pierre burst out in anger. The ministers looked shocked and whispered angrily among themselves.

"It would, after all," de Grève went on, motioning for silence, "be a way of working your way back into the King's good graces."

"I see. Yes. It's too bad my mind doesn't run that way, but it doesn't." Pierre looked down at them with fierce pride.

There was a silence, then de Grève continued, after a glance at his colleagues, "No, I don't believe it does. It would have been a clever trick, to pretend to want to leave for England, knowing full well it was impossible, as you would have known if you'd been with the King's forces and had observed the situation. It would have been cleverer than pretending to be a convert to our Religion and our cause. More believable. I thought it was possible that you were that clever. But now that I see you, I believe that you are too honest to be that clever.

"Do you all agree?" he looked around at his colleagues again.

Heads nodded, some reluctantly.

"But as it is now," de Grève resumed, "now, you are stuck here with us and we are stuck with you. The English have gone. There will be a blockade soon, very soon. That's what de Retz's papist monkeys were up to, I've no doubt, measuring our throat for an iron collar with which to choke us, bit by bit. That is their hope. But we can hold out and we will, until the English return, the navy, I mean, with soldiers, arms, and food. Then perhaps you will be able to travel again, if you still want to. But in the meantime, you must throw your lot in with us. Can we count on your assistance?"

Pierre thought a while, then shook his head slowly. "I will not take up arms against my King. I have no reason to fight my own people. Your cause is not mine. I do not believe in it. Great injustice was done to you, and I will not add to it by fighting against you. But it would not be prevented, nor would further injustice be prevented, by my fighting for your world against my own. I'm sorry, I can't explain it any better."

An outraged babble broke out from his listeners. Pierre could make out phrases. "He cannot stay." "We will not feed a useless mouth." At last, de Grève silenced the debate with a commanding voice.

"Messieurs, surely we are being petty, worse than petty. This man saved our people, and for that very reason his own life is in danger. If we send him out, he will fall into the hands of his enemies, and he will die. I wish he saw fit to join forces with us. We could dearly use his help. But I believe we must respect his decision. He has spoken well and honestly. I admire a man who does not betray his own people. We should not betray our own, either, and as I see it, this man here earned the right to be considered our charge, for we owe him a debt of gratitude, for which the sharing of our bread is little enough recompense."

"Easy to say now," one of the others broke out, "but wait 'til we're starving. He'll eat as much as five of our children."

De Grève looked coldly at the speaker and continued, "You do not always take my advice, nor do I think of my word as law, but I feel honor bound to speak my mind on this." An ominous silence brooded over the room. At last de Grève said, "Shall we put it to a vote: 'That the Duke de Galle be allowed the freedom of the streets of our city and such food as we can provide, until he can depart in safety.'"

Reluctantly, hand after hand was raised in favor, and the measure passed unanimously, if without enthusiasm.

The meeting broke up. Some of the younger ministers hurried from the room, giving Pierre as wide a berth as possible; others clustered in small groups, talking in low voices and eyeing him covertly. Pierre began to move toward the door, but de Grève, having concluded his business with the others, overtook him and placed a hand on his arm, both to slow his steps and to make a gesture of friendship. Pierre was surprised to see a smile warm the face which had been so grim throughout the meeting.

"I wanted to make sure that you did not take offense at some of the things that were said here," de Grève began.

Pierre shrugged, almost indifferently.

"Our accusations, our fears, were no reflection on you, but rather reflect the situation in which we find ourselves."

"I assure you, Monsieur, that I understand you have cause for a certain — distrust, shall we say?"

It was not a word that de Grève liked, and his face looked stern again.

"But just as you look at it from your point of view," Pierre continued, "I look from mine. Selfishly, perhaps. And all I can feel is bitter disappointment at being trapped here." Pierre's voice rang with the chagrin and anger which boiled up within him, overcoming all considerations of courtesy or caution.

At first, de Grève's face reflected a matching anger, but then his expression softened again, and he spoke sympathetically, "I know. You had a plan and a goal, and they were blown apart by circumstances beyond your control. But now, I urge you to reconsider your ideas. Give up your thought of England. La Rochelle is as safe a haven as there is on earth, and here you are among your countrymen. This city is impregnable, and our people have the will to resist far more than the popish forces have the will to attack. Our faith burns bright and gives us courage. Our enemies will sue for peace on their knees, long before we think of surrender. And when peace comes, all those of the Religion and those who have been our friends will be free to pursue their lives without interference. You will see it, I promise you. You are safe for now, and in the end, you will be free. You've reached a port in the storm."

"I hear your words," Pierre said, "but may I tell you frankly how I feel?"

De Grève nodded.

"I feel more of an outsider, a foreigner, here, than I believe I would have felt among the English."

De Grève looked at him gravely for a while, then smiled. "Who knows? Perhaps you will find it more congenial than you think."

* * *

A week later, in early December, Pierre stood on the wall of the outer fortifications, looking out over the inlet to the Atlantic. To his left and right, silent throngs of men and women, in clothes muddy up to the thighs, stood watching, as he watched, the harbor's mouth and the wide bay.

In the distance, where the bay narrowed to a mouth, two forts glowered, one on each side, both now occupied by royalist forces. Near the forts they could make out the masts of a large flotilla. Directly below, in the middle of the bay, the waves washed around the hull of a huge vessel filled with stones and sunk to make a platform for the guns now trained to fire from close range on the city's walls. Piles of hay stacked on it gave it the look of some mad barnyard in the midst of the bay. Some of the bales were still smoldering and smoking. The watchers on the walls had seen the bales smolder, smoke, and then go out. Sadly they realized that their superhuman effort of dragging the tinder all night across the sludge of low tide had been for nothing. Their hope had been to set fire to and destroy the menace beneath their walls, but their torches could not prevail against its solid bulk and soaking environment.

All day, they came and went, to peer down as the royalists worked like ants in the construction of a blockade between the new fort and the port's entrance. Boats were brought up and sunk in a line and connected with floating beams. All day, Pierre stood and watched as the Rochelais came and went beside him, until by evening the royalists' work was done, and the blockade was complete.

At dusk, there was a flurry of activity on the sunken ship. A glow, then a puff of yellow smoke followed by a muffled thump. A stone ball arched toward them, then struck the rocks at the shore with a crack. "They are getting the range," Pierre observed to no one in particular. "They are in no hurry. They think time is on their side now."

Chapter XLIII

lone in the study of his Paris Hotel, the Count de Retz, Albert Gondi, sighed with weariness. He felt not just the fatigue of the long, difficult journey he had just completed; it was the constant pressure of events, too much to handle, too little time. He turned back from the window overlooking the garden now rapidly filling with the gloomy shadows of the late January afternoon. It looked as he felt, he thought. This morning's ceremonies at Court had brought home to him that his weariness was not of body, but much, much deeper.

He could not deny that he had spent an agreeable morning making his formal report to the King and Queen Mother and had basked pleasurably in their obvious satisfaction with his accomplishments.

His visits to most of the German princelings had left these foreign gentlemen, if not happy about St. Bartholomew's Day, at least not unhappy enough to go to war about it. The Emperor in Vienna had fumed, but he still hoped for French help against the Turks. The election of a new king in Poland was a confusing process, but Gondi's efforts had left the Duke of Anjou as the front-runner, if not the odds-on favorite. Finally, the fortifications of his newest territory, Belle-Île, off the coast of Brittany and not far from La Rochelle, which the King had elevated for him to a Marquisate, were coming along well. On all of these matters he had been petted and applauded.

Yet he could see that the King's face, never healthy, had a drawn and haunted look. He laughed too quickly and without merriment. The Queen Mother was even more disturbing. She looked older, more careworn, but at the same time even more determined, as the captain of a garrison might appear after many weeks of siege of a position that he has vowed to hold to the death. He recognized that the King, slightly fey at the best of times, could be unpredictably violent and dangerous. But the Queen Mother, hard pressed, would be even more demanding and even less tolerant of failure. She had sent word immediately after the audience that she would be pleased to be received at Gondi's hotel that very evening.

Success, it was surely success, everyone was telling him he was a success. He was the man of the hour. And all he could think of was, Thank God it's over. It was luck, fortunate circumstances, and he had been able to profit by them. Yes, he had understood them and had brought long experience and personal charm to bear. And yes, he would have been blamed for failure, yet it seemed so empty, pointless. As a reward, he thought, I get to play again and again and again until — until I lose. He sat down behind his desk, wrapping a fur-lined silk cloak more tightly about him. A servant entered and lit the candles. "Her Majesty has left the palace, my lord. She will be arriving in a quarter of an hour."

"Yes, thank you," Gondi replied wearily.

The beautiful room smiled at him in the candlelight, the marble caryatids seeming to sway in the firelight as they effortlessly bore the mantelpiece. Gondi buried his head in his hands. If only he weren't so tired. If only he could leave these burdens for a respite, however brief. He knew only too well that it was his own energy that kept him climbing the slippery ascent. He knew that any relaxation of vigilance would let events get out of his control. He laughed mirthlessly. As if these great events, wars, rebellions, religion, could be controlled by anyone. But he knew that he must at least seem to control them; knew, too, that this seeming, and his talents, had allowed him to parlay his good fortune into, into what? This? He looked around the room.

He helped himself to some wine from a carafe. He knew he would get a second wind soon, that this black mood would pass, that he would feel buoyed up by his successes and the honor, indeed pleasure, of supper with his royal mistress. At least he would be able to stay in Paris for a while to see his wife, to deal with his own affairs.

Turning to the pile of correspondence accumulated during his absence, he pulled out the letter from Maurice de La Renaudie. The letter, typically, was not without its problems, but informed him that at least in regard to Athalie matters were once again under his control.

As he reread the letter, he suppressed his involuntary annoyance at its pretensions and tried to concentrate on its mixed bag of good and unpleasant news. Athalie was safely installed at his wife's château of Ancy le Franc in Burgundy, a secluded, rural place where the truant could be dealt with at leisure and without undue risk. The baby, the source of so much nuisance, had been taken care of by Augustin Pascal. He was not informed and did not care to know how. In resolving this major dilemma, so far La Renaudie had not disappointed him. His henchman had merited gratitude. But there the problems began again.

Maurice was useful, but he was plainly getting ambitious. Gondi thrived on advancing men who could thereafter be grateful and useful to him. But Maurice had, it seemed, as much or more risk of becoming dangerous than he did of being useful. Yet the question of what to do with him was becoming acute. Ward of the de Galle heirs' estates? That was quite a plum for someone like Maurice, whom Gondi would have shrugged off a year earlier. And demanded, if you please! Well, that could be dealt with, he reflected. It wasn't a bad idea, as by arranging it, he could reward Maurice at no cost to himself. Moreover, as he had good cause to know, the de Galle debts would rob Maurice's plum of most of its sweetness. That, he smiled, would serve him right. But it wouldn't do to let one like Maurice get too big for his boots or seem to be able to demand things. In that respect, his failure to follow orders and bring back Pierre de Galle for trial was a useful blunder to hold over his head. And a curious business it was, too.

Maurice had plainly captured de Galle, but then de Galle had been killed, or died. It was very odd and apparently not exactly his fault. Still, he would have to explain it to the Queen Mother. He reread Maurice's account:

I had spent some pleasant days with the Duchess de Galle before her unfortunate accident.

If I didn't know as much about you, and she weren't so pregnant, I'd read a bit more into that, Gondi thought wryly. The letter went on:

As a sister, she unburdened herself to me of her horror at the baseness of de Galle's flouting of the King's orders. She suspected him of all manner of treason and shuddered at the thought of seeing him again. She fully cooperated with my ruse of luring him to her side. Then when her child was born and she was so ill, she seemed to be keeping herself alive to see him. I found it odd, but even near her death, no man could resist her bidding. I now realize it was all to accomplish her own sort of revenge. I know not with what honeyed words she did it, but somehow she persuaded him to attempt to flee down an ancient tunnel. We found it quickly enough and pursued him. When he heard our approach, he attempted to swim a flooded part, but it was too long and we know he perished, as she knew he would. What a woman! I know she would warmly approve of my wardship of her little son, and I think it fitting that I should at last be master where I was treated so basely. And it is fitting, too, that she and I...

She and I, that's a good one, thought Gondi.

...were able to show our family's love for King Charles...

Our family! Was there no end to his pretension?

...by eliminating such an unworthy member as my late and unlamented stepbrother.

Well, the Queen Mother would have to be told and she would suspect foul play. Fortunately, it seemed to be Anne de Galle who had actually done in Pierre. That let Maurice and himself off the hook, and the Lady Anne was presumably beyond the reach of the Queen Mother's displeasure. But it was an odd business. Anne, the lovely, seductive pleasure-seeker murdering her husband for political reasons? He shrugged. At least de Galle was out of the way. He rose to see to the arrangements. If the Queen Mother felt herself sufficiently en famille, she might be mellow enough to broach the subject of Maurice's damned wardship. At least his wardship of Athalie seemed secure for the moment.

Gondi rose and walked briskly through the hall, cast a practiced eye over the table setting, strode out into the elegant entrance foyer, studied the flowers, called for four more torchbearers, glanced over the musical list proposed by the majordomo, scratched two pieces and added three more. He stopped by a window and admired his reflection in the dark glass. He adjusted his cloak of deep red velvet, took off a gold chain, looked at himself, then put it on again. Menu, wine,

467

music, flowers, he ticked them off again on his fingers. The Queen Mother had given him short notice, barely two hours, but, he smiled to himself, it ought to come off well enough. He found the overseeing of these familiar tasks soothing, and he felt his earlier gloom begin to dissipate.

From the courtyard, the muffled sounds of horses being reined in reached him, and with a final glance at his cloak, he strode briskly out through the main door in time to help his royal mistress from her mount.

"Welcome, Madame," he smiled and bowed. "You honor my house by your presence. I hope the simplicity of my hospitality will not seem too mean for you."

Startled as he was to see Augustin Pascal bring the Queen Mother's bodyguard to attention before marching them off, Gondi gave no indication and offered the Queen Mother his arm.

"Alberto mio," she replied in Italian, a good sign, he thought. "I have no fears about your hospitality. It is such a relief to me to come here to your lovely home and escape for a few hours from the babel of the European princes. Alberto, Alberto, talk to me of Florence, play me some real Tuscan music, let me relax a bit. Ah, how good it is to be here, where I can feel at home."

"Come in, please, Madame, the night is chill. Let us sit in my study with some wine, and you shall have from me anything my poor abode can offer."

Gondi led her into his study where the cheery fire and spiced wine could most effectively produce the mellow mood he hoped for. Catherine de Medici quickly relaxed and chatted volubly about family matters, but suddenly turned sharply, though still smiling, and said, "You noticed my new guard's captain?" She smiled sweetly at Gondi. "If I weren't so pleased with all you have accomplished in Germany and Poland, I would be a bit annoyed with you. You were really very naughty to have played such a dreadful trick on Augustin Pascal."

"But, Madame, I saved him; he had made a fool of himself with the King."

"Rubbish! The King can't remember money for ten minutes, let alone overnight, as you know better than most.

"Pascal came to see me last fall while you were away," she continued. "He was most polite. He told me, or rather t-t-told me, I find his stutter absolutely charming, don't you? Anyway, he told me that you had told him that silly gambling debt was in deadly earnest and only you could save him from the King's displeasure, in other words from ruin. Alberto mio, I see your fine Italian hand getting another poor sod to do your dirty work."

"But, Madame..."

"No, let me finish. He very generously told me that a business venture of his had rather prospered and he was prepared to settle the debt, and then some for the unfortunate delay. You knew nothing of this?" She eyed him sharply.

His dumbfounded expression told her all she needed to know.

"Yes, indeed, ten thousand gold ducats is a princely sum, isn't it, Alberto? I'm sure you never expected it to be paid. Well, neither did the King, so when I, at Pascal's request, discharged the debt, the King was quite bowled over. Took it as a gift, which I'm sure won't hurt the advancement of the family Pascal. The whole thing was elegantly done, Alberto. Oh, come on, now, don't pout. It amuses me so to see my master of intrigue outmaneuvered by a family of bankers! So Pascal shall guard me, and I have taken him into my own household. You have no objections?"

"No, of course not, Your Majesty," he replied weakly.

Catherine de Medici stared for a moment into the fire, then reached for more wine, which Gondi hastily poured.

"I'll tell you, Alberto, I didn't know whether I could stand it while you were away," she said, suddenly serious. "Walsingham, the English ambassador, came to see me and was positively rude. When I mentioned the proposed marriage of my dear little son Alençon to Queen Elizabeth, he was polite enough, but he looked at me as if I were crazy. And about the religious troubles! We told him again and again that we had had to move against the Protestants to save the royal family from Coligny's murderous plot, but all he replied was that we would have to wait to see what the investigation concluded! Alberto, he didn't believe me! I could see it in his eyes. All fall I have written to Elizabeth. Lately there have been some hopeful signs, but it has made things very difficult." She wrung her hands and looked about to cry. "Ah, my poor young Hercules — and how unfortunate to have given him that name! Fate has teased me by making him frail and marking him with sickness. Where else can I find him a crown?"

"Calm yourself, Madame," Gondi replied smoothly. "You can forget Walsingham for tonight and enjoy a quiet evening with my family. How it pains me to be of so little help to you with these matters."

"You could have helped deal with this," she said, eyeing him sharply. "Look at this letter I received from the Emperor in Vienna. He demands details, reasons, justifications for actions against the Protestants. He says if it was an act of self-defense, why did the killing go on all over the country. Even now. Here, look at these reports from the cities in the south — Lyons, Toulouse — killing, killing, killing. I know my son sent strict orders to these places that there was to be no bloodshed, but look at what I was getting." Her voice was rising to an emotional pitch.

"Your Majesty, it was out of love for you and your son, the King, that the people rose up throughout the land to kill the heretics. When they heard of the outrage the Protestants had planned in Paris, their hearts impelled them to rash, but understandable, anger. They are simple people, Your Majesty, and have not the greatness of heart of King Charles, who pardons even his enemies when the immediate danger is past."

"It is good to hear that, Alberto mio," she said. "But do you not think that foreign agents, or perhaps people of the Guises, are stirring up trouble, trying to take advantage of the confusion in the country?"

"No, Madame," Gondi replied too quickly. He rose and offered his arm. "Let us go in to dinner."

She rose and smiled. She squeezed his arm affectionately.

"It is good, I say, to hear that, Alberto. I only half believe it, but I wish it were true. Oh, God, what a disaster that night in August was! I foresaw trouble, but nothing like this!"

"Please, Madame, at least a Spanish invasion was averted. That was your worst fear. Here," he said, noting with pleasure her obvious delight at his supposedly impromptu arrangements, "you shall sit here in the place of honor. My cook's son has just returned from Florence. He brought some things with him I think you will like." He nodded to the musicians in the gallery, and the pleasant strains of the viols floated down.

"If you please, Your Majesty," he continued, "the Spanish are delighted with our forceful determination to rid ourselves of the Protestant threat once and for all. It has been said that disloyalty to the Church is often followed by disloyalty to the King."

"Albert," she said, "Spare me your philosophy. I don't know whether you believe that, but I do not. Nor do I trust the Spanish. I think they are provoking this awful business."

"Surely not," he replied. "Why, I had word only this morning from my cousin, Jerome, that all Madrid rejoiced for weeks. He says someone even saw King Philip laugh, which had never before been seen at all. No, the Protestant princes may snap and bite, but Spain is solidly on our side now."

"Do you think so, Alberto? Then riddle me this: those captured men that fool Genlis led into Mons last summer, with illusions of French control of the low countries, and also of gaining favor for Protestants in France. My son King Charles wrote to the Spanish that as far as he was concerned, the Duke of Alba, who maintains full Spanish control there, could hang every last one of them. He wrote, I think, at your suggestion."

Gondi nodded. "It seemed a small way of tossing something to the Spanish, and what would we have done with those men if they all returned?"

"Well, wise one," she continued, "after you left for Poland, we received word that the Duke of Alba, who has never been known for being tender-hearted, set them all free, let them march out, with their weapons, if you please, with full military honors. My son then gave orders that these men should all be tracked down and killed like beasts. Do you know what I think, Alberto? I think Spain is isolating us. Spain will be happy if we are perceived as bloody-handed fanatics, while Spain with all the horror they have inflicted on the Netherlands, appears to be kind and merciful. I don't wish to carp, I know this is a family supper and I am a guest in your house, but I don't think your plans have worked as they should."

Gondi had stopped eating. A chill of fear washed over him. As his hand gracefully beckoned the lackeys to bring on the roast, his mind raced. The Queen Mother was relaxing, feeling at home, obviously pleased with his hospitality, but all that would count for little if he did not address her real problems. These, as ever, were crowns for her children. He sighed.

470

"There is no question, Madame, that in the short run the measures we had to take against the Protestants will cause criticism. It is easy enough for the Emperor to lecture you on magnanimity. He didn't have them massing a few streets away planning to cut his throat in the middle of the night."

She grasped his arm. "You know how to say the right things, old friend. Yes, you are right. We must not let their insults plunge us into despair. You shall speak for me on those matters."

"And do not forget Poland, Your Majesty. They, too, have been upset, but my wife and I have excellent relations with the leaders. I don't mind telling you, it's no credit to me, of course, but my wife has been most helpful. They were appalled, it seems, that we don't all speak Greek and Latin every day as they do. Come to think of it, I suppose we would, too, if the choice were that or Polish."

Catherine de Medici laughed out loud. "It isn't that, Albert. It is that they are fifty years behind the times. In King Francis' time, Latin was popular here for lovers' sonnets. So I suppose it would be still in Poland."

"At any rate, Your Majesty, my good wife is something of an amateur of the classics, and on several evenings has conversed for hours with the Polish lords in the ancient tongue. Whether it was the pleasure of her company, or that it made them homesick, I don't know. But I do know that she has their ear. I think I can manage them. That means that the chances of an election of Anjou as King of Poland seem to me to be as good as they ever were, that is to say, excellent."

"That is good news indeed, Albert. The scorn of nations I can bear, indeed I must bear it for the good of my sons, ah, if only we can be successful. It will, I suppose, take money?"

"Alas, yes, Madame, unfortunately it will not only be the noble character of your son which will sway them. I fear many of the Electors will be quite expensive."

"Well, Alberto, you can see to that, too, can't you?"

"Madame," he hesitated. "The amount may be substantial. I am not sure..."

"So will my gratitude be substantial," she said, eyeing him sideways. "I have been much distressed by the horrible events that have gone on since August, events you assured me could be controlled. Yes, Alberto, I feel quite easy about asking your help on so small a matter, but one so close to my heart."

Gondi paled slightly and helplessly drank some wine. He felt outmaneuvered and boxed in. The wine did no good. A glance showed that Catherine de Medici was enjoying the music, which gave him a moment to think. There were assets he had from which he could raise the necessary consideration. There was the promised Spanish gold, and, his thoughts raced, yes, of course, there was Athalie, Athalie with her rank and properties. Suitably pruned, of course, Athalie could be wed to one of the up-and-coming Polish electors, a reward to him far greater than money and one that would cost Gondi himself nothing.

Then, too, King Charles' lovely little queen had just had a daughter. Her failure to produce a son naturally caused Anjou's stock as heir apparent to rise, as

471

it was not thought that Charles IX could live to produce any more children. Helping Anjou would be a prudent long-term investment and Gondi was nothing if not prudent. Yes, Athalie would be a way out of several problems at once.

"It will not be easy, Your Majesty," he said finally, and kissed her surprisingly slender and beautiful hand. "But I think I can manage it. I know only a part of your heavy burdens, and it rejoices my heart that I can lighten one of them."

Catherine de Medici beamed benevolently at her counselor, her eyes as inscrutable as a cat's.

"And now, Alberto," she paused as if unsure of herself, "now I must ask an even greater service of you. I want you to go to La Rochelle and bring that siege to a quick end."

Gondi slumped slightly. Before he could reply, the Queen continued with a voluble torrent.

"I know, I know, you have done much already, your galleys got invaluable information on their harbor, but Marshal Biron has been there for two months and has accomplished nothing. My dear son, Anjou, will head a new expedition, but he has not your experience, Alberto. And that city must be taken! I will not have another of these endless civil wars! Ever since last summer they have refused to accept the King's orders to abandon their religion! They won't even take orders from Henri Navarre as you said they would; Alberto, you must!"

"Madonna," he was finally able to say. "I live to serve you. But, it is much you ask. That city is impregnable. It will have to be starved into submission. That cannot be done quickly."

"No, Alberto. It must be taken. You must take it. We cannot afford for this thing to drag out for months. I will give you men, guns, whatever you need, but it must be stormed and brought under control quickly."

"Your Majesty, I will do my best," Gondi replied softly, needing all his skill at diplomacy to disguise his dread of La Rochelle's bristling ramparts and chilly swamps lashed by winter storms off the Atlantic. A more uninviting prospect would have been hard for him to imagine. And somehow, without saying so, she had contrived to imply that La Rochelle was his fault! He sighed inwardly. Failure would be his, and victory, if it could be contrived, would be Anjou's. But then if Anjou was to be King of Poland, gratitude for Gondi's services in enhancing his prestige might be a valuable commodity. In any event it was not in Gondi's nature to weep over spilled milk, nor to pay grudgingly what he could not avoid. He rose, bowed, and kissed his Mistress's hand.

"It shall be as you wish, carissima Madonna."

As Gondi escorted the Queen from the hall, she turned and said, "Your supper was splendid and your hospitality as ever magnificent, Alberto. You will not find me ungrateful. I know how weary you must be," her eyes held genuine concern, "but we must all make sacrifices for the good of the state."

Gondi smiled weakly. He had learned long ago that resistance to this sort of entreaty was useless. As they strolled together toward the door chatting pleasantries, he wondered idly if she had not arranged the whole evening to maneuver him into agreement with the project.

Just before she reached the door, the Queen Mother turned and impulsively embraced him. He felt the admiring gaze of his household and her people. He decided to save La Renaudie's report and the mystery of Pierre de Galle for another day.

Chapter XLIV

A March gale lashed sheets of rain against the Cinq Cochons, the principal, indeed the only, inn in Nieulle, a village just north of La Rochelle. Midmorning seemed hardly lighter than dawn. Cinq Cochons, grumbled Julio, as he replaced a spent candle with another. Five pigs, they called it, and to be sure, there were five complacent-looking porkers on the hostelry's sign, now nearly horizontal and creaking noisily in the wind. They had seen little enough of the succulent roasts the sign promised. Three days ago they had arrived, his master, Albert de Gondi, in a litter, a Protestant bullet in his side. A royal surgeon and his assistant had removed the ball, and Julio had to admit he admired his master's seeming nonchalance at what must have been excruciating pain.

Julio looked down at the sleeping form on the miserable bed. He was worried. For three days, Gondi's fever had been high. That was too long, Julio thought. Why did Gondi have to take such risks, why lead charges at La Rochelle's impregnable walls? Every time Gondi appeared, every Protestant on the walls took a shot at him. Finally, the inevitable had happened, and he, Julio, might soon be out of a job. He sighed and stretched. Might as well see if dinner would be anything more than fish again. He looked once more at Gondi's sleeping form and left.

Gondi moaned and tossed in feverish sleep. He woke suddenly, thinking someone had come in. When he saw that it was Blaise, the Duke de la Roque, he relaxed. Only his friend, old Blaise. The Duke was silent, regarding him with distant grey eyes. Slowly the thought formed in Gondi's mind that Blaise was dead, dead these three or four years. Idly, he noticed that he was not afraid, but curious.

"Well, Blaise, you see they got me, too."

The Duke said nothing.

"Not like the old days in Italy. Then it was summer, and a man could fight in the sun, not in the damned rain." It had rained the day the Duke had fallen at the battle at Moncontour; somehow that made him feel a strange companionship.

"Well, it was good of you to come. But why won't you speak?"

Gondi tried to pull himself up a bit. The vision wavered, dissolved. Gondi was burning with fever. His wound ached. He reached for the goblet of wine on the table. It seemed very heavy, but at last he held the cup to his lips and tasted the sour, local wine. He took a few sips and replaced the cup. He miscalculated, and it fell to the floor.

"I wonder why I was thinking of old de la Roque," Gondi mused. He supposed it was on account of being wounded, being treated by doctors. Athalie, was she involved? No, he hadn't thought of her for weeks. De la Roque couldn't reproach him. For all the trouble she had caused, he had managed to save a good deal for her. Marriage with the Polish leader, Count Wierzka, now that was not so bad. Service to the state, gratitude of the Queen Mother, and the possibilities of great things in the Baltic, if Anjou were elected king. Why, wasn't that a splendid outcome to the mess she had got herself into? He'd have her brought up to Paris come summer, and if the Count liked what he saw, well, that problem would be solved.

He forced himself into wakefulness. He had been dreaming. De la Roque was dead. It had been a dream. He winced as an unplanned movement stabbed white-hot pain into his side.

He ran his hand over the dressing on his left side, wanting to press the wounded part, as if that could stop the pain; he refrained, knowing it would only make things worse. The doctors said no vital organs were touched, he said to reassure himself, but they would say that whether it were true or no. The only statement a doctor makes that can be believed is when he declares that his patient is dead. Bowing and scraping, behaving more like valets than men of science, they kiss your heinie before they wash it. Ugh! And yet, one is in their hands.

No, not true, one is in the hands of God. "And I'm the one I'm talking of, not some mythical 'one'! I am in the hands of God. May God be merciful!" he whispered. But why should He be merciful? Because I have defended His Faith, He must see it that way. Gondi shuddered and tried to free his mind from the fears which preoccupied him.

If only Ambroise Paré were here. The King is lucky to have such a man, a doctor who can be trusted. Still, one could hardly expect that physician, a Protestant, to minister to the Catholic besiegers of La Rochelle. And anyway, he is getting old. I'm getting old, too, Gondi thought, but not old enough to die, please God! I am weak, weak as an old man, helpless. All my strength has seeped away through the hole in my side.

He lay still for a while, exhausted, then his mind began to flail again. It was not just death he feared, but helplessness. He had promised the Queen Mother to crush the resistance at La Rochelle, to end the war and to bring her peace — and he had promised to accomplish this miracle rapidly. In January, when he left Paris, he had promised it, and again in February, during a brief visit to the capital, when she had been even more insistent. And here it is March, and no progress made. Gondi groaned from frustration.

Nothing seemed to bring results: we have cut off their fresh water, but they drink from their wells; we have prevented any supplies reaching them, but they have eaten their livestock, their dogs, and now shellfish, grubbed from the living mud that surrounds that horrible place; and we have attacked and attacked and attacked, but they have resisted every attack. He thought sourly of the bastion before which he was shot. How fitting! The Protestants put their faith in the Scripture, and the bastion they call the Gospel stands firm against all assaults. This siege is deadly for highborn Catholics. The Duke of Aumale died a few weeks ago attacking the bastion, and now, I — no, I'm not dead, not dead yet.

But this helplessness is almost worse than death, he mused. I should be in control, I should be thinking of ways to end this mess, so that the Queen Mother will have peace and her darling, Anjou, will be able to proclaim himself the military genius who subjugated La Rochelle. At the very least, I should be thinking of explanations, excuses for my failure. I can't even do that. With a start, he realized that the Queen Mother's unwanted generosity with men, cannon, and ships made excuses difficult, indeed impossible.

"I can't even write, I am cut off, with no news, vulnerable," he sighed, and with another surge of self-pity, he gingerly lowered himself for more rest. He closed his eyes, wondering vaguely where that damned Julio had gotten to.

The door creaked open on a badly adjusted hinge. Gondi looked around and saw Maurice de La Renaudie enter the room silently, as usual. His heart leapt with joy. Here, at least, will be news. He felt a flush of gratitude to Maurice, the faithful servant in time of need.

"What news?" Gondi asked impatiently.

"The Gospel bastion holds. We cannot take it. There are hundreds dead in the trenches. The defenders mock us from the walls, sing hymns, and laugh. Even their women fight us, pouring molten lead on our heads. It's quite hopeless. You should just face up to it."

Maurice spat out the last words contemptuously, enjoying the unguarded look of panic that crossed Gondi's face. Gondi closed his eyes. Maurice watched him in silence. After a while, he resumed, "One of the reports we've gotten from La Rochelle says my stepbrother, Pierre, is there. It's a little vague, a passing reference. Of course, that wasn't the point of the report. But I always thought it was possible he had survived. If so, this is the only place he could be."

Gondi opened his eyes and shrugged.

"See here, what are you going to do about it?" Maurice asked as abrasively as possible.

"I? I'm not going to do anything. Man, can't you see," Gondi waved his hand desperately, "can't you see? I'm..." He was going to say 'dying,' he was going to give voice to his great terror, but he stopped, too shrewd to parade his fear and weakness before Maurice, and yet he saw, in La Renaudie's eyes, that the younger man had read his thought.

Maurice laughed harshly.

Gondi continued more firmly, "Man, I've got bigger things to worry about than your stepbrother. I've got a war to worry about."

"Do you?" Maurice sneered. "Do you have bigger things to worry about? I don't know. If Pierre gets to England, that's where he's heading, surely, then what? His mother's family is powerful, you know."

"I know, La Renaudie, I know."

"He would not find it difficult to get Queen Elizabeth's ear, and the chances are that Elizabeth would believe his tale. You told the English there was a Protestant plot against the lives of the royal family, and that stopped their rage.

But if Elizabeth found out the truth? Where would all the Queen Mother's schemes for an English marriage for her little Hercule, Duke of Alençon, go? To Hell is where they'd go!"

"Yes, yes, I know."

"So, you'd better worry about dear Pierre."

"Yes, I do. I will. But he can't get to England while the blockade is in place."

"What if someone runs the blockade?"

"That isn't possible."

"So you say, but your predictions haven't been so good lately, have they?"

Gondi stared at Maurice, startled.

"May I?" continued Maurice, assuming a sweet tone, and without waiting for an answer he sat on the end of the bed and leaned against the bedpost. "You know, you're right when you say you've got worse problems to worry about than my stepbrother. But it's not the war I'm talking about."

Gondi half-hooded his eyes and watched Maurice fearfully. "You've got me to worry about, after all. Pierre isn't the only one who knows the truth. Who knows it better than I?"

Gondi laughed harshly. "You speak, you sign your own death warrant."

"Not necessarily. I sign yours for sure, but..."

Gondi forced himself to laugh out loud.

"Ah, you don't agree?" Maurice settled himself more comfortably. "You think you are above danger, don't you? Perhaps you used to be, but look at yourself now. Apart from the fact that you're a physical wreck. I don't mean just that, though it doesn't help you.

"But even assuming you recover, you're still in a pretty pickle: your little massacre last August didn't bring peace, it brought war, and the little war, well, you don't seem to be able to win it, do you? My guess is that you aren't very popular back at Court, and it wouldn't take much to bring you down. Suppose Montgomery, who enjoys the protection of Queen Elizabeth and supports our La Rochelle Protestants, attacked Belle-Île? Belle-Île is your charge, but when I went to inspect it a month ago, I wasn't much impressed with its defenses and neither was Anjou.

"Suppose Montgomery, or some English pirates, or anyone, ran the blockade and brought food to La Rochelle? You can't take the city. You can only hope they'll give up. And they won't, 'til they're starving. Or suppose I told the truth about St. Bartholomew's Day, so your royal mistress knew what you did? Any of those things could cost you your life."

Gondi pushed himself up higher on his pillows. The effort brought another stab of pain to his side, but his anger was such that he hardly noticed the pain and had totally forgotten his fears.

"You little swine," he hissed. "You think you know it all. You think this old ram has had it and you can prance in and become king of the shit-heap. Well, let me tell you..."

"Don't get yourself all worked up," Maurice cut in. "You'll do yourself damage." And indeed, at his words, Gondi fell back on the pillows, drained and gasping for breath.

"You've got it all wrong," Maurice continued softly. "I don't want to do you in." He leaned toward Gondi, and the hatred in his eyes belied his words. "It's just that I can, and something will have to be done in case the temptation becomes too much for me."

"Even if you could harm me," Gondi whispered, "you would do yourself more harm."

"Oh, no. I don't think so. I have powerful friends, you see, and after all, I was only following orders." Maurice rose, poured himself some wine, then handed another cup to Gondi. Gondi's hand shook as he grasped the cup.

"But I'm reasonable," Maurice smiled. "You can buy me. I'm not like my stepbrother. I have a price."

"Oh, yes?" Gondi whispered, sarcastically.

"I want to be set up for life — respect and property, that's what I want."

"You already have the de Galle wardship, you are greedy."

"An empty bag," Maurice cried bitterly, "as you knew full well, my lord de Retz. I'll tell you what I want, I want your niece's hand in marriage."

Gondi's burst of laughter sprayed wine all over the bedclothes. Maurice darted a look of intense hatred at him. Choking with laughter, grimacing with pain, Gondi recovered himself.

"My dear fellow," he wheezed at last. "What an idea! Even if I could or would try to help you in this fantasy, and believe me I'm not that senile yet, my hands are tied. The Queen Mother has to approve, and she would never, never give her consent to such a union."

"Why not?" Maurice asked. "I've served her well. She has every reason to think so. And if you were to explain what I have done, the risks I've run..."

"I'm sorry, Maurice." Gondi's eyes twinkled with malice. "How shall I put it? The Queen Mother doesn't like you. No, that's not right. She can't stand you. Well, even worse — she sees you for the slimy, crazy, untrustworthy bastard that you are." Gondi collapsed in weak laughter, then mastered himself with an effort. "I mean it, La Renaudie." His tones were icy. "I've told you the truth."

Maurice had gone red, but at Gondi's words, the blood drained from his face, leaving it a white, stiff mask of rage. "That's too bad," he said softly, "because that's my price. I've thought about it a lot. I know what I can do, and I know what I need. So, you'd better think about it, too, and you'd better think fast."

With two lithe strides, Maurice crossed to the door. As it groaned open, he looked back. His eyes and Gondi's met like two swords. For a moment, the two men were silent, and still as two swordsmen locked in a parry. Then Maurice lowered his gaze and was gone.

Chapter XLV

t was May Day, 1573. In the square before La Rochelle's town hall, a young oak had been recently planted and festooned with garlands and ribbons. Bagpipes rang and wailed, filling the square with rhythm, and around the tree crowds of dancers leapt and whirled. It was a mild day, vivid with sunlight. The new grass gleamed and the sky was blue with a brightness that would have seemed impossible even a month before.

This is a brave show, Pierre thought, feeling once again a grudging admiration for these stubborn people. The faces of the dancers were haggard and their clothes hung loosely on wasted frames, but they danced, as tradition required, more in defiance than in joy, perhaps, but still, they danced. Joy, he thought — these are not a joyful people, these followers of Calvin. Is it their Religion which makes them joyless, or is it the other way around?

Then Pierre chided himself. Who could be carefree in such a situation? Their confidence, which he had found on his arrival, had suffered rude attacks, though things had seemingly gone well for a while. The King had sent as his envoy a prominent Protestant, François de la Noue, called Iron-Arm. That had been a good sign, and even better had been the fact that Iron-Arm had been persuaded to abandon his attempts at conciliation and to assume military command of the city. Some said the King had even consented to this, and La Noue himself denied that his action was a betrayal of the King's trust, yet the Rochelais still proclaimed it a great coup. La Noue's coming, which followed Pierre's arrival by a matter of days, had made Pierre's ambiguous position even more difficult. If La Noue, the King's envoy, can join forces with us without dishonor, what is to stop you from doing the same? people had asked him. To point out that La Noue was, after all, a Protestant and he, Pierre, was not, merely intensified the scorn and distrust of those around him.

December and January had been times of hope for the Rochelais. Under Iron-Arm's directions they had strengthened the fortifications, while the King's forces, under Marshal Biron, were quiescent, waiting for reinforcements and filling up their time with trench-digging and construction. It was not until February that things began to be difficult.

Though they had suspected the worst, still the Rochelais were filled with consternation at the arrival of the main royalist army, 40,000 men, some people said, headed by the Duke of Anjou and under his command, his younger brother the Duke of Alençon, as well as the Dukes of Aumale and Nevers, the Princes of Condé and Navarre, and the Count de Retz.

The negotiations, if they could be called that, which followed, had served more to discourage the Protestants than to advance the cause of peace. England was not to be counted on, the royalists told La Noue; La Rochelle was on its own. La Noue returned to the Rochelais and argued that they should sign a peace treaty, but the ministers, remembering all too vividly the fate of their leaders the prior August, refused. Using further negotiations as a pretext to leave the city, La Noue joined the Catholic forces. Thus, the glee his arrival had occasioned was blasted, and the city's morale received a great blow.

There followed attack upon attack. The walls of the city were so long that the defenders could not man every point at once. Yet the surrounding lands were so flat and exposed that the royalists could rarely mass a surprise attack. The King's army tunneled trenches at night, only to find the Rochelais at the openings at dawn. Anjou used brute force; the Rochelais, men and women alike, resisted desperately. Especially around the bastion called the Gospel, bitter, intense fighting followed day after day. And always the Rochelais resisted.

The first assault had marked the beginning of a new way of life for Pierre. As the tocsin clanged and the citizens rushed to the walls, Pierre had idly wondered how he could keep out of the way of not just the hurrying soldiers, but more their looks of withering disdain. They think I am a heathen, a coward, and a parasite, he though glumly. Unable to shelter away from the walls, he finally mounted, unarmed, to the walls to watch.

The scene was one of sharp, brutal ferocity. And in the weeks ahead, it was to become hatefully repetitive. The royal forces, seemingly innumerable, rushed forward with ladders, while a fusillade of arrows, cannon, and arquebuses kept the defenders behind the parapet. The royal forces swarmed up, and only when their covering fire had to stop could the defenders begin. It seemed to favor the attack, but it was not so. For as soon as they could move, the defenders were able to rain down a withering blast of projectiles. Ladders toppled, men screamed, and the dead piled up at the foot of the walls.

A shout at his left, and Pierre saw that the royal forces had gained a foothold on top of the wall. Instantly their number increased as men cut, swore, fell, and cut again on the narrow parapet. Suddenly, Pierre saw Michel de Brossan fall, a sword thrust in his side. Without thinking, Pierre dove into the mêlée, and dodging blows, dragged Michel to safety. Seeing that he was badly hurt, Pierre lifted him gently and bore him off to a nearby inn which had been designated as an infirmary.

He was oblivious of the grumble of gratitude as he left Michel to be tended by one of the surgeons, and he returned to the walls. Three times that day he rescued wounded men, although one had died before he could be brought down from the walls.

In subsequent days Pierre took the precaution of wearing a helmet and breastplate, and soon his great form came to be expected on the walls. It began to be observed, then remarked upon, that where he was, the defenders fought best, perhaps because the slight hope of being pulled out alive led them to take greater risks. While Pierre did not find himself popular, the looks of disdain gave way to grudging respect and occasionally admiration. He might be a papist, but he was no coward.

The worst moment occurred suddenly one day as the royal cannon succeeded in breaching a large irregular hole on the south side of the rampart. The fighting had gone on fiercely most of the day, but again the royal forces had not been able to capitalize on their precarious advantage. Fighting on the rubble was doubly treacherous because of the uneven footing, and casualties were high on both sides. Toward evening, the royalists fell back, and the Protestant commander, perhaps rashly, ordered a counterattack. The ruse worked at first and a large body of Protestants were soon far down the rubble toward the foot of the wall. Suddenly, the Duke de Nevers launched a flank attack. It was short and bitter. A ball from the wall all but killed the Duke outright, but his men cut off a score of Protestants. Surrounded, these men fought with the desperation of those whose lives are forfeit, and perhaps because of their courage, or perhaps because the royals, dismayed by the loss of their chief, fought less well, the majority drew back, and the Protestants were able to retreat slowly back up the pile to safety. Without any preliminaries, Pierre sped like a shadow through the defenders, down the pile, into the royals. Quickly he seized two prostrate Protestants, and one under each arm, began the painful ascent to the ramparts.

With a roar, eight royal attackers were upon him. Arrows glanced off his helmet, and a sword stroke clanged off his back plate. Yet he continued up, until covering fire was able to drive off his pursuers. On the top of the wall, he set down his burdens. One was dead and it was plain the other soon would be. So drenched in their blood was he that Pierre did not notice for a few minutes his own blood dripping from his left side.

"A nasty gash, Monsieur de Galle, but it isn't deep," said the Protestant leader. "I never saw anything like what you did. Two men, uphill! You have God's protection it seems." Pierre, exhausted and in pain, allowed himself to be led away without protest.

So they had fought on, even when lack of food began to sap their strength, as did the inevitable losses in the number of fighting men. Fresh vegetables had long since disappeared; salted meat and fish and pickled vegetables were low; grain was nearly gone. The women went out at night to gather mussels, oysters, and clams, and the staple of their diet had become shellfish eaten raw, eaten in soup, eaten in stew. Pierre's stomach turned at the thought. This had given them food through mid-April, but now even that was gone. The Catholics had one day surprised the bands of scavenging women and had carried away the prettiest of them.... The next day, soldiers from La Rochelle, dressed in skirts and bonnets, had given the Catholics, who had returned for a second raid, a nasty surprise. It was a good joke, a pleasant revenge, but it did not put food in the stomach.

The city would have yielded, Pierre thought, and there would have been none of this dancing around the May Day tree, if help, unhoped for, had not arrived. The previous day, the news had come: a small fleet, filled with French Protestants commanded by Montgomery, with provisions and arms from the English, had taken the island of Belle-Île north of La Rochelle. Like the spring sunlight, hope, and with it, courage, had returned to the Rochelais. The winter of despair, like the winter of cold, was over. Montgomery would raid the coast. Montgomery would stop provisions from reaching the royalists. Most important, Montgomery would bring food and arms to La Rochelle. A raid on an island 70 miles up the coast did not put food on the evening's supper table. Yet he might come, he might bring food. They might not starve, or worse, capitulate. That was worst of all. Pierre had heard it again and again: "If we surrender, we die. Remember Paris. Better starving in our own walls then being cut down like animals."

Pierre watched the wan faces of the crowd, sunlit and animated. My feelings are not theirs. I am not one with them. I only want to be away. And yet, he thought, my future is bound up with theirs. I will starve with them or surrender with them, unless Montgomery brings us food. And if Montgomery comes, I can escape with him to England.

At this thought, the first stirring of feeling penetrated Pierre's apathy and exhaustion. To leave this alien, hostile atmosphere, to escape from these claustrophobic walls, to be allowed to do, to act, to be — he realized, suddenly, that he wanted his freedom passionately, even more than he longed to gorge himself with food and rid himself of the constant, numbing, hypnotizing ache of hunger.

Pierre's rambling thoughts were abruptly interrupted by the raucous clanging of the tocsin. The bagpipes stopped their noise, the merrymakers froze, rooted in sudden fear, and then, pandemonium broke loose. Men rushed for their armor; women rushed for the walls. Pierre, too, ran through the narrow streets and up the vertiginous steps to the top of the ramparts. It was, as he expected, a new attack on the Gospel bastion; he could see hundreds of small forms, a confusion of colors and glimmering armor, massed below the bastion, hanging from ladders, and yes, climbing onto the top of the bastion itself. My God, he thought, we were so busy living in our dreams that we let them surprise us at last. As he watched, the flag on top of the bastion was ripped off its pole and passed down the ladder to greedy hands below. He could hear the distant shouts of triumph.

Pierre got down from the rampart's ledge and began to run along the walkway toward the bastion. As he ran, he saw in the streets below crowds of armed Rochelais rushing to the defense. Let them be in time, he prayed, silently at first, then puffing the words out audibly with gasping breaths. He heard, at last, the welcome sound of the Protestant cannon booming, and, as he approached, the battle cries of the defenders and the screams of the wounded. He climbed back onto the ledge of the rampart, and leaning over, looked across at the tower. The royalists who had climbed the bastion were gone, dead or withdrawn, he could not say. Protestants had once more manned all the defensive positions, the same positions they had occupied for months; the same cannons fired from the walls, and were answered, as always, by heavy fire from below; the bloody turmoil returned to the pattern which was all too familiar to Pierre's eyes. His heartbeat slowed, he took a deep breath and turned to go to visit the wounded.

The Duke of Anjou, quivering with rage, burst into Gondi's room at the inn, his brightly burnished corselet, unstrapped, hanging loosely about his chest and shoulders. Not just rage, but fear as well, made him look vicious and terrifying. His wrath at first made him barely coherent, but he had subsided into a piercing litany of failure that bored into Gondi's skull like some hideous drill.

Perspiring freely in the May warmth, Gondi tried to shield himself, to somehow soften the impact. But as fear gnawed his own innards, he was far from successful.

"This," Anjou stormed, "this is the last straw, de Retz. With Belle-Île in their hands they'll slip supplies in and we'll batter our swords to pieces on those damn walls before they yield. I tell you, you'll pay for this. Why in the name of all the saints in heaven didn't you see this one coming! I'll tell you why, you scheming, thieving Italian bugger, because you were lying in bed, probably going over your accounts, while Montgomery was raiding your most important responsibility!"

"But I was wounded, wounded and even so, leading a charge," Gondi interposed.

"So you were. I know that. But the charge was futile, like all the others. And expensive, like all the others! The Rochelais were supposed to be kissing my feet months ago. And now this!" Anjou gestured grandly in the direction where he supposed Belle-Île to be.

"I tell you, de Retz, people are saying you've lost your grip."

Gondi paled. Maurice, standing well to the rear of the retainers in Anjou's entourage, smirked. Gondi vowed to himself that at the first opportunity he would cut La Renaudie's throat.

"Monsieur, if you please," Gondi tried again, as the Prince, momentarily out of breath, paused.

"I have launched three galleys to reconnoiter Belle-Île," Gondi continued. "The fortifications are damaged, and the raiders led by Montgomery cannot hold it. We will soon have it back, I assure you."

"Then why did you lose it in the first place?"

"One of the survivors said they came during a storm. It was a surprise. If we had had more..."

"If you had had more!" Anjou shouted. "You would have had more if you hadn't been lying in bed! Look, de Retz. I'm sorry I shouted at you. But I have to have a victory here fast. And I don't see how this isn't a very bad setback."

"Well, yes, but it has been my experience that a little success often allows the weaker side to see the wisdom of seeking a treaty."

"Does it really!" Anjou's voice dripped with sarcasm. "I suppose you'll say next you planned to lose your new fortress of Belle-Île to the English so that these Protestants would want to talk peace with you?"

"No, Monsieur, of course not. But one must try to succeed even in adversity. They have to know that we can't be beaten, that in the end they must surrender."

"Well, de Retz, I'll tell you what I think. I think we haven't hit them hard enough. Tomorrow we'll try again. I'll take that damn Gospel bastion of theirs if I have to blow it down stone by stone!"

"Monsieur, as you wish. But I think that these charges are telling the Protestants something. They say the Duke of Anjou is in a hurry."

"Well, damn it, I am in a hurry!" he shouted. "So would anyone be, whose subjects are holed up in a walled city refusing to admit their governor."

"I'm sure, Monsieur, you meant to say your royal brother's governor."

Anjou looked quickly from side to side. "Of course. But my haste is obvious."

"If you please, Monsieur," Gondi continued evenly. "Our haste tells them that time is perhaps on their side, not ours. It tells them that if they can hold out, your will may crack before theirs. Thus, it might be prudent to act as if we didn't care about a boatload of provisions. Let them think we plan to stay here all summer and all winter, too. Let them not forget in their joy that they must consider not just this boat, but the next and the next."

"What you say may be good strategy, de Retz, but the time for strategy is short. I've had one letter from the King and two from my mother saying we must end this siege. We have to do something now!

"Anyway," Anjou said after a long pause, "you have been lying here since March. Get up, man, get moving. You have three of the best galleys in France. Get them out to Belle-Île and get it back!"

"Monsieur, I still cannot move without pain."

"What is a little pain when your duty calls. No doubt you are stiff from lack of exercise. Look, I'll give you two weeks. If you can't get your own fortress back then, I'll ask my brother to find someone who can! We just can't wait for you, de Retz."

They left with a clatter of armor and a buzz of talk. Maurice, dawdling behind, grinned unpleasantly at Gondi.

"I won't add to your burdens by inquiring about my little matter," he said. "But don't let all your military problems push it out of mind. I haven't forgotten." He closed the door and was gone.

"Julio," Gondi bawled. "Get me my armor. I've got to try to stand. Got to do something."

* * *

Gondi hated sea travel at the best of times, but this was to be no moonlight sail. The great covered poop deck of Gondi's best galley, La Marquise, heaved under his feet. It was the second night out from La Rochelle, and the evening breeze, chill once they had stood out from the shore, made his wound ache. Gondi resolutely bade his stomach be silent as he drew his cloak more closely about him. The breeze, at last, fresh from the west, promised a swift completion of their passage. But a whole day, wallowing and rocking in a dead calm! To the right and left, about a quarter of a mile on each side, the sleek hulls of his other two galleys, captained by Strozzi and Copri, could be seen in the dark. Each galley held more than a hundred men-at-arms, and with luck and darkness, they hoped to catch Montgomery's raiders as they had caught the original defenders. Damn it, Gondi swore, I'm too old for this.

The breeze freshened, and the night wore on. Gondi slept fitfully, wishing he were warmer, wishing it were over. In the middle of the ship, the armed men huddled, catching sleep, looking to their weapons. There were few sailors among them. A surprise attack by sea was not their usual business and many were apprehensive, if not frightened.

Gondi cursed again as the ship rolled with the swell. Where had it all gone, the banners, the white horses with rich trappings, the bright shields and polished armor of his youth? Somehow he used to associate battle with sunlight. Hadn't it always been sunny in Italy? Now it was always fog, rain, cold, and fighting one's own countrymen. He laughed at the irony. He, an Italian, had been happy fighting Italians for France. Now he fought Frenchmen for France. Bah! There was no glory in it. That was the problem. It was more like patching a leaking roof, or fighting a disease. Survival was the only reward, not fame, riches, or glory. And failure was so easy. He rose and gazed into the night.

The moon, which had lighted their way, had set after midnight. There was a light mist on the water, but stars were clear above. "How long, Captain?" he asked.

"We're dead on course, sir, I reckon we'll make the island before daybreak just as you wanted."

Gondi grunted with satisfaction. So far, so good. It was essential to catch them before they suspected anything. His intelligence, a fishing boat, two days ago had reported two galleys and about 80 men. Gondi peered through the mist. If the wind held, they would be able to approach in silence without having to use their oars.

"We'll have to break out the oars soon, sir," the Captain said later. "I can't get her around to the harbor side on the wind."

"As you must," Gondi replied, "but quiet! Where is Strozzi? Damn the mist, I told him to keep close."

A shape appeared in the gloom.

"Ahoy, Strozzi," Gondi called. "Follow me in, muffle your oars."

"Right you are," came the muffled reply.

An hour later the land could be made out, a darker mass in the darkness. The oars made a rhythmic clunk as the men pulled with a will. They rounded the landward point just before dawn, and as the sun rose, Gondi's galley bore into the harbor. But before they reached shore Gondi knew there was trouble. Copri's vessel dutifully followed, but Strozzi was a speck on the horizon. The harbor, silent, was empty of English or indeed any foreign vessels.

They swarmed ashore, and in a few minutes had command of the island, an easy task as there was no enemy at all. A fisherman, rousted from his hut, reported that the English had been there the night before.

"But they go out, before dawn every day for the last three or four days, they go out, then mid-morning they come back."

Gondi left a force to secure the island and ordered the rest back on board.

"They must be close by," he cried. "We'll catch them out of port."

They were just about to cast off when Strozzi's galley passed into the harbor, its men pulling as though the devil were behind them.

"Why in God's name didn't you follow me in?" Gondi yelled. "You said you would."

"I never saw you after midnight," Strozzi called back, across the still water.

"You acknowledged my call."

"It wasn't me. It must have been someone else, but I have worse news. I saw two galleys at dawn. They were heading the wrong way, so I knew they weren't your ships. They must have been the English!"

"Damn. They must have passed us!"

In a flurry of haste they cast off and cleared the harbor. The morning sun, bright, made the work hot. The breeze fell again and oars alone moved the boats. They seemed made of lead. Gondi ground his teeth in frustration. It might be two days before they could get back to La Rochelle, and the English had several hours' head start. The English would have all the time in the world to slip into the port. They would be no match for his three galleys, but could easily overcome the slower, smaller ships that made up the rest of Gondi's blockade. Gondi stared helplessly at the morning glare on the water and wondered when his miserable luck would turn.

Chapter XLVI

ierre found the cheering crowd at the quayside even more bizarre than the gathering around the Maypole. Could two ships make such a difference? He saw more than one unfriendly glance. As usual, he thought, they imagine I'll stuff myself and deprive them. Word spread that the pastors had decreed a feast in honor of the brave English captains who had borne in the precious cargo. Pierre was turning away when Michel de Brossan, recovered from his wound, ran out of the Hôtel de Ville. "Pierre!" he cried, "Monsieur de Grève sent me to find you. Hurry!" Pierre shrugged and followed, mildly put off for no reason at all, perhaps because he disliked being summoned.

He found the old pastor alone, as was his custom, in a small, sparse room, just off the main chamber where Pierre had been examined many months ago.

"Come in, Monsieur de Galle," he began, "I have asked you to hear the decision we have reached. The English ship is going to slip out tonight. We offered to let them stay but they refused. I fear their capture but they say they are willing to run the risk." He paused. "I'm telling you this so you will know the facts. I told them about you and they are willing, if you wish, to take you out to England."

Pierre's face suffused with joy. Eagerly he seized the old man's hand and pumped it up and down.

De Grève gazed at him for a moment in silence. "I am not surprised at your reaction. Nor, I must say it, will all of us be sorry to see you go. For every one who has seen your work, indeed your heroism, in rescuing the wounded and in putting out fires, there seem to be two who have seen you eating our meager stores of food, and three who curse your obstinate clinging to the old religion."

Pierre's smile died. "I have done what I could, without actively taking up arms against the King. I have never eaten more than my share."

"Please, monsieur, I know that. And I think I know a little of the hard path your conscience has set for you. But I called you here to offer you a choice. We debated it this morning when the ships arrived safely, for which God be praised."

"A choice?" Pierre was incredulous. "You can't mean staying here where I am a misfit and unwanted? If there are dangers at sea, I will face them." Suddenly he smiled. "Oh, I see, you don't want to force me to risk capture by de Retz's galleys. You are very kind."

"No, young man," de Grève said quietly, his eyes steady. "I mean much more than that. I believe you could well serve both God and your King if you help us seize this chance to make peace. I ask you, if you will, to stay and talk to our enemies under a flag of truce. You can describe not just our new supplies, but our will to fight for our lives and our faith. They will believe you. They will see that their hope of starving us out is folly, and our walls they have learned about already."

Pierre lowered his eyes. A great feeling of desolation swept down on him. The golden green vision of England splintered in pieces. It was preposterous. Why should Gondi and Anjou listen to him? And if he missed the boat...? He had already spent seven months gazing vainly at the sea. And these people hated him, barely tolerating his existence. Even that, he imagined, was in part due to his size and reputation.

"Monsieur de Grève, I, I cannot help you this way. You must see how important it is for me to leave. And what could I say that your own pastors cannot say?"

De Grève sat slowly down on his bench. "I feared that would be what you would say. I said as much at our meeting this morning. Why, I said, should one who can escape to ease and pleasure forbear to do so? Why should he lift a finger for those who grudge him his crust of bread? But I had to ask you."

"Monsieur," Pierre said slowly. "Why me?"

"Because you are one of them, even if they suspect you. They may revile you, but in their hearts they will know you speak the truth. And that truth in their hearts will help more than ships to change their minds. Slowly the certainty that they cannot prevail will grow on them, and then they will grant that we be left in peace. I have watched you, Monsieur de Galle, for some months. I have never seen you shirk danger or ever utter a false word. No, they may hate you, but they will have no choice but to believe you. And it is written in the gospel, 'Blessed are the peacemakers, for they shall be called children of God.'"

Pierre walked slowly to the window. He grasped its bars high up, and rested his head on his arm. Below, the unloading of the ship was almost complete. The pastors had carefully supervised removal of the food to the nearby warehouse, where it was kept under constant guard.

With a sigh, Pierre turned back to the old man on the bench. He is old, Pierre thought, yet he defies the King of France, lives on moldy bread, and may yet be burned or hanged. All he wants is to be left in peace. Pierre knew he had no choice. Duty required it, but more than duty, it was right. It was the way things had to be. England, with the rank, riches, and safety it held for him, seemed somehow tarnished if while he was at ease there, this brave old man had to be butchered like his fellows in Paris. I saved some of them, so I suppose I must try again, he concluded.

"I will do as you ask," Pierre said simply. In the dim light, he could not see the tears glistening in de Grève's sunken eyes.

"Monsieur de Galle," de Grève spoke at last, "God's ways are not our ways. In His own providence He sent you here and kept you here against your will. How many times have I thought when I saw you on the battlements, 'A thousand shall fall at thy side, and ten thousand at thy right hand, but it shall not come nigh to thee.' I argued this morning and I am sure of it. The Almighty has chosen you for a great task. I hope and believe that this will be it. In any event, I believe that you are in His hand."

"A man must do what he must," Pierre muttered, confused.

"I'm sorry, I presumed too much, Monsieur," de Grève said quickly. "I recognize that you would not wish to speak of these things with me, a Protestant."

"No, you misunderstand me. I do not believe that there are no good men among you. I do not perceive God's will clearly as you seem to. But in a dark place, I will hold onto my honor, at least."

"As you wish, Monsieur de Galle," de Grève said, smiling, "but I am not sure that we are speaking of such different things."

Early June saw more savage attacks against resistance of redoubled vigor, now that the defenders had food and ammunition. Signals for a parley were exchanged and on a fine day in mid-June, the great Porte de Cougnes gate opened, and a delegation under flag of truce emerged.

The group, two military men and four black-clad pastors, would have roused no interest as they passed through the Catholic lines if it were not for Pierre, gaunt from lack of food but still towering above them.

Word of the blonde giant sped back to headquarters like wildfire. Maurice looked uneasy. Anjou looked incredulously at Gondi. Anjou's brother-in-law, Henri, Prince of Navarre, much against his will a Catholic captain, sat silently on the edge of the gathering.

When the delegation arrived at the tent, Anjou could scarcely contain himself. "Monsieur de Galle," he cried. "We had not expected you. First a traitor, then dead, now it seems doubly a traitor. What do your black masters hope to gain by sending you as their spokesman?"

"I am no traitor, my Prince," Pierre replied, "and they will speak for themselves. I agreed to come to report to you what I myself have seen of their resolve. That is fact, and you would do well to consider it. But I am not here to argue their cause, with which I do not hold."

The Protestant pastors glared balefully at Pierre. "I told you de Grève was an old fool," one of them hissed to his companions.

"In any event," the Duke of Nevers said, "let us begin the discussion. As I understand it, there are six issues..."

There was a terrific commotion outside. Trumpets blew, men shouted, and before Nevers could continue, an aide de camp entered and spoke hurriedly to Anjou. Anjou rose and faced the doorway.

Two messengers in the Queen Mother's livery entered, then knelt and prostrated themselves at Anjou's feet. "Receive, Sire, the grateful congratulations of your servants. The Lord has been pleased to award you election as the King of Poland."

Pandemonium broke out in the camp. Wine was liberally served out, cannon were fired and men shouted for joy. In the tent there was much congratulating of the new King; even his Protestant enemies joined in wishing him well.

Anjou clapped Gondi on the back and whispered, "Don't think I'm not aware of all you did in this. I'm prepared to overlook that Belle-Île business. Perhaps we can get something settled quickly here. I can't waste my time smoking these rats out of their hole."

"Shall we send them away for today?"

"No, let's see what can be accomplished. It would be a great thing if I could ride in triumph into La Rochelle while the eyes of Poland are upon me. It would get things off to a good start, if I have the reputation of a great general."

The discussion dragged on for several hours while the sounds of merrymaking grew louder throughout the Catholic camp. Pierre duly gave his account of the Protestant determination. It was received with frank hostility.

He resumed his seat thinking that he was perhaps a better judge of Catholic mentality than de Grève.

At about four, it became plain that no progress was being made. The Protestants whispered among themselves and suggested an adjournment. Gondi strolled to one side and hissed to Maurice. "Get some men and seize de Galle." Maurice raised an eyebrow, but hurried off to obey. The Protestants rose to leave, bowed, but as they were about to leave the tent, six burly archers entered and surrounded Pierre.

Maurice, holding aloft a much-stained warrant, shouted, "Pierre de Galle, you are arrested in the King's name for high treason and other crimes."

"See here," shouted the Protestant captain, drawing his sword, "We are here under a royal safe conduct. You can't touch one of our delegation."

Anjou cocked an eye at Gondi.

"Oh, but we can," Gondi replied. "The safe conduct applies to Protestants; this man is no Protestant, he is a renegade Catholic."

"We offer him the protection of our religion. It is we who asked him to come with us."

Gondi looked at Pierre, "Are you a Protestant, de Galle?"

"No," Pierre replied.

"Wait a minute, Monsieur de Retz," Henri Navarre strode forward. "This man has risked his safety, perhaps put his head in a noose, to bring peace to La Rochelle. I'm sure his sympathies are with the Protestants. They have to be. I think he should have a choice now, to become one officially, if he isn't one at heart already."

"My lord," Pierre gave Navarre a wintry smile. "I thank you for your good will. But I am no more a Protestant than..." he checked himself, just as he was about to say, "than you are a Catholic." He ended lamely, "...than the Pope is.

"I would not say I am a Protestant if it were not true, even to save my life. For this much I do believe, they are wholly sincere, and it would be wrong falsely to pretend belief in what they hold at the cost of their own lives."

Navarre turned away, clumsily brushing his eyes.

"Then I'm afraid it's out of your hands," Gondi said briskly, turning to the Protestant captain. "We are, of course, grateful for your help in apprehending this felon. Such good will may even improve the climate for negotiations."

"Monsieur de Retz," the captain bristled, "This is an outrage. Were it not preceded by so many others, I would say your conduct was shocking. As it is, it is no more than we should have expected. What you can expect is this: It is all as Monsieur de Galle has said. We will never yield to you on trust of your good faith! Never, never, never! You had better tell the Poles to appoint a regent, Monsieur d'Anjou. You will be occupied here with us for many, many months."

With a pitying glance at Pierre, for they were too few to help him, the Protestants turned and slowly made their way back to the city through the Catholic camp, now becoming wild as the wine flowed and pipes played.

"We should hang him right now," Maurice volunteered.

"No you don't," Anjou snapped. "This is a great day for me and I won't have it spoiled. This is a matter for my brother, anyway. De Galle, once dead, now alive again, is one of the great magnates of the kingdom. He will have his justice, but it will be on the Place de Grève in Paris, not on some tree here. Send him back to Paris, de Retz. I don't mind saying that your bit of police work came at a damned inconvenient time. I tell you right now I want this siege ended fast!"

Gondi motioned Maurice aside. "Don't let him out of your sight this time. Take him to Paris, that's what the Queen Mother wanted anyway. Of course..." Gondi lowered his voice. "If he should try to escape, you'll have to prevent it."

Gondi had expected Maurice's usual glow of anticipation, but Maurice remained impassive.

"You must think I'm a fool, Gondi," Maurice rasped. "You told me last fall the Queen Mother wanted him alive. Now you hint that I should dispose of him. You think you're too clever by half, but I'm on to you. I kill him, which shuts his mouth, then you get me for disobeying the Queen. Neat, but as my lord Anjou, I mean His Majesty the King of Poland, once said, 'Gondi is losing his grip.' I'll take him to Paris and he won't be harmed, and he won't escape. And you had better be prepared to deliver."

"La Renaudie, you are a fool! And I am not. Sooner or later, I'll finish you, that is a promise."

"Words, old man, words. I'm a friend of the King of Poland, and I'm going to cook your goose if you don't take care of me."

Maurice had just left with his guard escorting Pierre when cries and shouts arose from the south side of the camp. "They're coming!" was the cry. A glance revealed a massive Protestant sortie, falling upon the drunken Catholic lines. Guns boomed, men screamed as they tried desperately to buckle on their armor. Maurice watched for a moment then summoned six more guards. "Mount up," he ordered. "We leave for Paris at once."

As pandemonium raged in the camp under the long midsummer twilight, Pierre, his arms bound behind him, found himself once again en route to Paris.

Chapter XLVII

It was just at dawn that Pierre, his arms shackled behind him, surrounded by La Renaudie's men, crossed the Seine and entered Paris by the same gate he had used to flee nearly a year before. The early July day promised to be fine and warm after the morning chill had passed. The bird and forest sounds gave way to the sounds of the city stirring, stretching itself for another day — bells of dozens of churches, the first high, thin cries of the street vendors, the rattle and clank of shutters and gates being opened.

Pierre smiled on the lovely day. How beautiful Paris was. How beautiful this morning was. He looked up at the sky, pink giving way to blue. How beautiful, he thought again. He had no illusions about his fate, indeed had had none since Gondi's men had seized him. He would be jailed for a brief time and then beheaded. It had all been arranged. There might be the form of some sort of judicial process, but it would just be show. Gondi and La Renaudie had rigged it all, and it was pointless to worry about it.

Pierre was not surprised at his own attitude, nor was he resigned to his fate. He had lost and been stripped of everything, lands, estates, titles, but he was still de Galle, the de Galle for the moment, and he could still die well. To die well, to approach certain death with utter aplomb — that seemed to him not only important, for really he had nothing else left, but instinctive dignity. He had been captured by his enemies. Well, so had many of his ancestors. He was unjustly accused, certainly he was not the first. His young life was to be snuffed out, well that was what his duty had required. He wished it could be otherwise, but he did not delude himself.

He wondered off and on whether he should seek a royal pardon, demand to talk to the King, get his and his father's friends to try to bargain. It all seemed pointless now as they rode slowly down the rue de Tournelle. Somehow, he supposed, de Retz will have rigged it, and the thought of the pleasure his stepbrother would have thwarting him made his stomach turn. No, better to maintain his dignity in silence.

The early sun gilded the peak of Montmartre. He thought again of Athalie. Where was she, what had they done to her? He sighed as he thought of their dreams of England dashed during the dreary winter at La Rochelle. He sighed again, how much he would give to see her again. But no, it would be better thus, for he knew how his death would pain her. Better that she should be far away and hear of his passing in a letter.

He woke from his reverie to find the company halting in front of the gates of the Conciergerie, the ancient dungeon where what passed for justice was meted out by the criminal chamber of the Parliament of Paris. After a brief exchange, the great gate swung open and they passed inside. The color, it seemed, went out of the day.

There were some further exchanges as the guard dismounted, and Pierre was marched by the warden's guard up a long winding flight to a bare stone cell in the north tower. The warden bade him adieu and left. The window was too high for him to reach and he sat down on the wooden bench. He chafed his wrists but the manacles had rubbed the skin raw during the long ride. He smiled thinking how absurd it was to fret over such a small matter when it was his neck that was in real jeopardy.

At about nine o'clock, he judged, the door opened and an escort, led by La Renaudie, called him out. "Now you'll have some fun, Blondel," Maurice said as he smiled and licked his lips. "I've been waiting a long time for this moment. You'll squirm. Bring him along, lads."

They marched him down and down, past the entrance level to one lower. They entered a large bare room with a large fire roaring on the hearth. One look at its grisly apparatus revealed its function. Pierre's cheeks whitened a bit, but he gave no other sign of interest.

"So, Blondel, this is one of the best-equipped establishments in France. I intend to introduce you to all of its amusements. That great constitution of yours will stand plenty, and what fun it will be to give it to you. I can't make up my mind; shall we start first with something big like the rack, or something exquisite like the thumbscrew? What do you think? It's only fair to ask your preference."

At that moment a tall, hawk-faced man in a long black robe entered, followed by an entourage of clerks and heavily built men in leather aprons. Maurice doffed his plumed cap and bowed gracefully.

"Good morning to you, First President de Thou," he said. "May I present the prisoner, Pierre de Galle. He and I were just discussing the merits of beginning with thumbscrews. What do you think?"

"Ah, yes, good morning, Monsieur, eh, eh…"

"La Renaudie," whispered one of the secretaries.

"Ah, yes, Monsieur La Renaudie. May I know your business before the tribunal? We have a rather busy day ahead of us."

"I have here, my lord President, Pierre de Galle to be tortured. I was told by the Count de Retz, whom I have the honor to serve, that I might assist and suggest the order of things."

"Well, Monsieur, er, er, you are apparently here under some misapprehension. We speak here of the 'question,' not torture. In any event we are to interrogate Laurent Dumont, a highwayman, this morning. I have no de Galle on my agenda."

"But I was told he was to be put to the question," Maurice protested. "The Count de Retz…"

"Monsieur," the President snapped icily, "this is the criminal tribunal of the Parliament of Paris. These matters must be done according to law. I have just told you we are occupied this morning with another prisoner. If it is urgent, perhaps we could take Monsieur de Galle late this afternoon. But I must tell you straight out that there will be no thumbscrews for him. This is a judicial process. The rules are quite clear and I'm surprised you don't know them, if, as you say, you have any business here at all. We must start with the water first, four gallons for the ordinary question, and eight for the extraordinary. The prisoner is entitled to two brief respites and to be warmed before the fire between each session. At the discretion of the tribunal we can use the boot instead, four wedges for the ordinary question and eight for the extraordinary, and the same respites. Nothing else is allowed. You should know that. I say, what did he do?" he concluded, turning to his secretary.

"Treason and lèse-majesté," Maurice volunteered eagerly.

"Is that so?" said the President, impressed. "Well, in that case I suppose we might have to use the boot. I generally try to avoid it. It needs more men and generally takes longer. In any event, the secretaries will be occupied transcribing the testimony we get this morning, so we can't possibly begin with him until late afternoon." A secretary whispered something about "...supper, President of the Parliament." De Thou nodded then turned back to Maurice.

"No, I'm afraid we can't finish this afternoon, anyway. These things take time, you know. Perhaps we could start tomorrow morning, then we could make a proper job of it.

"Now if you would please clear the chamber. I like to begin these hearings on time. We must keep to our schedule. We are very busy, you know."

Maurice had no choice but to march Pierre back the way they had come. "Don't worry," he snarled as he prepared to slam the door of Pierre's cell. "Tomorrow will come soon enough. That old coot is a meddling busybody with his rules and procedures. I'll get the King to show him a few shortcuts." The door swung to and Pierre was left alone.

Pierre paced back and forth, four of his great strides one way and four back. Never a word should they have! He smashed his left hand with his right fist, hampered by the heavy manacles. La Renaudie gloating over him, licking his lips with satisfaction... Pierre ground his teeth. He thought of his father and began to calm down. His father, groveling before La Renaudie, begging mercy? It was unthinkable. It could not happen. He set his jaw firmly. There was simply no choice, he had to resist to the end. The trick was to remember that he was a dead man. If he was dead, then none of it would matter. The grim-lipped image of his father in his mind seemed to approve of this course.

Back and forth he paced. Somehow the waiting seemed the worst part. He smiled wryly to himself and resolved to try to remember tomorrow, after they finished, if he still thought waiting was the worst part. Suddenly a great wave of sadness washed over him. There was so much to do, to see, to be. His line might continue, but he would never see the sky, feel the rain, see the flowers, see Athalie again.

Athalie — her lithe, dark form overwhelmed his mind for a moment. He could feel the soft strength of her body, see the wisdom in her dark eyes. He found himself imagining that somehow she knew of his plight, somehow she had prevailed on someone, and had been allowed to bid him adieu. She would understand and bless his rock-like resolve of silence, come what might. He imagined the heavy door opening, Athalie, gorgeous in the doorway, then flinging herself upon him as the door slammed shut behind her.

Pierre would blink stupidly, as one might awakening from a sound sleep into blazing light. A moment later they would be in each other's arms, and Pierre would be raining kisses on her weeping eyes and black hair. He would lift his arms together so his manacled wrists could clear her head.

"Dearest Lie-lie, how did you...? How could you? Oh, never mind, you are here. That's all that counts. I guess you know about the fix I am in."

"I know."

"I am available, as it were, only because my stepbrother seemingly failed to get some forms filled out for my torture. You must not come again. I couldn't bear to have you see me after I, after they..."

"Pierre, this can't happen. We must stop it!"

"Lie-lie, please, if you love me, no, I know you love me, but please. I have accepted my death. It doesn't frighten me much. But when one has prepared for death, it is a disservice to speak of hope."

"But there is hope, there has to be, they can't do this to you."

"Lie-lie, don't you see, they have to do this, and my esteemed stepbrother will relish every minute of it. If I struggle, it will only give him more thrills. The only way I can diminish his pleasure is to act as if I didn't care, to show no fear, to show them all what it means to be de Galle."

"Pierre! Damn you, Pierre!" Athalie cried. "All you can think of is your pride, your family honor, and that worm, La Renaudie. He counts for nothing. For that matter, your precious family counts for nothing! But don't I count? Can't you save yourself for me at least?"

Pierre would gaze sadly past Athalie, then place a manacled hand on her shoulder. "What use would it be, dearest? It is all rigged. What use would it be to proclaim my innocence even if someone could be found to listen to me. Don't you see? All I have left is my honor. That they cannot take from me. No matter how they break my body, they shall not have a word from my lips, I swear that to you, Athalie, not one word."

"Oh, Pierre," she cried sobbing, "I don't want your oath, I don't want your honor, or your title, or your family. I want you! I want you! Please let me help you. I shall help you, no power on earth, not even you, can stop me!"

"Athalie, please, you will only upset yourself."

"Don't 'Athalie' me," she retorted. "You will see it done. I shall not stop until your head rolls off the scaffold! Not for one instant. Now I shall go and I shall not rest!"

In Pierre's imagination, Athalie flung her arms around Pierre's neck, kissed him, and ran to the door, shouting, "Guards! Guards!" In a moment she was gone, the silver tinkle of her voice calling for a horse drifting back down the corridor as the heavy door closed once more.

Pierre sat on the bench, his head in his hands. He felt lost, drained, and helpless, whereas he had been so proud and defiant. Can my love unman me so, he wondered.

Chapter XLVIII

hat same cool morning in early July, Athalie was strolling idly among the roses of Gondi's Hôtel de Perrin in Paris. Tiring of her promenade, she sat on a bench in an alcove and took out her needlepoint. She had spent nearly a week in Paris, but had as yet seen no one but her uncle Gondi's wife, her aunt the Countess, and of course, the servants. Her aunt had been evasive, but from the servants' gossip she knew that she had been brought from Burgundy to be presented to a Polish nobleman. Her chief joy at the moment was the news, also gleaned from the servants, that La Rochelle had successfully wrested a peace from Anjou, now King-elect of Poland. That meant, she thought happily, that Pierre would soon be in England. Softly she felt for the scrap of parchment in her sleeve. She was never without it — it was all she had of Pierre. It was perhaps all she would have, if the gossip were right and she was to be packed off to Poland.

Her reverie was disturbed by a commotion at the gate. She could distinguish her aunt's voice. It sounded first subdued, then shrill. Then she heard a bell-like laugh — Margot! Could it be Margot?

It could be and it was, and with her usual refusal to be balked, the Princess soon made her way past guards, servants, and aunts, to the garden.

"So you see, cousin," she said, embracing Athalie, "I have come to let bygones be bygones. Though I won't deny I've been very angry with you — never a letter, never a word. Of course, even now, no one is supposed to know what happened — except Mother, of course. But I can tell from what she does, what must have happened. If you'd just gone away for a rest cure or some kind of spiritual retreat, you'd be back at Court now, as a lady-in-waiting or married or whatever. If you're in disgrace, it can mean only one thing — a baby — and Mother's waiting 'til she marries you off to forgive you.

"But really, Athalie, you could have confided in me. I, of all people, would have understood."

"Oh, Margot, forgive me," Athalie cried. "If I could have written to anyone, I would have written to you. But you see, all through last year, there were commitments that made me keep silent, and since I've been here, I've been unable to communicate with anyone. My aunt would never have let me write to you, of all people. She knows we were friends.

"Margot, dear, I began to think I'd never see a friendly face again. I've been so miserable. The worst of it is the baby. If I could have my child with me, I could bear anything." She turned away in tears.

Margot put her arm around Athalie. "There, there, little cousin, I know it must be very hard. But, you know, Athalie, in reason, a woman in your position can hardly keep a baby around."

Athalie shook her head violently and sobbed.

"Well," Margot paused, looking for a new subject. "I can't say I've thought about you a great deal. I've had my troubles, too, as you can imagine, if you've kept up with things at all. Navarre is pretty ghastly — all garlic and sweat and humps like a bull, but I think the way they've treated him is really awful. All that prating about peace, and no sooner are we married than they kill all the Protestants in their beds, and would have killed Navarre, too, if I hadn't saved him. Well, that's all supposed to be in the past. Navarre is a good little faithful Catholic now — or so we're supposed to believe. I don't mind telling you, though, I don't think he's anything like the buffoon they think he is, for all he's a little rough around the edges.

"And how can we put religious dissension behind us, while the fight goes on? I thought it was over when my brother had to give up on La Rochelle. Such a fuss. Mother was furious, but at least they are all back at Court. It was so dull with them away fighting all spring. And they didn't even win." She giggled.

"But it just never seems to end. Why, just this morning, the most amazing thing happened. They brought in Pierre de Galle, under a guard headed by his brother or stepbrother or whatever he is. Last winter they said he was dead. Now it seems he's alive and has been arrested at La Rochelle on a warrant that goes back to those horrible days in Paris, and your uncle Gondi has written a letter all about treacherous activities with the Protestants since then — at La Rochelle and other places — and advising my brother to have him put to the sword.

"Well, what a furor! You know, my brother the poor King can't bear any mention of St. Bartholomew's Day, so the letter threw him into a frenzy. Dear thing, he became really ill — of course, he's almost always ill — so needless to say, nothing could be decided. But I mean, really, what a shame: on the one hand, we're supposed to forget about it all, and on the other, we're not allowed to forget anything.

"Athalie, what is the matter?"

Athalie was absolutely white and stared out with a fixed, horrified gaze.

With a struggle, she mastered herself and turned slowly to Margot. "Margot, if you love me as you always say, you must do something for me. You must return at once and get your mother to send for me immediately. However, you can, you must do it. It is a matter of life and death. Please, Margot..." Her shoulders began to shake.

"But of course, Athalie dear, I would do much more than that." She looked quizzically at Athalie. "I begin to see the light, cousin dear. Could it be? Oh yes, it could be! Well, well." Athalie shook her head more in despair than negation, and tears began to roll down her cheeks.

Margot sat beside her and cradled Athalie's head against her body. "It's all right, dear little friend. I won't blackmail you into telling me your secret. I understand.

"There, there. I'll do you better than taking your message. I'll take you."

Athalie looked up.

"Oh, my aunt would never allow it."

"Will she not? My dear, will you never learn to appreciate the uses of power? Come," she took Athalie's hand and pulled her up.

Athalie snuffled and wiped her nose on the back of her hand. "Oh, Margot. I got the front of your dress all wet."

"Never mind, silly. Now come." With a purposeful stride, Margot led Athalie across the courtyard and into the house.

Athalie had barely time to snatch up a cloak as Margot, holding her firmly by the hand, swept her across the hall toward the door. An ashen-faced Countess de Retz barred their way.

"But, Madame," she squeaked at Margot, "the Count gave express instructions that the Duchess should remain here. She has conducted herself very badly and as her guardian, he has considered it in her best..."

"Madame," Margot cut in. "I think you forget to whom you are speaking. I do not care a sou what the Count de Retz considers are my cousin's best interests. She shall see my mother immediately. Stand aside, you are becoming tedious."

The Countess, her cheeks crimson with rage, her mouth working uselessly, had no choice but to obey. Athalie found herself outside, with Margot issuing a string of forceful if sometimes contradicting orders to her attendants. "You, ride on ahead. The Queen Mother is at the Château de Madrid! No, the Duchess will ride with me. No, she does not need a litter. Hurry!"

Soon they were off, along the rue de St. Honoré out through the suburbs, past the rolling green Montmartre, dotted with windmills, and into the Bois de Boulogne, the Princess's whole entourage of ladies, men-at-arms, and lackeys being urged on at a most undignified speed by Margot's imperious shouts. They had no sooner clattered to a halt in the main courtyard of the Château de Madrid than Margot again seized Athalie's hand and pulled her through the groups of courtesans and ambassadors, oblivious to curtseys, bows, and curious stares directed at Athalie. Catherine de Medici was dictating a letter as Margot, having knocked timidly at the door, then burst in anyway, Athalie shrinking slightly behind. The Queen Mother stopped, looked up at Margot with annoyance, then with a baffled look at Athalie, a mixture of amazement, pleasure, wrath, and embarrassment at her momentary loss of self-control. She dismissed her secretary and stepped slowly around her writing table.

"Well, well, well," she said, "I see you have caught the truant who was too ashamed of herself to see me. I won't ask you, Margot, how you coaxed her out, but I thank you for it. I have wanted to give her a piece of my mind for some time."

"I did not coax her, Madame," Margot giggled. "I captured her from her uncle's prison and from his wife, the warden of the jail."

"Please, Madame," Athalie spoke up. "They told me you would refuse to see me. Only now I must see you. You must help, oh, please, help me." She stopped, choked with sobs. Margot put a reassuring arm around her shoulders.

"Do I understand you to say that she was restrained, and that my councilor, her uncle, told her I would not receive her?"

"Just so, Mother," Margot replied.

Catherine de Medici lowered herself into a chair. A practiced observer, Margot noticed the certain extra smoothness in her motions as she arranged her dress. She was rigidly mastering her anger, which, judging by the lengthening silence, was considerable.

Margot braced herself, as she was not completely sure that she was not the target of at least some of the royal ire. Athalie broke the silence by falling at the Queen's feet, wracked with sobs, begging her to help. "Help me, oh, please, save him. Save him!" she cried.

The Queen Mother slowly, then with assurance, stretched out a jeweled hand and pulled Athalie toward her. She pressed Athalie's face, oblivious of the tears staining the black silk of her skirt. "Athalie, my child, don't be afraid. I am not going to hurt you. I am so very, very happy to see you. I have missed you. Oh, why didn't you write or speak? But no matter, now you are here and there is much that can still be done about your future. Now, now, Athalie, stop crying. It is all right. I will speak to your uncle. What did you say?"

Athalie, oblivious to the Queen's affectionate chatter, had continued to choke out, "Save him," between her sobs.

"Save whom, child?" she asked softly.

"Pierre, Pierre de Galle," Athalie said with force.

The Queen Mother rolled her eyes heavenward. "Yes, dear, it was very sad. He was a great disappointment to me. But it is you we must think about. Just the other day your uncle and I were discussing Count Wierzka as a possibility. He is said to be rather good-looking and he has an immense property near Cracow. He was no end useful in getting Henri the Polish crown. He would be so flattered at a connection with you, and well, he should be, that I am sure he could be made to overlook, er, the events of the last year. What did you say, dear?"

Athalie raised her head. "Yes, I said yes! I will do anything, go anywhere, but save him, you must save him!"

"She is overwrought, Margot. Perhaps you should take her home. We could talk next week. This business of de Galle is absurd. The wretched man has been dead nearly a year. Come now, Athalie, get a grip on yourself."

"Mother," Margot broke in. "He isn't dead, but he soon will be. De Retz captured him and he is now in the Conciergerie. I heard he was to be tortured this afternoon."

"What are you saying, Margot?" The Queen Mother jerked erect. "He drowned. Who told you this?"

"La Renaudie, at the Louvre, was bragging about it this morning. Apparently de Galle escaped, or something, to La Rochelle. They caught him two weeks ago and brought him here in irons. Why don't you ask Athalie why she cares so much."

"Yes, I shall do that. And I shall also ask Monsieur de Retz a few questions. Well, Athalie?"

"Please, Your Majesty, send for him and speak to him yourself. He isn't a traitor, he is the most loyal man in France."

"But what is he to you, dear, even if he is such a paragon, which the facts indicate he is not."

"He is..." she stammered.

"Oh, come on, Athalie," Margot giggled. "Don't be such a goose. He was her lover, the secret lover and the father of her child."

"Is it so then?" Catherine de Medici said slowly. "I see. I see a great deal." She rose and walked to the window. The warm summer breeze fluttered the papers on her table, and only the rhythmic swish of the gardeners' scythes outside broke the silence.

"Pierre de Galle," the Queen Mother began, "was accused last summer of very serious crimes." She paused, then rose and faced Athalie. "Athalie," she said, "I am not almighty God, but on this earth I have certain powers. I can and will do this much — Let him be brought at once. Let him first be cleaned and dressed. Let him know it was I who sent for him."

She rang a small bell, and to the serving girl who appeared she gave a string of orders. Horses, they would return to the Louvre at once, the Count de Retz was to be summoned to meet them there no matter what the excuse. The corporal of her guard was summoned. The serving girl hurried off and the Queen Mother sat down at her desk and picked up a quill. She dashed off a note and was just sealing it when Augustin Pascal entered.

"Take this to the warden of the Conciergerie and give it to him or to the First President of the Parliament if the criminal session is still sitting when you arrive. Take some men with you. This letter authorizes you to take the prisoner, the Duke de Galle, to my chambers at the Louvre. No power but the King's own can stop you. He is hunting at Vincennes, I imagine, at this hour, and if you hurry, de Galle will be at the Louvre before they can get the King to act.

"Now, dear, dry your eyes. You shall stay here with Margot. We will return this evening."

She embraced Athalie, holding her close for a long minute. "Pray God that we may be in time."

* * *

Pierre's pacing around his cell was abruptly disturbed in midafternoon by the clump of men-at-arms and vociferous argument muffled through the heavy door. The huge key rasped hoarsely and the door swung open. Pierre squared his shoulders and awaited his fate.

La Renaudie, his face troubled, entered, followed by the warden and Augustin Pascal. The latter bowed ceremoniously to Pierre, then turned back to the others, continuing an argument that had been going on for some time.

"Now, s-s-s-see here, Warden, we're wasting time. My m-m-m-Mistress ordered him brought at once. I insist that you obey."

"Well, it looks all right, but I don't..."

"It's outrageous," cried La Renaudie. "He is a dangerous traitor. He has killed men and escaped time and time again. My orders from the King were to bring him here for trial and execution. It would be madness to let him out, even under heavy guard."

"Well, I don't know," said the warden. "It's all most irregular, but it is Her Majesty's signature." He looked imploringly at La Renaudie.

"Warden, there has to be some mistake," Maurice responded. "Somehow the Queen Mother was inveigled into this. She would never ask anything so foolhardy if she were properly informed."

"Monsieur Warden," Augustin cut in, "You have here the plainly written order of Her Majesty. I d-d-d-don't suppose you are so foolish as to refuse to obey it."

The warden looked more miserable as Maurice drew breath to start in again.

"Well, it seems I have no choice. It is an order, after all."

"Damn it, man!" La Renaudie shouted. "When I tell the King about this, he'll have you flayed alive!"

The warden, suddenly angry, bristled. "Look here, Monsieur de La Renaudie, maybe you have the King's ear and maybe you don't. But I follow orders, see, and this man here has an order all signed and sealed. You there, take off his manacles."

"You fool," Maurice hissed. "If he escapes, you're done for."

"I'll wager you're the one that's done for," the warden shot back. "If you are so afraid of his making off, why don't you go along as extra guard. There is nothing in the order that says you can't."

"Perhaps I shall," said Maurice softly. "You'd like my company, wouldn't you, brother mine?"

Pierre, who was being hurriedly garbed in a fresh doublet, remained silent.

A few minutes later, they descended the circular stairs and in the courtyard mounted for the short ride to the Louvre. As they rode slowly up the quai toward the bridge across the Seine, Maurice dropped back so that he was riding at Pierre's side. Suddenly, his long dagger flashed in the sunlight as he drove the blade at Pierre's exposed side. Just as suddenly, with a whistling clang, Augustin Pascal's sword knocked the blade from his hand.

Without a word, Maurice spurred his horse and disappeared.

* * *

"So, Monsieur de Galle," Catherine de Medici said quietly, "at last we can have a little chat." Turning to the guards, she said more forcefully, "Leave us."

"But Madame," Pascal protested, "he's said to be dangerous. The Count de Retz has said..."

502

"Leave us," she snapped. "I will answer to the Count de Retz, if indeed he does not answer to me!"

Obviously uneasy, but having no choice in the matter, Augustin Pascal retired, followed by the guard. The door closed.

"You may sit, Monsieur," the Queen Mother said. There was a long silence, not awkward, because the Queen was appraising Pierre as a doctor might a patient, or a merchant a valuable antique. Pierre, resigned, felt nothing at all.

"I do not generally converse with attainted traitors," she said slowly, as her eyes took in his great form, shabby and bent a little, but still proud, his grey eyes steady, his mouth firm, but not defiant.

What a wonderful specimen, she thought, almost in spite of herself. Involuntarily coquettish, her face softened a bit. "However, I wished to hear certain things from your own mouth.

"Have you been put to the question yet?"

Pierre moved heavily, then said, "No, not yet. Tomorrow, I think. They said they would try the boot. I don't care. Where I am to go, I shall have no further need of feet or legs."

She looked at him sharply. There was something incongruous, horrible, about this magnificent man seemingly resigned, almost passive, before his fate.

"Monsieur de Galle, I must hear from your own mouth what happened the night..." she groped for words, "the night of the Protestant revolt."

"It was wrong," he said, "so I tried to stop it. I couldn't and I fled. Now I am to die. What more is there to say, Your Majesty?"

Damn the man, she cursed inwardly. "Don't you realize I have the power to put you to death or set you free?" She winced as she recognized the quotation after she had said it. "What you did is well known. I want to know why you did it."

"Madame," Pierre replied, "with greatest respect, I am, as you say, an attainted traitor. Of what use would it be to you, or anyone, what I say, or why indeed should you believe it?"

"I may believe it because you are de Galle, and moreover, because you seem determined to be killed. Your attitude is not that of one who would say anything to save himself. As to why I want to know, it was because your action made no sense to me at the time, and I do not like mysteries. I think I have some discernment of human nature, I thought I knew you. Indeed, as we sit here, I think still I know you. Now please, tell me why you bolted."

Pierre looked up at her pale, puffy face. Utter weariness overcame him. What use was speech? What good would it do? Could it wipe out one drop of the blood that was shed that night, blood that he himself had shed? He sighed and remained silent.

"Pierre!" she shouted. "For the last time, speak, or will you defy that order, too?"

"Madame, I mean no discourtesy, and I thank you for seeing me, but..."

"Speak!" she ordered.

"Very well, but you will not be pleased at what you hear. If you know of this already, I can be no more dead than I shall be. If no, then I have done you an injustice, and I would not go to my own doom with that on my conscience."

Ah, these nobles, the Queen Mother sighed to herself. Was there ever a more pompous, stuffy race on earth? Yet the awesome stillness of his courage could not be blinked at.

"I learned, Madame, shortly after I set out on that, er, night, that the supposed threats of the Protestants against you and the royal family, indeed the whole idea of the rebellion, had been made up by La Renaudie, my stepbrother. He had shouted the threats at the Protestant meeting and had been shouted down by Coligny and the others. Then he came here and said it was they who said what only he had urged. So I saw it was all a terrible mistake and tried to stop it. Then I found that it was no mistake to the Count de Retz. I knew that I knew too much, and I fled to save my life. I saved a few other lives on the way, but that was but a drop in that boiling cauldron of murder."

"And you were not a Protestant sympathizer?" she asked.

"No," he replied. "That was what my late wife could not understand. It was the underhandedness of it. The King had been deceived, that was all there was to it." He fell silent.

"You had the information from one of the Protestants, I presume?"

"Yes. He was my friend. De Retz had him killed as soon as I brought him to the Louvre."

"Why did you not come to me?" she asked. "No, don't say it. I know the answer."

Catherine de Medici sat back on her chair, suddenly felt cold, and pulled her robe a bit closer around her shoulders. Accuser and accused had suddenly changed places. And she knew beyond a shadow of a doubt that Pierre was telling the truth.

She rose heavily and walked to the window. The westering sun gilded the rooftops rose, and birdsongs floated in on the breeze. She turned back toward Pierre, her face invisible against the bright sky.

"I, too, was deceived," she whispered, "although I don't know whether you have it in you to believe me. I let myself be deceived in part for the good of the state, but for the rest, I did not know. I thought we had no choice. Oh, my poor Charles, he must never know of this," she concluded, wringing her hands. "I made a mistake. Can you forgive me?"

Pierre met her eyes without a word.

"Pierre, if anyone is, you are France. I know somehow that your forgiveness would be forgiveness indeed."

"Forgiveness, Madame? I don't understand."

"Yes, Pierre, forgiveness. I need it and I beg you to give it to me." She sighed and turned away. "For if I was deceived, it was because I was not unwilling to be deceived. I wanted Coligny out of the way, of course I did. It was not personal; he

504

was a great man in many ways, and in some ways an old friend. Yet he was at once too powerful and not powerful enough. His weakness forced him to take risks with the state in order to control his followers. If he had been stronger, he would have been less dangerous. As it was..."

She shrugged and spread out her hands.

"A ruler must make hard choices. I could not risk a Spanish invasion, because Admiral Coligny's followers were hot for war in the Netherlands. So much was necessity. I make no apology for it.

"But for the rest," she turned away, her eyes downcast. "It was so horrible. I tell you I knew fear that night. I knew that a beast had been loosed that was far worse than my wildest imaginings. A beast of no mind, no principle, and strong, Pierre, so strong, far beyond our power to stop, let alone control." She crossed herself. "I pray God never to see that fury again. I pray that the princes of the future will remember that it is unstoppable and pitiless.

"That was a mistake, a blunder, and blunders in a prince are sins, Pierre. For this, I accuse myself. I made a mistake and people died, and other people killed. For my penance I must bear the memory of that night and those days, and no one must ever tell my poor son the King that it was a horrible mistake. It would be the end of him. He is not well, you know," she said earnestly, "and these bouts of illness make it hard for him to show his real greatness. Ah, my poor son." She sighed heavily and sat down. Pierre remained silent, but his face bore a look of pain that reflected repugnance as well as compassion.

"Well, Monsieur de Galle," she said, suddenly all business, "something must be done. You realize, of course, that having told the Pope and the King of Spain that we lured the Protestants here to kill them, we can't very well say now it was all a mistake, can we? As it was, we had to seem worse than we were, because I didn't want them to know we were powerless, powerless to stop the Catholic mobs. So you see, the truth is now awkward."

"I supposed all along that it was awkward, Madame. That is why I am to die. It is unjust, but it seems the world is unjust."

"No, no, you damned ninny!" she shouted. "If I didn't have excellent grounds for knowing you are no monk," she said, as she arched an eyebrow coyly, "I would swear you had taken holy orders! It is not how to kill you that occupies me, it is how to save your all-too-stiff neck!

"If you swear to silence, will you keep your word? No, of course you would, but will you swear to silence? You must see what fools we will all seem if word of this got abroad."

"Yes, I see," he said. "Moreover I can't see what difference it makes. The dead are dead."

"Pierre, we are ruling a kingdom of the living. And part of our duty is keeping the Spanish out of our land. They must never know that if they whistled, Paris would revolt in a holy war against anyone but the Catholic extremists. You do see, don't you?"

"Yes, Madame, I will swear. I am glad you were deceived." He bent forward and kissed her hand.

"That leaves the details of your predicament. I shall propose this to the King. You will buy a pardon by ceding that great tract you have in Touraine north of Plessis Gaillard. It's great hunting there, and the King will love it. That will explain how the pardon came about, without getting into whether you were really innocent or not. You agree?"

"Madame, a few minutes ago I expected to be dead in a few days. I supposed my estates were confiscated anyway. I shall manage somehow. I shall raise a company and go off to fight the Turks or for the Turks."

"Pierre," she said, beaming, "you are too good to be true. You will not mind the loss of some estates, as I have it on excellent authority that you are about to acquire a considerably larger property."

Pierre's stupid look was only partly compounded of fatigue.

"If you are not to be beheaded, you can be of use in other ways, and you can repair a bit of damage you have done to my own plans. I refer," she paused, glaring severely at him, "to the Duchess de la Roque. Through your wicked philandering, she is no longer suitable as I had wished for a marriage that would be of use to the state. I have decided that she may as well marry you, and serve you right. Now we shall all return to the Château de Madrid where I shall arrange the details. Meanwhile, Pascal will see to your needs and act as your guard. You have not been pardoned yet, and some zealous subject might attempt to injure you."

She then rang the little bell, which produced one of her ladies as if by magic.

"Send for the Count de Retz. Tell him to come at once, no matter what he is doing."

Chapter XLIX

aurice de La Renaudie reined up at the crowded intersection at the Pont Notre Dame. He glanced over his shoulder and saw only the typical horde of men, horses, and pack animals of an ordinary Paris day. It was plain that Pascal was more concerned with escorting Pierre than pursuing Maurice. He turned right and moved slowly toward the parvis of the Cathedral. There, where the crowd was a little less, he paused to reflect.

Pierre was soon to meet the Queen Mother. It was possible that she would leave matters as they stood, but he sensed otherwise. She had herself sent for Pierre. Gondi could not have arranged it, as his whole plan had been to wring a confession from Pierre before she learned anything. No, something had slipped, and if it had, it was every man for himself. Gondi would be no further help and was no doubt his enemy. Maurice had no illusions about the mercy he could expect from Gondi, the same, he thought with amusement, that he would offer to the Count de Retz if the occasion presented itself.

Calming himself, he forced himself to think. If the Queen knew the truth, her wrath would fall on Gondi first and himself second. Gondi is done for, he mused. He himself could plead, as he had told Gondi, that he was only following Gondi's instructions. But Gondi had said she despises me, he thought.

No, the best place to go was right back where he started, to the Duke of Anjou, now, by the grace of God — and, he imagined, not a little French gold — King of Poland.

He made his way across the bridge and thence back up the right bank to the Louvre. He found the new king emerging from his private oratory, his eyes red with tears.

"Alas, Maurice, I was overcome in prayer by the magnitude of the sins of the world. I sometimes wonder if even God is infinite enough to forgive so much sin. Come, let us get some refreshment. I have been fasting all day for penance."

He led the way into his sumptuously appointed apartments on the first floor. When a cold supper, wine, and music had been arranged to his satisfaction, he mused, "Well, I suppose that brilliant commander de Retz will set you up in some new intrigue or other. Damn me, if he didn't make a mess of things at La Rochelle."

"I do not wish to continue with him," said Maurice. "He has lost his grip. He is over fifty, you know, and well, at La Rochelle he really let you down. He just couldn't seem to do anything right. It's sad in a way to see someone who was once reported brilliant make a fool of himself."

"Yes, I noticed that, too, but of course you were at his side and better able to see it. I saw only the results, or rather, lack of results. I'll never forgive him for that stupid business of seizing de Galle. I'm sure the Protestants would have agreed to our terms before that. Afterward..." Anjou shrugged eloquently.

Maurice watched appalled, as his dream of a triumphal entry with his newly-granted Polish vassals looking on evaporated, leaving only the sour smell of failure. It was obviously Gondi's fault.

"But I detect, do I not, a bit more urgency in your unannounced, though most welcome, visit?"

"I need your help, Your Majesty," cried Maurice, suddenly kneeling at Anjou's feet. He noted with pleasure that Anjou much liked being addressed by his new title.

"You're not really supposed to call me that here, Maurice, but entre nous, it does have a nice ring to it, don't you think?"

"Indeed, eh, Sire, you were born to be a king, and not just of Poland."

"Hush, Maurice, you go too far!" His thin, aesthetic face crumpled into a broad smile. "But your loyalty is precious to me. Now, what is the matter?"

"I'm not sure how it's going to fall out," Maurice said, "but my mission last summer with the Protestants is going to cause trouble. I hardly need tell you, it is all Gondi's fault."

"Last summer! But what you did was... why, it was heroic, spending months with those stinking Protestants! It broke my heart when you renounced our faith." Anjou looked mistily into the distance.

Maurice's face was pale. "Your mother has sent for de Galle. She is going to interrogate him herself."

Anjou looked at him closely. "Well, what of it? De Galle flunked the test, all brawn and no courage when it came to it. Why does she care anyway?"

"I suspect that de Galle will tell some lie about me to save his own neck. It's the kind of thing he would do in a second. And you know she has never liked me, despite all I have done. She'll believe de Galle, and I will be the goat as usual."

"That hardly seems fair. What do you want me to do?"

"Take me into your service. Protect me. I'll gladly go with you to Poland!" Maurice's words tumbled out in a rush. "Sire, Poland is cold and filled with, well, Poles. A man of your refined tastes will be bored, and you will need distraction, amusements of the finest sort. I will provide them. I will occupy myself day and night with turning that frozen desert into a garden of delights for you."

"Yes, I have been worried about that. Could you, Maurice, would you...?"

"Sire, I am yours. I have always been yours."

"Then of course. I'd love to have you in Poland. I hadn't dreamed of asking you, you seemed so well fixed here. Still, if Mamá doesn't like you, it makes things awkward. Well, she can't mind if I take you to Poland. Indeed, what right has she anyway to mind? I am the King of Poland. I can do as I like and have about me whomever I choose!" He rose and adopted a regal pose. "Your fix doesn't sound very serious to me."

Maurice looked furtively toward the door.

"May I stay here, Sire, until we find out what is going on? I'm afraid of de Retz's agents."

Anjou cocked an eyebrow. "Well, you have better reason than most to know about his agents. I'll speak to Mother this afternoon. They told me she had suddenly returned here to the Louvre. You stay here, you'll be perfectly safe."

* * *

"Ah, my dear Count," the Queen Mother purred as Gondi bowed. "You are prompt indeed. Let us stroll together and admire this fine evening."

The old garden of the Louvre was an odd place to find the Queen Mother, he thought. But the evening light across the Seine made the most of it. Gondi followed, walking a little stiffly from his wound. She eyed him appraisingly, but said nothing.

"I suppose, Madame, you wish my own assessment of the peace we now have at La Rochelle."

"No, Albert, I think I know enough about La Rochelle. Besides, it is all past now. Actually, I was thinking of reviewing with you the entire business of that siege, to see if it might not afford us some lessons for the future."

Gondi licked his lips nervously. His limp became slightly more pronounced.

"Here is what happened, my dear Count, correct me if I overlook anything. "The siege began in November when one of your galleys was captured in their harbor; the negotiations you launched in March came to nothing; in April you lost Belle-Île because the defenses were inadequate; while attempting to recapture Belle-Île you let Montgomery slip past you and re-provision the defenders; and that left us with no choice but to make peace with the Protestants on their terms. The alternative would have been interminable delay and more dead. We lost nearly 20,000 men, you know."

The Queen Mother paused to admire a statue of a satyr. "The light at this time of day is so lovely, Alberto." Gondi had paled during her recital.

"But Alberto, I do not wish to reproach you for all of these things. I am too old a campaigner, even if only an armchair general, not to know that the vicissitudes of war are unpredictable and uncontrollable. Indeed, there may have been no point in going over these somewhat mournful and unpleasant facts. War is a game of chance. Unlike many inveterate gamblers, I do not believe in a pattern; events do not repeat themselves. No, the only pattern is in the characters of the actors. Hence, the only constant I see in the siege is that your hand, my dear Count, was behind every important occurrence. I must be lucky that a man I can trust is at the crux of events, exercising whatever control is, in fact, possible."

A flock of swallows, cheeping madly, raced overhead, turned round a tower, and sped back.

Gondi wished to believe in the good will her words implied, but panic gripped him. He recognized that the lack of overt anger was a danger sign.

"However, enough of that," she continued. "Here, sit a bit, I see that your wound pains you. I wish to speak to you of another matter altogether: your niece, Athalie. What of her?"

Gondi leaned forward, greatly relieved. "I also wished to talk of that."

"How convenient."

"Since the winter I have kept her in the protection of my house, in my wife's custody."

"A prisoner of sorts."

"For her own protection."

"Of course."

"I have brought her to Paris so she could be presented to Count Wierzka as we discussed. But now that your son has won the Polish Crown, that worthy's help is no longer needed. I wish to propose another, and I think better, use for Athalie."

Gondi paused, and glanced at his mistress. Her face was impassive.

"My faithful servant," he went on, "and yours, Maurice de La Renaudie, has petitioned me for her hand, and I am inclined to grant his request. His origins are... unfortunate, but he has done more than enough to expiate the sins of his father and to merit advancement. He has the King's favor. I believe he will go far, and with my niece's fortune behind him, his greatest dreams will be realized. We have discussed the matter in depth, and he recognizes that aspiring to the Dukedom is out of the question. I believe that problem could be solved — if Your Majesty permits — by my purchasing the Duchy de la Roque."

"I see," Catherine purred, "and thus will both my faithful servants be rewarded — la Renaudie with possessions and a fortune which should have been beyond his wildest dreams, and my little Gondino with a Dukedom."

"If Your Majesty is kind enough to look at it that way."

"Somehow I am confident that you will be able to find the funds to recompense your ward for the loss of la Roque," she arched an eyebrow at him.

"I think I could manage."

The Queen Mother rose and faced him. "Look you, my friend, I had a somewhat different idea. I thought to marry your niece to Pierre de Galle."

"Pierre de Galle!" Gondi turned white.

"His rank is entirely suitable. There would be no need to truncate her estate. He is widowed. There is no obstacle there. Moreover — he is the father of her child."

Gondi realized in an instant that she could know this only from Athalie's mouth or Pierre's.

"Are you not going to protest that he is a traitor — and should be executed?" she asked.

"Indeed, Madame."

"And yet I have it on good authority that he is not the traitor, but you, my dear Albert, you and your La Renaudie. The plan to eliminate Protestant nobility, rioting and killing, the civil disturbances, the siege of La Rochelle — all our misery of the last year followed from a Protestant plot wholly invented by your agent.

"How much did they pay you, Gondino?"

"What, Madame?"

510

"How much gold did you get from the King of Spain?"

"Madame, you accuse me falsely." Gondi rose, pale but determined. "I do not deny that with La Renaudie's help, I set in progress the execution of the chief Protestants. It was the only thing to do after the attempt on Coligny's life. They were a danger, Madame, and we had to strike first."

"And the attempt on Coligny's life?"

"I will tell you everything, Madame, since you ask me. That also was planned, but it, too, was essential. Indeed, Madame, in your heart, did you not know it was essential? Did you not wish it?"

She was silent for a moment. "It is true, but I did not wish for an attempt, Alberto, as you know."

"In both cases, Madame, I did what I had to, for the good of France. My only fault was not confiding in you. But Madame, often in the past I have brought about things which you desired but in which you did not wish to be implicated. I thought this was another such situation. You have always said you wanted your people to act with discretion and authority."

"When the whole future of our Kingdom depended on the outcome, you thought you could act on your own discretion? your own authority? Sirrah, do you think you are King?"

"Madame, I misjudged the outcome. But if I had succeeded, would you not have rewarded me?"

"Indeed," she snapped. "Even if you are telling the truth, and even if you did not mount this scheme entirely at the Spanish behest, it nevertheless was a disaster for our objectives. A blow at the Protestants might, might I say, have worked for the peace I desired, as last summer the Protestants were all for war.

"But Albert, your ruse failed. We had war anyway, bitter, stupid, expensive civil war, and moreover, we lost it. In addition, we nearly lost every diplomatic initiative in Europe. It is a miracle that anything was saved."

She paused and looked at him for a long time.

"I do not know what to believe, Albert. My instinct tells me you are a traitor — yes, truly, a filthy traitor. Save your golden words — I've heard enough of them. Yet, you have been my confidant, no, more than my confidant, my friend, no, even more than my friend... for oh, how many years. But you know all this, and you know that if you have betrayed me, it is a triple betrayal. Yet I know that if your story is true, I must forgive you. But how am I to know the truth?" She gazed deeply into his eyes.

He looked away.

"La Renaudie knows," she mused. "I could have him put to the torture."

Gondi started. "No, Madame!"

"Ah, Albert, such fear!"

"He would say anything. I have seen it too often."

She shrugged. "So! I will never know your heart."

She turned away from him.

"Well, what is to be done? We have told the world we killed the Protestant leaders in self-defense. England half believes it. The Germans wish to believe it. What is more important, my poor son King Charles believes it. He dreams of the massacre, the screams, the stench. His mind can barely face the reality he knows — self-defense, necessity, royal prerogative. He believes his salvation hereafter depends on this — that he acted without choice or malice. He can never be told otherwise."

Gondi smiled.

"Four people know, Your Majesty: you and I, Maurice, and de Galle. The only outsider is de Galle. He can be sentenced without anyone the wiser."

She looked at him and returned his smile. "So, I should spare you and your pawn, though I know you may be guilty, but I should condemn a man whom all agree is innocent?"

Suddenly she turned on him.

"Well, I will not do it! I do not trust you. Know this: I will never trust you. But I trust young de Galle. As much as anyone, he has the honor of a gentleman. He will go free and marry your ward. Yes, Albert, your wardship is gone, you shall account for it — your Dukedom is gone. Think no more of it. You say I am unjust? You have certainly failed me, and probably that failure was intentional. I will not reward you by giving you what you most covet. You will be Marshal — that is expected by everyone and I will not openly disgrace you, but do not expect any other rewards from my hands.

"As for La Renaudie — his mouth will be shut for him. See to it.

"And Athalie's child, I trust its whereabouts are known to you?"

"No, Madame," he replied weakly. "That was a matter I left to La Renaudie." He saw with fear that her eyes had become hard. "But wait, your own captain, Pascal, he was there, he would know. I am innocent, Madame. It was he and La Renaudie."

"Albert, shut up," she snapped. "Ho, Pascal!"

Pascal appeared on a dead run, his sword unsheathed. He dropped to one knee before the Queen.

"Do you know anything about the child of the Duchess de la Roque? Is the child...?"

"Indeed, Madame. I myself gave her to my brother Aimeri's people. She is alive and thriving."

Gondi expelled a deep breath.

The world seemed to move again.

"Send someone to your brother at once. Let the child be brought here." The Queen Mother was firm but kind to the trembling Pascal.

"Now Albert, you are excused. See that you don't bungle the assignment I gave you."

* * *

Gondi's mount screamed and bucked as he kicked it savagely and rode off at a gallop. He knew the full enormity of his dismissal by the Queen Mother would soon hit him. Now, momentarily beside himself, he could think of only one thing and on that he focused with maniacal intensity. Kill Maurice de La Renaudie. He would not use poison or an assassin. No, right now he would take six men, break Maurice's door down, and throw the wretch's carcass into the Seine. And God help anyone who tried to stop him!

Chapter L

The hours after the Queen Mother and her entourage had galloped out of the Château de Madrid were the longest Athalie had ever passed. Horror and fear such as she had never known washed over her in sickening waves. They alternated with waves of almost passionate love and gratitude toward the Queen Mother, the feel of whose bulky body as she had embraced Athalie stayed in her mind. Hard under the bulk, strong, and how fast she had ridden off. Ridden off to what?

Athalie choked back her tears. What if she were too late? What if the king ordered...? The Queen had not promised anything, and she had left in such haste. She did not often hurry. She must have known that only haste, only immediate action, could save him.

Athalie found she was praying, praying without ceasing. "Oh, save him. Let her be in time."

Time passed with agonizing slowness. Outside, the soothing summer sounds, the breeze, the buzz of an insect, a bird, a dog barking. Inside, the familiar afternoon sounds, chairs moved, dishes put on tables, orders given as the servants went about the routine for the evening meal. Two gardeners passed in the path below, their great straw hats hiding their faces, their voices soft and slow in the warm afternoon. They don't know, she said to herself. They don't know that in that awful prison, rope and iron are biting into my beloved. She began to pray again, and the time passed so slowly.

Margot looked in twice, then three times. But even her irrepressible chatter was stilled in the face of Athalie's agony. This was not something words could help. If she had been in time, but if she had not been in time.... Margot blew a kiss at Athalie and closed the door softly. Poor little cousin, she thought.

At about eight o'clock a troop of horses clattered into the courtyard. As soon as Athalie heard them, she ran through the dim halls and burst out into the golden westering sun.

There he was, sliding down from his mount. There he was, he saw her, grinned foolishly, and in three seconds Pierre and Athalie were in each other's arms.

"It's all well for them," Catherine de Medici grumbled as Augustin Pascal helped her to dismount. "I, however, have ridden twice as far as Monsieur de Galle today and have much further business before sunset if he is to remain at liberty. However, I imagine we could all use some sustenance. Monsieur de Galle does not seem to have dined well among the Protestants. Let us go in to supper."

* * *

"Well, well, well," Anjou said, draping his cloak over a chair. "You seem to have been in rather a storm center." He looked appraisingly at La Renaudie. "My mother didn't tell me all, that's plain, but what she did say was quite enough. It seems we are all to keep things just as they are about the Protestants last summer. I never could understand what the problem was, or why we needed an agent like you, when all we needed to know was that they were heretics.

"But Mother always coddled them, it was sickening how she went on about Coligny. And my brother, the King, why, it was disgraceful. Anyway, it seems you were right." Anjou yawned and sat down. "She told Gondi to cut your throat."

Maurice was completely still. There was a sour smell of fear in the room. "But I talked her out of it," Anjou laughed easily. "She is so proud of my new crown that she isn't likely to refuse me.

"But it was damned hard and there are conditions. You are to leave the country at once and then remain with me in Poland. Another condition you won't like at all: de Retz is to be pushed off as well. You two can keep an eye on each other. I'll tell de Retz that we impale criminals in Poland, and I'll impale him if anything happens to you. I'd think Mother was sending him along to spy on me, if she weren't so angry with him. You were right, too, about de Galle. He is, or will be, pardoned, and he is going to marry that little Duchess de la Roque. I wondered what ever had happened to her.

"You are to produce de Galle's infant son at once," Anjou continued. "I'll just send some people for it, shall I, save you the bother? And we are all, you as well, to attend on Mother tomorrow noon at the Madrid."

* * *

Early the next morning Athalie and Pierre, arm in arm, strolled through the gardens down to the Seine. The scene was one of complete tranquility. The sky held but a few puffy clouds, the swans patrolled majestically on the river's broad, smooth back. The air was rich with the perfumes of summer. Every few steps Pierre stopped, bent, and kissed the top of Athalie's head.

"I love you, Lie-lie," he murmured.

"Dearest," she replied, "how crazy to have had such commotion, then to be finally washed up here in the morning, on the banks of the Seine, with nothing to do but love you."

"Yesterday at this time I was a dead man," Pierre murmured.

"No, hush," she said, putting a hand on his mouth. "That is past. Today is the day for love, just love, no past, no future, just love now with you here."

A discreet cough interrupted their reverie. Aimeri Pascal approached, beaming. Behind him came a rosy-cheeked, plump woman.

"Gabrielle!" Athalie cried, flinging herself with joy upon the woman who held out the infant. In a second, laughing, weeping, raining kisses on the puzzled infant, Athalie held her most precious treasure. Pierre smiled bashfully at Aimeri.

"Your arrival was most fortunate."

"Not at all, Monsieur de Galle, I have had the honor to serve Her Majesty on some financial matters. Augustin sent word yesterday that the child should be brought at once. She is a beautiful and healthy little girl. I'm told she has a bit of a temper, but she has been good as gold this morning.

"This I have for you. I met with the King before he went off hunting this morning. It is your pardon; all is well. You are completely free. The King was quite pleased about getting the forest north of Plessis Gaillard. He told me your father said the deer were great there. He is going to move Court there in two weeks. But he doesn't always do what he says he will.

"I suppose you will miss it, but Rocher de la Roque is a much better place and in much better condition."

Pierre continued to smile.

"I say," Aimeri went on, "I hope I'm not putting my foot in it."

"No, no, it's not that at all, Aimeri dear," Athalie said. "It's just that I want us to live at Islette. I want to finish it as my mother would have. I wonder if there will be enough money to live on if we do that."

"You have no worries on that score," Aimeri said, smiling. "The Queen asked me to look over the books last night after she revoked your uncle's wardship. I'm glad to say he was most cooperative; of course, he and my father go back many years together. Anyway, everything is in order. I have to say he managed your property as if it were his own, which I suppose is how he looked at it. Fact is, he has done very well by your properties, always selling the poorer ones, always buying better, always keeping everything up, and with good stewards to collect the rents and see to things. You'll have enough to turn Islette into Chenonceau if you like."

"What I would like," said Athalie, "is to ask you to handle these affairs for me, I mean for us." She smiled at Pierre.

Aimeri doffed his cap and bowed gracefully. "I am yours to command."

* * *

The arrival of Henri, Duke of Anjou and King-Elect of Poland and Lithuania, instantly dispelled the unpleasant tension that crackled among the persons gathered on the upper garden of the Château de Madrid. The Duke, resplendent in green and white, dismounted gracefully and warmly embraced his mother. Beaming at him, she exchanged pleasantries and thanked him for his presence. She bowed cordially to Henri Navarre and Margot, who had accompanied him.

Anjou disengaged himself and, putting an arm around Albert de Gondi, drew him aside. "Now see here, Albert, I've talked it all over with Mother and I think I have it sorted out. There's no getting around the fact that she is, how shall I put it, disappointed in you, but I think I can help you out. I'm not one to forget someone who has done me a good turn, and you certainly did your best as far as Poland is concerned. So I've decided to make you one of my advisers at Cracow. That will get you out of Mother's line of fire," he whispered conspiratorially. "Let someone else take the heat for a while." He flashed a radiant smile. "Besides, I need you. What's more, I like your company."

Gondi's eyes could not conceal the pain and disappointment he felt. Poland was very nearly the end of the world. It was said to be, certainly, a center for scholarly and scientific pursuits, but of refinement, taste, and fashion, well, it was very far from France. Moreover, to be away from France would allow his enemies to make it all but impossible for him to regain a position of eminence. Still, he mused, to be away from France is one thing, but would it be truly away from France?

If King Charles were to die, then this man, Anjou, the brand-new King of Poland, would be France. To have his ear, to have been with him in his own exile... Gondi's mind began to flow in familiar channels.

"My Prince," he whispered, kissing Anjou's hand. "Your kindness is more than I deserve. I would follow you to the ends of the earth."

"Then it's settled," Anjou breezed on brightly. "One thing. I want you to make it up with La Renaudie. He is a friend of mine, as are you, my dear Albert, and I don't wish bad blood among my friends."

Anjou beckoned Maurice forward. La Renaudie emerged from Anjou's entourage, oddly inconspicuous in Anjou's livery rather than in his customary black. He was completely subdued.

"I humbly beg your pardon, my lord de Retz," he said, bowing to the waist. "I bitterly regret the words between us, and I, for my part, and for the love of His Majesty, King Henry," he lowered his voice reverently and gazed adoringly at Anjou, "I offer you my true love and devoted service."

Gondi suppressed simultaneous urges to laugh or vomit. So, he thought, the snake becomes a spaniel. Still, he was too experienced not to realize that actors were playing parts, and that he must play his as well. Even, he thought, if it is to be a farce and not a tragedy. Still, we have not yet played the last act, Monsieur de La Renaudie.

"With all my heart, and for the love of this wise and gentle prince," he said, grasping Maurice's hand, "I do accept your words as honest as your face, and your love as true as your deeds."

Anjou, pretending to be oblivious to the irony, embraced both men, then dismissing Maurice, turned back toward his mother. "But where is the Duke de Galle, for whose benefit I suppose we are all here?" The Queen Mother gave a sign, and a bell chimed in the bright morning stillness.

"I don't mind telling you, Albert," the Prince continued. "I was glad to see de Galle pardoned. I didn't agree with him on the religious business, but it was just like him to get mixed up with Protestants without holding with them. Still, I always liked him, even if he is a snob about that damned long pedigree of his. And that magnificent wife of his — what a pity she is with the angels! Must have bowled you over to find that he was tumbling that funny niece of yours." He dug Gondi in the ribs, noting with pleasure that Gondi was not amused.

"I have arranged to fetch his son by the lady Anne. I suggest, Albert, that you be the one actually to turn the child over to him. You take the credit, no harm trying to get back in his good graces. If he isn't to be executed, he'll remain a powerful man."

"Yes, of course," Gondi managed weakly, "You are most kind."

* * *

"Athalie!" Margot's call reached the banks of the Seine. Margot appeared at a run, dragging her grinning husband, Henry King of Navarre, in tow. "Athalie, darling Athalie," she cried, as she embraced her and then drew off, clucking admiration for Gabrielle, while Pierre looked on.

"Well, Monsieur de Galle," Henry said. "I had not expected to see you again in this life. I am glad to the bottom of my heart that you are safe. Margot has told me of her exploits yesterday. I rejoice that my family was able to help you."

"Your Majesty is most kind," Pierre mumbled.

They regarded each other in silence for a moment. Both had changed. Both had known sorrow, war, and danger. Both had looked death in the face since the mock tourney a year before. Navarre's eyes were thoughtful, like a model prisoner who bides his time, knowing that eventually his jailers will slip and he'll be ready to seize his chance. Pierre's frame, still gaunt from his short commons at La Rochelle, matched his eyes, grey steady eyes that had seen the complexity, or perhaps the simplicity, of love and death.

"So, Pierre," Henry said at last, "we are to have your nuptials this morning."

"Yes," Pierre smiled broadly. "It should, of course, take place at St. Gatien's at Tours. But the Queen Mother said she wanted Athalie's position regularized at once; she even made me promise to recognize our daughter." He grinned. "As if my bride would have allowed otherwise. As if I did not already cherish little Gabrielle as Athalie does. As well, I have a son and heir by Anne."

A bell chimed above. "We are summoned," Athalie said. "Stay by us, Margot and Henry," she said. "Her Majesty has insisted that, for form's sake, my uncle must give me away and, and," she whispered, "La Renaudie must be best man. But you, Henry, can stand with Pierre, too, and Margot, you can walk with me."

Pierre put an arm around Athalie and drew her close. "Don't be afraid, Lie-lie. It's all right now."

A hush fell over the crowd as Pierre and Athalie appeared in the gate. Athalie's gown of sky-blue silk, intricately embroidered with seed pearls, emphasized her creamy skin and dark hair. She was ignorant, of course, that the rather expensive garment had been ordered by her aunt for her presentation to the unlamented Count Wierzka.

Commandeering that gown from Gondi's hotel on instant notice had been another of those matters the Queen Mother had somehow found time to attend to. There were not a few gasps as various lords and ladies recognized the splendid diamond and sapphire necklace that graced Athalie's neck. It had been given to Catherine herself by François I shortly after her own marriage to his son, the late King Henry. The royal heirloom, as a gift to the bride, did even more than the

Queen Mother's frosty glance to stifle the beginnings of a titter, as some ladies in Anjou's entourage caught their first glimpse of the scandalous young duchess.

Pierre was clad in white silk, but despite his broad grin, the festive effect was diminished as his white doublet, which would normally have set off his ruddy golden complexion, now rather emphasized his pallor, the result of months of deprivation. The doublet and hose, borrowed for the occasion, did not fit his huge frame as well as they might have. His eyes, too, were grave, thoughtful, as they surveyed the crowd, nearly the same, he thought, as would have surrounded my scaffold. Only his carriage, his graceful powerful stride, gave unmixed proof of his resilience. He nodded to Anjou and Gondi. He did not appear to see Maurice.

With great gentleness, he took Athalie's arm and led her forward, followed by Margot and Henry Navarre. They approached the Queen Mother and both knelt. She bade them rise, then embraced first Athalie, then Pierre. Afterward, people said there were tears in her eyes as she gruffly ordered the procession to enter the chapel. She mumbled something about having made the Archbishop come all the way from Paris and not wishing to keep him waiting.

Following her lead, the bridal pair entered. In the end there was a press of nobility trying to squeeze through the doorway after the bride and groom, for the chapel at the Château de Madrid was not large, and no one wanted to miss such a remarkable event. Maurice brought up the rear, his normally mobile face devoid of expression. They can't very well start before I arrive, he mused, as he entered the door. Pierre de Galle may be lord of the present. But the future, I think, is going off to Poland, and I am going to be part of it.

THE END

Made in United States
North Haven, CT
05 February 2022

15725246R00287